Praise for Jeff Salyards and the Bloodsounder's Arc Trilogy

"*Scourge of the Betrayer* is a literary appetizer that will undoubtedly captivate anyone who enjoys fantasy, be it epic fantasy, adventure fantasy, military fantasy, etc. If you're a fan of Cook's Black Company, or GRRM's *A Song of Ice and Fire*, or of classic fantasy sagas like Leiber's *Fafhrd and the Gray Mouser* and Moorcock's *Elric*, this is a debut novel that is, like Jagger said, 'what you need.'"

—Paul Goat Allen, *B&N.com*

"*Scourge of the Betrayer* by Jeff Salyards is my Debut of the Year and Fantasy of the Year. It is also one of the finest debuts I have ever read, instantly converting me into a fan and follower."

—Nick Sharps, *SF Signal*

"*Scourge of the Betrayer* offers an interesting twist on the military fantasy pattern. . . . If you're in the mood for a solid gritty fantasy, give *Scourge of the Betrayer* a try."

—Stefan Raets, Tor.com

"*Veil of the Deserters* is everything I was looking for in the highly anticipated follow-up to *Scourge of the Betrayer*. What Jeff Salyards has crafted here is a rare sequel that actually manages to outdo the first. . . . Paced exceptionally well throughout, it also has the kind of killer climax that manages to completely satisfy, while still leaving the reader desperate for more."

—*Beauty in Ruins*

"5 of 5 stars. . . . Seriously, why aren't more people reading Jeff Salyards?! He's outdone himself with this one."

—*BiblioSanctum*

"Long story short, you need to read this series. The second book is every bit as incredible as the first . . ."

—*Bibliotropic*

"Last year Jeff Salyards came out of nowhere and gave us the amazing debut *Scourge of the Betrayer*, a novel that was one of my personal favorites for the year. This year, his follow up novel *Veil of the Deserters* outdoes his debut. . . . 9.5 out of 10 stars."

—*Speculative Book Review*

"*Bloodsounder's Arc* is shaping up to be one of my favorite fantasy book series of all time. 5 stars."

—*Elitist Book Reviews*

"With *Chains of the Heretic*, Jeff Salyards presents an engrossing tale of a military company forced to flee their homes. This is a journey of survival and personal ambition you don't want to miss."

—Jon Sprunk, author of the Shadow Saga

"Jeff Salyards' great conclusion to his Bloodsounder's Arc trilogy. . . . Continues the gritty realism of the military action of the first two books while adding in a whole new creepy and very cool element that I don't want to spoil for anyone. If you enjoy military fantasy, jump on these books."

—Courtney Schaefer, author of the Shattered Sigil series

CHAINS *of the*
HERETIC

CHAINS *of the* HERETIC

Bloodsounder's Arc Book Three

JEFF SALYARDS

NIGHT SHADE BOOKS
NEW YORK

Night Shade books may be purchased in bulk at special discounts for sales promotion, corporate gifts, fund-raising, or educational purposes. Special editions can also be created to specifications. For details, contact the Special Sales Department, Night Shade Books, 307 West 36th Street, 11th Floor, New York, NY 10018 or info@skyhorsepublishing.com.

Night Shade Books™ is a trademark of Skyhorse Publishing, Inc.®, a Delaware corporation.

Visit our website at www.nightshadebooks.com.

10 9 8 7 6 5 4 3 2 1

Library of Congress Cataloging-in-Publication Data is available on file.

Cover illustration by Ryan Pancoast
Interior layout and design by Amy Popovich
Map illustrations by William McAusland

Print ISBN: 978-1-59780-813-2

Printed in the United States of America

To my amazing and lovely wife, Kris

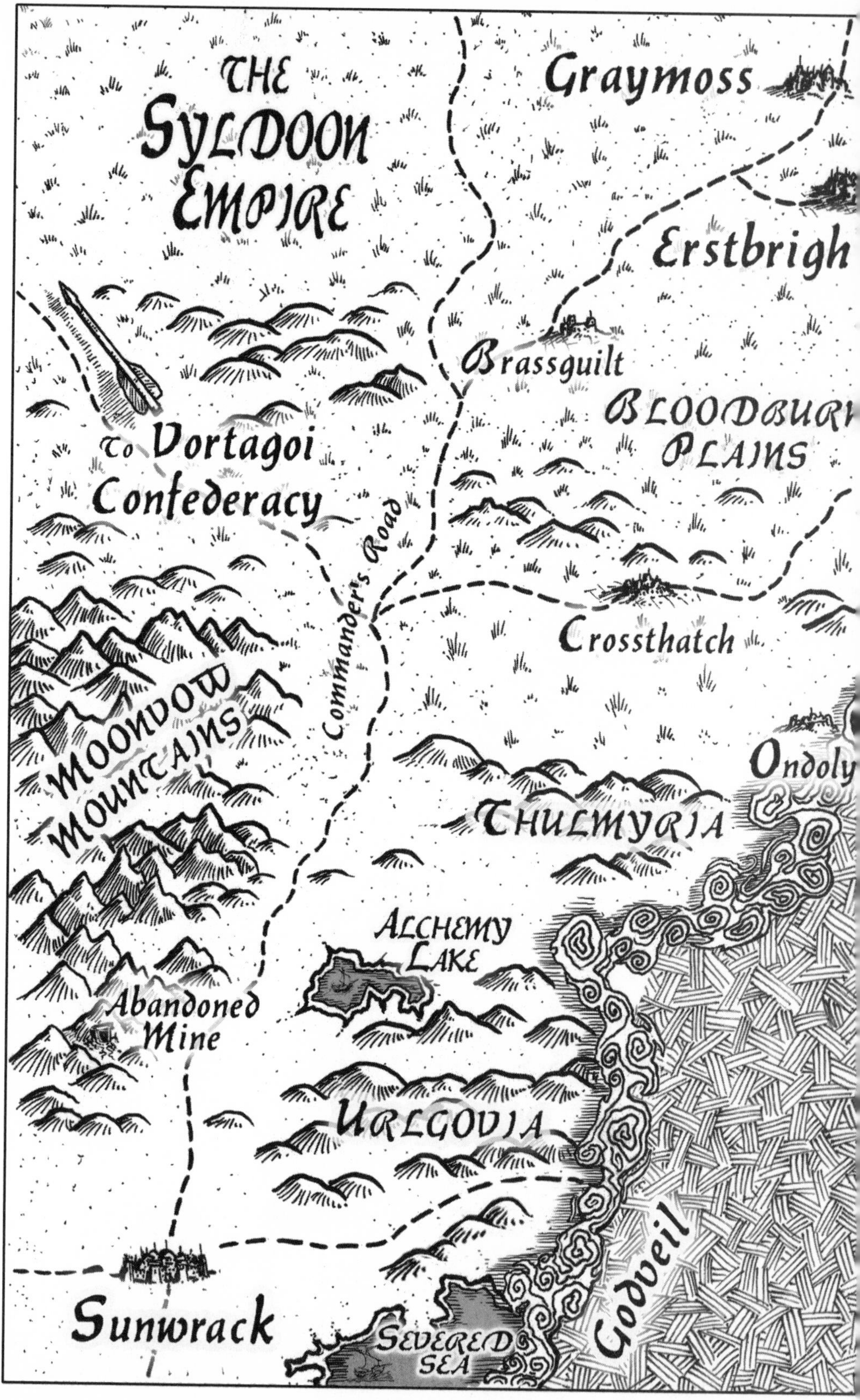

THE
SYLDOON
EMPIRE

Graymoss

Erstbrigh

Brassguilt

to Vortagoi
Confederacy

BLOODBURN
PLAINS

Commander's Road

Crosstnatch

MOONDOW
MOUNTAINS

THULMYRIA

Ondoly

ALCHEMY
LAKE

Abandoned
Mine

URLGOVIA

Godveil

Sunwrack

SEVERED
SEA

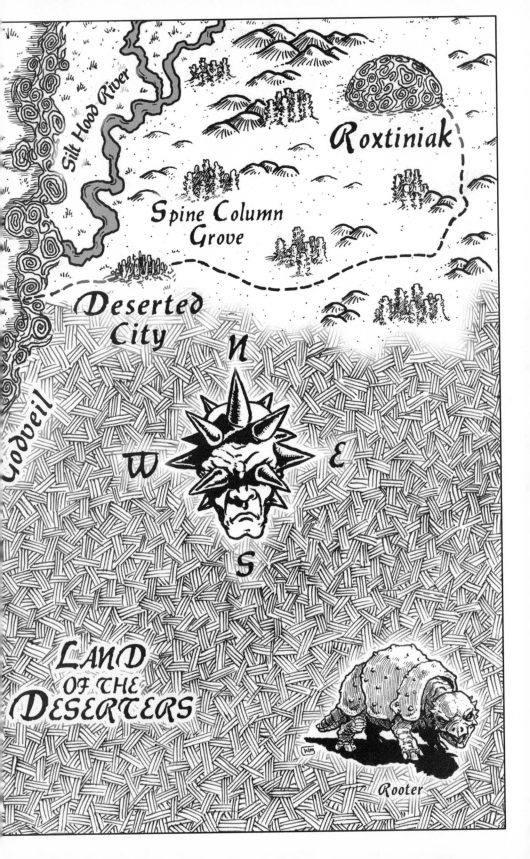

Silt Hood River

Roxtiniak

Spine Column
Grove

Deserted
City

Godveil

N

W   E

S

LAND
OF THE
DESERTERS

Rooter

CHAINS *of the* HERETIC

I sat in the wagon bed as we bounced over the uneven earth, having left the flat and well-maintained road behind miles ago. Sweat poured down my brow, dripping onto the pages, and I was irritated at the necessity of having to wipe it constantly, but it was that or risk the sweat fouling my marks on the page or staining the ancient manuscript in front of me.

Besides the heat and the air so heavy it seemed to clog the throat, it was difficult to concentrate at the task at hand for other reasons—my mind kept drifting off, seeing those Jackals trapped on the bridge out of Sunwrack as it rolled out from underneath their horses' hooves, seeing them desperately fighting on despite knowing there was no reprieve or rescue, their shields up to deflect the arrows raining down on them, several getting through, their armor and bodies bristling with shafts, and then, finally, hearing their screams as the Jackals fell into the Trench when there was simply no more bridge left to support them.

We'd left the Jackal Tower with over two hundred men. We'd left Sunwrack with nearly a quarter of that dead or dying in our wake. The only upside to such slaughter was that we were unlikely to run out of ammunition or supplies soon.

Even when I managed to block out that horrible scene, I found myself thinking about what a fool I'd been, allowing Skeelana to get close to me, fostering it even, in my own fumbling fashion. I'd been warned again and again, and still, against that and what passed for my own better judgment, I'd not only encouraged her to treat Captain Killcoin, but nearly invited her into my own head. No, I *had* invited her. The peculiar thing was, she had resisted. She could have mined me for more damning information, and yet, despite betraying the captain and his Jackal Tower, she had chosen not to. Well, after kissing me deeply and bonding with me, of course. There was that.

Damn me, but I was a colossal fool.

There was a reason I really didn't have very good luck with women. I'd befriended Lloi, though we had backgrounds as disparate as could be, and I didn't truly understand her. I respected her, found myself caring for her, and then, without warning, I'd been cradling her in my arms when she died. That should have discouraged me from opening up to another woman any time soon, especially a Memoridon. And yet, I'd warmed to Skeelana, and that had stirred feelings far more dangerous than those allotted to friendship. Even if she hadn't betrayed the Tower, the infatuation would have been the height of foolishness. But of course she had, and in part thanks to me, so I managed to make foolishness an art form.

I forced myself back to the documents, penning my translation, though it felt pointless. The likelihood of discovering our salvation in the brittle pages was, well, nearly nonexistent.

The hours and miles rolled by, and while I didn't unearth our salvation, I did encounter many interesting lines and references. When we finally stopped to rest the horses, I stood as much as the wagon allowed, hunchwalked to the front, stepped over the bench, and rolled my neck around, eager to share my meager findings with the captain.

Vendurro had already jumped down into the grass to tend to the horses. I was surveying the barren area, the ground mostly small thorny brush, stones, a few twisted trees that looked tortured and tormented and the last of their kind, and not much else. I was about to jump down myself, when I noticed something exceedingly strange. We had settled near the shore of a lake. That in itself wasn't all that unusual—after leaving the road several days prior and trekking through the hilly province of Urglovia, we came across quite a few bodies of water, both large and small.

But something about this lake seemed different. I shaded my eyes and looked across it; the surface was less blemished than most mirrors, perfectly reflecting the sky above. And it was as quiet as it was still, with no birds in the shallows, nor any flying overhead. The small trees around the shore were bare and stumpy, thorny brambles mostly, with sparse undergrowth. There should have been some animals, some semblance of life or activity. Lakes always drew animals and settlers to them, and yet this lake and the land around it were utterly deserted.

I got down and walked closer, leaving all the Syldoon soldiers and their horses behind near the wagons. Some sticks and jagged rocks broke the surface of the lake near the rocky shore, but there wasn't even the slightest ripple around them. It was only when I was a few strides from the water's edge that I noticed something even more peculiar. A raven was lying on its side in the rocks, clearly dead, but not rotten or decomposing. While its eyes were gone, the body itself was in remarkably pure condition, like a grisly gray statue. I knelt down and examined the bird, turning it over with a stick. It was as well-preserved as some animals I'd seen in Highgrove University that had been fished out of tar pits, presumably hundreds of years after meeting their demise. The contours, the skin, the teeth and claws of those mice and squirrels were all intact, as if they had just met their end.

This bird was equally hardened for all posterity, its wings still folded along its sides, though not by having fallen into any tar or anything else except perhaps the water itself, and it wasn't blackened, but the color of stone.

I nudged the bird with my boot, expecting it to be heavy, but it left a small chalky smudge on my toe, and one brittle feather crumbled a little at the edge, but otherwise it remained the same. After looking up at the encampment, I decided to walk along the shore a bit, and in the span of a hundred yards, came across several other animals equally preserved—two small sparrows, a bat, three mice, and a large crane, the vane and barb in its feathers perfectly intact. In each case, they all appeared dead for ages, and yet none had rotted like usual carcasses, which was decidedly odd since any dead creatures above ground were subject to scavengers and elements. I even encountered what appeared to be a calcified eagle of some sort, its bearing still lifelike and proud, even if it was on its side in the sand. It was in such pristine condition I almost expected it to unfurl its wings and take flight again.

I walked the shoreline, wondering at this dead lake and its lifeless denizens. I'd never seen anything like it, or even heard of such a thing. It certainly wasn't natural. I knelt on some pebbles and sand, grabbed a large stick, and very slowly slid it into the unmoving water. I realized I was holding my breath, and cursed myself a fool as nothing happened—what did I expect? A flash of lightning? A dead man to rise from the depths and claim me as another mummified victim? I tossed the stick into the water, watched it disappear, and even those small ripples looked reluctant and weak, as if the lake would not abide any disturbance, or was slumbering and not easily woken. A moment later the mirror-like flatness returned.

I reached forward, debating dipping the tip of a finger in, when I heard, "I would advise against that, archivist."

Nearly falling in, I planted a hand on the pebbles before standing and looking at the captain. "Is it truly that dangerous?"

Braylar was staring at the once regal eagle at his feet. "This predator thought so. I don't imagine you will instantaneously turn to stone, but the water is as caustic as you will find anywhere. They call it Lake Alchemy."

"I've never seen its like. If I didn't know better, I'd suspect some sorcery at work," I said, not entirely sure I did know better.

He looked up at me. "You are a learned boy. A scholar. I expect you would look to the natural for explanation first, yes?"

I stood up and dusted off my hands. "Well, before riding with you and witnessing the effects of Bloodsounder, and seeing a Memoridon blind a battalion of Hornmen or Imperial troops, I wouldn't have put much stock in magic at all. But clearly some things in this world extend beyond the pale."

Braylar drummed the fingers of his left hand on the flail. "There is truth in that, I grant you. And yet, I'd wager this lake is not cursed at all, not in any kind of supernatural sense at least. Something in the waters here did this." He pointed at the eagle. "Unusual? Yes. Magical? Doubtful."

After hardly speaking to the captain the last few days, I was reluctant to provoke him, but found myself saying, "Well, regardless of the cause, this is the most blighted body of water I have ever seen."

A half smile came and went like a flicker. "That we agree on. Where we truly diverge is whether or not we consider it folly to stick our fingers in a blighted lake. Awfully difficult to write if acid eats the flesh off your finger bones or turns them to chalk. If you must satisfy your curiosity, at least use your off hand, yes?"

He turned and started heading back to the convoy when I said, "I discovered more. In the second chest."

Braylar pivoted and walked back towards me. "And yet instead of informing me immediately, you chose to play with dead things?"

"Well, given what you said, the other night that is, I wasn't sure when the right time to approach you would—"

"If you cannot abide being berated occasionally, you really should have stuck with chronicling the exploits of wheat merchants rather than accompanying the most hardened military band in the world." The return of the twitch-smile told me that was as warm a response as I was like to get. "Now. What have you discovered?"

"I need to have my notes and translations to give you a full report, and it is nothing so good as explaining how Cynead did—"

"Enough qualifiers."

"Well, the last time I mentioned some accounts like this you were skeptical, so I waited until I compiled several of them, and—"

"If you do not arrive at a point immediately, I will throw you in the lake and watch you turn to alabaster."

I pointed at Bloodsounder. "I came across several more references, in independent sources, describing weapons like that, called Sentries. Most of them called the wielder and the weapon itself by the same name, like Grieftongue that I told you about."

"And?" he asked, none too collegially.

"And there were several more accounts, with multiple witnesses, of weapons like Bloodsounder allowing the wielder to pass through the Godveil."

"There are also accounts of manticores and winged women who cannot bear children and steal them from new mothers. What of it?"

I folded my arms across my chest. "I thought the same reading Anjurian accounts of Memoridons."

The captain looked ready to skewer me again and stopped himself, with some effort. "Point taken. And still, even if true, this has little to do with the here and now, and helps us not at all."

"Perhaps not," I conceded carefully. "But do you recall the high priest of Truth I told you about, Anroviak?"

"The one who dismembered memory witches to plumb their secrets? Yes, the name is not easily forgotten."

"Well, I came across a later account by a high priest named Luzzki. He'd read Anroviak's account of the Grass Dog memory witch who'd purged herself at the Godveil. He was no less skeptical than you—"

"I like this one already."

"But it was balanced out by curiosity. And judging from his tone, he was the sort who had to see a thing with his own eyes before disparaging. Or believing."

Braylar's eyes narrowed. "My threat to throw you in still stands. I do hope you are spiraling towards something remotely relevant."

"Well," I said, wishing I had my notes with me but not wanting to risk greater wrath by running off to get them, "it took him some time, but he managed to capture a memory witch of his own."

"I imagine they were more plentiful then."

"Yes, her name was Kinmerra. And he took her to the Godveil, though with fewer witnesses than his predecessor had. The first time."

Braylar seemed, if not outright intrigued, at least mildly curious. "Go on."

"Well, Kinmerra had heard all the tales, of course—anyone who approached the Veil was driven mad or simply snuffed out—and she begged him not to force her towards it, promised to do anything else he asked, but her pleas were not answered."

"I assumed not, or you would not be wasting my time with this tiresome tale. Please proceed to the heart of this, Arki."

"Luzzki made it sound as if he was of two minds, but he still ordered her to walk towards the Veil, exactly as Anroviak had done, fully expecting her to perish, but wanting to be certain for himself."

Braylar scowled, "You do know what a heart is, do you not, scribe?"

"Well, Kinmerra didn't have her wits stolen, and she didn't fall down dead. She got within five feet of the Godveil, and while she went towards it with tears streaming down her face, she returned calm. Serene even. And when Luzzki pressed her for her impressions, all she could say was that she had been cleansed." I paused for effect. "Clean—"

"Yes," he said, "I did hear you the first time. And I am aware of the meaning of the word. What of it? Perhaps she never possessed the ability to fletch dreams or walk among memories in the first place. All we have in this instance is the word of a priest—"

I opened my mouth to object, and he pressed on. "Fine, several priests, then. But all of them long dead. I assume Luzzki didn't want to anger his clerical fathers by having a dozen notarized witnesses in attendance when he performed this test."

"True. That would have certainly been impossible. But Luzzki, feeling that he'd truly discovered, well, rediscovered really, a secret about one of the heretics of their order, chose to explore it further. To repeat the experiment. As I said, this was the first venture. The second, he did have witnesses, and the third, more still, and each time Kinmerra survived. It was only after the fourth that he presented his findings to some elder legates in his order, substantiating what Anroviak had claimed at least a century before."

Now Braylar's curiosity was piqued. "Hmmm. And did they burn this exceptionally thorough holy man at the stake, for forgetting the cruel lessons of history?"

I shook my head. "According to his own account, the order dismissed his research, and commanded him to discontinue under threat of protracted death."

"At least they are consistent. And did he comply? Or was his record cut short as well?"

"Wisely, Luzzki didn't push the issue, no doubt valuing his skin over any zealous pursuit of proving his point. He had no wish to be a martyr. But he did privately harangue them for being skittish fools. Even as he discontinued. Or at least he stopped jotting down his impressions or discoveries if he didn't heed the warning."

The captain knelt down, picked up a flat round stone, turned it over in his hand, and tossed it into the air. "I will admit, regardless of whether these accounts are mired in falsehood or fiction or delusion, they are intriguing." He cocked his arm back and sent the rock flying, watching as it skipped six times before sliding under the surface, the ripples leaden and disappearing quickly. "But even if true or accurate, they still do not help us in the here and now."

I countered, "If they are true, perhaps they could help you cleanse yourself when you are flooded with memories. Maybe you don't need a rogue witch or Memoridon at all, you only need to approach the Godveil. Now, that won't help you defeat Cynead or reclaim the Memoridons, but if it's true—"

"If, if, if. You would have me gamble my life on the suppositions of some poorly substantiated claims from a millennium ago?"

"Centuries, not a millennium." I resisted the urge to grind my teeth together. "Why have me sift through all these tomes at all if you're simply going to dismiss everything I uncover?"

Braylar gave me a withering look. "You overstep, archivist. As always, your job is to simply translate and relay. Mine is to make sense of the findings and determine what, if anything, to do with them. You have done a solid job on the whole, though somewhat slow. But do not mistake my small praise for license to question my every decision."

I was about to protest that his praise was mean indeed, when I saw Vendurro coming down the small hill. "Cap," he called out.

Braylar turned and looked at him. "Sergeant. What can I help you with?"

Vendurro appeared ready to say something when he suddenly took notice of the rocky shore and slowly scanned the well-preserved animals near the water's edge. "Got to say, you do have a soft spot for all kind of places dead, deserted, and otherwise queer."

Braylar's eyes narrowed to slits again as he stared hard at the younger man. "I do hope you didn't jog all this way to discuss aesthetics? If so, jog right back up that hill."

The sergeant shook his head. "Can't say that I did, Cap. Just kind of hit me, is all. But thinking you'll want to be done gazing at the waves and getting all aesthetical yourself. Well, if there were waves to speak of. Which there ain't. That's the real peculiar thing, if you ask me. Which of course you didn't."

"No," the captain said, slowly and with great effort. "I did not. What I did ask is why you are here."

"Begging your pardon, Cap, but that weren't quite what you asked. Implied, maybe, but what you—"

"I'm not sure if you are deliberately being obtuse or if Mulldoos was right in guessing that you had been kicked in the head by your horse. Report, Sergeant. Immediately."

Vendurro nodded. "I'm here on account of Mulldoos, Cap. Something's got to be done."

"Oh?" the captain asked. "And what would you have me do, precisely? Do you imagine that I can undo Rusejenna's memorycraft and restore him? Make the sands in the hourglass flow up instead of down?"

Vendurro looked to me and I shrugged my shoulders and gave him a sympathetic look back. "Well, maybe no undoing what's been done, but—and this ain't me telling you how to captain, Cap, make no mistake—thinking it might be a good idea for you to talk to him."

"Talk to him," Braylar repeated without inflection.

"Ayyup. Little while ago, Sergeant of Scouts came back, the little one, Rudgi, with the freckles and upturned nose?"

"I am aware who my Sergeant of Scouts is, Sergeant of the Obvious."

"Right. Well, she reported to Mulldoos, or tried to anyways. He looked ready to rip her in half. That is, if he had two good arms—hard to do much ripping with just the one. Anyway, he cursed her out, still slurring, and while she took it well enough, he dismissed the hells out of her before I heard what she saw or didn't see."

The captain looked displeased, though whether because of receiving a half-report, hearing his lieutenant's condition, or something else, it was impossible to say.

I'd seen Rudgi once or twice before. She was one of the handful of women in our company. In Anjuria, a woman might be pressed to fight if her home were invaded, but I'd never heard of any being part of the military. The Syldoon had no such compunction, and while they didn't have a large contingent of female soldiers, they certainly existed here or there. I wondered how they dealt with being surrounded by coarse men, especially those prone to violence. But I assumed they must have been able to hold their own.

"You do realize," Braylar said, snapping off every word, "that the advantage of having officers at all is that they can handle issues themselves and only alert me to the ones that require my immediate attention."

Vendurro nodded. "I hear you, Cap. I tried talking to Mulldoos, to find out what Rudgi reported, and he near bit my face off too. Worse than usual, I mean. Never seen him like this. And when he dismissed the hells out of me, just went back to closing his eyes and propping a tree up with his back like he's been doing. Figured you'd want to know about it, is all." Then he pointed at the rushes. "Awww, plague me, hate to see that."

I looked where he indicated and saw a mummified bird of some kind. "What's the matter? Why?"

"That's a duck," he said, as if that explained everything.

"And what is the significance?" I asked. "Why is that worse than a crane or any other dead thing on the shore?"

Vendurro replied, "Just got a soft spot for them, is all."

"Ducks?" I asked.

"Ayyup. Back where I come from, my tribe, they put a lot of stock in ducks. Our totem, as it were."

I thought he might have been putting me on, but if so, it was masterful, as his face was as flat and expressive as the lake. I asked again, "Ducks?"

"Ducks," he said. "You name another animal that can walk, swim, and fly that well. Go on. Name one. Can't, can you? That's because there ain't another. Leastwise that I know about. Kind of special, like that, ducks are."

I had to admit—I'd never thought about it like that before. Still . . . a totem?

He turned to Braylar, "Always struck me as odd there weren't no Duck Tower. In Sunwrack, that is." As soon as the words were out of Vendurro's mouth it looked like he wished he could recall them.

Hearing the name of the capital city we were all fugitives from, the captain's already dark mood went all black. Without another word he stalked up the hill, one hand on Bloodsounder.

Vendurro kicked a piece of driftwood. "Plague me. Just never know when to shut my plaguing yap." He started up the hill as well.

I glanced around. Vendurro did have a point earlier—between haunted tombs, forsaken temples, deserted plague villages, and now desolate and deadly lakes, the captain did seem to be drawn to the strangest and least hospitable locations in the world.

And with that, I followed the two of them away from the eerily still water and the odd bestial corpses that ringed it.

Braylar, Vendurro, and I walked through the pickets and tents, and Syldoon nodded or saluted the sergeant and captain and pointedly ignored me. Though Skeelana was a manipulative viper, she at least had been one other person in the company I could chat with who was also an outsider of sorts. With her gone, I was relegated again to the fringes, or even farther, given the captain's foul mood and Vendurro doing double duty of late.

When I saw that we were heading towards Mulldoos, I nearly walked off towards the wagon instead. He was difficult enough to deal with under the best circumstances, and the last few days had *not* been the best. Despite all their bickering, it was clear he and Hewspear were close, and no change in the older Lieutenant's condition had to be weighing on him. But even if Hewspear had been back on his feet, Mulldoos himself was hardly better, still stricken by whatever Rusejenna had done to him in Sunwrack before Braylar brained her.

Still, if calamity were approaching, it was better to hear about it now than to sit in the wagon and wonder, dreaming up the worst scenarios imaginable. So I followed the captain and sergeant. Vendurro looked at me and whispered, "Best not to mention the eye. Or the face. Or really anything about him. Ayyup. Best not to say much of nothing."

Sound advice.

The pale lieutenant was ignoring us as we approached, back against the gnarled trunk of one of the odd twisty trees, his eyes closed.

Captain Killcoin asked, "So answer true, Lieutenant, how are you faring?"

I was fairly certain Mulldoos wasn't sleeping, but he took his time opening his eyes and replying, and I understood instantly why. The left side of his face was still immobile, and his words came out slurred, "Plaguing fantastic, Cap. Never been better. Can't barely use this arm for shit. Sight's all blurry. Got the balance of newborn colt, the energy of an old man. I—" he swallowed hard, and it looked like it took real effort. "Yeah. Real plaguing good."

Mulldoos closed his eyes again and leaned his head back, and I was secretly glad of it—seeing that drooping eye on one side and murder in the other was as disconcerting as it got, no matter what warnings Vendurro gave.

For once, Braylar seemed at a loss for what to say. Slowly, he went down on one knee and laid his hand on the big man's shoulder. "You know as well as I, the effects of some memory magic aren't permanent."

Without opening his eyes again, Mulldoos slurred, "Ain't like you to deal in false hope, Cap. Figure you owe me better than that."

"Very well. No one knows if you will regain what you've lost. But you are alive still. That's something. And so long as you manage to remain so, you will have the chance to visit some measure of vengeance on Cynead. Hold on to that, if nothing else."

Mulldoos laughed, though with only half his mouth working, it was a broken, ghastly thing. "Hate's the only thing keeping me going right now. That, and trying hard not to shit myself. Got no time for nothing but those two things."

Braylar grabbed Mulldoos by the arm that seemed nearly paralyzed and shook him hard. "You will make time. You are still an officer of the Jackal Tower. The men depend on you. I depend on you. Do your job. Stew in your self-pity all you like, but maintain and do your job, Syldoon. I owe you the truth, yes? Well, you owe me your service, and you will perform your duties to the best of your abilities, even if they are halved. You might very well shit yourself, and if you do, you will wipe it off and keep doing your duty, as you have always done. Do you understand me?"

Mulldoos opened his eyes again, and the good one was focused and hot as he jerked his shoulder away. "Duty and performance, is it? That's rich, coming from you. How many times did me and Hew, Ven, even your plaguing scribbler there, cover for you, prop you up when your flail was doing its best to lay you low? More times that I can plaguing count is how many. And now Hew is husked and me . . . well, I can barely sit the saddle, or walk twenty paces without getting spinny like I been drinking half a day. All I ever been good at is fighting and teaching other whelps how to fight, but now I couldn't hardly take Arki there. Even jawing at you now is winding me. Lot of plaguing good hate does when you can't even—"

Braylar buffeted him across the chest with the back of his hand, rocking the beefy lieutenant into the tree. Mulldoos started to push off the bark, mostly with the right arm, when Braylar backhanded him in the chest again.

I'd seen Mulldoos angry a hundred times, but for the first time witnessed naked fury contorting half his face, with the other oddly slack. I thought for sure he would strike the captain back and looked around, noticing Vendurro was doing the same.

Braylar hissed, "We are as we are, Mulldoos. Damaged, diminished, yes, but not dead. Not yet. And until such time, you will get your ass out of the dust and do your duty. I do not care if the men see you wobble, or curse, or struggle, but they will not see you succumb. I thought we were damned in the streets of Sunwrack, penned in as we were against overwhelming odds. And I was willing to offer myself up, just as you were, for a chance to spare the men. Our men. But that was a mistake. We fought free at tremendous cost, Lieutenant, but free we are. And now . . . now we die with weapons in hand or readying the troops, no matter what else befalls us. We do not surrender. We do not succumb. And we do not lie in the dirt bemoaning our fates. Have I made myself clear?"

Mulldoos glared at him, and I half expected him to reach for his falchion or try to grapple the captain, but instead he turned and spat into the dirt. Or tried. At least half the spittle landed on his chin, and Mulldoos laughed then, reached up with his good arm, wiped it off with his fist, then shook his head. "Real plaguing inspiration to the troops I am."

Vendurro said, "They don't look to you for spitting lessons, Mull. Just being there, among them, that will go a long ways. They just need to see you, is all."

Mulldoos glared at the sergeant as Braylar stood back up. "You think so, do you? Just me tripping amongst the troops going to boost morale, is it?"

Vendurro didn't hesitate. "Not the tripping part so much, no. Maybe you ought to just settle for standing for now. Leaning against something. But ayyup, telling it true. We need you. So do what Cap here says. For once." He smiled. Mulldoos did not.

Braylar offered his arm and Mulldoos glared at that too. But the captain left it hanging there until Mulldoos finally clasped forearms and Braylar hoisted him to his feet. Mulldoos hadn't been exaggerating his condition—he did look besotted. But he found his footing and nodded once.

The captain gave his big shoulder one more squeeze. "Very good. Now then, let us check—"

Vendurro interrupted. "Cap." He pointed and we all looked and saw a Syldoon running towards us, covered in the dust of the road. He thumped his chest and spun his salute.

"Report, Syldoon."

The soldier replied, "Way's clear ahead, Captain. Far as we can tell, that is. But we got company from the rear."

Braylar said, "I imagine if it was the Imperial army on our heels, you would have a bit more urgency in delivering the news, yes?"

The soldier nodded. "Sorry, Captain. Couple of scouts ought to be here straight away."

Braylar took a step forward so that the soldier was close enough to smell his breath. "Are you trying to tell me that the only Syldoon who can actually inform me of anything have yet to arrive? I do hope you didn't interrupt us here just to tell me that. Because then I would be left thinking you are either a simpleton or you are intentionally doing your best to frustrate me, and neither option will do."

The solider turned crimson and stared straight ahead. "No, Captain. That is, I only meant to say that the scouts are escorting your sister. They'll be here shortly."

The captain stepped back and nodded.

Mulldoos shook his head and said, "Well, ain't that a hard kick to the jewels."

The reporting soldier glanced at him after hearing the muddled words and then quickly looked away, but not before Mulldoos noticed. "You got anything else to say, you dumb prick? That the sum total of your report? Anything else you want to add just now?"

The soldier kept his eyes fixed straight ahead. "No, Lieutenant."

"Good. Then get your poxy ass out of here, you stupid whoreson. Dismissed."

The soldier saluted again, spun on his heel, and headed towards the rest of the troops with the fastest walk possible, clearly glad to be away from his temperamental officers.

Vendurro puffed out his cheeks and exhaled loudly. "What are you supposing that means, Cap? Soff following us, showing up?"

Mulldoos replied before Braylar could, "Can't be nothing good, I'll tell you that plaguing much."

The captain locked his hands behind his back and started walking. "I cannot say what she intends. Or what motivates her from minute to minute. I never could. But we would not have escaped Sunwrack without her surprising intervention. That much is certain."

Mulldoos said, "You can't seriously be thinking of welcoming her with open arms, Cap? Been betrayed by one Memoridon bitch already, and they all lick Cynead's rings now, every last one of them. Mems are the enemy, every last one."

Braylar gave a twitch-smile. "Perhaps. But I doubt very much the Emperor authorized her to help destroy an Imperial battalion. She acted on her own. I reserve judgment as to what game she plays, but she did aid us. No doubt for her own purposes. But there is a good chance we would all be dead or in irons if she hadn't assisted us. There is no disputing that."

Mulldoos spit again, and managed it only slightly better now that he was upright. Then he slurred, "Mistake to trust her, is all I'm saying, Cap. Plaguing huge mistake."

The captain started walking to the camp. "That is entirely possible. We shall see."

Three riders crossed the field towards our camp, and with her scaled cuirass and red cloak and hair, it wasn't difficult to pick out Soffjian in the middle. The two Syldoon escorting her were hanging back slightly, whether out of fear, distaste, or healthy respect, it was hard to say. One of them I recognized as the beak-nosed Benk, an impudent soldier whom Braylar had to browbeat earlier when we captured Henslester. The captain, Mulldoos, Vendurro, and I waited for the trio to rein up.

Azmorgon was there too, impossible to miss, as he towered over every human I'd ever seen and made Mulldoos look svelte, thick with muscle and fat. When I first saw him in the Jackal Tower, I hadn't realized he was a lieutenant, and it was only after we fled Sunwrack that I saw he was in our company at all. Being unknown, and massive, and with a mean smile mostly hidden in a bristly beard that could have been home to several small animals, he was intimidating, and made me wish Hewspear was standing in his place instead. And hope against hope that he might recover.

The horses halted in front of us. Braylar said, flatly, "Sister."

"Brother," Soffjian replied. She looked over her shoulder at Benk just behind her and then back to the captain. "While I do appreciate the armed guards, it was hardly necessary. I do not require protection. And if I'd intended to attack, I can assure you they would hardly have slowed me down."

Mulldoos looked ready to spit, and then reconsidered, given how challenging that was proving of late. "Memoridons got no immunity to weapons. Just ask your dead sister."

Soffjian took Mulldoos in, head cocked slightly, and if he felt uncomfortable beneath her gaze, he gave no sign. Then she said, "Well, Rusejenna cannot argue your point. Though it appears she struck first, and hard. Let me guess. Limbs not working properly, blurry vision, dizziness, fatigue, half that horrible mouth of yours frozen to muddle your words, and an even worse disposition?"

Mulldoos laid his hand on the pommel of his falchion. "Only need one good limb, you mouthy bitch."

"And I need less than that to dispose of the likes of you." She eyed him up and down. "Especially in your current condition. You have spittle on your chin."

Azmorgon boomed a laugh. "She's got you there, Mully. Sounds like you got wet mushrooms in your mouth, and you been hamstrung real good too."

Mulldoos didn't bother looking up at the lieutenant. "Watch your plaguing tongue, Ogre."

"Sure thing, Mushrooms. Sure thing."

Before Mulldoos could respond, Soffjian turned her attention back to her brother. "But I didn't come here to squabble with you or your men or to do battle. In fact, I could do with a rest. I've developed an unhealthy habit of coming to your rescue, though it appears I did not do nearly enough. How many men do you have remaining?" She looked back at the Jackals soldiers. "One hundred and fifty? Perhaps a few more than that?"

Braylar smiled, or snarled; sometimes it was difficult to tell the difference. "Perhaps. But depleted or not, you clearly have assisted us. There is no doubt on that count. The question, as always, is one of motivation. Just as you did in the plague village, and on the road home against the Hornmen, you do nothing without being driven by the ulterior. So. Why did you help us escape from Sunwrack, sweet sister?"

She swung her leg over and dropped from the saddle, as ever, with grace and no small amount of haughtiness, despite being covered in dust and looking tired beyond measure. "I'd pretend to be wounded, but I simply don't have the energy for games. Helping you escape was the least of it, really."

Braylar looked intrigued. "Oh? And how is that?"

She pulled her ranseur out of the long leather sleeve on the side of her horse and dropped it over her shoulder. "Would you be so kind as to have one of your men tend to my horse, Bray? I'm afraid I didn't think to bring a second mount, and he could do with some care. I'd do it myself, but beyond fielding your questions, I will also need to rest. And food. I've been in the saddle for most of the last two days, and have barely closed my eyes."

Mulldoos was not sympathetic. "What makes you think you're riding with us? You're licking Cynead's hairy jewels now, which makes you the enemy, no matter what you did in Sunwrack."

"Which makes me doubly glad you are not leading the troops," she replied. "While my brother is stubborn to the point of madness, he does very little without considering things from all angles. One of his few redeeming qualities, really."

Azmorgon spoke, his voice rumbly and growly and difficult to discern, like it belonged to a brown bear that had somehow learned human speech but utterly failed to master enunciation and clarity. "You going to let her squawk at you like that, Cap."

"Her squawk, loathsome as it is, has the ring of truth to it." Braylar pointed at one of the soldiers who had dismounted and was standing at attention. "Many thanks for escorting my sister. Please take her horse and treat it as your own. While her tenure here could prove incredibly short, let it never be said we are poor hosts for the duration."

The Syldoon saluted and while he looked none too happy, said, "Aye, Cap," before taking the reins.

Soffjian nodded. "Many thanks." And then she seemed to catch herself as she looked at our small group. "I see the Ogre there, of course, but where is Hewspear? I do hope Rusejenna didn't strike him down. Of all of you, I enjoyed his company the most."

Vendurro replied, "Alive. But Rusejenna husked him good. He hasn't come to at all. Not even stirred a little. Can you help him with that?"

Mulldoos gave the sergeant a black look with his good eye and Vendurro held up his hands. "Memory magic done him in, maybe it can help him, too. You ain't seen him lately, Mull, but it's bad. Real bad."

Soffjian gave a small, sad smile. "I can take a look at him. But I am skilled in the art of rending, shredding, and destroying. Repair is best left to those with more tender talents. If Skeelana hadn't proved herself a serpent, she would be my first suggestion." Vendurro's face fell and she reiterated, "I will look, though. I will look."

Mulldoos used his good arm to push Vendurro back. "Sergeant here ain't speaking for us, witch. Cap'll decide who looks at what around here. It were me, you'd get a good look at the bottom of my boot and nothing more."

"I'm sorry," Soffjian said, "I couldn't quite make that out. It sounds as if you have half a loaf of soggy bread in your mouth."

"Go fuck a leper, you haughty—"

Braylar shouted, "Enough, the both of you!" When Mulldoos and Soffjian remarkably held their tongues, he continued, "Now. As much as I enjoy and even admire a good dissemble, Soff, the laws of hospitality dictate that good guests would do well to answer direct questions with direct answers. You said there was more beyond clearing our path. Explain."

Soffjian nodded. "So I did. I have been following you the last two days, trying to scrub the land clean of any of your memory debris you leave behind." She looked at Vendurro. "As I said, far better at obliterating than healing." Then she turned back to Braylar. "While I was there when a good chunk of this company was hung, there are Memoridons bonded to the rest, and surely Cynead has them trying to track you. So I cleared your trail as much as I could, and picked up pieces of it and scattered them around further afield, hoping to prevent any other Memoridons from hounding you. I cannot promise it will work. You have a lot of men. And while I disregarded any memory trails I could have hunted myself, that still left a large number. Have I mentioned that I haven't slept?"

"You did," Braylar replied. "And yet you still haven't answered my question, sister. And I'm afraid until you do, you cannot remain in this camp. Why do you help us? You are beholden to Cynead now. You are either attempting to betray him or play us, and neither would prove a wise move."

She turned back around and faced us, the lightning bolt of a vein pulsing in her forehead. "No. Forgive me. As I said, I am exhausted." Soff lowered the ranseur and stuck the butt spike in the earth. "I would have guessed my actions in Sunwrack spoke for themselves. But I will not live under Cynead's yoke. It was difficult enough being controlled by a Tower Commander, but at least Darzaak is a fair man. Honorable, if hard. Now that Cynead is unopposed and unchecked, his ambitions are limitless. He will lead the Syldoon to ruin, and with them, all Memoridons leashed to his hand. You are fighting against that, as is Thumaar, I suspect. So I fall in with you. Not out of any loyalty to you, of course. I have none. But because I see no other choice."

Braylar twitch-smiled and said, "You do know that's exactly what we would have done, if we had somehow made the discovery first? We would have bound you all to Thumaar."

"I have no illusions, brother, and I am no fool. Of course I assumed such was the case. And perhaps all men would become tyrants with unchecked power in time. Still, the deposed emperor is more temperate and less likely to abuse. With Cynead, it would be immediate. Irreversible. He will lead us to ruin. That, I am certain of. Your outfit might possess the means of stripping him of that power."

"Horseshit," Mulldoos said, sounding drunk. "Ain't buying it, Cap."

Soffjian looked at him. "Careful, Lieutenant. You are slobbering again."

"And you got caltrops in your cunny. But you're holding back, sure as spit."

"There you go again with those troublesome esses."

The captain snapped, "Enough of this. I share his skepticism, Soff. While I have no doubt that you do not want Cynead holding the chains that bind you, I strongly suspect you want no chains at all."

She nodded slowly. "Who among us wants chains, brother? I risk a great deal on this gamble. Everything, in fact." She pulled a sealed scroll out of a pouch on her belt and handed it to her bother. "Darzaak assured me you were close. That your scribe there," she said, looking at me with those intense and disconcerting eyes, "was on the cusp of unraveling mysteries, unlocking the secret. So I agreed to throw my lot in with you, broke the blockade in Sunwrack, and I am here now."

Braylar cracked the wax seal, flicked the pieces off, and began to read. "That seems decidedly rash, for one so prone to evaluating everything coldly and deliberately. The good Commander might have oversold our ability to break any chains, let alone reforge them."

Soffjian laughed. "Be that as it may. What's done is done. I am here now. And as you can read, Darzaak promised that if I aid you, I will be freed forever."

Braylar passed the scroll to Mulldoos. "And how long do you have, sister?"

She returned his hard look in kind. "Two tenday. Maybe less. I've never tested the limits before."

I asked, "How long until what?"

No one answered right away, and then Vendurro cleared his throat. When that was met with more silence, he said, hesitantly, "Memoridons got to report back to the Tower that controls them. Or this case, Emperor. While Syldoon always had Memoridons to chase them down if they went missing, the Memoridons themselves got a whole different reason for having to fly back to the coop."

"OK. What does that mean? What compels them? Clearly it isn't loyalty."

As soon as the words were out of my mouth I wanted to recall them, but Soffjian laughed a short mirthless laugh and replied, "Isn't that the truth. No, it is forced fealty, Arki. A Memoridon has to return to the frame, in this case, held by the Emperor."

"And what happens if she doesn't return?"

Soffjian favored me with a mirthless smile. "If a Memoridon goes too long without reporting back, convening with the frame, there will be a surge, and one of two things will happen. Her powers will be burnt out of her forever. Or she herself will be snuffed out. So. I do hope you translate quickly. Now I need to rest before continuing to scrub our trail clean. With your leave, brother."

Soffjian gave a small bow and turned on her heel, and began striding away before actually waiting to hear what Braylar said.

Mulldoos held his tongue until she was out of earshot and then turned to Braylar. "You ain't really thinking of trusting her, are you, Cap?"

Braylar was watching a hawk circle lazily far above us as he replied, "Can you trust a viper to sheathe its fangs?"

"Well, maybe not the smartest move to wear one around your neck then." It was difficult to hear his words eliding wetly, but while most people would have been self-conscious, Mulldoos soldiered on as if he weren't afflicted at all, only looking more prone to violence than usual as his mouth betrayed him, but making no move to talk less or pay attention to how muddled he sounded. Perhaps Braylar's speech had inspired him, but I suspected he would have kept talking out of pure spite regardless, especially after Soffjian taunted him.

Braylar tore his gaze away from the circling hawk. "She is dangerous, there is no dispute, but she has proved invaluable on two occasions now, instrumental in saving us."

"And you," Vendurro offered, and then looked sheepish as the captain glared at him. "Well, it was mostly Skeelana on that score. But—" the captain's glare sharpened. "Yeah, she saved us all twice."

Mulldoos shook his head, and that much at least without impediment or difficulty. "Can't train a snake, Cap. Only a matter of time before she sinks her teeth into your neck."

Azmorgon rumbled. "Aye. Me and Mushrooms agree on that score."

Mulldoos flashed the massive lieutenant a hateful look as Vendurro said, "I saw a Gurtagese once, had a box full of snakes. And they seemed to mind him well enough. Doing tricks, even. Tying themselves in knots on command. Never seen anything else like it. People throwing money at him, dumbfounded they were."

The pale lieutenant looked ready to spit and thought better of it. "If it wasn't a horse that kicked you in the head, it I can't figure what knocked your brain box loose." He returned his attention to the captain. "Hew were here, he'd say just what I'm saying. I didn't like having her around when she was a Jackal. But now—"

Braylar cut him off, "Now her fate is tangled with ours. Soffjian has broken with the Emperor just as we have, though for reasons of her own. She is no less an outcast and branded traitor. And for the now, that makes her a useful tool and uneasy ally. One that could prove valuable again."

Mulldoos shook his big head again. "Tools don't hate, Cap. Same ain't true of your sister." And then he walked off, though with one leg seemingly at odds with the other.

Azmorgon shook his hoary head, chuckling. "You got a bitch of a sister, Cap. Right bitchy, she is. But she gives Mushrooms the business. Entertaining as hell, that."

Vendurro said, "You got a queer sense of fun, you do."

Azmorgon replied, "Wouldn't be the first I've heard that, Squirrel."

There was a silence as we watched both lieutenants leave. Vendurro broke it by saying. "Weren't making that up. About the snakes. Saw it with my own eyes. He had them doing tricks that just weren't snakelike at all. Unnatural. But Mulldoos got one thing right—a brass viper bit the handler right in the eye. Poor bastard's whole head swelled up, skin turned black and purple. Died screaming. So, yeah, snakes are real dangerous."

Braylar laughed, and while it was abrupt and disappeared so quickly it was easy to think I'd only imagined it, it sounded like he was genuinely amused. But then he stood there silently, gazing off towards the placid polished lake with so many dead things littering the shore, like sacrifices made by foolish locals. Or perhaps by the lake itself. And the levity was gone as he said, "Nothing is certain, save death. The only mystery is the means and who bears witness."

With that, he turned and walked away as well.

Vendurro waited until he was out of earshot before giving a low whistle. "It was just a snake."

I replied, "This animosity between the captain and his sister—"

"Hatred, more like. Animosity sounds way too plaguing polite to cover it."

"Hatred then," I agreed. "But it is obviously more involved than a failed attempt to revenge his father. They were only children, and Soffjian mentioned something that sounded like it occurred years later, with the Syldoon. Do you know anything about that?"

"Happened before I was a Jackal," he replied. "Cap was never one to talk about it. Which meant no one else was one to talk about it either. So can't rightly say. And you'd have bigger jewels than the snake handler if you ask him about it." He slapped me on the back. "Come on. Figure you got some penning or reading of some kind to do. Best get to it and get some rest. Figure tomorrow won't be no shorter than today."

I returned to the wagon and recorded the events of the day and then translated by lamplight until I couldn't fight sleep off any longer and collapsed into an ink-stained heap. But as usual, my bladder got the best of me and roused me sometime before dawn. It always seemed to conspire against me like that, no matter how exhausted I was or how little I drank before collapsing.

I tossed and turned under my thin blanket, hoping I could fall back asleep, but my bladder was insistent, so I cursed quietly, threw the blanket aside, and clambered out of the wagon. As expected, most of our makeshift camp was asleep, some in the handful of wagons, but most in small wedge tents or huddled masses around the campfires that had died out.

There were plenty of guards posted around the perimeter, and I knew Captain Killcoin had mounted men screening the countryside to alert us of any hostile advances. Still, even with those assurances, it was peculiar to walk among a sleeping camp. All these violent men in repose, the entire camp silent. A few Syldoon who were guarding a line of picketed horses saw me, one nodding, the other two ignoring me. And again I was reminded that soldiering seemed to be nine parts boredom—waiting, training, erecting or pulling down camps, tedious chores, moving—and one part horrible, sudden, and irrevocable violence.

I shivered and headed into a thicket of reeds. I was unlacing my hosen when I looked down the small incline towards the placid lake and saw a lone figure there along the shore, still as stone.

After relieving myself, I nearly walked back towards the wagon to get back under the covers, hoping for one more blessed hour of sleep before Braylar gave the command to pack up and get moving again, but as usual, my curiosity got the better of me just as often as my bladder.

I walked towards the lake, wondering who else found it as fascinating as I did. As I got closer, I should have guessed. Even with everything in shades of gray, I saw moonlight glinting off the tines of the ranseur. That should have stopped me immediately and sent me back up the hill, but for some reason my feet kept me moving forward.

Soffjian surely heard my footfalls and the tiny cascade of pebbles, but didn't seem especially alarmed or concerned. She was also much better at guessing. Still facing the water, she said, "My brother does have a talent for finding lonely locales. And you seem to have a habit of meeting Memoridons in the dark of night. I would curb that if I were you."

That seemed designed to drive me off, and should have really, but failed. I took a few more hesitant steps, knowing I wouldn't have too many opportunities to speak with her without arousing suspicion or animosity among the Syldoon. "No, you Memoridons are dangerous to be certain. But I don't think I was the only one surprised that Skeelana threw in her lot with the Emperor like that."

"No," she replied, smiling ever so slightly, "but you were the only one to be seduced by her. Or were you hoping it was the other way around?"

I felt my face flush as I stammered, "There wasn't any . . . she didn't seduce me. It was . . . it was only a kiss. One. Singular. How did you—"

"Your boyish infatuation wasn't lost on anyone with half a brain. Which means I was the only one who likely noticed. So I hazarded a guess."

"You . . . you didn't know?"

"Not until now. How interesting. Though hardly shocking. Skeelana won many people over with her plucky charm. Why should an overtrusting boy prove any different? But you are right about that—it turns out she was far more devious than anyone suspected." She snapped her wrist and made a stone skip across the waveless water, just as her brother had. "So, young scribe, back to our original point, I have to confess I am surprised you sought me out here. Clearly, not driven by romance this time. Why are you not abed, as you obviously should be?"

"I was about to ask you the same. I came out to, well, it doesn't matter. But not seeking anyone out, that's for certain. I saw you down here, and was curious. Are you riding out now?"

She dragged the butt spike of her polearm through the gravelly sand, flicking some out into the water, resulting in more of a plonking sound than any kind of splash. The water was heavy indeed. "Soon. I wanted to look at this very unusual lake once before I did though. I'd heard rumors of it before but never had cause to visit." She turned and faced me, grounding the ranseur in the loose soil. "But you did not come down here to ask after my sleeping habits or to discuss peculiar lakes, did you? If you have more to say, do so now. Otherwise, leave me in peace."

Yes, they were family.

I considered that coming down here might not have been the wisest course for any number of reasons and nearly excused myself to rush back to the wagon, but here I was, and the opportunity was there as well. "Captain Killcoin told me about your father. How he was murdered. And how he, your brother that is, how he fled when your priest called on you to attend him in the deadroom."

While she had been flitting around amusement before, a mask seemed to slide into place as she said, flatly, "Did he?"

I pressed on. "He did. Though the thing that struck me was, it sounded as if you two were close. Closer, anyway. Which surprised me, given your . . . relationship now."

"Oh? And how would you quantify our relationship now, scribe?"

After thinking about it for a moment, I replied, "Severed. Or severe. I'm still trying to figure it out. But unpleasant for sure. "

That actually earned a laugh, but it was short and clipped and harsh around the edges. "I do so appreciate your forthrightness. Remarkable. And as to my brother's flight from the deadroom, well, it must be so very painful to admit that your sister is stronger. I am surprised that he chose to reveal even that much. How very loquacious and generous of him. And what else did my brother say?"

"Not much," I admitted. "He stopped there."

"As well he would. It is one thing to admit some failure of courage. Permissible in one so young. Expected, even. But the subsequent failures? Revenge unfulfilled, that's one thing. Again, feckless youth can be blamed. But an entire people betrayed? No. That admission doesn't flow out of the mouth so easily, does it?"

I thought of a way to dip the question in honey but then simply replied, "How were your people betrayed? What is it you think he did?"

She pulled the ranseur out of the stones and sand as if yanking it from the body of a fallen foe and then laid the haft on her shoulder. "Not think. Know for a certainty. And you will need to ask him that, scribe. I do wonder what he will tell you. Now I have miles to ride and trails to clean."

She started up the incline, towards the camp. I was tired, and fought off a yawn, but I knew if I held off recording the latest entry and tried to sleep any more, the details would be lost come dawn. So I sighed and headed back to the wagon, resigned to lighting the lamp and uncorking some ink again.

I fell asleep sitting up, quill still in hand, my head leaning against the wooden rib that held up the canvas frame, and was jostled awake the next morning as I felt the wagon shift into motion and heard the familiar sounds that told me our company was on the move again—the creak of the axle, chains rattling overhead, pots jostling each other, the clomp of the horses' hooves all around us, men shouting orders up and down the line.

And of course, Braylar calling me out, "Attend me, Arki."

I made my way to the front of the wagon, hunchwalking as ever, dodging the swinging pots and tools, and climbed over the bench awkwardly as the wagon rolled over a rut and nearly sent me tumbling.

He said, "I would have thought you'd have mastered that by now, archivist. You've spent more time in a wagon than most drovers."

I took the dried goat he offered and stifled a yawn as the captain added, "And little better at getting rest when the opportunity affords itself. I assume you were up working. Any progress last night?"

I confessed that the forays into journals and scrolls and ledgers hadn't proved revealing, beyond some oblique references to things I'd already uncovered.

The captain nodded, clearly expecting that, but no less irritated to hear it. "Very well. Sup on our fine road fare, wash it down with some watery ale or equally watery wine—the choice is yours—and get back to your pens then."

I continued chewing, working the meat from one side of my mouth to the other like sinewy cud. "At least it makes the ale taste good. Or the wine. That's something."

Braylar allowed himself a tiny smile that wasn't burdened by a twitch but lasted so short a time it was easy to imagine it was merely a trick of the morning shadows. "I find your cheery disposition endlessly entertaining, Arki. I do wonder, though, if you will be able to maintain it, in the face of what

30

you witness and partake of. I hope you can, but it would be disingenuous of me to say I expect it. And I do know how you loathe falsehood. I almost feel some semblance of guilt for having lured you away from your quiet and tempest-free life."

I lifted the flask, drinking old wine that had a nasty vinegar bite to it, and swallowing the meat cud, trying not to choke. I considered Vendurro wrestling with his grief, and the difficult task of relaying the news of Glesswik's death to the widow and children, and how his walk, his stature, had changed. Was it irrevocable? Would he ever recover the spring in his step, or the carefree demeanor, having lost his best friend and being increasingly more burdened with more responsibilities, and witness to more loss? Why should I prove any different?

Lloi dying in my arms, killing not only one man, but now more, being betrayed by Skeelana . . . I said, "You told me not so very long ago that having tasted a touch of grief, I was that much closer to living a complete life. Perhaps I am just further along the road now."

He gave me a long evaluating look, then shook his head once. "I do say quite a lot of things."

"And many decidedly untrue or manipulative. But not that one. You spoke true. Didn't you?"

Braylar flexed a gloved hand, the leather stretching and creaking, and leaned back against the bench. "You are young still, but not daft. There are many cruel truths in life. I spoke but one. When you know what you can endure, then and only then do you know what you are capable of." He reached into a bag and handed me a wedge of cheese. "Now, fill your belly and get back to work. We—"

He stopped as he spotted a horseman riding hard down the road towards us, hooves kicking up dust. I assumed it was a scout returning, but the haste didn't bode well at all. Braylar stopped the team and called out behind us orders to halt, which were relayed down the line.

When the Syldoon reined up and saluted, red-faced, sweaty, and staring straight ahead, suspicions were confirmed—he was loath to deliver his news.

"Report," Braylar ordered.

The scout remained rigid in the saddle. "Screeners sighted a big company closing in on us, Cap. Two, in fact. North, and a little further northwest."

"Well, that is not welcome news, is it? How many in each?"

"Screeners didn't give an exact count, Cap, but—"

"An estimate then."

The scout looked as uncomfortable as you could just relaying information, but his posture didn't melt in the slightest. "More than us, for certain. Twice as many. In each company, Cap. Urglovians. The one directly ahead looks to be Governor Pinchurk's. And the one northwest—"

"Yes, yes, Governor Wezlik's. Thank you for the geography lesson. And how far away?"

"Half a day. Little more maybe."

Braylar scowled. "Dismissed. Rest yourself and your horse, Syldoon. Send another back down the road to fetch the screening party."

The soldier nodded and saluted again. "Aye, Cap," He rode down past our wagon quickly, clearly relieved to be relieved.

I asked, "How did they prepare such forces so quickly?"

Braylar turned and snapped at me, "Memoridons can send messages in an instant. Not all of them shred people's minds like my sweet sister. Our supreme advantage in intelligence is but one reason the Syldoon have been a superior army on nearly every battlefield we have tromped across. Only now they are no longer working in our interests, are they?"

Vendurro and the massive Azmorgon rode up alongside side us, with Mulldoos pitched at an odd angle in his saddle behind and Hewspear next to him.

Mulldoos said, "Telling you, you shouldn't be in the plaguing saddle, you old goat. Holy hells, you just got husked—you ought to be resting."

Hewspear's eyes were a little sunken, and there was a waxy sheen to his skin, but he sat the saddle better than Mulldoos, back straight, and had an uneven smile. "While your concern is amusing, I've napped long enough."

"Plague me, I want you in a wagon so I don't have to hear your smacking gums, you wrinkled ass."

Braylar gave Hewspear a long appraising look. "I am very glad to see you among us again, Lieutenant. Glad indeed." Then he looked at the other officers. "I do hate to ruin a good reunion, but you all saw the scout, no doubt?"

"That we did," Mulldoos slurred, and immediately looked furious that his mouth was still betraying him. "Bad?"

"Certainly not good. The Urglovians are out in force ahead of us."

Vendurro asked, "Too many to take on, expecting?"

"You expect right," the captain said. "We will not engage unless we have to. I didn't break free of Sunwrack only to let the men die in the wild."

Azmorgon boomed, "Sure would like to take on somebody somewhere. Yeah, maybe they weren't the ones that laid into us and killed our brothers on the bridge, but they're aligned with those whoresons. Leopards, Anjurians, Urglovians, no matter. Like to make somebody bleed a lot of blood. Lot of blood."

"Yeah, ours," Mulldoos replied, again siding with the captain so long as someone else seemed to be opposing him. "Cap says we change course, we change course."

Azmorgon dwarfed Mulldoos, no easy task, and even his huge stallion looked like a pony underneath him. "You telling me you don't want to cut up some witches, Mushrooms?"

Mulldoos urged his horse closer and laid his hand on the hilt of his falchion. "Keep calling me that. Go on. One good arm is all I need, you ogre fuck."

Braylar slapped the side of the bench. "We do not bloody ourselves and we don't throw our lives away simply in the name of misbegotten revenge. When the time and place is right, we will cut them deep, but that will be ground of our choosing and when the odds are in our favor. For now, we veer west and work around the Urglovians."

Hewspear waved at some gnats, doing no good at all. "I imagine they have some Memoridons in their company, Captain?" He said this nonchalantly, as if he hadn't had his brains nearly melted the last time we all saw him in the saddle.

Braylar nodded slowly. "They likely do, so they will report our movements for certain to the Imperials. But we have mobility as the advantage for now."

I wondered what he meant by that, since we had so many supply wagons that slowed our convoy down considerably, but it didn't seem prudent to ask just then as he announced, "We head back south, then west, slip past them."

I heard Soffjian's voice coming up behind us. "That would likely prove a very bad idea, brother."

Everyone turned and looked and saw the Memoridon with three soldiers, one of them Benk, looking none too happy to be accompanying Soffjian again. Braylar said, irritation smoldering, "And why is that, sister?"

She smiled at Hewspear. "So. Not dead then? That at least is some good news."

"How many, how far?" Braylar asked.

Soffjian pointed a long finger at Benk. "I saw the young Syldoon here on their way to you, in a hurry from the looks of it. I accompanied and asked this one very nicely to explain the urgency."

Braylar said, irritation flaming higher, "So forthright, my men."

Benk colored up. "The wi—" He stopped himself, cleared his throat, and tried again. "The Mem here, your sister, I mean. Real persuasive. I hurried though."

"Why, of course you did. And what is the news then?"

Benk looked at the other two soldiers and then replied, "There's a large company of Urglovians coming in from the west. Big one. Three or four hundred."

Braylar drummed his gloved fingers on the bench. "How many miles apart they are they from the other forces, and how distant from us? Is it possible for us to slip between them?"

Benk looked at the other scout and shrugged. "What do you think? A dozen miles, maybe?"

Hewspear said, "If they have Memoridons, as seems likely, then slipping between or past doesn't seem viable."

The captain looked at his sister. "And to the south?"

Soffjian replied, "Near on a thousand, half a day. And there was no time to clean all your tracks. Go west or south and you go to your death and destruction."

Braylar slapped his thigh. "Well, as appealing as destruction sounds, it appears we have no choice. I have heard enough. East it is."

Mulldoos looked around at everyone, waiting for someone else to object, and when no one did, took it upon himself. "East, Cap? Nothing that way except for the Godveil. And that ain't any kind of way at all."

Before Braylar could reply, though, Soffjian did. "Astute, as ever. But my brother is right. Our only chance is to slip around the Urglovians and then continue north again."

Mulldoos glared at her, and with one eyelid sagging, it was hard to tell if that enhanced or diminished the effect. "We'll be penned in. And I wasn't speaking to you anyway, witch."

Braylar wrapped Bloodsounder's haft on the wagon bench to reclaim their attention. "We are penned in now! It is a broad enclosure at the moment, but they are clearly coordinating and that pen closes in tighter every moment we delay. Alert the troops. We go east—not to the Godveil, but east until we are clear."

Azmorgon, Mulldoos, and the scouts rode off one way and Soffjian another.

The captain sighed and then looked at Hewspear closely. "I have seen men felled by Memoridons who never recovered, so it is something of a miracle that you are in the saddle at all. I must say, you do look much better than expected, Hew. Is that deceptive?"

Hewspear smiled. "I do not profess to be fully healed, Captain. There is some dizziness, some nausea. But no, I am in much better condition than Mulldoos."

"I need you alert, competent, and capable, yes? Can you do this, Hew? Tell me true. If not, the best thing you can do for all of us is to heed the advice of your crass nursemother and get some rest."

Hewspear nodded, the coins in his beard clacking. "I will not do my duties unless I am confident I can ably perform them, Captain. I am well."

Braylar smiled. "Very good. See to it then."

Hewspear saluted smartly in that twisting, odd way the Syldoon had. "Aye, Captain. I will ascertain what we need from the scouts."

He held himself erect as he turned his horse about, but I suspected he had to be keenly and acutely feeling the aftereffects of Rusejenna's attack.

Vendurro must have been thinking the same thing. "Got to say, glad to see him up and moving and all, but . . ."

The captain glowered as only he was capable of. "He is as forthright as they come, and not half so mulish as Mulldoos. Hewspear will do nothing to endanger the men—if he says he is fit, he is fit, and there's an end to it."

"Aye, Cap." Vendurro rode back towards the rest of the soldiers as well.

I looked at Braylar and couldn't help gulping as I asked, "Captain, if we get trapped against the—"

"The Godveil is my concern. Translating is yours. Back to it, Arki."

I climbed back in and tried to focus on my job.

Our convoy changed direction and we rolled over the uneven terrain. While it wasn't as hilly as it had been in the first stretch of Urglovia, it was a far cry from the flat plains of Anjuria. The captain wasn't interested in any company at all, even silent company, and ordered me back into the wagon to continue translating. He didn't add "while there was still time," but then again, he didn't have to. Escape wasn't looking promising, and he had made it clear that we were not going to surrender. I tried very hard to focus on the worn pages in front of me, hoping to distract myself from envisioning mad charges to our doom, but I found myself rereading the same passages over and over again. Hours passed by and I made only halting progress.

It didn't help that most of the recent documents were exceedingly dull and mundane—more lay subsidies, catalogues of public works by some priest of Truth or another, and endless inventories of larders documenting depleted this or that at one temple or another. Even worse were manorial or baronial records and other texts written by secular parties, as there was almost no likelihood of encountering anything related to Memoridons, frames, cursed weapons, or anything else of interest. Still, I pressed on, but it was so odd to be reading the most boring tomes ever drafted while every mile likely brought us closer to obliteration.

When we broke to feed and water the horses, I took the opportunity to get out of the stifling wagon and stretch my legs and clear my head. I saw Hewspear standing alone in a field, running his palm across the very top of the feather grass as it blew gently in the dry breeze.

I was uncertain if he preferred to be alone, but in my experience, the only way to be certain was to ask. I approached and when he heard me he turned and favored me with a smile. He still looked waxy, and tired, and more bowed than usual, but his eyes were alert. I said, "How do you fare, Hewspear?"

The tall lieutenant replied, "I am alive, Arki, and that always beats the alternative."

"So it does. What I meant to ask was—"

"How am I recovering from having my mind nearly torn apart? Rusejenna wasn't able to complete her attack, thanks to the captain, which is the only reason I am alive at all. All things considered, I am actually remarkably well, in truth."

He reached up and tapped a long finger against his temple. "Some physicians at your university surely studied our brains, but so far as I have ever gleaned, no one has much of an idea of how things work up here. I'm not even sure Memoridons do. And they alone have the ability to deconstruct, dissect, and distress what the gods saw fit to give men for minds. It is an awesome and terrible power, and I am glad I was not cursed with it. More glad still I was not blasted apart by it. I am better off than Mulldoos, as it happens." He looked immeasurably sad saying that. "An admission that leaves me feeling unsettled. And guilty."

I'd never really considered it in that light before. I glanced back at the convoy and then said, "Can I ask you something?"

"But of course, young scholar."

I said, "It's clear why memory mages have been feared and hunted for millennia whenever they were foolish enough to be discovered, and why some priests and all Syldoon have sought to control them. They are terrifying, or at least intimidating. But I can't help notice that even before Rusejenna, Mulldoos harbored a very special hatred for Memoridons. Why is that exactly?"

The older officer turned to me slowly. I thought he might not answer at all when he finally replied, "I would suggest you pose that question directly to him, but we both know how that would likely end."

"With me on my back, gasping for air, or with his boot on my chest."

Hewspear smiled. "An accurate assessment. So I won't point you in his direction. But you must never mention that I told you this, or mention it at all really. Because a boot on your chest would be as good as it got. Understood?"

"Understood," I replied.

"Good. Walk with me for a bit then."

We moved off further away from the company, and Hewspear said, "You recall the manumission ceremony in Sunwrack?"

"The hangings? Yes, it's sort of seared in my memory. Nearly impossible to forget that."

"True. And doubly so when you are directly involved. I was witness to Mulldoos's ceremony, standing in the small crowd of Jackals. And this particular manumission was tragically similar to the one you yourself were witness to. Only both Memoridons seemed to struggle that day. It was clear from the start that someone would choke to death, possibly several someones."

"I meant to ask about that, Hewspear."

"Hew is fine, Arki."

Nodding, I said, "Hew, then. Why do the Syldoon hang all the men at once? Why not one at a time, so that there is less chance of the Memoridons allowing one to strangle to death?"

He continued walking at a leisurely pace. "An astute question. While there are some who posit that those recruits whom they sense will be hardest to bond with must be brought closer to death, that still doesn't entirely answer why they don't do them singly. The answer is terribly Syldoonian, I am afraid."

"Which is?"

"The manumission does have an element of gruesome pageantry to it, but it isn't simply for show, or even a ritual. For those slaves who elect to stay, to become full-fledged members of the Tower from that day forward, it is important they understand the weight of that decision. As well as the inherent dangers. They all accept the noose, knowing that there is a chance, however small, that they could die at the end of it moments later."

"So . . . this ensures that no one stays without seriously mulling over the consequences?"

"Correct. It is a decision that will impact the rest of their lives. Whether that proves to be decades or moments. They don't want anyone in the Tower who has not pledged their body and heart to their Towermates and the survival and success of the Tower itself."

I shook my head slightly. "That does make a rather terrible sort of sense. So, that day, when Mulldoos was hung, someone died? Or someones?"

Hewspear stopped walking. "Yes. Two, in fact. But it was the boy alongside Mulldoos, closest to the center, the last to hang, that scarred him."

I was suddenly wondering about the wisdom of pursuing this questioning at all. "He was close to the boy?"

Hewspear nodded. "Aye. Recruits are brought to the Empire from the hinterlands on all sides. Many have nothing in common at the start, possessing a variety of cultural trappings. Most don't speak the same language. But after ten years, they develop a kinship, a brotherhood, that is tougher than the best-forged steel. And nowhere was this more evident than between Mulldoos and Vreelan. I watched the two of them, and while the pair hated each other at first, no doubt too similar and hating the reflection, they grew to become closer than any two people I can recall seeing."

Under the gruff, belligerent, crass exterior, I suspected there was something . . . more relatable. Hewspear continued, "So when Vreelan went purple and dropped, Mulldoos was the first there to rip the noose free, and the first to know it was too late. The boy was dead."

Yes, some questions were better left unasked. "I can see how that would do it."

"Yes. To be fair, Mulldoos never liked the Memoridons before—his clan had hunted memory witches to near extinction time and time again in his land. But seeing his truest friend die because of their slowness or negligence? Yes, that branded his heart with an unwholesome hatred that has cooled little to this day."

I had trouble imagining a connection with another person like that. "That's tragic. I can't even fathom. But at the same time, it's the Towers themselves that order the Memoridons to perform this ceremony, correct? Aren't they more responsible, really?"

Hewspear started heading back in the direction of the convoy. "Oh, indeed that is the truth. But grief isn't always beholden to the truth, and is not especially fond of gradient or distinctions of subtlety. Mulldoos pledged his life to the Jackals the day he was hung and saved—he couldn't very well assign them responsibility. He blamed the Memoridons then, and will to the end of his days."

I nodded. "I can understand that. Truly. But what you just said brings up another point. Vreelan himself chose to be hung, knowing full well the risks that something could go horribly wrong. As you mentioned, that's part of the severity of the choice—risking your life for the promise of more, when you could simply walk away with less, but the surety that you will in fact walk away. Surely Mulldoos can't blame the Memoridons completely. Can he?"

Hewspear gave a small, sad smile. "Oh, I am sure he harbors some resentment for his dead comrade. He does have an impressive capacity for anger. But while the dead can make good scapegoats, they make poor targets for bile and bubbling hatred. Especially when the Memoridons in their multitudes are very much alive."

He looked down at me and said, "Which is precisely why I tell you to never speak to him of this. You think you have seen him in a state before? Ha. That is nothing at all. The years cool passions for some men, neutralize poison, soften the edges of grief and rage and prejudice. But for others, they hold on even tighter to the things that burn their insides out regardless of the passage of time, or even in spite of it, as if to curse the very world itself. Mulldoos is such a one."

He started back towards the camp. "Be grateful you have a moderate temperament and keen appreciation for subtlety. I hope they are never tested. Thank you for the walk."

⊕

After relieving myself I returned to the wagon, opened my case, and began again, despairing of ever finding anything else remotely useful to anyone. But I delved into a small book with a warped wooden cover and finally came across some passages that caught my interest. It was another account by an underpriest of Truth, Santrizzo. There was nothing immediately arresting— various descriptions of his duties and excursions to various villages in the vicinity of his temple. But Santrizzo mentioned more than once an acute curiosity for those things arcane. He chastised himself for it on more than one occasion, admitting that he would likely only bring down the wrath of the order by pursuing that line of thinking. And yet, he seemed drawn to all things peculiar or beyond the pale.

I pressed on, excited again to be translating something that appeared to be leading somewhere. Three hours later, I was nearly done recording and making notes, and couldn't fight a smile off my face. Finally, something noteworthy to share again.

And that's when Braylar called me back to the bench. I pulled the canvas flap aside and started to throw my leg over when he looked up and said, "No, span the crossbow and then take your seat here, along with a quiver."

I looked ahead and saw a village coming into view. It was larger than the plague village we'd occupied near Deadmoss, but not much. Though this one was clearly not deserted, as I saw several villagers running from the olive trees, dropping their baskets as they fled down the road towards their homes.

"Are we riding through the village?"

"We are. Crossthatch."

"Why?" I asked, suddenly as worried as if we'd just run across the entire Imperial army.

"Because that's where the road happens to go. Which is where wagons go. When they wish to travel. Which is what we are doing. Now span that bolter and be quick about it."

I wiped an ink-stained hand across my brow, mopping up sweat with my sleeve, and did as commanded.

When I stepped over and joined him on the bench, careful not to accidentally knock the trigger and discharge the bolt, I asked, "Do you want the blanket to cover the crossbow?" Before realizing the absurdity of the question, as we couldn't blanket an entire convoy. "Never mind."

He stopped whatever rebuke he had in mind and nodded. "Simply have the crossbow at the ready. Casual, but visible. Villagers do not pose a threat. They will likely hole up in their hovels until we pass. But one can never be too careful."

It was better than a battalion blocking our way, but I still felt uneasy, and more so as we approached the outskirts and the first few buildings. While a fair number of villagers might indeed have been hiding, many were out, and staring openly at the convoy as it rolled up.

A large party of villagers were walking down the road towards us, and every whitewashed house with thatched roofs we passed revealed more of them standing and watching, their hosen rolled down to their knees, broad straw hats everywhere, dirty linen, lean figures, spare and sinewy. Most were holding some agrarian instrument or other—sickles, scythes, pitchforks. While they couldn't be blamed for holding the tools of their craft, I found it hard to believe they had all been using them just then. And they did not look especially welcoming.

Braylar halted the wagon and his lieutenants rode up on either side, along with Soffjian, her ranseur propped on the shoulder of her scale cuirass. Casual but threatening.

Mulldoos was just next to me and pointed at a burly man in the group approaching who was holding a staff longer then he was, with two iron loops at the top and a shorter stout bar hanging down. "Now *that* there is a proper flail, Cap." And he laughed, but his mouth made it sloppy.

Captain Killcoin ignored him, eyes locked onto a short figure in the middle of the small band in finer clothes than the rest. He had a bald pate, gray hair that looked like horse mare glued to his skull that fell to his shoulders, and a sober expression on his pocked face.

The leader of the welcome party said, "Name's Fellburn. The mayor of Crossthatch. Folks hereabouts call me 'Mayor Fell' on account of that. Hard to figure, but there it is."

Braylar nodded once. "Well met, Mayor Fell. I am Captain Braylar Killcoin."

"Sort of had a hunch you would say that. See, word arrived just yesterday that there was a big party of Syldoon in the territory here, might pass through, might not. Led by one Captain Killcoin. Jackal Tower, am I right?"

"You are indeed." Braylar turned to me. "You see. No finer intelligence and communication talent in the world than the Empire's." He looked at Mayor Fell again. "I imagine, then, that this messenger might have also mentioned that we are in quite a hurry. Given that we are fugitives now. It is a relatively new status, so it still rolls off the tongue strangely. But there it is."

Mayor Fell smiled, tight and small. "Aye. Word was you were deserters."

"And how do you feel about that, Fell? I do hope you aren't thinking of trying to apprehend us."

The mayor shook his head. "No, nothing like that. Imperial squabbles, well, those are for you and yours. We're clearly no soldiers. Or fools. Won't be trying to stop you. I just came out to tell you we want no trouble is all."

Braylar looked around at the scattered populace of Crossthatch. "That's good to hear. And yet, I cannot help but notice a surprising amount of shears and scythes and pitchforks and, why yes, that man there does indeed have an impressive flail." He laughed. "That sort of thing tends to attract trouble, Mayor Fell."

The mayor looked a little sheepish. "I told the folks that much as well. But I ain't emperor, just a humble mayor, and my people, well, they felt real uncomfortable letting a big armed party come riding through without making some show of being able to defend themselves if it came to it." He extended his own hands, open, palms up. "Course, I tried explaining that if you came through with evil in your hearts, a show of spades weren't like to dissuade you. We're simple folk. But proud. So there it is."

Braylar started to reply when we heard hoof beats, coming fast. A rider came up on our right, reining in right before the captain, the Syldoon breathing fast, the horse frothy around the muzzle, its chest pumping.

"Report!"

The soldier said, "Big company coming in hard, Cap. Four, five hundred." He continued panting.

"How far?"

"Mile. Maybe less. We missed them. Came out of an abandoned quarry, south of here, looks like."

Braylar's eyes narrowed and he grabbed the crossbow from my hands, turning back to the mayor. "How much did they offer you to delay us?"

The mayor was backing up, holding up his hands, shaking his head.

"We had to—"

The crossbow bolt in the chest stopped him short and he fell over backwards, his plea severed.

"Pity you won't get to spend it." The crossbow hit me in the stomach and I reached for the quiver to reload it when Braylar shouted and got the team moving again.

The villagers ahead of us jumped out of our way and ran for cover of the buildings as crossbow bolts began to fly as the convoy picked up pace. I looked to my left and saw a small girl peering up over the edge of a window—a bolt slammed into the adobe a foot away and she ducked back down.

We rode hard through the remainder of the village, brick and clay buildings flying past, but didn't encounter any resistance. The road curved to the east, and we rounded a barn where we nearly slammed into a hastily assembled blockade of barrels and wagons and cairns.

Braylar halted the troops as the dust the horses and wheels had kicked up billowed ahead of us. "Thirty men, off horses, move this shit out of our way! Now!"

Mulldoos and Azmorgon echoed the order and Syldoon dismounted and ran forward, cursing and shouting as they shoved and pushed everything aside.

Braylar slammed the heel of his hand on the bench. "I wish I had time to burn this humble little village to the ground!"

Soffjian rode alongside, waving her hand in front of her face as she coughed on some of the dust. "How is the fugitive life treating you so far, brother? Even the farmers have turned against us. What next, the weather?"

He swore at a soldier struggling with a barrel and said to his sister, "You'd do well to remember that our fate is yours as well!"

"Oh, it isn't lost on me, Bray."

The captain hit me in the arm, "Span it, boy!"

I shifted the lever forward to release the claws, dropped the bolt in place, and folded the devil's claw back onto the stock.

An arrow thunked into the side of our wagon, and another struck the wall of a building to our right, plaster flying. Everyone looked around, and one Syldoon saw the attacker in the loft of a barn, spun in his saddle, and loosed a bolt. It missed wide but frightened the archer enough that he ducked down. When he rose back up to take another shot, two more bolts didn't miss, both striking him in the chest.

The soldiers had most of the debris clear when I heard shouting from behind us. A moment later another Syldoon rode up. "Nearly to Crossthatch now, Cap!"

Braylar stood and bellowed, "Enough! Mount up!"

Most Syldoon ran back to their horses, and a few pushed a final wagon aside.

The captain got our team moving and we lurched forward, maneuvering around a small cart, the side of our wagon smashing against a barrel as we passed.

And then we were through, several Syldoon riding ahead of us through the last of the village as the rest of the convoy followed our wagon. No more villagers challenged us, and it looked like we would be back on the dirt road and on the move again when one of the advance screeners returned.

Braylar slowed the team enough to hear him. "What now?"

The long-faced Syldoon replied, "Got us a big problem, Cap. War wagons ahead, nearly set up, about ready to link the final chains, looks like. Twenty, thirty maybe. Pickets of cavalry on the perimeter. There's a ravine to the east. Not a pure blockage. But real snug."

Vendurro was riding next to us and said, "Plague. Me. It's like they knew we was heading this way. Sprung the trap good."

Braylar considered for a moment, then asked, "Memoridons?"

Long-face said, "Didn't see any, but like Sergeant Ven said, they knew we was coming. Got to figure they got at least one in tow."

Braylar said, "Very well." He turned to Mulldoos, Hewspear, and Azmorgon, who all reined up. "War wagons linking ahead. Ready the men. Loose what bolts we can, but no one is to engage. Is that understood? We force our way past, then ride hard for the north."

They said "Aye, Cap" almost in unison and turned their horses about before heading back down the line and relaying the order.

Braylar turned to me. "We are about to head directly through a withering rain of arrows. Get inside, get behind a barrel, and keep your head down. We cannot afford to lose you."

I finished spanning a second crossbow with shaky fingers and stopped, stunned at his comment. "Another crossbow would help, wouldn't it? I'd prefer to stay."

The captain shook his head. "You have as much chance of shooting one of our horses in the back of the head as an Imperial. Behind a barrel. Now."

I slapped the devil's claw on the stock, harder than I meant to. "You know that's not true. I'm no marksman, but every bolt flying in their direction will help, correct?"

Braylar thought about it for the briefest moment. A twitch-smile later, he said, "Very well. But you will get behind the bench at least. We need to at least outfit you in a filthy gambeson if you continue to play hero, but for now, take some cover." Then he spread the aventail of his helm out, slipped it up over his head so the mail draped across his shoulders, and strapped down the embattled shield on his left arm.

The captain worked the leather lines again, manipulating the horses of the team with subtle movements as he got them moving again, and the rest of the convoy followed. As Braylar used the lines to communicate to the beasts and we wound through the carts and cairns, several horsemen sped ahead, those in the very front with shields at the ready, and the second group armed with crossbows, presumably trusting their scale and lamellar cuirasses to be enough protection.

We rode through the remainder of the buildings, picking up speed, and one or two townsfolk poked their heads out to watch us pass, but not so much as to present a target. That was an astoundingly good idea.

I crawled over the bench, nearly racking myself as we rolled over a rut, and took position just behind the captain's shoulder. I built a quick tower of sacks of grain on one side, and rolled a barrel onto the other.

I expected a hail of arrows like those we experienced fleeing Sunwrack. Which proved entirely inadequate, as far as expectations went.

The last of the buildings of Crossthatch whipped past, and our wagon rattled over a short wooden bridge as we crossed a shallow ditch, and that's when I saw the war wagons ahead. They were impossible to miss, and as I looked over the top of the bench, I felt my breath catch. The Urglovians probably had fewer soldiers than we did, but they had erected what amounted to a fortress on wheels ahead. The wagons were chained end to end and created a long, insurmountable wall across the road—each looked extremely heavy and sturdy, larger than our own, built of thick planks, tall, and they had an extra wall deployed to protect the wheels and gaps underneath on the broad sides facing us, and the section above had arrow loops.

There must have been dozens of soldiers on platforms just on the other side, relatively protected, able to loose with impunity those wicked-looking composite bows. Several of the wagons also appeared to have ballistae as well, or some similar engine, just visible over the upper edge of the wooden walls.

In the very small gaps between the wagons, I could make out some Urglovians wielding longspears, halberds, two-handed maces, and a number of other nasty weapons. There was absolutely no going through the wagons, and with the ground falling away in a ravine to the east, and stony ground to the west, that left a relatively small alley that we had to pass through. The Urglovians didn't have enough wagons to blockade our entire path, but enough to make passage deadly.

Braylar worked the leather lines in his hands and shouted encouragement to the horses, and we rolled forward at close to a gallop, making our way for that narrow open space. A dozen or so horsemen veered off to the right, intent on trying to round the wagon fortress on the ravine side, or at least present more targets and draw arrows their way.

I knelt and held the crossbow at the ready, hand away from the steel trigger until we got close enough for me to pick out a target that I would likely miss, cursing myself for not accepting the captain's offer to simply burrow beneath all the supplies we had and hope for the best.

We were about three hundred yards out when the first arrows arced over the top of the wagon wall, flying high in the sky. With the clouds dark and imposing, I lost the shafts in the gloom above us, but even with the creaking and rattling wagon and clamor of the horses' hooves, I heard the arrows as they came down. It was like an awful wind, and then I saw them again as they struck. Most hit the ground around us, a few slammed into shield faces or ricocheted off lamellar plates of soldiers ahead of us, but one horse was hit and slowed before continuing forward. Our horses were unharmed, but one arrow tore through the canvas above me and thudded into a barrel behind me.

All of the Syldoon took aim as they galloped, loosed their bolts, and then spanned the crossbows again, almost without losing any speed at all. But the bolts were ineffectual, especially at that range, all striking the wooden walls of the war wagons or into the ground beyond.

Another barrage of arrows was already flying, a little shallower as we had closed the gap, so I was able to see them a bit more clearly. Which only made it worse, really.

The ballistae shot their bolts as well, which were easy to track, as the missiles were nearly as long as a man was tall. The ones I saw flew between riders and disappeared, but they would not be deflected by armor or helm if they found a target.

Then arrows hit everywhere at once: the ground on either side of our convoy, the road between riders, into several Syldoon themselves, although only one fell from the saddle that I saw. I heard a horse scream next to us, and the sound of canvas tearing again, this time right alongside me. An arrow ripped through and stuck into a sack to my right. I watched the grains start to trickle out and had to force my eyes forward.

More arrows filled the sky, though again the trajectory was less parabolic. I rested the crossbow against the bench, sighted along the length, picked out an Urglovian in lamellar and a nasal helm standing between two wagons, took a deep breath, and loosed.

Between the rocking wagon, the distance, and my own poor skills, there was little chance of hitting him, but I saw the bolt slam into the broadside of the wooden wagon not too far off, and hoped I at least startled someone. Then I ducked.

Again the arrows rained among us, one striking the bench inches from my face, puncturing it and spitting splinters into my hair. I scooted back as I picked up the other loaded crossbow, nearly discharged it as the terrain suddenly got bumpier and I flew off the floorboards. We'd left the road.

I repositioned myself and tried to pick a target, and saw the majority of our company had veered as well. I expected us to slow, since the ground was less even and I imagined we could break a horse's leg or shatter an axle or a wheel on one of the wagons, but we seemed to speed up if anything.

That's when I looked up and saw the arrow sticking out of Braylar's shoulder. It appeared to have penetrated the lamellar. Braylar turned and grabbed me by the arm. "Loose another bolt or present a smaller target, but stop sightseeing, you shrunken cock!"

Only seeing his eyes in the helm, I couldn't tell how badly injured he was, but I did as commanded as the arrows fell again, this time one striking the lead horse in the flank, two hitting the side of our wagon, and a third shredding canvas and landing inside somewhere.

I cranked the lever back and was nearly finished reloading when I looked at the war wagons, now much closer, and saw that arrows not only flew over their walls, but shot out of the loops in the broad sides. I aimed for one of those as best I could, squeezed the trigger, and fell behind the bench again to reload, this time being sure not to lean against it.

I heard another scream just behind us, though couldn't be sure if it was human or animal, and Braylar cursed. When I looked back over the bench, I saw that one injured horse had fallen and crushed its rider, and another horse, wild with fear and pain, had reared and thrown the Syldoon from the saddle. Another soldier was struck square in the chest with a ballista bolt and flew backwards off the horse, the large bloody head sticking out of his back like a spear, having lanced him through and through. And then we rushed past those fallen. Several other riders were riddled with arrows.

The arrows whizzed all around us and it seemed a few more volleys would take out half our company before we even cleared the war wagons. Soffjian galloped past us on our right, arms stretched out, ranseur in one hand, fingers splayed in the other. But before she had a chance to perform any memory magic, an arrow struck her in the chest and ricocheted off, the shaft broken. But it had disturbed any concentration she needed and it was everything she could do to keep herself in the saddle.

I spanned and dropped the next bolt in as quickly as I could, rose above the bench, and quickly sighted one of the Urglovians operating a ballista, working furiously on the winch to reload the large weapon. After squeezing the trigger on the crossbow, I dropped back down and began spanning again instead of tracking to see if it had managed to hit anything.

The Syldoon all around us were shooting crossbows, but the Urglovians unleashed their composite bows faster, even with the Jackals using the devil's claws, and while we were galloping we also had no cover, whereas our enemy might as well have been in a fort. If we inflicted casualties, they were negligible—the best we could hope for was making them hesitate behind their walls, or shoot too quickly.

And then suddenly we were rumbling past the war wagons on the uneven ground, bouncing so much I bit my tongue and spit and tasted blood. The war wagons were in a rectangle, and while we were only fifty yards away now, we passed the short side of the mobile fortress, so fewer arrows struck our company as we raced past.

One arrow flew through the canvas panel just above my head and out the other side. And as we cleared the war wagons, I felt our own vehicle shift crazily as we broke for the road again, careful to keep my tongue well away from my teeth as my jaws clamped shut when we launched over a lip in the earth and rumbled onto the packed dirt.

I nearly let out a whoop before hearing an arrow strike the gate at the back and two more flew through the canvas, one puncturing a crate right near my feet. I dropped the crossbow, grabbed my writing case, and hid behind it as best I could as more volleys fell before we were truly out of range.

Grabbing the crossbow again, I crawled to the rear of the wagon as I clumsily worked the lever. Some of the Urglovian cavalry that had been inside the protection of the war wagon came pouring out to pursue, but the Jackals finally had the advantage again, expert at shooting and reloading their crossbows even at full gallop.

I saw several Urglovians struck by bolts before they called off the chase and circled back to the wagon fort.

Really, all we managed to do was to ride fast and not all die, but that itself felt as rewarding as routing the enemy, considering how quickly that trap closed around us.

Despite my throbbing tongue, sweat pouring double time from every pore, and my heart racing faster than any horse's, I couldn't suppress a huge smile. Survival was the greatest prize of all. I wanted to yell, to cry, to drink, and yes, to whoop, loudly, maniacally. We'd lost men, we'd been bloodied and injured, but no matter what, we survived. And that felt as sweet and wonderful as anything I could imagine.

I started crawling towards the front of the wagon—we'd slowed down to avoid blowing the horses, but were still going too fast to maintain anything resembling balance—when my elation was suddenly pricked. The captain had been hit, his sister as well, and I had no idea who else among us had survived. Was Vendurro fine? Hewspear? I was even anxious to hear that Mulldoos was alive. Just because I'd survived didn't guarantee anyone else had. And then I felt selfish, small, and foolish. Who knew how grievous our casualties were.

I grabbed the bench and was about to haul myself over and check on the captain when I suddenly stopped short.

A phantom smell tickled my nose, wafted into my mind, though I knew it wasn't really there. Musky, dusky, and unmistakable, though I was sure it was emanating from somewhere miles away.

Like a ballista bolt through the chest, it suddenly hit me why the trap had closed so quickly, how our enemy had so easily predicted our path.

Skeelana.

Bile bubbled in my throat and my head spun, and I tried to convince myself I was mistaken. It couldn't be.

When Skeelana told me in Sunwrack that she bonded with me, I thought it was only to torment me. I never imagined it was true, that a single kiss, no matter how pleasant or terrible, was enough to truly establish a bond. After all, I wasn't helpless, dangling from a noose, fighting off death. How could it be?

And yet that smell was real. Her scent. As strong as if she were sitting on my lap, running her fingers through my hair, using me all over again.

I had to come clean. I'd withheld information before, about the Hornman boy recognizing me in Alespell, and it had nearly doomed us all.

I had to confess what my heart told me now. Or our survival might prove very short-lived indeed if I failed again. Of course, my own life might be hanging by a thread if I admitted the truth, especially if Mulldoos was in hearing distance. Even slobbering and off balance, he could still kill me with one arm. And Azmorgon could probably strike me down with his beard alone.

But I wouldn't repeat the same mistake again, damn the consequences.

W e rode hard well into the night, long after it seemed safe, given how rocky the terrain was. The company had surely already sustained a fair number of casualties riding past the war wagons, though I was reluctant to ask the captain if he knew the severity of the damage. In fact, after I inquired about his injury and was shouted at, I was reluctant to ask him anything at all, and stayed inside the wagon for several hours. At first, it was the pretense of recording what happened, but I knew I just didn't possess the courage to talk. So I tried to sleep, which proved nearly impossible given how crazily the wagon bounced and jittered along. When we finally did stop sometime in the pitch black, I considered approaching Braylar then to talk about Skeelana but hesitated, just as I had when we were in Alespell and I knew the Hornman we spared had recognized me.

Only this time, it wasn't simply the captain's wrath or utter disapproval I risked, but the entire company's. And it suddenly hit me how badly I craved their acceptance, how badly I had the entire time. While it was abundantly clear I was not and never would be a Syldoon soldier, and so couldn't be a true member of their brotherhood, I had started to prove myself of late, to earn some measure of respect, even from those least inclined to give it, like Mulldoos. And while that could never confer the sense of belonging they shared amongst themselves, even the shadow of it was better than nothing at all. My whole life, I had been essentially an orphan, an outlier, a mute witness to things, but never partaking, never involved, never invested. Sold off by my whore of a mother, a reluctant scholar, and finally, bouncing from one city to the next, accepting short-term employment devoid of even the semblance of friendship and belonging, I never truly recognized just how deeply I had longed for that. I'd hidden my own depth of loneliness in the practicalities of the jobs, the integrity of the work.

But growing to know these rough and tough soldiers, hearing their stories, garnering their trust, I felt an unexpected comradery. It made no sense. Truly.

A tenmonth ago, I would never have even imagined accompanying such a group, let alone feeling myself drawn in, caring about what befell them. When I took the assignment, it was purely for the possibility of some adventure, the opportunity to record something of import, a desire to have a purpose.

What I failed to realize was that there was more underpinning it. It wasn't just vocational purpose I craved, but that belonging. And I had finally and against all odds begun to find it here, with these hardened, coarse, crude, but also cunning, brilliant, and fiercely loyal men. Some respect, friendship, integration, settling into their violent rhythms and understanding their harsh cant. I had not hung with them, would never be entrenched as a Syldoon. But against all odds, they (or at least some of them) had adopted me just the same. And I was loath to jeopardize that.

And so I lay there, pulling my blanket tight, trying to convince myself that with the harsh reality of morning light, I would have the courage to speak up, to admit what I knew once again, as failing to do so might imperil us all. I cursed myself for speaking to Skeelana at all, for allowing myself to open myself to her in the slightest. Ironically, it was that same craving for true kindred companionship that might ultimately cost me all whatever it was I had gained with the Jackals. Only I was too stupid to recognize that hers was false, whereas the Syldoon kind was edged and dangerous but still undeniably real and true. I cursed her, cursed myself, and was no doubt in the middle of some other curse when I slipped into oblivion.

Just after dawn, I woke, stiff, achy, and miserable, limbs leaden as I climbed down off the wagon. I saw that the injured swing horse from the middle of the team had already been swapped out with a fresh one, and wondered how many beasts and dead men we left behind us.

I saw Braylar off to the side. He'd exchanged the damaged lamellar cuirass and byrnie for a mail haubergeon that had three rows of steel plates down the back and chest. The captain was leading his lieutenants, Soffjian, Vendurro, and a woman with a pug nose I recognized as Rudgi—she was shorter than me, in soldier's garb and a lamellar cuirass, with coiled hair the color of honey and thick eyebrows the hue of bark. They were all heading away from the rest of the convoy, arguing amongst themselves, no doubt angry at being trapped and nearly annihilated again, and fire churned in my gut. I emptied my bladder, doing little to help my belly, and then slowly walked in the same direction, knowing that every moment I delayed would only shred my resolve further, and it was slight enough as it was.

Sure enough, the first thing I heard as I approached the group was Mulldoos sounding a bit slobbery as he jabbed a finger in the direction of Soffjian. "Your fault. You wiped the trail clean, like you ought to have, like you said you did, we wouldn't be in this fix."

She stabbed the butt spike of her ranseur into the dusty earth. "Syldoon, you would be dead already if I hadn't risked everything to travel among you. Yes, I cleared the trail, and yes, I did it as competently as could be managed. Is it possible I missed something? Yes. It is a large company and I am one Memoridon. But it is just as possible that someone picked up your physical trail. A lot of broken twigs and hoofmarks in our wake."

"Sure, fine, maybe behind us. But that don't explain how they got ahead of us, laid that trap in that pissy little hovel town, got the war wagons set up real nice just waiting for us."

Soffjian measured her response, though only barely. "You are a brute, but I gave you credit for a modicum of cunning. Surely you know that there are Memoridons conveying messages out there. They probably gambled on a few likely routes and planted ambushes, hoping to snare us."

Not shockingly, Mulldoos wasn't exactly mollified. "Sure. Could be that's it. Or maybe you're playing us. Maybe you wanted your witch sisters and those imperial horsecunts to ride us down. Maybe you've been coordinating with them the whole time. Come to think of it, that makes a lot more sense." His hand fell to the pommel of his falchion.

She spun her ranseur, the tassels whirling like a dancer's skirt. "It pains me to admit it, but I gave you far too much credit on the point of cunning. You are an absolute idiot. I am here at your Commander's behest, and risking everything on your behalf, as it happens to align with my behalf."

"You're nothing but a faithless bitch who—"

Braylar stepped between them before Mulldoos had a chance to say or do anything else and raised his hand. "This serves no purpose, Lieutenant. You forget too quickly, my sister helped us escape Sunwrack. Why do so if she only intended to see us destroyed? Far more convenient to side with Cynead then and simply be done with it, yes?"

Mulldoos didn't have a solid rebuttal to that one, which seemed to only make him angrier. "Fine. Fine, as you say. But that still means she did a shit job covering our trail. What's the point of having her with us if she can't even manage what she's been trained to do?"

Azmorgon said, boomed really, "Don't much care how they trapped us. Point is, they got a good idea where we are and where we're going. All I want is a chance to deal some damage back to them. Maybe instead of running like rabbits, we ought to stand and engage. We run from Sunwrack, we run from Crossthatch, that's what they expect. Run, run, run. But I say we take the battle to them. Surprise those whoresons and engage, crush them, kill the plaguing lot of them and piss on their corpses."

Hewspear shook his head. "We would need a full company of giants like yourself to have any hope, Az. We are outnumbered, woefully, and our only hope is to slip free of this net and then rejoin Thumaar."

Azmorgon waved a huge hand at the older man. "Bahh. Horseshit. I only brought my boys with this sad little outing thinking we'd get a chance to cut down some of those Imperial bastards. So far, all we done is tuck tail and get whittled down. It's horseshit, it is. Nothing but a stinking load of—"

Braylar said, "You brought your boys with us because you were ordered to, Lieutenant. Our mandate is to get to Thumaar, above all else. We will have our vengeance. Make no mistake. But at my conviction and command. We will not waste the lives of everyone simply to satisfy your oversized bloodlust."

"Weren't saying that, Cap, just saying—"

"I know precisely what you are saying. But I will pick the time and place for us to strike back at them, and just now is neither. Just now is the time and place to consider how we can avoid any further ambushes or blockades and win free once and for all. And thus far, none of you has produced anything resembling a remotely useful strategy." Azmorgon stared at his much smaller commanding officer and looked ready to argue his point, but instead rolled his massive shoulders and gave one small quick nod.

Braylar turned to his sister. "Soff—sweep behind us again."

She pulled the ranseur out of the dirt and started to object but he raised a hand. "Yes, they know roughly where we are, but they can only coordinate amongst themselves with true and recent intelligence. Let us make that as difficult as possible. Redouble your efforts and cleanse our trail, yes?"

Soffjian sighed before slowly nodding. "I'll do what I can, brother."

Mulldoos said, "Best do better than that. Can't afford another ambush up the road."

Braylar said, "She will do what she can." Then he looked at Vendurro and Rudgi. "Sergeants, make sure our men scour the landscape ahead. Send more scouts, and ensure that they appreciate that they must account for every possible place a battalion could be lying in wait. Another lapse will not be tolerated. Is that understood?"

Vendurro replied, "Aye, Cap. I'll pass the word. Impress the gravity and whatnot. But seeing how fast we been riding, hard to look into every nook and cranny."

"An abandoned quarry is hardly a nook though, is it, Sergeant?" The captain was spitting venom now.

Rudgi said, "Begging your pardon, Cap, but I have to agree with Ven here. It's a lot of territory, and we're moving fast. It—"

Braylar stepped closer to the pair, spitting spit now. "Do you think for an instant I am somehow unaware of our present circumstances? Do you?!"

Vendurro and Rudgi both shook their heads. "That is correct. I am painfully aware. If the scouts need to rotate out faster, they do so. If they have to take spare mounts to ensure a full gallop, they do so. They will investigate every deserted quarry, village, outpost, or temple, and doubly so any inhabited place. And you will be sure to mention that if they fail spotting the enemy again, they better hope the entire company is wiped out, because if not, my wrath will be far worse than anything our enemies can muster. See it done, Sergeants! That is all."

Vendurro ran his hand through his hair, and Rudgi nodded. Together they said, "Aye, Cap."

Soffjian and the sergeants started to walk away, and I took a deep breath before saying, "It might not help. None of it."

The rest of Braylar's retinue was accustomed to my presence by now, but Azmorgon looked at me as if I were a dead animal he'd just stepped on. "And what's this runt know about it? Why don't you stick to your quills, you little shit, and let the soldiers do the soldiering, eh?"

Braylar ignored him, and fixed me with that oh-so-disconcerting gaze. "What are you driving at, Arki?"

The entire group looked at me. I tried to focus on the friendlier faces, Hewspear, Vendurro. I realized that might be the last time I saw them so inclined. Still wondering if I was being courageous or making a colossal (or fatal) error, I said, "I don't think Soffjian or the scouts are really to blame."

Braylar arched an eyebrow. "Oh? Is that so? Do go on. You have my unadulterated attention."

"Well, that is, I think I know how they've been tracking us so well. I don't know for certain, but—"

Mulldoos slobbered, "Quit your hemming, scribbler. Get on with it already."

Yes. Colossal error. After another gulp, I said, "It's Skeelana. She must be in a group that's following us."

Soffjian gave me an impenetrable look. "And why would you say that, oh reedy scribe?"

Her gaze made me as uncomfortable as her brother's, perhaps more. But I forced myself not to look away as I replied, "She told me something in Sunwrack. Just after we met the Emperor in the Circus. But I thought she was simply trying to unnerve me, and didn't take it all that seriously. At the time. But now . . ."

Braylar snapped his fingers. "Out with it, Arki. What did she tell you?"

"She said she could follow me. Just as her sisters could track all of you."

Braylar eyes narrowed almost to slits. "That bond requires an intimate, strong, almost fevered connection. You were not hung, so please, do explain why this wasn't simply a bluff."

"In Sunwrack, before the Caucus, she came to my room. Our room. And—"

"Gods and devils, boy," Mulldoos said, slapping his meaty thigh, "Tell me you weren't stupid enough to mount a plaguing witch."

"No," I replied, looking at Soffjian. "But we did kiss. That was it. I never imagined that would be enough, so I assumed Skeelana was . . . could that be enough?"

Mulldoos's pale face went red, Braylar gave me his scowliest scowl, Vendurro shook his head sadly, Rudgi only looked confused, and Soffjian laughed. But Azmorgon took three long strides and struck me across the face with the back of his hand. Unlike the buffet Braylar delivered to Mulldoos a few days ago, this one sent me flying off my feet and sailing backwards. I struck the ground, blasting the wind out of my lungs, and stared up at the flat gray sky, unable to move, wondering if he had dislocated my jaw or cracked my skull.

And then Azmorgon was standing above me, blocking out the sky, the world, the future, his face practically purple. "You stupid shit! You know how many men we lost yesterday, on account of you? Do you, you plaguing bastard, you stupid little fuck? Do you?!"

I thought he was going to stomp on my head and finish me off, but then two blades crossed underneath his chin, a falchion and the head of a slashing spear.

Mulldoos spoke slowly, eliminating some of the slurring. "Settle down there, Ogre. He might be a stupid bastard, but he's our stupid bastard. Can't let you crush him into jelly."

Hewpsear nodded from the other side of the giant, his spear in both hands. "Perhaps the captain didn't explain things to you fully—though I seriously doubt that—but our archivist here has essential utility to this mission. He is young, foolish, and has poor amorous taste, but his health is paramount to our success. And what's more, no one pressed him for this admission—he willingly volunteered the information. Late, as it were, but of his own accord. So I advise you to step back and breathe deeply a few times until you have mastered your passions."

Azmorgon looked at the other two lieutenants as if they were mad. I probably was too. He said, "This is how it is, huh? Siding with a stupid plaguing cunt over your own kind?"

Mulldoos tapped the falchion blade against the slashing spear. "I ain't seen you in years, Ogre. Never much liked you before, can't say what's changed for the better in the last few days. You're a horsecunt and a half, but you're my Towermate and brother, and I'll defend you against any threat that comes. Any and all. But while the scribbler might have horseshit for judgment, he's no plaguing threat to anyone but hisself, and we're wasting real valuable time talking right now. So why don't you listen to the old goat here and take a step back and gentle up right quick? Play it smart."

If Azmorgon was bothered overmuch by the steel at his throat, he didn't show it at all. Maybe he thought his dense beard would preserve him. "You talk mighty big for a squat little man who's gone half to mush." Then he looked at Hewspear. "And you, Walking Stick—I respect my elders, but only so long as they ain't got addled brains. Yours are churned like butter, old man. Seems to me the witch castrated the both of you in Sunwrack. Now, you lower those blades right plaguing now, or I'll take them from the pair of you and bury them in your bungholes."

Then Braylar was there, and while he didn't have Bloodsounder in hand, he didn't need it. "Lieutenant, while I don't have anything against a little scrap amongst the men now and then, this is neither the time or place. You will shut your mouth and do your duty. The archivist is my concern, and I alone will attend to him. Have I made myself abundantly clear?"

Azmorgon slowly stepped back and Mulldoos sheathed his falchion and Hewspear propped his spear on his shoulder. "Real plaguing clear, Cap. Got to ask, though, did that bitch Rusjenna mess with your head, too?"

Mulldoos reached for his falchion again but Braylar put his hand on the lieutenant's wrist. "Enough, the lot of you." Then he turned to Azmorgon. "I consider myself a consummate communicator. But perhaps 'shut your mouth' was somehow ambiguous, yes? Do I need to elaborate or unpack that command for you, Lieutenant?"

Azmorgon looked down on his captain and shook his head. "Nope. Got it, Cap."

"Very good. Commander Darzaak appointed you lieutenant, but it is well within my purview to strip you of the rank if warranted. And failure to obey direct orders will do nicely as justification. How about that—is that clear as well?"

Azmorgon nodded once, spit in the dust, and then stalked off back towards the convoy.

Hewspear shook his head and looked at the sergeants. "Let this be a lesson to you junior officers. Discussion is permitted. Encouraged even. But insubordination, gross or slight, will never be tolerated."

Mulldoos walked over to me, squatted with some effort, and leaned over me, wobbling a little.

He reached out his hand, and for moment it seemed he meant to help me up, and I started to rise, holding my face. But then he placed his palm on my chest and pushed me back down. I flinched and he said, "Don't worry, scribbler, I didn't save you from the Ogre just so I could kill you myself. Not yet anyways. But you don't pull your head out of your scrawny ass and quit chasing after witch slit, and we'll be having a real different conversation next time. You understand me, boy?"

I nodded.

"Alright then." Mulldoos withdrew his hand. "You are without question the dumbest little overeducated shit I ever met." He stood unsteadily and sauntered off, cursing.

Vendurro came over and did offer me his forearm. I clasped it and he hoisted me to my feet, then swatted some dust off my tunic. "Got to say, Arki, hoping you held back. You did more than kiss the witch, didn't you?"

I hesitated and then figured the truth had gotten me in as much trouble as it could, so a little more wouldn't hurt. "No. I did not."

"Well then," he said, "got to agree with the previous assessment. Dumb was fooling about with a Memoridon in the first place. Dumber was not at least getting your pecker wet for the trouble." Vendurro gave a crooked smile, swatted my back, though whether to clear more dust or congratulate me on my stupidity, I wasn't sure, and then headed off to brief the scouts.

Braylar turned to Soffjian. "Well. You are vindicated at least. Can you sweep behind us to prevent her from tracking our resident buffoon here?"

Soffjian was still grinning, finding the whole situation morbidly amusing. "I will need to spend a few minutes with him, to register his 'footprint' as it were." She showed her teeth in a predatory smile, and I felt myself shiver. "Have no fear, archivist. I won't kiss or hang you, I promise."

The captain said, "Do it. Immediately." He gave me a dark look. "We will speak of this later, Arki."

Braylar walked past me, brushing my shoulder with his own, before I had a chance to reply. I turned and watched him stalk back to the wagon.

Soffjian said, vulpine smile still in place, "You and Skeelana really are full of splendid surprises, aren't you?"

offjian led me away from the convoy, through short scrubs and dust and rock, the dark rich soil of Anjuria giving way to a drier, hillier landscape in Urglovia. She said, "You really are going to develop a sullied reputation, consorting with she-devils like this."

I intended to keep my mouth shut, as it only seemed to get me in trouble, but found myself saying, "I never meant to . . . that is, I never imagined that my . . . dalliance with Skeelana could possibly endanger anyone in the company. At the time, I thought, like all of us, that she was a Jackal."

Soffjian put the butt spike in the dirt in time with her right foot coming down. "Surely the boarson warned you against even glancing at our kind, did he not?"

"Boarson? Mulldoos?"

"The very same. He is a brute, to be certain, but also possesses some cunning. So I imagine he would have told you it's not clever, getting entangled with a Memoridon. And less clever still, failing to report some critical information after she betrayed the Jackals."

I noticed she didn't say "us" and was reminded that she bore no lasting loyalties to anyone in the company now. "Well, as I said, I thought she was simply trying to needle me, or get a rise. I didn't think briefly kissing her would be . . . never mind."

We stopped midway down a small hill, with the battalions hidden behind us. "Must have been some kiss," she said, seeming to enjoy my discomfort, as she offered that disquieting smile again. "This is far enough. Now then, as I said, this shouldn't cause you any undue discomfort. I have no wish to bond with you, I only need to peruse some of your memories to get a feel for the kind you will likely leave in your wake."

She stood next to me, and I felt my breathing and heart both speed up. Mulldoos was right—any man inviting a Memoridon this close was a colossal fool indeed.

Soffjian reached up and put her hands on either side of my head—the right cheek was sore from the back of Azmorgon's hand, and between that and my trepidation, it was all I could do not to flinch. "That's going to color up nicely tomorrow," she said, closing her eyes.

I wasn't sure if I was supposed to do the same, so left them open, watching the lightning-bolt vein in the middle of her forehead start to pulse faster. She didn't press on my skin, but it felt as if her hands were carved from cold stone, and I suddenly felt dizzy. She might have been able to disguise her presence in my mind if she chose (although she admitted that, being a war Memoridon, subtlety wasn't her strength), but whether she lacked the skill to do so or simply chose not to use it, I suddenly understood why memory witches were found out so frequently. I sensed her there, moving among my memories, inspecting, tagging, cataloguing like a curator or librarian. It was like hearing footsteps in a hall, only seeing no one when you turned to try to find out who was following you.

Only this occurred over and over, the intense feeling of being watched, observed, but unable to see the silent witness, no matter which direction I looked or how quickly I spun. I knew she was in me, observing silently, even if I couldn't see her.

A Syldoon topped the hill behind her, saw us, and came running down. I said, "Soffjian, uh, we have company."

He had ten thousand freckles on his face—a mottled mask—and he was breathing heavily, the pale skin between freckles flushed. "Cap says you two need to return, and right quick, too."

Soffjian took a step forward and stared him down, clearly irritated. "Your captain was the one who just sent us down here. But do tell him that his interruptions do nothing but distract and delay, and we will be along shortly."

The Syldoon went redder still but stood his ground. "Begging your pardon, but Cap said you'd say something like that. Scouts come back. From two fronts. We got trouble. He said I ought to tell you that you wouldn't be needing any broom just now."

The soldier clearly didn't understand the message, which made him like delivering it even less, especially to an irritated Memoridon who could churn his brain to butter in a blink.

"Very well." Soffjian grabbed me by the back of the elbow and pushed me forward as she started to run. "Come along, Arki. It seems your days of dalliances are at an end."

She sprinted up the hill and the Syldoon and I followed. Soffjian put her long legs to good use and stayed ahead of us the entire way, the bobbing head of the ranseur angled over her shoulder.

The captain had gathered the retinue again, as well as three soldiers I assumed were scouts.

Azmorgon looked at the pair of us as we ran up to the group and spit into the dust at his feet.

I caught Hewspear in mid-sentence. "—numbers are not good, to be certain, but there must still be a chance to slip past one group or the other."

Soffjian asked, "Brother, what's happening?"

Azmorgon spat again. "What's plaguing *happening* is that little shit you all seem so fired up about protecting might have just fucked us all in the unsuspecting arses."

She matched him glare for glare. "I was directing the question to your captain. You can be sure when I have need of information from you, I will give you a verbal cue to let you know, so as there is no confusion on your part. Or I will simply slip into your oversized skull and take what I need."

Braylar was staring north as he replied, "Scouts, bring my sister up to speed." His left hand fingered the chains on Bloodsounder, and while I couldn't see his face, I wondered if his eyes were closed.

A young scout with reddish stubble on his face said, "There's a large party to the north. Outnumbering us two to one."

The scout standing next to him unbuckled his helm and pulled it off, hair soaked with sweat. "Battalions to the west are greater in number still. Must have some wit—, uh, some Mems with them too, as they're closing in but not leaving too many miles between them and the troops ahead. Real coordinated, they are."

"And," Braylar said, now drumming his fingers on the chains, "there is no need to try to erase any more of our tracks just now—the Imperials following us have closed the gap. And without wagons slowing their procession, they are in no danger of falling further back. So. We have convened to discuss which group we are going to try to slyly slip past or cut our way through. The trap is shutting, and we have little time, and less."

Mulldoos said, "Got to be north, don't it, Cap? Northeast anyway. Ride close to the Veil, we might be able to get past them. Especially in the dark. Nobody wants to go near it, they can help it."

Hewspear nodded. "And if escape proves untenable, they are the smallest of the three contingents. Better chance of fighting through them than the other two."

Azmorgon said, "Ears all waxed out, or your wits just crumbing to dust? Ain't no chance of being slippery now. Only option we got is to fight. Fight and win free, fight and die, but either way, we get some Leopard blood on our blades, and it's about plaguing time."

Mulldoos replied, "Escape, fight, whatever we plaguing do, it's got to be north, either way. And it's got to be now."

"I done told you, Mushrooms, running time is over. Fighting is the only chance we got."

"You call me that one more plaguing time, and I'll cut your plaguing tongue out."

"What's that? Couldn't quite make that out, what with your mouth all mushy and—"

Mulldoos started forward, and Hewspear and Vendurro stepped between.

Braylar spun around. "Enough. We head north. We try to slip past them to the east, and if they block the way, we cut through them. We did so in Sunwrack, and Crossthatch. We will do so again. Ready the men."

Given how the previous meeting nearly ended up with me choked to death, I was reluctant to speak again. But it was my reluctance to speak that got us into this mess, and I was hungry to possibly redeem myself. "There is another way," I said.

Everyone looked at me. I tried not to look at everyone, but focused on Braylar. "A way no one will expect. And a way, frankly, you might not like, but I would still urge you to consider."

Braylar looked at me, as telling as a statue. "I am listening."

"In the translations, there have been several times when a weapon like Bloodsounder was mentioned. The Sentries of Sentries, they are called. And while there was paucity of detail about origins or intent, one thing that cropped up several times was that the wielder was able to pass through the Godveil."

Azmorgon boomed out a laugh and said, "Plaguing fairy tales ain't getting us clear of this mess, you little shit. We got to move, Cap."

Oddly enough, it was Mulldoos who jumped to my defense first. "Only chance we got of untangling what Cynead did is this little shit. So why don't you keep your furry plaguing mouth shut until he's done explaining what he's plaguing talking about."

Vendurro asked, "What are you talking about, Arki? You think, what, that Bloodsounder—"

"You too, saddle sore. Let the scribbler talk. Got no time for this horseshit."

Azmorgon stepped forward, though made no immediate move to choke me. "Exactly. We got no plaguing time at all and you addled idiots want to sit here and—"

"Silence," Braylar ordered. Then he looked at me again, still with a stony expression. "Are you saying you have encountered more accounts since we last spoke of this? Incidentally, since I last told you that I wanted to hear no more about this?"

"I have," I replied. And added for Azmorgon's benefit, "And from credible sources. Not storytellers or poets or sensational romances, but learned, sober men, critical and even cynical men, who found what they witnessed incredible, but still very much real. Men separated by centuries, but the accounts remain consistent. Men wielding weapons like Bloodsounder not only passed through the Godveil, but returned, and in some cases, with several men accompanying them. I wouldn't suggest it if I didn't believe it was plausible and true, or if our situation weren't so dire."

Everyone was silent for a moment, until Vendurro gave a long, drawout whistle, and then Azmorgon shouted at Braylar, "You're not really putting any stock in this horseshit, are you, Cap? We got to ride. Now. Or we'll be cornered. We can fight through one group, but no chance of two or three."

Hewspear ignored him and asked me, "You said men accompanied. In these accounts. How many? How many men crossed over with the wielder?"

"I can't plaguing believe this," Azmorgon said. "The lot of you are plaguing mad. Why not just summon a demon to fight for us?"

Soffjian said, "You are right. It is utterly preposterous. Witches and artifacts wielding memory magic? A power-hungry emperor syphoning control of all the witches in the entire empire to his control in one fell swoop? A Veil that isn't a physical barrier but prohibits anyone from approaching? All of it is absurdly ridiculous, really."

I ignored the pair of them and replied to Hewspear. "Only a handful. They apparently held onto the wielder as he passed through. I have no idea what the limit might be. But even if it is only a small group, the captain could lead them through and come back for other groups. And if it works, the Imperials couldn't possibly follow. We could make our way away from them and reemerge miles and miles away from being cornered."

Soffjian turned to her brother. "On the road to Sunwrack, I implored you not to order your men on a mad charge against odds that would certainly doom you. I was . . . convinced to assist, and evened those odds considerably. I was wrong then. It pains me to admit, but there it is. But now, each of the companies we face has Memoridons, and if any are war Memoridons, the chances of me turning any battle in our favor are remote. And I do not say so out of false modesty. So again, I urge you, consider what your archivist says. You can save all your men. If you try to win free, you will die, and all your men with you. You will have failed your Tower and Thumaar and whatever else it is you purport to fight for. You will all die."

Mulldoos said. "Cap, you know how I feel about all this mystical horse-shit. Godveils and witches and your thrice-cursed flail there. The whole lot of it. Give me a blade and a man with bone and blood to fight. That's all I long for. But like you said, we got to pick and choose our ground. Might be, this fool idea works, and gets us out of this so we can rejoin Thumaar and take the fight to those Imperial bastards when you plan for it, instead of trying to gnaw your foot free like a bear in a trap. Might be, too, it kills us all dead. But small chance is better than none."

Soffjian nodded, and Hewspear and Azmorgon both started talking at once, arguing over each other. Braylar raised a gloved hand. "Enough. All of you." He had to say it a second time, louder, before he finally got silence.

Everyone looked at him, waiting for his pronouncement. Braylar tapped his index finger on the top of Bloodsounder's haft and looked down at it, one long silent moment stitched to another and another before he looked up again and said, "We head northeast at haste. If we can make it around Urglovian forces, we will. If not, we try our hand at madness and I will attempt the Godveil. If I fail and fall . . . well, I would say you could make a glorious final stand, but glory depends on someone recording the tale for posterity. And I'm sure the first thing you do will be to strike down my archivist here, so the record will be at its conclusion."

The captain twitch-smiled and said, "Ready the men. We move out. Now."

His lieutenants and sergeant marched off, with only his sister remaining, as she had no one to ready but herself. Soffjian said, "I am a bit stunned, I have to say, but you exhibited restraint and wisdom just then, Bray."

Before he could offer a jab or jibe in return, she turned on her heel and walked back towards the convoy. Braylar watched her go and shook his head. "Be glad you have no known siblings, Arki. Be very glad of it."

⊕

We rode for the remainder of the day and well into the night, trying to at least maintain the distance we had between us and pursuing forces, and to increase the chance of us angling past the Urglovians ahead.

The company stopped briefly to feed and water the horses, but we didn't make camp. Men ate and dozed in the saddle as we pressed on in the dark, the great ringed moon creeping out from behind dense clouds now and then to offer its light, but then slipping away as if taunting us.

I slept for a time in the wagon bed, though it was broken, fitful, and barely counted as any kind of rest. I spelled the captain for a few hours before morning, and he told me to wake him the moment any scouts returned. I expected him to lay into me, to unleash a torrential downpour of insults, barbs, and derision, but we exchanged the lines without a word.

Miraculously, he was snoring within minutes and slept like the dead. I rubbed my eyes and pinched my wrists and sprayed brackish water on my face to stay awake as I maintained our northeastern course until dawn finally approached. While I didn't have mastery of the lines like Braylar (and never would—it was surprisingly complicated to issue commands to so many horses, much like playing a foreign instrument), he'd taught me the fundamentals of guiding the team of horses and I could hold a steady enough course well enough, provided we didn't need to take any evasive action. But I had orders to wake him immediately if anything unusual happened at all.

I was half asleep, watching the sun slide over the horizon and wondering what was closer now, our foes or the Godveil, when I felt the captain's hand on my shoulder. He climbed over the bench and took his place alongside me. We sat in silence for a time, listening to the axle creak and the iron-rimmed wheels roll over rocks and uneven ground, when he finally said, "I could have paid for a whore, you know."

I looked over at him, uncertain what he meant and he added, "I wouldn't have even dipped into Jackal coffers to do it. Truly, it would have come out of your commission, but all you needed to do was ask for the coin and I would have seen it done."

I was still confused. "A whore, captain?"

"For companionship. So that you didn't feel the need to jeopardize our entire operation by nuzzling a Memoridon in the dark."

I felt my cheeks go hot and steeled myself for the barrage.

Instead, he only sighed and said, "What is done is done. But going forward, I suggest that if you happen to come across Skeelana ever again, you forget your cock for a moment and stick something else in her, yes?"

I'd thought about that thing more than once, especially now that she was hounding us, but held my tongue, nodding only. Braylar clapped me hard on the back. "Very good. Now hand me some goat."

I pulled the sack of dried meat out from underneath the bench and asked, "You struck down Rusejenna." I stopped, unsure how to phrase what I meant to say.

"Is that intended to be a question? It had the inflection and rise of a question, and yet, strangely, was very much a declaration we both know to be true."

"Have her memories, have they begun, that is—"

"Assailing me? Seeping into my skull? Haunting me?"

I nodded quickly and grabbed some meat. It tasted like bark and was no less easy to chew.

"No," he said. "In fact . . . there have been no memories washing over me at all. I feel remarkably . . . cleansed. More so than even after Skeelana purified me."

I thought about that for a moment. "Do you think killing a Memoridon works differently? With Bloodsounder, I mean."

"I understood the question, Arki. And the answer is, I do not know. I never killed a Memoridon before."

I looked at his hip, at the flail sitting there like a sleeping snake with two heads.

"Do you have another statement in the shape of a question, Arki?"

"I have something I've been meaning to ask, only it never seemed to be the right time."

He looked straight ahead, expression unchanged. "Oh. And does now seem like the right time?"

"No," I admitted. "But it is no worse than any other time."

"Astute," he said. "Speak then."

"I know that when you are separated from Bloodsounder you are tormented."

"That is true. And also not a question. It might not even be a preamble to a question, the way you are proceeding. Spit it out already, archivist."

"Why use Bloodsounder at all? If you have to fight, why not simply leave it hanging by your side, choose another weapon? I realize that Bloodsounder warns you of impending violence. But at times the cost seems . . . prohibitive."

Braylar nodded. "More than you will ever know. But you see, Bloodsounder torments me if we are separated, and it torments me when we are together, but it is a jealous thing. In all respects, it is very much like a woman."

"Jealous? What do you mean?"

"You've seen me use a crossbow, a suroka, dispatch men in other ways, yes? And yet when I do, this cursed flail wracks me with pains. Not the sickness of being lost in a swamp, like the sludgy wash of stolen memories. But sharp, biting pain, deep in my skull. Bloodsounder will tolerate me flirting with another weapon now and then, but if I tried to set it aside for good, to leave it out of the fight too long, it would torment me no less viciously than if I tried to bury it in a box and leave it in my wake." He looked down at the flail. "We are wedded, this horrible thing and I. Only my death shall sunder our delightful little bond."

I tried to stymie a shiver and failed. "I will get back to the pages, captain. Maybe there are some clues there about severing the bond. I will keep translating until I find—"

A horseman came riding hard towards the convoy. I'd been with the Syldoon long enough to know that rarely boded well. Scouts never galloped up to report that our enemies had been swallowed up by marshland or stricken by the plague.

Braylar called out, "Report, Syldoon."

The scout sat straighter in the saddle as he saluted, the morning sun giving him a golden silhouette, totally at odds with the news he delivered. "Urglovians are moving to intercept us, Cap, heading southwest. And Denvin reports the army to the west is closing in, too. Can't see slipping between them, not if they got any brains at all and got men patrolling ahead."

Braylar pulled Bloodsounder off his belt. "So be it. Ride down the line, and tell the lieutenants we head due east now."

Braylar's personal retinue felt comfortable disclosing doubts and arguing tactics with him, but the men were a different story. Still, some reservations crossed the scout's face, as if he wasn't sure he heard the order correctly. But before Braylar could berate him for dawdling, he replied, "Aye, Cap. Due east." Clearly, the rank and file didn't know much about what bedeviled their captain, so they had no reason to suspect he was about to march us straight into the Godveil.

As the scout rode off, Braylar gave me a long look. "If your assertion proves correct, you could very well rescue all of us from doom. And if it proves false—"

"I will be the second man to die," I said, wondering if I would keep the goat in my stomach.

The captain twitch-smiled. "You are beginning to think more and more like a Syldoon. It is time you dress the part. I asked the men to put a spare gambe-son and nasal helm in the wagon. They should be somewhere in the back."

"Captain?"

"Put them on, you dolt. If we do somehow survive the Godveil, we have no idea what to expect on the other side, and I would like to keep you alive long enough to congratulate you for your mad, mad plan."

I stood, nearly falling off the bench as the wagon rocked over the hard ground, and my heart felt like it was trying to beat its way out of its ribcage. I swallowed hard. "Aye, Captain."

He said, "Oh, and Vendurro jiggered together a scabbard to fit Lloi's blade. Syldoon don't favor sabers or curved swords in general, so it took some work. So buckle that around your waist as well and be sure to thank him later. You have no competency with the thing, I know, but should you find an enemy in your face, it will prove more useful than trying to club them with an unspanned crossbow. More importantly, I don't want you damaging any more crossbows."

He laughed at his own joke and then said, "Well? Get to it, Arkamondos. It is uncharted territory ahead for us all."

The gambeson was a simple thing, a thick quilted linen coat that laced together at the front. It wasn't a terrible fit, but part of me wished it had been, as I could have put a dead animal on my shoulder and it would have stunk less. It smelled like a thousand soldiers had worn it before, and was stained with sweat of the ages. I wondered if the stench drove off fleas and lice, but I suspected not. Still, so long as I rode with the captain, there were bound to be arrows flying in our direction and men trying to kill us, so it was a foul comfort. The helm was little better, as the padded lining was stained with the sweat and oils of more men than I cared to think about. No blood at least. That was something.

After belting Lloi's curved blade at my waist, I rejoined Braylar on the bench, rather clumsily, unused to armor and weapons.

The captain inspected me briefly and nodded curtly. "I don't want you deluding yourself into believing you are fit for combat—you should still hang near the rear and do your best not to attract attention—but those might just save your life when that proves impossible. As it likely will."

We crossed some dry gulches and gullies, short grass beneath the horses' hooves, with strange rock formations that seemed to burst out of the harsh landscape like stone fountains, something dreamed up by a drunken sculptor. Larger copper and salmon-colored rock layers seemed precariously balanced on smaller ones, or leaning crazily but somehow still not falling. Some striated stones formed asymmetrical arches and miniature towers for reasons that perhaps only the rocks understood. Perhaps these were the leftover dreams of mad gods. Had the Deserters' left these behind as some signal or warning?

Our team struggled as we ascended a hill after passing through another ravine. I thought Braylar was going to have to turn us around to find a different route, but we continued climbing and climbing.

When we reached the top, I felt my breath catch. The other side of the ridge descended into a small valley, with the Godveil winding its way across the floor, warping everything that lay beyond. What I hoped lay beyond. Our options were limited, but if this gamble failed, we would be well and truly trapped, and I had no illusions about Azmorgon sparing me a second time. A padded jacket would certainly not stop his wrath if the captain lost his life on this venture, and I didn't imagine any of his retinue would be especially interested in protecting me a second time.

I looked up, and it was as if two disparate skies had been stitched together. Almost directly above and stretching to the west, it was dark blue with fluffy white clouds scattered about, unmoving as if pinned there. To the east the clouds gathered together, dark gray and dense like wet clay, blocking out the sky and growing darker still until they were nearly black and then obscured entirely by the warp of the Godveil.

Those storm clouds didn't seem especially fortuitous. But with the Syldoon it was hard to gauge—perhaps a black and heavy sky was actually a good portent.

Braylar called a halt, and his retinue rode up alongside us.

Vendurro tipped the broad iron brim of his pot helm back. "Well, plague me, this would be a pretty sight, wouldn't it? That were, if that forsaken Godveil weren't running right through the middle of it like that and our enemies weren't closing in to crush us."

Braylar asked Mulldoos, "How many miles away are the Urglovians?"

"Main body is a ways out, still. A few miles. Their war wagons are keeping them slow, but guessing their scouts are close. Don't have much time."

"Any," Azmorgon amended, towering over everyone. "Don't have any plaguing time. We're pinned down here, Cap. Pinned. Out to make a break for it and ride right into the Urglovian bastards right now, before we got no chance at all."

"Your opinion is duly noted, Lieutenant," Braylar replied. He turned to Hewspear. "And how far back are the Imperials?"

The older lieutenant had a distant look in his eyes, and it took him a moment to realize he'd been asked the question. "Several miles still, Captain. But they have no wagons, so they will close soon now that we've stopped. We ought to make our play now."

The captain said, "I'll ride down to the Godveil. This hill is as good a place as any to make a stand. Block as much of the pass with the wagons as you can. We'll be leaving them behind, either way. Unload whatever supplies and provisions are absolutely necessary, and distribute the weight on spare horses. When I return, I'll start leading the men with me, as many as we can manage at a time. We will need to hold this position until we have crossed the company through."

Azmorgon spit a phlegmy mass at a thorny bush. "And if you fall down dead at the Godveil? Which seems real plaguing likely. Almost a surety, really. What then?"

"Then," Braylar said very slowly, "You will have your foolish charge into overwhelming forces after all, and you can gloat in the afterlife when you see me anon."

The captain jumped off the wagon, his mail and plate harness clinking and slithering, and mounted Scorn. The officers were shouting orders at the men behind us, ordering them into position, and I felt the wagon rock as several climbed in the back and began unloading.

Braylar rode next to the bench and turned his helmet in my direction, the aventail obscuring his face. There was a beat before he said, "Of all the archivists who have ridden with this company, you annoyed me the least."

He started down the hill and I called after him, "I'm coming with you."

The captain reined up and spun his horse around to face me as I jumped off the wagon and ran to the rear. When I returned on my irascible mount, Braylar said, "Going to throw yourself into the Veil if this gambit fails?"

"It won't fail," I replied, not entirely believing it. "I am so confident, in fact, that once you return, I will be the first you lead over. To prove to the others it can be done."

Braylar tilted his head slightly, regarding me for a moment. I couldn't read his expression and could barely see his eyes, so I wasn't sure if they were hot with anger, wide with surprise, or implacable as usual. "Very well," he said. "Let us put your theory to the test."

He rode down the hill and I nudged my horse to follow. It wasn't nearly as steep as the hill the men had hurtled down at the temple ruins the last time I'd seen the Veil, but I still felt myself clutching my reins tight and leaning back as we descended, trusting my horse not to kill either of us.

As the ground leveled out and we closed in on the Godveil, I felt its ceaseless tug, even from fifty yards away. The compulsion to keep going, to approach the Veil, was almost overwhelming. I looked at the captain and asked, "Do you feel it? The draw?"

He dismounted, Bloodsounder in his hand. After a beat he said, "I feel nothing."

I swung my leg over and dropped down. "Good. That's a good sign." I didn't have any idea if that was true. It could have been an awful sign.

I heard Braylar laugh. "You really ought not to lie, Arki. Being the most ingenuous creature alive, you truly haven't the slightest skill at it."

"Well," said, "I hope it's a good sign at least."

"As do I. Now, did the manuscripts describe how this was done with any specificity?"

I was tempted to try to dissemble, but it was pointless. "No, not really. They did all seem to agree that the Sentries approached the Veil with weapons in hand. One or two alluded to the fact that the weapon and man were of the same name now—the man who wielded Grieftongue was known as Grieftongue, the man wielding Wrathedge was known—"

"Yes, I think I have it. So did the man say the weapon's name or—"

"His name as well."

"Did this Grieftongue absurdly say 'Grieftongue,' or announce his presence before entering the Veil?"

"I don't know. The records made no mention of it. But it couldn't hurt."

"Couldn't it? Even if this isn't just the fabrication of legend and someone actually passed through, I could still very well die by failing to know exactly how it was done, yes? So, you know of nothing else said or done, no incantations or bizarre gestures, nothing mentioned at all, besides the twice-naming?"

"No," I admitted. "Not that I encountered."

"Very well," he replied, as he started walking forward. "If I should die because you simply didn't translate far enough to learn a magic word, my wrathful wraith will hunt you."

I looked back up the hill and said, "Azmorgon would crush my skull right after. So you'd have to hunt in a hurry. Captain Bloodsounder." I forced a laugh, but it felt even hollower than it sounded.

The captain walked forward, holding Bloodsounder at his side, the twin chains and Deserter God heads swinging alongside his leg, not quite hitting the ground. It was a purposeful stride, as if marching forward to engage a foe, though this one was a millennium old, created by inscrutable gods, and deadly without reprieve. Even if the manuscripts were correct and someone had managed to pass through unmolested, that was centuries ago. What if the gods had changed the locks, as it were, or whatever latent powers were in weapons like Bloodsounder no longer functioned? What if I had just convinced the man to walk to his death, on nothing more substantial than my powers of translation and interpretation?

I nearly rushed forward, shouted for him to stop, but forced myself not to. We had no choice. It was this way or Azmorgon's, and at least this option had the possibility of our surviving.

Braylar didn't slow his pace at all. He might have gripped his weapon tighter, might have felt his cold heart beat faster, but none of that showed in his stride, and I respected him enormously for it—whatever else his faults, he was decisive and brave. I held my breath, praying that Braylar didn't simply crumple into a heap as he closed in on the Godveil.

But he did not. He walked straight ahead, slowly raising Bloodsounder as he did, and though it was difficult to tell from that distance, it seemed like the warping bent and shifted faster, and then it wove around him and he was gone. Well, not truly—his watery silhouette remained, but he must have continued walking, as even that disappeared.

I waited. The moments ticked by, and I found myself jogging towards the Godveil before realizing how deadly foolish I was being. I hadn't taken more than fifteen steps when the draw turned into a compulsion. I knew I needed to halt, to move back, but all I wanted to do was move closer, to reach out and touch the Veil, become part of it, join some small portion of myself to the immeasurable immensity of it. I tried to stop, but my feet carried me forward, and it was so beautiful ahead, the heat-wave intensity, the urgent tang of vinegar, the hum and thrum growing, that single final note of a harpist hanging in the air, but now louder, every step, louder, and then there were more notes, overlapping notes, and I raised my hand as I walked, outstretched, wanting to even graze it, and I felt my body respond as I closed in, vibrating as well, as if my very bones shook my flesh and tried to throw it off, as if my skull wanted to slough off my own skin, and it should have terrified me, but it was amazing.

Every step brought me closer to something wondrous, miraculous, sublime, and—

Braylar grabbed my wrist and suddenly the thousands of thrumming notes were gone, and so was the urge to walk towards total oblivion. There was only the wildly warping Godveil twenty paces in front of me, extending in all directions.

I shook my head, but was careful not to pull away from the captain. "Was I—"

"About to have your life snuffed out? Yes, I imagine you were very close."

"You survived. I mean, of course you did, you're standing here. Unless you are a wrathful wraith." I tried to smile, as it was better than nearly vomiting. "What did you see? On the other side? How—"

"The stolen memories are gone. As to the other, come along. See for yourself. Let's test your second part of your theory and find out, yes?"

I nodded once, quickly. Now that I was no longer under the Godveil's spell, I wanted nothing more than to run off in the opposite direction. But I forced myself forward, and then had to keep his pace to avoid him losing his grip on my arm.

He stopped right before the Veil. If I reached out I would have touched it. I did not reach out.

Braylar turned his face in my direction, his eyes in shadow, his face behind the mail curtain. "Are you ready, archivist?"

"Yes, I think—"

He pulled me through and I gasped. But I didn't feel anything. One moment, the pulsing Veil was in front of me, and the next, it was simply behind. And directly ahead was . . . terrain exactly like that on the other side, dry, scrubby, russet stones. While the physical details were utterly lacking in drama, I still shouted, "It worked! I told you it would!" My voice broke with relief.

Braylar held onto my wrist and led me another forty paces forward. Then he let go. I resisted the urge to grab him, like a drowning man clutching at debris in the sea. While I felt the tug of the Veil behind me, it wasn't irresistible. Aside from being dizzy, there were no aftereffects at all.

He looked down at Bloodsounder and shook his head. "I was sure one of us would die. I've never been more happy to have been proven wrong." Then he grabbed my wrist tight and we started back towards the Godveil. "Come. I have a small army to bring across."

Braylar led me back through to the other side, and besides another bout of dizziness and nausea, the small trek did no harm. When we were far enough away from the Godveil that I wouldn't succumb to its song again, he mounted Scorn and said, "A battle half won is no victory at all."

"What does that—?"

Braylar had mounted Scorn and was racing past me up the hill. Glancing up, I saw the Jackals looking down at us. Soffjian stood out among them, a slash of scarlet like a wound.

By the time I'd mounted my own horse and scaled the hill, Braylar had already dispatched orders and summoned his officers, who were all on horseback around him.

Then the Syldoon began arranging into an orderly column. Their efficiency truly was a marvel. Sometimes disturbing and terrifying, but never less than a marvel.

Braylar and his retinue were off to one side, out of earshot. As usual, it sounded as if there were an argument brewing. Hewspear had his slashing spear across his saddle. "The scouts reported their outriders close. We are running out of time. There are surely other routes into this little valley, but most are goat trails that are nearly impassable to horse. They will come this way."

Mulldoos nodded vigorously. "Aye, time's slipping quick now. And it will take some time to get the boys through. How many did you say you could take at a time, Cap? Five? Ten maybe?"

Braylar nodded. "Arki confirmed a handful. We will try to exceed that, of course—I suspect if someone isn't protected in the chain, we will know immediately without losing life."

Soffjian had the hint of a smile on her face. "Well met, Bloodsounder. You are shorter than expected."

Vendurro was looking down the hill at the Godveil. "Still can't believe you made it, Cap. The both of you. I mean, I watched it, my own two eyes and everything, but still hard to fathom. What did it feel like? Was—?"

"You shall know very shortly. Our primary concern is making sure the Imperials do not run us to ground before we are through. Fire alone won't do."

Vendurro replied, "I could throw some caltrops down. Sure, they won't come riding over them like idiot Hornfuckers, but even taking time to clean them up will slow them some."

Mulldoos nodded. "Couldn't hurt. See to it, Sergeant."

Vendurro rode off and tasked a few men with returning to the wagons with him.

Rumbling as usual, Azmorgon said, "I'll hang back, Cap. Need twenty or so men. Rearguard. Hold the pass. Prick any of those pricks if they try to close, keep them at bay until you clear out of here. Light the wagons behind us. Sound good?"

Hewspear interjected before the captain had a chance to respond. "It is a sound plan. But—and I do hate to pull seniority—but it should be me who commands the men."

Azmorgon leaned forward in his saddle, his lamellar clattering. "Jealous of anyone stealing your glory, you old wrinkled twat? That it?"

"Mind your tongue, Ogre," Mulldoos said.

The stout lieutenant's normal intimidation tactics were lost on the giant, who laughed. "Or what, Mushrooms?"

Braylar clapped his hands together. "Enough. I am heading down to start leading troops over. Azmorgon, Soffjian, accompany me—the men need protection on the other side."

Soffjian said, "Brother, I can do more at the rearguard here to protect your men. You—"

"We have no idea what truly awaits us on the other side of that cursed Veil. You will go in the initial group." He turned to his other lieutenants. "Mulldoos, Hewspear, hold the line here at the base. When it's clear the majority are safe on the other side, light the wagons and ride hard to join us." Then he turned to me. "Your supplies are likely still in the wagon. Get your gear and then meet me at the base, yes?"

I nodded. "And the manuscripts?"

"The men spread out the remaining scrolls and parchments among the horses already. The pages you translated will be burnt."

"Burnt?"

He threw his hands in the air. "Why is it no one understands how fire seems to work? Yes, Arki. We ensure it doesn't fall into the Emperor's hands, in case his researchers see something in them you missed."

"I missed nothing."

"Very good. Then you won't cry when they are burnt." Then he turned and started riding down the hill.

He might have been wrong about the crying. It seemed a tragic waste—all the ancient knowledge and records, turned to ash and lost to the wind. But it couldn't be helped. Still, it ran counter to everything I had spent my life doing—compiling, recording, and now translating accounts intended to be read and read again.

Shaking my head, I earned a curse from a passing Syldoon as I rode too close, and his horse snapped at mine as well. I moved away, leaned over my horse's neck and apologized for being a poor rider, and then we headed towards the wagons. They were positioned front to end across the pass to block as much of it as they could. The Syldoon had stripped the wagons of most of the necessary supplies and tools they could carry, with only a few soldiers checking the remains to be sure nothing vital was left behind before dousing most of them in oil.

Vendurro was heading back with the handful of soldiers he had taken to spread the caltrops across the trail further up. He said, "Got to say, Arki, maddest plaguing thing in the world, crossing the Godveil. Like thumbing your noses at the gods, ain't it?" He shook his head, a melancholy smile on his face. "Wish Gless could have seen this. He would have shit himself."

Then he laughed and kept riding.

Rudgi was rolling a barrel of oil past and looked up at me. "Best get done whatever it is you're doing here, scribe. We've got orders to get these alight right quick. Unless you want to stand around and scribble something down for posterity. Then by all means, hang back, watch the wagons burn, maybe take a plaguing nap."

"Posterity can wait," I said, as I dismounted and then climbed up onto the captain's abandoned wagon. The interior looked well and truly looted, the bed littered with nails, a half-empty sack and a trail of grain from the hole torn in the canvas. The crate that had contained the scrolls I hadn't gotten to was thrown open and completely empty.

It was truly sad that this wagon felt like more of a home than any city I'd visited or even lived in. But there was no denying the pang of loss I suddenly felt. It was nothing but wood and canvas, cramped and uncomfortable, filled with stenches known and mysterious, and generally sweltering, but I was loath to leave it. I sighed, and grabbed my brass writing case from the corner of the wagon, slipped the strap over my helm and shoulder, and started towards the front again.

I stepped onto the bench when I heard hooves. A galloping horse. A Syldoon sped past, riding hard, and headed down the hill towards the Godveil.

Rudgi ran up to the wagon and ordered me out. "Get down there with the others, Arki. Burning time."

The Imperials were upon us.

I rode down the hill as quickly as I could, but not so fast I risked breaking my horse's legs or flying off to break mine.

It was difficult to get a head count, but the captain had led about half the company across, maybe less. He must have been ready to guide another group across when the scout reined up and reported, as now he seemed to be trying to settle a dispute between Hewspear and Mulldoos.

I dismounted and ran up as Mulldoos finished a thought as only he could, "—and there's an end to it, you plaguing walnut. No way you stay behind. Wagons are on fire, so make a stand here until Cap gets the boys through, and that's it."

Hewspear shook his head. "Even if the Urglovians and Imperials failed to realize that we were transporting troops through, they outnumber us two or even three to one. And they'll have the added range up on that hill. They'll shoot us to pieces. You know they will. And once they do see what we're up to, they'll likely come storming down that hill and destroy us to a man."

"Let them try," Mulldoos said.

Hewspear said, "Captain, you can only take, what, ten men at a time, correct?"

Braylar nodded. "We tried eleven and nearly lost a man. The number is ten."

"And you have to lead them far enough in that they don't run right back into the Godveil. Meaning, we wouldn't have the numbers to withstand them at full strength, which is why we tried this gambit in the first place, but with most of the men through, the remainder will be slaughtered. You know this, Mull. Our best chance is to hold the pass on the high ground with a small group. Twenty ought to do. That will ensure the rest of the men get through."

Mulldoos shook his head. "You ain't staying behind."

Hewspear countered, "It has to be an officer. Azmorgon is through already. And it obviously can't be the captain."

"Me then."

"Or me," Vendurro said as he approached.

Hewspear replied, "Ven, you are able enough, and this is no aspersion, but you are only a sergeant." He turned to Mulldoos. "And it pains me to say it, but in your current condition, you aren't the best choice either. It will be me."

"Bite my hairy jewels, you old bastard. With your ribs stove in and your skull rattled by Memoridon bitches, you're in no better shape."

"I am. And what's more, I am your elder."

Mulldoos pulled his helmet off his saddle and worked the aventail out before slipping it on his head. "There's dirt plaguing younger than you. But I'm leading the men."

Hewspear appealed to Braylar, "We are running out of time, Captain. Quickly. Reason with the stubborn fool. Or I'll hit him in the head with my mace and you can drag him through the Godveil."

The captain was staring up the hill. Black smoke was coiling up slowly, hardly bothered by a draft. "That won't deter anyone for long. Hew is correct—time is short. And you can't both go."

Mulldoos stalked up to him. "I've got it covered, Cap."

Braylar looked at both his lieutenants for several moments, but it was impossible to gauge his expression behind the mail. Then he said, "Hew, take twenty men. Hold the pass for as long as you can. Once I get the last of the lads through, break for the Veil. I will come back and guide you through."

Hewspear nodded slowly. He shifted his slashing spear in front of him. "Aye, Cap. We will hold."

Braylar clapped him on the shoulder. "Very good. Now go."

Mulldoos started to object again, slurring his words more than usual with rage, and Braylar grabbed his arm and leaned in close to say something I couldn't hear. Mulldoos continued shaking his head, but less vehemently.

Hewspear propped his slashing spear on his shoulder and then walked forward to address the remaining Syldoon. "The Imperials are nearly upon us. I'm going back up that hill to keep them at bay long enough for our brothers to make it through. I need twenty lads to accompany me. Who will it be?"

It took only a moment, and then dozens and dozens of hands sprang up closest to the lieutenant, and those gave rise to others, rippling back away from Hewspear until the entire assembly had volunteered.

Hewspear said, "I see you bastards are going to make this difficult then." He smiled. "I expected nothing less. Very well—you five," he pointed at a group and then another, "and you five there, and you, and you brave lads there." He looked up the hill and into the sky. "Follow me. The rain's held off—it's still a fine day for crossbows. Let's go fill some Leopards with bolts, shall we?"

The men cheered as Hewspear walked back to his horse. Braylar saluted him from atop Scorn and then rode to the group of the soldiers waiting to cross next. I watched men clasp his wrists on either side as he held Bloodsounder aloft, and then men clasping wrists down the line until ten were in a row and moving into the Godveil.

Turning back to the officers, I saw Hewspear pat Vendurro on the shoulder twice. The younger man nodded and then headed to his horse.

Mulldoos was slumping more than usual in the saddle as he looked at Hewspear. "Never met a man more stubborn than you."

"That's only due to the shortage of mirrors. Which in your case is a good thing."

"Plaguing old goat."

"Plaguing boarson."

The pair laughed, and Mulldoos said, "Don't dawdle on the hill any longer than you have to, you wizened bastard."

Hewspear shook his spear. "You must have mistaken this for a walking stick." Then he called out to the twenty he selected. "Let's ride, Jackals."

The Syldoon started up the hill, and halfway they passed Rudgi and the few soldiers who'd stayed to light the wagons ablaze, riding down the hill. A few words were exchanged, Rudgi saluted Hewspear, and then both groups continued on.

I stood there watching Hewspear and his twenty go, once again amazed at the depth of that brotherhood. They were all riding up to face a much larger force, and they did so not only willingly, but with jokes on their lips and defiance in their hearts.

Hewspear's group crested the hill and rode out of view, no doubt taking up position behind the burning blockade.

I turned to see if Mulldoos was there, but he had disappeared into the throng of soldiers in front of the Godveil, though I still heard him bellowing orders and curses.

Braylar returned again, rode up to the line of soldiers, and repeated the steps in lining up a new group of ten. A few times a horse balked and tried to turn from the course, but the Syldoon, being expert riders, managed to maintain control. Each passage to the other side seemed to take an eternity. There were about fifty soldiers left when I heard a distant scream up the hill.

I looked over my shoulder, but there was nothing to see. The top of the hill was empty. The Imperials likely thought us trapped, so I hoped they were content to sit back and exchange bolts and arrows in the pass, rather than risking a charge against burning wagons and who knew how many men holding the position. As Braylar led another group of ten through, I thought the strategy might just work, and Hewspear and his men would have a chance to rejoin us after all.

But then I saw them on top of the dusty rise, on horseback, slowly retreating as they loosed bolts and then moved aside to span their crossbows as more Syldoon took aim, sort of a reverse of the "rolling gears" they'd employed against the Hornmen after we had captured Henlester.

Only the Imperials had far more composite bows, and even in the crowded pass, they could still shoot them in ranks, arcing them high into the sky, and as they'd proved in Crossthatch, much more rapidly.

A barrage rained down, and while the Jackal armor protected a good number of them, deflecting arrows, saving lives, some horses were struck and took their riders down, and some riders fell from the saddle, having sustained grievous wounds from arrows that found unarmored spots. One Syldoon with an arrow in his neck rolled down the hill, snapping the shaft and kicking up a cloud of dust before coming to a stop.

The Jackals retreated further, loosing what bolts they could, but another barrage of arrows came down, black shafts pinning men and beast, depleting their numbers, with those that missed the mark landing halfway down the hill.

I looked over my shoulder quickly, seeing Braylar lead another group through and silently urged them to hurry.

The tall lieutenant waved his hands and his men fell back, shooting once more before coming down the hill ten or twenty paces, safe from direct assault for a moment. Arrows filled the sky again, but they overshot the Syldoon and landed harmlessly in the scrub on the hill. The Jackals worked their devil's claws and spanned crossbows again, just as the first infantry appeared over the lip of the hill, their scale armor and helms shining in what remained of the sun, the dark clouds having wiped most of the blue away now.

Hewspear and his men loosed their bolts, and the infantry loosed their arrows, and men fell on both sides. The infantry were drawing more arrows from the quivers at their hips when the remaining Syldoon at the bottom of the hill loosed their own crossbows.

Many in the first wave of infantry were struck by bolts and wounded, several falling to the ground, but those that remained pulled their shields off their backs and stepped forward, allowing more infantry to file onto the hill. Those in front had the long shields up, covering most targets, and those behind began shooting arrows with impunity, at both the Jackals midway down the hill and us at the bottom.

One arrow flew close enough to my head that it sounded like an angry wasp buzzing by. I instinctively ducked, though the only meager cover I had was my horse's neck.

Braylar was leading another group through, and one soldier's horse was struck in the flank by an arrow. The animal reared and the Syldoon lost his grip on the men on either side. He fell to the ground, clutching his head, rolling as if he were on fire, and then falling still, and the man to his right at the end of the line thrashed twice with no tether to Braylar before falling dead from the saddle as well.

The captain and the others parted the Godveil and disappeared from sight. There were still more than ten men left on this side. I'd never wished there were another Bloodsounder around, but I did now.

I looked back up the hill as I spanned my crossbow, expecting to see Hewspear and his remaining men galloping down to join us now that they lost the hill, but instead, they dropped their crossbows and pulled their swords and maces and axes, and one slashing spear, and charged up into the three lines of infantry who'd taken up position protecting the archers.

The Imperials had their shields, but weren't expecting the small number of men to charge, and didn't have their longspears at the ready. If they had, they would have pierced every Jackal galloping up the hill at them, or broken the charge completely.

As it was, some of them were drawing their own sidearms when the Jackals burst into their line, blades flashing and falling, cutting, slashing, crushing.

The front lines were in complete disarray, several injured not only by steel but by the hooves and mouths of the horses suddenly among them. But more infantry poured over the crest of the hill.

Hewspear bought us time, as Braylar led the second to last group through. But the infantry kept coming in waves. The lieutenant slashed and stabbed, cutting down men on all sides, spinning his mount as they flanked him, his slashing spear thrusting and arcing around him. His horse kicked out, likely crushing the skull of a man who didn't even scream before falling to the earth. But even with his horse and the bloodied head of his blade whirling everywhere, one of the soldiers rushed in and grabbed Hewspear.

The lieutenant struck the soldier in the face with the haft, slashed him across the neck as he fell back, but that Urglovian was replaced by five more, and they pulled Hewspear from the saddle. I sighted down my stock and squeezed the trigger, hitting a nearby Urglovian spearman, hoping against hope that they might only capture Hewspear, but weapons rose and fell, rose and fell, bloodier and bloodier, and then stopped as the infantry formed up to attack the other remaining Jackals.

I felt a hand on my shoulder and nearly swung out with the crossbow.

Vendurro's eyes were locked on the final Jackals on the hill who were cut down to a man. Not one of them tried to run, to escape. They stayed, they fought, they died.

Vendurro said, "Come on, Arki. Out of time." I blinked several times. The captain was about to lead the last of us through.

I nudged my horse forward, furious, helpless, and joined him at the end of the last line Braylar was leading through, grabbing the sergeant's wrist.

Several arrows fell around us as we rode forward.

I was waiting to feel an arrow pierce my back, or for my horse to buck and throw me as we approached the Godveil, resisting the urge to look back up the hill. And then we were through. I saw that the remaining company had ridden several hundred yards away, which was smart, as the Urglovians continued to shoot at us, even after we disappeared.

Mulldoos was the only one who was waiting for us right on the other side. "Hew? The rest?"

Vendurro shook his head once as he released my wrist. We all started forward to get out of bowshot. All save Mulldoos.

As I passed him I heard him say to himself, a slurry growl, "Every last Leopard. Killing every last plaguing one."

Just then, I believed him wholly and silently pledged to help him in whatever way I could.

Mulldoos jerked on his reins and spun his horse around and raced towards the company as another hail of arrows fell all around him.

We rode away from the Godveil in utter silence, out of range of even the closest archer on the other side as shafts fell in our wake until they stopped falling altogether. It wasn't unlike the mood that pervaded after we fled Sunwrack. Crypt silence filled with futile thoughts of murder hanging heavy in the air. The thrum of the Godveil disappeared behind, and then there was only the clop of hooves, the creak of leather, and the occasional jingle of harnesses or cuirasses nearby. A number of Jackals had lost their lives as we escaped, and there was absolutely nothing anyone could do to avenge them just now.

It was awful watching the Jackals fall on the bridge at Sunwrack, but doubly so watching Hewspear get cut down. I didn't know the man nearly as well as Vendurro, Mulldoos, or Braylar had, but I respected him—even broken and ailing inside, and older than any of the Jackals among us, Hewspear was twice the man of almost anyone else in the company. And he always dealt with me fairly. There was a nobility there, too, and a graciousness. While Hewspear could be firm, unyielding even—I thought back to his words about exiling his daughter-in-law if that's what it took to secure a place in his grandson's life—he was gentle and kind as well. And less rash or driven by his appetites than most men. Especially Mulldoos. I shuddered to think how his comrade was going to deal with the loss, and kept picturing Mulldoos dying as well, over and over, as he tried to avenge his fallen brother.

I shook my head, feeling a hollowness that refused to give way to pure sadness, at least so far. I tried to hold out hope, to convince myself maybe the lieutenant had only been badly wounded and captured rather than killed. But I've had no better success lying to myself than to anyone else.

Even if no one spoke, Syldoon frequently looked around uneasily, as if expecting monsters or the gods themselves to suddenly swoop down on us, and the scouts Braylar sent ahead seemed a little more reticent than usual. We obviously ventured somewhere humans weren't intended to go, but at least we'd done so with a large if depleted armed force. That was some minor comfort.

The terrain was identical to what we left behind on the other side, which shouldn't have been shocking, but somehow was. It felt alien, even if there wasn't anything visible to indicate it was. Between the muzzled rage and the anxiety, there was a horrible sense of tension and foreboding in the company that I was sure wasn't mine alone.

We rode for another hour and then stopped as the black clouds finally opened up. As they had outside Sunwrack, the Syldoon conducted their duties without complaint, but also without any hint or merriment, revelry, or even crude barbs and asides. I'm sure many had been close with the twenty who had just died to save our lives, or the few who didn't survive the crossing. I wondered if they wished that Hewspear had selected them so they would be spared the guilt and remorse they surely felt. While I was no soldier, it was a terrible thing to witness men sacrificing themselves for your behalf, even if they had accepted the charge willingly.

I did what I could to help, caring for and feeding the horses, but it was small distraction and no balm at all. By the time camp was set up, such as it was, the rain finally subsided, though clouds remained, blocking out the stars and moon completely. Braylar took up residence away from the rest of the company, and his small retinue was sitting in a circle around the fire he prepared. I was a bit surprised, partly that he had found anything dry enough to light, but also assuming he didn't want to attract the attention of whatever might roam this side of the Godveil. But maybe the captain was itching for a fight, or the chance to confront his makers and accuse them of being the uncaring and hateful deities they were.

I wasn't sure how much wine or ale was left, or when we might see more of it, but they all seemed to be drinking freely. After seeing who sat where, I took a spot between Soffjian and Vendurro. Rudgi, Mulldoos, and Azmorgon were on either side of the captain. No one was in a hurry to speak.

Finally, Vendurro said, "What's the plan, then, Cap? How far you going in here? And will we still be heading northish?"

Braylar didn't respond right away, staring into the sputtering flames. No one pressed him, and the silence stretched on so long I thought maybe I imagined the question being asked at all.

Then the captain replied, "I do not know."

Vendurro looked around the group, scratched at the tuft of hair on his chin, and when no one else thought to reply, said, "I know it's a bad time, so don't mean to press, but, well, we've gone to somewhere nobody ever imagined they'd ever see, me included, and the boys, well, they'll be wondering what you have in store, Cap."

"Will they?" Braylar asked, both syllables over-enunciated, weighted with dire consequence.

Vendurro nodded but said no more.

The captain took his eyes away from the small fire and said, "I will announce our intentions on the morrow. The men will simply have to try to sleep without knowing them in full."

After another long silence, Azmorgon shifted his immense weight on a damp log and said, "Probably no good time for this neither, but who do you have in mind to promote? To lieutenant, that is. I got some good boys who—"

Mulldoos drew his suroka. "That's the beauty of a blade. It don't care what neck it slices across—giants bleed no slower than runts, just a lot more."

Azmorgon's laugh sounded like two stones being rubbed together. "I know you two were close, but Squirrel there is right—Cap's got to think about practicalities now. So it might hurt to hear, but we got to consider—"

"If you open your giant mouth again without showing the dead the proper respect, I swear I'll drive this through your jaw and shut it myself."

Azmorgon leaned forward. "Hew died saving us. Good man. Fool of a man, too, same as you all. I told you we shouldn't have headed for the Godveil. It was a fool notion, and I was against it from the start. And if you had to leave someone for rearguard, should have been me, like I done told you, but—"

Mulldoos sprang off his rock with surprising speed and had the point of the suroka pressed to Azmorgon's neck before the huge man could do anything to stop him. "Shut. Your. Plaguing. Mouth. You hear me, Ogre? Shut it. I lost my best friend just now, so you want to try your luck, you make a move or say one more plaguing disrespectful word and see if I don't ram this into your skull and watch the gallons of blood leak out. You hear me, you whopping huge horsefucker?"

Vendurro and Rudgi had their swords halfway out and Soffjian had a dangerous focus on her face.

Braylar stood and walked over to the lieutenants. "Azmorgon, you are right on one count. The men need to see their leaders acting decisively, especially in a time of crisis and chaos. From this moment forward, Vendurro is the company's newest lieutenant. If you have any suggestions for nominating a new sergeant to fill his vacancy, I will hear it on the morrow.

"Because Mulldoos is also right. We lost one of our best today. Along with more than twenty other good men. And a failure to afford them the proper respect will incur my wrath no less than the man with a blade to your throat just now. So I suggest you follow the good advice you just received and shut your mouth before someone really loses their temper and things end badly. I cannot afford to lose any more lieutenants today. I have made myself clear, yes?"

Azmorgon hadn't flinched away from the blade, his eyes locked with Mulldoos's, and he was weighing something for several tense moments before replying, "Aye, Cap. All clear."

Mulldoos slowly lowered the blade and took his place in front of the dying fire again. Azmorgon reached up, touched his jaw, fingers coming away with some spots of blood. Apparently his immense pelt of a beard offered little added protection.

The Ogre got to his feet, looking larger than ever, and he stared down at Mulldoos. The pale boar ignored him and Azmorgon walked off into the dark.

When he was gone, Rudgi laughed quietly. "Good thing nobody really lost their temper, eh?"

Vendurro looked at Braylar and seemed miserable. "Cap, what you said, it's—"

"Overdue. Hewspear was intending to retire soon, before Cynead played out his most recent coup and forced us to the road. Did you imagine we kept you close simply because we craved your wit and company?"

The younger man shook his head slowly. "No, Cap, but—"

"You were being groomed for the position. You simply find yourself in it a little earlier than expected. It is done. Congratulations, Lieutenant."

Vendurro nodded, and it was the most sorrowful promotion I'd ever seen. He didn't bother wiping away the tears that fell down his cheeks or pretend ash had flown into his eyes. "Aye, Cap." He took a long swig from his costrel.

Rudgi leaned over to Vendurro and said quietly, "Timing is lousier than lice, but good on you, Lieutenant. You deserve it."

Vendurro gave one quick nod, tried to respond, then stopped himself.

The group lapsed into silence again. Eyes lost in the shrinking flames once more, Braylar said, "We have spoken at length about what constitutes a bad death, a good death. I have seen many, men die, in my charge and by my hand. Too many of both, truly. But today a hero died. Many, in fact, but we would have lost half our company or more if it hadn't been for Hewspear. He had ever been stalwart, courageous, and true, an exemplary soldier and leader, and I've spent most of my life chiding myself for not living up to his example.

"Was his a good death, saving so many? I do not know. I no longer pretend to know. But he was one of the finest officers to ever have the honor of calling himself Syldoon, and one of the finest men I've ever had the pleasure of calling friend. That much I know for a certainty." He slowly hoisted his costrel and said, "To Hewspear," before taking a drink.

Then he passed it to Mulldoos who did the same. Voice cracking, he said, "To Hewspear" before tipping it up.

Mulldoos handed the costrel to the new lieutenant. Vendurro's eyes were wet as he said, "To Hewspear." After taking his drink, he held it out for me.

I started to reach for it but stopped short. "I . . . I'm not a Syldoon. I—"

Mulldoos said, "You don't drink to his honor, you skinny whelp, and—"

I accepted the costrel, said, "To Hewspear," and took a swallow of bitter wine.

Tears started to well up and I looked at Soffjian, then back to Braylar and Mulldoos.

Braylar gave a short nod and while Mulldoos glowered, he said nothing, so I handed the flask to Soffjian. "To Hewspear," she said, taking her drink before getting halfway up to hand it over the fire to Rudgi.

The short sergeant accepted it and completed the ritual with the repeated toast and drink.

We sat in silence again after that, as there was nothing left to say as we watched the fire until it was dead and gone.

The next morning, the company continued heading north, not straying too far from the Godveil. I rode near the front of the column, behind Braylar and his men. I suspected this always irked the other soldiers, but Braylar commanded it, and what's more, I enjoyed not choking on the dust kicked up by over a hundred horses.

The first day was mostly uneventful. Every time I climbed out of the saddle, stiff and aching and with new blisters, I tried to find time to continue translating, but I had little energy for it. A somber mood still held sway over the company, so I was in no hurry to trouble anyone and kept to myself.

That wasn't true of everyone. I was walking back from the most secluded spot I could find to relieve myself when Soffjian startled me. "Pity, isn't it?"

Having nearly jumped out of my skin, I replied, "What is, exactly? I can think of many things that would fall in that category just now."

She gave a small, rueful smile. "Very true. But just now," she looked off to the east, away from the Godveil, "I was thinking that this is the first time in half a millennium or more that humans have ventured on this side of the Godveil, and assuredly the first time ever in force like this. So it strikes me that it is a true pity your captain is pressing so hard driving north."

"What would you have him do?" I asked. "Deviate from his mission to go exploring in the wild?"

She laughed, brief, almost a bark. "Oh, that wouldn't exactly be out of character, now would it? I know he is tempted. He must be." She pointed east. "We have no idea what lies out there. None. It is the greatest mystery to ever befuddle mankind. Where are the gods? Why did they truly leave? Was it really profound disappointment in us? That seems bad form, as hosts, doesn't it?"

I looked east as well, and admitted, "I would love to know. To explore. It is a terrifying thought. But also an exhilarating one. And maybe it's a pity it isn't possible. But it isn't, is it?"

She faced me again. "Possibilities are more water than stone, wouldn't you agree?"

"Maybe to a Memoridon. To the rest of us mundane folk, burdened as we are by expectations and limitations, things are not so fluid."

Soffjian cocked her head to the side. "I can't decide if that is flattery or insult. But either way, I would suggest you are the one limiting yourself here."

"Oh?" I asked, intrigued despite myself. "How so?"

"My brother dismisses input as often as not, but I know he values yours." I started to object, but she continued. "I would have no chance at all convincing him to head east a bit, to deviate slightly to see what we see, and would be shouted down by the rest even if he was inclined to listen. But you might not fare so poorly."

I shook my head. "You know your brother—better than most, I warrant. He has a mind for vengeance now, as does the whole company. They want to reunite with Thumaar and then bloody the Emperor as soon as possible. He won't listen to me on that point. Even if he believes it a pity as well."

Her face hardened to stony impossibility. "Vengeance is it? He ought to be very careful then. While Bray has undeniable intelligence, when it comes to matters of orchestrating vengeance, his skills leave something to be desired."

She turned to leave and I blurted out, "That seems a bit harsh. He was a boy, still. And at least he tried, didn't he?"

Soffjian looked over her shoulder. "Tried? Oh. Yes. He did. And in truth, I advised him, mapped out almost the entire plan really, so I was equally inept at vengeance. At least when it came to my father. I have improved considerably since then."

Then she walked away.

The next day proved much like the last, only I was more sore and uncomfortable. It was largely uneventful as well, with the only real exception occurring when we stopped to rest the horses in the afternoon.

I was walking away from the company, trying to find a good rocky outcrop to offer some shade, as the sun was beating down and reflecting off the parchment and giving me an awful headache. Mulldoos saw me and altered his course to intercept. I considered pretending that I hadn't noticed and continuing a touch faster, hoping he would think it too much work to cut me off, but it was pointless, and would likely result in an uglier dressing down or encounter than it otherwise would have been, so I stopped.

Mulldoos had that odd hitch to his step, as his left arm and leg both seemed reluctant to cooperate most of the time. When he caught up, the pale boar stood in front of me, looked me up and down, and said, "Put those plaguing pages and case down, scribbler."

I was instantly nervous. "The pages? But—"

"Yes, you leprous boil, the plaguing pages."

I thought about reminding him that the captain had tasked me with that job, but knew that wasn't likely to help the situation resolve without me getting elbowed in the gut, so did as he commanded, setting the case on top to keep the pages from fluttering away.

Mulldoos said, "You'll never be a soldier. Never even be halfway competent. Obvious to everybody, ain't it? But if you're going to go around dressing the part, you better pick up a few things to avoid getting that helm all dented up or that gambeson skewered and bloody. You ready?"

I was a little dumbfounded—I always assumed if anyone would tutor me at all, it would be Vendurro. I was afraid to ask, really, as I knew I would be a target for mockery if I even attempted to swing a blade. "Did Captain Killcoin, uh—"

"What? Ask me to take you under my wing and regurgitate martial knowledge into your tiny little beak like a maternal mother bird? No. He plaguing didn't. But he's got a use for you, and it's miracle of miracles you ain't been killed already. And I figure since you keep on throwing yourself in harm's way, you best do it with at least some small chance of survival. If you got to die, at least look good doing it. So, asking again, you plaguing ready, scribbler?"

I looked at him. Face flushed, one eyelid drooping, half his face slack, posture torqued. Maybe he needed this as much as I did. I nodded, and Mulldoos did as well.

When I started to draw Lloi's blade, his hand shot out and clamped around my wrist. "Whoa, there. Who said anything about you wielding steel, you overeager bastard? Nobody, that's who. Plague me, but you're in a hurry to get yourself killed."

"I thought—"

"Well knock that shit off straight away. Obey orders. That's all you got to do here. Think you can manage that?"

I straightened and nodded, wishing he hadn't seen me at all.

"Right then. First thing, if you're going to get into a scrap sometime, you'll be needing something in the other hand." He pulled the buckler off his belt and handed it to me. It was steel, with the handle wrapped in stained leather. "Might be we give you a proper shield at some point, but best to start with something simple, easy enough to get used to."

The buckler did seem small and easy enough to wield, but it was surprisingly heavy.

"What's the most powerful muscle in your body?"

I thought about it for a moment and then tapped at my helm.

Mulldoos laughed, and then hooted. "And here I thought you were supposed to be half clever. It's your legs, your hips. You get in a fight, everything you do starts there. Stance, movement, generating power and follow-through, controlling range. Legs. Now, you got the legs of a wee chicken. But truth is, almost anybody can learn to defend themselves a little. We got girls in the company no bigger than you who manage not to get killed. Rudgi for one. So I ain't given up hope entirely. Stance first, as that's your base. Get those legs a little wider than shoulder width."

I did and he looked me over. "Hmmm." Then he pushed me with one hand and nearly sent me toppling over. "Got to have a solid base. Widen it a bit. Nope. Too wide. You got to be able to move as well." I adjusted and he said, "There you go. Now drop that sword foot back some, angle the toe out."

He circled me and inspected. "Could be worse. Now bend the knees. Little more. Keep the weight on the balls of your foot. Right. How do you feel?"

I felt my legs in a completely unnatural position that made me look an ass, but said, "I feel like . . . a coiled spring."

He slapped me on the back, and while it wasn't done with malice, it still almost knocked the wind out of me. But at least it didn't knock me over.

"Right. So let's see you hold that buckler."

I held it out away from my body, arm nearly straight.

"What are you plaguing doing? Warding off a moth? No. Bring the elbow back, now tuck it close to your hip. That's it. Not too tight, but cocked, coiled like you said. With a little shield like that, you're going to be doing active blocking. Know what that is?"

I shook my head and he said, "Course you plaguing don't. Because you know shit all. Your best bet is to avoid a blow altogether, but sometimes that just ain't realistic. Active blocking means you'll be moving the buckler around a lot."

Mulldoos adjusted my arm. "Getting ahead of myself here though— we'll get to blocking later—but the only way to do that is to have the buckler close to start. You can shove it out, intercept or deflect a blade, smash someone in the mouth real good, but first, keep the shield elbow anchored like that. Don't want to start overextended to start, plus, it'll get heavier quicker than you can imagine, so waving it around like that will sap your strength."

I didn't want to block anything and wanted to hit somebody in the mouth even less, but he made sense, so I nodded.

"Right. Now, slowly pull that barbarian slasher free."

I reached for it and he added, "Slowly. I'd tell you to go get a blunt, but none of them got the curve like the Grass Dog thing there, and the balance would be different. Got to train with something that matches what you'll be using when you get stuck in, so that one it is. But it ain't a toy, ain't even a knife. It's a sword, and even if savages made it, you'll treat it with respect or I'll knock you in the dirt. You hear me?"

I nodded and held it out in front of me.

He said, "Now, we're a long way from talking about how to wield it—we'll get there sometime if you don't get yourself dead first—but in order to have a proper stance, you need to feel the weight of the whole kit. So. How do you think you should hold that?"

I thought about seeing Vendurro fight, or Mulldoos, or anyone else who wielded a weapon or a sword. While there were variations, depending on the weapon, most favored a cocked elbow tucked in, and the weapon angled out above the shoulder, so I tried to approximate that.

Mulldoos looked me over, walked around me, pushed my arm here, changed the angle of the curved blade, kicked a foot, forced me to readjust a little, but not much really. I smiled and he scowled. "You been riding with us more days than I would have liked—if you didn't somehow manage to pick up one plaguing thing from watching us gut Hornmen and Brunesmen, I'd think you were worse than useless. Wipe that plaguing smile off your dumb face, scribbler, or I'll pound you to paste, you hear?"

The smile was gone in an instant. Sweat dripped down underneath the helm padding and into my eyes, and I reached up to wipe it off, forgetting for moment that I was holding a weapon. I clanged the small hilt off the bridge of my helm and Mulldoos laughed. "Serves you right for getting cocky, you green bastard. Now, you got a stance of sorts going on here. But you stay in one place rooted to the ground, you'll be dead quicker than spit, so we got to build some movement in. We'll start real plaguing basic, so I don't have to repeat myself a dozen times. You ready?"

And so it went for the next hour. Mulldoos showed me how to take small steps on the balls of my feet, keep my knees bent, maintain my balance. All of which I did poorly and with a great heaping of derision.

When we were done, Mulldoos said, "Moving out soon. That's a start. Not a great one. But it'll have to do."

He started to walk away, and after sliding the sword back into the scabbard without stabbing myself, I said, "Thank you. For helping me today, I mean."

Mulldoos stopped. "Won't just be today. You got a whole lot of learning to do before you stop embarrassing yourself and this outfit."

"Fair enough. But why? You could have told Vendurro or one of the others to—"

"Because," he said, the rest of the sentence hanging unsaid for a while, as if he were deciding whether or not to actually speak the words. Then, "That old goat was plaguing right. Just now, I'm not much good in a fight. Not like to instill confidence or steel nerves. The bastard wounded my pride on the other side of the Godveil, but as plaguing usual, he spoke true. Hated hearing it. But there it is. Only thing I ever been real exceptional at was cutting down enemies myself or inspiring the boys to do it. Knowing I couldn't do either back there, well . . . like eating hot stinging nettles, and then shitting them out."

Mulldoos looked at me, and while the left eye was half-hidden by a droopy eyelid, the right was fever bright. "Only other thing I got any real gift for, besides drinking copious amounts of alcohol, is turning tender recruits into hardened sons of whores. Still better at that than any man here. So it's me. You plaguing lucky bastard."

He headed back to his horse. I picked up my brass case and did the same. As we started riding again, I considered moving up alongside the captain and gently bringing up the idea of exploring further east on this side of the Godveil, as Soffjian suggested. But I knew how he would respond, so there was nothing to be gained except another earful, and I'd had enough of that for one afternoon. The rest of the day's journey was without incident.

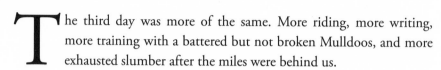

The third day was more of the same. More riding, more writing, more training with a battered but not broken Mulldoos, and more exhausted slumber after the miles were behind us.

But the fourth day on the other side of the Godveil, it looked like everything might change.

A scout rode up, not galloping, but definitely a canter. I recognized him from some of the other reports he delivered, a lad named Dunkiss. Usually his long face gave him away, but this time it was difficult to tell what lay ahead.

Braylar said, "Report, Syldoon."

Dunkiss replied, "There's a city, Cap. Ahead. Big one."

Vendurro, Soffjian, and Mulldoos all started talking at once, and Braylar shouted, "Silence, the lot of you!" Then he looked at Dunkiss again. "Populated?" He asked with the same tone you might inquiring after something mythical or supernatural.

"No," Dunkiss said. "Dead. Long time, from the looks of it."

Mulldoos shook his head. "Next time you lead with that, you dumb cock. Instead of 'there's a big plaguing city up yonder.'"

Braylar said, "The lieutenant has a point. You are certain it's empty then? If it's large, you couldn't have explored all that far."

Dunkiss took that as the challenge it was. "Had four men combing over it half the day. It's older than dirt. Thousand years at least. And abandoned near as long from the looks of it. The wall and stone buildings are still standing, some of them leastwise. Though some are collapsed here or there from disrepair. And anything wood or wattle has gone to waste, falling over, warped, overgrown with weeds and whatnot.

"But that's the queer thing. Usually, you see something like that all abandoned on the other side, temple or whatnot, it's been picked over. Scavenged. Other settlements steal lead roofing, stones that could still be used, whatever. But not this city. Just old, dead, and falling over all on its own accord.

Nobody took nothing that I could see. And there's nobody there, Cap. Not a plaguing one."

The captain remained skeptical and wanted to ride close enough to see for himself.

Two hours later, we crossed a rise and looked down a shallow valley at the remains of what was once a city bigger than Rivermost but smaller than Alespell.

Dunkiss's assessment had been accurate, as far as I could tell. Sections of the stone curtain wall had collapsed, the rubble core spilling all over the broken stones like a gaping wound, but one delivered by the siege of time rather than any invading army. While there wasn't enough thick vegetation in the area to completely overtake the structures, nearly every standing building was covered in unchecked ivy or moss or fronds or weeds.

All men had seen deserted places before on the other side of the Godveil—temples, small villages, forts. But I'd never heard of an abandoned settlement this large, and it was exactly as Dunkiss described—haunted looking, as if the occupants had simply disappeared at the exact same time and left the city to fall beneath the weight of ages.

Even from far away, it was far more unnerving than the plague village we rode through, and I couldn't suppress a shiver.

Mulldoos looked at the captain. "We going in, Cap?"

Braylar shaded his eyes, scanned the dead settlement, and shook his head in the negative.

The company rode by at a distance, every soldier staring at the empty, abandoned city, mumbling or cursing but unable to look away.

And on the fifth day on the other side of the Godveil, everything really *did* change.

Rudgi had been accompanying the scouts, and she came riding back earlier than usual. I moved ahead so I was within hearing distance when she reported, "There's a forest ahead, Cap."

Braylar asked, "And you thought this worthy of my attention, why exactly?"

She sat up straight in the saddle, despite having ridden hard to deliver the news. "Oh, I'll wager this isn't like any forest you've seen before, Cap. Or heard."

"Heard?"

"Aye, Cap." She maintained a level expression, but there was a strange tightness in her voice as well. Nervousness?

Azmorgon shook his huge head and said, "Is the Sergeant of Scouts getting scared by trees? Is that what I just heard?"

She stiffened and replied, "We're on the wrong side of the Godveil, Lieutenant. Every little plaguing thing makes me jumpy. But these trees, or columns, or whatever they plaguing are, they aren't natural."

Azmorgon rumbled out a laugh. "Lasses being in armor ain't natural. But it don't make me quiver in my boots."

Mulldoos said, "What are you plaguing going on about, Sergeant? What did you hear?"

She took a deep breath and addressed the shorter lieutenant. "First off, these trees, if that's what they are, don't look a thing like any trees I ever seen. Tall, but no limbs—just big trunks covered in some purplish moss. But that's not the strange thing. Well, it's a touch strange—whoever heard of trees with no limbs—but the strangest thing is the sound coming from the grove. From the tree columns."

"What kind of sound?" Vendurro asked.

She looked at him. "Kind of a keening."

Braylar said, "Did you say 'keening'?"

"That I did, Cap. My people, my clan, they had this awful dirgeful wailing thing they were wont to do anytime anyone died. Went on for weeks at a time, day and night. Just terrible, a pox on the ears really. This sounds a lot like that. Only my people weren't tree columns. On the other side of the Godveil."

The captain replied, "Well. Now my curiosity is piqued. Is it due north?"

Rudgi said. "Northeast. That's the other thing—there's a big sluggish river ahead, heading out of the Godveil. Not moving fast, but pretty deep. Probably the Silt Hood, but hard to say. Either way, it will be tough to cross without a ford, so it's going to force us east some. This grove is east of the river."

"Very good, then. Northeast we go."

We heard the forest before we saw it. *Keening* was an apt description. It immediately reminded me of something I hadn't heard in many years. I don't remember a great deal from my childhood at the inn with my mother, but there was a traveler who frequented it, who always brought a strange wooden horn with him, nearly as long as he was tall. It produced a grief-stricken baleful sound, and he sang sad tunes to accompany. He was not popular.

The noise sounded like a cross between that peculiar horn and a chorus of women wailing, as Rudgi described. She gave Azmorgon a smug look but he didn't say anything. Though he did draw his long polearm out of its sheath and prop it on his armored shoulder.

We heard the sound increase, one wail intermingling with another in a horrible chorus. And then the incredibly odd forest came into view as well. If the sound it made was disconcerting, the "trees" themselves were no less so. We came around a bend and saw the first of them. Rudgi had done a good job describing those as well. The trunks were completely limbless, with every inch covered in a dusky purple moss, and they rose up higher than dreadshade pines. They did resemble columns more than trees, and I would have mistaken them for as much until we got closer. They were asymmetrical, some growing almost perfectly straight, others curved slightly, with a few of the shorter ones bent and contorted as if they were trying to get out of the shade of their larger siblings to drink up some sun.

And if the oddity of limblessness and complete coverage by moss weren't enough, as we rode up to the first, I saw what must have been making the noise—each tree column was marked by hundreds or even thousands of holes, most the width of a few fingers. Whenever the wind blew, each column took the sound, amplified it, distorted it. The whole forest was a morose chorus.

The company rode around the outskirts of the forest. While there were a few stray columns close to us, and some even further west towards the Godveil, they grew tallest and thickest and most crowded to the east in the grove Rudgi mentioned. The horses were nervous, and their riders weren't much better. Judging by the murmuring and exclamations behind me, no one had ever seen the like either. While the company wasn't exactly used to the Godveil or easy around it, it was something they had seen, or at least heard about, all their lives. But these tree columns were completely alien.

I looked over at Soffjian and saw awe and pleasure on her face.

Braylar sent Rudgi ahead again to rejoin the other Syldoon who were scouting. After the initial chatter died down, we rode in silence for two more hours. Human silence, anyway. The tree columns continued their endless lament, crying out for some loss that had wounded them immeasurably. It was disquieting in every way possible.

We were about to rest the horses when Rudgi came galloping back to us, horse lathered, her freckled face flushed and sweaty.

She stopped in front of the captain and didn't even wait for the order to report, but started right in, speaking fast. "Never going to guess what's ahead, Cap!"

He sighed. "No. I expect I won't, and I'm not especially in the mood for riddles, so let's dispense with the clue-giving and cut directly to the specifics, yes?"

"Men!"

"Men."

"Climbing trees."

"Men climbing trees."

She nodded, still looking excited. "Ayyup. Or columns. Whatever you want to call them."

No one said anything. Mulldoos looked at Vendurro, Azmorgon looked at the dusky columns around us. Soffjian looked at me and smiled, only slightly less rapacious than usual.

Finally Braylar said, "And why, pray tell, are there men climbing these extraordinarily sad columns? To jump to their deaths?"

Rudgi replied, "Looks like they're working. In harnesses, pulling some weird spikes out of the trunks, putting them in bags. That's where all the holes came from."

Braylar leaned forward. "And did they see you?"

"Cap, I have to say, I'm kind of insulted. I'd be a pretty piss-poor Sergeant of Scouts if I got got that easy."

"How many?" he asked.

She thought about it. "There were a handful working the columns on the edge of the forest, but couldn't see deep in, and didn't want to risk getting too close. On account of the not wanting to be seen thing. So I raced back here."

Again, there was a long stretch of silence as everyone considered the unexpected revelation and what it might mean. I had read of a small handful of men parting the Godveil, separated by centuries, and while the accounts specified them coming back, some must have stayed on this side for some reason. But why? And how many? Had they repopulated this side of the Godveil? Why had the gods not expunged them as well, or struck them down as interlopers?

Finally, Mulldoos said, "Looks like the plaguing Deserters didn't abandon the whole lot of us, did they? Kept some on this side to go spike picking on the weirdest plaguing tree-things ever seen. Makes total sense."

Soffjian looked at Braylar. "It seems we didn't have to stray far from your chosen path to see the exceptional after all. Marvelous, isn't it?"

Braylar ignored her and turned to Mulldoos. "Convey the order—the main force will follow, but at a discreet distance. At least until we've ascertained what is afoot ahead and if it poses any threat."

"Aye, Cap."

As Mulldoos started down the line and Braylar and Soffjian started riding ahead, Azmorgon called back, "Speak slow and sure, Mushrooms."

Mulldoos paused, looked about ready to turn and confront Azmorgon and then kept riding.

Venduro said, "You might think you're just jolting his jewels. But I'm pretty sure Mulldoos ain't thinking the same thing at all."

Azmorgon regarded the much smaller man. "Look at you. A few days in the mighty officer's club and you gone and forgot who your elders are. Let me clear it up for you, Squirrel. I don't much care what that damaged fuck thinks, and got even less of a concern what weird little stones you got spinning around in that hollowed out gourd of yours, Lieutenant. Keep it to yourself."

The Ogre rode ahead to catch up to Braylar and Soffjian. Vendurro looked at me and shook his head. "Plague me, but there's some sour whoresons in this company."

"Don't worry about it, Ven," I replied. "I, for one, am always interested in what those weird little stones are doing."

He laughed and hit me in the shoulder. "Come on, then. Let's go see what these monkey men are doing on the wrong side of the world."

With the remainder of the company a hundred yards behind us, Braylar and his retinue had dismounted and walked among the mournful columns. Most of us had crossbows in hand, though Soffjian had her ranseur and Azmorgon his massive inelegant chopper that looked like it could cleave a horse in twain.

Rudgi said, "There's a clearing ahead. More of these columns on the other side. Though like I said, most have spikes sticking out of them, running up and down the length. That's where we saw them."

Braylar asked, "And you saw no men in armor? You are sure?"

"Sure as I could be, Cap. Like we talked about, I didn't want to get in too close. Still some sun left this afternoon, and not enough good cover—didn't want to give up our location. But I didn't see any glinting on anything else. So, nobody in metal armor close, that's for certain."

"Very good," Braylar said. "Take Dunkiss and circle around, further into the forest. Make sure it's just us and the workers in the columns of woe, yes?"

"Columns of woe, eh?" She smiled. "Funny, Cap. Right funny."

He sighed. "Just go."

As Rudgi set off on foot, Braylar regarded his men and his sister. "I'd hoped to find only squirrels and thrushes in our path, but it seems we have more to contend with."

"This is a priceless opportunity, not to be squandered," Soffjian said. "You are something of a master squanderer, so I do hope you embrace this one."

Vendurro asked, "What are they plaguing doing here, Cap?"

Braylar looked at the columns around us. "Besides harvesting the most bizarre trees in the world, you mean? I have no idea whatsoever. Like you, after seeing the ruins of the city, I imagined we were the only men tromping about on this side of the Godveil. Clearly, that was an erroneous assumption. But it is important we raise no alarms here. The forest has pushed us as close to the Godveil as we dare go."

Mulldoos said, "Maybe it's time to quit worrying about plaguing opportunities and head back through?"

Before Braylar could reply, Soffjian added, "That is the definition of squandering."

Braylar glared at her and said, "It is too soon, Mulldoos. The Imperials could be camped just on the other side. And if they get our trail again, we will have the glorious and suicidal end that Azmorgon there seems to be clamoring for. No. We do not return yet."

Azmorgon said, "So what's the plan, Cap? Going to kill these climbers?"

Braylar shook his head. "They are not soldiers. I don't kill unarmed men. Well, unless absolutely necessary. Or they have provoked me. Which is not the case here."

Vendurro asked, "What is the play then, Cap? Capture a few? Question them?"

"And then kill them," Azmorgon offered.

Mulldoos said, "Even for a plaguing Syldoon, you are a bloodthirsty bastard, you know that, Ogre."

"Aye. Best remember that, little man."

Braylar said, "Depending on who they are or where they come from, we might not even have a language in common. Putting one to the question could be fruitless."

Soffjian pointed at me. "You are forgetting, Bray, that you have one here who speaks a myriad of languages, both alive and dead."

I replied, "I read them well enough, and can write several, but speaking is something else altogether. I'm not sure how much of an asset I would be."

But Braylar made up his mind. "When Rudgi returns and we confirm there is no immediate threat, we will approach them. Weapons in scabbards. We have no idea what kind of response we will get, but even the dullest lout in the world knows a weapon when he sees one, and this is one time we do not wish to terrify or subjugate."

Azmorgon replied, "Got to speak my mind here, Cap, but thinking—"

"I know your mind already. We proceed as I say we proceed. If you have a problem with that, you can leave now and try your hand parting the Godveil on your own."

Even the Ogre shut up after that.

The captain, his retinue, and a handful of Syldoon crossed the clearing and approached the spiked columns on the other side. As Rudgi reported, there were a few men at various heights, shirtless, skin like bronze, covered in sweat as they swung on leather harnesses, pulling strange, almost translucent spikes as long as their forearms out of the dense mossy trunks and slipping them in satchels around their waists. The men were working with some tools—chisels and small hammers—as the spikes were lodged in tightly.

None of them saw us approaching, and the horses' hooves were muffled by the carpet of moss that littered the floor between the tree-columns. We were twenty paces away when the closest worker finally saw us. His eyes went wide, and he would have fallen twenty feet if not for the harness, as he lost his grip on the trunk and slipped before yelling something.

The other workers turned and saw us, and then they too started yelling to each other, eyes filled with terror as if they were seeing monsters rather than men with horses.

Mulldoos said, "Huh. Didn't figure on that. Good thing we aren't holding steel—they'd be shitting themselves just now. Might do it anyway."

As Scorn pawed at the loamy earth, Braylar raised both hands to show he wasn't armed. "Well met. I should begin by asking if you understand what I am saying, yes?"

The three men in harness continued shouting at each other, gesturing wildly, swinging on the trunks. One tried to climb higher before realizing he risked impaling himself if he did. Another seemed to be trying to move and hide on the other side of the column, for all the good it would do him.

The captain tried again in Anjurian, but had no better results. If anything, that only seemed to frighten them more, as they were nearly jabbering to each other.

Braylar turned to me. "Diplomacy will die an untimely death if we cannot communicate. Can you make out anything they are saying?"

As terrified as the men were, it would have been hard to understand them even if they were speaking fluent Syldoonian. "I can't be sure with all the shouting, but they might be speaking some kind of Old Anjurian. Or some variation of it. Though I stress *might*. As I said, I—"

"Speak inadequately, yes, yes. I was listening. But poor fluency is better than none at all. Try to calm them down and see if you can make anything out. Otherwise, I might be tempted to let Azmorgon chop them down from there so my sweet sister can interrogate them. And no one wants that. Especially the tree men, yes?"

I nodded, removed my helm, and handed it to Vendurro. After taking a deep breath and running my hand through my damp hair to stall for time, I walked my horse forward slowly, arms outstretched, trying to frame different statements in my head in Old Anjurian, and finally settling on the simplest one. I looked at all three men in turn "Hello," I said. "My name is Arkamondos."

The climber closest to me stared, his large nose flaring, sinews cording and rippling on his lean body. While he still appeared mostly terrified, it was tinged in something else as well. Confusion. He had understood something. Or at least it looked as if he had.

I tried again. "We intend you no harm," I said, haltingly, and then rephrased, as the first construction had been wrong. "What are your names?"

All three were silent now, no longer yammering, but not speaking either. "Your names?" I asked. "My name is Arkamondos. Arki. What are your names?"

The closest climber looked back at the others nervously. He whispered something, and another shook his head fast and said, "No!" and then something else I couldn't understand. It wasn't Old Anjurian, but it sounded like some derivative.

The third man pointed at the Syldoon behind us, arm waving, finger wagging, speaking quickly as he shook in his harness. Most of it was lost on me, but it sounded as if one word was "beast" or the equivalent.

I looked over my shoulder, and then back to the man who was pointing, listening as he said something else and then "beast" again, his eyes bulging, stubbly face almost a rictus of fear, the muscles in his thin ropy arms all standing out.

I rode back to the captain. "It's not us they're terrified of. Or not just us. They are afraid of the horses I think."

Mulldoos barked out a laugh. Vendurro said, "The *horses*? What are they plaguing afraid of the horses for? It's not like we're riding rippers."

Soffjian said, "Horses are not frightening. If you are familiar with them. But what if they've never seen them before?"

Everyone looked at her. Azmorgon said, "What are you plaguing going on about, witch? They're men. What do you mean they ain't seen horses?"

She regarded the belligerent giant. "You truly are a dull oaf, aren't you? Men from our half of the Godveil know horses. We've ridden them for millennia. Even those who couldn't earn enough in a lifetime to buy and care for a horse have seen others on them. But this side? We have no idea what's familiar to them, or how long they have been here. But what if they have no horses here? What if they have never seen their like before? Perhaps they think we are beasts ourselves with four legs. Or they are creatures of myth, monstrous or alien to them? Who can say. But I suggest we dismount."

Azmorgon said, "What you're saying is you got no plaguing idea, do you?" He turned to Braylar. "Let me chop them down. Then we'll have a nice little talk, up close and personal."

Braylar replied, "We dismount."

We all did as commanded, all of us watching the men in the columns as we did. When we set our feet on the ground, one gasped, and the three of them began talking quickly to each other.

Braylar said, "Now try it again, Arki. Tell them we are not horse monsters and mean them no harm. Find out who they are, and where their settlement is."

I gave Vendurro my reins and walked forward, saying in inelegant Old Anjurian, "Please tell me your names and where you are from. We will not harm you." I didn't add, "unless you take too long to gather your courage and speak to us," as that seemed less than productive.

The closest climber looked down. The two behind him nearly hissed, urging him to be silent from what I could tell. But he finally spoke to me. "We are farmers. Only farmers. Do not hurt us."

I wondered if this was how Old Anjurian was meant to sound, or if the dialect had changed so much to muddy the words, but I was pretty sure I understood the gist of what he said, even if that was no kind of farming I'd ever seen and they weren't holding radishes. Maybe the Old Anjurian word meant harvester.

"We will not hurt you," I said. "Will you come down please, so we may talk more easily? We mean you no harm. I swear it."

The lean leader looked back at the other two and they shook their heads in unison. Then one suddenly twisted around to look deeper into the column forest.

It took me a moment to make out the sound of hooves over the low keening sound the columns made, but then I saw a Syldoon weaving between them, riding hard for our position.

Whatever meager progress I made with the column climbers disappeared in an instant as they pointed at her and started yelling something at me again.

But Rudgi was no less frightened than they were—her face was pale, and her expression and demeanor sent a shiver up my spine.

Braylar saw it as well, and asked sharply, "What is it, Sergeant? Are we under attack?"

"Yes. No. I don't—I can't say, Cap. I can't, I don't—"

He stepped closer to her and drew Bloodsounder off his belt. "Report! What did you see?"

She stuttered, "Cap, it was—" and then she shook her head as if to clear it. "Two of them coming that I saw. Two. Two coming. Got to do something."

He reached up and snapped his fingers in front of her face. "Master yourself, soldier! At once! What approaches? Be quick about it!"

She looked at him, blanched, swallowed hard, and tried again. "Can't say. Huge. They were huge. Never seen anything so big."

"Men?" Braylar asked, though from the tone he knew the answer already.

"No. No, Cap. I can't say what they plaguing are, but not . . . they aren't men."

I heard the closest climber say in a heated whisper, "Overlords. The overlords come." It was hard to tell if it was a threat or a warning.

I looked at Braylar and told him what I heard, finishing with, "Maybe we should go."

The captain pulled his helm over his head and mounted his horse. "Whatever they are, there are only two of them. Still, it never hurts to be prepared." He pointed at Vendurro. "Get the company here. Now."

Vendurro mounted up and rode off as the remaining Syldoon climbed into their saddles as well. Braylar ordered, "Syldoon, ready crossbows and switch to sidearms if and when they close. These columns are too crowded to get off more than one good shot."

Soffjian said, "And what would you have me do, oh puissant warrior?"

"Your range is no less than our own. And might even be more. Work your memorycraft on whoever—"

"Or whatever."

"*Who*ever approaches. Take them down without killing them if possible."

"If possible," she said, holding her ranseur above her head with one hand, flexing the fingers of the other outstretched hand. "I make no promises."

I mounted up, fumbling a bit with the crossbow as I spanned it, but a little less so than usual.

The men in the harnesses were all frantically trying to look behind them. I just finished dropping the devil's claw on the stock when I heard something—it sounded like a faint drum beat. I realized with my gut churning that they were probably footfalls of some kind. And then I saw movement between columns fifty feet away.

A huge shape appeared and disappeared, weaving its way towards us. Whatever it was, it was half again as tall as any man save Azmorgon, maybe taller, and it was coming fast.

Braylar called out, "One shot, then draw weapons and spread out!"

The Jackals all raised their crossbows and I did the same.

My horse blasted air out its nose as it jerked its head side to side, and it was all I could do to keep in place as he stamped about.

I heard the nasty twang as three crossbows loosed around me, and then two more, and I looked up. And wished I hadn't.

Seeing the ripper for the first time in Alespell was like watching a monster emerge out of a nightmare to walk among us. But this was so much worse.

The creature was at least ten feet tall, broad and densely muscled, body and limbs much larger proportionately than any human's, its skin the color of ash. It wore some kind of thick, hardened leather armor affixed with irregular brass plates, moving faster now as it charged towards us, dodging between columns for cover, wielding some sort of gigantic spiked club. But more bizarre and awful than its monstrous size was the head. It had no eyes, with small spikes protruding from where they would have been as part of a crown of horns that wrapped around its head.

My bladder nearly set free as I recognized that head from temple ruins and the flail heads on Bloodsounder, and I almost dropped my crossbow.

One of the bolts struck the giant in the shoulder, with the other two sinking into the mossy columns behind it, and the creature bellowed so loud and fierce, I froze. Off to my right, Soffjian closed her eyes and splayed her fingers. The creature halted briefly, and I raised my crossbow, hoping she would fell it. But the giant slowed only for a moment, shook its horned head twice, and then came on again. My fingers were trembling as I took aim, and I squeezed the long steel trigger. The bolt skidded off a brass plate on its harness.

I dropped my crossbow, felt for Lloi's sword, missed it, and looked down to wrap my hand on the hilt as I drew it so quickly I nearly sliced my other arm and my horse's neck. I unhooked the buckler Mulldoos had given me, wishing it were larger, wishing I were hundreds of miles away, limbs feeling weak as something beyond nightmares bore down on us.

The creature bellowed again as it loped between the final columns and came on, and my horse started to turn away, and I desperately wanted to let it. My first instinct was to jerk on the reins when I felt the horse spook, but remembered Vendurro telling me that would only unnerve the beast more, so I reached forward and put my hand on its neck—it didn't do much, as it probably sensed I was terrified, but at least it didn't bolt.

The Syldoon had spread out, and there was a moment when the giant was unsure which of us to attack first. It raised the thick haft of its weapon above its head, and I saw that the spikes were the translucent things the climbers had been harvesting, and three protruded from either side at the end. While the giant had no eyes to see, it moved its head around until it fixed on me, being the closest. Then it charged at me.

I froze, knowing nothing I could do could possibly hurt this mammoth monster, that I was surely dead, when two more bolts struck it, one ricocheting off, the other embedded in its chest inside the leather armor, but only enough to make it more angry. It plucked the bolt out with one huge hand like a tiny thorn, roared, and then changed direction for the one who shot it.

That soldier made the mistake of trying to span his weapon with the devil's claw rather than drawing his sword or riding away.

The creature took three massive strides around a column and swung its club. The blow hoisted the soldier out of the saddle and his body went flying, blood spraying from the three gaping holes in his chest from the spikes. They had punctured the lamellar as if it were wet parchment.

Azmorgon rode past the giant, looking small for the first time, his chopper in both hands. But the giant started pivoting, and he had to veer off delivering a blow.

As the giant turned, Mulldoos came at it from the other side, slashing at its legs before riding past as well. The giant spun but didn't even try to deliver a blow, knowing it was too late, and then it moved around another column, bearing a shallow gash—it seemed its hide was nearly as thick as its armor.

The giant charged at Braylar, club raised high, and two more Syldoon rode between to protect their captain, one wielding a sword and shield, another a mace and shield.

The eyeless giant couldn't have seen them, shouldn't have been able to see anything, but it moved and reacted as if it knew exactly where everyone was. It took one quick stride and brought the club down in a vicious arc, striking one Syldoon at an angle across the collarbone.

I heard it snap, and saw the spikes bite down deep, again puncturing armor.

The horse reared, hooves flailing at the monster in front of it. The giant struck the horse with a backhanded blow across the head that felled it. The soldier was ripped out of the saddle as the giant pulled the club and finally freed the spikes again.

The other Syldoon rode forward, striking the giant in the arm with his mace. As the rider tried to move off, the giant spun with surprising speed, grabbed the soldier by the back of the head, hoisted him out of the saddle as if he were a child, and swung him against the nearest column. I heard the man's neck or back break as the body hit the mossy bark and dropped to the loamy earth.

Braylar charged from the other side, the twin flail heads striking the giant in the ribs as he passed.

Again, the creature knew that assailant was too quick, and turned to face another, blood oozing from another small wound, but showing no signs of slowing.

As soon as the captain was clear, several more crossbow bolts struck the giant, two sticking, the rest flying off in different directions.

The giant roared, clearly furious at having no foe close enough to destroy.

I saw a blur of red next to me as Soffjian rode at the monster's back, ranseur cocked near her shoulder.

She called out something, and the massive creature turned to face her, but she had no intention of closing—she threw her weapon and veered off before it could strike at her.

The ranseur hit the giant in the throat, and while it seemed to strike deeper than the bolts, it reached up, pulled the polearm free and tossed it away, bellowing in fury and pain.

Two more bolts struck it in the back, one ricocheting off a brass plate, another puncturing the hardened leather, but not biting deep. The giant sprang off to its right, using the columns for protection as it closed on another soldier who hadn't had the time or sense to ride away from it. The giant swung its spiked club, and the Syldoon instinctively tried to block the blow with his shield, which erupted into broken wood and a shattered steel rim. The giant brought the haft up, reversed direction, and caught the wounded Syldoon in the side of the helm.

The spikes didn't penetrate the steel, but they didn't need to—the force of the blow dented the helm in half a foot and caved in the soldier's skull. The Jackal was dead before he hit the ground.

I realized I was rooted to the spot, paralyzed, and cursed myself, sheathing my sword, putting the buckler back on my belt, and drawing the crossbow again.

Another Syldoon rode past, slashing one of the giant's thick exposed legs, and he got clear just as the spiked club swooshed behind him.

More quarrels were loosed, one striking the creature, one splintering against a brass plate, and one also hitting one of the Syldoon who was riding past the giant. The soldier changed direction for a moment, ducked, and tried to ride away from the creature, having missed the chance to strike at it, but the eyeless giant was too quick. He only caught the soldier with a glancing blow in the side, but even that crumpled him in the saddle. The Jackal rode past, hunched across his horse's neck, and disappeared into the purple columns.

Mulldoos and another soldier screamed together as they rode at the giant, and he spun to face them, bleeding from a dozen wounds, bolts sticking out everywhere, but the attack was a feint, and they raced off to the right and left.

But Azmorgon came in fast from the giant's rear and brought the long blade of his chopper across the creature's lower back as he passed. The blows would have severed any man in two, but the giant didn't go down. The huge club arced out, but Azmorgon ducked and rode clear.

The giant tried to take another step and then screamed in pain, reaching back to feel the newest wound. Its hand came back covered in blood, and another step caused it to grimace as it wobbled slightly.

The Syldoon around it used that opportunity to unload their crossbows, a handful of bolts striking the giant in various spots. Even though they didn't all stick, and the ones that did might not have struck deep, the massive creature bore wounds everywhere, with the one delivered by Azmorgon being the worst. It staggered, shuffled sideways, reached out to break its fall on a column, and then dropped to its knees.

Braylar called out, "Loose! Loose, you whoresons!"

Five more bolts struck, and the giant toppled over, dropping its flat club on the earth next to it.

Braylar ordered everyone to hold. With the sounds of battle over, there was only the low keening from the columns and the moans from those who were wounded but still somehow miraculously survived being struck by the eyeless creature.

The captain dismounted, and several others around did as well, though I noticed most of the company behind us stayed on their horses.

I climbed down too, shaking, breathing fast though I'd done next to nothing. The captain, his sister, Mulldoos, and Azmorgon all slowly approached the giant, and I did as well.

Braylar raised his hand and everyone stopped several feet away. We all stared at the massive body sprawled and bloody in the moss leavings. Even dead or dying, it inspired awe and terror. Its skin looked as thick as the rooters we had seen on the Green Sea—while it hadn't deflected all bolts and blades, the skin was nearly armor on its own, and kept penetration to a minimum. It was covered in some bizarre asymmetrical design that I mistook for a tattoo of some kind, but looking closer, I saw that it was some scarring or carving in the skin itself.

The plates on the hardened leather were odd as well, each slightly different in size, not affixed in a regular pattern, and engraved with some asymmetrical line pattern that echoed what was carved into the giant's pale hide.

The giant had what looked to be two black manes winding between the spikes on its head and down its back, disappearing into the armor.

Soffjian had reclaimed her ranseur. "Should we make sure he isn't napping?" she asked with a crooked smile.

Braylar nodded. "An excellent suggestion. We've already lost too many today. No need to take anything for granted."

Soffjian took a step closer, and stabbed the giant in leg with her ranseur. The creature stirred, one huge arm flailing once, before growing weak and dropping to the moss again.

Mulldoos said, "Plague this!" He took three awkward but quick strides, and then the falchion came down on the back of the giant's neck. The creature convulsed once and started to shift slightly, but even though Mulldoos was damaged, he was also incensed. Three more blows and the falchion finally crunched deep enough into its spine to kill the hulking thing.

Braylar looked around quickly before sighting Rudgi. "You said two, yes?" She nodded, eyes still fixed on the dead giant. "Aye, Cap."

He shouted, "Be ready, Jackals. There is another. Reload and—"

Vendurro called out, though flat and sad sounding. "No need, Cap."

Braylar looked at the younger lieutenant as he rode up and dismounted, waiting. Vendurro pulled off his helm, looked at the captain and said, "Came in from the side when you were fighting this one. Tore into the troops right quick, took out ten, maybe more, before we felled the plaguing thing."

Then Vendurro looked at the one Mulldoos had just hacked into, and his eyes darted over to Bloodsounder and back to the dead giant. Then in an almost reverent whisper, he said, "Plague me. Did we just . . . did we just get attacked by gods, Cap?"

Mulldoos was wiping off his falchion. "Think gods bleed, boy? Or get killed at all by the likes of men?" He glanced down at the huge creature. "Monster, maybe, demon even, but this ain't no plaguing god, no matter how many horns it's got sticking out of its plaguing head. Might be it's a Deserter, might be it's not. But whatever it is, it ain't a plaguing god, that's for damned sure."

We all stared down at the huge body. I had no idea what the others were feeling, but I was still stunned. The ripper we set loose in Alespell was a terror, to be certain, but it still was just an animal. A large, vicious, incredibly fast animal with no fear of men, but an animal just the same.

But this . . . this was something else altogether. The leather armor was elaborately tooled and showed amazing craftsmanship; the flat haft of the spiked weapon wasn't simple, but adorned with slight but intricate carvings along its length. This creature was the most terrifying thing I'd ever seen, but it was no animal, and even "monster" seemed insufficient. Mulldoos did have a point—no matter how easily the giant ripped through the soldiers or how tough it was, it could be killed, and was no god.

But what was it?

Rudgi demystified things, though, as she walked around and stopped near its legs that were bigger around than most trees. "Gods. Can you imagine the size of the cock on this thing? He'd plaguing kill a rooter if he fucked it." She looked around and stopped at Soffjian. "Come on, you can't tell me you aren't the least bit curious. How big do you reckon it is?"

Mulldoos gave Rudgi a cold pale stare. "The thing makes Azmorgon look like a dwarf, managed to see us plenty fine without any plaguing eyes, must weigh more than a laden wagon, and killed near on ten men all by its lonesome, and you're worried about its *cock*?"

Rudgi shrugged. "Legitimate question, isn't it? I mean, every male something or other has a cock. Most natural thing in the world, really. Even monsters or demons or gods. In fact, you all seem more fixated on your packages than us most of the time, so it sort of comes as a shock you all didn't make the observation first."

Mulldoos shook his head, Soffjian chuckled, and Azmorgon said, "A dwarf? What's that make you, little man? A plaguing possum?"

Mulldoos started to respond but Braylar cut him off. "We need to move. We have no idea what alarm was raised, or how many more of them are out there. If nothing else, we need to clear this forest before nightfall so if we are attacked again we can use our crossbows to good effect. Make sure the wounded are tended to and get them back in the saddle. Now."

Soffjian glanced around at some of the other crumpled and bloodied bodies. "And what of your dead, brother?"

She asked this with no inflection, almost casually, but watched him very carefully as he directed his response to Vendurro. "We don't have time to bury them. Throw them across their horses. They come with us."

Azmorgon said, "Better if we just leave them." Then added a belated "Cap" as if that made the sentiment better.

Mulldoos spit against a column. "Those are our plaguing brothers, you whopping big horsecunt."

"Our plaguing dead brothers. And they'll only be slowing us down. Look, if it makes you feel any better, if you somehow outlive me, you can dump my body in a gorge or leave it for the crows. Couldn't give a toss either way, because I'll be a plaguing corpse."

"No worries, Ogre. I'll be sure to piss on your dead face."

Azmorgon's big bushy eyebrows drew closer together, and there was murder beneath them for a brief moment, but it disappeared as he smiled. "Like I said, do what you plaguing want, Mushrooms. Pretty sure I'll be the last man standing, but either way, the truth is the truth. Better to leave them. Say a few pretty words if it makes you sleep better."

Braylar said, "The Jackals do not desert our own. Alive or dead. Not now, not ever." He turned away and slipped Bloodsounder on his belt. "They ride with us until we have a chance to bury or burn them in honor. And I think we have overstayed our welcome here on this side of the Godveil. Mount up, you whoresons. We have some riding to do." The Syldoon started back towards their horses. Soffjian continued looking down at the behemoth we had finally felled. The victory was a costly one. We certainly couldn't survive too many more victories like that.

I glanced back at the columns where we'd first sighted the climbers. They were long gone, having fled sometime during the melee. Turning back to Soffjian, I said, "Perhaps some places are better left unexplored."

She gave a quick nod and then said, "Perhaps so, Arki."

There was sadness there, though it was impossible to tell if it was more for the lost opportunity or the lost lives.

We headed north to clear the columns and were forced further east by the bend in the broad sluggish Silt Hood (assuming Rudgi was right). As the forest receded and disappeared behind us, the ground to the east grew hillier. Scouts scoured the countryside ahead of us, as those closest to the river looked for a place to ford it.

It didn't seem to matter which side of the Godveil we were on—we were harried and cut down, and attrition was taking its toll.

Vendurro was riding alongside me and his mind was obviously occupied, as there was no idle chatter at all. Which was sort of disconcerting. Sort of like a bird without a beak. I sensed he wanted to be left to his thoughts, despite being only a few feet away, so I was reluctant to say anything. But as it turned out, I didn't have to sit in silence for more than a mile before he said, "Queerest thing, ain't it?"

"What's that?" I replied. "There's a lot of queer things happening."

"Well, that's just it. Thanks to you and a bunch of crumbly parchment, we parted the plaguing Godveil. Or just Veil, if there's not gods hereabouts. Whatever we end up calling it. Point is, we led a small army through. Never been done before, right?"

"Not that I know of."

"So there's that," Vendurro said. "And on this side, we see a dead city, and the strangest greenery that ever grew anywhere, only it ain't green, but purplish, and covered in even stranger spikes, with a bunch of skinny pricks climbing up and down like trained monkeys, plucking those spikes out like some kind of rare fruit. So yeah, as if just being on this side weren't off-putting enough, there's the plaguing scenery.

"And then, just in case those two things didn't make a man mighty uneasy all by their lonesome, well . . ." he started speaking faster, "a couple of Deserters mosey on up and lay into us, shredding us like we were only so many straw dummies in a training yard. Only we managed to kill a couple, so they ain't gods. We don't think. Don't rightly know. Maybe they're priests to the gods, maybe monsters or demons like Mull says. But who plaguing knows? All we got for certain is they ain't men, and likely something a lot more than men. So we're a long way from home, in a place we got no place being in, confronting things way beyond our understanding. And dying way too plaguing fast."

Vendurro shivered and cast a quick look behind to make sure the other soldiers hadn't overheard. "I know I shouldn't be talking like this. Ain't very . . . lieutenanty."

It hit me then that getting promoted when you hadn't been expecting it, might not have even wanted it, would have been challenging enough even under ideal conditions. And these were not ideal conditions. I said, "It's a natural reaction, Ven. These are incredibly . . . unnatural circumstances. And I guarantee every man in this company is wrestling with the same thoughts you are."

"Maybe, maybe not. But officers ain't supposed to let on they wrestle with the same things as the rank and file." Then more quietly, sounding young again, he added, "Hewspear never did. Model officer right there, if there ever was one."

I looked behind briefly as well before saying, "Well, be that as it may, he'd be thinking the same thing as you just now. And you didn't reveal it to anybody but me, and you know I'm not talking to the rank and file. Most of them want to punch me in the face."

Vendurro laughed, chuckled really. "You're giving yourself too much credit. More like all of them."

I did laugh, but it was stopped short when I heard a gut-wrenching scream from somewhere behind us, a shriek truly, something that didn't sound like a response to pain, but fueled by the most irresistible terrors imaginable. The last time I'd heard a scream like that, Soffjian was driving a man mad as we fought the Hornmen in Alespell.

My first thought was that we were under attack by Deserters again, or something worse if possible. But there was no enemy to be seen.

Braylar, Mulldoos, Azmorgon, and Soffjian raced down the line, and Vendurro and I followed close behind. It didn't take long to discover the source of the scream.

Several Syldoon had gathered around something, and Braylar ordered them out of the way as he dismounted.

A soldier was lying in the stones and scrub, one foot still in the stirrup. Braylar shouted, "What happened? Who is this?"

Benk said, "Name's Guntro, Cap. His, not mine."

"I know who you are, you ass. I say again, what happened?"

"Nothing," Benk said, sounding surly and stupid. "That is, nothing I could see. He wasn't acting peculiar like at all. Just quiet. But we all been quiet. Then all of the sudden, starts hollering like his bones was on fire or his skin were melting something fierce, then clutched his head like he been hit with an invisible bolt."

Braylar glanced at Soffjian as Benk continued, "That was it. Fell out of the saddle. Is he dead? Not looking real alive, is he?"

Vendurro had dismounted and was kneeling next to Guntro, checking for any signs of life. He looked at the captain and shook his head.

Braylar asked, "Does he bear any serious wounds? Signs of infection?"

Vendurro felt Guntro's head, his palms, looked his limbs over. He pointed to the bandage on the dead man's forearm. "Cool as can be. No stink of rot anywhere. Only wound I see is this one." He looked up at Benk. "What happened to his arm here?"

Benk replied, "How should I plaguing know, Sergeant? I ain't his nursemaid."

Vendurro stood and said, "That's Lieutenant, you dumb plaguing bastard, and you've been riding along with him."

He said it with conviction and some bile, and Benk backed down. "Pardon, Lieutenant, but can't rightly say."

Vendurro said, "Well get down off your horse and inspect him, then, you whoreson. Get the rest of his armor off."

Benk dismounted, looking none too happy, but Mulldoos had a big crooked grin on his face.

As Benk started removing the dead man's armor, Braylar called out. "The wound on his forearm. Does anyone know anything?"

Another soldier rode up, weaving between the other Syldoon, and said, "Aye, Cap. One of them Deserter giants clipped him a little. Only a glancing blow, though. Wasn't deep at all. Someone else distracted the Deserter before he could finish Guntro off. He got off lucky. Well, until now, that is. Not so lucky now I guess."

Mulldoos ordered that soldier to get down and give Benk a hand undressing Guntro.

"Anyone else know anything? Did Guntro say or do anything out of the ordinary before screaming and falling down dead?"

The soldiers looked at each other, and no one volunteered any information.

When Benk and the other soldier were finished, Guntro was dirty and dead, but without any other wounds to speak of.

Everyone looked at the corpse.

Soffjian approached and said, "May I?"

Mulldoos stepped in between, scowling and slurring, "You may get your ass back up on that horse. Or you may walk in any other direction. You may do any old plaguing thing you may think up, so long as you stay clear of us and ours."

Braylar walked over and put his hand on the pale lieutenant's shoulder. "I don't think she can do any more damage here. Do you?"

Mulldoos still had a black look, but slowly took a step back. A small step. But a step.

Soffjian nodded to her brother and approached the corpse. Benk and the other soldier got up and moved back as if they'd just seen a brass viper slither out of a hole.

She squatted alongside, closed her eyes, placed one hand on Guntro's arm, and moved her other hand over his chest, his head, without touching him.

Some soldiers leaned forward in their saddles, others shifted nervously, and no one looked comfortable. Especially Mulldoos.

Soffjian opened her eyes. "It is hard to tell with the dead. But there is residue here to be certain."

Azmorgon rumbled, "What are you plaguing talking about? Residue?"

She said, "Memory magic. I strongly suspect that's what killed him just now."

Benk said, "Ain't no Memoridons hereabouts. Excepting you. Are you saying you killed him?"

"Yes, you simp. I struck him down for saying something stupid. Who might be next, I wonder?"

Vendurro said, "So . . . the Deserter then?"

Soffjian stood up. "Or his weapon." She pointed at the small wound on his forearm. "I can't say for certain."

Vendurro asked, "But why didn't it take him out when he got wounded?"

Soffjian looked at Braylar as she responded. "I imagine it was memory poison of some kind." She turned back to Vendurro. "I do not pretend to know definitively. I know as little as you do of Deserters, in fact. But do recall—memory magic did not originate with men, but with the gods. Or their proxy."

She walked back to her horse as Mulldoos said, "Plaguing legends. Told you, those things we killed weren't gods. And we got no idea what came from where. Nothing but legend. Which is the same as real old horseshit."

Soffjian climbed into the saddle and swept her arm around, east to west. "You aren't the most observant type, so perhaps you failed to notice, but we currently find ourselves in the land of legends. At least their chosen sanctuary. But believe what you believe. I tell you, no blade or infection brought that man down. That much I am certain of. It was memory magic. Unlike anything I've seen before, but memory magic. Ascribe what you will to that, Syldoon."

She rode back up the column. Braylar watched her go until Azmorgon said, "Guessing you'll want this one on a horse, too?"

The captain turned back to his monumentally surly officer. "I will want this man dressed. I will want this man back on his horse. And I will want you to see to it. Yes?"

He didn't wait for a response, but got into his own saddle and called out to his soldiers, "Death is death. Our enemies caused it. That is all that matters. Perhaps someday we will return when we are at strength, and visit untold vengeance upon the massive bastards here. But for now, we continue north until we can cross the Veil again and leave this cursed place behind. That is all that need concern you. Understood?"

When Vendurro and I were mounted and riding to the front of the company again, I looked over at him and said, "That was quite lieutenanty, how you handled yourself back there. I am sure Hewspear would be proud."

Vendurro glanced over at me, then away quickly. "You think?"

"I think."

He allowed himself a small, somewhat sad smile, but it was brief, and gone almost as soon as it arrived.

Trying not to dwell overmuch on more cursed weapons, monstrously huge eyeless overlords, or the increasing number of enemies we made no matter where we went or which side of the Godveil we were on, I threw myself into translation at every opportunity. With Braylar always hounding me for updates, there was a heightened sense of urgency, but now, without the wagons, and with our numbers dwindling by the day, the exigency had doubled. Every moment I pored over another lay subsidy roll or some account of a depleted larder, I wanted to scream. It was everything I could do not to skim and rush in the hopes of finding something of substance relating to Sentries, early Memoridons, even the Godveil. And I knew the more I rushed, the more opportunity to miss something. Still, there weren't that many tomes and pages left to sift through, and I despaired of ever finding anything remotely relevant or useful.

But then I opened a new ledger and immediately recognized the precise, clipped, and straightforward script. It was in the hand of Vortniss, the Temple of Truth priest who'd studied Anroviak or Untwik's writing on the subject of controlling memory witches. Unlike Luzzki, who pressed his witches to approach the Godveil and didn't specify how he maintained a hold on them, Vortniss's other account I'd seen had provided some tantalizing if incomplete details about the construction of the first frames.

I was expecting more of the same here—oblique references lacking explicit description— and got it for a fair number of pages. But then a new entry began describing the "frames" in greater detail as a means of building on the experiments the earlier priests had performed in controlling memory witches.

Slowing down for accuracy was nearly impossible, but I knew when I presented my findings to the captain there would be a reckoning if I couldn't answer all or most questions confidently and in full, especially if Mulldoos, or worse, Azmorgon, was in attendance. Hewspear's absence was still sharp in many ways, but he always proved level-headed and deliberate when assessing new information, and I was afraid how it would be received, even if I was thorough and exhaustive in my interpretation of the words written so many centuries ago.

I hadn't gotten nearly as far as I would've liked when the captain ordered us to get on the move again, and translating in the saddle was impossible. Still, I couldn't help scanning the pages as we rode, even if I couldn't piece everything together or write down anything I found. I nearly bumped into the horse in front of me more than once.

Braylar noticed and fell back until he was alongside me. "You do seem more distracted than usual, Arki. And that's saying something. What have you found?"

I glanced over at Vendurro, behind me slightly, and kept my voice low. "I don't have enough to say for certain, Captain. But it is provocative. And I'm hopeful."

He wasn't wearing his helm so I could see his eyes, which somehow managed to both narrow and register some excitement at the same time, which was quite a trick. "Oh? I do presume you have enough in hand to warrant such a declaration, yes?"

"I do. I think I do," I said. "I'll need more time to be certain. But yes, this is the most fascinating and germane writing I've come across yet. I can't promise it will explain how Cynead managed to syphon control of all the Memoridons in one fell swoop. But I also can't promise it won't." It was difficult to moderate my tone and enthusiasm.

"Very good," he replied. "Light a lamp when we make camp this evening, and don't bother helping with the horses and gear."

"Truly?"

"Truly. Our need outweighs any caution at this point. And besides, I don't think the Deserters will see it, do you?" He twitch-smiled and resumed his place at the head of the line.

Vendurro nudged his horse a little closer. "You really think you got something good, Arki? Something we can use to take that pompous prick down?"

There was no disguising his enthusiasm, which was one of the reasons I was growing to like him so much. "I might. I just might."

Vendurro nodded three times in quick succession. "Well then, best wipe that goofy smile off your plaguing face and get back to it!" he said, with a goofy smile on his face.

And so I did.

When we finished riding for the day, I earned some foul stares from some of the other Syldoon as I continued scribbling by the lamp, but Vendurro kept watch as I continued poring over Vortniss's record, and sent anyone away who asked what I was doing.

Even when Azmorgon came by, towering over Vendurro, and said, "Hey, little shithead, douse that wick."

Vendurro replied, "He's doing what he needs to be doing, Ogre."

"I was talking to the other little shithead, Squirrel. You his champion now?"

Vendurro stood up to him. "Operating with Cap's say so. You got an issue with it, you take it up with Cap. Go on. Wake him up. I'm sure he'll be really plaguing happy to have a chat and explain his motives and whatnots. Loves to have his sleep broken like that, he does."

The Ogre stalked off.

Much later, I saw Soffjian pause as she walked by, watching me for so long that I grew incredibly uneasy before she finally moved off into the dark.

I continued on long into the black evening, my quill scribbling furiously, pains in my back growing, hand aching, a dull pounding behind my tired eyes, watching the watch change in the middle of the night, and still pressed on.

When I finished translating the journal, I revisited key passages again and again to be sure I'd gotten it right, or at least not absolutely wrong. Satisfied, I finally doused the lamp and fell into a fitful slumber for a few hours, exhausted but still jittery with the discovery, rolling it over in my mind, stunned that the answer might truly be in these pages, and frustrated that I hadn't happened upon them much earlier.

After waking, splashing some water on myself, and forcing myself to eat something, I changed into a slightly less sweaty and sticky tunic, made myself as presentable as you could after sleeping on the cold ground, gathered my writing case and notes, and found the captain.

He saw me coming and summoned his officers and Soffjian.

When we were all assembled, Braylar said to me, "Well, Arki, I do hope you have roused us for good reason. Mulldoos is in a foul mood when he hasn't broken his fast yet, and judging by his expression, he is long on hunger and short on patience."

Vendurro looked at Mulldoos as he took a bite out of a boiled egg and offered another.

Mulldoos said, "Plague your egg. That ain't no way to break a fast. Give me a plaguing chicken or two. At least a plump quail. Anything but something that dropped out of the hindquarters of a bird."

Vendurro replied, yolk in his teeth, "I ain't positive, but don't think chickens shit the eggs out, Mulldoos."

"You don't put that egg in your mouth or back in the pouch, and I swear I'll stick it up your ass and you'll be the one shitting it out."

Braylar folded his arms behind his back. "You see. Foul temper. Either way, you should begin now before things get worse."

"This better be good," Mulldoos said.

I was nervous, especially with Mulldoos snarling, Azmorgon staring holes through my skull, Soffjian looking on critically, and Braylar with a shorter temper than ever of late. Only Rudgi and Vendurro looked encouraging, and his cheeks were stuffed with egg so he actually did look like a squirrel.

My news was as fulsome as anything I'd discovered, and I wanted to launch into it directly, but also wanted to be sure they had context. "As you might recall, Vortniss was a Priest of Truth hundreds of years ago, who was fascinated by the memory witches, and like some of his predecessors, sought to control them rather than destroy them. And he was far more methodical than some of the earlier priests in the order who had done the same. Or at least luckier in not getting found out. He—"

Azmorgon said, "Got no interest in a plaguing history lesson. Thinking I'll get the troops ready to move out, lest you got a problem with that, Cap."

Braylar gave the much larger man a measured stare before replying, "This history lesson, as you call it, might be the key to regaining control of the Memoridons and bringing Thumaar back to the throne. But if you would rather resaddle a horse, by all means."

Azmorgon shrugged his massive shoulders, looking more bear than man. "They ain't going to resaddle themselves." Then he walked off, scratching his ass as he went.

Soffjian said, "I obviously missed out on your earlier discoveries as well, Arki, but you can bring me up to speed another time. Please do continue."

I said, "Vortniss suspected that the memory witches and the guardians— the Sentries who had weapons like Bloodsounder—that they were all tied to the Godveil somehow. The witches were able to approach much closer than anyone else, and returned unburdened, their powers in check for a bit. And the guardians—"

"For not rehashing," Braylar said, "you are doing an inordinate amount of rehashing. Proceed. Quickly."

I pressed on. "Well, it's all relevant. Because Vortniss figured out that if he could somehow harness the energies of the Godveil, draw some of it away, that he could bind the witches to him without needing the incessant pilgrimages to the Veil. And after a great deal of experimentation, mostly failures, and some lives lost in the process, he finally hit on the solution. A frame."

Soffjian asked, "So this Priest of Truth was the forerunner then?"

"One of them. But it doesn't really matter if he hit upon the idea first. What does matter is that he not only perfected it, but served as a model. From his account, it sounds as if another priest found out about his experiments and, rather than reporting him to the legates, stole the secret, as he too framed a small portion of the Godveil and used it to bind witches to him."

Mulldoos said, "And Vortniss couldn't very well go squawking to the high priests about it, as they'd both get their bellies ripped open and their guts strewn across the temple courtyard."

I nodded. "That's right. But Vortniss was cagey. And vengeful. He schemed and continued his experiments, though with far fewer witnesses who might be able to betray him. And while it took him several years, he finally uncovered a way to steal the portion of the Godveil his brother had procured in his own binding."

Braylar twitch-smiled. "At long last, you come to the marrow of the matter. What did he do, Arki?"

I tapped my brass writing case twice. "It is actually quite brilliant. Or at least exceedingly clever."

"You are exceedingly annoying. What. Did. He. Do."

I said, "He had several memory witches in his service and—"

"Service!" Soffjian laughed. "Such a lovely and dishonest euphemism."

"Control then," I amended.

"Try slavery."

Braylar said, "It is hard enough getting a straight answer out of him without you needling him, sister. Be still."

I tried again. "Vortniss released one of the witches from his frame, and bound her to an underpriest with a new frame, and—"

Mulldoos interrupted, earning a black look from the captain. "He did what now? Why would he plaguing do that? Thought he was a jealous horsecunt?"

"An experiment," I replied. "He wanted to see if he could steal the energy back to his own frame, reclaim control."

Braylar turned his slitted mossy eyes on me. "I am unsure how many different ways I can ask how this was done." Then he surveyed the rest of his retinue. "And if anyone else utters a single word, I will let Azmorgon saddle you."

No one else spoke, so I said, "It seems it required . . ." I glanced at Soffjian quickly. "Sacrifice. He killed two of his witches in doing so, but he managed to syphon off the bit of Godveil in the underpriest's frame, drew it back to his own, and the control defaulted to him once more."

"And this sacrifice, did he reveal specifics on how this was accomplished, precisely?"

I nodded. "He did. Apparently he ordered both of the witches to focus day and night, meditating without food or respite, until they succeeded in drawing the swath of Godveil back to his own larger one."

Soffjian said, "And in doing so, snuffed out their lives."

"Yes. Though that's a soft euphemism for murder."

She smiled as Vendurro said, "So we can ask questions now?"

Braylar sighed but didn't deal out any more threats, so Vendurro said, "So Cynead must have a whopping big frame hidden somewhere, biggest ever, right? Must have, to have all the Mems bound to him like that."

Soffjian said, "He does. In a tower in the Citadel. He must have sacrificed—apologies, murdered—a fair number of his Imperial Memoridons to accomplish it."

"These were hedge witches Vortniss used," I replied. "Not fully trained Memoridons."

"Yes," Soffjian said levelly, hinting at something dangerous under the surface, "but that was to reclaim something from one small frame controlling one witch. Cynead usurped control over fifty Tower frames in Sunwrack alone, and who knows how many in other provinces, each frame controlling hundreds of Memoridons. So it's safe to assume that the cost was still quite high, training or not. Memoridons were sacrificed."

I could only nod.

Vendurro rubbed the tuft of hair on his chin like it was a small mouse he hoped to win over, and said, "So . . . we just got to find and destroy the frame, right?"

Braylar replied, "No, young Lieutenant. That's exactly what has prohibited the Memoridons from simply doing the same and freeing themselves for centuries. Destroy the frame, and there would be a horrible surge unleashed that would slay every Memoridon bound to it. Isn't that right, sweet sister?"

Soffjian gave him a hard look and cold smile. "If only severing our chains were so simple, brother, you can be sure we would have shattered our frames centuries ago." She looked at Vendurro. "Three hundred years ago, give or take, there was an uprising in the Badger Tower. Memoridons turned on their Commander, took him prisoner, and destroyed the frame, despite his warning them several times that they were dooming them all. They ignored him, opting to risk it, hoping that such stories were only a myth designed to keep them cowed. As it turned out, they really ought to have been more open-minded. The moment they shattered the frame, they all fell dead."

"Commander too?" Vendurro asked.

"Commander too. So you see, destroying the frame is out of the question. And you can be sure, even if a hateful wretch like Mulldoos here got it in his head to try, it is exceptionally well protected, to prevent just such a thing."

Mulldoos rubbed the pale stubble on his face with some knuckles. "Much as I'd like to take all witches out, Thumaar will be wanting you for his own, and we got orders to make that happen. Which means reversing what that quivering twat of an emperor done." He looked at Braylar. "Big problem there, though. How in the plaguing hells are we supposed to do that without having Memoridons of our own? Kind of brings us full circle back to this fuck-all place we're stuck in, don't it?"

Braylar gave his sister a long, pointed look, until she noticed and shook her head vehemently. "In case you have forgotten, I am not beholden to the Jackals anymore. I am not your Memoridon to command, brother. And even if I were, while I appreciate your boundless confidence in my abilities, I couldn't possibly undo what a circle of my sisters managed to accomplish. Not on my own. And I have no wish to die trying."

Rudgi looked at Soffjian. "You and your sisters are Leopards by default now, right? But through no choice of your own. There must be others like you who got no wish to be his tools, especially if you spread the word the bastard's got no problem offing you to further his plaguing agenda."

Soffjian replied, "Perhaps. There will be some Memoridons still loyal in their hearts to their former Towers. Slavery has a peculiar way of distorting fidelity like that. But that presents its own problems. Even if I somehow got word to some who might be inclined to side with Thumaar as the least loathsome option, the chances of the plot being discovered and squashed are very high indeed."

Vendurro asked, "Can't you just . . . ?" He wiggled his fingers quickly by his ear.

Soffjian laughed. "Ahh, you are delightful, Ven. But no. Unlikely. That's one area of memory magic in which I have very limited skills. I would need to practically be in the Trench to manage even the humblest of efforts. Beyond which, you can be sure the Imperial sisters will be poised to intercept any such unsanctioned communication. I'm no less a deserter than you, just now. Even if I somehow reached another Memoridon inside Sunwrack, the chances of me being reported would be quite high. But even if not, I would need to meet sisters face to face to truly orchestrate any kind of counter coup. That simply is not my talent."

Mulldoos looked at Soffjian. "Fat plaguing lot of good you are, witch," he said.

She turned on him. "I am the only witch you have, Syldoon, and apparently I need to remind you, not an especially forgiving one. Mind your tongue."

Mulldoos started to reply when Braylar cut him off. "We are allies, and will comport ourselves as such. Both of you."

I tried to break some of the tension and bring us back to point by saying, "What about hedge witches?"

Instead I only drew Mulldoos's squinty-eyed ire. "What about them, scribbler?"

"Well, the priests of Truth managed to syphon the energy using them before, so maybe it could be done again. Until we do get control of the Memoridons, we'll need to find another way to ensure the captain doesn't succumb to any more stolen memories anyway. Who's to say we couldn't locate a handful more?"

"Me. I'm the one saying it. Finding Lloi was a fluke. You see how plaguing hard it was to find a replacement? And you're talking about finding a handful?" He waved his good arm at me. "Piss on this, Arki, but we ain't in any better position than we were an hour ago, except I'm hungrier, and we still got no idea how to get control back."

Braylar said, "Both paths are likely fraught with failure or death. But we will need to choose one if another doesn't present itself." He looked at me. "You have done good work here, Arki. Let us think of this some more, yes, and see if we can concoct a third option."

The company broke camp and started winding north again according
to the curves of the river, but I didn't have long to bask in the small
heaping of praise the captain had dealt out.

We'd only put a few miles behind us when I saw Braylar slow his horse,
one hand slowly dropping to Bloodsounder, his head tilted to one side.

I recognized that position too well now, and while I knew he wasn't about
to stand in the stirrups and start swinging the flail in circles above his head
and announce his affliction to the entire troop, I was sure he must have been
getting some warning of impending violence.

After nudging my horse ahead to catch up, I sidled alongside. "Captain?"

Mulldoos and Vendurro recognized the signs as well and also approached,
with the pale boar saying, "What do we got, Cap?"

Braylar held the haft of Bloodsounder with his right hand, slowly pulling
the weapon free from the hook on his belt. "It will be soon. Before midday, I
am thinking." He had that faraway sound to his voice that only came when he
was sifting through his own memories that hadn't quite been made or those
the flail had stolen from a dead man.

Vendurro asked, "Deserters? Something worse? Can't be something worse,
can it? A flock of rippers would probably be better, wouldn't it? I mean—"

Mulldoos glared the younger man into quiet and then Braylar responded.
"It is . . . hard to say. There are Deserters coming for us. But men, too."

I said, "Not Syldoon though?"

"No," he replied slowly, and then released the flail. "Something . . . else. It
was difficult to make out."

Mulldoos asked, "Should we keep on north, Cap? Can't say I like the idea
of heading further east, but we could double back south, try to get around
whatever's plaguing ahead."

Braylar shook his head, partly as rebuttal, partly simply to clear Bloodsounder's ripples out. "There are two groups, I believe. Not huge numbers. Then again, even a small party of Deserters could prove problematic, yes? We will wait on reports and decide from there. Until then, we continue north, though moving further east so we aren't trapped against the river."

I hoped this warning would prove false, as they were sometimes wont to do, but an hour later, a rider came galloping towards us from the rear. Since there didn't appear to be horses on this side of the Godveil, I assumed it was a Jackal. But galloping scouts never brought fair news.

The soldier stopped at the head of the company and saluted. He was breathing fast and hard through a narrow nose, though it was difficult to tell if it was from strenuous riding or nerves. His report confirmed the latter. "Deserters, Cap. Moving up on us fast. Small party, about five miles or so."

"Define small, soldier."

The scout steadied himself, took another deep breath. "More than ten, less than twenty, Cap. They might night have no eyes, but still see plenty good, so I didn't want to hang around. They had a couple of outriders. Well, walkers, as they weren't riding nothing. Gave them a wide berth, crept up and saw the party. Brought word straight away."

Vendurro said, "Even ten could still mete out a wicked bunch of damage. Two of them put a big hurt on us back there in the columns."

"True," Braylar replied. "But that was with no room to ride, and less to shoot. This terrain is hilly, to be sure, but we could pick a spot that was to our advantage if it comes to it."

Mulldoos spit into the stones. "Aye, but they can take a lot of damage too. Might have to plug them a dozen times each before they close."

Braylar said, "And with nearly a hundred Syldoon remaining, that shouldn't prove impossible."

Mulldoos asked, "We going to just keep heading north, see if they can keep up then?"

Braylar nodded. "That seems prudent. No sense engaging them if we can avoid it. Even greatly outnumbering them, we have nothing to gain by meeting them in a pitched battle."

The scout took a drink, rinsed the dust out of his mouth, and spit some water in the dirt. "Something else, Cap." He didn't look eager to deliver this last bit of news, but obviously had no choice.

"Yes, soldier."

The scout shook his head slowly. "Queerest thing I ever did see. Or near about. The Deserters, well, they got some sort of baskets or barrels on their backs."

"Baskets or barrels? And why is this so peculiar?"

"Not the baskets so much, but what's in them."

Braylar scowled. "Dog heads? Gourds? Hot pies? What is it, man?"

"That's just it, Cap. Men. They got men in the barrels."

Braylar blinked twice. "Men. In the barrels."

"Ayyup, Cap. Though unless they got them folded up real good, these men got no legs. No room. Barrels are only big enough for the torsos. The upper half, Cap."

"I know what a plaguing torso is, you idiot. Is that all?"

The scout nodded and said, "The barrels had quivers full of javelins on the side. And some of the Deserters, they got what looked like staff slings, in addition to their spiky clubs and whatnot."

I asked, "What's a staff sling?"

Mulldoos looked at me, one eyelid unhinged. "Gods, but for all that learning you sure are a dumb shit sometimes. It's a plaguing staff with a plaguing sling on the end."

Braylar ignored us. "Anything else?"

The scout replied, "Nope, Cap. That covers it. Want me to head back?"

"No, you are relieved. Ride with us and take a respite. Send Dozzwik in your stead. Tell him to monitor their approach and give word immediately if they encounter anything else."

After the scout rode down the line, Mulldoos asked, "So what do you reckon, Cap?"

"I don't know if they can overtake us, or if there are more parties ahead, but I am relatively sure we will encounter them. That much felt certain. The best thing might be to simply pick ground of our choosing to engage."

But before Mulldoos could reply, Vendurro called out that another scout was riding hard in our direction from the north.

Braylar swore as we watched the rider approach, his hand on Bloodsounder again.

Soffjian watched him carefully and said, "That vicious thing truly is a prescient piece of work, isn't it, Bray?"

The captain kept his eyes on the scout. "Would it were otherwise, but yes. It would appear so."

The scout arrived and reported another party of Deserters closing in on us, slightly larger, at least twenty-five in number, similarly outfitted with barrels and slings.

After Braylar dismissed the scout, Vendurro said, "What do you reckon they got legless men on their backs for anyway?"

Mulldoos replied, "Why don't you canter on up and ask real nice? Maybe they'll lop off your legs and let you take a ride."

Braylar looked at his officers. "We head east. Further from the Silt Hood. Advise the outrider to find the most level open ground that will favor our maneuverability. Presuming that is still an advantage."

The officers conveyed the order down the line as we turned away from the river and the Godveil beyond it.

We continued east, but several hours later another scout reported that the Deserters to the south had changed course as well and were closing the gap. They were only two miles behind now.

The captain increased our pace after letting the horses rest only briefly in the middle of the afternoon. But as dusk closed in, it was clear we weren't losing them, and they continued only to slowly make up ground. Braylar found the area he was looking for, generally flat, with no trees or columns or anything else to interfere with bolts or offer our enemies protection.

Whether or not maneuverability was an advantage, speed no longer seemed to be. The Deserters continued gaining until Braylar ordered us to hold and spread out, preparing to face our pursuers.

Not long after, we saw the enemy on the horizon. The Deserters stood out as huge, stark silhouettes.

I heard Vendurro say, "Plague. Me."

The Deserters began marching forward. They were still several hundred yards out, beyond crossbow range, but not by much. Braylar spun his horse around and addressed his officers. "We fight them here, take them out from a distance if possible, and then head back south, as the north seems blocked."

Azmorgon slid his helm over his huge hairy head. "About time. Been spoiling for a fight."

Vendurro put his pot helm on and said, "You don't say. Never would have imagined."

It was hard to tell with the massive beard, but I think the Ogre smiled. "Try not to get crushed, Squirrel."

I pulled the crossbow off the saddle, started spanning it. When I glanced up, the Deserters were spreading out into a single line, and Braylar called out orders. "I'll lead the crossbows from the center, staggered. Mulldoos, you take half of the remainder on the left wing, Azmorgon, you do the same on the right. Once we start loosing, they will likely come hard, realizing they can't sit at distance. And they will probably make for the crossbows to eliminate that threat. We will take out as many as we can, fall back with rolling gears, and draw them in, though not too deep. With any luck we will rout them and drive them off, but if they survive the bolts, the wings will collapse, flank them, and—"

"Crush them," Azmorgon finished. "Got it, Cap."

Braylar likely took issue with the tone and interruption, but didn't bother dressing him down. "Soffjian, ride with one of the wings. If they close, see if you have any better luck with your memorycraft. Vendurro, stay with me. Ready the troops, get them in position, relay the directive about gears."

Everyone started moving off, issuing orders, splitting up the company. As expected, they responded immediately with practiced precision, even though we were across the field from a sizable battalion of demons, monsters, or at the very least, giants.

For the hundredth time in the last few days, I wished Hewspear were here to help put me at ease, even with the likelihood of death looming. I looked to Braylar. "Where do you want me, Captain?" It was all I could do to ask without my voice cracking.

Braylar glanced at me as he fitted a bolt in his crossbow. "While you have improved as a shot, marginally, you can barely ride in a straight line, and you certainly can't maneuver and loose a crossbow at the same time. You would only get yourself killed. Head off with Mulldoos. He won't be your nursemaid, but with any luck it won't come to that. If you see a Deserter, shoot it." He slapped the devil's claw on the stock. "And if things go sour, I don't know that surrender is an option—they might not honor such things—but you could end up climbing columns like a monkey. Better than death, yes?"

I shaded my eyes and looked at the Deserters, barely able to make out the small human heads behind their horned ones. "I could also end up having my legs cut off and being stuffed in a barrel."

Braylar twitch-smiled. "Who can say? You could always turn the crossbow on yourself. I'll leave that decision to you." Then he rode over to the crossbow cavalry lining up behind us. Vendurro had them in position already, three lines, the horsemen staggered so they would all have a clear shot ahead at the Deserters who were slowly approaching.

I rode over towards the Syldoon on the left wing. Mulldoos was the only other one with a crossbow loaded and ready—the rest had their shields and weapons out, except for a few who favored polearms.

Mulldoos saw me and trotted over, eyeing the crossbow in my hand. "You going to accidentally shoot one of my boys here, scribbler?"

I shook my head fast. "No, Lieutenant."

"That's good. Because you can be sure I'd break your skull with your crossbow if you did, you got it?"

With most of his face hidden behind mail, and one eye drooping, that wasn't a visage to be trifled with.

I nodded, mouth dry, and he continued. "Stay on the far edge so you don't trip up any real soldiers. Loose if you got a shot, but if they make it to the center, or veer off and take us on, get the hells out of the way and wait for us to save your sorry ass again. Don't even think about drawing that Grass Dog cutlery, as you'll just end up slitting yourself open somewhere. You got that?"

I tried to take breaths. "Don't shoot any Syldoon, and don't gut myself with Lloi's sword. Got it."

"Good. Now get your ass in position."

I rode to the far edge, keeping my horse always a few feet from the soldiers. I'd seen some temperamental horses kick or bite if crowded by other horses, and while the Syldoon were masterful horsemen, I expected that the beasts mirrored the character of their riders.

The Syldoon waited as the Deserters slowly marched forward, nearly in range now. I imagined Braylar would hold until he was sure every bolt would strike home somewhere and do some damage.

Several Deserters had staff slings at the ready, and the name was just as self-evident as Mulldoos made it out to be—a staff nearly as long as they were tall, with a sling at the end. I wasn't sure what the range would be for one used by a man, but these were obviously much longer, and would have the benefit of their strength and four more feet of elevation. Still, there looked to be fewer than fifteen slings to four times as many crossbows on our side. Even with ranges being equal, we would certainly win that battle. The only question was how many bolts it would take to bring down an armored Deserter. But then I thought about projectiles—I'd never seen a regular sling used, but I'd heard they used stones or lead shot. From the size of the pouches at the end of the cords on the Deserter's version, their staff slings were like miniature trebuchets.

I tried not to think on the possibility of a huge stone punching a hole in my chest as the behemoths continued closing. Drumming my fingers on the side of the stock, I kept looking back and forth between the Deserters and Braylar and his Syldoon in the center, waiting to see the bolts filling the sky and arcing down on the enemy. They all had their crossbows up and ready, sighting down the lengths, preparing to loose, and so I did the same.

The Deserters kept coming at the same deliberate, maddening pace.

I heard Braylar call out, "Steady. Nearly there, lads."

However, before we shot any bolts, the Deserters stopped, crouched slightly, the staff slings up in the air and cocked over their shoulders, held in two hands, and suddenly those long staves were all whipping forward, with one cord slipping free as the pouch loosed the projectiles hurtling high into the air.

Unlike an arrow or bolt, these didn't appear to be the most accurate weapons, and with the size of the ammunition, easy enough to sidestep, especially since there weren't that many. Five or so seemed to be heading to our wing, five to the middle, and five to the far wing, dark spots in the bright blue sky arcing towards us. None of them were directed towards me, and I watched the Syldoon in the wing nudge their horses away from the stones, some lifting their shields to be sure they weren't struck.

But as one projectile hit the ground ten feet to my right, I realized they weren't stones at all—the projectiles were ceramic and shattered on impact, releasing a cloud so thick and black it was nearly tarry.

Syldoon starting coughing as the smoke rose everywhere, mixing together, forming a dense dark fog. My horse whinnied and started to shy away, and I wasn't about to stop her. But it was too late. Even as we shifted sideways, more ceramic projectiles struck the ground, and then there was no escaping the smoke.

I sputtered as I felt it rise up around me, stinking like burning hair, and I gagged, my horse jerking her head around, stamping the earth, shifting sideways. I tried to turn to get to fresh air. We moved off to our left, away from the wing of Syldoon, when I heard more objects whistling through the air. They sounded different than the pots or canisters though, and as I watched through teary eyes, I understood why.

Several large stones crashed into the ground amid the horses' hooves, nearly setting them into a panic, and one struck a Syldoon in the head. His helm was crushed as he flew from the saddle as if a giant hand had pulled him from behind, and he was surely dead before he even hit the ground, blood pouring down his face from his ruined skull under the stove helm.

The smoke was dissipating, but still stung my eyes and nose, even as I was away from the worst of it. Several Syldoon were bent over against their horses' necks as they led them towards me.

I heard crossbows loose, though not in unison, as their ranks had likely broken and their visibility had to be worse than mine.

Another volley of large stones rained down, and while most missed, another Syldoon was struck in the shoulder, and even from fifteen feet away I heard bones under the armor crack, followed by his single scream.

But that sound was immediately rendered unimportant by another terrifying noise—pounding, getting louder by the second.

More crossbows loosed, and I looked through the gray haze, trying to find a target myself, but between my eyes still watering and what remained of the smoke, it was nearly impossible. I aimed in the direction of the Deserters anyway, squeezed the long trigger, and hoped for the best as another volley of stones struck, one bouncing five feet from me, half the size of my head.

There were more screams far off to the right as some unfortunate Syldoon must have been hit, and then I saw a Deserter emerge from the ashy smoke, charging the nearest soldier, the staff sling held high.

The Syldoon saw him, tried to control his panicked horse, and raised his shield to block the staff as it swung down.

The planks shattered, and the arm probably did as well, as the soldier spun his horse and swung his axe.

It sliced into the giant's arm and drew some blood, but not enough to do more than anger it.

The Deserter whipped the staff around, the long cord trailing behind, and it slammed into the soldier's side, knocking him from the saddle.

I grabbed a bolt, forgot I hadn't spanned the crossbow yet, and dropped the quarrel into the stones as I fumbled with the devil's claw.

Looking up, I saw two more Syldoon ride forward, slashing at the Deserter as they passed.

The giant's thick hide-armor deflected one blow, and the other drew more blood, but the Deserter had the staff moving again and caught the passing Syldoon in the back.

I finished spanning, grabbed another bolt, and took aim at the Deserter.

Another Syldoon rode out of the thinning smoke between me and the Deserter, and I stopped short of shooting just in time.

The Deserter swung the staff and the thick haft cracked against the shield, but the Syldoon was smart and didn't try to block the blow directly, only deflect it off line a little.

He led his horse forward, swung his sword as he passed, and the tip caught the Deserter below the jaw.

The giant stepped back, brought one hand up to try to stanch the blood, and swung at the Syldoon, but he was already clear.

Blood flowed around the Deserter's thick fingers and the giant wobbled a little, turning and swinging the staff in a semicircle with one hand to ward off other attacks.

I sighted down the stock, held my breath, and squeezed. The bolt was a blur and struck the Deserter in the side of the face. It opened its mouth to roar, but no sound came out, as more blood pumped between its fingers.

The giant fell forward, and a Syldoon rode past on either side and slashed it again before it toppled.

I was spanning the crossbow again, terrified, but thrilled I actually hit the giant where I hoped to, when another appeared, two of the three spikes on its club bloodied, a human in a barrel on its back.

A Syldoon was racing for the pair, shield up, mace tucked behind it.

The Deserter turned to face the Syldoon and the soldier wisely veered off, but while he narrowly avoided the swipe from the club, the legless man in the barrel reared back and let a javelin fly.

The tip struck the Syldoon on the edge of the shoulder outside the lamellar cuirass.

As the Deserter spun to face another horseman galloping past, the human on its back spun as well, and I saw that there were actually two cylinders, a smaller one just inside the outside barrel, so he spun the one inside all the way around until he was facing directly behind the Deserter.

Right at me.

He drew another javelin from a quiver on the outside of the cylinder, and I dug my heels into my horse to present a moving target.

I ducked low as I tried to work the devil's claw and felt the javelin sail past right over my head. Rising up, I dropped the bolt in place, tracked the pair as they moved off, aimed for the man in the barrel, and loosed.

The bolt struck the cylinder just below the rim. Considering my restless horse and the moving Deserter, that was frankly amazing, but just then I really wanted to put a hole in the legless man who so narrowly missed driving a javelin through me.

As I started to reload the crossbow again, I glanced up and saw the man in the barrel grabbing the Deserter's shoulder and then yelling something at him.

The Deserter turned around, saw I was the closest opponent, and started forward, huge legs pumping.

I knew I couldn't reload fast enough to loose a bolt before the Deserter caught me, and even if I could have, there was no chance of me hitting him in the throat or anywhere else that might have slowed him down, so I was just about to give my horse my heels and try to ride clear when three more Syldoon attacked him, one racing by on either side, striking at his exposed legs as they passed, and the third attacking him from the rear.

The Deserter was badly wounded, or hobbled anyway, and struggled to spin to face his foe.

The Syldoon turned with him, and while I couldn't see every strike, he must have been slashing the barrel more than the sightless giant itself.

As the Deserter took another halting step, the straps on its back gave way, the barrel overturned, and the legless man fell out, dropping seven feet to the earth, slamming his head on the ground.

The man was using his arms to turn over when the Deserter stepped on him, no doubt caving his ribs in, as he gave one short gurgling cry before it was cut off.

The three Syldoon circled the Deserter and cut him down without any of them sustaining an injury, and as I finished spanning the crossbow I looked around the still-smoky battlefield.

Any organization had completely broken down, and Syldoon were fighting Deserters everywhere in random clumps, a chaotic tableau out of the worst nightmare. I saw Azmorgon ride past a Deserter engaged with another Syldoon, his chopper extended to the side to allow him to strike from as far away as possible. The Deserter struck the Syldoon full in the chest, carrying him out of the saddle, the long translucent spikes buried to the haft for a moment before the body flew free and the spikes pulled out, trails of blood streaming behind. Azmorgon arrived too late to save him, but angled his blow up, the tip of the odd polearm catching the Deserter in the side of the neck as he passed.

The giant dropped to a knee, reached out a hand to steady itself, but Azmorgon circled back around and slashed again across the giant's face.

I turned away as the Deserter fell backward, dead or dying, crushing the man in the barrel on its back. Part of me hoped the man died immediately, and part of me hoped he suffocated slowly.

Twenty yards away, I saw a Deserter swing the spiked club, striking Mulldoos's horse in the neck. The poor beast screamed and fell to its side. Mulldoos managed to free his feet from the stirrups and roll as the horse toppled, but the Deserter was nearly on him as the lieutenant tried to regain his feet, unsteady and wobbling.

A bolt struck the Deserter in the hand, pinning it to the flat haft of the club, and another hit him in the shoulder, missing the armor, but still not buried deep in the exposed flesh.

The Deserter roared and turned to face its new foes, while the javelin thrower was pulling another from his quiver, presumably to throw at Mulldoos.

However, even teetering and robbed of some of his dexterity, Mulldoos acted fast. He took three ungainly steps, launched himself off the dead horse and into the air, and slashed at the man in the barrel with his falchion at the height of his leap.

It was clumsy and awkward, and he bounced off the barrel and hit the dirt hard, but the javelin thrower was slumped over the edge of the barrel, blood pouring down the planks in a curtain, arms dangling, the javelin on the ground.

The other two Syldoon took out the Deserter as Mulldoos got to his feet and moved off at a crouching jog, looking for another horse or a new Deserter to attack.

While the Deserters were massive, several times stronger than any man, had reach, and hardened leather and brass armor in addition to their already thick hides that gave them inordinate protection, and many had men in barrels throwing javelins from on high, the Syldoon outnumbered them greatly. Men and horses were brutally struck down, but the Syldoon were overwhelming the Deserters, regaining their cohesion, sweeping past and staying out of reach, flanking with coordinated attacks, or using the crossbows to good effect now that the smoke had dissipated enough to see more than five feet.

It looked like Braylar's company was going to survive this battle, no matter how severe the casualties. They were going to defeat the hulking monsters.

And that's when I saw the first female Deserter, fifty yards away, surveying the carnage. Though she was a foot or two shorter than the male Deserters, and spindly where they were preposterously huge, I was still sure I couldn't have missed her earlier—unlike the warriors doling out horrible damage among the Syldoon, she wasn't outfitted in any kind of armor, but had on a bright green robe that flowed loose about her limbs.

I suddenly felt my skin tighten and the hairs on every part of my body stand on end, and I scanned the field until I saw Soffjian, her blood-stained ranseur at her side. I cupped my hands in front of my mouth and screamed her name.

It took two tries before she heard, and a third before she identified the source, and once I had her attention, I gestured wildly at the robed figured and then hurried to span my crossbow.

Soffjian looked in her direction as the robed Deserter slowly raised both arms, several strips of green cloth fluttering from her thin limbs. I fumbled with a crossbow bolt as I noticed her four thick fingers splayed on each outstretched hand.

I was nearly done cranking the lever back when I saw Soffjian extend her ranseur in front of her in one hand, with the other splayed as well, but just as I released the claws and was about to drop the bolt in place, I suddenly saw nothing but horrible, blinding, flashing light everywhere around me, so intense that each pulse was like a physical blow to my head.

When I was a child and left to my own devices, I tried to see how long I could look directly at the sun on a cloudless day, testing myself to go further each time until even shutting my eyes left the afterimage of the fiery ball still there, searing. My mother caught me at it once, spun me around by the shoulders, and slapped my face, telling me my foolishness was going to give her a blind, useless son.

This was similar, only a thousand thousand times worse.

The pulsing white light was so painful it caused me to reel, and I nearly fell off my horse. Eyes closed, the assault still continued, and then it was combined with a shrill whistling noise that grew louder and louder.

I brought my forearms up to my ears, desperately trying not to let go of the crossbow as my head swam and my stomach roiled.

It felt like the Deserter was assaulting me from the inside out, and my whole body was rebelling against me, and I was sure I was going to pass out or die when it just as suddenly stopped.

I blinked, sparks and black spots filling my vision in equal measure, bent over, clutching my stomach with one hand. Still queasy, it was all I could do to try to sit up straight.

Everywhere around me, Syldoon were suffering as much as I was, disoriented, in pain, trying to figure out what had happened and why it had stopped. The javelin throwers on the backs of the remaining Deserters fared no better, and even the eyeless giants seemed to be struggling to regain their balance. But they recovered much faster, and proceeded to roam the battlefield, some striking down disoriented Jackals, though most were using the flat of their hafts of the staves of their long slings to subdue them. Only one or two killed Syldoon with the spiked clubs.

I looked at Soffjian—she was still in the same spot, her arms outstretched, but shaking now, and her face was nearly as red as her cloak and hair.

The robed Deserter was in the same position as well, though she was slowly pivoting until she fixed on Soffjian.

I dropped the bolt in, hands shaking, bile in my mouth, head spinning, and slowly raised the crossbow, looking down the length, trying to keep the weapon steady as I aimed at the robed Deserter, which was nearly impossible.

Out of the corner of my eye, I saw Soffjian suddenly drop her ranseur and collapse, falling over onto her horse's neck.

Taking a final breath, I squeezed the long trigger.

And watched the bolt whizz just over the robed Deserter's shoulder.

Having dispatched Soffjian, she turned her attention back to the rest of the Syldoon company, arms rising up again.

Braylar was the only Syldoon who hadn't seemed affected by her attack. He charged, embattled shield on his arm, Bloodsounder held high. The female

Deserter saw him coming, pivoted and faced him, arms outstretched as if she were going to push him from fifty yards away.

The captain tilted slightly in his saddle, but kept galloping. I was spanning the crossbow again, watching him, sure he would kill this giantess just as he had Rusejenna in the streets of Sunwrack, and knew we would triumph again, thanks to that cursed flail.

But then two massive Deserters stepped in his path to intercept him, one with a staff, the other with a spiked club.

Braylar changed direction, tried to race past the one on his right, and nearly made it. But the Deserter swung the staff wide, extended it with his hulking left arm stretched completely.

Braylar might as well have run into a huge tree branch. The staff struck him across the chest and vaulted him out of the saddle. Scorn kept galloping.

Then the blinding light and deafening sounds erupted again.

I did drop the crossbow this time. Even with my eyes clamped shut and my hands over my ears, there was no stopping it. The blinding light and shrieking whistle were deep in my skull, threatening to explode it from the inside out.

Turning to the side, I vomited and gagged and vomited again, and my horse started forward as I toppled from the saddle, falling as if the ground had opened up underneath me and I were dropping through an endless abyss.

I heard screaming, and wasn't sure if it was mine or someone else's.

My final thought was a curse directed at myself for being such a poor shot. If only I had been four inches lower.

And then all was black, the abyss absorbed the light and the sound and left me in the absolute dark with only the thumping of my heart beating fast all around me, and faster still, pounding at a frenzied pace like one of the oversized drums in the hippodrome back at Sunwrack.

Until that stopped too.

I woke up and felt the ground shifting and rumbling beneath me, and thought I must have still been in the grip of the spell the spindly Deserter had cast. But then I realized it wasn't the ground at all, but us, as I ran my hands over the wooden planks of a broad wagon bed. All around me, Syldoon were crowded close, some curled into balls as much their armor allowed, a few groggily leaning up against the wooden side of the wagon, some supine, staring vacantly into the cloudless sky. There were nearly twenty of us packed in there.

My head pounded a thousand times worse than anything wine or sickness had ever accomplished—it felt as if a Deserter were squeezing my skull in its humongous hands, intent on crushing it to pulp.

I tasted blood and my tongue felt raw and bloated, and I realized I must have bitten it at some point, likely when I screamed myself into oblivion.

The wagon stank of sweat and piss and vomit and shit, one awful stench knotted with the rest, and it was all I could do not to vomit myself. I couldn't tell if I had or not. My gambeson was soaked in sweat, but I didn't think the vomit was emanating from me. The wagon shifted again, and my bones shifted with it, feeling as brittle as glass. I tried to reposition myself to get slightly more comfortable and discovered that my wrist was shackled to an iron loop on the side of the wagon, and there weren't even enough links to stand up.

I leaned against the boards and looked over the edge as much as the short chain allowed. We were on a road, and while the overall terrain hadn't changed much, the position of the sun said we had been traveling for half a day. Or longer. I imagined I would have pissed myself if it had been more than a day, and it didn't feel as if I had, and my bladder ached. Every time we jostled over the smallest stone or a crack in the road, I thought my head was going to explode like a melon dropped from the highest battlements.

It was so very difficult to think, but it suddenly hit me that this was the largest wagon I'd ever seen, and since the humans feared horses, I assumed some other beast of burden must have been pulling it. I craned my neck and rose as much as the shackle permitted and looked ahead, feeling dizzy and then nearly throwing up as my stomach lurched when I saw what was harnessed to the wagon.

Four swaying rooters, or something closely related to the beasts I'd first seen in the Green Sea with Lloi and Braylar, each two or three times the girth and length of an ox or a bull, their knobby hides broken up by tufts of bristly hair here and there. There was a human walking alongside in simple linen trousers, goad in one hand, whip in the other, his own scarred back sweaty and dirty. It didn't look like he fared much better than the rooters, who also bore whitish scars on their flanks. One of the beasts grunted and snapped its huge mouth at the rooter alongside it, and the whip snapped out across the hilly backside. The whip would have torn a man's flesh from his bones, or drawn blood at the very least, but it didn't even leave a mark on the rooter's thick flesh.

I heard the Deserter before I saw him, his footfalls heavier than any creature's in the world. Or at least the other half of the world—who could say what was normal or common on this side?

The sun shone off the brass plates, giving it an almost wet look, and for some reason that made me nauseous, and I started to look away as the giant ambled past, but stopped when I saw the man in the cylinder case on its back looking down, his hand next to the quiver of javelins, as if he were just looking for an excuse to pluck one up and pin someone to the wagon with it.

Vendurro said, "Starting to really develop a strong kind of dislike for those legless bastards."

He was a few prisoners away, and looked as green as I felt. That should have provided a queer kind of comfort, but I hurt too much to feel anything good at all. Knowing he was alive was some true consolation though.

Another Syldoon next to him said, "Probably got no choice, Sarge—uh, that is, Lieutenant."

Vendurro glared at him. "I don't care if the Deserters lopped those legs off at birth or yesterday—a man's always got a choice, especially when it comes to who he kills or who he don't. He killed his own kind."

The Jackal persisted. "Deserters would probably lop off his head if he didn't do it, is all I mean. And we're nothing to him, Lieutenant."

"We're plaguing human, you ass. That one, who just went by in the basket? I saw him put a javelin through Minks. Right through his throat, before that she-devil Deserter took us all out. You can bet, I get a chance, I'm lopping off that bastard's arms and leaving him alive to roll around and wish he had let the Deserters kill him when he had a chance."

That shut the other soldier up. We were moving around a gentle curve in the road, and I stretched to look above the short wooden wall of the wagon to see behind us—there were two more identical wagons pulled by rooters, the first as full of prisoners as our own, the second not nearly as much. So what had been over one hundred and fifty men leaving Sunwrack had been cut down to about a third of that number.

All the horses were tethered and trailing behind the third wagon, and Deserters marched alongside the whole procession. There were a handful of humans as well around the wagons, servants or slaves, there mostly to goad the rooters along, walking with staves and costrels.

While they'd left us in armor and allowed me to keep my writing case, assuming it wasn't a weapon, I hoped my translated pages and the remainder of the texts were still on the horses back there, and then felt guilty for worrying over ink and parchment when so many lives had been lost so quickly. I wasn't even sure who among Braylar's retinue was still alive besides Vendurro.

With so many bodies turned and contorted, it was difficult to tell even in our own wagon—I didn't see Azmorgon's bulk or the captain amongst the men. Though there was no mistaking Mulldoos's pale stubbly scalp on the other end of our wagon, his head slumped over his knees, which were pulled up to his chest.

Half of the soldiers around us were still dead to the world, possibly for good, though if so, I imagined the Deserters would have left them behind with the rest of the corpses.

I called out to the Lieutenant, whispering as much as I could, but loud enough to carry, "Mulldoos . . . the captain?"

He looked up, with half his mouth still curled in a nearly permanent snarl, and said, "Can't say. Saw him still struggling against that robed bitch when I went black. Him and his witch sister. Last thing I saw was the pair of them trying to stay upright." He called out loud enough for everyone in the wagon to hear. "Anybody seen Cap?"

Those that were awake and moderately alert looked around, and one at the rear of the wagon said, "Pretty sure I seen him back there, Lieutenant, looking around a while back."

"Pretty sure? That's what you're plaguing telling me, you scabby twat? *Pretty sure?*"

The Syldoon looked like he wished he never spoke. "Think so."

I looked at Mulldoos. "Azmorgon? Soffjian?"

He could only muster evil in the eye that wasn't obscured by a sagging lid. "If you think I give two shits about the Ogre or the Witch, then the Deserter witchcunt churned your brain something awful."

I was glad I hadn't been closer or he might have clubbed me with his big arm.

It struck me that this was how Henlester must have felt, trapped in his wagon. Well, he wasn't surrounded by creatures long presumed to be deities, or hulking rooters, on the wrong side of the Godveil. But the sensation of having had everything taken from him—possessions, future, possibly life— and traveling to a destination he had no knowledge of; that I could absolutely relate to. And there was no likelihood of anyone riding to our rescue. I had always assumed getting captured by the Imperials was the worst thing that could happen to us.

I was so very, very wrong. If they suddenly materialized and somehow overwhelmed the Deserters, taking us captive in their name, I imagine most of the Jackals would have been relieved.

Human captors, even vengeful or furious ones, were a known evil. We had no idea what terrors the Deserters might visit upon us. It was clear they had no qualms about severing men nearly in half and using them for their own purposes.

A soldier next to me roused, convulsed, then got his legs underneath him enough to rise up and vomit down the side of the wagon.

The smell made another Syldoon a little further gag, but he managed to keep the contents of his stomach inside (or had already emptied it, it was hard to tell), before saying, "Gods, Kithrik, what did you plaguing eat, rotten yak?"

One of the human slaves (or very poorly cared-for servant) walking along the side of our wagon handed the closest Syldoon a leather costrel of some fluid or other. The Jackal grabbed it, sniffed the short spout, and then figured if our captors wanted us dead, they could have done the job easily enough when we were all unconscious. He took a swig as we all watched, waited just to be sure he hadn't been poisoned anyway, and then handed it to the soldier next to him.

The slave was watching the Syldoon drink, apparently waiting to reclaim the costrel after it made the rounds. He had a narrow face and a nose bent in several directions, as if uncertain where to go. It looked nearly useless to breathe out of. Half his head was shaved and the dark hair on the other half was in multiple braids that formed a curtain on his shoulder. There was intelligence in the close-set yes, even as he looked wary and skittish, and a disturbing design branded or scarred onto his cheek. I scooted as close to him as I could, earning a curse from the Syldoon next to me who'd just vomited, and then said in my best Old Anjurian, "Where are they taking us?"

The slave's expression turned nearly to horror when he realized I spoke his language (or some butchered version of it anyway) and he started to sidle away.

I said, "Wait. Please. Tell me your name. Please."

The man looked uncertain, perplexed, possibly still frightened; it was hard to be sure. He took a small step back towards the wagon as he kept walking alongside, but not so close that he could be grabbed by anyone inside.

Staring straight ahead, several moments passed. Finally, he whispered, "Bulto." And then again, with slightly more force and volume, as if he hadn't told anyone his name in a long time, and had forgotten how to do so. "Bulto."

I lowered my voice. "Arki. I am Arki. Where are we going, Bulto?"

Bulto looked immediately ready to bolt again. But after deliberating and looking around as he kept pace, he said, "Roxtiniak. You go to Roxtiniak. To see the Matriarch." Or what I assumed meant "matriarch," or "mother." It was hard to be sure.

"Roxtin—?"

"Roxtiniak," he repeated, slowly.

"That's a—" I struggled to think of the word for "region" so I tried, "City? Or a place? Is it a place?"

He seemed to understand city and he nodded. "Big," I think he said, though there was more to it than that. But that seemed to be the gist. Big.

"Thank you, Bulto," I replied, and tried to smile.

He was staring at me when we both heard a Deserter bellow something at him I couldn't understand, clipped and guttural. The man's face went pale, except for his crooked nose, which appeared incapable of changing hue. He spun around and raised his arms above his head.

The Deserter took three broad strides, covering a remarkable amount of ground very quickly, and backhanded the man across the face.

The giant hadn't put much force behind the blow, but Bulto still slammed into the wagon and fell to the road, looking up, his nose rebroken, blood on his lips as he opened his mouth and pleaded.

While the Deserter didn't strike him again, he bent down low, grabbed Bulto, and lifted him to his feet the way a father might a disobedient child that had suddenly gone limp.

Bulto was still babbling so quickly I couldn't make any of the words out even if they were some variant of Old Anjurian.

With thick lips curling, the Deserter shouted something in Bulto's face, pointed at our wagon, scolded him a final time, and then stalked off.

Bulto sagged slightly, knees weak, and I thought he might fall to the ground again, but he steadied himself against the wagon, wiped the blood off his chin, and walked away without another word.

Apparently he no longer cared about the costrel.

I heard Mulldoos say, slur really, "Learn anything useful before you went and nearly got that scrawny prick killed?"

"I asked where they were taking us," I replied.

"And?" he asked.

I looked down the road, not knowing what the answer meant. "He said we're heading to a big city called Roxtiniak. At least I think it's a city. To see 'the Matriarch.'"

Mulldoos grabbed the costrel from the soldier next to him. "Matriarch, huh?" After a large swig, and with water dribbling down his chin, he added, "Prefer to look a person in the eyes before gutting them. Guess I'll have to forego that pleasure when I off this giant Matriarch horsecunt."

We rolled along for a few more hours, and what struck me most was how unpopulated the area was. There were the skeletal remains of some ancient human villages and small towns, mostly fallen to the ground with the remaining structures reclaimed by nature, almost entirely obscured by bramble and vines and moss and thorny trees and grass. But no Deserter holdfasts of communities, and no sign that men lived on this side of the Veil except for the few slaves traveling among us and those workers we first saw climbing the columns.

After passing a few more long-dead settlements, our road connected with another broader avenue, and not long after, we saw some populated farming settlements at the base of some hills, though at some distance from the road. The dwellings themselves looked simple and sparse, but what caught the attention was the hilly land beyond. I'd only seen agriculture and farming on level land, but here, the hillside had been cut into terraces, the face of each covered in stone, and the crops on each level going up the entirety of the hill. The figures or farmers were difficult to make out, but I saw straw hats.

No matter what side of the Veil you were on or who your overlords were, the sun was the sun, and the floppy hat your friend.

An hour later, we rounded a bend and I saw something that stopped my breath in my chest for a moment.

There was the same warping, twisting, alien energy that composed the Godveil, only this time instead of being shaped into a towering curtain, it was bent into a massive dome in the middle of the plain.

And the road led directly towards it.

It was only after gaping and feeling the nausea return that I realized there were several large carts coming towards us and away from the dome, pulled by single rooters and with Deserters seated in them and human slaves goading the beasts. As they got closer, I saw the Deserters weren't dressed like our captors at all in their leather and brass armor, but outfitted in clothing that was utterly plain in color (having none at all, being undyed linen and wool and silk) but gaudy in design, nonetheless—voluminous sleeves adorned with bells and tiny strips of cloth somewhere between fringe and streamers, belts crisscrossing their chests, festooned with metal baubles and strangely patterned badges.

The giant horned occupants of the cairns gawked as they passed our procession, or at least gave that impression—without eyes it was difficult to say for certain. But while they were a different caste or profession than the giant Deserter warriors escorting us, their chalky skin was equally marked in those faint swirly designs, asymmetrical and elaborate and arcane. One slim female in a cairn shook her head slowly as she took us in, her lips curled in what could only be distaste, and she ordered the slave to hurry the rooter along.

When our convoy was a hundred yards out, the tang of vinegar reached our noses, even more intense and powerful than the smell approaching the Godveil, and as we got closer I saw that the dome was somehow more tangible. Where the Godveil masked what lay beyond, disguised it in the shifting currents of energy like heat waves, you could still discern the shape or outline of things. But this dome was less translucent, and the rippling was more like the shifting waves in a deep lake than the eddying energies of the Godveil, more substantial somehow, nearly opaque, and not even showing the silhouette of what lay beyond.

I swallowed hard as we rolled closer, and felt the same trepidation as I had approaching the Godveil. There was the horrible compulsion to continue towards it, a drawing that was nearly irresistible, as well as the certainty that doing so would only bring madness or death, except the choice to continue or turn back was no longer ours. And we no longer had Bloodsounder to protect us.

I was sure the Deserters hadn't captured us for any other reason than to sacrifice us to this thing, and I looked around and saw similar fears, even on the faces of these hardened and oft-times brutal soldiers.

The Deserters heading the other way must have been making a pilgrimage or a sacrifice or something else, but I felt absolute terror wash over me just then, absolute and irrefutable.

We were being led to our slaughter. That was the only explanation.

But then our procession stopped, and a Deserter continued on ahead, walking down the road, closing in on the oscillating mercurial dome.

I pulled my chains tight to try to get a better vantage point, and I wasn't the only one.

The Deserter raised a fist, shouted something that would have been unintelligible even if I had understood the tongue, and then turned and slowly walked back to rejoin his massive brethren ahead of our wagon.

I waited, straining, feeling the pull of the rippling surface of the dome, and the terror of it too, and then suddenly another Deserter appeared, walking through the wall of the dome, approaching our procession, and even from a distance I noticed the obvious difference in size and physique. She was outfitted like the other female we'd seen during the battle, the one who had ensorcelled an entire company of Syldoon, the one difference being she had a long spine projecting up between her shoulders and above her head, fitted to a harness on her back.

She gave a cursory and arrogant nod to our Deserter captors—it was odd but still comforting in a way to see these giants exhibiting behavior that wasn't completely alien to our own. Apparently there would always be castes and hierarchies, even among demons, demigods, or monsters.

Our captors bowed low, maintained the deferential pose for several beats, and then rose again. One of them exchanged a few words with the slender female, and she seemed to be looking us over as she listened. Then she strode past the warriors. Every Deserter bowed as she moved past, and it was clear they afforded her a great deal of respect.

The Deserter with the spine stopped alongside our wagon, and I shivered as she slowly turned her head—even eyeless, it was clear the giant was examining us.

From behind me, I heard Mulldoos say, "Think the bitch will understand Old Anjurian, scribbler?"

I didn't turn around as I whispered, "I don't know. The slave did, somewhat, though the language has diverged from what I studied. Why?"

Mulldoos said, "Well go on and tell that massive ugly devil we're an exploring party from the mighty Syldoon plaguing Empire. Diplomats. Envoys. Representatives. However you want to plaguing put it. Make it real plaguing clear that fucking with us is a real bad idea."

"Is that wise? Maybe . . . maybe we should . . ."

The Deserter continued scanning us, looking over each prisoner in turn, head cocked slightly to the side, exhaling deeply every time she finished taking in one and moving on to the next.

Mulldoos almost shouted. "Just plaguing do it, ink stain. Right quick. Don't like the look of this bitch one bit."

I conveyed the lieutenant's sentiments, minus the profanity and unveiled threat.

She turned and regarded me, and my words practically turned to dust in my mouth as she cocked her head to the side. Though shorter than the males, she still towered over all of us. Her lips peeled back in what could have either been a sneer or a smile or a snarl. Then she slowly raised both arms above her head, cocked at the elbows.

Mulldoos yelled, "Did you plaguing tell her, Arki?"

I nodded slowly as in a dream, watching in terror as she grasped the spine in both hands, feeling a mystical draft rolling over me, lifting the hairs all over my body.

"Well tell her again, you skinny prick!" Mulldoos rasped. "Tell her whatever she's about to plaguing do is a real bad plaguing—"

But the moment ended. The charge of whatever esoteric thing she had worked was gone.

The Deserter released the spine, turned her head to Mulldoos, and said in halting Syldoonian. "This one understands you well enough, white worm. The Matriarch said deliver alive. She said nothing about you having your tongue. Easy enough to pluck it out by the roots."

Mulldoos somehow went paler than usual, but he leaned forward, pulling the chains taut, before saying, "You just crawl in this wagon and try it, you behemoth bitch."

The Deserter grinned, predatory, and gave a clicking chuckle of sorts before moving down the line to the next wagon.

Mulldoos fell back against the side of the wagon and slammed the heel of his hand into the floorboards several times.

The Deserter went through the same motions at the wagon behind us, examining, then grasping the spine.

Vendurro leaned over and said to me, "Well, at least you won't have to struggle none trying to figure out how to tell them to go fuck themselves in Old Anjurian, eh? Mulldoos can do it just fine in perfectly good Syldoonian."

When the Deserter finished approaching each wagon in turn and examining everyone inside, she walked to the front of the procession once more. The human slaves got the rooters moving again, and the wagons continued rolling over the well-paved road that led directly into the dome.

The tangy sting of vinegar grew more powerful as we moved towards the oscillating and scintillating surface of the dome. Only we weren't clasped hand-to-hand to Captain Killcoin or protected by Bloodsounder at all.

But the Deserters and human slaves walked forward nonchalantly, clearly not worried about madness or death. The first of them parted the warping, gently curved veil, disappearing from view entirely.

The rooters at the front of the wagon moved through as if the veil dome weren't there at all.

As we approached, I didn't feel the tug that I had when we crossed the Godveil—I felt nothing at all. At least until the wagon moved me into the pulsing weft and weave itself. Then it was if my mind were being cast about in a tempest, twisted, torn, consciousness stretched. I saw thousands of flashes of human memories, each a separate current flowing against the rest— powerful, awful, in danger of pulling me under and swallowing me completely. There were sensations I recognized as they washed over me—sounds of animals growling; splashing water and children crying; cries of joy and fury; the scent of lemongrass; the feeling of an embrace; the pleasure and bite of pain as a blister popped and tore; the shock of icy river water up to my thighs; the howling of wind that precedes a hellish storm; the smell of rooter dung, piled high.

There was also a rush of some other alien sensations that were so overwhelming and beyond the scope of anything I'd ever experienced, I nearly vomited.

It felt like an eternity of being churned in the eddy, and then we were suddenly through, though it was clear we had only physically traveled a few feet.

I shook my head, trying to clear it, feeling nauseous and faint and hot, as if struck by sickness. It seemed to pass quickly, and then I saw what was inside the dome, a few hundred yards away . . .

A wondrous, massive, and completely alien city that could only serve as sanctuary for the Deserters.

Roxtiniak.

We continued rumbling towards it and the first thing that stood out was that while the city was walled—with much higher walls than any human settlement—there was no dry or wet moat. The road led to a simple but massive gate, open wide, and a gatehouse, but no drawbridge or portcullis, and no flanking towers nearby, no hoardings or battlements, no siege engines on top of wide towers along the walls, no arrow loops in the few towers that did break up the wall. In short, none of the defensive constructions or developments that would have marked any human city of this size.

But of course, with a mystical dome preventing approach, all that was rendered irrelevant—had the Deserter with the spine not examined us and somehow marked us as able to pass through, I was certain we would all be dead. As we rolled towards the open gate, I wondered why there were any walls at all.

I looked over at Mulldoos, who was scowling, of course, but appraising as well. But he shared his thoughts with no one. With a wrenching sadness, I realized I'd never hear him and Hewspear banter over how they would broach a city's defenses again. No bristly arguments about possibly tunneling under the veil surrounding the city or capturing a she-devil to breach its defenses, or any other method they might weigh and discard.

We rolled between the stone walls and while there was nothing there as marvelous or sublimely horrible as the warping dome, Roxtiniak itself was nearly as overwhelming. Simply the scale and size of things, all built to accommodate the giant inhabitants. I felt like a very small child again, overcome with awe and fear and wonder.

The buildings ahead were never square or perfectly round or symmetrical, but curving in odd shapes, and resembled the terraced farm we'd seen. Each level had a flat roof that was covered in undulating grass, with every upper story always smaller than the one immediately below, which gave the effect of the structures being carved out of a hill rather than built solely of stone and wood and stucco.

The rooters pulled our wagons into an expansive plaza directly on the other side of the wall that was bordered by neat rows of purple moss columns, though all empty and devoid of spikes. While they weren't so crowded as to provide a true wailing, there was a low lament as the breeze blew through the holes.

There were Deserters milling about everywhere in the plaza, some on large stone benches, but the majority standing or walking. Most wore flowing robes with sleeves so long and billowy they nearly trailed to the ground, and odd sashes and strips of cloth and rectangular cloaks and a hundred other accoutrements that were obviously designed to add flourish or "texture" to the clothing, having no functional purpose at all, and looking like they would only catch on things and prove problematic.

Not surprisingly, given the horns, none of the Deserters were wearing hoods, hats, or cowls of any kind. And the backs of the gowns, robes, and free-flowing tunics were open halfway down the back, I presumed to show off the dual and triple "manes," and the myriad ribbons, bells, and assorted doodads that were worked into them, or how they crisscrossed each other.

All of them had similar designs on their skin, as if they were inscribed somehow by brand or knife or chisel, scarred and marked forever.

I mentioned as much to Vendurro. He ran his hand over the inked noose at his neck and muttered, "Kind of makes our efforts look sort of amateurish, don't it?"

There were only a few Deserters armored like our captors, and every single one of them turned in our direction and adopted the postures of those who would be staring if they had eyes.

It seemed obvious they either had never seen so many human captives at once before, or had heard that we were all armed and had killed some of their own. They turned to each other and had hushed, guttural exchanges, and one female pointed.

But the most noteworthy thing wasn't the presence of so many more Deserters milling about, the excessive cut of their cloth, or their behavior as they gawked at us as we rode past, but the colors. Or lack of. I'd noticed it before, but now with so many Deserters, the effect was striking. While it was hard to tell the caste or class from the style of clothing, one thing they all had in common was that their garb was undyed. Belts, robes, trousers, cloaks—one and all, they were the natural hue of the material, pale grey, cream, bone, tan, and devoid of the slightest hint of any dyes.

The Anjurians had favored earth tones, and muted colors on the whole, but the Deserters made their fashion seem garish and gaudy in comparison.

While the clothing had many folds, and studs, and strange physical flourishes, it was clear that, not having eyes, they had no cause to appeal to that sense at all. The Deserters were completely washed out.

And that's when I noticed the same of the architecture—while many buildings had discs near the doors that were like mosaics of some kind, they were done only in tiny grey tiles or stones arranged in what might have been a pattern of some kind, but didn't cohere to form any kind of image. And while the surfaces of the buildings had hundreds of small grottos, alcoves, carvings, or other peculiar projections I assumed were ornamental, they were utterly devoid of color as well. Unlike a human city, there were no painted facades or murals, no doors of different hues. The buildings were remarkable because of the sheer scale, and how asymmetrical everything was, especially compared to any human construction—but there was no effort made to distinguish, enhance, or distract with color. Most of the buildings were terraced, and some had huge bulbous towers, oddly angled promenades, and a hundred other things that made them unusual compared to human dwellings, but it was difficult to take that in, with all of the colors bleached out entirely. Or never added in the first place at least.

It was like seeing an alien otherworld.

A few soldiers around me gave voice to similar thoughts, commenting quietly as we rumbled down a broad avenue away from the plaza. One looked at a terraced building we rolled past. "Just keeps getting queerer and queerer, don't it?"

Vendurro replied, "Looks like it was built by plaguing ghosts. Giant ghosts."

The only flashes of color were small rows of mossy columns here or there, lining the avenues or glimpsed through the arched openings of walls, though the moss was so dusky purple as to be almost black, and were a result only of nature's artistry rather than something chosen by Deserter botanists on account of their color, which they must not have been able to see anyway.

As we rumbled down another large avenue, gawked at by countless sightless Deserters, I noticed that was another oddity—the moss columns we encountered out in the wild were present in several manicured gardens or perfectly orchestrated rows as well, their translucent spikes shimmering in the sun.

I gawked in turn, looking at the severe faces of the Deserters, the stern and somewhat bewildering facades of the buildings. Vendurro said, "Plague me, but for not having eyes of any kind, they sure do stare a lot."

Benk nodded. "Makes my skin crawl, it does. Plaguing bastards."

Several soldiers mumbled agreement, and Mulldoos said, "Spend less time yapping, you sorry sons of whores, and more time marking things. The number of streets, landmarks, any barracks you see. We're going to get out of this plaguing city, fighting or sneaking, and we got to know where to go. You hear me?"

Benk lifted his head from his knees and laughed. "You saw that dome, Lieutenant. Like the Godveil, it were. Ain't no getting out on our own, unless they decide to let us out, even if we painted ourselves a path right back to the gate."

Mulldoos gave him the one-eye glare and balled his hands into fists. "Give me lip one more time, you little fuck, go on and do it. And the second we get unhooked from the wagon here, I'm going to beat you senseless. You hear me, Benk?"

No one challenged Mulldoos before Rusejenna struck him down, especially when he was glowering and working himself into a lather. Even Azmorgon might have thought better of it. But Benk returned the stare, long and hard, and everyone in the wagon watched to see if the lippy soldier was about to grow bold enough to challenge that threat, now that it was less likely that Mulldoos could actually carry it out.

Finally, Benk said, "Aye, Lieutenant. Marking the city. Right." Then he turned and spit out the side of the wagon before looking at the large oblong granary we passed.

Even more than their control of the Memoridons, or their system of recognizing and rewarding talent over heredity, or their cunning or viciousness, the thing that had ensured the Syldoon triumphs over the centuries was their discipline and devotion to the brothers in their own Towers. And just now, that was all we had to sustain us. If that failed, we were well and truly doomed.

I leaned back against the wood as we jostled over the cobblestones, trying to force myself to breathe and not succumb to panic or despair.

We made our slow trek through the streets, and everywhere it was the same. The Deserters that were out already stopped to take us in, the same way humans might if a menagerie of exotic animals were on parade, and word preceded us, as some of the groups were large indeed.

But as different as their physicality and fashions were, they still had shops, and traded, and haggled over the price of a bolt of (undyed) cloth or a tray of strange meats on a corner. They were disturbingly human in that respect.

Beyond the pronounced asymmetrical and terraced aspects of most of their architecture, and the lack of color, the other thing that stood out was that, like their clothing, the surface of almost every Deserter building was textured in some way, without a smooth surface to be seen. There were indentations and alcoves, ribbed paneling and exotic stucco relief, filigree of stone and metal, holed surfaces that seemed perfect for nesting birds, and a thousand other features designed to add variety and appeal to tactical senses as much as visual ones, which was odd, considering the Deserters couldn't see them or possibly reach most of the surfaces.

And while there were fewer rows of harvested mossy columns this far into the city, so the low lament was faint and barely audible, there was another noise that sounded like metal chimes of some sort, but with a whirring or humming that accompanied it. As the thoroughfare curved, I saw the source—there were square stone columns periodically lining the street, and they had open sections carved into them where some bronze objects hung. I strained to make them out as we rode past—they looked like spheres composed of strips, with narrower bands inside, and narrower still inside those, and all of them spun when the breeze blew through the obelisk, causing them to hum and whirr and chime.

We crossed another broad avenue, and I looked in both directions. The left was much as the rest of the city—gray or white, marked by unusual-looking buildings and monochrome Deserters. But to the right, far down at the end of the avenue, there was an explosion of color—bright, brassy, lurid even, and the size of the buildings made it clear they housed humans.

I wished Bulto were around, as I wanted to ask someone what that meant. But after the blow he had received already today, he probably wouldn't have been overly inclined to dole out information even if he had been nearby.

We moved on, the street far more winding than anything in Sunwrack or even Alespell. While the Syldoon capital was the height of order, and Baron Brune's city was haphazard and confusing, the roads generally ran straight. Here, they meandered and curved for reasons that had little to do with geography or any other easily discernible reason.

But I saw a massive building in the middle of the city several blocks ahead, rising above the two- and three-story buildings we passed. I caught glimpses of it at first, and as we got closer, it was easy to pick out.

Looking up, I noticed for the first time that the Veildome wasn't complete—there was actually a large hole in the center that made it possible to see the sky above.

With the rooters rocking side to side as they pulled our wagon train along, I heard a noise that continued growing louder. At first, it sounded like fast-flowing water, which was strange, as I hadn't seen any rivers near this city, and I doubted there was one running through the middle of it.

The sound of rushing water grew louder and more insistent as we neared the central building that dominated Roxtiniak, rising much higher than any Tower in Sunwrack.

The avenue opened up to another broad plaza, and then the largest construction I had ever seen was laid bare in front of me. It curved off in either direction, and it must have been round or oval in shape, though it was impossible to tell, being so close to it. It was like an inversion of the style of so many of the terraced buildings throughout Roxtiniak—each story extending out a little further than the one below. The extensions weren't all that pronounced themselves—the principles of engineering didn't cease to apply on this side of the Godveil, and you wouldn't build something that was inherently unstable—but there was no denying that each story jutted out slightly more than the preceding one.

As we approached the huge structure, this seemed to give it a looming, bulging presence.

Several dozen armed Deserters were waiting for us in front of some broad steps that led up to colossal double doors on a landing, their wide, flat clubs on their armored shoulders, the spines glinting in the last day's light, seeming to both reflect and absorb the sun.

The wagons came to a rest. The human slaves or servants bowed low and slunk back away from the Deserters who approached. One of the warriors who had been our escort seemed to be reporting, in their odd guttural, pointed, and rigid-sounding language, to a Deserter who had an ugly human in the container on his back.

The giants spoke for a few moments, and then the leader of our escort barked some orders and several slaves sprang back to work, running up to each wagon with keys, unlocking the backs, climbing in, and releasing the chains from the loops inside but ensuring we were still very much chained together.

It felt good to stand again, even though I was now a prisoner or slave. At least I still had legs, unlike the poor bastards on the Deserters' backs. Though, I had to remind myself, they would throw a javelin through me in a blink if I misstepped, no matter what common ancestry we had.

My muscles were cramped, and I was bending over to rub my thigh when I heard a shout from behind me.

I looked back at the other wagon to see what was causing the commotion.

Azmorgon had his forearm around one of the slave's necks, and the man's face was turning a garish shade of purple as he was hoisted into the air. Azmorgon shouted, "Give me the key, or I break his scrawny neck."

Mulldoos muttered, "Plaguing ass. These giant horsecocks don't give a single leaky shit about their chattel. Bastard's going to get us all killed."

I almost pointed out Mulldoos had nearly done the same at the gates with the female Deserter, but held my tongue as the large males closed in, spiked hafts at the ready, and some half-humans in barrels holding javelins, arms cocked back to release.

Mulldoos shouted at Azmorgon, "Drop that skinny prick, you dumb plaguing bastard!"

But it didn't look like Azmorgon was in any mood to comply as he spun to face the Deserters and repeated his demand.

Then Captain Killcoin stepped forward and said something quietly to the huge lieutenant. Azmorgon shook his furry head, the slave wriggling in front of him, kicking weakly as his air was running out.

Braylar said something else, louder this time, though I still couldn't make it out. But the look on his face made it clear he was not in the mood to suffer insubordination.

The Deserters closed in, weapons still ready, and there was a moment when the Ogre's face looked doubtful, but it passed quickly and his expression hardened—clearly he wasn't about to back down, even if his pique and pride brought down Deserter wrath on every Syldoon prisoner.

Braylar kicked the much larger man in the back of the knee, and as he buckled forward a little, the captain struck him in the temple with his elbow three times in quick succession, the first two as Azmorgon released the slave and dropped to a knee, and the final one as he started to rise and spin to face the captain.

That third elbow to the ear stunned the Ogre and sent him to the floorboards. But the captain wasn't taking any chances—he dropped on top of the lieutenant, pinned a massive arm behind Azmorgon's back, and leaned over to say something, presumably to reacquaint him with the necessity of following orders.

Vendurro gave a long whistle. "And here I thought Mulldoos had the sharpest elbows in the company."

Mulldoos laughed. "Where do you think I plaguing learned it from?"

Another Syldoon with two missing teeth said, "Begging your pardon, Lieutenant. That is, Lieutenants. But ought the captain be putting a hurting on Azmorgon like that? I mean, he was only doing what he thought he ought to to get us out of this fix."

Mulldoos turned and looked at the soldier, stared him up and down with his one unhooded eye. "Were you begging pardon for rank stupidity? I'm guessing that's it, am I right? Must have been. Although ain't no apology big enough to make up for a shitdumb comment like that. Because there were three things real plaguing wrong with what Azmorgon just pulled there.

"First, you don't go rogue and put any play in motion without Cap's say so, even if you are a lieutenant, and even if that play were plenty thought out and like to put us in a better situation than we currently find ourselves. Second, that play by Azmorgon makes your stupidity look pretty inoffensive on the whole. Wasn't going to accomplish much except to win us beatings, lashings, or beheadings. Or whatever other awful thing these Deserter bastards can dream up for a man."

The soldier took the berating in stride. "And the third thing?" he asked.

Mulldoos glanced at the wagon behind us as the captain got off Azmorgon and helped him back to his feet. Then he turned back to the tooth-deprived soldier. "You don't ever disobey a direct order from superior officer. You do, and an elbow to the ear is about the best thing you can plaguing hope for."

He didn't look at Benk when he said it. But Mulldoos did say it loud enough for everyone around us to hear.

The Deserter warriors pushed the human slaves out of the way, grabbed the chains, and started leading us out of our wagons, none too gently, striking some of us about the shoulders with the flat of their spiked hafts. They shouted at us as we jumped off the backs of the wagons onto the stones. We couldn't understand a word of it, but the warning was no less clear than the lieutenant's.

Still, they felt the need to drive the point home. In the wagon behind us, a Deserter was watching an injured Syldoon struggling out of the back, favoring what looked to be a broken or badly sprained leg. The Deserter stepped up, a massive elbow shot out just as Braylar's had, only when it struck this Syldoon in the temple, it sent him flying to the stones, and it was a blow there would be no getting up from. Blood dribbled out of the dead Syldoon's ear, and the Deserter looked at Azmorgon and Braylar, still inside the wagon, and he click-laughed, then pulled the next soldier out.

I was still staring at the corpse when a Deserter's shadow fell over me, and he screamed something, spittle flying down, and I got my feet moving instantly, walking towards the steps of an entrance to the overwhelmingly large palace or keep.

They led us through a huge arched entrance and down a long corridor. There were enough Deserter guards around that even Azmorgon wouldn't be foolish enough to try anything else. If the outside of the buildings in Roxtiniak had impressed me with the level of detailing in the facades and stone carving— wild whorls, scrollwork, and other stonecraft—the interior of the citadel was something else altogether. While it was just as devoid of color as the rest of the Deserter buildings, there didn't seem to be a wall, panel, grotto, or door frame that wasn't elaborately worked, sometimes with abstract designs, other times with incredibly detailed scenes of Deserter life—warriors clashing, legless humans sometimes in the barrels on their backs, robed female Deserters with the spines sticking up above their shoulders, as well as others dressed in garb and in vignettes I couldn't discern the meaning of.

The level and sophistication of carving was dizzying. And perplexing. Did the Deserters enjoy rubbing their hands over the artistry? They navigated just fine without walking sticks or guides, and attacked the Syldoon without any obvious impediment, so they clearly possessed some ability to sense their surroundings. But could they appreciate such intricate stone and woodwork without the use of eyes? It seemed impossible.

The scale of everything inside was also designed to accommodate our giant captors, and contributed to my feeling of being a disobedient child summoned to accept punishment from an angry adult. Well, if the punishment was exaction of limbs.

We shuffled along, injured, exhausted, starving, foul-smelling, our chains clinking, until we reached the end of the hall and the Deserters directed us up a huge flight of winding stone stairs. Luckily, the Deserters had prepared the stairwell for human slaves as well, as there were sconces periodically, though not as many as if the humans had had a say in lighting the way, as it was very difficult to make out anything in the gloom and deep shadow.

After several landings and entrances to new floors, I lost track of how many we passed. All I knew was the muscles in my legs were burning and cramping, and my breath was coming ragged and almost wheezing. The hardened Syldoon weren't showing the effects as much, accustomed to discomfort and pushing themselves to the limit as they were, but it was some small consolation that I heard lots of heavy breathing around me as well.

Finally, we reached our destination, or at least floor, as the stairs continued up, but we were ushered through a large arched doorway and down another hall.

My head was spinning, so my sense of direction, suspect on the best days, told me nothing about where we were headed. There were several more armed Deserters towering above us as we were directed down the hall and through an open doorway.

That was another architectural oddity—the lack of actual doors inside the building. Every human domicile I'd ever been in had doors, for privacy or security. But most rooms here had none.

We walked through the doorway two at a time, and I had no idea what to expect—were we being presented before some ruler, sent to an interrogation room or cells of some kind (unlikely without a door), or something else?

The interior didn't exactly answer the question, except for eliminating another possibility—there were no rulers to be seen. There was a series of interconnected rooms, all without doors, and it seemed they were quarters of some kind, though mostly empty. All that was left in most of them were human-sized sleeping mats, and a few woven screens here or there. Whatever chests or wardrobes or other usual furniture had once been housed here had been removed.

The human slaves moved amongst us, unlocking our manacles, pulling the chains free. I saw Azmorgon rubbing his wrists and glaring at a slave as if he were considering backhanding him, but he managed to restrain himself.

The Deserter guards stood at the door while the slaves kept releasing us, making as little eye contact with the Syldoon as possible. We started moving off away from the door, looking into the other rooms connected with the main chamber. I had just stepped around a corner when the last Syldoon was unchained, and one of the hulking guards started yelling in their opaque tongue, miming as if he were removing his own armor.

While they had stripped us of helms and weapons, and taken bolts out of quivers, they hadn't bothered to take our armor until now. No Syldoon seemed in a hurry to remove their gear and the Deserter bellowed again, spittle flying off his thick sallow lips.

Braylar said, "You hear our host. He wants us to be more comfortable. Everyone, be good guests, yes?"

Several muttered and Azmorgon went further. "Plague that, Cap. Ain't giving these bastards nothing! And none of you whoresons should neither!"

Braylar nodded. "As you will, Lieutenant. But for the rest of you who presumably want to live and not have your skulls caved in like Wincer in the yard, I suggest you do not test our host's patience." He started unbuckling the straps on his splinted vambrace.

Everyone else started doing the same.

I ducked behind the wall for a moment, slid the strap of my writing case over my head, knelt down, and slid the brass case under a dirty sleeping pallet. Then I stepped back in the room as quickly as possible and started taking my gambeson off.

When we were done, the slaves gathered our gear and nearly ran out of our barless prison.

The Deserters waited until all the slaves were gone, then turned and left the main entrance as well.

As Syldoon set off to explore the extent of our limited quarters, Rudgi stared at the open doorway. "Is this some kind of a trap, then? Leave the mice in a maze, wait until they try to leave, then smash them with a boot or let a cat gut them?"

Vendurro replied, "Least they could do is give the plaguing mice some cheese first."

Braylar walked over to us, face pale and drawn, his eyes nearly slits, and he seemed to be wobbling a little.

Mulldoos asked, "Glad to see you made it, Cap. Though you kind of look like shit just now. If you don't mind me saying."

The captain replied, "Now how could I mind that, Lieutenant? If you started doling out disingenuous compliments, now, that would make me suspicious."

While he aimed for a jest, the strain in his voice and rigid posture belied that.

I glanced at the hook on his belt. I'd never seen it empty unless he had Bloodsounder in hand. "Is—" I lowered my voice. "Are you feeling the absence . . . explicitly just now?"

Braylar looked at me. He was clearly suffering, though not as with the barrage of stolen memories he usually had to contend with. He seemed as lucid as ever, only more pained than usual. "That is one way of putting it, Arki. It is not as sharp as when my men buried the weapon miles behind us. The flail isn't nearly as distant. But yes, there are . . . pangs. Explicit pangs."

Mulldoos said, "Last thing I saw before we were captured was you still standing, fighting off the she-devil Deserter."

Braylar pulled the gloves off his hands and stuffed them in a pouch. "Bloodsounder afforded me some measure of protection, it seems, though not so much as when Rusejenna attacked us. The Deserter woman was . . . far more powerful." He looked around us, peered at the rooms where Syldoon stood wondering what to do or say. "My sister. She is not among us, then?"

Mulldoos declined to answer, maybe not trusting himself to hide any glee he felt, but Vendurro replied, "Nope, Cap. She went down when you did, from the sounds of it. Nobody seen her since. Weren't in the wagons."

The captain nodded slowly. "I thought not. Well." There was some emotion threatening to rear up just then, but he gave it no opportunity. "Let us take stock, yes? How many have we lost?"

Mulldoos and Vendurro looked at each other. The pale lieutenant said, "This is the first we got all the men together again to take an accurate count. I'll get on it."

"Do," Braylar replied. "Get Azmorgon as well. Give that impulsive bastard something to do to occupy his—"

We heard something behind us and looked over to the doorway. One Syldoon was standing above another soldier lying on the floor, curled up, body quivering and quaking, eyes rolling back into his skull. It took me a moment to recognize that it was Benk, as his face was contorted into a rictus.

Vendurro ran over to the soldier still standing. "What plaguing happened?"

The Syldoon was still staring down at Benk, shaking his head. "He just looked. Just looked is all."

Braylar approached as well. "Just looked at what?" he asked, already angry as if he anticipated the answer.

The soldier pointed at the door. "Weren't trying to leave. Just wanted to peer out a little. Of the door. But he never got there."

Mulldoos managed to growl and slur, "What do you plaguing mean he never plaguing got there?"

We all watched Benk convulse another time, eyes still mostly white, as the soldier quietly said, "He was walking towards it, the door that is, and when he was five steps away, he flew back like he got hit with an invisible battering ram. Ain't such a thing. Not saying it was that. Only that's what—"

Braylar raised his hand. "Yes, soldier, we understand. So he screamed and flew back. That is all?"

"That, what he's doing now, jerking around like that."

Vendurro knelt and held Benk in place until he finally stopped shaking and floundering, and his eyes came back down. He spit out some blood and saliva and looked up at us, confused, angry, and scared. He shook off Vendurro's hands. "What—"

"Guess that answers the question about the trap," Rudgi said.

"Quite," Braylar replied.

Mulldoos looked down at Benk and shook his head. "Guessing you didn't hear a plaguing thing in the wagon, did you? No play without Cap's say. You dumb fuck."

Benk got up into a sitting position, still shaky and weak, eyes unfocused. "I was just looking, is all. Investigating like. Just . . . that's it. All I was doing."

Vendurro stood up and asked, "What happened to you?"

Benk stared at the doorway as if it were an animal that attacked him. "Walked towards it. Towards it a bit, is all. Then . . . it was like every light and sound in the world hit me at once. Don't remember nothing else."

"Wasn't much else to remember, you prick," Mulldoos said. "Except you nearly biting your tongue in half as you jerked around like a fish on a dock."

Benk rubbed his head. "Hurts. Bad."

"Good," Mulldoos said. "Plaguing good."

Benk looked at the captain, voice somewhere between pitiful and plaintive. "Just trying to help. Nothing more. Can't blame a man for that. Just—"

Mulldoos said, "You ever been taking a shit, and it's lodged in there good, and you push and your ass makes an awful squeaky noise right before things work themselves out? That's what you sound like right now, Benk, a whiny annoying shit. Shut your mouth."

Braylar looked at his lieutenant. "So. Take stock, and also tell the men to stay well away from the door."

Mulldoos and Vendurro nodded and set off into adjacent rooms and the captain started walking away with me in tow. When we were far enough away not to be heard, I asked, "What do you think they intend to do with us?"

Braylar pressed his lips tight and closed his eyes for a moment, and tremors rolled over his eyelids and seemed to find a path down his cheek. The captain clenched his jaw and waited it out until whatever ailed him passed or lessened. Then he opened his eyes again and said, "I have no idea. And even if I concocted a notion, it would likely be proven wrong. So we will simply wait and see. They didn't summarily execute us as they could have, so that could bode well. Or it could be they are only saving us for something worse. We cannot know until they make their intentions clear. But until then, I intend to do my best not to fall over wracked with pain as we assess and try to formulate a plan of some kind."

He walked towards the other rooms, arms crossed at the wrists behind his back, head down slightly, bowed under unseen and immeasurable weight. I wasn't sure what would prove more of a burden or torture—the presence of stolen memories that ordinarily afflicted him or the absence of the weapon itself that he contended with now.

When it was clear the Deserters weren't coming back, I pulled my writing case out from under the pallet, cracked it open, and recorded the awful events of our capture. When I was done, I walked into some of the other mostly empty rooms, moving through them, drawn forward by the distant sounds of the city of Roxtiniak. While it was an alien place to be sure, perplexing and foreign and disturbing, there were still voices, shouts, what sounded like curses, and the rolling wheels of gigantic cairns pulled by rooters.

It suddenly hit me that I had no idea what became of our horses. Would they kill them? Eat them? Given the reaction the humans in this land had to the beasts, I doubted they had simply set them free, and they certainly weren't going to ride them. I felt guilty I hadn't stopped to think of it before. While I hadn't spent my life around the creatures, or formed any kind of bond the way these Jackals had with their own mounts—being crossbow cavalry for the most part—I had grown to appreciate the animals in my short time, saddle sores and all. I even looked forward to those moments of brushing my own horse, caring for her. They were beautiful, strong, smart beasts.

If the Deserters had killed them off, I was glad I at least hadn't seen it.

Sighing, I looked out the window. Unlike the door, the windows were barred, so I didn't think I would set off a trap like Benk had, but still held my breath as I got closer. Not being thrown across the room, I peered out—given the construction with the upper floors extending out slightly more than the ones below, even if there weren't bars, it would be impossible to scale the walls down, especially without a rope or any kind of tools.

The city view was breathtaking, though, even more so than the view of Sunwrack from the height of the Jackal Tower. But as I surveyed the oddly shaped and asymmetrical buildings around the city, something arrested my attention unlike anything else. I'd caught a glimpse of it from the ground level, but now with this vantage point, I saw it clearly.

There was a small quadrant of smaller dwellings, mostly walled off from the rest of Roxtiniak. Even with the sun setting somewhere beyond the city's Veil, the colors of this little sector were awesome to behold—garish, outlandish, brighter than any dwellings I'd even seen, and undeniably human. They might have been slaves, but they seemed to delight in expressing themselves in the one way that couldn't possibly offend their eyeless masters. While the Deserters had a way of sensing their surroundings I couldn't fathom, they clearly couldn't see the color of anything.

In the extraordinarily muted and neutral tones of the rest of the city, this riot of color was the greatest silent protest I'd even seen.

I heard someone approaching and turned. Vendurro said, "There you are. Thought you must have been off roping the unicorn again."

I started to protest and he chuckled and hit me in the arm, "Plague me, Arki, but you're tighter than a priest's bunghole sometimes. It might actually do you some good if you let off some of that pent up . . . whatever it is you got pent up, and took matters into your own hands. Hand, anyway." He laughed at his own joke, and I couldn't help smiling. Then he turned to go, took a few steps before stopping and looking back at me. "Well, come on then. Didn't think I came out here just to harass you, did you? Cap wants us."

I followed him through the rooms I'd seen, passing several with Syldoon reclining against the walls, staring vacantly ahead or with their heads resting on their knees. Curiously, none had fallen into the cots that filled most of the rooms. Perhaps the captain had ordered them not to, or possibly they didn't trust that gesture as benign or truly generous.

We turned and moved off through an open doorway that led to another suite of rooms, and I noticed the rumbling sound of rushing water was louder here.

A few rooms later, Vendurro and I joined the captain, Mulldoos, Azmorgon, Benk, and Rudgi. My stomach twisted as it hit me anew than Hewspear was going to forever be absent from the captain's council.

The group was facing a broad open but barred window, silent, looking out at whatever lay beyond. As I settled in line next to Vendurro, I witnessed something that made the colorful human commune seem completely insignificant.

The Deserter palace was in the shape of a ring and was so large it was difficult to imagine how long it would have taken them to construct it. That alone would have been impressive, as it dwarfed even the most magnificent of human dwellings, but what lay in the expanse in the middle was so utterly unlike anything I'd ever witnessed, it was impossible to even understand it at first or believe my eyes weren't betraying me.

At the base of the palace, there was a broad lake surrounded by a wide strip filled with more of the spiked columns and other foliage and footpaths, but it was the lake itself that drew the eye immediately and revealed what the odd watery noise was. In the middle of the lake, there appeared to be a . . . giant drain of some sort, fifty yards across. It was as if a round waterfall occupied the center—the water ran over the edge of what must have been a deep circular cliff of some kind, though I couldn't see how deep it went down, even from this height and vantage point, as the rushing water disappeared in mist and spray in the drain.

I stared, shook my head, and turned to Vendurro. "That's . . . impossible. Isn't it? I mean, if a river goes over a waterfall, the water is replenished from the source. But this . . . it's a lake. Impossible."

Mulldoos replied, "Impossible is something that can't exist, right, scribbler? Seems like this queer lake is mighty strange, but it sure as hells exists, don't it?"

I couldn't take my eyes off the water disappearing into the huge drain in the center. "Fine. Clearly it does exist. But have you ever seen anything like this, then?" He didn't reply right away, and so I added, "Anyone? Because real or not, such a thing shouldn't be possible."

Vendurro offered. "Kind of like a fountain, ain't it? How does a fountain plaguing work?"

"It is like one," I admitted. "Only ten thousand times larger. And not man-made. Or Deserter-made. It is a *lake*."

"Right you are. Still want to know how a fountain works though."

Mulldoos shook his head. "Your head is a plaguing fountain."

Braylar leaned against the small stone window ledge, eyes fixed on the bizarre lake as it emptied into itself without running dry, the crashing water a dull roar in the background. "We are in the land of the Deserters. Whatever these beings are, we do not know what they are capable of, or what sorcery or sophisticated engineering unknown to us they possess or employ. Perhaps they have shaped the land, or created this themselves. Or perhaps it simply is. There is no telling what exists or does not on this side of the Godveil, or why." He stepped away from the window and walked towards the opposite wall as we all started following. "And what needs concern us just now is trying to understand our captors as quickly as possible and figuring out the best strategy to getting out of this."

Mulldoos said, "Ogre, why don't you try just walking out the front door. Maybe Benk cleared the way for you."

Azmorgon glared at him. "Yeah. Real plaguing funny. Plaguing hilarious, you are, you squinty little fuck."

Rudgi said, "Who knows, maybe if you got to running first, you could—"

"Shut your hole, she-cunt." Azmorgon rumbled.

Vendurro said, "On account of a lady having lady bits, and Rudgi there being a lady, the 'she' is redundant."

"I'm no lady, Ven. But you're right about the redundancy. It is pretty plaguing redundant."

Azmorgon glowered down at both of them. "The whole lot of you, plaguing riotous. But now that Squirrel's been elevated, these two bastards are my peers. You, though?" He jabbed a huge finger into Rudgi's collarbone, knocking her back a step. "You don't watch that stupid tongue of yours, you'll be cleaning my chamber pot for weeks. Just see if you don't. Maybe with your stupid tongue even. Cleaning it with your tongue. How's that sound, you lippy little she-cunt." He caught himself. "Regular cunt. Whatever I plaguing feel like calling you." He looked around, daring anyone to correct him.

I never thought it possible, but Azmorgon really did make Mulldoos seem like an erudite orator.

Braylar appeared to be ignoring the entire exchange, eyes fixed on the lake that really shouldn't have been a lake, but when a Syldoon came running over to the window, the captain spun around, hand reaching for Bloodsounder even though the flail was nowhere near.

The soldier said, "Your sister, Cap. She's alive. Well, mostly."

He turned and moved at a quick walk towards the main entrance to the quarters and we all followed.

When we got to the main common room and the arched doorway, Soffjian was on her hands and knees about eight paces into the room, and two Deserters were standing behind, surveying the Syldoon around them. They each had their spiked hafts in hand, though not immediately threatening, held relaxed at their sides, and they stood there, towering over the unarmed humans as if challenging them to bull-rush the pair.

None did, of course, so the Deserters turned nonchalantly and strode out.

Soffjian tried to get to her feet and fell, barely catching herself before slamming her head on the stone floor. She was far enough inside the room that she didn't set off the trigger near the doorway, but no one was in a hurry to go assist her, just the same. Several of the soldiers looked around, and a few muttered.

Finally, Braylar walked forward until he stood next to his sister. Soffjian could barely raise her head, but either recognized his boots or gait, as she slurred, "Well. Seems roles are reversed a bit. Must be fantastic for you." Then she collapsed.

Braylar knelt down and rolled her onto her back. She didn't seem to have any bruises or contusions of any kind, no noticeable wounds. The captain lifted her torso off the stones and then called out, "Vendurro. Give me a hand. Let's get to a cot, yes?"

Vendurro ran up and they hoisted her to her feet, one arm over each of their shoulders, and lifted her limp weight off the ground enough to carry her into the closest room with bedrolls.

I watched them disappear around the corner. It was disturbing enough to see Braylar succumb to Bloodsounder, or Mulldoos and Hewspear laid low by Memoridons. But to see Soffjian, a powerful Memoridon in her own right, overcome so easily by the Deserter witch . . . well, that was truly frightening.

At least she was still alive. For now anyway. That was something.

Rudgi was standing nearby and looked at me. "What do you suppose they did to her? And why did they keep her singled out like that this whole time?"

I shook my head. "I can't say. Interrogated her? Tortured her? Toyed with her? They are a totally foreign species—it's impossible to know until she can confirm anything."

"Well. That's real uplifting."

"You did ask. But I am only guessing."

Rudgi was still looking at the room they'd taken her to as the rest of the Syldoon dispersed. "Didn't have a mark on her though, did she? You saw that, I'm guessing. Or didn't, as it were. You know what I mean."

"I do," I replied. "And you're right. It didn't appear that they physically hurt her."

"Sooooo . . . do you suppose they must have used the same sort of witchery on her she uses herself? Something like that?"

I turned and looked at her, noticing for the first time that she was the same height as I was. Her dark eyes were startlingly earnest. There was no mockery there, no mischief that I could see, no hint of anything but pure curiosity. "I can't say for certain, Rudgi, but—"

"On account of not being witness to what they did, and not being a Deserter, and not a bunch of other things. I got it. But I'm asking you to suppose with me. What do you suppose?"

"I suppose they were exploring. Her memories. Her mind. They probably saw that she had some defenses against their sorcery, and put up the best fight. And I *suppose* that would make them very curious."

Rudgi nodded twice and looked back to the room. "That's roughly what I was supposing myself. I sort of feel like I ought to be glad, on account of the damage she's doled out. Kind of a cruel sort of justice. But then again, she's Cap's sis. And what's more, he needs her, it seems like. Though what for, exactly, is hard to say, isn't it? Cap's never real forthcoming about the particulars, is he?"

I didn't answer right away, as it hit me that the rank and file Jackals didn't likely know the full scope of what Braylar or their Tower Commander intended for them, or how or why Soffjian was accompanying us at all.

"It is hard to say," I replied, and before she could ask anything else, added, "Excuse me."

I walked away, though now with the scrolls gone, I had no real pretense for needing to have any space to myself. Still, better than deflecting questions or revealing more than I ought to.

It was a very odd feeling to possess more knowledge of our purpose than most of the people around me, when the reverse had been true for so long.

I would have reveled in that notion more if we hadn't been trapped in a prison without bars by a giant race who could march through that open door any moment to kill us or shred our minds or toss us in Lake Drain or whatever else they felt like doing.

Being in the know for once brought no pleasure at all. That hardly seemed fair, as the opportunity to enjoy that position might never come again.

The captain kept close counsel with his lieutenants and occasionally sergeants, waiting for his sister to wake, or arguing over potential plans, or
doing who knew what. Without translation to occupy my time, after
recording a bit more, I didn't know what to do with myself. And without weapons, I couldn't even ask Mulldoos for any more welt-filled lessons on how to wield
one. The Syldoon seemed just as restless, having no chores, drills, preparations,
or reconnaissance to occupy them. I overheard some grumbling quietly to each
other, though they always quieted whenever I came near. But we were all in the
same position—nothing for it but to wait. At least for the moment.

So I took a cot as far from everyone as I could manage and laid back, my
mind buzzing with how unreal it all seemed, being a prisoner in a Deserter
city on the other side of the Veil.

And before I knew it, I fell into a sleep. A depthless, dreamless sleep like
the dead, as it happened. Much more soundly than I could have possibly
imagined, though abbreviated. I woke sometime in the middle of the night
to the sounds of dozens of snores of varying patterns around me, disoriented,
in the dark, and it took me a moment to remember where I was.

My bladder was full to bursting, so I carefully got out of my cot and made
my way to the nearest chamber pot that our captors had provided, scattered
in the corners of rooms. It sounded like a furious storm when I released, and
I was certain I would wake someone, but if I did, no one gave a sign.

I considered heading back to my cot, not knowing how many hours of
night might be left. But now alert and roused, I knew I'd only lie there staring
up into the black, mind whirling and spinning itself silly, and likely unable to
fall back asleep anytime soon.

So I shuffled out of the room, moving slowly and carefully to avoid waking anyone around me, and biting my lip to avoid yelping when I banged my
toes on the doorframe leaving the chamber.

I wasn't sure exactly where I intended to go, but my feet had their own ideas, and I found myself drifting towards the dull roar of rushing water. It was a miracle that didn't have everyone running to the chamber pots twelve times a night.

A small breeze was blowing, dry, cool, and I looked down at the lake that should not have existed, constantly running into its own drain in the center. While I couldn't see much below, I looked up through the hole in Veildome to see that the horned moon occasionally broke free from a cloudbank and threw a flash of silver on the water that was constantly flowing away from the shore in the most unnatural fashion possible.

I heard a voice behind me, "Sleep, elusive as a ghost, plaintive as a widow, and as easy to hold as the wind."

I turned around as Captain Killcoin stepped up alongside me. "It is good to see I am not the only one so plagued." He sounded exceptionally tired, and not a little far away, as if he were talking more to himself or a phantom and expected no reply.

"Captain. You should try to get some rest."

Braylar turned towards me, though the clouds had conspired against the moon again, and I could see little of his face and nothing of his expression. "Should I? Truly? I hadn't considered it before, but you very well might be onto something. Shocking that no one else has thought to suggest it to me." He spoke with a surplus of sarcasm, and the rebuke was only barely below the surface.

"That is, I only mean, since—"

He waved a hand. "Oh, desist. I know what you meant, and why. Believe you me, if it were possible, I would be doing it. But it is precisely the pain I'm experiencing just now that makes it untenable. Bloodsounder's absence burns. Burns fiercely, Arki. The cursed thing torments me whether I wield it or not. And the pain is like a wound that has gone sour, but inside my body, a sickly flame that spreads and consumes."

We sat there in silence for a bit, both of us watching the rushing water, listening to the cascade and spray as it flew down its own peculiar well. Finally, I asked, quietly, "And has there been any change? With Soffjian, I mean."

If he looked in my direction, I couldn't see it. "You have such concern for my entire bloodline. Incredibly touching."

It lacked some of its usual sting, though, being less pointed, and more a rebuttal by rote than driven by any passion or innate irascibility. So I pressed on. "She is still out of it, then?"

I expected that to raise his ire, and was ready for it, but instead he only exhaled slowly and said, "She is the same. Yes."

Braylar said nothing else, so I dropped the subject, and was weighing whether to ask about anything else now that I had his undivided attention, or to return to my cot and resume sleepless staring, when he abruptly said, "You asked once what was the true cause of the rift betwixt us, which I rightfully silenced you about. But you guessed correctly at the time—it wasn't simply my inability to kill our father's murderer that sits between us like a poisonous puddle. That was the start of it. But only just the start."

I said, "I asked her. What the origin of the rift was. She told me you were. Though she admitted some culpability in failing to help you avenge the murder."

That seemed to simultaneously agitate and amuse the captain. "Did she now? And what else did she tell you then?" Finally, there was the telltale edge to his voice, but still muted. Somewhat.

"Nothing, really."

"Nothing, really, or really nothing?" He was looking at me, and his face might as well have been obscured by the mail drape of his helm for all it told me in the dark.

"She said the two of you conspired to bring down the murderer, but stopped there, and said that if I was ever curious, I should risk your wrath by asking you myself. She'd say no more about it."

He thought about that for a moment before replying. "Curious. I would have expected her to take the opportunity to spew all manner of truths. More damning than lies in this case, as it happens."

"So I know you tried to kill your father's killer and failed. But I don't know the particulars."

"Nor shall you," he replied. "They are pointless to rehash. I will tell you only this. Soffjian had no intention of leaving me to carry out the deed myself. She simply didn't trust me to do it successfully."

"And by your laws, she couldn't do it herself."

"Yes, that is correct. But that didn't stop her from concocting strategy and assisting in carrying it out. It was a foolish enterprise underpinned by a shortsighted plan carried out by idiot children. Failure was a foregone conclusion."

"What was the plan?"

"I do sometimes admire your quiet relentlessness. Sometimes."

I said, "But not now?"

"Not especially."

"Should I stop?"

"*Will* you stop? Unless I gag you, I suspect not. But you should know enough by now to be sure that gagging someone will trouble my conscience not at all."

I knew that to be true but pressed on anyway. "So you tried to murder the Syldoon murderer and failed? What happened?"

"You know about the Choosings, yes?"

"When the Syldoon recruiters choose candidates from among far-flung tribes? Yes."

"Well, the Syldoon are insurmountably stubborn at times, and the Jackals more so than most Towers. This outfit insisted on meeting my people for the Choosing, as if murdering the chieftain's brother and nearly doing the chieftain in himself as he sought vengeance was no deterrent whatsoever."

"But your priests, they must have objected?"

"Oh, certainly," Braylar replied. "My sister and I were counting on that, you see. As I hid in the woods nearby, Earthpriest Grubarr and Sunpriest Hordomin marched out to parley with the Jackals, to demand justice, in truth. They ordered the Syldoon captain to turn the murderer over to them, so he might be tried by our laws."

I chuckled. "I'm sure the Jackals were really receptive to that."

He might have laughed, though it was short and hard to hear above the distant roar of water. "Astute. The captain insisted the murderer would be tried according to Syldoon law and none other. They continued shouting, as the Syldoon soldiers and Orlu looked on, weapons at the ready, but no one especially eager to bloody them. The Syldoon were greatly outnumbered, but the priests knew that if they slaughtered this platoon, the wrath of the Empire would fall on them, and their own doom would be sealed."

"And so you did what, exactly?"

"I stepped into the open, out of the treeline, where I'd been watching, waiting, my head and heart filling with these swollen ambitions, my blood pumping like a war drum. For a moment, and for the first time in my life, I felt powerful. I was not meekly following my sister, I was not continuing my father's weakness and passivity. I was powerful. A part of me began to hope that my sister didn't interfere as we planned—it was a small part, and undoubtedly crazed, but part of me felt as if I could actually beat this soldier, strike him down with the sword in my hand."

"Sword?" I asked. "Wait. You didn't have one of your own, did you?"

"No, but do you suppose there was only one blade on the island? It was my father's, if you must know. I stole it before he was put in the ground."

"I see. And so you marched out to do, what, slay the murderer in front of an entire Syldoon company?"

Braylar leaned over further, holding tightly to the bars. "I walked onto the grass and towards their line, towards the murderer. Their captain had not rejoined them yet, his back to me, occupied as he was with the priests of my tribe. But many of their soldiers saw me. How could they not, a lone figure walking across the grass bearing a sword? They saw me, and I knew that my own people could see me as well. There were shouts from both sides.

"The captain turned to see what his soldiers saw, and he smiled, hands on his hips. And then I heard laughter, snickers. And suddenly, I no longer felt powerful. In fact, I suddenly felt like revenge and redemption were overrated. But I told myself that this is what we had planned for, Soff and I—we had anticipated their reaction and would turn it to our advantage."

"I still don't understand. I expected you might try to slip into their camp, catch them unawares or something. Surely, you didn't think this plan was going to work. Did you?"

He gave a tired shrug. "We were foolish children, Arki. Yes. In fact, we did imagine our plan was going to work, as Soffjian had engineered most of it, and as I had most of my life to that point, I trusted her implicitly. We were counting on them not expecting this at all."

"Well, I imagine you nailed that true."

"Yes. Now, would you like to use your extensive imagination as to how the rest of it played out, or shall I continue?"

I nodded, and then when it was clear he might not have seen me, I said, "Please continue."

"Many thanks," he replied, laden with sarcasm. "As I closed the last few paces the captain lifted a hand to silence his troops, and he spoke to me.

There was no doubt about the smiling now. He said, 'Little man, why do you come to us so armed and battle-ready? We are about to hold a Choosing, and this is a peaceful affair.'"

I said, "May I ask one more thing?"

I felt Braylar's glare more than saw it. "If you must."

"I noticed before, when you were talking to Ven and me about your father's burial preparations, that you seemed to recall words spoken decades ago by Earth Priest Grubarr as if you heard them just yesterday. I wasn't sure if Bloodsounder had somehow made your memories sharper, in relief, or . . ."

"What? Me playing fast and loose to capture the spirit of how things actually happened?"

"Yes. Something like that."

He snickered. "Unfortunately, that cursed flail has gifted me with an unnatural memory nearly as potent as a Memoridon's. So, as much as I would like to forget the awful moments of my life, they remain clear and precise. Anything else then?"

I shook my head and he must have seen that much as he continued, "I wasn't sure if I should respond to the captain—I didn't know if I had courage for many words, and I hadn't rehearsed any for him, so I saved them. I took four steps and stood before the murderer."

"No one stopped you?"

"No one stopped me," he said. "They saw a scrawny youth who was more comical than threatening. They no doubt were curious what I intended. My father's killer was clearly a dullard, because no recognition was etched on his face. He was shorter than I remembered, and with his hands bound, he didn't seem so fierce or brutal. I held the sword in front of me, with both hands, and addressed him, praying I would get the words right and that I had the strength for all of them. 'Five days ago, at a Sanctuary, you struck down and murdered my father. I was there, I was witness. I am here today to claim the vengeance that is mine by custom and law. I challenge you to a duel.'"

I shook my head. "That was your plan? Challenging a trained killer to a *duel*?"

The captain ignored me. "It took a moment for the words to register, but when they did they were met with hooting laughter. It took the dullard an additional moment or two, but then he seemed to find the humor as well.

Even with my confidence aswirl, even though we had hoped for such a reaction, this still infuriated me. I didn't feel powerful, but I felt a surge of anger, and I knew it would be enough to carry me through.

"I didn't take my eyes off the murderer, but I sensed the captain walk closer to me. He said, loud enough for all his troops to hear, 'Vengeance is a heavy task, little man. You might consider waiting a few years. Why don't you come back to us when you have some stubble on your chin?'

"I did face him then, and though I hadn't planned to speak to him, my rage emboldened me. 'I'm here now, I claim it now. Or is he such a coward who would only face old, unarmed men?'

"The murderer took a step towards me, but two of the other soldiers restrained him. The captain spoke in Orlu for all to hear, 'You declare a duel with one breath and call the man a coward with the next. You are an amazing boy.' He called out to his troops, though his eyes did not leave mine, 'There is a reason we take their children—there will be fewer to grow up and kill us.' And then he said something in Syldoonian. He directed his next words to me in my tongue. 'You are brave, little man, but you are misguided. Your father was not murdered, and there is no vengeance to—'

"But I surprised both of us by interrupting with an emphatic, 'Liar!'"

He said this loudly, as if he were speaking to this captain again rather than his archivist, and I was worried he was going to wake some nearby soldiers.

Braylar continued, "I called him a liar again, and then said, 'Did you ask the Lemonman? Did you? He saw it! I saw it! My father did nothing—nothing!—and he killed him. Your soldier there, he killed him!'

"The captain still smiled, but he seemed infinitely less amused. 'Called a liar to my face, twice in one day. You are an incredible people, truly.' He looked over my shoulder. 'But if I cannot convince you to stay your blade today, perhaps one of them will.'

"I looked over my shoulder as well, at the three priests closing, and panic began to well up in me. An exchange with the captain was not part of the plan, Soffjian taking this long to loose an arrow was not part of the plan, and I suddenly felt small and ill-suited to this task. But it was too late to go back to the trees.

"Hrodomin was shouting at me to return to our lines, this was no place for a boy. A hand fell on my shoulder, sweaty and heavy, and I turned—a Syldoon soldier was standing before me, his helmeted head towering above me. He said, 'Give us the blade, boy. It's over.' His beard was like a stiff brush and his breath reeked of eels. I had no more time to think this through—I simply reacted. I lowered the sword as if I were about to hand it to him. He released my shoulder, and when he did, I took a swing at him."

"Were you really trying to cut him or—"

He replied, "I was trying to get space. Which I got. He stepped back and I darted past. Before anyone could do anything I moved in and thrust the sword at the murderer's belly, just as he had done with my father.

"He saw me coming and tried to retreat but bumped into the solider behind him. Trapped, he raised his bound arms and blocked the blow—I stabbed him in the forearm. He jerked his arms away and I stabbed again, this time hitting him in the chest, and while I was but a lad, I felt it slide in several inches."

I asked, "You'd never attacked anyone before, had you? What . . . how did it feel?"

He gave me a long look lost in shadow. "I expect you know the answer to that now, Arki. Just as it had during Sanctuary when my father was killed, time seemed to freeze. I was two feet from this man, could see his eyes, his mouth, just as he had seen my father's. There was shock, and pain there—his mouth was open, his shoulders were rolled forward. But when time began to move again, the similarity ended. He did not collapse immediately as my father had. The murderer bent forward and grabbed at the sword with his bound hands, wrapping both of them around the blade."

Even though this was an incident that happened decades ago, and Braylar obviously survived, I still felt my pulse quicken. "What did you do?"

"Instinctively I tried to pull it away, out of his body, away from his hands, but I'd caught the blade on a rib. My father's sword was stuck fast, and I couldn't wrench it free. I grabbed the hilt with my right hand and pulled again, but it was stuck fast. Seeing the soldiers stepping forward to stop me, I did the only other thing I could think of."

"You ran."

"I pushed. Hard," he said. "With both hands and all my weight. And the murderer screamed. I pulled again, digging my heels in—the blade slid towards me, stuck again on the same rib, and then, with one more heave, came free, sliding out of his chest and slicing his other hand almost to the bone.

"The bastard screamed again, shrill this time, and doubled over, blood from his chest and hand pouring down the front of his trousers. I stepped back, looked at him, looked at the sword in my hand, and for that moment, it was as if we were alone, alone in the world, just the bleeding murderer and me. I didn't hear anything. There was movement all around, on the periphery, but none of it registered, or mattered, not at that instant. I had stabbed a man, sawed at his insides, slashed his hand almost in two, and I wanted nothing more that moment than to stand there and watch him, to see what feelings would develop in my chest. Pleasure? Hatred? Disgust? Bloodlust? But I shook it off, knowing every instant was precious, and turned to run."

"You said something about Soffjian shooting a bow, for distraction, I assumed. I'm guessing she must have, or you would have been struck down or captured already."

"How remarkably perceptive. You must be a scholar of some kind," Braylar said. "I turned to flee and almost ran right into a spear. A soldier was ready to skewer me, and had I been an instant slower I would not be relating this to you now. But I turned in time, and by blind reflex alone managed to sidestep the thrust. He drew the spear back to thrust again, but then he spun, his torso whipping around before his legs could respond. He turned to face whoever struck him and I saw an arrow sticking in his shoulder, just outside his scale cuirass, a small circle of red growing around the shaft.

"And it was then that I heard the noises around me—the sound of feet and hooves on the ground, men shouting orders, the hum of another arrow. It was then, too, that I noticed that there were already two arrows in the ground, one on either side of the murderer, who was now starting to stagger in small circles. Another arrow flew over my head, missing by only a foot or two, and foolishly, instinctively, I tuned to see where this last one was heading. There was a soldier behind me, clutching his thigh, the arrow sticking out between his fingers, its white feathers bright in the sun."

"So that was your plan, you would attack him while she shot enough arrows for you to escape in the confusion?"

He paused, and I could only imagine the twitching going on there, but then heard humor in his voice. "She took longer than I expected. But yes, she was finally doing her part to help me escape. And so I ran as hard as I could, knowing I was running for my life, knowing I might have waited too long, with all that sword sawing. I flew past a soldier who was on one knee, his shield in front of him facing the woods where the arrows were coming from. He saw me, and shouted, as if anything he could say would make me stop. Another soldier turned away from the woods, took a few steps to cut me off, a broadsword drawn, shield slung on his back. I started to change direction, but it turned out not to be necessary—an arrow skidded off the top of his helm, shearing the feather plume as it went, and the soldier dove to the ground, rolling out of my way.

"There were a few soldiers on either side, but no one in front of me. All I had to do was pump my legs and make it to the trees before I got cut down. I pushed harder, trying desperately not to slice something off with my father's blade, and I was suddenly sure I was going to make it—I was too fast, they would never catch me, not so long as Soff kept shooting. I'd done it, I'd stabbed the murderer, watched his blood gush, and now I was going to sprint to freedom. I started to laugh. The laugh of a man who has faced demons or death and won.

"My joy was short-lived indeed, however," he said. "One moment I was running full speed, the next, I was flying, my feet taken out from beneath me, the ground rising up to smash me, plugging my mouth and eyes with dirt. And then I felt it, an awful pain across my left shin, and I thought for a moment that my leg had been severed, that my foot must be somewhere behind me. I planted a hand on the ground, tried to rise up, discovered that both my legs were whole, even if the left was throbbing with fire, and so I started to run again, but my leg wouldn't cooperate, buckling underneath me. As I fell again, I saw who had struck the blow—there was a soldier on my left, behind me, kneeling behind his large shield, and there was a spear in the grass alongside him—he had swung out and struck me with the haft as I ran past.

"The Syldoon was glancing into the woods, eyes searching for the archer or archers out there—the arrows had been coming so quickly even I had begun to wonder if Soff had recruited others. He was measuring, weighing the risks against the rewards, when I heard the 'thunk' of another arrow, followed by a scream—it had hit a wooden shield and pierced the arm that held it. I forced myself up again, told myself that I would make it, on one leg or two, it wouldn't matter. I had to make it to the woods. We had horses there. I grabbed my father's rib-loving sword and started to rise again. The pain was sharp, up and down my shin, and I felt blood dripping into my shoe. Still, it wasn't broken—I was hobbled, but still moving, and with each step the woods got closer.

"Suddenly I was bowled over, again landing face-first in the dirt, the air blowing out of my lungs in a rush. A body was on me, heavy, and a splinted vambrace was on the back of my neck. I struggled to move, but I was gasping for air, and it was useless. The soldier lifted his forearm long enough to crack me in the ear with his elbow, and then he dropped it on my neck again with more weight behind it. The sun and sky were blocked out and a shadow fell—he must have swung his shield over the both of us, although I couldn't really see, my eyes filled with dirt, tears, and more dirt. His sweat dripped on me, and then I felt his breath, just next to my ear. He said something in Syldoonian that I of course didn't understand."

"Did Soffjian give herself up?"

"I had no idea just then. I was somewhat occupied. The solider on me was much larger, much stronger, and my arms were pinned underneath me. I hoped silently but very fervently that I hadn't stabbed myself when I landed. I turned my head, if only a little, spit grass and dirt and a little blood out from a bitten tongue, and still unable to breathe, began to wriggle with panic. He mistook this for struggling to escape and smashed me in the ear again with his elbow, again demanding something which I interpreted to mean 'stop struggling' or 'plague yourself.'

"I reined the panic in enough to stop fighting, and though I'm sure he was doing me no favors, he shifted his weight a little—no doubt to swing his legs further behind the shield and keep them arrow-free. But it was enough of a shift that I managed to gulp in some air. All I could see of the world was a small strip of grass beneath the rim of the shield. I managed to pull in a few more breaths, hoping that I lived long enough to know that my father's murderer was dead.

"And so I stared at that slit of light, taking what breath I could. The soldier leaned over me and whispered a question, which marked him as an idiot that he hadn't realized that we spoke no words in common. Not understanding, I told him as much, but he seemed as equally frustrated with our communication problem so I got another elbow to the ear. He repeated his question, whatever it was, as if I were being intentionally dense or enjoyed being beaten."

I asked, "Did you try to struggle?" before realizing how foolish it was.

Irritated, he replied, "If there had been any way for me to lash out at him I would have, but I was helpless. 'I hope she shoots you in the face' was all I could muster. He might not have understood the words, but the tone was clear, and it earned me another elbow to the ear, the hardest so far. Everything went black. When my vision came back, I was unsure how much time had passed, but he was still on me, still breathing the same, and nothing else had changed, so I guessed little. My head was throbbing, my ankle was on fire, and I'm sure my ear was the size of a horseshoe.

"I tried to look underneath the rim of the shield, hoping to see something, anything. It wasn't long before I was rewarded. I heard boots, several of them, and in a few moments I saw four of them in front of my strip. And then a voice, the captain's. He issued an order in Syldoonian. Though it belonged to a small man, this was a voice that was accustomed to being obeyed, and it was, immediately. The arm lifted off my neck and I was pulled to my feet. Dizziness buffeted me—whether from lack of good air or being beaten in the head, I don't know—and I almost fell, but the soldier who had so generously pummeled me grabbed my shoulders and kept me upright. There were three more soldiers positioned between us and the woods, their shields locked together. I could see none of their faces, but their helms swiveled left and right as they searched the trees.

"And then the captain wrapped one arm around my chest and put a dagger to my throat. For a mad moment, that seemed more humorous than terrifying, and I had to stifle a laugh. The captain called out, 'It's over. Step out now.' The seconds passed, all of us peering into the woods, and nothing happened. Part of me hoped Soff had fled already, another part hoped she loosed one more arrow, nailing the captain in the face.

"But a moment later, Soffjan stepped out of the trees, bow raised above her head. The captain looked at her, and called out, 'We have been ambushed by two children? Remarkable.' And that was it. We seemed to be on the edge of victory, but we were both captured. Still, we recognized that possibility. Embraced it even. While we both hoped to escape, the true goal was to ensure the murderer lay dead."

Almost sadly, I said, "But he didn't, did he?"

Braylar waited a long time before answering. "No, Arki. He did not. The captain told the soldier to pick up my father's sword, which had been lying beneath me. The soldier held it up for inspection—the tip was covered in blood and dirt. The captain clicked his tongue in the roof of his mouth. 'A fine weapon,' he said. 'Truly. Very fine. Where did you steal it?'

"I didn't answer and felt the dagger on my skin again. 'I don't toy with you, boy. One of my men lies bleeding—maybe dying—because of it. I would know where you got it.'

"By now Soff was ten feet away, and she heard the question and provided an answer. 'Don't hurt him. The man your murdering dog shot—that was our father. The sword is his. Will your man die?'

"The captain replied, 'A family affair, is it? How interesting. He very well could die. You would do well to pray to your gods to prevent it, because if they don't, there will be no saving you. No, no saving at all.'

"Soffjan stopped a few steps away. Hands still on her head, she said, 'I hope he dies. But I hope he dies slow. He deserves worse than my father.'

"To the soldier holding my father's sword, the captain said, 'A remarkable people, but not altogether intelligent.' To Soffjan he said. 'Perhaps you did not hear me girl. If he dies, you die.'

"Soffjan dropped her hands to her side. 'My father is dead. And my uncle—the one you shot as he tried to avenge my father—he might die too. If he does, he will have taken five days. I hope your man takes a tenday.'"

"That does sound like her," I said.

"Indeed. It does. But her desires were immaterial, as were mine. The man did not die by my hand, not that day, not ever. He was killed in a raid along the Anjurian border years later. I was captured, and though not selected in the traditional Choosing, became a Jackal slave. And as you surely guessed, being scholarly, a Memoridon in the Jackal camp identified Soff's latent abilities and claimed her."

"And your priests, your people, what did they do?" I asked. "They must have cried out against not only the lack of justice but your abduction."

"They did. But they did not attack that day. It was only the following year, when the Syldoon returned to the islands. My uncle, tough old root that he was, somehow recovered from the wounds he endured. He led the Orlu seeking vengeance, and wiped out the entire Syldoon Choosing company."

I thought about the tale, and how painful it must have been to relive it—the murder the other day, the botched revenge and abduction today, especially since Bloodsounder enabled him to recall it with cruel clarity—but that alone didn't explain all the shared bitterness that had unspooled between the siblings in the years to follow.

Soffjian had mentioned the conflict years later, and Braylar's lapse or failure there. I turned to ask the captain about that, but he was gone, his departing footsteps drowned out in the rush of the bizarre lake below.

It took ages, but it felt like my mind had finally quieted enough to let me slip back into sleep when commotion woke me up again. I blinked and rubbed my eyes, and it was early morning, judging from the sun on the floor outside the chamber. The Syldoon were mostly up already, and then I realized the cause of the upset. Dozens of human slaves had arrived bearing food, as the Deserter guards towered silently, watched them hand the bowls and trays out.

No matter how awful a situation you found yourself in, an empty stomach only made it worse. A few of the Syldoon had attempted to speak with the slaves as they accepted the food, but the language barrier shut that down quickly enough, and when a soldier persisted, the sudden presence of a looming Deserter stopped any conversation attempts immediately.

I stood, stretched, and was about to walk over to the nearest slave when I saw Bulto a little further away and changed my path.

He recognized me when I stood in front of him, and after glancing around to be sure no Deserters were paying attention, whispered in the odd variation of Old Anjurian that I mostly understood. "You still live? That is good. You eat?"

He handed me the bowl, which appeared to contain some kind of thick soup, a spicy broth filled with diced roots and crescent-shaped beans, and I took a robust chunk of dark bread as well.

I made sure the Deserters weren't paying any attention, and said as quietly as I could, mouth barely moving, "The trap, by the door. Is there a way to avoid setting it off?"

He seemed uncertain about my use of "trap," so I tried again. "The alarm. Noise, sound, when you approach the doorway. Can we stop it?"

Bulto turned pale, handed out a bowl to another Syldoon who eyed me suspiciously, and then said, "Don't ask. Leave the door alone."

I said, "I have to. We must escape."

Bulto shook his head and pursed his lips as he knelt down to the large tray he'd carried in to retrieve more bowls and bread to hand out. After another Syldoon moved off, he said, "There is no escape. You cannot."

I wasn't sure if he meant that we shouldn't try or that it was pointless to. Looking around I caught Vendurro's eye on the other side of the room and gave him a pleading look and then inclined my head to the slave. It took him a moment to understand what I meant, but then he gave a small nod and walked a little closer, bowl and bread in hand.

Turning back to him I said, "We cannot stay here, Bulto. We have to return home. There must be a way."

Bulto handed out another bowl and some bread, and there was only one more bowl left. He shook his head again, more urgently this time. "There is no return. No escape. You—"

I heard a crash and looked around. Vendurro had "accidentally" dropped his bowl, no doubt to attract the attention of the closest Deserter who must have noticed me lingering near Bulto.

Vendurro was kneeling down to pick up the wooden bowl, but two slaves rushed over, obsequious but insistent as they began to clean up the soup with rags and another approached to offer the lieutenant a new bowl.

The Deserter grabbed the slave by the shoulder and made him cry out, then shoved him back, soup sloshing over the edge of the bowl.

I saw a terrified expression on Bulto's face, and then felt the presence behind me. I was turning around, knowing a Deserter was there, trying to think of something to say. The Deserter gave me a lazy slap to the side of the head that sent me spinning once before I was flat on the floor, my skull feeling like it was split in two and spilling my brains all over the stones.

The giant took two steps and stopped right in front of me. I thought that was it, that he intended to step on my chest and crush every rib I had, but he took another step and grabbed Bulto by the back of the neck and shook him. The Deserter was hardly ferocious about it, but still nearly broke the poor boy's neck before shoving him onto his hands and knees, barking something I couldn't understand, and then all the slaves began to withdraw in haste.

I reached up, felt the wetness on the back of my head, but it was just a smear of blood, and not as bad as I feared.

Vendurro was there then, offering me a hand. "You alright, Arki?"

I reached up and grabbed it with the hand that wasn't sticky with blood. "Just a little shaken up."

Mulldoos was standing nearby, and between the hunk of bread in his mouth and the slurring, I could barely understand him as he said, "What were you plaguing asking that little rat about anyway, you dumb bastard?"

I replied, "I was asking about the trap. By the doorway."

"Course you were." He helped hoist me to my feet with his free arm. "Figured it was good to start the day getting slapped around like a lippy whore, did you?"

Braylar walked up, eyes red-rimmed and bloodshot, and it was clear he hadn't gotten any more rest. "You are the only one in the company with the ability to communicate with our hosts, so I do hope you show a bit more discretion next time, Arki. Did you at least learn anything useful?"

My head was throbbing, and my stomach was still grumbling, and I said, "The slave was frightened."

"Sure he was," Mulldoos said. "Didn't want to get flung around like a wet rag. Like he did. On account of you. Guessing he won't be in a huge hurry to have any more chats, eh? So what did he say?"

I looked at the captain and lieutenants and was about to respond when Azmorgon, Benk, and Rudgi joined us.

Rudgi said, "Heard we missed some excitement."

Mulldoos replied, "Yeah, scribbler here decided to pester one of the slaves to see if he had an escape plan hidden in the folds of his funny-looking tunic and got slapped silly by a Deserter. You know, like you'd expect."

Azmorgon laughed as Braylar asked again, "Did he reveal anything useful, Arki?"

I shook my head and immediately wished I hadn't as that made the throbbing more pronounced. "He said there was no escape. And he was scared."

"For good plaguing reason," Mulldoos added.

"But I got the sense that he was just terrified to talk at all. There still could be a way to bypass the trap at the doorway."

Azmorgon said, "What was it you whoresons suggested? Running through the doorway fast? That was it, wasn't it? Running. Fast."

I ignored him and said, "The slaves aren't affected. They don't set the alarm off. Just like the veil around the city. The Deserters have a way of marking who is allowed through certain portals. We can't do anything about that.

Short of capturing a Deserter who can get us through. But maybe there's a mechanism involved, in the stones, the door itself. Maybe we can bypass that somehow."

Azmorgon glared at me, his massive beard seeming to almost bristle. "Or maybe you just shut your fool plaguing mouth and break your fast and leave the thinking to the likes of us."

Mulldoos swallowed his bread and turned to the huge man. "Arki saw an opportunity and he took it. Was it smart? No. Plaguing weren't. But we ain't getting out of here by trying nothing at all."

Azmorgon's eyes narrowed. "Used to respect you. Little bit. But you gone soft. Softer than plaguing sand, you are."

Vendurro said, "Sand ain't really all that soft." Everyone looked at him. "Just saying. You get it in your boot, or worse, in your smallclothes, ain't any kind of comfort at all. Kittens are soft. A woman's tit is soft. But sand is three kinds of scratchy. Especially up in your backside."

Azmorgon started to reply, but Captain Killcoin cut him off. "Arki, while I applaud your initiative, you truly do pick the most ill-advised moments to express it. Next time, you will not operate independently. If there is another opportunity to speak to the slaves, we will coordinate the entirety first—diversions, questions, approach. I can ill afford to have your brains splattered against the stones. Are we clear?"

He might have dressed me down further, if not for the blood about to drip in my eyes. "Yes, Captain," I replied, wiping it off with the back of my hand.

"Good." He handed me his bowl. "Break your fast, and then clean that wound. We will talk more later."

I moved off away from the others, towards the windows facing the rest of Roxtiniak. I was curious to observe the Deserters some more, to try to ascertain anything that might prove useful. I heard the rain falling before I saw it, though it was really a gentle shower.

The streets and avenues were strangely empty, save for some human slaves who walked here or there. There wasn't a single Deserter. Which seemed peculiar on the face of it. But then again, knowing nothing about our massive captors, it really shouldn't have surprised me. Perhaps it was a religious holiday, or some arcane rule that governed when they could move about freely.

Though it still seemed strange that the humans were allowed to roam, navigating around puddles, carrying their parcels, leading livestock, or bearing messages. There were far fewer of them about than in any human city, even a small settlement, but they weren't prohibited access of the street. Heads down, yes, and not speaking to each other if they could help it, but not guarded or watched.

I heard footsteps and turned around. Vendurro walked up to the window, peered out into the rain. "Sorry I didn't see what you were up to earlier. Might have been able to save you that goose egg if I'd acted a touch quicker."

"No," I replied. "The captain and others were right—it was foolish to try to get information alone. If I'd been smarter, I would have waited, but I recognized that boy, had spoken to him earlier, and didn't know when I might get the chance again."

"Ayyup," he said. "Foolish. But gutsy too. Often one in the same, ain't they?"

"I suppose so."

Vendurro looked at the rain falling and said, "Got to admit, Arki, never cared much one way or the other for your kind. You know, the bookish sort, I mean." He looked at me and added a smile. "That is, we had plenty of learning to do in our tenyear before the hanging, all manner of things. But I only did enough to get through. Never took to it like Cap or Hew. And sure as hells wasn't my plaguing vocation like yours. Those other company archivists we had, they were bookish, to be certain, but never liked or trusted a one of them. And they sure as hells had no guts to speak of. Unless you count the one risking his neck to betray Cap as gutsy. Which I suppose it is. But not the good kind."

I wasn't sure what he was circling towards. "Thank you. I think."

Ven smiled, then slapped me on the back.

I winced, as my head was still connected, and he said, "Sorry about that. What I'm driving at is, Cap is spot on—you proved yourself five times over so far, and got more to contribute besides, so you're an asset, to be sure. Don't want to lose you on account of foolish gutsiness. But more than that, just don't want to lose you period. Got enough of that going on."

I considered that for a moment. "But I heard Mulldoos say that everyone outside the Jackal Tower is either a tool or an enemy."

Vendurro said, "Even he's warmed up to you some. Defended you against Ogre more than once, and started training you a bit. Maybe Azmorgon's right. Maybe we are going soft. Like a kitten." He laughed. "Not plaguing sand. But more like, seems you found a way to be a part of the Jackals, even without being amongst us the whole time or going through what we all gone through. You proved your mettle, is what I'm getting at."

I nodded, and while even that sent my skull to aching some more, it felt good.

He was quiet for a moment before looking over his shoulder. When Vendurro didn't see anyone immediately around, he said, "Got to say, and it hurts some to put it to words, but really miss hearing Hew and Mull squabble like a couple of old women. Truly do. When we get back to our proper side of the Godveil—" he looked at me and added, "—and we will. Going to really enjoy killing me some plaguing imperial Leopards. Those whoresons are going to pay three to one for every Jackal they struck down."

I resisted the urge to say anything, afraid my pessimism would sour the moment. First we had to escape this ring palace, and if Bulto were to be believed, that simply wasn't going to happen.

We stood there in silence for a while, watching the steady but soft rain coming down, and all I could think of was the comrades I'd seen fall now, and how I had no right to grieve them like Vendurro or any of the other Jackals. I made a silent pledge then that if we ever did make it back somehow, I would find Skeelana, and I would make her pay. I might not be a proficient killer like the other Jackals, wasn't truly one of them, despite what Vendurro said, but I would make her pay for her betrayal and my failure and foolishness. I could do that much.

Vendurro's stomach rumbled. "Think they got chickens on this side?"

"Chickens?" I asked, perplexed.

"On this side of the Veil? Ain't seen none, but you kind of have to figure they didn't kill off all the chickens. Though who knows. Ain't got horses. Maybe they done away with chickens too."

I looked at him. "Why do you ask?"

"Could really go for a boiled egg right about now. Where there's chickens, there's eggs."

I laughed, and said, "When the captain gives me leave to talk to Bulto again, that will be my first question. Where, oh where, are the chickens?"

He chuckled and replied, "Yeah. Do that. Important question, that."

There were more footsteps, coming fast this time. We both turned around and saw Rudgi running up to us, face flushed. "We got more visitors. Quit counting raindrops and come on!"

Vendurro and I looked at each other and then ran to follow her.

We entered the main chamber by the door and saw all of the Syldoon gathered, the captain and his officers at the front. Vendurro and I made our way through and joined them.

When we were near the retinue, Vendurro asked, "What's— " but he stopped when he saw the two Deserter guards in full regalia just outside the doorway.

I peered out and saw armored Deserters lining the walls the entire way down the hallway, still as statues.

Vendurro whistled and then said, "How long have they been like that?"

Mulldoos replied, "Few minutes now. Marched up, took their positions, and been standing there ever since."

"Huh," Vendurro said, capturing all of our collective confusion and amazement in that single syllable.

Braylar ran his hands through his hair and looked pained, as he seemed to be fighting off pain or nausea. "I suspect we might finally meet someone of import. Arki, be ready to translate," he called out over his shoulder, not taking his eyes off the doorway. "I will be the only other person speaking in this room. Is that understood?"

There was a chorus of "Aye, Cap" from behind us.

I watched, waiting with the rest, wondering what could possibly happen next, sweating as time dragged on with no movement from the Deserters. Was this a prelude to execution? Torture? Our legs being lopped off? Something worse?

And then I saw four figures emerging from the stairs we had taken to get here—a slim human trying to keep pace with three giants, one in front, the other two trailing just behind.

The Deserters lining the hall remained still as the figures approached our room. The human was female, garbed in a close-fitting charcoal-colored robe, marking her as different from the other humans we'd seen in Roxtiniak. The color and cut was simple and severe, and her expression did nothing to diminish the effect—a small, clenched mouth, lines on her face (though I suspected not due to smiling), narrowed dark eyes, and pewter hair pulled back tightly away from her face, compacted into some chambered bun. But while she was afforded nicer accoutrements and carried herself differently, she still had the carving or branding on her cheek that seemed to mark her as just a more respected slave.

The three Deserters were female as well, shorter and slimmer than the male counterparts, though still much larger than even Azmorgon, and certainly towering over the human female. The two Deserters in the rear were dressed in robes and strips of cloth, with a single spine in a harness on their back, and I recognized one who had accompanied us to the palace and issued orders.

But it was the lead Deserter who distinctly stood out from the entire group. She carried the longest spine I'd seen, tapping it on the ground every few steps like a staff or longspear. But more than the singular spine, it was the costume and bearing that marked her as unlike any other Deserter we'd encountered so far.

She had on a robe, somewhat similar to the females behind her, but the cut and layering was different. For one, it left her left breast bare. I'd seen illustrations of women like this at university, from distant and long-forgotten tribes, and being a young boy, couldn't help but stare with hot eyes. But here, the effect was more disturbing then arousing.

While the materials were undyed like all the other Deserter garb, hers had far more intricate patterns and subtle textures woven into it or embroidered on the surface, it was difficult to tell.

Over her shoulder and trailing a yard in her wake, she wore a cloak that seemed composed entirely of dead and dried flowers—thistles and caspia, lavender and flax, and probably a hundred other flowers I'd never seen before. Given that gardens appeared to be rare as far as I could tell, the fact that she had a long cloak covered in dead flowers certainly stood out, as did the rustling, sashaying noise it made as she walked, leaving bits and pieces in her wake, like a snake constantly shedding its skin.

She had a beaded headdress on that must have required quite a bit of tailoring to fit it precisely around the horns that projected from her head. It covered the front of her scalp down to her narrow hatchet-like nose, which seemed to only reinforce the fact that these giants navigated just fine without eyes.

Mulldoos whispered, "Now who the plaguing hells is this . . . rootercunt supposed to be?"

Braylar threw him a black look, and the pale boar shut his mouth again, but it was a legitimate question.

As the Deserters and human approached the doorway, the Deserter warriors finally moved, entering in front of her, and taking position on either side. Two or three could have killed every man and woman in the room, especially with the Syldoon trapped and unarmed, so it was more for effect to demonstrate respect than anything.

The cloaked Deserter with the headdress entered next, followed by the other two giants and the human female, and she made directly for the captain and our small group at the front of the Syldoon.

Braylar stood straight, rigid, presenting as formal and confident a posture as he could.

The human female surveyed our company, nodded once, and said, in near-perfect Syldoonian, "You are in the presence of Vrulinka-Antovia-Lilka, the resident Matriarch of Roxtiniak, Guardian of the Veil, the Great Wielder. You may call her Matriarch Vrulinka, if you wish. Less taxing on your tongue, I should imagine." She looked at Braylar. "And you must be Captain Braylar Killcoin then."

I'm sure every Syldoon in the room gaped, all save Braylar, who maintained his composure. "You speak Syldoonian . . . with impressive fluency. And what do we call you, then?"

The woman replied, "You are over kind, I think. I speak passably, at best, not having much opportunity. Certainly not so well as one born to it. Clumsy? Is that the word? It is a challenge for our tongues, you see." She turned to me and said, in nearly flawless Anjurian, "More so than some languages, though. Anjurian is less . . . cumbersome? Is that how you say it?" I nodded as she said, "You must be Arkamondos."

I didn't trust myself to speak, so only gave another small nod.

She continued in Syldoonian, "As to who I am, it is hardly important. I am but a humble servant to the mighty Matriarch. You may call me Nustenzia. As to tongues, Matriarch Vrulinka insists that a few of us study the most prominent languages of your land. We do get such infrequent visitors in this age, but you just never know who might decide to visit. And the Matriarch places a premium on good communication." She looked at the rest of Braylar's retinue. "And let me see . . ."

Nustenzia turned her head in Mulldoos's direction. "And these are surely your lieutenants, Mulldoos, the newly appointed Vendurro, and the hulking Azmorgon there." She gave a frosty smile. "Relatively speaking, of course. On the human scale."

She inclined her head towards Rudgi. "I'm afraid I don't know your name. I offer my apologies," she added, not sounding particularly apologetic.

Vendurro blurted, "How do you plaguing know our names at all?"

Nustenzia smiled, as a condescending mother might fielding an obvious question from a not-so-bright child. Then she pointed.

We looked and saw a shaken Soffjian standing in a doorway behind us, leaning against the frame, as the herald or priestess or whatever Nustenzia was said, "The Matriarch was very intrigued to have a Memoridon amongst us, you see. And one who could withstand a direct assault, no less. They were eager to interview that one. And to test her. And such tests can be . . . well, less than forgiving. Especially to one not especially . . . what is the word? . . . compliant? Acquiescent?"

Soffjian spoke as if drunk, words furry and lacking her normal precision. "Let them never accuse me of acquiescing."

Nustenzia smiled again, chilly and edged. "But when the Matriarch wants to know something, the Matriarch will know something."

She looked at Braylar again. "It was very educational. So we are glad of your visit, but—"

Mulldoos said, "We didn't come on a social jaunt. Those giant fucks attacked us and killed half our company."

Nustenzia gave the lieutenant a level disquieting look. "Plain speaking, is it? Very well, broken man. You were on this side of the Veil, were you not? You do know my masters constructed it for a reason, I presume. So venturing on this side, uninvited, unannounced, well . . . that makes you trespassers. Interlopers. A pestilence, to speak plainly.

"And as such, you are lucky in fact that my masters didn't simply slaughter the lot of you. So given that you are guests in the Matriarch's house, alive at her whim, I do recommend you show a bit more gratitude and respect. Your presence here is not welcome, and has caused quite a stir. My masters, you see, they are far less forgiving of your kind suddenly arriving like this. The Matriarch could simply let them dispose of you or . . . how do you say it? Husk you? Yes. Her advisors urged both and the

Veil must be carefully maintained. So . . . are you feeling more grateful now, broken man?"

Mulldoos started to step towards her, but Braylar put his forearm across the lieutenant's chest and said, "We didn't know your masters even existed, so you can perhaps forgive us for inadvertently stumbling across their land, regardless of the regard in which they typically hold us. And guests are not usually accustomed to being sequestered. Or," he glanced at Soffjian, "viciously interrogated. Which is to say nothing of the soldiers you killed. Where are their bodies? Did Matriarch Vrulinka command they be left behind to fertilize the fields with their blood? You see, mayhap, why gratitude might be in cheap supply just now."

Nustenzia nodded very slowly, took two steps back towards the Matriarch, and bowed her head. She said something in the Deserter tongue, and the Matriarch replied, somehow both slithering and broken up by unusual clickish noises.

"What did you plaguing say?" Azmorgon asked, no less brusquely than Mulldoos.

Nustenzia regarded him. "I said, you ill-mannered troll, that the lot of you were going to prove no more compliant than your stubborn Memoridon there. It is my opinion that collegial communication will prove . . . problematic, at least until my master has taken you firmly in hand. Which is what I recommended."

Azmorgon said, "You tell your plaguing bitch mistress that she can cup my huge jewels in her hand—"

"Azmorgon!" Braylar shouted. "Shut your mouth immediately!"

The large man looked at the captain. "Or what?"

Mulldoos and Hewspear had argued with the captain before, but never in front of the men, and never outright challenged him like that, but before anyone could respond, Matriarch Vrulinka snapped the spine down on the stones, stopping the conversation cold.

She surveyed the Syldoon, smiled, showing gently pointed teeth, and started speaking Syldoonian. "I detest your tongue, truly. Awful. Heinous. Painful to hear, worse to speak. But I need no interpreter, human. Now, we have much to discuss. There are things I would know about you. Captain, you and your retinue will follow. That is a command you understand, is it not?"

The Matriarch started for the door without waiting for a reply, saying something to the two Deserters directly behind her.

Braylar looked at us. "Lieutenants and chronicler only." He turned to Soffjian. "If we fail to return—"

"You always return," she said, still somewhat shaken. "It is one of your more annoying qualities. But yes, if you somehow fail to, we will do our best to kill as many of the giants before they take out the rest of us."

Braylar nodded. "I expected no less." Then he turned to follow the Deserters and Nustenzia.

Vendurro was closest, and started after the captain, and Mulldoos and Azmorgon filed in behind, with me taking up the rear. Mulldoos turned to his much larger companion. "I'm only going to tell you this once, you hulking horsecunt—"

"Save your breath. Can't understand what you're saying half the time anyway."

Mulldoos replied, "You disrespect Cap in front of the men again, you and me are going to have a serious falling out."

Azmorgon laughed. "Didn't realize we were all that cozy."

Mulldoos replied, "Ayyup. But we're about to get a lot less friendly in a hurry if you pull a shit stunt like that again."

"You couldn't beat me in a fair fight even with two good arms, you plaguing mushmouth runt."

"Nobody said shit about a fair fight." Even hobbled, slurring, with the droopy eyelid, and facing a much bigger man, Mulldoos still managed to hold his own; when Azmorgon couldn't think of a reply fast enough, he moved ahead to catch up the captain.

We approached the doorway, and paused right before the spot where Benk had been rendered senseless.

Nustenzia was waiting in the doorway. "No need to be skittish. The Matriarch could have killed you at any point. She still might. But be assured, she would not let a door do it. You shall pass. Come."

Despite hearing that, I still held my breath as we walked through the portal, but whatever wards were there permitted us to pass through. Unlike at the Godveil or the barrier around the city, I felt nothing but an involuntary shudder.

The doorway didn't strike us down with unseen magics, but I'm not ashamed to say the pending interrogation terrified me. I had no illusions about being half as powerful as Soffjian—if we were subjected to anything remotely close to what she endured, I knew I would be husked or worse.

The armed Deserters fell in behind us as we marched along. The Matriarch and her silent robed companions were a dozen paces ahead, and Nustenzia fell in alongside the captain.

I overheard Vendurro ask her, "So, the Deserters, they ain't gods at all. Are they?"

Nustenzia replied, "Gods? That all depends on how you define the term. Are they far more powerful than we could dream of being, wielding magicks beyond our comprehension, creating something where there was once nothing? Yes. Does that make them gods? That is for you to decide. But you would do well not to call them Deserters. It is something they are . . . sensitive about."

Mulldoos said, "They ain't gods. And I can think of plenty of riper words for them than Deserter."

Nustenzia shrugged her bony shoulders. "Do not call them gods then. But, as I said, I would suggest not calling them the latter either."

"So," Vendurro asked slowly, the word stretching out. "Are there any gods on this side of the Veil at all, that the Des— . . . that your giant masters up there serve?"

"None that I have seen, no," Nustenzia said.

"So what do you worship then? Them?" Vendurro pointed at the Deserters ahead.

Nustenzia said, "Why would we worship beings who are not gods?"

Crunching some dried flowers underfoot, I said, "But they might be. Gods, that is. That it depended on how you defined the term."

She replied, "I said it depends on how *you* define the term. I do not presume to instruct you on religion."

Mulldoos slapped his thigh. "See! Told you they weren't plaguing gods! Even Runeface there can plaguing see that."

Vendurro turned to the captain as we rounded a corner. "Huh. Well, ain't that a kick in the crotch. This whole time, a plaguing thousand years and then some, and folks been pining for something that never existed at all. Can't say if I'm sad or glad."

Mulldoos gave a wet-sounding laugh. "We ever make it back, you can evangelize to every dumb plaguing bastard we come across, spread the word, see how they like hearing they been frauded since the beginning of time. Love to see that. Right before they stick a spit up your ass and roast you over a fire."

Nustenzia said flatly, "I would not worry overmuch about leaving."

The Matriarch led us down another long hall until we came to a stairwell with a massive Deserter on either side. As always, there were no doors.

As we approached, Vendurro said in a rough whisper, "You're human. Why do you plaguing serve the Deserters?"

"Tsk. That word. Unhealthy word for you. Do not use it. And as to why—they have longer legs, and there is nowhere to run. Now be silent."

The Matriarch allowed us to catch up, then she started down the spiral stairs, and Nustenzia indicated we should follow. Even though going down was easier than up, my legs were still wobbly when we finally reached the bottom. There were some scattered sconces on the walls, obviously to aid any human slaves that had to use the stairs, but fewer than in any normal human castle or tower, and I proceeded carefully to avoid slipping and twisting or breaking my ankles in the deep shadows.

But I was about to discover I had no idea what dark was.

There was a single doorway at the landing. And unlike all the others in the citadel, this one had a thick wooden door, currently open. I heard something beyond that took me a moment to place. Gently lapping water.

The Matriarch and the two attending Deserters kept walking into the chamber beyond, along with four guards. Nustenzia moved closer to the captain, lowering her voice as she said, "Your eyes will be useless beyond. Stay close to each other. And remember, whatever befalls you, she did not bring you here to kill you. You should survive this. But do not fight it. It will go easier."

Braylar said, "Are we supposed to believe you're suddenly looking out for our overall health and happiness?"

She gave him a chilly stare, her face mostly obscured in shadow with the torch on the wall several steps above us. "We are all still humans, are we not?"

A Deserter near us hit Azmorgon in the back with the flat of the haft of his spiked weapon. The brute nearly spun around to confront the giant, but Vendurro and Mulldoos both restrained him. Braylar said, "Well, it is rude to keep a host waiting. Let's follow without any incidents like getting impaled or bludgeoned to death, yes?"

We walked through the doorway and into another stone hallway. I looked back, and whatever weak flickering light was showing along the bottom was quickly snuffed out as well, and the last thing I could make out at all was that the hall took a sharp left. Feeling my way along the wall, I walked blindly until the hall disappeared. We were in some underground vault or chamber, but beyond that, the blackness was now absolute, and I couldn't even see my hand in front of my face. I had no idea about dimensions or what could possibly be waiting ahead. The sound of moving or splashing water was louder.

Vendurro said, quietly, "Plaguing dark, ain't it?"

Mulldoos answered, just as quietly, "Real plaguing astute."

The Syldoon in front of me took a few hesitant steps, and I forced myself to follow, though walking into the inky unknown was as terrifying as anything I'd ever done.

Matriarch Vrulinka called out from somewhere thirty or forty paces ahead, her voice alternating between rasping and sibilant. "Step forward. The problem with Foci is that they do sometimes overstep, but Nustenzia was absolutely correct about one thing. I did not bring you here to murder you. Intentionally at least. Step forward, step forward."

I heard some more footsteps in front of me, small ones from the sounds of it. I moved forward slowly with my arms straight out in front of me, shuffling along until my hand hit something and I nearly yelped.

Azmorgon said, "Quit playing grab ass, you tiny fuck."

The voices echoed wildly here, but that still did nothing to tell me about how large a space it was really. I waited until I heard Azmorgon move. Part of me wanted to stay as close to the Syldoon as possible, but my fear of the unknown in the chamber was balanced out by my fear of Azmorgon's temper.

After a moment, I scuffled forward again, listening, straining to hear the captain and his men in front of me. There was more soft splashing ahead, rhythmic, like small waves. Was it an underground lake? A pool connected to the bizarre lake in the center of the citadel compound? Something else?

My mind started racing, one fear colliding into another—what else might be in the room besides our Deserter hosts; how deep was the water ahead and what might be lying beneath the surface; what did the Matriarch intend to do to us; if this was what Soffjian experienced; if I would live to walk back out of this room.

Vrulinka said, "There. Stop."

There were no more footsteps in front of me, and it sounded like I had fallen a little further behind, so I took a few more steps until I closed in on the sound of someone breathing heavily and then stopped as well.

No one else was moving—there was only the breathing, and the still distant sound of water striking some unseen shore.

The Matriarch called out, "You have entered my land, uninvited, and I would know why."

After a pause, Captain Killcoin said, "We were fleeing enemies on the other side of the Veil. We had no intention of entering your lands, being unsure if even attempting to do so would prove mortal folly, but we had no other options at the time either. So, desperate and trapped, we crossed the Veil."

The Matriarch's disembodied voice seemed to come from everywhere at once. "And yet you did not cross back at the first opportunity."

Braylar said, "That is untrue. We intended to continue north until we were confident we wouldn't encounter our enemies on the other side again. We were forced to navigate around a river. And that is when we encountered the grove. And your . . . kin. They attacked us on sight, and we defended ourselves."

There was a laugh that was jagged with clicks not made by a human mouth. "So, a large armed band of humans, all defenseless victims. Is that what you would have me believe, fragile human? Perhaps you understand my . . . skepticism."

Braylar said, "You do forget. We humans from the other side revered you as gods. Well, revered and hated, on account of that abandoning business that features so prominently in our theology. But gods nonetheless. Do you really suppose we armed ourselves, crossed the Veil, and went hunting for gods for sport?"

Vrulinka was still chuckling and clicking. "I am unfamiliar with the subtleties of your awful tongue, but that struck me as somewhat . . . thornier than expected."

"You prefer straightforward and unadorned?" Braylar asked. "Very well. We did not cross the Veil to challenge, assess, or explore, and certainly not with intent to create more enemies. But some blood was spilled on both sides—mostly ours—and then you wiped out half our company with a much smaller group and imprisoned the rest here. So perhaps you can see why I am skeptical that you consider us any threat at all, Matriarch."

No one spoke right away, and the sound of breathing and rippling water was magnified. With each passing moment, I began to fear the worst, when Vrulinka finally replied. "The Focus was correct. You are a pestilence. Or plague carriers. Much like the birds or vermin that on their own could not damage you, but have proven over time to carry a disease that nearly wipes you out. A simplification? Yes. Entirely accurate? No. But that is how the majority of my people view you. So you see, when an armed band crosses over for the first time in history, there is bound to be some alarm. My council has already called for your execution. Many times in fact. So, your very presence here is something of a conundrum. That is the word, is it not? Conundrum. So I must ascertain the state of things."

Braylar asked, "You are not speaking of the plague that ravages our land from time to time, are you? What pestilence do we carry that can harm the likes of you?"

Vrulinka's voice seemed to somehow expand, as if coming from all directions at once, and even seemed to be echoing in my skull. "Your memories, Syldoon. Your virulent, turbulent, colorful, poisonous memories . . ."

But before anyone could respond, I experienced the oddest sensation—though my eyes were still useless in the deep black of the chamber, I suddenly saw an image in my mind, or several flickering shards of images, though unlike anything I had seen before. I "saw" the outline, the texture, the contours, of a long four-fingered Deserter hand, flexing, closing, flexing, closing.

It was as if I somehow saw the hand, but bleached of all color, and with a wealth of details I could never have seen with my own eyes—the tiny individual hairs that made up the Deserter's hide, shifting, rippling, as the muscles underneath moved to form what passed for a fist, the veins in the flesh taking on new trajectories as the flesh clenched.

I heard someone, probably Vendurro, say, "Plague. Me." But it sounded very far away, as if it were an echo of something he said from hundreds of yards away, something distant and weak and immaterial, or possibly something I recalled from a distant time, though part of me knew that wasn't the case.

I had the powerful feeling of being a Deserter, looking at its hand, but that was impossible too, as they had no eyes to do so. And then the sensations shifted further, and I felt utterly unmoored—the image of the hand seemed to become less substantial, ghostly, until only the faintest flicker of an outline remained, and then it shot out away from me, quicker than a bolt, quicker than anything. Not just directly in front of me, but on all sides all at once. A hundred thousand outlines of that hand, maybe more, loosed into the depth everywhere around me.

I felt my stomach churn and twist and was immediately nauseous, as my mind had difficulty making sense of what it was experiencing—it was like when you spin around as a child so many times, you can't see anything on your final twists and it feels as if you are looking everywhere at once.

With human eyes, it was impossible, and yet the sensation remained—the outline of the phantom hand flying off in all directions, faster than anything, and suddenly returning, so forcefully I raised my hands in front of my face to protect myself.

I knew it wasn't real, or at least wasn't a physical thing that could harm me, but it felt as if countless wasps were flying at me from every direction at once. This happened again and again, and the nausea increased, and I gagged and dropped to one knee, closing my eyes as if that would somehow stop what was happening, though it had nothing to do with human sight.

And it kept repeating, over and over, the phantom hand flashing out and returning, absolutely disorienting, and my mind fought against the utterly foreign sensation, resisting it the same way you might try to wake yourself in the middle of a horrible nightmare and continue to fail.

But then something even stranger began to occur. It wasn't the phantom hand flashing out and back too fast to track, but I started to sense the dimensions of the chamber we were in, about fifty yards wide, and several hundred yards long, with two rows of columns supporting the roof, and I saw the silhouette of three Deserters some distance away—it was like catching the outline of something as a lightning storm raged, and you managed to identify bits and pieces in the briefest flashes of light, to make sense of what was out there. Only there was no light at all. Just the phantom hand, flashing out and back repeatedly, and each time, I saw, or felt at least, the shape of the room, the shifting ripples in the distant water, the figures of the other Syldoon, all kneeling or bent over, save the captain, and between us and the water, the three Deserters observing us.

I still had to fight off the urge to vomit all over myself, and while it wasn't getting easier, it had plateaued and didn't seem to be getting any worse. There was only the disorienting dizziness, the failure to completely understand what was occurring, and the ability to somehow feel the shape and texture of everything around me.

The Matriarch's voice again seemed to be ricocheting inside my skull. "You see. We are very different, your kind and mine. We might not be gods. But we are more than men. And still, we are susceptible. So susceptible."

The phantom hands and the contours of the room and its inhabitants suddenly disappeared, and I was plunged back into the black, as if a thick hood had been thrown over my head, and it was a relief, as I no longer tasted bile in my throat, but it felt crippling as well. What I experienced was a sense far more precise and voluminous than sight, and having it stripped away felt like the greatest loss imaginable.

I started to rise slowly, experiencing a blindness that was even worse than having my eyes plucked out, but glad to at least be trapped in my own limited senses again, when they were ripped asunder.

It felt as if I had been torn from my body, and was devoid of any sensations at all—the queasy stomach, the sounds of breathing and gagging and the gentle water lapping at the other end of the chamber, the stench of sweat despite the cold damp, the damp itself, everything was stripped away.

The Matriarch's voice was again everywhere and nowhere. "You. You are limited, deviant, destructive, lustful creatures. Doomed. You are doomed. We are not your gods, though if we had been, I imagine we would have destroyed you. But it was not your doomed nature that drove us away. But this. This and this and this . . ."

From nothingness, a total void of sensation at all, I was suddenly overwhelmed, oppressed, trampled under an onslaught of images, sounds, smells, feelings, so many feelings, like walking through the Veil surrounding Roxtiniak again, only tenfold more potent and devastating . . .

A woman, face pale, drenched in sweat, hair slick strands all over the pallet she lay on, reaching up, arms trembling, tired, exhausted, her body a pulsing oven of pain, and still she was driven by desperation, fear, and the sliver of hope. Eyes wide, she told herself that the silence was fine, it was normal, it didn't mean anything at all. Every birth was different. Some babes just took longer to adjust to their new world, to work the sweet air into their lungs. That's all it was. That's all it could be.

She called someone over . . . the midwife? An older woman with a face like a dried up riverbed appeared above her, lips pressed tight into a white slit. The exhausted woman shook her head, mouth opening but not emitting the slightest sound, tears and sweat streaking down her trembling cheeks. "My child? Please. Where . . . bring me my child . . . please . . . don't . . ."

The midwife slowly handed her the dead body of her blood-smeared child and the woman screamed, a wretched, searing sound as hope bled out . . .

Two men grappled in the filth and debris of an alley, rolling over each other, trying to get purchase, both fighting over a dagger. The larger man ended up on his back, losing control of the blade, smelling the sour stench of ale and garlic on his assailant's breath. He blocked several slices with his forearms and hands, tried to grab the smaller man's arm again, missed, started to flail, twisting his torso, trying to roll the other man off with his legs, his head half-submerged in a puddle as he thrashed. The man on top straddled him, trying to cut him again, cursing as he hit nothing that would end the fight, and got his elbow in on the fat man's jowls, pushed him to the side, tried to drown the bastard if he couldn't stab him to death.

The fat man was panicking, choking on mud and piss and unknown sludge, and stopped worrying about the dagger or the pain it was inflicting and punched blindly, hitting the smaller man in the throat. His assailant fell off, and the fat man rolled to his side, sputtering, panting, wondering if the piss he tasted was his own. He looked at his assailant struggling as well and thought about getting up and running for the broad avenue nearby, calling for the guard, but his fear gave him a surge of strength, and he crawled towards the smaller man, struck him in the shoulder with a fist, the chest, and finally the head again. His assailant was on his back, eyes fluttering, the side of his head bleeding into a puddle, but the larger man got on top of him, choked him with his fat, short fingers, turned the smaller man's head, and drowned him in three inches of water as the rain continued to fall . . .

The grandmother had lost her son to a skirmish along the Anjurian Syldoon border. She never cared much about borders before, and had no more cause to care now. They were just lines in the dirt greedy men drew to say this is mine and that's yours. All she knew was having her son stationed near one meant there was more chance for him to get cut down.

She tried to prepare herself for that, to steel herself for when the news arrived that her boy was dead, killed over a line in the dirt. But you just can't. No amount of telling yourself a thing can happen over and over is ever enough when the real thing comes.

They say a parent should never have to put her child in the ground. And that's the truth. But it happens all the time. The plague, an accident, some other disease. Children die, especially little ones. But once they reach adulthood, you hope it will be them burying you and not the other way around.

So when the news came, she was no less devastated for expecting it. She wasn't sure she could survive it herself. Until she saw her granddaughter a tenday later. Gangly, sassy, smart as a whipcrack, but not a woman yet, and damaged, lost, and needing her grandmother as much as a person could need anything at all. The grandmother knew then she had to be strong, that her loss, awful as it was, wasn't the only one, and maybe not the worst. That girl has been even more broken. So the grandmother took her in. They were each of them the only thing the other had left in the world. The grandmother took her in, taught her to avoid men who cared more for lines in the dirt than how to till it or to make something of it, and did her best to do right by her.

So, years later, the grandmother looked at the woman that gangly girl grew up to be—strong, feisty, brighter even then before, a journeywoman arkwright, and she wept, smiling, her heart full of a fierce pride and love that might not had happened, had it not been for the loss they shared . . .

A young woman watched, hidden behind a tree. She fidgeted, shivered against a biting wind, pulling her cheap cloak tight, and continued watching, cursing herself a fool, furious with herself for every horrible choice she'd made, for her weakness, her blindness, her stupidity. She smelled the wood burning in a nearby fireplace, and told herself she just needed to leave, to head home and pick up her meager belongings she had packed already and simply leave the bastard, knowing even as she thought it that she was lying to herself again. And then she saw them.

Him.

Tall and angled and lanky, arm draped around the girl as the pair walked down the dirt path. Despite the cold and the random snowflakes carried in every direction at once, they laughed.

The young woman hugged herself as the pair embraced, and the lanky man kissed the other woman, once, long and slow, and then again, a fast peck, and again, the way new lovers do, and then again, as they started to part and pulled back together. The young woman watched, so cold she could barely feel her limbs, as the woman finally gave one more kiss and pushed the lanky man away, laughing, eliciting a laugh from him as well as she entered her home. The man started walking down the lane, wrapping his hands in the folds of his tunic, whistling, and the young woman stayed hidden for a moment.

She had her proof. The lanky man was a faithless bastard. She knew she should rush home and make her escape from him, but instead, she found herself turning around the tree as he came, keeping it between her and the bastard who had made such an awful fool of her. And then she knelt and picked up an ice cold stone with her hands, shivering.

But shivering not from the elements, but the hot rage coursing through her, the humiliation, the emptiness, the failure and foolishness not to have seen what he was earlier. And she moved through the trees, holding the large stone with both hands, catching up to the lanky man with the disarming smile who always seemed to know just what to say to her, to flatter her, to appease her. The man whom she felt most comfortable with of everyone in the world, who had convinced her to reveal her truest self without even seeming to try. And she ran up behind this man, breath ghosting is front of her mouth, and cried out once, not a name, but simply a shrill anguished scream, and as he started to turn around, she struck him in the back of the head with the stone as hard as she could.

The lanky man fell to the earth and she nearly fell as well, tripping over one of his long legs, losing her balance, ending up in front of him. The man looked up, holding the back of his head with a bloody hand, trying to rise, limbs not cooperating, eyes unfocused, and that made the young woman even more furious, as if he was willingly looking past her, and she screamed and brought the stone down, but only struck a glancing blow to his temple. The lanky man slumped forward, raised his red hand to ward off more blows, and tried to crawl the other way, and to the young woman, this was just his rank cowardice made flesh. She thought she only meant to hurt him, to match the damage he had inflicted on her, but now, snowflakes landing on her eyelashes, a bloody stone in her still hands, she knew that was no longer enough.

She brought it down again, and again, no longer screaming, but with calm drive and insistence. As his hands dropped to the ground, and his limbs jerked, and blood spattered the snow, she lifted the stone again and told herself it was just like churning butter . . . just like churning butter . . .

And the memories came, faster and faster, distinct at first, but then jumbling together, one awful, tragic, wonderful thing after the next, poignant, beautiful, mundane, shocking, gut-wrenching, a storm of human memories, lurid, passionate, horrific, sublime, potent surge after surge, and I reeled and again fell to my knees, but no amount of clenching my eyes tight stopped the deluge, and I bit my tongue as I hit the stones at my feet, hearing the Matriarch's voice as from a wraith, "You carry the plague . . . it is who you are . . ."

And then everything was lost, replaced again by the void.

When I woke up, my eyes were crusted over with gunk, my mouth was dry and sore, my muscles hurt everywhere, and my stomach felt like it had heaved everything out a tenday ago, empty and acidic.

Rudgi's face appeared above me, and I realized I was back in our prison quarters again. She turned and called out, "This one's up, too." Then she glanced back down and wrinkled her nose. "He'll be needing a soapy bath as well. Pissed himself good."

I should have been mortified, but I was too disoriented and sore to care. "What . . . ?" I licked my cracked lips.

Rudgi handed me a ladle full of water out of a bucket. "Easy does it, now. Take a drink or two, would you?"

I did, spilling half of it down my shift with shaky hands, not caring about that either. "What happened? How long have I been . . . out?"

She took the ladle back. "That wasn't quite the bath I had in mind. And as to the rest, the Deserter bastards brought you and the others back two days ago."

"Two . . . days?" I shook my foggy head and tried to sit up, but my arms barely supported me. "The rest of us? So we all made it?"

Rudgi smiled. "You all made it. Caked in vomit, crying out in your sleep, pissing yourselves like buckets with no bottoms, but yeah, you're all here. I have to say, makes me real happy Cap didn't invite sergeants too."

I immediately thought about Braylar, and how he had suffered bombardments like this so many times before. "And everyone . . . we're all awake now?"

She nodded. "Aye. You were the last. You doing OK? I mean, aside from everything I just mentioned?"

The water I managed to get down nearly threatened to come right back up as I burped, but I nodded. "Yes. Couldn't be better. Why ever would you ask?"

Rudgi looked at me closely and then looked towards the wall, and then the ceiling.

I glanced in that direction and started to turn away when I saw something out of the corner of my eye, like a spider crawling or a shadow slipping past. I looked longer, and nearly scooted back away from the wall—images flew across the surface, ghostlike, silhouettes, emerging from nowhere, sliding over the rough stones, and disappearing.

"What . . . ?"

"And . . . there it is," Rudgi said. "Vendurro said you might be seeing things too. Well, seeing what's there, maybe, that no one else can."

I looked at her quickly in time to see her shiver, then back to the ceiling. More faint outlines coalesced on the surface, held sway, and then disappeared. And as I glanced around the chamber, I saw the same thing on all the walls and the rest of the ceiling, now that my eye was picking them up. "Memories," I said quietly, somewhat horrified. "The Matriarch . . . being with her allowed us to see them. Memories of slaves who have been in this room, and that one, and . . ." I stopped myself. "We all see them?"

"Every one of you poor bastards that accompanied those Deserter fucks. Ayyup."

Horror and fear gave way to fascination, until I couldn't do anything but stare, to try to make out what the images or sensations were, oddly flattened and stripped of most of their substance as they raced across the walls and ceiling. It was like seeing ghosts flitting around the room.

"Come on, Arki," Rudgi said, chuckling as she helped me to my feet. The muscles in my calves seized up, and I had to stretch and reposition several times to finally work the cramps out before I could walk.

Soffjian entered the room, looked me up and down, and gave a thin humorless grin. "So good of you to join us again, Arki. We were beginning to wonder."

"Your kindness is, as ever, uh . . ." My mind was seizing up as well.

That seemed to bring about some actual mirth. "Bountiful? A deep comfort? Effervescent?"

"Right. Something like that." I was staring at the wall again, as what looked like the pale outline of a rooter rumbled past.

Soffjian laughed. "Don't worry, Arki. It goes away eventually."

As odd as it was to see the memories of slaves smeared on the wall, appearing and disappearing like the surface of a lake touched by the wind, I was almost saddened to hear I wouldn't be able to see them soon. "Was this . . . is this what they did to you? Is that why you were unresponsive when they returned you?"

"Yes and no. I've spoken with the others—well, not Mulldoos, as he was disinclined to discuss—so I've heard enough to recognize that they tried something similar with me at first. But I have defenses and training for resisting that sort of thing, and managed to rebuff them. A bit. So they had to . . . escalate their efforts."

Rudgi started to leave when I said, "Could I have some more water, please?"

She handed me the ladle, standing clear to avoid the smell and any spillage. When I finished taking a few more gulps without vomiting, I handed it back.

"Get yourself some soap, Arki. A lot of it," Rudgi said, softening it a little with a crooked smile before leaving.

I tried to imagine what Soffjian had endured and was glad I couldn't. "What were they trying to accomplish? Why did they subject us to that?"

Soffjian said, "I can't answer for certain, not being a Deserter, or whatever they call themselves. But I suspect they were trying to overwhelm you, overcome you so as to better sift through your memories once you were helpless. I imagine they were trying to ascertain whether we were telling the truth or if we actually were a feeler of some invading army." She shrugged. "Though they could have been doing anything, truly. It wasn't all that different from the manumission ceremony, though far more hostile and invasive. When a man is at his most helpless, you can work unimpeded."

I nearly threw up again. "Do you think they . . . bonded with us?"

"No," she said. "I do not."

"Why?"

Soffjian gave me a long look. "I imagined you would have pieced that together by now, being at least passably clever. While these giants are far more powerful than us in every way, and fancy themselves quite a bit above our kind, they can't abide us in great numbers, and though I doubt they would ever admit as much, they fear us."

I considered that, and it made sense with what the Matriarch had said before invading our minds. "Or detest us."

"Or detest us," she agreed. "They clearly have some use for our kind still—while they erected the Veil behind them, they allow small communities of humans to serve them here. But very small. A controlled population. Tightly controlled, from the looks of it. Whatever calamity befell them on the other side before they left the teeming realms of men behind, they have no desire to see it repeated. Which is why our unexpected arrival here is a stone thrown at a hornets' nest."

My stomach grumbled and churned, though I wasn't sure whether with rebellion or hunger. "What do you think they mean to do with us now?"

Soffjian pursed her lips and took a deep breath. "I haven't the slightest idea. But I suspect it will not be anything we like."

She turned and left and I followed, though slowly, stepping carefully to be sure my legs weren't going to cramp up and betray me again. When they finally seemed to behave themselves, I walked out of my room.

There was a bathtub that didn't have the cleanest water in it, but it was at least tepid, and much better than a urine-soaked shift. I cleaned myself off, dressed in what passed for a fresh tunic, and timidly ate some bread, hoping it would stay down. When it didn't catapult back up, I looked for Braylar and his retinue.

A few of the Syldoon soldiers who saw me gave me a small nod, but most ignored me, which was all for the best really.

I found the captain, his officers, and his sister in the room with windows facing the city of Roxtiniak, arguing over something. It wasn't raining, but the clouds were spread thick and wide, covering the entire sky like a shroud.

Azmorgon saw me first and said, "Look who's back. Figured you were a goner, little flower, all your petals crushed into powder. Or whatever petals get crushed into."

Mulldoos looked at the huge man and shook his head. "You're a plaguing idiot."

"What? Ain't that what herbalists do? Crush things into dust or powders or whatnot with a thistle?"

"Pestle, you plaguing—never mind. Not even worth it." Mulldoos looked me up and down, and while he didn't welcome me, he didn't mock me either, so that was something.

Vendurro said, "Good to see you, bookmaster." He leaned in close as I passed, conspiratorial. "I would have gone with 'pages of a scroll crushed into powder' myself, if I was a plaguing mean-ass bastard. Which I ain't. Most of the time, leastwise." Then he winked and clapped me on the back. "Still seeing whispers on the wall?"

I nodded slowly, realizing I was looking past his shoulder as one crept across the stones and disappeared again. Whispers on the wall was apt.

Vendurro said, "It'll pass. Did for the rest of us."

Braylar seemed to be assessing me as well before continuing the conversation they were embroiled in. "We don't yet know their intentions."

Mulldoos replied, "We know they cracked our heads open like rotten nuts, played around inside worse than any Memoridon witch would do, and nearly husked the lot of us. I'd say their intentions aren't so plaguing mysterious as all that."

"None of that is false," the captain replied. "And yet, they did not in fact husk us. And they could have killed us instead of capturing us in the first place, or at any point after, including in the bowels of this citadel. They chose not to. Let us not forget that."

One side of Mulldoos's lips curled in a snarl. "Fine. They didn't off us or husk us. Yet. But even if they don't, you seen the dumb bastards they got under their big boot heels. Men are little better than dogs or cattle here. The worst of the lot are riding around in baskets, thinking they're some kind of elite chosen ones when the truth of it is they just ain't got legs to run away."

Braylar rubbed his fingers under his jaw, across the heavy stubble. "I am not suggesting we offer to kneel and paint their impressively large toenails. I will be no one's thrall."

"Good. Then it's settled," Mulldoos said.

"Nothing is settled. What I am saying, not to be mistaken for suggesting, is that we should not act rashly and ensure our deaths. We will escape this place. But we must be tactical and measured about it."

Azmorgon said, "Measured this, measured that. Hate to say it, on account of him being a needle stuck in my cock most of the time, but the pale bastard there has the right of it. We got to bust out. Got to."

Soffjian sneered as well as anyone I have ever seen. "Marvelous plan. I would love to hear the specifics."

"Specifics?" Azmorgon asked. "What are you plaguing going on about? We lure some in here, kill them, make a break for it."

"Oh, yes, an incredibly sound plan, as expected. I imagine, then, that you have already begun construction on the tunnel that will get us out of this room, since the door is impassable, and from there, under the walls of the city, since it is surrounded by a barrier no less deadly than the Godveil itself. Because if not, I suggest you start. That will take a good bit of time."

Azmorgon stood to his full, impressive height, as if that might cow the Memoridon. "Listen, you lippy bitch, nobody asked for your plaguing input."

"I did," Braylar said. Then he surveyed the group. "I asked all of you here, as we need to discuss a strategy. But as my sister so keenly points out, that requires forethought, planning, and measured consideration."

Vendurro said, "Maybe digging ain't so practical, but why not climb out of here?"

"Atta boy, Squirrel!" Azmorgon said, never one to pass up an opportunity to add an insult to an otherwise collegial conversation.

Mulldoos said, "You seen those inverted walls, Ven. A spider could do it, maybe even a squirrel. But we ain't climbing down."

Vendurro replied, "Not with our fingers and toes, we couldn't. Never said we were plaguing monkeys. But maybe we could tear up some cots, work up some ropes or harness of some kind, scale our way out of here."

Soffjian said, "Even if we did manage to scale down with jury-rigged ropes, there are still things to contend with. On the interior of this round keep, you have only the lake. No escape there, unless you expect to swim down the drain in the middle. But we know all too well where that leads. And on the other side—"

Mulldoos finished. "Hundreds of eyes. Or horns, in the case of the Deserter cunts. We'd be seen by somebody for sure."

Vendurro wasn't quite ready to admit defeat. "Not at night."

I said, "But they can see at night. Or sense. They aren't reliant on light like we are—they see another way. Just like they weren't affected by the smoke when they attacked us. They aren't limited like we are."

Mulldoos nodded. "What the scribbler said, it's spot on. They'd see us at night as clear as if the sun were riding high."

Then it hit me. "Rain," I said, quietly, more to myself than anyone, thinking out loud.

Azmorgon gave me a beady glare. "What? What did you plaguing say?"

"The Deserters. They're foiled by rain."

The captain had the briefest hint of a smile on his face, but it wasn't twitching and didn't disappear. "Elaborate."

I said, "The other day, when it was raining hard, there wasn't a single Deserter out, was there?"

Azmorgon said, "So what? So plaguing what? Maybe they don't like plaguing water? What's that got to do with—"

"Let him plaguing talk, you big floppy twat." Mulldoos said.

I gave Mulldoos a surprised and grateful nod. "When we were in the water chamber, the Matriarch showed us how they see things without needing eyes. The hand. Remember the hand?" Vendurro nodded, and I said, "That was a memory. Of theirs. They somehow project their memories out, feel them rebound off everything around them, take in the contours, shapes, textures of all the objects, in all directions."

I began to talk faster as everything started to fall together, my hands waving as I gestured. "That is how they perceive the world. They send out memories, and see what they bounce off."

"Makes no plaguing sense," Azmorgon growled.

Soffjian replied, "Yes, as if a barless prison created by eyeless giants who are just south of being gods makes a tremendous amount of sense."

Rudgi had a broad grin, her top lip so thin it nearly disappeared, and she suddenly looked lovely. "*That's* why they have all those layers and baubles and embroidery on their clothing! They can't see a blue sky, but they see texture, and to them, that's attractive, am I right?"

Vendurro added, "And the buildings, with all those grooves and panels and carvings and grottoes and whatnot. Same thing."

"And probably," Rudgi said, excited, "why they carve those runes or designs into their skin, scar themselves like that." She shook her head. "Textures. The eyeless bastards see textures. With memories. Huh. Queerest thing ever, isn't—"

"Rain," Braylar said, clearly impatient. "What of the rain, Arki?"

"Well," I said, "They don't need light to see the shapes of things. But rain . . . the raindrops are objects too. Tiny, fast moving. And if there are a lot of them, falling hard enough, I bet that effectively blinds them. That's why they all fled inside when it rained. They'd be wandering around blind otherwise, or close to it."

Everyone silently chewed on that for a few moments. Azmorgon was the first to speak, such as it was. "Sooooooo . . . ?"

"So," Vendurro said with a big toothy grin, "If we waited to climb down during the rain, they couldn't see us."

Mulldoos wiped some spit off the corner of his lips. He did not look lovely. "Maybe the scribbler's right. Maybe. Makes sense. Well, as much as anything can plaguing make sense on the wrong side of the world. But even if the Deserters couldn't see us, the lickspittle thralls down there might, and they could raise an alarm. And then there's the other thing. Even if no one paid us any mind at all and no alarm went up—real plaguing unlikely, but for the sake of arguing here—the chances of us climbing hundreds of feet down with no wall to brace ourselves, on rain-slicked makeshift ropes, when all it takes is one man to slip and bring the whole lot of us down to the stones . . . Well, worse than plaguing slim. Pretty much impossible. So there's plaguing that."

Vendurro said, "Alright, can't climb down. Suicidal, like you said. But we can go *sideways*."

Mulldoos started to object but Braylar said, "Sideways?"

Vendurro looked at the captain. "Got to figure they keep the wards on the doors for prisoners or slaves, right? Ours, maybe some others. But betting they don't have traps on all of them. Storage rooms. Something like that. So, supposing someone climbs along this level, works their way around to another window, climbs through. No slick ropes. Less chance of being seen by human folk. So it stands to reason that someone could sneak out of whatever room that is, and . . ."

"And what?" Mulldoos asked. "Get killed in that other room instead of this one."

"Nope," Vendurro replied. "But we got to bust out of here somehow, don't we? Seems the window to window could work."

Soffjian added, "I like an impossibly ambitious escape plan as much as the next person, but before we go too far, there is one other rather annoying wrinkle."

"What's that?" Vendurro asked.

"Two, actually. Even if we somehow escape this keep—premature, I know, as we've only just gotten someone into another room. But even if we escape, we have the Veildome around the city to contend with in this daring scenario. And even if we somehow circumvented that, we still have the Godveil beyond. Without Bloodsounder, we are still very much trapped on this side of the Veil." She managed to say this flatly, but the blunt reality of the statement still delivered a vicious blow.

Mulldoos said, "She's got a point. You thinking our wall climber's going to sneak around peeking in every door on every floor until he finds that blasted thing without getting caught?"

Vendurro was at a loss, but Braylar wasn't. "You all forget something. According to the manuscripts and even our captors, I *am* Bloodsounder. I can feel it. It's not far. Certainly not half as far as when you all stole it once and stashed it back in the earth. It might even be on this level somewhere."

Soffjian gave her brother a long look. "You fell out of a small tree and broke your arm when you were a tenyear, Bray. It had a lot of branches. It might as well have been a ladder—a one-armed man could have climbed it blindfolded. As much as I would enjoy watching you make the attempt, do you really think you are in the best shape to scurry around a stone wall with scant footholds or toeholds, in the rain, while your mind is clouded and limbs weak?"

Braylar twitch-smiled. "I do hate to disappoint, but I am not so enfeebled as all that, sister. I will manage."

Mulldoos raised both hands in the air. "Whoa, whoa, before anybody gets out on that wall, I got some other objections."

"But of course you do," Braylar replied.

Mulldoos said, "Let's say you or someone else can find your blasted flail. That gets us through the Godveil, but that still doesn't get us out of this plaguing domicile. Still got the ward on this plaguing door."

Azmorgon said, "Maybe it'll do the same with the ward. Bypass it."

"And maybe you got a brain no bigger than a walnut," Mulldoos said. "If you had said it could get us through the barrier around the city, I might be nodding—similar thing. But I'm guessing this ward is something else altogether." He looked at Soffjian. "You know anything about that, witch?"

Soffjian replied, "Seeing as you asked so cordially, you pale ass, I will offer my expertise. I have no idea. Memoridons have never erected a Godveil or built an invisible memory trap, so far as I know. But so long as we are bandying about guesses, I will say that it seems likely they are constructed differently, and would require different mechanisms to bypass them."

"Guessing, guessing, guessing," Azmorgon said, waving a big hairy hand in slow circles. "How about less of that and more doing, eh? We got to do something. We all agree there, don't we? Got to *do* something."

Mulldoos replied, "Got to *do* something, yeah. But something that makes some kind of sense and doesn't get us all killed. While the rest of us figure that out, why don't you go run into the doorway. Maybe you'll have better luck than that plaguing idiot Benk."

Azmorgon was about to reply when I said, "What if we captured someone who could undo the trap? Release the mechanism somehow, or free us to pass, as it obviously only prevents some from passing?"

Mulldoos said, "Like who, scribbler? One of the Deserter bitches accompanying that Matriarch? You figure one might just be strolling the halls, ripe for abduction by an unarmed Syldoon?"

"I thought you told me a Syldoon is never truly unarmed?" His eyes were narrowing and a hostile rebuttal was building when I continued, "But no, I didn't mean one of them. Far too dangerous and unlikely. But what of the women, one of the human Foci? They have short leashes and aren't as powerful as Memoridons, but they are skilled in some memory magic. Perhaps one of them could walk us through, or stop the trigger."

Mulldoos was chewing on that idea when Soffjian added, "It is possible, Arki. Perhaps even likely. But then we come full circle—we have no idea where they reside in this keep, or how well guarded they are."

"Not yet," I concurred. "But we could. I'm sure Bulto would know."

Vendurro said, "Last time you tried talking to him, you nearly got your brainpan stove in."

"That is true. But that was before they interrogated us." I looked at Rudgi. "The last slaves who came did so with a light guard, you said."

Rudgi nodded. "Aye. Guessing they figure they got us well cowed now."

I looked at Braylar. "I'm willing to try it, Captain. The next time he comes with food, I'll see if we can find out where the Foci reside, where our weapons and armor might be, especially Bloodsounder, to make hunting easier."

Braylar gave me a long look as everyone waited for his response. "We might not be cowed, but that lad is. He will not be in any hurry to reveal anything to you, if he opens his mouth at all."

"But it is worth a try, isn't it?"

Braylar gave the smallest of nods. "Perhaps." He looked at his council. "I would hear your thoughts before deciding on a course. All our lives are on the scales."

Azmorgon said, "We'll be trimming the sails and manning the oars, or the other way around—never did understand nothing about sailing—but you got to captain, Cap. Tell us what direction to go in here, and we're going, but I'm with the pale bastard. We can't wait around and list into the plaguing reefs. You got to steer the ship. We'll do the rest."

"Downright nautical," Vendurro said. "You sure you never sailed?"

Braylar didn't give him a chance to respond, and thankfully discontinued the muddied sailing metaphors. "What say the rest of you?"

Vendurro looked at the older lieutenants, then at the captain. "You know I'll follow your lead, Cap, and if your lead is to sit tight and think things through a bit more, I'll be right there, watching you think. But I got to agree on one point—the longer we wait, the less chance we got of making something happen the way we want it to. Better to act, than react. Ain't that what you always say?"

Braylar gave a wry smile, however brief. "Always is a bit extreme, but point taken. And you, Rudgi?"

Rudgi winked at Vendurro. "Better to act than react."

Braylar nodded and looked at his sister and me. "And what of you two?"

Azmorgon started to say something, certainly no compliment, but Mulldoos elbowed him in the side and the huge man shut his mouth, reluctantly.

Soffjian said, "The last time you asked my counsel was nearly three tenyear ago. Forgive me if I am a bit stunned. But we can safely surmise that now that the Deserters are confident we are not the vanguard of a human invasion, we will either be killed outright, husked, or enslaved. I suspect killed outright. I say we act as soon as possible."

Braylar gave a small nod, then looked out the window as he asked, "And you, Arki?"

Azmorgon couldn't contain himself anymore. "Asking a pen monkey and mind witch for advice? Plague me."

I ignored him as I replied, "Better to act than react. I think."

"Very good." He looked at Azmorgon. "Have the men alternate watch on the door. We might not have much time, so we need to know the moment that boy returns."

"Aye, Cap."

"We see what information we can glean. And we go from there, yes?"

Everyone said "Aye" or saluted.

Mulldoos only nodded, not liking this plan at all, but seeming to know more rebuttals weren't getting him anywhere. He stood, joints creaking, wobbling slightly, and spoke to me. "Best see if you can glean a knife or fork from that skinny bastard too. Real hard to abduct someone with a spoon or just your elbows."

I was about to say his elbows would likely do just fine, but bit the reply back and nodded. I looked back and saw the captain staring out the window at the shroud of clouds, and couldn't help feeling glad not to bear the burden of responsibility, in addition to whatever other unseen devils sought to malign him.

Slaves came with food and to change chamber pots two more times that day, and the Deserter guards were lax, standing just outside the door one time, and barely inside the other as the slaves went about their business. But there was no sign of Bulto, and I began to fear he'd been permanently reassigned (or permanently disposed of).

The next morning, Rudgi alerted me that Bulto was among the group of slaves that showed up. I entered the main chamber quickly, saw that the Deserters were standing just outside our deceptively barless cell, and not especially interested. But I knew any delays would alert them to something, so I moved over to Bulto as quickly as I could manage. Vendurro and Mulldoos were lingering nearby, eating dark bread, ready to cause a distraction if necessary or alert me if I needed to withdraw.

Bulto saw me heading towards him and immediately started shaking his head and looking around, anticipating the next blow.

Looking nervous, he kept distributing plates of food, and after I accepted mine and made sure none of the Deserters had entered the chamber, I said, "I need your help, Bulto."

He shook his head again. "Do you like pain? I don't."

I said, "We need to leave this place, and we need your help. Where—"

"There is no leaving. None. No leaving."

"We *are* leaving, Bulto," I said as urgently as I could while whispering. "But we need to know some things." I glanced at the Syldoon monitoring the door. No sign yet. "Where are the weapons and armor we had when they brought us here?"

Bulto's hands were shaking as he handed out another plate of squash, peppers, and bread, and his face and neck had turned a violent crimson. "I . . . I don't know."

"You do," I pressed. "I know you do. You know things. Where is our gear? And where is Bloodsounder? The flail? The captain's flail?"

His head jerked up at the name, and I knew he had heard it before. But he maintained feigned ignorance. He said, "I do not wish to die," or something close to that—he spoke too quickly for me to entirely follow.

"Neither do we, Bulto. And we will if we remain here. You must help us."

He glared at me. "Must I? Or must I tell the Matriarch and earn favor?"

I pressed on, even as his too-narrow eyes challenged me. "Please. A few questions. Tell us where the arms are. The flail. And our horses. And tell us where the Foci sleep."

His head jerked around as he nearly dropped a plate looking back to the door. "You must not speak of them. Do not."

"I have. And I will. Tell me." I suddenly remembered another important detail. "And the other rooms. Are they warded like this one?" He didn't seem to understand so I tried again, "Trapped? With the memory trap, by the door? Sound, light?"

Another Syldoon nonchalantly took the proffered plate and moved off as if I weren't risking my neck, maybe all of ours, with this illicit conversation.

Bulto's lips were a tight line, nearly disappearing. "Why? Why should I help?"

Without thinking it through at all, I blurted out, "We'll take you with us. Away from here." I had no idea if that was true, but tried to will the uncertainty away from my face.

Bulto looked around nervously again, fidgeting, as if merely hearing such a proposal might spell his doom. "Away?"

"Yes, help us escape, and you escape with us," I said, hoping I wasn't lying.

Bulto handed out another plate, slowly. He only had a few left. The other slaves were nearly done distributing the food. He seemed to be wrestling with himself. I waited, glancing at the door as he handed out two more. Finally, whispering, Bulto said, "Only rooms for prisoner are like this one."

"What room is next to us with a window? Down the hall?"

He thought about it for a moment and said, "Storage."

"Good. And our horses." He looked confused and I added, "The four-legged beasts that came with us to Roxtiniak."

"Your beasts? I do not know. I assume in the rooter pens. East of here. Due east."

"Excellent. And our gear? The Foci?"

He was so skittish, I thought he might bolt at any moment, but after a quick look to the door he said, "Your gear is one floor below . . . ten . . ." he thought about it and nodded. "Ten doors down. West. West of here. In a storage room. Lakeside. I do not know if the flail is there. Bloodsounder. It might be. They . . . they do not like it." He looked at the other slaves heading back to the door. "The Foci, they are in several quarters. They separate. Our masters keep them separate."

"A woman," I said, "Nustenzia. White or silver hair."

Bulto started heading back to the doorway. I grabbed his arm, and he said, "You will take me? How?"

I had no idea. "Tell me where she is. Then tell me where you are. When we break free, we will find you."

It was hard to tell which was more evident on his face, boyish hope or seasoned skepticism. "She is on this level. Halfway around. Four doors from the stairwell. Lakeside."

I released his arm. "And you?"

He gave me a plaintive look. Hopeful won out. "Three floors below. Cityside. Four doors from the stairwell." But then some bitterness reclaimed his expression and he shook his head. "But you will die before you get one floor down." Then he turned and nearly ran for the door to catch up with the rest of the exiting slaves.

I neglected to ask about cutlery. But I hoped Mulldoos would forgive me.

I was too anxious to even eat as I walked with my plate to find Braylar. Several Syldoon looked at me as I passed, and it felt as if they knew that I carried some news of portent. But that might have simply been my imagination or an uneasy and empty stomach.

The captain and his retinue, however, were all gathered together near the window facing the ever-draining and refilling lake, and there was no question they were expecting me.

Mulldoos spit out several globs of food as he said, "Well? What did the little bastard have to say? You were talking to him long enough, I was sure you were both going to end up dead. Or betrothed."

"He was reluctant," I replied. "As predicted. But he was forthcoming about a few things. He wasn't positive about Bloodsounder, but he was sure the rest of our weapons and gear are one floor below. And the Focus we are after is on this floor."

Braylar pushed a mottled pepper around on his plate for a moment before replying, "You said a few things. That was two. And the third?"

"Four, really. Our horses are allegedly in the rooter pen. East of here."

"And the fourth?"

I hesitated before replying, "The location of his room. Bulto's room."

Soffjian said, "And why, pray tell, would we care about his room?"

I forced myself to meet her unnerving stare. "I promised him we would bring him with us."

Mulldoos barked out a laugh; Vendurro gave a long, slow shake of his head, and Braylar said, "Did you?"

"He wasn't going to help at all. Even asked why he shouldn't just report us. So I played the only thing that came to mind that might be compelling to him."

Smiling crookedly, Rudgi said, "You are betrothed."

Braylar was less amused. "And what makes you think he did not simply lie, or that he isn't laying our secret plot bare to the first Deserter that will listen?"

I resisted the urge to reply immediately, knowing I would simply flounder or make an ass of myself, and took a moment to compose my thoughts. "It is a gamble. For certain. But then we knew that. We can sit here and wait for the Deserters to potentially swoop down on us, or act on the information, hoping for the best. He seemed earnest. And I believed him. But can I swear to the veracity or accuracy? No. I can't."

Braylar maintained the same opaque expression, but Mulldoos smirked and said, "You got stones, kid. Grant you that."

The captain lifted a finger from the plate, looked at whatever was on the tip, popped it into his mouth and said, "Anything else?"

"No," I replied, and then amended, "Oh, and ours should be the only doorway that has a trigger of any kind, or a trap. Presumably."

Braylar stood, dusting his hands off on his trousers. "Very good. So then. Assuming this information is accurate—which is quite a leap, truly, as we have no way to corroborate any of what's been told, but let's presume it is in fact on point—let us examine this course of action more carefully. Even if everything is golden truth, we need to coordinate our escape while it is raining or just before it is set to, as that is the only way to cover our flight."

"Assuming that little bit of supposition ain't rife with errors too," Mulldoos said. "We have no proof rain blinds. None at all."

"Fair point," the captain replied. "But for the sake of this exercise, let us assume all our assumptions are without fault. So, that means our intrepid wall climbers have to make the trip across wet stones, without falling, and without raising alarm."

I said, "If it is raining, even a little, and we're right about that reducing their visibility, sight, whatever we want to call it, that would at least provide cover for the climbers."

"Cover, yes, and a slick surface as well," Braylar replied. "But even if not raining yet, it would need to be at night, to reduce the chances of a Deserter looking out one of a hundred windows and seeing a few humans clinging to the wall like ivy. They don't need light, but presumably they do need sleep.

"So, our scalers make the trek around the inside wall of the citadel into the storage room undetected. They creep down a hall. Undetected. They dispatch any guards around the Focus. Unarmed, of course. They abduct her. Without detection. And then they return here first to release us—the Focus can do this, yes, as we have surmised—and a large group of Syldoon roam the halls in the night without raising alarm and then break into our weapons larder. Which, we duly hope, has Bloodsounder in the tally."

Vendurro started to say something, but Braylar raised his hand. "Wait. I have not concluded. So, after breaking free from our prison and obtaining our weapons and armor once more, our still-sizable troop fights or skulks our way free of this damnable ring keep without being captured, cornered, or killed off completely, and into the rain, which has begun falling at precisely the perfect time to cover our trek to the rooter pens, where our horses have not yet been slaughtered for meat or out of fear. We then proceed to ride through the downpour, and I lead us out through the Veil, seeing as I am Bloodsounder, and reunited with my namesake."

Braylar looked around at his retinue and then concluded with, "Yes. A most excellent plan. What could possibly go wrong?"

Vendurro scratched the back of his head. "Well, when you lay it out like that . . ."

Azmorgon slapped his meaty hand on the wall. "You know my plaguing mind. I still say we act. And act some more. Better than sitting here and waiting for the axe to fall."

Soffjian said, "The plan is fraught with unknowns and dangers. There is no denying that. But it galls me to wait for our captors to decide our fates. I find it difficult to admit out loud, but the Ogre's oration is compelling on one point—it is better to make a move and have it potentially end in spectacular disaster than do nothing and have the Deserters decide things for us."

Braylar seemed amused by that. "I know your mind, Mulldoos. What of you, Vendurro? Rudgi? Do you still feel we should proceed?"

Vendurro pushed his bottom lip out with his tongue, thought about it for a minute and said. "It was my fool idea. Could go tits-up in a hurry, that's for plaguing sure. But better than sitting here staring at each other until the Deserters slice our throats or husk us or lop off our limbs or whatever. I say we do it."

Rudgi nodded. "Aye. I'll volunteer to make the climb. The stones have crevices, and I have small feet and hands. Grew up in the mountains. And smaller on the whole—harder on the whole—harder to spot. I'll go."

Soffjian looked at the young Syldoon with what might have been respect. "I will accompany. While not small, I am far daintier than the rest of your brutes. And they did nothing to snuff out my abilities. The Deserters have some resistance to my memorycraft, but I can still take one out. And I certainly can stun one of the Foci."

Vendurro said, "Aye, and I'll be going as well."

Mulldoos said, "What do you plaguing know about climbing walls, you dumb prick?"

"No more nor less than anyone else here. But a lot of crevices, and I got thin fingers. And it was my plaguing idea. I'm going."

Azmorgon laughed. "I knew calling him Squirrel would pay off!"

Mulldoos ignored him and stared at the younger man. "Just made Lieutenant. Real bad time to go playing hero."

Vendurro shrugged his shoulders. "Never a good time, really, but it ain't like scaling a mountain. Just got to go sideways a bit and climb in a plaguing window. How hard can it be?"

The hooded eye didn't reveal much, but Mulldoos gave a lot away with the other one. For the first time since I met the man, he seemed truly unnerved, maybe even afraid. Then it occurred to me that with Hewspear gone, Vendurro was likely his closest Towermate, and he was in no hurry to see another one die. But it was obvious to all that he couldn't take Vendurro's place, and would have been a lousy choice, even before Rusejenna had struck him down and robbed him of some of his dexterity.

"That settles it, then," Braylar said. "Ven, Rudgi, my sister, myself."

Mulldoos said, "Cap, I thought we covered this. You're—"

"We did. And I am the only one who can find Bloodsounder. We do not know for certain where it is, but I can tell as I get closer. I go." He glanced out the window. "It's cloudy now, but not raining. We'll monitor as the day goes, and if it seems like rain is coming in, we'll do it tonight. If not, tomorrow night. But we can't afford to dally and delay. Perhaps Vrulinka is keeping her council at bay, or perhaps they simply deliberate slowly, but they could decide our fates at any moment. We go the moment the rain falls."

Sometimes fortune favors fools and their folly. And sometimes it acts arbitrarily and favors no one at all, or according to some design mortals are not privy to.

While the clouds rolled in and out the remainder of that day, it was clear rain was holding off. But as dusk gave way to night, and the hours dragged on, darker, heavier cloudbanks finally moved in and laid claim to the entire sky, inking out the last of the stars. The whole company was anxious, in part dreading the arrival of the Deserters before we could see our mad plan to fruition, in part hoping the rain was going to show but not so early as to make the stones treacherously slick.

There couldn't have been more than two or three hours before daybreak when the rain came at last. It was hardly a deluge, but certainly enough to make the climb far more dangerous.

The tension was a dense thing, as the captain had briefed his men on what they intended to do. While the prospect of escaping here no doubt buoyed their spirits, the equal possibility of losing half their officers in the attempt or being executed to a man if it was thwarted weighed heavy enough to sink the spirits entirely. Everyone was short, on edge, or surly—even Vendurro seemed to want to wait out the day by himself, so I did the same, recording events and then stowing my brass case under my sleeping mat again.

While waiting might have been a large part of soldiering, this seemed different somehow, even more difficult to bear than waiting for a battle to begin. At least then I might have been able to do some small part to help, to affect the outcome. The majority of the Jackals had to resign themselves to simply waiting and hoping as well.

Finally, with the sun long gone and the moon somewhere above us obscured by dense cloud foliage, Braylar gathered his retinue close to the window. The Deserters had been keen to leave nothing in these quarters that might be converted into a potential weapon, except one thing: the clothing we wore. Azmorgon had torn strips from several shifts and twisted them tight—Braylar, Soffjian, Vendurro, and Rudgi had the makeshift garrotes tucked into their clothing and stood before the dark, watching the rain gently fall.

Three of the iron bars that had been in the sill were now in a pile leaning against the wall beneath, with the dust and rain turning into a paste. Azmorgon seemed entirely too pleased with himself. I'd seen him testing their strength earlier in the day, and heard him working at the bars a couple of times in earnest. He might not have been half as strong as a Deserter, but he was twice as strong as any normal man.

I looked out the window. It was spitting rain, but wet was wet.

Mulldoos moved back from the small puddle on the floor. "Hard to tell, on account of the Deserters not needing light to navigate at all, but ain't seen any movement in any of the other windows for a while. Seems those huge fuckers need to sleep at least. Clear as it's like to get." It sounded as if he'd hoped to report a battalion of Deserters wandering the halls at night to force Braylar to call off the climb.

The captain looked at his small crew. "We go slow. No need to end up splattered on the footpaths below due to haste. Make sure you have a good foot and handhold before moving at all. The façade is textured, as Ven pointed out, so there should be no shortage of edges to hold onto, but they are wet. Proceed cautiously. Understood?"

They all nodded, but Rudgi added, "I hail from hills and mountains. Done a fair bit of climbing, when I was a kid. You've got to go slow all right, but not so slow your muscles cramp up. Make certain your grip is sure, but don't freeze in the same spot too long. Steady, but keep moving."

Braylar took a deep breath. "Excellent advice. But for any of us not sired by goats like our diminutive sergeant here, if anyone should fall, the body will be discovered by morning, and they will certainly kill every Jackal left in these cells. No matter what happens, it is imperative we press on. No matter what. Is that also understood?"

Sober nods all around. Braylar might have twitch-smiled, though the darkness made it even more difficult to tell than usual. "Very well. It is time to roll the dice, yes?"

Rudgi was the first to start climbing over the windowsill. Vendurro reached over to steady her arms and hold her but she shook him off. "Nuh-uh. If I can't manage to climb out a window without falling, the dice are loaded the wrong way."

He stepped back, and Rudgi placed her feet on the wall, then reached over to find a handhold. "Nothing to it," she said, though it was hard to tell how much bravado there was there in the dark. "Keep your eyes on the stones in front of you and not the ones below, you'll do all right."

Everyone watched her stretch, find a new hold, move slightly, and reposition herself. I can't speak for the others, but I felt as if I might throw up. I did look down, and it was a long, long, unforgiving fall. The dark waters moved below, heading towards the drain in the center of the lake, but the trees and footpaths were directly below the windows. At that height, the water might not have been any better anyway.

Even with a light rain, it didn't take long for Rudgi's shift and curly hair to get damp, then soaked. I was glad it was dark and I could barely make out her silhouette—even with lives literally hanging in the balance, I was tempted to see how the thin material clung to her and cursed myself.

After Rudgi had moved five feet away from the edge of the window, Vendurro turned to Mulldoos. "Got no family but my Towermates. All for the best, really. Hate to have someone pining, wondering which fool way I went and got myself killed. But if falling's the way, or getting squashed by a Deserter in the hall, make sure Gless's widow keeps getting her coin. And mine."

Mulldoos grabbed his shoulder. "You trying to shirk responsibility, you little shit? Plague you. You'll make certain of it yourself, you hear me?"

"Aye," Vendurro said. Mulldoos released his arm and Vendurro followed Rudgi out onto the wall. He moved more slowly than she, less certain, feeling his way by inches until he disappeared in the darkness after her.

Braylar looked at Soffjian. "Let us hope I am better at clinging to wet stones than I was at climbing ladder trees, eh?"

She gave him a tight-lipped smiled. "Yes. Let's."

Then she watched as he made his way out. I saw him flex his hands after he was a few feet away from the window, and he moved no more quickly than Vendurro, but his silhouette slowly disappeared as well.

Soffjian rolled her head around on her neck, stretched her arms and legs, and then stepped out on the wet wall.

When she too was cloaked by the night and rain, Mulldoos stepped back from the window and said to no one in particular, "Dumbest plaguing plan ever."

Azmorgon was still leaning out, his big hairy hand a meat shelf above his eyes. "Should have plaguing said as much when you had the chance, shouldn't you?"

"I did, you monstrous bastard. I plaguing did, but you idiots didn't want to hear it."

The huge lieutenant moved back from the window and shook the water out of his bush of a beard. "Oh, everyone heard you complaining about something, mush mouth, but nobody heard you suggesting any other real plaguing alternatives, did we?"

Azmorgon was half a man heavier, towered over Mulldoos, and had full use of his massive limbs, but none of those facts seemed to cow the pale boar at all. "You think it's such a great plaguing idea, why don't you climb out and see if you can cram those ham hands of yours in those tiny holes."

Azmorgon laughed. "Your mother said the same plaguing thing."

Mulldoos's fist shot out and slammed into the larger man's nose, and even though he was maimed and hindered, he stepped in and landed an elbow on either side of Azmorgon's ribs.

Anyone else would have collapsed on the spot, but Azmorgon simply grunted and brought his giant fist down on the crown of Mulldoos's head.

The shorter lieutenant dropped to a knee, but as Azmorgon raised his tree trunk arm to strike him again, Mulldoos sprang up with his shoulder right into Azmorgon's crotch.

That did faze the Ogre—Mulldoos was smaller than him, but still thick with muscle and pride, and no man was immune to such a shot. Azmorgon grunted again and staggered back, doubled over, and Mulldoos's body betrayed him as he lost his balance and almost fell over himself.

I yelled, "Stop!" and then remembered it was the middle of the night and lowered my voice, trying it again as a harsh whisper. "Both of you! The captain needs us ready!"

Mulldoos regained his footing first and came forward, his fists up. The Ogre was still hunched over but when the smaller man was nearly on him, Azmorgon's arm swept up and he caught Mulldoos with the back of his hand, sending him sprawling towards the wet floor by the window.

I tried to grab Azmorgon's arm, but it was like trying to restrain a rooter. He shrugged me off and nearly sent me spilling to the stones, but I regained my balance, ran in front of him, and positioned myself between the two men as Mulldoos tried to get back to his feet and slipped, falling on his side.

"This is madness!" I said. "When the captain and the rest make it back here—" I looked at Mulldoos. "—and they will make it back here, no matter how stupid you think the plan is—they will need every able-bodied man to fight free of this place. Do you think for a moment Captain Killcoin will be merciful to idiots who started fighting the second he was out of sight and bloodied or murdered each other? No! The answer is no."

I thought Azmorgon would bat me out of the way like a gnat, or worse, turn those huge fists on me before attacking Mulldoos again, but he stopped, wiping some blood off his nose and mustache. "Just a friendly scrap. Men blowing off steam is all. Ought to try it sometime. Against a sack of leaves or something."

He walked away, chuckling at his own joke, licking blood off his hairy fingers.

I turned to Mulldoos and offered my hand as he made his way to his feet again, but he shook his head. "Don't need your plaguing help, scribbler. Had it under control."

"Uh-huh," I replied. "Of course. Just like Braylar did against that big spearman when we rescued Henlester. How silly of me."

Some anger flashed in his one good eye and I was sure he was going to strike me, but then he stopped and reached up to rub the knot forming on his skull. "Ayyup. Just like that."

I said, "That wasn't just a 'friendly scrap,' was it?"

Mulldoos shrugged his shoulders. "Do you mean, would one of us beat the other to death? Nahh. Likely not. But there weren't nothing friendly about it neither."

I nodded and then said, "You don't like each other much, do you?"

Mulldoos spit some blood on the floor. "We're brothers, Jackals. I'd die defending him, and him me, when it came down to it. But no, we don't like each other much. That's for certain."

I shuddered, imagining how quickly Azmorgon could have turned me into a bloody puddle if he wanted to. "That shot to the groin should have felled him. I was amazed he kept going."

Mulldoos replied, "The Ogre's the biggest bastard I ever seen. Leastwise, before this side of the Veil. Takes a lot to take him out. And I didn't hit him square as I would have liked. Got a lot of thigh."

"I guess you better hit him right in the jewels next time."

Mulldoos favored me with a bloody smile. "Guessing so."

I watched the candle near me burning, wick flickering and hissing, wax very slowly melting. It was a torturous way to pass the time, but I knew sleep would prove impossible. It amazed me that so many of the Syldoon were able to close their eyes with such apparent ease, but that seemed to be a skill inherent or nurtured through years of potentially having death around every corner—eventually you must simply get inured to such things.

Vendurro and Braylar had both cautioned me to try to get some rest whenever the opportunity was there. But all I could think every time I shut my eyes and tried was the likelihood that someone had plummeted to their deaths climbing the wet stones outside, their scream lost in the sounds of running water and rain, or been impaled on one of the Deserters' massive flat-hafted clubs, or otherwise dispatched in gruesome fashion.

Still, I must have possessed some innate talent for sleeping while stressed, as I managed to drift off when a hand roughly shook me awake.

The candle was still lit and hadn't burned much lower, so it couldn't have been that long. "Wha—? Are they, did they—?"

Mulldoos said, "They're back. And they brought a friend. We're moving."

I rubbed my eyes, still tired but suddenly very alert, and joined all the other Syldoon who were gathered in the main chamber by the open door.

I was relieved to see all of them had returned. Their hair and clothes were still damp, but they were very much alive. Braylar and Vendurro were each holding a short blunt candlestick they had procured, with long spikes where the candles would be mounted; Soffjian was carrying a lit lamp; and Rudgi was propping an unconscious Nustenzia against the wall opposite the door.

All of us inside the room stopped just short of the trigger that set off the memory trap and waited. I had a hundred questions and was glad I couldn't approach or I might have simply spewed them all at once.

Braylar was looking down the hallway when Mulldoos said, "A lantern, Cap. Ain't that a bit . . . obvious?"

Braylar replied, "Better that than stumbling about in the dark." Then he turned to Soffjian. "Time is of the essence, yes? Wake our dreaming Focus. Now, if you please."

She looked at Nustenzia as she set the lamp down. "I will try. I wanted to be sure she didn't raise an alarm, so I took her out somewhat more . . . forcefully than I intended." Soffjian tilted the woman's chin up with one hand, and pressed her other hand on the side of the Focus's head. She closed her eyes, lips moving the way a mumbler's might, barely perceptible, and a moment later Nustenzia's eyes flew open and she jerked as if dunked in cold water.

Rudgi held her tight as Soffjian said, "I am tired, anxious, and peckish, so there is a very good chance I won't take you out so gently a second time. I suggest you behave yourself."

Nustenzia looked at the Memoridon and three Syldoon, then through the door at the rest of us watching. "Well," she said, then wiped some spittle off her lip. "This is a surprise. I'm not certain what you possibly hope to gain by abducting—"

Braylar said, "You seem a moderately clever woman. I am sure you can piece things together. You are going to help us escape."

Nustenzia laughed, and then lifted her hand to cover her mouth as if it might continue if she didn't stifle it. "Oh, no. No, I am sure you are mistaken. You could not—"

Braylar loomed over her. "You are going to either remove that trap, or you are going to guide us through the door. I don't particularly care which. But you will do one of those things, or I will beat you to death in this hallway. Now, tell me again, am I very much mistaken?"

Nustenzia blinked several times and slowly lowered her hands. "I would like to live. Truly. But I do not possess the power to undo what my masters have done." She looked at Soffjian. "Your own flesh and blood here possesses far more potent abilities than my meager skills. I have seen it. I assure you."

Soffjian grabbed the woman's face with both hands and pressed hard. "And I assure you that getting beaten to death will be a far kinder fate than what I can do to you. And will, if you do not cooperate. Now, you have narrow scope of ability, it's true, but what the Deserters have not neutered is quite impressive indeed. You forget, I too have seen what you do. You amplify power. That is something no one in my order has managed, and you can do it with the Deserters' memorycraft, which is several times more potent than what I can do. So you will tell me how to manage this, and you will assist, or you will suffer immeasurably, and then I will let my brother finish you off with his barbaric fists. Do you understand, Lady Focus?"

Nustenzia looked at Soffjian, saw the truth in the threat, and nodded, or as much as she could while her head was mostly immobilized.

Soffjian let go of her and said, "Good. Now tell me how to do this thing."

Nustenzia pushed herself off the wall and stood. "The spell is woven into the stones itself. We cannot shut it down entirely. Only the Matriarch or one of her sisterhood could manage such a thing. But we might be able to bypass it long enough for the Syldoon to walk out. But I do not know for sure, and even if we manage this, you are still trapped—"

"Let us worry about what comes next," Braylar said. "You will be kept alive only so long as you prove useful. I suggest you begin proving yourself now. And I don't suppose I need to tell you what will happen if you betray us, delay us, or lie to us, do I?"

Nustenzia gave a rueful smile. "Oh, no, I am moderately clever. I believe I know." Then she took Soffjian by the hand and stepped forward, stopping just outside the door. "We cannot stop the trap. But I believe we can stop it from reacting to you."

"Like the Veil around Roxtiniak?" Soffjian asked.

"Yes. Precisely. So, we will enter, and I will try to help you, to give your soldiers a temporary mark. It won't hold long, but—"

"Long enough," Soffjian finished. "Go on. What do I need to do?"

The older woman said, "Concentrate on me, bonding with me. Do you think you can do that?"

Soffjian gave her that vulpine smile she and Braylar shared. "Oh, I do have some experience at that."

The pair walked through the large doorway holding hands. I half expected the light and sounds to explode anyway, but the two women made it through without the slightest ripple or reaction.

When they were inside the range of the trap, Soffjian asked, "And now?"

"Now," Nustenzia replied, "it becomes more . . . elusive. I cannot create the mark the door recognizes. But if you can figure it out, the mark in me, I can assist you in tagging each man in this room with it."

Soffjian looked puzzled, Braylar irritated, and Azmorgon and Mulldoos seemed like they were ready to put aside their differences to pummel the woman to death.

And then something hit me. "It will be something raised, or textured. Something the Deserters could sense after they had marked a human with it. Like the brand on Nustenzia's face. But probably buried inside them."

Soffjian favored me with one of her rare heartfelt smiles. "Yes, Arki. I suspect you are right." She looked at Nustenzia again, closed her eyes, and for a moment I thought the Focus might try to run back out the door, but she closed her eyes as well, thin arms slack at her sides, and accepted the examination.

A few moments later, Soffjian opened her eyes and took the older woman by the hand again. "Open yourself up. I will show you the mark. But you will need to help me apply it to the Syldoon."

Nustenzia gave a curt nod. "As you say. I will try."

The two women stood silently, hand in hand, facing the Syldoon. Several moments dragged by, and I heard Benk whisper, "What are those witches playing at? What's taking so plaguing—"

Mulldoos growled, "Shut your mouth, soldier."

Benk glared at Mulldoos but wisely said nothing more.

Soffjian opened her eyes, as did Nustenzia, and the Memoridon said, "Benk, since you seem so eager to walk out of here, you will be our test subject. Walk through the door."

Benk looked like he very much wished he had kept his mouth shut, and he turned to Azmorgon for guidance. The Ogre said, "Get to it, you little bastard." Then he slapped Benk on the back with an open hand and sent him flying forward.

Benk flailed, arms waving as he tried to grab purchase but there was only air, and he nearly landed on his face. When he finally stopped himself, he was only a foot from the door. Well within range of the trap, which had not been activated.

Braylar asked, "Are the rest marked?"

Nustenzia nodded, and Braylar said, "Two at a time then. Out you come."

The Syldoon lined up and began walking through the portal. Each time, they seemed to hold their breath or flinch, and each time they exited unmolested. I ran back to my sleeping roll, snatched my writing case, and made it back just in time to walk out with a soldier ahead of Mulldoos and Azmorgon, the last Syldoon.

When they were all clear of the room, Soffjian and Nustenzia walked out as well. The Focus said, "I would continue proving my worth. What would you have of me?"

Braylar said, "Are there patrols in the middle of the night?"

"No," she replied. "What need?"

"And guards at the stairwells?"

"Again, no. "

"And on the floor below, am I to believe that the storage room full of our arms and armor is unguarded as well?"

Nustenzia's brow wrinkled. "I have never checked. I could not say."

Braylar said, "And if you had to hazard a guess?"

She gave him a cold, level look. "The room itself? No. Not likely. But it is near the barracks. They occupy three floors in the palace—the one below ours, and two below that. So if you are asking if you will run into my masters, I would say yes, even in the middle of the night, you just might."

Judging by the gleam in her eye, she was looking forward to that prospect.

Braylar said, "Bloodsounder. My flail. It is close. I can feel it. Is it housed with everything else they took from us?"

She gave him a long look and then the tiniest of smiles. "You are Bloodsounder. You would know better than I."

He appraised her as well, and then decided her sarcasm wasn't worthy of a rejoinder, and instead addressed his troops. "We reclaim what is ours, and we kill anyone who tries to stop us. Then we are free."

It sounded so deceptively simple and singular.

We left our quarters—Braylar, his officers, Soffjian, and Nustenzia at the front, with the rest of the Syldoon following. I was in the group of soldiers just behind Braylar's retinue. Nustenzia was bound with strips of cloth but left ungagged, presumably to mine her for information as we proceeded. I overheard snippets of conversation about our horses, and the shifts of Deserters. Braylar didn't seem especially worried about her giving us away—if someone encountered a group of Syldoon prisoners wandering the halls, it wouldn't much matter if Nustenzia shouted or not.

We made it to the stairwell without incident and started spiraling down, with the single lantern taken from Nustenzia's quarters lighting our way and throwing shaky shadows on the walls. While our numbers had been thinned considerably since leaving Sunwrack, it was still a large party to sneak through a sleeping citadel, and the sound of so many feet moving at once seemed like drums to my ears. I expected we would alert the Deserters of our passing any moment.

While I hadn't grown accustomed to weapons and could only use them with something just below competency, I couldn't help wishing I had something in my hands to defend myself with. It was ridiculous, really—if we were discovered, we were doomed, as a handful of Deserters could take out what remained of our company even if we were fully armed and armored. But I had never felt more defenseless in my life walking down those gigantic halls and stairs.

The doorway to the level below was open, as seemed to be Deserter custom. Braylar held up a hand, and we all stopped walking down, though several soldiers bumped into each other where the lantern failed to keep the darkness at bay.

I strained to hear as the captain whispered something to Mulldoos and turned and grabbed Rudgi by her small shoulder. The sergeant moved around him on the oversized stairs and made her way to the doorway. She and Soffjian crept out onto the floor and moved off in opposite directions.

Braylar was leaning close to Nustenzia, speaking in her ear and listening to her whispered response. He nodded and waited until the two women returned and reported.

I assumed the way was clear, as we started to file out, heading to the left. The soldier ahead of me shoved me off with his elbow as I nearly fell over him in the dark. "Watch it, you skinny bastard. Keep your bony bones to yourself."

With every step, I imagined Deserters suddenly roaring and charging out of their barracks quarters to crush us into red sludge, and I felt my heart hammering like a cornered animal's.

The company walked by several open doors as quietly as we could, and I was sure the light from the lantern, however shuttered, might wake the Deserters until remembering that they couldn't see light or dark. But their legless human basket riders or slaves were another matter. And I had no illusion about them not waking their masters if they did.

We followed the gently curving corridor around the round keep, and then Nustenzia pointed further ahead.

Braylar called a halt and Rudgi again did the advance scouting, creeping forward at a crouch as she disappeared into the dark, and we waited. I looked behind us, though there was nothing to see save the illuminated contours of hardened faces.

Rudgi came back a minute later, and I thought I saw her hold up two fingers.

Braylar nodded, and he huddled with his officers. They exchanged some signals with their hands. Soffjian interjected herself, grabbing her brother's arm as she shook her head. She pointed at herself.

They clearly didn't agree, but without being able to throw verbal barbs at each other, they managed to resolve it fairly quickly. Another hand-signal exchange occurred between captain and men, and they nodded silently.

Soffjian straightened up and pressed herself close to the wall as she began sidling along it towards whatever lay ahead. The keep was so large, and the curve of the hall so gradual, it would be impossible to truly sneak up on anything. If there were Deserter guards ahead, I didn't see what hope we had of continuing, but then again, I wasn't the one issuing hand-commands.

Vendurro and Braylar followed, wielding the carved candlesticks as short weapons, then the other officers and a few other soldiers. They all stopped twenty or thirty paces from Soffjian, who was still pressed up against the wall ahead.

Then she stepped away from the wall, though it was difficult to see anything more than the faintest silhouette in the dark. Nothing happened, and she took a few steps ahead and raised both her hands. I knew her fingers must have been splayed, though they were impossible to see. She continued walking, and then I heard something scuffling from somewhere further down the corridor, but it was immediately lost in the footfalls of eight Syldoon rushing forward.

Mulldoos grabbed Nustenzia's arm and held up a hand.

I couldn't make out what happened in the gloom ahead, but I heard fighting, and some guttural grunts, then a pronounced thud that could have only been a Deserter hitting the floor, followed closely by another.

Mulldoos lowered his hand and the rest of the company approached. I saw the Deserters' arms and legs on the ground while Vendurro and Braylar continued bludgeoning them with their candlesticks. One Deserter's four-fingered hand jerked and the other one shifted his limbs a little, but it was clear they weren't putting up a fight, and with their thick skin, it took multiple blows before the captain and lieutenant delivered enough to make sure they didn't get up again. Braylar had chosen to crack open a skull and Vendurro was using both arms to drive the spike of the candlestick into the other Deserter's neck. I forced myself not to gag as I saw a large pool of blood that looked as black as ink in the pale flickering light, and I nearly stepped in it before seeing it. Blood was dripping off both slender spikes of the candlesticks the captain and lieutenant were holding, and splattered on their forearms and chests.

Nustenzia looked at Soffjian, then at the Deserters, and back to the Memoridon. Her voice was measured, but not disguising some awe along the edges. "You . . . stunned them?"

Soffjian was massaging her temples with two fingers. "Something like that. Though differently than I had tried before when they captured us." She glanced at me and then looked at her brother. "The Wielders can shape human emotions, manipulate them, but they also detest them, and can only abide them in small doses. And the Deserter warriors are no Wielders. I assaulted them with human memories. *Lots* of human memories."

We all walked around the bodies and into the storage room, except for several Syldoon who remained behind to pull the huge bodies inside after us and stay by the door to monitor the hall. I expected to see racks of Deserter weapons and armor, but those must have been in the rooms the Deserters bunked down in, or at least a different storage room than this one. Here, there were several rows of orderly wooden shelves, with crates, barrels, and other miscellaneous containers organized neatly.

Braylar held up a flat hand and stared straight ahead. To himself he whispered, "They didn't separate it after all." Then he moved away from the light and into the gloom.

I strained to see what he was doing as his silhouette disappeared. We all waited, no one patiently, until he finally returned. And then I saw the lantern glint off the steel in his hands, and heard the dull rattle of chains.

I couldn't make out his face, but then I heard Braylar rasp, "Our gear is in the back. Come on."

He led us further into the room, and along the back wall were several tables, all lined with various pieces of armor, helms, swords, axes, surokas, a falchion, a ranseur, and whatever that massive half-blade, half-haft polearm Azmorgon favored was called.

It took several minutes for everyone to find their gear, with a great deal of clinking, clattering, and muttered cursing that could have woken the dead. It took even longer for the Syldoon and the Memoridon to strip out of the shifts the Deserters had given us, put on old clothing, and then arm themselves. After dressing as quickly as I could, I wiggled into my gambeson and nearly choked on the stench, having forgotten what a rank, sweat-stained, mildewy piece of armor it was. Still, it was much better than wearing no protection at all. I didn't see the dented nasal helm I'd worn before, but there was an unclaimed kettle helm with a brim on the table. I tried not to think about the former owner as I plopped it on my head. It wasn't a bad fit, and the lining in the helm wasn't as foul as what I had dealt with wearing the last helm.

I gathered a belt and quiver of bolts, buckled it around my waist—with our numbers reduced, ammunition was the only thing that wasn't a problem just now. I was about to grab a crossbow when I saw Lloi's curved sword and scabbard in the shadows. Ridiculous as it was, it nearly brought tears to my eyes as I buckled that around my waist.

Vendurro grabbed me by the shoulder as I selected a crossbow from the three remaining. He had a lamellar cuirass over his mail haubergeon that seemed to be reserved for the lieutenants or higher officers—it would still take some getting used to his change in rank, and I didn't like to think on it, as that meant dwelling on why the promotion was necessary in the first place.

He gave me a big toothy grin. "Not bad, bookmaster. Sling that writing case and you might actually be protected for a bit."

I followed his advice, and while I felt awkward with everything strapped, slung, and shifting as I moved, it was the best kind of clumsiness in the world. Looking around, I could almost feel the Syldoon's spirits rising as well. They were still every bit as grim and determined, but if they died now, it least it would be with steel in their hands and going down fighting.

That thought almost spoiled things, and I tried to remind myself that we were going to win our freedom, not be slaughtered in the attempt.

Braylar said, "We make for the stairs. There is only one direction after that. Down, down, down. We kill anyone we encounter."

A soldier asked, "Human slaves?"

"Anyone," Braylar replied as he slipped the aventail of his helm over his shoulder, his face all but hidden behind the mail curtain. "We cannot afford an alarm being sounded, or anyone reporting our presence, and the slaves are most certainly more terrified of their masters than us, so we cannot depend on any promises they might make to keep silent. If fortune favors us, we won't have to wet our blades at all. More likely, she will give us a poison kiss. Either way, we descend to the main floor, dripping red or otherwise." He looked at Nustenzia. "From there, we sprint to the rooter pens and pray they haven't slaughtered our horses, or this escape will prove short-lived."

Mulldoos added, "And if any of you plaguers are prone to prattling to the gods begging favors, you might want to ask them to keep the drizzle coming a while longer yet too."

With that, the depleted but fully armed Syldoon party started for the doorway.

Rudgi had replaced one of the other Syldoon by the door so they could get their gear on, but she came running over now. "Three of the big bastards coming this way, Cap."

Braylar said, "Are they hunting us?"

Rudgi shook her head. "Doesn't look like it. But once they see that big old puddle of red out there . . ."

Braylar ordered everyone away from the door and to take position out of sight. He hisspered, "On my word, we storm out, three at a time."

We crouched and waited, listening for the unmistakable heavy footsteps approaching. I heard the Deserters while they were still somewhere down the hall, but the pace and rhythm changed, then stopped altogether.

There was some muffled discussion in their gruff language, and then more footsteps, this time receding.

Braylar lowered his fist, and the first of the men poured out of the storage room, all with crossbows loaded and ready to loose.

I heard the twang of the crossbow strings and zip of the bolts, followed by a cry, and then more bolts loosing with the next wave of Syldoon stepping into the hallway, and more with the third and fourth.

The Deserters cried out and grunted. While the giants had thick skin, they hadn't been wearing any additional armor, and at that range most of the bolts had no trouble penetrating them. Still, it would take more than that to bring them down. I came out and saw the Syldoon spanning their crossbows. Fifteen paces down the hall, one Deserter was bleeding everywhere as he leaned against the wall, having taking the bulk of the bolts, another giant was charging towards us, and the third had gotten away.

The Syldoon loosed several more bolts at both. The Deserter against the wall slid down, dropping to his knee, still taller than most men, but the closest one was only enraged as a bolt sank into the thick inscribed flesh.

Several Syldoon worked the levers on the devils' claws while others switched to hand-to-hand weapons, dropping the crossbows or flinging them over their shoulders as they brought shields and melee weapons to bear.

This Deserter looked even bigger than most, emerging out of the dark and into the pool of lamplight like a pale nightmare. He swung the giant spiked club, catching one of the Syldoon still spanning his crossbow in the chest, lifting him off his feet, and swinging the body into another soldier, knocking them both to the floor as he pulled the club free, blood spraying.

A Syldoon stepped into the space, thrust his sword up to try to puncture the giant's throat, but the Deserter sidled sideways, and the sword skidded off the huge pale neck, barely drawing blood. The Deserter backhanded the soldier and sent him flying, then brought his hand up to the haft, lifting the club high, about to bring the spikes down into two Syldoon who had their shields up.

Three more bolts struck the giant in the throat, and he gurgled and staggered back, lowering the club slowly as he reached up and snapped the hafts of the bolts. Another bolt slammed into the giant's face, between where the eyes should have been, and he fell into the wall and then down to the floor.

Four Syldoon marched up, shooting the giant again to be sure he was finished, and a handful of others did the same with the other Deserter who was sitting against the wall, head lowered on his massive chest.

When the bolts struck that body, the Deserter didn't even flinch.

The captain already had us moving out then. Vendurro ordered two Syldoon to watch the hallway behind us as we started for the stairs.

We stepped around the Deserter bodies, and I saw drops of blood on the floor far ahead of us, but I wasn't close enough to be sure. I was wondering how badly the third Deserter had been wounded when I felt something brush against my ankle. I jerked away from the huge boot and nearly pulled the long trigger of the crossbow.

Vendurro said, "Easy, Arki. He was just twitching a bit, nothing more." Then added with a good natured laugh, "Seen mice jump away from cats slower than that."

I stared at him, amazed he could joke in this situation. But then again, he could joke in almost any situation.

We filled out the rear, with the other two Syldoon hanging back behind us about twenty paces, and started forward at a quick walk to keep the jangling and clattering to a minimum, but there was just no good way to sneak in armor.

I didn't think we were going to catch the bloodied Deserter, not unless he dropped dead from the wounds. While I saw some more blood drops here and there on the floorboards, most smeared by the shoes in front of me, it was difficult to tell how serious the injuries were. I was no physician, but I knew a Deserter had a lot more blood pumping through its veins, which meant it could stand to lose quite a bit more before bleeding out, unless a vital organ was punctured.

We were still sixty or seventy yards from the stairwell when we halted briefly. I wasn't tall enough to make out anything that happened at the front of the line, but that didn't stop me from getting on the balls of my feet to try.

Vendurro slapped me on the back. Well, on the writing case. "Never met a curiouser soul in my life."

I regained my balance and was turning to respond when the line was moving forward again.

"See," he said, jogging alongside me, "that's the thing about soldiering. Real simple like. When you need to know something, you're told something, and when you don't, you ain't."

I was considering how to best reply to that when I saw the third Deserter body face down on the floorboards, dark circles around the multitude of bolts sticking out, mostly from its back and legs, except for what I assumed was the final bolt at the base of its skull between the twin manes that ran down its back.

I didn't have time to look at it beyond that as we raced past, closing in on the stairwell. And that's when I saw two more Deserters step out of a doorway ahead on our left. While neither was armored, one had the spiked flat-hafted greatclub in his hands, and they were no doubt checking on the commotion in the hall.

I couldn't make out much—the line stopped so abruptly I nearly ran into the man ahead of me. I heard crossbows loosed at the front and saw that the first several lines were staggered, with those in the very front kneeling, and those immediately behind fanning out to shoot over them.

A few bolts hit both giants and flew off at an angle, grazing them barely or not at all at that distance, but several struck true. One Deserter stepped back, fletching from a half-dozen bolts sticking out of his chest and stomach. The other roared as a bolt struck him in the shoulder, and he disappeared back inside the door.

The next line loosed, and four or five more bolts hit the Deserter still in the hall. The giant spun, grabbing for the wall, trying to stay upright as the Syldoon slowly advanced and the next line loosed as well. The Deserter did go down then, though he was on his hands and knees, one hand still on the wall.

Another volley finished him. And then we kept moving, those in the front tossing the crossbow straps over their shoulders and switching to melee weapons—mostly shields and one-handed weapons, except for Azmorgon, and of course Soffjian, with her ranseur. The other Syldoon kept their loaded crossbows at the ready, but I heard Vendurro say to me, "The second you shoot that bolter, you draw that blade. Might have need of it."

I kept my fingers away from the long trigger, hoping I wouldn't need to shoot the crossbow, knowing I would, and not wanting to accidentally discharge it into a Syldoon's back in front of me.

I looked back and saw Nustenzia near the rear, but not the last line where she could potentially run. Lamplight does queer things to expressions, but I was pretty sure she looked either horrified or terrified or both.

We closed in on the door, and four more Deserters started to come out, and this time they were wearing hardened leather and brass armor, or at least pieces of it, and they were all armed.

The Syldoon had two very small advantages—the Deserters apparently had no shields, and none had the javelin throwers on their backs. Braylar called a halt, and the Syldoon in the front rows dropped down while those behind them loosed.

Most of the bolts struck the targets—they were huge and hard to miss—but a few hit the stone walls behind the Deserters, and some ricocheted off the brass plates. The four giants started running down the hall, the first two with several bolts in them already.

The second row of Syldoon switched to melee weapons as the row behind took aim and loosed. One of the Deserters that was struck in the throat stumbled, and a Deserter behind him tripped over his fallen comrade, but the other two came on, roaring and cursing us in their tongue.

The next two rows of Syldoon did the same, and the other Deserter in the front slowed down, wobbled, and then fell against a wall, scrambling for support before sliding down to his hands and knees.

The other Deserter came on, with only one bolt in his barrel of a bicep, and the one who stumbled had regained his footing and wasn't far behind.

The Syldoon in front had their shields locked edge to edge, forming a small wall in the hallway, while those behind them continued reloading and shooting over them.

The first Deserter hit the shield wall, throwing his hip into the soldiers, knocking several Syldoon back as if they'd been hit by a battering ram, limbs and shields flying, and then the giant started swinging his greatclub in all directions. The three spikes blasted through one shield like translucent spear heads, driving that Syldoon to his knees until the Deserter kicked him in the chest and sent him flying back.

Swords and axes hit the Deserter, most deflected by the armor, with one axe seeming to cut deep above the Deserter's elbow. But the giant swatted that soldier away with the haft of his club, sending him spilling into the crossbowmen behind, several bolts shooting up at the ceiling. The Deserter caught a Syldoon in the side, wrenched his spiked club back out of the torso, tossed the body aside, and started swinging again.

The Deserter coming up hit a Syldoon as well, laying about with his greatclub—the three spikes drove through the scale cuirass and into the soldier's back as he tried to regain his balance, crushing him to the ground. The Deserter stepped on the body and ripped his weapon free before taking two long strides to rejoin his companion, still sowing chaos in what remained of the shield wall.

The Syldoon slashed and stabbed, drawing blood but delivering no incapacitating wounds. A Deserter blocked a blow from Azmorgon that would have destroyed any man, turned the long blade with the spikes, and stepped in, ignoring a sword slash and slamming the haft of the greatclub into the shields, sending several more Syldoon sprawling backwards.

The other Deserter paused and bellowed as a bolt slammed into his neck. While I was worried about hitting the Syldoon in front of me, the giant towered over all of them. I took aim and loosed, and my bolt hit the giant's cheekbone and flew off behind him. But he stopped moving long enough for several other Syldoon around me to do the same, two more bolts sprouting from the flesh just inside the collarbone, above the hardened leather, and another from the giant's head. That Deserter fell back out of sight.

Soffjian's ranseur shot out from the second line, the long middle tine driving deep into the Deserter's shoulder. She pulled it back as the giant grabbed for the tasseled haft. But that only seemed to enrage the Deserter more as he stepped in, the spiked greatclub coming down in an arc.

The Syldoon directly in front of him wasn't able to move back in time, and the spines drove through the wood and impaled his arm. He screamed, and the Deserter shook the greatclub, yanking the soldier forward as he slammed a fist into the shield and pulled the weapon free.

But instead of retreating back to the line, the soldier dove forward, driving his shield into the giant's crotch. The mighty Deserter bent over as three more bolts struck him, one ricocheting off a horn or the thick skull underneath, but the other two hitting him on either side of the neck.

The Deserter backhanded the Syldoon, sending him flying into a wall, but was still slow to stand back up. Then another bolt hit him in the middle of the throat and he fell backwards.

The fourth Deserter, who I thought out of the fight, came running out of the shadows at the Syldoon. Soldiers stepped up to protect their brother with the three holes in his arm, but the Deserter was faster to react and charged in, the greatclub crashing down. Even badly injured, the Syldoon still managed to get his shield up and deflect the worst of the blow, but even as the spikes skipped off the surface, he screamed in agony again, his arm likely broken as well as bleeding, and the shield didn't come back up in time to protect him from the next blow—three spikes jutted out the back of his hauberk.

Two more bolts hit the Deserter, but the Syldoon had had enough of fighting defensively—several broke the wall and ran forward, led by Braylar and Mulldoos, hobbled as he was.

The Deserter spun his greatclub with the body still impaled on it. The dead soldier flew into the Jackals, knocking one to the ground, but the others came on, surrounding the bloodied giant. He swung everywhere, the huge haft swooshing through the air as he tried to keep the Syldoon at bay, but like a bear flanked by wild dogs, he could only spin and cover himself so long.

Vendurro darted in from the rear, slashed the Deserter across the back of the legs, and managed to step away from the greatclub as the giant pivoted and tried to catch him with a two-handed blow.

Braylar and Mulldoos closed in then, the lieutenant chopping into the Deserter's legs again with his falchion, hamstringing one. The Deserter staggered and was slow to spin and attack—Braylar moved with him, and the twin flail heads lashed out, catching the Deserter on the underside of his broad chin.

The giant's head snapped back, and he fell into the wall, and then the other Syldoon were on him, weapons a blur as they attacked without remorse.

When they stepped back, the Deserter was in a bloody heap on the floor.

I heard someone vomiting and turned to see Nustenzia doubled over, weak in the knees from the looks of it, and then she sputtered and heaved again.

The Syldoon stepped away from her, but I felt sympathy, even if she was technically the enemy. I'd seen enough bloodshed with the Syldoon that my stomach no longer rebelled every time, but I remembered how awful and shocking it was to witness. Though I imagined she had seen her masters do far worse, and my sympathy dried up.

Azmorgon turned to Soffjian. "What's with the plaguing skinny poker, witch? We lost two good men on account of you! You should have—"

"You really are a massive fool. We will lose the entire company if I exhaust myself before we are free of this blasted city, you idiot. We still have the Veildome around Roxtiniak to contend with. Or had you forgotten that small detail?"

I thought Azmorgon was going to attack her when the two Syldoon who had been holding up the rear rushed forward, one of them stopping near me, the other running past and shouting, "Cap, Deserters coming. Coming fast. Pouring out of the doors behind."

Braylar got us moving again, with several Syldoon at the front pausing long enough to stab the prone Deserter bodies a few more times, conserving bolts, and several more Jackals looking at their fallen comrades as we ran past.

No more giants emerged from the last few doors, and we headed into the stairwell, taking stairs quickly as we spiraled down, shadows wild and chaotic on the stone walls. It was a relief when we passed the next two floors that housed barracks without being blockaded.

Did the Deserters have some way of sounding an alarm, alerting each other that their prisoners had escaped? They likely never expected it was possible, but the Matriarch and her ilk were incredibly powerful—they might have known the trap in our quarters had been bypassed already.

I was dizzy and winded by the time we reached the ground floor. I half-expected to find a full contingent of Deserter warriors there to crush us, but there were only a few slaves moving down the corridor, in between weak beams of gray dawn light coming through the narrow open windows along the wall. When the slaves saw us, they understandably fled the other way, and we jogged towards an unguarded doorway.

The rain was still falling beyond the columns of the entrance, but that sweet gentle sound was immediately broken by heavy footfalls coming from the stairwell as a large troop of angry Deserters closed in on us.

We ran.

As we cleared the columns, the falling rain was more than cleansing—it signified salvation. Potential salvation. That is, if I was right about the Deserters being blinded by it. If I was wrong, we would all be dead in moments.

The vicinity around the towering round keep was empty, just as it had been during the rain before. But that didn't necessarily prove anything. I swallowed hard, hoping I hadn't been a horrendous fool to suggest using the rain for cover.

Braylar ordered Syldoon to bring Nustenzia to the front. Benk grabbed her by the arm and dragged her forward. Braylar turned to her and said, "Our horses. They are nearby, yes, in the rooter pens. Direct us."

Nustenzia was still pale and shaken, and didn't respond, staring off into the rain. Braylar stepped directly in front of her. "If we are cornered in Roxtiniak, and I see the Matriarch or any of her ilk, I will do one last thing before they strike us down, and that is slit your throat. So. I ask again. Where are our horses?"

She blinked, then rubbed at her eyes, as if just now noticing the raindrops collecting on her lashes. "Yes. The pens, the royal pens. That is, I believe so, I believe they took your beasts there. I have not seen them myself. It isn't far from here. To the east." She shook her head. "But—"

"Good enough." He turned to his troops. "We move out."

We set off at a jog, not wanting to run headfirst into any opposition, but not wanting to dawdle if there was pursuit.

I looked over my shoulder and saw at least a dozen Deserters standing just inside the columns, protected from the rain, and wondered if they could sense us at all, or if there was some other reason prohibiting them from stepping out of the keep to destroy us. One or two started to walk out, looking disoriented, taking a few hesitant steps before retreating for cover.

We jogged down a broad avenue, and while there were no Deserters out, we did see a man carrying several clay jugs on a stick balanced on his shoulders. He saw a group of armed humans, dropped his stick, and ran away from us and his shattered jugs.

Vendurro said, "Gods. No wonder the cowards were so easy to plaguing conquer."

I might have countered that even the well-trained and armed elite of the Syldoon weren't exactly putting up much opposition either, and until very recently considered the Deserters gods as well, which tended to keep insurrection to a dull roar, but I was nearly out of breath and it wouldn't have done any good anyway. So I just continued to run, my case bouncing on my back, my quiver doing the same on my hip, my gambeson growing heavier with each drop of rain, as I kept the crossbow pointed up into the gray, drizzly sky and prayed to whatever gods might be listening that the rain would fall long enough for us to escape this terrible place.

We headed down a narrower cross street, encountering no one else, when we came to the huge barn that Nustenzia said housed the rooter pens. Azmorgon grabbed a handle and pulled a large door as it began to slide down a track. I was certain we would find only dead horses, or tack and harness, or nothing at all save the giant rooters staring stupidly at us, but I heard a distant whinny from somewhere deep inside. The captain led us through the opening and out of the rain, posting two men at the door.

While our eyes adjusted to the gloom, the usual smells assaulted us— horseshit, hay, and a musky stench that was so heavy it might as well have been a cloud, which I assumed was due to the rooters, who were bellowing from somewhere in the barn.

Four stable boys (stable slaves, I had to remind myself) saw us enter. One raised his arms above his head, two began backing away, and the fourth stared, motionless. Several crossbows were trained on them.

Braylar called out, "We have no wish to—" and then cursed and stopped himself. He turned to Nustenzia. "Tell them they will live, provided they do as commanded."

Nustenzia turned and gave the captain a hard look. "They are only boys," she said with disdain.

Braylar met her glare for glare. "And they will only be dead boys if you do not encourage them to comply."

It struck me then how inured to the Syldoonian methods I'd become, that she was the first to object to them, whereas I simply accepted them for what they were.

The Focus spoke to the four slaves, and the eldest stepped forward and replied in that oddly guttural and still sibilant Deserter tongue, then pointed back beyond the large rooter pens.

Nustenzia spoke to Braylar again in Syldoonian. "Your beasts are in the back. They have not gone near them."

Mulldoos growled, "They better have plaguing fed them. Or I don't give two plaguing shits how compliant they are, they'll still be dead."

Nustenzia began to reply, but Braylar cut her off. "And the saddles? Bridles?"

She looked at him blankly and he tried again, spitting each word out. "The gear they had on them, yes? Where is it?"

Nustenzia spoke to the slaves again and the eldest pointed towards the rear of the barn.

She turned to the captain. "Everything was stripped off them, put in an empty pen at the back."

Braylar addressed his men. "Find your harness, find your horses, and mount up. We will have some spare mounts now, so bring those as well. And ensure our silver-haired matron here does not need to run alongside." He looked at Nustenzia. "Have those jittery lads assist us. The sooner we ride out of here, the sooner they can return to shoveling rooter shit and being tormented by their overlords. Understood?"

She nodded and relayed the order, presumably, and everyone moved out. I walked past caged wagons, wondering which one they had used to haul us here, and several pens of hulking rooters, most of which ignored us, save for a bull that snorted and bellowed and looked ready to charge.

Our horses were all in three large pens, stomping nervously or excitedly as we approached, it was hard to be certain. I wanted to be sure my surly beast was among them but followed everyone else's lead in retrieving saddle and kit first, relieved to see that the untranslated pages were still in packs.

The slave boys moved among us, not sure what to do, looking like they were about to brown their britches at any moment, and the stoic Nustenzia seemed stiffer than usual, no doubt not looking forward to sitting on a strange creature for the first time.

I hauled the saddle back but didn't see my horse right away, but as others found theirs and narrowed the field, I saw her near the back. I'd never taken to riding, but seeing her again, the prospect of escaping here became a real thing, and it was hard to remember being happier. I patted her muzzle and stroked her neck and would have kissed her if her breath had been sweeter. It would have earned less scorn than kissing Skeelana.

I was climbing up and throwing my leg over when one of the Syldoon who had been at the front of the barn came running up and said, "Big company of Deserters coming this way, Cap."

Braylar threw me a hostile look before replying, "Oh? I was under the impression that navigating in the rain would be problematic for them."

The soldier replied, "They got some of them legless basket-riding bastards on their backs. At least fifteen of those, directing them, and another twenty or so Deserters falling in behind. Not walking real confident, but those prickless wonders are leading them through the sprinkle."

Whatever elation I felt was snuffed out like a candle between wet fingers. Azmorgon called out, "We just ride around them. Or over them."

Mulldoos replied, "You sure as shit got a tiny brain in that massive skull. They got over forty. Even if they're half blind, they can block the avenue off. No riding around that."

"Another avenue then, just take another one."

"And if that one's full of Deserters too?"

Azmorgon said, "Then we shoot the hell out of them. What other choice we got, Mushrooms? You want to plaguing surrender?"

Before Mulldoos could reply, Vendurro said, "The rooters."

Everyone looked at him and he said, "Drive them out in front of us. A stampede. Run the Deserters over, or leastwise out of the way, clear a path. We ride after them, break for the gate once we get through."

Soffjian said, "That could work, Bray." She gave a wicked smile. "And if nothing else, how often do you get to see a rooter stampeded?"

Braylar looked around until he spotted Nustenzia sitting rigidly on her horse. "Tell the boys to open the pens, herd the rooters towards the door, and we'll handle the rest."

The slaves seemed to sense what we intended and looked more frightened than before. Even the eldest who spoke for the rest was pale as he replied to her.

Nustenzia resumed Syldoonian. "Their masters will be furious if they allow anything to happen to the rooters. They might kill them."

Braylar pointed his crossbow as the closest stable boy. "But *we* will kill them if they don't. Do you see the difference? Make it very clear to them. Tell them to herd these beasts to the entrance and prepare to goad them out the door on my command."

Nustenzia's face was a mass of quivering frown lines, but she continued her conversation with the boys as Braylar spoke to his men. "On my signal, we will drive them out before us. They are already uncomfortable enough around the horses, but the creatures might need some additional encouragement to adopt the proper speed for a true stampede. But we do not kill any. Every raging rooter is our ally. Understood?"

The men all nodded or said "aye" as the boys ran ahead to unlock the pens. They looked so small and fragile moving amongst the enormous gray creatures. I worried that any attempt to set the animals stampeding was going to result in at least one or two of the slaves being crushed as well, but as harsh and brutally pragmatic as Braylar and his men were, I understood now that the safety of the Jackals outweighed everything else that might be dropped on the scales.

Some of the rooters protested loudly, snorting, bellowing, thick purple tongues lolling, but ironically enough, the boys seemed to know how to handle these creatures with skill and confidence, unlike the smaller horses that terrified them simply by being alien. The slaves used long goads to slap the thick hides and move them out of the pens, past the wagons, and towards the entrance, maintaining the correct distance to herd them without endangering themselves overmuch in the process.

Yet.

The Syldoon followed on horseback, also keen to maintain some distance, although the mere presence of the foreign beasts behind them was enough to make the rooters uneasy. I tried not to think about what would happen if the rooters turned and charged us. There was simply nowhere to run. We'd be dead before having a chance to even face the Deserters out in the rainy streets of Roxtiniak.

The boys knew their job and kept the rooters moving ahead. But the huge beasts at the fore were closing in on the half-open door, and then there was no telling how they might behave once goaded.

Braylar called ahead to the two Syldoon keeping watch, "The Deserters—how far now?"

A Jackal, not much older than the slave boys, tore his eyes off the approaching herd of rooters and looked out the crack, then reported, "Close. Real close. Eighty yards. Maybe seventy."

"Very good," the captain replied.

The soldier nodded quickly, though with rooters nearly to him and a huge party of Deserters coming from the other direction, I imagined he didn't really share that sentiment.

Braylar said, "When I give the word, pull the doors open wide. Wide as they go. And then get behind a wagon and wait for the herd to pass by. Once they do, Benk has your horse."

The Syldoon nodded again and Braylar yelled, "Nustenzia. When those doors fly open—"

"The boys will move the herd through them. Yes."

"No," he amended, "Not move. Drive. They must not amble down the avenue looking for something leafy to munch on. They need to be driven. Do you understand?"

She gave a curt nod and spoke to the stable hands again in that odd language.

Braylar cupped his hands to his mouth and shouted, "Pull, soldier! Now!"

The Syldoon pulled the doors, running them down the tracks as quickly as he could and then dodging to the side to hide behind the wagon. The boys took their cue and slapped the flanks of the rooters at the rear of the herd with their goads. The beasts roared protest, but barely moved. The boys tried again, whipping the thick pebbly hides more, but it still didn't have the desired effect.

As the rooters in the front started to slowly step through the door and into the light rain, Braylar raised his hand and lowered it quickly, and several crossbows discharged.

The bolts struck three rooters at the back end, and while they didn't penetrate deeply, it was enough to send them forward quickly, bellowing.

Braylar gave the signal again and four more bolts shot out. This time the rooters roared and charged, snapping their big square teeth on the flanks of the beasts ahead of them. The effect cascaded, the rooters at the rear rushing forward, biting and slamming their bulbous domed heads into the rooters in their way, all of them bellowing in fear or anger.

But one smaller rooter, still nearly the size of a normal wagon and with a single bolt sticking into its hindquarters, did not try to run out of the barn, but turned instead to face whatever was tormenting it. The closest thing it saw was one of the boys with a goad in his hand.

The rooter lowered its huge head and charged, legs as thick as trees propelling it across the shadow of the barn. The boy froze as the others screamed at him to run, and when he finally regained his wits and started to turn, it was too late. The rooter struck him in the lower back with its domed skull and sent him flailing over some wooden railings into a pen, limbs flying.

Crossbow bolts slammed into the rooter's side, but it was fixated on the boy and blasted through the railing after him.

Braylar shouted "Ride!" and squeezed his horse with his legs and got it moving in a hurry.

The other Syldoon obeyed, and we were all doing the same, galloping out of the barn.

I turned to my right and saw the huge humped back of the rooter in the pen as I flew past, and tried to block out the boy's screams.

We raced out of the barn and into the rain, with the rooters rushing down the avenue ahead of us. And it was a good thing they were—the men on the backs of the Deserters were pointing, shouting, and throwing javelins at the beasts.

Most of those bounced off the flanks of the stampeding rooters or missed completely, but they would have dented or torn through any of our armor. Some javelins did strike home and stick, but the rooters were too enraged now to think about turning back, and they lowered their heads and charged.

The Deserters swung their weapons in front of them, and some shuffled off to the side, clearly disoriented by the rain. They made easy targets for the rampaging rooters, who used their thick domed heads like rams.

Even the massive Deserters were no match for those colossal beasts, and they went down or were thrown into the grooved building facades on either side of the avenue.

The Syldoon galloped after the rooters, shooting any Deserters as they blew past and then spanning with the devil's claws.

Several Deserters were only knocked out of the way by the rooters, not crushed or trampled underhoof, but they were still mostly blind, and while some swung their greatclubs at us, most of them missed completely. But one connected with a passing Syldoon, impaling his shoulder and flinging the man out of his saddle.

I hoped he was dead. Because anyone stopping to help him would be.

One of the legless humans on the back of a Deserter called out, surely telling the eyeless giant where we were. I saw his face under his plumed helmet, and we locked eyes for a brief moment. The man reached for a javelin in the quiver on the side of the barrel as the Deserter slowly stepped forward, uncertain, head cocked to the side, listening, trying to get a fix on the passing horsemen.

I lifted my crossbow, sighted down the stock as best I could on a moving horse—which was to say hardly at all—and squeezed the long steel trigger as the man reared back to throw his javelin. I'd been aiming for the javelin thrower, but the bolt struck the Deserter square in the shoulder.

The giant flinched just enough to upset the throw and the javelin sailed over my head. Then I was racing past, dodging a Deserter body in the puddles and another Syldoon who was slowly crawling nowhere, blood pouring out of three holes in his chest.

We rode through some side streets, only occasionally encountering some men or women trudging through the rain and mud who jumped into alleys or doorways or pressed themselves against walls as we rode past. It was as if we were somehow worse than their memory-sucking overlords who bred them and kept their population tightly controlled. If they were smart they would have begged to ride with us. Although they would have been denied.

As we navigated the streets, I saw the Syldoon ahead of me holding the reins to Nustenzia's mount. She was gripping the saddle with white fingers, rocking wildly. I saw her looking back towards Vrulinka's keep more than once, though whether she was hoping for more pursuit or dreading it, I couldn't say. The stoicism hadn't crumbled completely, but it was clear it was cracked, and there was nothing but terror underneath.

But there were no more Deserters, and I began to hope we'd met the only opposition we were going to encounter before reaching the gate and Veil immediately beyond.

Braylar halted us briefly and ordered Nustenzia brought forward.

Soffjian wheeled her horse around to face her. "When we clear the gate, we need to pass through the Veildome. If we do not, cannot, my brother here won't have a chance to kill you, as I will do it myself. If there are any of the Matriarch's ilk here, I can resist them long enough to ensure you bleed to death on the stones. Do you understand?"

Nustenzia recovered some of her composure and haughty bearing. "I understand you perfectly. And I told you, I can only assist you in marking your warriors once we are close enough to the gate. When we are there, I will augment your attempts to do so and guide you, as I did in the keep. I am not sure what else you would like me to say. But please, threaten some more."

Braylar clenched and unclenched a fist. "And you are certain I can't simply walk us through with the flail?"

Nustenzia looked at him as if he were a child asking the same question for the fortieth time and expecting a different answer. "I do not know that for certain. I did not create the Veil. While it has a similar function as what you refer to as the Godveil, the design is different. Could you try? Yes. Could that actually kill you on the spot? Yes. Or it might do nothing. But I doubt very much that it would allow you to pass."

The captain turned and urged his horse forward again, cantering down the street, crossbow up, head on a pivot, and the rest of the Syldoon did the same.

As we rounded a multi-level terraced garden, we saw the gate ahead. It was far less fortified than anything on the other side of the Godveil, so we wouldn't have to contend with portcullises or moats or anything else. But it didn't matter.

There was a line of Deserters gathered in the rain in front of the gate. Several on either end had legless javelin throwers on their backs, as did some in the center of the line, and the rest of the Deserters wielded their great clubs or the staff slings they'd used out on the plain. And though it was hard to tell from that distance, I was relatively sure there was a thin female Deserter in robes in the middle of the line.

The javelin throwers started pointing in our direction, and though the Deserters were still stymied by the rain, they all turned towards us, and the slingers cocked their long staves back. With their incredible strength, their range outdistanced our crossbows, and while the rain helped cloak us, it could also foul the composite crossbows if they were subjected to water too long, and no one had any time to apply fat to the strings to protect them.

Braylar slowed the company long enough to spin and face us. "We ride fast and hard. Their shots will come before we close, but when we are in range, take out the javelin throwers. Those are their eyes. We do that, and they are essentially blind again. These Deserters are our final obstacle, but we must take them out to buy us time to go through the gate." He looked directly at Soffjian. "Do you have enough strength to overwhelm them as you did in the keep and still escort us through their Veil?"

Soffjian replied, "I will just have to, won't I?"

I'm sure under the mail drape Braylar twitch-smiled as he said, "Yes. Yes, you will."

One of the Jackals asked, "What about the she-bitch there in the skirts? What do we do about her?"

Braylar replied, "We don't play favorites just because someone forgot to bring a weapon to a battle."

There were some chuckles at that, but the same soldier said, "What I meant to ask, Cap, is—"

"I know precisely what you meant to ask. We hope she cannot attack us without being able to adequately target us."

"And if she can?"

Mulldoos turned and shouted, "If she can, you dumb horsecunt, then this will be the shortest plaguing fight ever. Any other plaguing idiot questions anybody is just dying to ask?"

The captain nodded at Mulldoos and then addressed the full company. "Once we dispatch the legless bastards, keep moving. And do not close with the Deserters unless absolutely necessary. We blind them, whittle them down, and then take them out when the odds tip in our favor." He looked up at the dark clouds. "It is not an especially good day for crossbows. It might be among the worst, truly, but it is still our day. We kill these giant whoresons and win free."

Vendurro muttered, "Just once, it would be nice to casually stroll out of a city without having to kill everybody."

I lifted the flap on my quiver, checked the crossbow, and silently agreed.

We started forward with Braylar setting the pace, first at a trot, and then picking up speed. I noticed something on the cobblestones, and then several somethings, and had the incongruous realization that there were worms everywhere, drawn out by the rain, now getting squished under our horses' hooves.

Then something whizzed by close, and then on the other side, above my head, though I couldn't see either. Most of the shots missed the mark, as we were still at the edge of their range, and they were using directional firing rather than trying to strike individual targets, but one or two lead balls ricocheted off a helm or some lamellar plates.

I ducked as low as I could, silently apologizing to my horse for using its neck for cover, and kept riding as more shot flew by. Luckily the staff slingers were still shooting blind, and their weapons were not as quick to loose as bows, but they had amazing range, and a few moments later another lead shot hit a rider in front of me in the chest or shoulder.

He nearly dropped his crossbow and wobbled in his saddle, slowing for moment, and I saw a large hole in his byrnie that was leaking blood that he reached up to touch, but I galloped past before seeing how badly injured he was.

The Syldoon changed direction, crossing back and forth from one side of the street to the other as they galloped on, doing their best to avoid the next volley of lead, and then they rose up almost in unison, tall in the stirrups, as they took aim with their crossbows and loosed.

I couldn't track the bolts in the rain, but I saw at least three javelin throwers jerk back in their baskets and drop out of view, dead or badly injured. Which was remarkable, given that the shooters were on moving horses and the targets mostly hidden behind the cover of Deserters.

The initial lead volleys had been arcing at a pretty high trajectory, but they came in mostly flat now, the balls zinging past, clattering off pale plaster, armor, the stones. A rider ahead of me went down when his horse was struck, crashing into the wall of a building and tumbling forward in a horrible mass of limbs that must have been breaking.

I rose up as best I could in the saddle, knowing I had no chance of hitting a javelin thrower, but doing my best to aim for the Deserter in the robes.

The bolt flew free, and while it didn't hit her, it made her jump and step back, and that was something.

I had to slow as I spanned the crossbow, lacking the skill and dexterity that came with hundreds of hours of practice, and I held my breath as I did, riding as close to a wall as I could, hoping a lead ball didn't suddenly rip through my chest or kill my horse.

When I looked up again, the Syldoon were far ahead of me, so I urged my horse on and nearly fell out of the saddle as she bolted forward. Several javelin throwers were dead or badly injured, as the Syldoon pulled up and wheeled around in a somewhat crowded version of the rolling gear formation Braylar and his men had performed against the Hornmen—they rode in, curling off just outside of javelin range, shot, and retreated.

But the staff slings kept whipping forward, and while the Deserters were still mostly blinded by the rain and unable to aim properly, they knew which direction to loose the lead, and either had some idea where the Syldoon were ahead of them or managed to get lucky, as three more soldiers went down, one crawling towards a building, the other two immobile in the street.

When the Deserters recognized that the Syldoon weren't riding close enough to engage them, they started forward slowly, using the remaining javelin throwers for directions, greatclubs at the ready. They didn't have any cohesion, but they were coming.

The thin Wielder stayed near the rear but followed the surging line of Deserters as well, hands outstretched, but turning her head this way and that, looking uncertain.

One Syldoon had the same idea I did and tried to take her out, riding closer than the rest and into range of javelins, his crossbow up near his chin as he dodged one javelin and took aim.

The bolt flew free and struck the female Deserter in the shoulder, but as the Syldoon turned and started retreating, a Deserter had run up several more paces to give his thrower a better shot, and that javelin arced through the air and struck the Syldoon in the small of the back. The soldier slumped over his horse, and the animal kept galloping.

Another Syldoon tried to grab the reins, but the beast had other ideas and raced between the soldiers, carrying the badly wounded or dead man along with him.

I raised my crossbow as I slowed down, careful to stay well out of range, and shot at the Wielder again as well, but hit a Deserter in front of her instead.

A lead shot rang off the side of my helm. Though it at least partially struck the brim and saved me from losing my head entirely, I still felt like I'd been hit in the head with a maul, and went black for several moments.

When I opened my eyes again, ears ringing, vision blurry, I realized my horse had slowed but hadn't changed direction. The staggered line of Deserters was fifty yards away and moving forward, inexorably.

Two more lead balls whizzed nearby, and I was about to jerk the reins and give the horse my heels when several Syldoon rode by, Braylar and his officers among them. Javelins flew, and more lead shot, but none hit the mark. Several Syldoon loosed their crossbows, and I saw one more javelin thrower slump back against the basket, a bolt in his face under the brim of his plumed helm.

But the Syldoon were only opening the way for Soffjian—she had her arms outstretched, the ranseur held vertically in one of them, and stopped about twenty yards from the closest Deserter. A javelin flew over her right shoulder, nearly striking her, and then two more Syldoon shot at the thrower, at least one bolt hitting him and causing him to take cover behind the bulk of the Deserter.

The rain was slowing, and the giants were close enough now that they must have been able to discern outlines, as several charged at Soffjian, their huge limbs churning, water and mud spraying with each thunderous step. She maintained her position, head tilted up, face in the rain, and the Syldoon halted around her, loosing the last of their bolts before they would have to ride off or draw their sidearms.

I fumbled with my quiver, drawing a bolt, and tried to work the devil's claw, my hands seemingly weighted down with iron shackles, my arms moving slowly, ears still ringing from the lead shot. I looked up and saw Soffjian tense, fearing the worst, that the female Deserter had countered her, or that she was hit by a staffslinger, but then the Deserters in the line stopped and then reeled, some dropping to their knees, others moving even more slowly than me, aimlessly, drifting away from the Memoridon.

The Syldoon closed in on them, shooting, reloading, shooting.

Even when the Deserters were hit several times, bolts sticking out every which way, they didn't react except to lurch further, or collapse. One by one they fell, as the Syldoon circled and shot them.

The female Deserter strode forward, the front of her robes a pink stain as rain diluted the blood dripping out her wound, and while she was unsteady on her feet, the thin giant raised her good arm and suddenly Soffjian lurched to the side, dropping her ranseur.

A bolt took the Wielder in the chest, and she dropped as well, but the damage was done. Several Deserters stood upright again now that Soffjian's hold on them was broken, and one swiped his greatclub at a passing Syldoon, catching him in the midsection and catapulting him out of the saddle.

Another Deserter swung at a horseman and missed, still disoriented or not seeing his opponent clearly, but pivoted and caved in the helm of another Syldoon with his backswing as the soldier tried to ride past.

The Syldoon rode off in all directions, putting distance between them and the remaining giants as they spanned their crossbows, all save Azmorgon, who charged ahead, his polearm in both hands angled back down the side of his horse. He galloped past one of the Deserters and used the long blade to slice a deep gash across the giant's thigh, just below a triangular brass plate. The Deserter was swinging his club but was too slow and then went down hard, his leg failing.

All the javelin throwers were dead, so even though two Deserters still had their staff slings, they seemed to have given up using them to discharge lead and were wielding them just like quarterstaffs as they moved off in the direction of the mounted Jackals.

Having taken out the ranged weapons or rendered them mostly useless, and with the Wielder down, the Syldoon could have simply ridden circles around them, filling the giants full of bolts until they were dead or weak enough to finish off.

But one soldier called out to Braylar and Mulldoos and got their attention, then pointed back in the direction of the center of the city and the round keep. Another battalion of Deserters was coming, guided by more half-men javelin throwers, and with another Wielder in their midst.

The captain ordered us to break for the gate. We were out of time.

Vendurro rode up alongside Soffjian, who was still in the saddle, but only barely, head forward, chin on her chest, and in danger of falling over at any moment. It was a wonder she hadn't already.

Braylar yelled, "Wake her!"

Vendurro shook her shoulder, and that did nothing except nearly unhorse her. He grabbed her arm, and shouted at her, but that had no discernible effect either. The young lieutenant looked at his captain and then grabbed Soffjian firmly and slapped her across the face with the back of his hand.

Soffjian's head finally rose up from her chest, but she looked drunk, barely responsive.

Vendurro wrenched her around, to no real effect. Then he pulled a costrel off his saddle, uncorked it, tilted her face up, and poured whatever fluid was there down her throat. She sputtered and threw her head side to side, then suddenly seemed more coherent as she grabbed his wrist and drew her suroka.

Vendurro said, "Sorry about that, but we got to leave. Oh, and you dropped your big sticker." He handed her the ranseur.

The Syldoon assembled near the captain, and I rode over and joined them as well. He looked at the half dozen Deserters still in the street further up, bleeding and wounded and unguided, but still very dangerous, slowly making their way towards us, though the light rain was still causing them difficulty.

Then Braylar pointed to the approaching battalion. "We have little time and less. So, we ride around those hulking bastards who have not obliged us by dying yet and make a run for the gate. They will likely shamble in pursuit, so while Soffjian prepares us to exit this wretched city, we will form up and shoot them to pieces. Then we ride out, never to return. Yes?"

Everyone nodded.

Braylar looked at the Syldoon bodies littering the street and said, "If you see any survivors, get them on the spare horses."

Azmorgon asked, rumbling like thunder, "And if they ain't fit to ride?"

Braylar gave him a long hooded look before replying, "Give them mercy. We leave no one for the Deserters to torture or slaughter."

The remaining Jackals started forward down the wet street, crossbows again spanned and at the ready, save for Azmorgon and Soffjian.

I still felt woozy as we rode forward, and prayed no one had to dispatch a broken or dying Syldoon soldier, as that would surely make me throw up. Luckily, the Deserters weren't much for half measures—if they struck you cleanly, there was an excellent chance you were dead.

We picked up speed, and the Deserters raised their weapons, hearing the hooves on the wet stones, but no horseman came close enough to strike down. Everyone shot a bolt, including me, though I missed badly, and I looked over my shoulder as we flew past. One more Deserter fell backwards with two bolts in its throat.

The wooden gate was still open, so that was something, but the Veil beyond was shimmering. Braylar looked at his sister. "Ready then?"

Soffjian was pale, and the lightning-bolt vein was pulsing in her forehead, but she nodded. "This would have been a pointless exercise otherwise, Bray."

She stayed in the saddle ten paces from the Veil and called Nustenzia over, who looked more shaken than anyone, despite not suffering a single wound. Soffjian said, "I will mark them, as before, correct?"

Nustenzia replied, "Yes. As before. Though I will need to help you. The mark must go deeper. Much deeper. If we do not embed it, I cannot promise what will happen."

Soffjian gave the Focus a grim look. "I can promise what will happen if we fail. We begin."

The first two Syldoon rode up, and Soffjian raised her hands and closed her eyes. Nustenzia did the same. Several moments crawled by, and I looked back down the main avenue, though I turned my head too quickly and had to bite back bile and close my eyes for a moment. When I opened them, I saw the broken Deserters coming for us and heard the heavy twang of the crossbows all around. One by one, they fell, and still the rest came on, either not realizing how depleted their force was or driven by compulsions that made no sense to a human mind.

As I took aim, I heard Soffjian say, "Go."

The pair of Syldoon looked at Braylar, but she repeated the order. "I believe I said you were ready. Go now."

Braylar nodded, and the Syldoon rode forward. I wasn't the only one who watched to be sure they didn't drop dead on the spot, but they disappeared into the woven, shifting whorls of air beyond the gate.

The captain shouted, "Enough, you gaping twats! Loose! Loose, plague you!"

The remaining Syldoon shot their crossbows and began spanning as more approaching Deserters dropped, huge bodies slumping to the cobblestones.

When half the remaining company had parted the Veil, the last of the nearest Deserters lay in a puddle of blood twenty paces away. But the other battalion was coming, guided by the javelin throwers, still beyond the range of lead balls, but not by much, and their force was at full strength. We could not possibly survive an assault, especially with two of our own leaving at a time.

Braylar finished spanning his bow and slapped the devil's claw on the stock. "By all means, sister, do take your sweet time."

She didn't reply but began preparing the next pair to leave.

There were only eight of us left when the first lead ball struck the wall ten feet above us, raining plaster down.

Soffjian ushered another pair of Syldoon forward. Braylar looked at Mulldoos. "You, Ven next, then Azmorgon and Arki."

Mulldoos started to shake his head, but Braylar stopped him before he could say anything. "That is a direct order. Go now."

"Cap, you—"

"I shouldn't have to suffer insolence at every turn. I will be right behind you."

Another lead shot struck ten paces to our left, followed by another hitting the cobblestones in front of us, spraying water and bouncing forward and nearly spooking Vendurro's horse.

Braylar said, "Now, Lieutenant. Unless you want me to get shot to death."

Mulldoos swore and grabbed his reins and headed to the gate, with Vendurro following.

Braylar looked at me. "My apologies for not sending you through sooner, Arki, but—"

"Jackals first," I said.

"What I was going to say was, I didn't even recognize you." He tilted his head in the direction of more lead striking, then looked at the last Azmorgon. "Keep moving, the both of you, but in no pattern. The cockless javelin chuckers are spotting for them, so let's make their jobs a bit more difficult at least, yes?"

We all started off in different directions as more lead struck the walls and gate around us, and it reminded me of dwarves at a fair, running back and forth as paying patrons threw rotten fruit at them. Only if we got hit now, it would be us splatted on the stones.

Several more lead balls ricocheted off the wall and street around us as we rode back and forth. Mulldoos and Vendurro went through the Veil, and Braylar turned to me. "Now you and—"

A lead ball caught the edge of the mail aventail on his helm. Had it struck cleanly, it would have crushed his throat, but even a glancing blow left him dazed for a moment. Braylar turned and shot his crossbow high in the air to achieve the greatest arc, then threw the strap over his shoulder as he pulled his shield off the saddle. "Go. Both of you. Now."

I rode up to the gate with Azmorgon, and as before on the other side, I didn't experience much as Soffjian lifted her shaky hands and held them alongside my face, except the waves of nausea and dizziness I was already battling.

Two lead shot struck nearby—Soffjian didn't waver, but Nustenzia ducked and looked around.

Soffjian hissed, "Concentrate, you stupid wretch."

Nustenzia closed her eyes again and lifted her hands. I suddenly felt an impact on my back, as if I'd been hit by a mace, and nearly fell out of my saddle. And then Soffjian ushered us through. The Syldoon were all gathered fifty yards from the Veil, and we rode over to them. I cursed every step my horse took, willing myself not to vomit, and hoping I didn't have a lead shot in my lung. I didn't see any exit wound, then remembered the writing case on my back. The thick brass panels might have saved my life.

No one said a word as we all waited, and it seemed too long. Much too long.

Mulldoos pulled his aventail drape up, turned, and spit into the grass near the road, and several Syldoon looked around nervously.

Vendurro said, "Plague me. Do you think—"

But then two more lead balls flew through the Veil, followed immediately by Braylar, his sister, and Nustenzia.

He rode up to us and said, "Ride, you whoresons! Ride!"

We rode clear of the Veiled City, and it was a good thing I wasn't in command, as I would have kept us at a wild gallop until every horse came up lame while Roxtiniak was still on the horizon. But Braylar maintained a measured pace, hooves pounding in the mud as we headed west, but at a controlled trot as the miles came and went, breaking on occasion to rest the animals, and then hopping back in the saddle as night came on.

If there was any pursuit, the drizzle continued to come down and thwart them for several hours, finally reduced to nothing more than a fine mist as the clouds broke free and showed the moon racing between them. We rode through the night, and the captain resumed his normal protocol of ordering scouts behind and riding far ahead, but we had established a solid enough lead that Braylar finally called a longer halt a few hours before dawn.

After removing my saddle and caring for my horse with eyes half closed and muscles aching, I was about to collapse when I felt an especially sharp pain in my back and remembered the shot that nearly did me in.

I pulled my writing case off to inspect it. Even though the shot had come in at an angle, the lead ball still punctured one side—which was hardly thin—tearing through the brass panel as if it were glass or gossamer. I flipped the case around, and the other side was dented where I'd felt the impact, but the shot hadn't made it out the other panel. I undid the clasp and opened the case and saw a hole through a stack of papers inside—the lead ball was deformed and flattened, pressed up against the last few sheets.

Vendurro was walking by as I pried the flattened lead out, careful to shield the pages and materials from what remained of the misting rain.

He gave me a blank look. "Lousy time to write, ain't it?"

I explained what happened and showed him the case, and we marveled at it together as he stuck his finger through the hole on the outside. Then he whistled and said, "Maybe we ought to start making armor out of thick paper, eh?"

He walked off, chuckling. I didn't have the energy. I nearly tumbled onto the least soaked ground I could find, laid back against the saddle, clutched a blanket around me to try to stay warm and dry, and then almost immediately slipped into black slumber. A battalion of approaching Deserters couldn't have woken me.

But sometime before dawn, Braylar's sharp tongue did. He ordered us to break our fast quickly and get back in the saddle. When we were all up and moving again, the sun joined us. The rain clouds had scattered, leaving behind wispy barges gently floating, suffused with the softest, sweetest colors imaginable, the pastels of comforting flowers and delicate gowns, confectioner's delights and exotic fruits.

Vendurro was riding ahead of me alongside Mulldoos, and I saw him tilt his head up and say, "Those Deserter bastards might be bigger, more powerful, maybe even smarter—"

"Definitely smarter," Soffjian said.

Vendurro continued, undeterred. "But they'll never be able to take in something like this. We got that over those giant horned whoresons at least. They'll never see a sunrise."

Rudgi was behind me as she said, "Or their own plaguing shadows for that matter. Or—"

"Or the color of their shit," Mulldoos finished. "The only thing I care about them seeing or sensing or whatever it is they plaguing do is the edge of my blade as I cut them down and murder them into bits."

Azmorgon turned around in his saddle. "We're riding the wrong way to do that, Mushrooms."

Mulldoos said, "Now, sure. Got no advantage. No chance. But someday I'm going to come back here and kill every damned Deserter we come across."

Azmorgon rumbled a laugh. "You are, are you? Cap in on that plan, or that just you bibble-babbling away on your lonesome?"

Mulldoos turned and spit, and seemed to be regaining some control of his lips and mouth, as he didn't splatter himself with it at all. "Every. Plaguing. One. I don't care how, but I'm doing it."

Soffjian said, "My, my, but that's an ambitious list. First, we have to cross the Godveil again and slaughter Cynead and every Leopard we come nose to nose with, and then we have to come back to this side and eradicate a race of massive near-gods whose only apparent limitation is that rain befuddles them and they can't see rainbows after."

Mulldoos slapped the helm hanging on his saddle. "There ain't anything godly about those giant horsecunts, and nobody asked you for help or even invited your plaguing input."

Vendurro shook his head. "And you say I've been kicked in the head too many times by a horse . . ."

There was some muted chuckling from Rudgi, and I smiled as well, but it was short-lived. Braylar silenced us with, "Now that the rain is gone, and likely for good, we'd best hope our lead suffices. They overtook us before, they can do so again."

Once again, there was a heaviness hanging in the air. Even if Mulldoos's dreams of bloody vengeance weren't remotely realistic, the reasons he had them were all too real and terrible. Braylar's company had been cut down by two thirds at the hands of the Imperials and then the Deserters. What began as a small army was now only a largish band, and it was too much to think on all the men and women who'd been lost already. And yet, that's all that seemed to occupy Mulldoos's mind mile after mile. Maybe all that sustained him.

That was one (and possibly the only) distinct advantage to being on the edge of the company, no matter how close I rode to the retinue—I had only recently formed indeterminate relationships with a small number of Jackals. I hadn't trained anyone, seen them develop, lived and fought and argued with them for years, hadn't hung alongside them or watched them transform from barbarian youth from the hinterlands of the world to some of the finest soldiers in the center of it. I would never be solidly in the Syldoon brotherhood, no matter how much they accepted me for what I could do.

And while that gave me some pangs of loneliness, that was far preferable than overwhelming hate-fueled grief.

The sunrise suddenly didn't seem so beautiful. In fact, it seemed mocking.

At midday we rested again, and the scouts reported that there was no sign of pursuers behind and no blockade ahead. After feeding and watering the horses and allowing them to graze in the stubbly, rough-edged grass, and then taking some sustenance ourselves, I had the chance to finally open my writing chest and began recording everything that had happened since the previous session. Some of it was still fresh in awful clarity, but I needed to ask Vendurro some questions to refresh some points and make sure I didn't leave out any important notes.

It felt so good to pick up a quill again. I might have been wearing a foul-smelling gambeson, and loosed a number of bolts that had ended life, but there was no question what my true vocation was, no matter how much I played at soldier and somehow survived another day.

And still, I hadn't put down four lines before my head started pounding, then swirling with dizziness, then pounding some more, and as I pressed on, it got nothing but worse, to the point that I felt nauseous and had to stop.

I wondered if I would have a chance to do any more translating soon, but with how awful I felt, I was almost relieved when Rudgi stopped by.

She started to say something, stopped, looked me over again. "You feeling all right, Arki? Looking kind of whitish and sweaty and, uh, not good."

I nodded, closing up my case, and even that small movement sent tremors of pain across my skull and down my spine. "I'm fine. Just took a shot to the head. I'll be fine." I corrected myself. Sort of. "I'm fine."

She nodded slowly. "Uh-huh. Fine it is. As you say. Anyway, Cap wants you."

I tried to stand, withstood another wave of nausea, and then steadied myself. "Well then. Best not to keep him waiting."

I walked slowly, taking stock with each step to be sure I truly was fine and not at risk to fall over unconscious or throw up on my feet.

Rudgi walked alongside me, eyeing me closely, which made me try to walk taller and wobble less. "I told you," I said, "I'm—"

"Fine. Ayyup," she said, sounding absolutely unconvinced. "So you did."

She led me away from the remainder of the company and around a small red butte.

When we were out of view, I came upon the captain and Soffjian standing together, which surprised me. They didn't occupy each other's company unless it was absolutely necessary or they were under duress. Neither of which boded well.

Rudgi stopped twenty paces off and let me continue the rest of the way unescorted. Which was just as well. The clouds had deserted the sky almost entirely and the sun wasn't doing my blinding headache any favors.

Braylar appeared ready to say something to his sister when he saw me approaching and waited. He looked at the case hanging by my side, then at my face. "Glad to be reunited with your old friend, I expect. Vendurro told me that case, or the contents at least, saved your life. Extraordinary, how things do play out sometimes. Are you whole, on the whole? You look . . . pained."

It might as well have been written on my face with red ink, though I felt foolish, given that countless others were dealing with more egregious physical wounds, and Mulldoos (and Hewspear, before his demise) had fought through far more debilitating abrasions of the mind. I nodded, careful to keep it small and slow, just the same. "A small head injury, Captain. Nothing serious. I am well." He continued staring at me in that entirely disconcerting way he'd mastered. "Truly," I added.

Braylar twitch-smiled. "You are a tragically bad liar. What is it— dizziness, pain?"

I gave a small nod. "Both. Yes."

"Anything else then?"

"Some nausea. And spots. I see spots on the edge of my vision, and it's a bit difficult to concentrate."

"That sounds less than auspicious. So now I ask with some trepidation: are you well enough to resume translating? That is the critically important question."

I nearly laughed at myself for thinking he had my interests at heart. "I believe so."

The captain shook his head and clicked his tongue in his mouth. "No, no, that will never do. Either you are fit to carry out your duties or you are unfit. There is no middle ground. Everyone in this company has a role to perform, and in many cases, others can step in to spell them or replace them entirely if they are lost. But you are rather more indispensable in your capacity. So I ask again, and recommend you do not dissemble or suffer undue bravado: are you fit to do this thing or not, Arki?"

"I am," I replied, hoping I sounded more confident than I felt. "I just finished bringing our account current. Which left me with several other questions."

He smiled again, a bit longer than usual, somewhere beyond wry and just short of humorless reflex. "But of course it did. For better or worse, that is your nature, is it not? Though in this instance, it is for the worse. We move with haste, so your questions, no matter how weighty and laden with import in your mind, will simply need to wait."

I glanced at Soffjian as she absently flicked over a small flat stone with the butt spike of her ranseur. She looked at me, and I said, "With respect, Captain, while my inquisitiveness might be a burr under your saddle most days, on this occasion I hope you will hear me out."

Braylar replied, "You have been taking far too many lessons from Vendurro of late. 'With respect' is an empty preamble designed to convince the listener to tolerate the absolutely impertinent point that immediately follows. I'm not sure which I despise more—that slyness or the blunt irreverence Mulldoos is so fond of."

"Or," Soffjian offered, "the near mutinous open stupidity of Azmorgon."

"Quite," he said. "At least Arki's foolishness is more tolerable on the whole." He gave me a hard look. "If barely. So, ask then. What is so pressing?"

I shielded my eyes from the sun, then moved around so I stood more squarely in the shade and tried to compose my thoughts.

"Be quick about it," the captain barked, no longer especially concerned with my well-being.

Still a little dizzy, I replied, "I suspect you two didn't amble out here simply to rehash pleasant family memories."

Soffjian said, "That would surely be a short rehashing, over before it really began, and requiring half the distance we took."

"So," I said, "I assume you are discussing our immediate future after we cross back over. And how we intend to, uh, reclaim the Memoridons."

"How very perceptive of you," Braylar said. "Any other clever observations to regale us with, or did you actually intend to arrive at these pertinent and pressing questions?"

"Well, this whole time we've been thinking that we would have to replicate what Cynead did somehow, use a cabal of Memoridons—"

"Really, Arki?" Soffjian asked. "*Cabal?* You sound like Mulldoos now."

"Fine," I amended. "Circle, or group, or whatever other name you prefer. We assumed we would need several Memoridons to reverse what he'd done, steal the control back and transfer it to Thumaar, correct?"

"Yes," Braylar said, clearly growing more impatient with each passing moment. "Another astute observation. And still no closer to anything resembling a question, much less one that demands my attention."

I swallowed, my temples throbbing. "But what if there were another way?"

The captain gave me a peculiar look. "You haven't resumed translating, so you couldn't have uncovered anything to suggest there might be. So now I am beginning to wondering if that head injury is more serious than you are letting on."

"No," Soffjian said. "Let him finish. What other way are you talking about Arki?"

I said, "I don't know, precisely. But it seems to be that we have someone in our midst now who might know."

Braylar and Soffjian were both quiet for a moment, and I went on. "Nustenzia. She is a Focus, an augmenter, correct? That is what you said, Soffjian, wasn't it?"

"It is indeed." She began to smile.

"Well," I continued. "If we can figure out the exact method of breaking Cynead's control and reclaiming it for ourselves, then perhaps we wouldn't need a cab—, that is, a group of Memoridons to help us after all, if Nustenzia amplifies what Soffjian does. She could serve. It might be enough."

Soffjian's smile growing marginally wider, and Braylar's scowl minutely less fierce. She replied first, "That is an outstanding idea, Arki. Brilliant, even."

I tried not to swell up at the unexpected praise, but she pricked it a bit by saying, "I should know—I was suggesting the very thing just before you arrived."

Braylar seemed less impressed. "It is an idea. Possibly good, possibly impossible. While we consider its merits, it is imperative you continue your translation at every opportunity."

When I didn't respond immediately, his eyes narrowed. "*Now* qualifies as one such opportunity, archivist. We ride soon, but you will need to use what little time you are afforded wisely."

"Yes, Captain."

He looked off towards where the camp was situated. "In the meantime, we will have a bit more dialogue with our resident Focus to sound her out on the topic."

Soffjian sensed he was on the move, as she fell in right beside him, which left me to follow, pleased I still had a purpose and had rediscovered it, but wondering how ably I would be able to perform it. Translating ancient texts was difficult enough without dealing with a crippling headache.

We rode hard southwest for the next two days, so there wasn't a lot of downtime to translate new material, which was just as well, as my headaches continued to arrive fast, hard, and often. I saw Braylar and Soffjian pulling Nustenzia aside to interview her, though they didn't invite anyone else to join them, so there was no way to tell what, if anything, they had learned. The one time I broached the subject with the captain, he snarled and snapped and that was that.

The scouts reported a large party half a day behind us. With the clouds white and sparse, there was no chance of any assistance from the sky. We rode harder, trying to maintain our small lead, resting only briefly enough not to blow all the horses, and riding on, exhausted.

But then the Godveil appeared before us on the third day out of Roxtiniak, stretching over the floor of a valley, shimmering in the distance as it had for a millennium, created by the giants who seemed intent on destroying or husking us.

I'd never imagined I'd be so happy to see the Godveil—or Demonveil, or just Veil, depending on what we started calling it now—in my life. A few of the Syldoon behind me whooped as they rode over the ridge and saw it as well.

Even as we rode down the gentle slope towards the Veil, though, everyone seemed tight, alert, heads on swivels, the scouts ahead of us riding back to the company unmolested to announce that the way was clear.

We halted thirty or forty yards out, as we had when we first crossed over, and while the proximity made the horses skittish, I felt the nearly irresistible urge to ride forward anyway, to approach the Veil, to feel the thrum vibrate through my body, to fill my nostrils with the stringent vinegar scent, to surrender myself to whatever happened.

Braylar turned and faced us. "As before, I will guide us through ten at a time. I regret to say, it will not take nearly as long as before." He stood in the stirrups and looked up the hill towards the ridge, causing some of us to turn and look as well, but there was nothing there.

He reclaimed our attention when he called out, "Imperials attempted to destroy us. They failed. The Deserters imprisoned us, no doubt also intending to eradicate us as well. We escaped, and they failed. A lesser company would be nothing but bones now. But we have survived, and will continue to do so until we carry out this mission, and the next, and every other mission our Tower Commander sees fit to give us. We live and die at the behest of our Commander, and our true Emperor once we reinstate him on the throne."

Braylar scanned the group, head slowly turning, mail aventail slithering. "But as you well know, a captain often has latitude in carrying out our missions. And this captain swears to you that one day, our dead will be avenged. We will make our enemies bleed for this. And bleed some more. But today," he said, turning and pointing to the Godveil, "We cross over again. Form ranks, first line, advance with me."

But as the soldiers started lining up, Nustenzia nearly fell off her horse as she shouted, "Captain! Captain Killcoin!"

The shrill noise and the rider's nerves, as well as the proximity to the Veil, nearly sent Nustenzia's horse bolting, but Vendurro managed to grab the reins.

Nustenzia quieted, if only a little. "Captain, a word! Please!"

Braylar didn't seem overly disposed to tolerate interruptions or delays, but after hesitating, he rode closer. "Yes, Lady Focus. What, pray tell, is so pressing?"

She looked at the Godveil and then back to him, face fallen, wrinkles somehow seeming to be carved deeper, any pretense of haughtiness broken. "I can't. I can't go."

Even with only his eyes visible, there was no question they registered ten kinds of irritation. "Oh, you can, in fact. It is quite simple. All you must do is stop startling your horse, hold hands, take a deep breath, and cross. I assure you, you can and you will."

Nustenzia started shaking her head, so quickly in fact I was worried she was going to hurt herself. "Physically. Yes. I don't doubt you. But I thought you were only keeping me as a hostage. You don't need to take me beyond here. I am no use to you."

Braylar laughed, a jagged, dangerous sound. "Oh, Lady Focus, you are very much wrong on that score. It could be said, is being said, in fact, that your worth has tripled almost overnight. We have great need of your services."

She looked back in the direction of Roxtiniak. "I have . . . I have a family."

Mulldoos said, "We all got a plaguing family. Most of them are horsecunts."

"A son," she said, still directing it to Braylar, hoping she might have better luck appealing to him than his gruff lieutenant. "I have a son. I can't leave him. Please. Let me stay here. Please. I—"

Mulldoos said, "Let me guess. Three tenyear if he's a plaguing day, am I right? Look at those wrinkles. No way you got a little one to look after back there."

Nustenzia did look at him then, and it was very good she didn't possess Soffjian's particular skills, or he would have been writhing in the dust, his mind carved out from the inside. "I had him late, if you must know. But no, he is no babe. Still, he is a lad. And he is . . . simple." She turned back to Braylar. "And he does need me. Very much. Please. Don't take me."

She was as plaintive as anyone I'd ever heard, but she might as well have been appealing to one of the stones nearby. I dreaded his words even before Braylar spoke them. "You are lucky, in fact, that you are still valuable to me at all, or I would likely cut you down here and now and leave you to feed the skullbugs. Serve me well, do as you are told, and perform the single task you will be assigned, and perhaps I will look more favorably on letting you return to your simple son. Until then . . ." and he directed the next to the rest of the company as he spun his horse around. "Form up!"

The soldiers obeyed, and Nustenzia leveled Braylar with the same sharp gaze she'd fixed on Mulldoos moments ago. It might not have been unwittingly, but he had clearly made himself another enemy.

I could cross the Veil a hundred times and never get used to the sensation, and it did nothing to lessen the ache in my temples, but walking out the other side was worth both the disorientation and the pain. The terrain was identical, of course, but it was the feeling that possibly, maybe, we could ride a single day without looking over our shoulders or facing a new foe who sought to impede or destroy us.

Closing my eyes, I tried to block everything out to see if I smelled a whiff of Skeelana's cloying perfume.

Nothing.

Of course, even if the way ahead was clear, that didn't mean we were remotely safe. What was to say the Deserters couldn't simply follow us? They'd created the Veil, after all, or their ancestors had. Even if they hadn't made an appearance on our side for a thousand years, it seemed overly optimistic to assume that was due to a lack of ability. If they hadn't needed something like Bloodsounder to create it in the first place, they surely didn't need an artifact like that to cross over. Perhaps they could part the Veil as easily as a silk curtain, with no repercussions at all.

I moved ahead a bit until I was alongside Nustenzia. I wondered if I had looked that wholly inept the first few times I was forced to ride with the Syldoon. It seemed like an awfully long time ago. I probably had, though at least I had *seen* a horse before. All things considered, she was doing far better than I could have in her position.

"Hello," I said, rather lamely, unsure how to begin, and falling back to basic greetings.

She glanced at me, and then back to the riders ahead of us, as if she might lose total control of the beast if she looked away for more than a moment. "Yes?"

Cold, but not entirely as hostile as I expected. "The captain, he does keep his word," I offered as some balm, consoling myself that it wasn't entirely untrue . . . he did keep his word—to his Tower Commander and Jackals. The rest of the world could burn and rot.

Nustenzia didn't glance my way again, or say anything, but I thought I detected a slight softening of her features, if only briefly. Then the composed and stoic mask was firmly back in place. "I expect you did not ride next to me simply to assuage me for being kidnapped, taken from my child, and transported into another world."

I nearly objected that it was the same world, but obviously that was a terrible lie. "No," I admitted. "I just had a few questions."

"Questions," she sighed. "Yes, you, the oathkeeping captain of yours, his relentless and insistent sibling, you all do so love to pose questions. I have answered theirs. I could answer ten thousand of them and not earn my way back to the other side, though. Isn't that right, Arkamondos?"

If she used my full name to make me feel more guilty or accountable, it worked. Extraordinarily well. "I can't speak for the captain, nor his sister, but he did promise your chances of returning weren't hopeless, provided you are compliant. I'm not sure this qualifies though. In fact, it seems downright uncooperative. I really would have to report that."

Rudgi was on the other side of Nustenzia and listening to our conversation, and she leaned forward to look past the Focus, shaking her head with a small smile that seemed a mix of surprise and appreciation. Four tenday ago, I never would have dreamed of shooting or even hurting anyone, tried to be forthright and ingenuous, and considered myself a better person for both. And now, I'd killed several foes, and here I was, manipulating and bullying a captive into answering my questions. I really was becoming more Syldoonian by the day.

I felt Nustenzia giving me the glare and ignored it, staring ahead, waiting her out. Finally she said, "Ask, then, disciple of devils. Ask as you must."

"I believe insults also fall into the category of failure to be pliant, but let's ignore that." I heard Rudgi chuckle and ignored her as well. "Your masters—who, by the way, are the only real devils, if you ask me, enslaving and husking and destroying countless humans for a thousand years—do they—"

"And do not your overlords enslave as well for half that time?" she countered.

Rudgi said, "She's got herself a fair point there, Arki."

Irritated, I pressed on, not wanting to argue semantics or degrees of deviltry. "As I said, your masters, the Deserters, what prevents them from passing through the Veil after us?"

Nustenzia gave me a long look, deep wrinkles across her forehead, a "V" between her eyebrows so pronounced it might as well have been another scar on her face. But otherwise the look was impenetrable, and I wasn't sure what she was weighing. Then she said, "I cannot say for certain."

"Cannot or will not?"

Nustenzia paused and replied, "Both."

Rudgi laughed. "You're quite the interrogator, Arki. Got some real talent for this sort of thing."

I forced myself not to respond to her and spoke to Nustenzia instead. "They created the Veil. Certainly the Matriarchs at least must be able to pass through. Maybe more."

Nustenzia stared straight ahead. "As I said. I cannot say. I suspect you are right. But I have never seen it done. And there is an edict that forbids any from trying."

"What? A punishable-by-death sort of thing?"

"Yes. Exactly that sort of thing. That is the way most edicts work, is it not?"

Rudgi laughed again.

I pressed on. "So it must be possible, if a hard mandate forbids it."

"Or was possible at one time," Rudgi said. "Some edicts are older than stone."

"Yes," I said. "So which is it? Do they still possess the ability? Do we need to worry about them following us to this side?"

Nustenzia did her best to maintain the rigid demeanor, but I had her horse on my side—it is nearly impossible to show disdain when bouncing around and fearing for your life. Still, she was moderately successful. "Never having seen it done, I cannot say whether it is lack of ability or ancient edict that prevents them from doing so."

Rudgi said, "Every rule ever made's been broken by somebody somewhere. If they could have done it, somebody would have, sure as spit. You ever hear any records of it happening, Arki?"

"No," I said slowly, drawing it out, wondering if I might remember something to refute myself. "But that doesn't—"

"No is the answer," Rudgi said. "That's why they're called the Deserters, after all—they left us high and dry. Never showed their horny faces again, am I right?"

I said, "True, no one claims to have seen them return or recorded it. But the Deserters are the memory masters, are they not, even dwarfing Memoridon skill. Perhaps they did, or can return, and simply eliminated any witnesses, or their memories of the event anyway."

Rudgi thought about that. "Possible, I guess. Just as possible that even if they could do it at one time, they lost the art of it at some point, and that edict is just to keep anybody from killing themselves trying."

Nustenzia had listened to our conversation long enough and snapped, "You do not know or understand them. Or us. I do not pretend to know what kind of deviants and lawbreakers you have on this side of the Veil, but humans do not disobey our masters. And the masters are the most deliberate race ever created. Whether they have the ability or not, an edict is the law, and the law was created by their ancestors to be followed."

"Or," Rudgi countered, "maybe they just drop dead if they try, same as us. But that would throw a huge old hole through your master worship, wouldn't it, like a stone through a pretty window."

Nustenzia bobbled and tried to right herself. "I. Cannot. Say. If you recall, that was and is my position."

"Fine," I said. "Let us try another tack, then. Why did they erect the Veil the first place? I mean, Vrulinka showed us that our memories are offensive, even poisonous to them. But how did they fail to recognize that? And if they were powerful enough to create the Veil and murder and enslave half the world on the other side, why not simply take out the bulk of the human race everywhere?"

Nustenzia glared at me, lips tight, wrinkles deepening. "Do you imagine I was there?"

"I imagine," I said, biting off the words, "that you are a Focus, and serve the Wielders, so you must be familiar with the history."

Nustenzia didn't respond right away, and I was about to ask again when she finally said, "My masters were in remote holdfasts on this part of the world. They did not live among humans, and preferred their own company. So while they understood there were differences between us, and that we were certainly inferior in many respects, they also knew our memories were potent. But they assumed this was simply another difference, and the volatility of our memories was simply another weakness."

"So," Rudgi said, "they didn't know they were poisonous?"

"I expect not," Nustenzia replied. "Or they might have wiped you out when they were still numerous enough to do so." She said this with bitter regret, seeming to forget if that had happened she never would have been born.

I asked, "So what happened? How did they discover it?"

"Humans live shorter, more violent lives. But breed faster. You encroached on them. Crowded them. It was only when your populations had swelled too large, and their members began to grow sick and die off, that they realized you were responsible."

"You say that as if it were malicious."

"No," Nustenzia replied, growing angrier, the runes carved into her face flushed. "But we are a sickness. And when a limb is infected, you have no choice but to excise it or die. So that is what they did."

I nodded. "So they weren't powerful enough to eradicate us, but they somehow had the strength to erect the Godveil."

"They killed off as many of you as they could, siphoned off your memories, and used that to prevent you from following them to the other side. They did what they could. What they had to. What you would have done, if you had not been so gruesome and weak."

"We," I reminded her. "What *we* would have done. Or are you something more than human, Lady Focus?"

Nustenzia gave me a hateful stare but said nothing, so I changed direction. "What are the tree columns? And those spines? Why do the Deserters—apologies, your *masters*—need those?"

She said, "I would have thought you had deduced as much already. You know how they perceive the world. The spines simply help them focus that ability. Refine it."

"Is that why the Wielders favor the long staff-like spines, rather than spiked clubs? They are simply the largest of the spines?"

Nustenzia replied, "I tire of this. Do you have any other questions or will you finally be silent?"

Four tenday ago, I would have stammered an apology or felt guilty for bothering her, regretting asking her anything at all, sympathizing with her plight. Instead, I found myself feeling a surge of anger and saying, "I understand you have left the only home you have ever known, and don't know your fate. I understand that you have left behind a son, and dread never seeing him again, and leaving a simple lad to who-knows-what-fate awaits his kind in Roxtiniak.

"Nustenzia, I am the kindest, most tolerant soul you will meet in this company. You'll be hard pressed to find anyone to treat you more fairly. But

I will tell you this, too—I have the captain's ear. He trusts me, values my opinion. And if I tell him how belligerent you're being, how difficult, you can be sure he will not take it kindly. I would like to see you return home to your loved one. But that will be impossible if you continue to prove overly averse. Think on that the next time I ask you a question."

I let them trot a few steps ahead and fell back, careful not to disrupt the horsemen behind me. My heart was pounding, my headache had reasserted itself, and I was sweaty. I felt one awful pang of guilt. But I also felt some exhilaration to say what I really thought instead of dousing it in politeness.

More Syldoonian by the day, indeed.

Over the course of the next five days, no Deserters thundered down the plains after us, no Imperials caught our scent and intercepted us, and the company started to lose some of the tension that had hung so oppressively and to fall back into normal rhythms. There were more coarse jokes and the occasional song when we stopped to feed and water the horses, and we didn't slip saddles back on them immediately, but took longer breaks as we had before. My headaches became less intense with each day, and I managed to get some translating in, though without discovering anything particularly useful or noteworthy.

Mulldoos continued to train me, though he mostly ran me through movement drills and made me practice my blocking. While I was in no hurry to get covered in welts or knocked to the dirt, I asked him once why it seemed like we were going so slowly, despairing of ever approaching anything resembling competency. He replied, "You're a shit student. Historically bad. But even if you were a natural, there's no plaguing shortcuts. So shut your mouth and be glad I'm not letting the soldiers use you as a pell. Because you sure as shit wouldn't block any of their blows. Get that shield up and resume a proper plaguing stance, scribbler."

So the miles came and went as we passed through plains the color of dried blood and hills dark and brambly. We were far from the seas or any significant rivers, and the whole world seemed to turn dustier and rockier, broken up occasionally by red cliffs jutting out of the dry earth, small copses of twisted trees that looked wretched and tortured, and thorny, prickly brush that seemed designed to capture travelers or at least blight their legs.

I was riding between Vendurro and Rudgi when I asked, "Where are we headed, anyway?"

"North," Rudgi replied.

"How incredibly helpful," I said. "But what I meant was—"

"Our destination?" she asked, smiling sweetly.

"Yes, that was sort of what I had in mind."

Vendurro said, "Heading to a village, a few days ahead."

"A village? One loyal to the deposed emperor, I hope. That seems a poor choice, for discretion I mean."

Rudgi said, "These villages are only beholden to one thing—the earth, the seasons, the weather. Well, that's three things, ain't it. The point is, so long as the lords of the land don't tax them to starvation or rob them blind if a company comes through on campaign, they don't much care what colors they're flying or which Tower they hail from."

"And gold," Vendurro said. "Maybe true loyalty's got little to do with it, but amazing what kind of temporary loyalty some jingly coins can buy."

I thought about that and replied, "But that's sort of what I'm getting at. What if Cynead's men come by, looking for us, or Thumaar, willing to pay more? Aren't we still in Thulmyria? Don't these people have some loyalty to the sitting emperor?"

Vendurro said, "As to the last, have to look at a map, but thinking we left Thulmyria behind. Not that it would matter. And as for them looking for Thumaar, they sure as spit might be, but nobody expects him back in the Empire. See, that's the beauty of meeting here—Cynead's not likely to reckon he even needs to be looking for the man. Figure's he's still in exile."

"And us?" I asked. "Surely he hasn't given up looking for us. What if Skeelana or another party comes riding in, hunting us, asking if any villagers would actually like a gold chamber pot instead?"

We passed by a small stand of warped-looking trees, and several crows took flight, cawing down at us as they lazily circled a few times before flying off.

Rudgi said, "Well, see, you got bought loyalty, like Lieutenant Ven here said—" She looked at him. "Still going to take some time to get used to how that sits on my tongue." He nodded, smiling, and she continued, "That might or might not keep villager lips nailed shut, depending on the next offer. But where that ends, fear takes right on over."

"Fear?" I asked.

"Ayyup. Unless it's Emperor Witchstealer himself comes riding up, which isn't likely at all, any villager knows Thumaar will kill every last man who betrays him. And a deposed emperor will outweigh a sitting emperor's boot-licking minion on the scale of fear every single day of every single year."

"But he is deposed, exiled. How many troops does he have left?"

Vendurro replied, "Can't rightly say. You can ask him yourself soon enough, if you like. But it's more than any imperial hunting party is like to have. And plenty enough to raze a village to the ground, that's for plaguing sure."

We continued heading north on a small dirt track that passed for a road, with deep wagon wheel ruts, and clumps of dirt and mud stirred up from a thousand thousand boots and shoes over the years. It was remote, and a far cry from the stone imperial roads connecting the major cities in the Syldoon Empire. Of course, those were exceptional—most of the rest of the world was connected by dirt paths or none at all.

"I have another question," I announced.

"That's right shocking, Arki. Right shocking," Vendurro said, grinning.

"Well," I replied, "Of course there are several, really. But you knew that. I was wondering, how did Thumaar get ousted in the first place? Obviously, that seems to be the Syldoon way, but what happened to him in particular?"

Rudgi slapped her thigh. "The Syldoon Way? I like that. That's funny, Arki. I'm going to have to remember to use that sometime."

Vendurro said, "Thumaar was, still is, I'm reckoning, a hard man. Don't get to sit yourself on the throne in Sunwrack without it. But he was fair, too, and quick to laugh, drink. His reign was long, and for the most part went about as well as could be expected, considering he got a plague and its ravages to contend with, some famine in there, with farms fallow and empty on account of half the farmers dropping dead, uprisings in far-flung lands. So, he had a lot going on, but the thing that did him in was he turned an eye from the Anjurians."

"What do you mean?" I asked. "Wasn't it Thumaar who authorized Darzaak to send the captain and your company into Anjuria to stir up trouble and weaken them around the edges?"

"Ayyup. Sure enough. But that was on the sly. Didn't announce that to most Towers. Nobody but Thumaar, some of his Eagles, and us Jackals knew about those operations. And that's a far cry from invading."

I said, "It sounds like he had plenty to deal with. Were Tower Lords still clamoring for war with Anjuria so loudly, even with all the rest going on that you mentioned?"

Rudgi said, "The Empire has been at war with Anjuria on and off for a hundred years. More. So there were always voices clamoring for another offensive."

Vendurro nodded. "Some, a few, loud voices belonging to crafty, ambitious men."

I thought about it for a minute. "Cynead."

"Ayyup. One of them," Vendurro said. "That sneaky bastard was Tower Commander of the Leopards at the time, even helped Thumaar take the throne years back, but the longer Thumaar sat on it, the more Cynead figured he was the wrong man for the job. He started coveting that sun throne for hisself real, real bad. And the thing was, Thumaar was a great general—the kind that led from the front, shucked off arrows and blows at the head of a charge, the sort men would do just about anything for."

"And women," Rudgi added. "All his troops. A lot like Captain Braylar, when it comes to that. Inspired that true loyalty Lieutenant Ven was espousing that coin can't buy."

Vendurro said, "Thing of it is, though, those traits make a plaguing good commander in the field, but ruling, especially ruling in Sunwrack, well, you got to be savvy with the politics too. And Thumaar, he preferred to be out there himself, quelling rebellions, leading the troops."

"Which might not have been terrible," Rudgi said, "only Thumaar led them the wrong plaguing direction."

Vendurro said, "Problem was, we hadn't softened up Anjuria enough, and in the meantime, there was an uprising in the Vortagoi Confederacy about the same time, to the far north."

I tried to recall maps I'd seen, and the snippets of history about the borders of the empire and which neighbors maintained sovereignty, like Anjuria, and which were allowed to govern themselves, in theory, but owed the Syldoon tribute and allegiance.

"The Vortagoi Confederacy, they were a principality, correct?"

"They were," Vendurro replied, "until they decided they weren't. Seems they were hit by the plague even harder than the Syldoon, claimed they couldn't make the payments, so Thumaar got on his big emperor horse and rode an emperor host up the stone road to the plum plains of Vortagoi, intent on putting that rebellion down before it could start, remind the upstart Confederates who really ruled."

"The only problem was," Rudgi said, "it proved to be a longer campaign than he figured, and costly, and he was away from the capital too long. The Syldoon like generals who lead from the front and emperors who shine the throne with their royal asses, remind the folks who's got the reins in the reigns."

I said, "So Cynead took his opportunity, convinced other Commanders to join him?"

"Ayyup," Vendurro replied. "Started poisoning some ears, spinning rhetoric, winning supporters who thought if the emperor needed to be marching off anywhere, it ought to have been a plaguing army into Anjuria. Thing of it was, Cynead never had full sway, from what I heard, so he got a little more drastic. Did what we always done when honeyed tongues and speeches ain't winning the day."

"The Syldoon Way!" Rudgi slapped her thigh again and laughed.

Vendurro smiled, and said, "He led a midnight coup in the Citadel, killed Thumaar's proxy, a general by the name of Lusvitt, and cut down or imprisoned the rest of his Leopard leaders. Oh yeah, and slaughtered the emperor's wife and son. There was that."

Rudgi shook her head and turned and spit into the tall brittle-looking grass. "Plaguing dishonorable cock, is what he is."

"That's awful," I said, so quietly I wasn't sure if either heard. "Why . . . why did Cynead do that, what purpose did it serve?"

Vendurro's grin was gone, his mouth now set in a small line. "Message. Just a plaguing message. Let the other Commanders know he wasn't one to be trifled with, and they better drop those knees and name him the new emperor right quick, or the streets of Sunwrack would be bathed redder than red."

"That smug fuck is a right royal whoreson, for sure," Rudgi said, "but it plaguing worked. Got to give him that. Commanders folded, kissed his ring, pledged fealty, and the empire branded Thumaar an exile, promised him a noose or sword if he ever returned."

We all sat in silence, riding along, occasionally coughing on the dust kicked up from the horses ahead of us.

Finally, I asked, "So where has he been?"

They looked at each other. "Nobody knows." Then Vendurro corrected himself. "That is, nobody's told us grunts. Commander Darzaak, some of the others who served Thumaar, helped him to the throne in the first place, they must have had some idea, or leastwise how to get word to him. Because this is the first time he's been back in the empire since the coup. No telling if he'll still be waiting for us, though. Didn't figure on getting chased all over the earth and right on through the Godveil. Devilveil. Whatever it plaguing is. We're plenty late, is what we are."

Rudgi shook her head. "He'll be there. He wants Cynead's heart, and he needs us to help give it to him. He'll be there."

Two days later, around midday, we approached a small beaten-down village in the middle of nowhere. While it wasn't abandoned like the human settlements on the other side of the Veil or the plague village we had stayed in overnight when hunting Henlester, the place had clearly seen better days. Years ago, from the looks of it. The walls of the buildings had been whitewashed once, but most of it had chipped and blown away on a dry breeze, leaving bare baked clay that seemed ready to crumble if you leaned on it. The roofs were buckled, a busted windmill that must have stopped spinning ages ago stood silent and still, and the farmers who lived here must have had an incredibly difficult time coaxing anything out of the dry and dusty ground.

I wondered why we were stopping here. Certainly Thumaar was somewhere else ahead. Were we getting more food? Supplies? It seemed a risk since we were fugitives, especially after our last adventure heading through a village. But then Vendurro unbuckled his helm and pulled it off, running a hand through his sweaty hair, and said, "We made good time. Looks like this is it."

I looked around at the first dilapidated building we passed and the faces of two small children clutching their mother's skirts. I asked, "This is what?"

"It," Vendurro said.

"Uh, what it? What do you mean?"

He stretched his back, smiled big and broad to a man in a broad thatched hat who didn't return it in the slightest. "It it. Brassguilt. Where we're meeting the big man himself."

"Thumaar?" I asked more loudly than I meant to, surprised. "Here? He's here?" I looked around again in amazement. "Why is he in Brassguilt?" I'd expected an exiled ruler to be whiling away his hours in some foreign court, a pampered guest (or, in this ruler's case, longing for his lost throne and concocting vengeful plans for recapturing it). But when Vendurro said Thumaar was in a village, I'd assumed it wasn't a dusty town on the edge of nothing, eating beans or roots or whatever else they dug up here.

"I expect you'd have to ask Cap that," Vendurro replied.

"Does he, that is, he doesn't *live* here, does he? He just arranged to meet us here?"

Vendurro tried his smile out again on another local with no greater success. "Expect he's been camped here for some time. Hoping we'd show. Scouts said he's here though, so we're here, and that's that."

Well. That was definitely that. I glanced around at a leaning barn. "But, where is his army? This place isn't big enough to hide, well, anything."

Vendurro grinned. "Too bad questions ain't stones."

He waited, knowing I would have to ask another. "Oh? Why is that?"

"You keep piling one on top of the next, by now you could have built yourself your own Tower. I'm thinking . . . Quill Tower. Ayyup. Tower Commander Arkamondos. Got a real fine ring to it, don't it?"

I glanced at the bland expressionless faces of some of the other villagers as they regarded the arrival of a band of armed soldiers with all the interest you might give some leaves blowing past you. "They don't seem especially welcoming, do they?"

Vendurro hung his helmet from this saddle and laughed. "Just can't help yourself, can you, Commander Arki?" I started to protest and he said, "Quill Tower is about up to the clouds. You can take a breather for a bit."

I still had a dozen more questions, but I could tell after long days in the saddle Vendurro was no longer in the mood to humor any, so I left the next question unasked and took off my own helmet as well.

We were here in a dusty village on the edge of nothing to meet a deposed emperor. And that was that.

Some children were curious about our arrival until their parents grabbed them by the ears or swatted them on the back of the head and told them to go somewhere else. But the adults, by and large, maintained the same level expression. Some made effort not to look at all, as if a band of armed soldiers rode down their rutted dirt street every day, and others seemed only vaguely interested.

A short man with a pronounced nose and paunch approached. His face looked like something unearthed from the unforgiving land as well—hard, pocked, as lumpy as a potato. He looked at the captain and his men, then singled out Azmorgon. "Would you be Captain Braylar, then?"

Azmorgon boomed out a long laugh, and kept right on laughing even though no one else was, as if he'd just heard the most uproarious jest in the world.

Braylar said, "You see, that is the benefit of being a man of average size. If a man had a mind to assassinate 'Captain Killcoin,' he might aim for that large bastard as well, giving me time to bring my shield to bear or ride for the russet hills. And even if he knew me by face, well, I am certainly a smaller target. In fact, I might make it a point to ask Lieutenant to precede me down all streets and through all doors from this day forward."

Azmorgon stopped laughing and Braylar addressed the paunchy man. "So. We have learned that it is dangerous to make assumptions. So I ask, are you the mayor? Village elder? Chief gourd grinder?"

The lumpy man gave the captain a stony stare. "Me? Nothing important about me. No sir. Not with the likes of you and would-be emperors prowling about. Expecting you'll be wanting to see that other man of great import now, huh?"

Braylar said, "It is always good to meet someone shrewd. Such a rarity these days."

The man wisely chose not to draw the conversation out further. I wished more men could have shown such restraint. Bloodsounder—the man *and* flail—would have consumed far fewer memories. "This way then," he said, starting off.

He led us down a winding dirt track, away from the rest of the village, such as it was, past a pen of goats, some graves, and towards a barn that looked to have been abandoned a century before but remarkably somehow still stood.

The man of no import stopped near the entrance and faced Braylar again. It seemed like he had something else to add, weighed the words against what they might cost him, and then settled on, "Sunwrack's a long hike from here. Might as well be on the other side of the Godveil. I got no quarrel with one emperor nor the other. Nobody here does. We want no trouble. But . . ." He wiped his bulging brow, and again seemed to be mulling over what words to choose, if any. He took a step closer to Braylar and lowered his voice. "We offered what hospitality we can, no grudges, no complaints. But it sure would be nice if you convinced the emperor of old in there to do his meetings in some other village from now on."

Azmorgon said, "Count yourself lucky we don't raze this horseshit village, raze it good, raze it some more, just because razing is so plaguing fun, turn this place to ash and burn those ashes too."

Mulldoos said, "Can't set fire to ashes, you whopping huge horsecunt. And even if you could, you think they're worried about what you'd do to their plaguing ashes? Plague me, but you got a queer way of doling out threats."

Braylar turned back to the gourdy man. "Your request is duly noted. I cannot promise my overlords will be receptive, but I will pass along the sentiment. And there will be no razing. Not today, at least."

Then he dismounted and said, "Officers, sister, Nustenzia, Arki, with me. The rest of you, settle here for a moment." He gave a twitchy smile. "Though don't take off your boots to stretch your toes. We will ride on soon enough, I am thinking."

"You are right on that score," someone behind Braylar said.

We all turned and looked, and for a moment my breath hitched in my chest, lodged there. The resemblance was only nominal, really—a long braided beard fixed with coins, a bare upper lip, and skin like dark wood. But while the beard was full gray, and the man was nowhere near Hewspear's height, and had a bald pate besides, there was no mistaking that they hailed from the same lands. The man and his gear were both weathered and aged— the face deeply lined, with the largish nose and ears that only came with poor luck or advanced seasons, the clothing no better than our own and possibly in a worse state, the mail cuirass patched in several spots—but neither seemed anything less than sturdy.

Braylar stepped forward and gave their quirky Syldoonian salute, fist twisting this way and that before slamming emphatically into the chest. "General Kruzinios."

The general returned the salute. A bit overly formal, more at place in court than a discreet meeting in a far-flung, flea-infested village. "You're late," he said, letting the statement hang there, half recrimination, half flattened question.

Braylar replied, "My apologies, General. Unavoidable, I'm afraid, and not for lack of effort to be punctual, I can assure you."

"Imperials?" Kruzinios asked.

"The Leopards were not entirely keen to see us reconnect with Emperor Thumaar, as you might imagine."

The older man nodded. "Imagination has never been my strength. But in this case, it does not require much. I should warn you: Thumaar has nearly paced himself into a ravine. His patience is even weaker than my fancy." All the wrinkles seemed to delta towards his nose as he squinted. "I'm assuming you had to outrun them, fight through them. But that still hardly explains the delay, even with precautions for making certain you weren't followed."

Braylar replied, "You are right, General. If that had been the full extent of our opposition, we would have arrived sooner. There were . . . exceptional circumstances."

"Exceptional?" he asked. "Explain, Captain. Quickly."

Braylar said, "We were trapped and had to cross over the Godveil, General. Though after discovering what is on the other side, we might need to de-deify that name a bit. No longer fitting, really."

I expected some dramatic reaction—amazement, skepticism, fear, anger, anything really. What I saw instead was the slight arch of an eyebrow, followed by a wildly understated, "Well. That would cause some unexpected delays then, wouldn't it?" Kruzinios's eyes dropped to Bloodsounder, but only for the briefest moment, before returning to the wielder, flinty as ever. "Looks like that whoreson Cynead was right to hound you then, wasn't he? So then. What's so ungodly about the Veil then?"

Braylar crossed his arms at the wrist behind his back. "Not the Veil itself, General. But what lay beyond."

"Beyond," the general said with no obvious inflection.

Most men would have shrunk a size under that weathered, flinty stare. But Braylar, in Braylarian fashion, did no such thing. "That's right. We did encounter Deserters on the other side. We unfortunately ran afoul of them early and often. But they are not gods. Giants for certain, and possibly monsters, demons, or something else, depending on how you classify such things. But the Deserters are not gods. So we have taken to just referring to the border as the Veil now."

Kruzinios finally allowed a touch of something besides impatience to creep into his voice, thought it was hard to tell whether incredulity or awe. "So. You crossed the Veil. And you encountered Deserters. Giants, you say. Only they are no more gods than you or me. Is what you are saying?"

The captain uncrossed his arms. "Yes, General. That is a fine summation."

If that irked the older man, he gave no sign. But he did give a long sigh, and followed that with several seconds of silence before saying, "Well. That is a tale and a half. For certain. But right about now I am just wishing you had stuck with, 'Imperials trailed us. We led them astray. Killed them, even. And now we are here.' And do you know why, Captain?"

For the first time, Braylar seemed ill at ease. "Because it would be a shorter tale?"

Kruzinios reached up and fingered the coins on the bottom of a braid, and I was again reminded of Hewspear and felt a sharp pang that couldn't have been mine alone. "I am trying to warn you, Captain Killcoin. I'm not even sure I should." He hazarded a look over his shoulder. "You will need to tread lightly. Especially as far as this topic is concerned."

"Oh?" Braylar asked. "I do not recall the Emperor being especially religious. Or sacrilegious for that matter. Why is this a dangerous topic, then?"

Kruzinios looked at the captain and his retinue, and it was clear for the first time that there was something warring on his face. "First, call him only deposed emperor or nothing at all. He detests the honorific while he is absent the throne. And second, these years have . . . not been generous. Be hard on any man, really, accustomed to power. But you hear of some rulers in exile eating dates, wearing perfumed slippers, whiling away their days, happy to have simply survived a coup. But a man like Thumaar? Ambition. Ambition is all. Teeming with the stuff. Well. These years, this man, his ambitions thwarted but not blunted, sharpened even in the interim. There have been changes. He's turned to the old gods. Now more than ever. That's all I will say for now. It's hard to predict how he'll take that news. You crossing over. Hard to say. He might even be excited. Always had a curious mind. But that business about the Deserters not being gods? Well. The less you say about that the better. You've been warned."

He turned and started towards the barn, and then stopped. "Oh. One other thing. You mention my warning at all to the man, and you'll be hanging from the rafters, and not even your sister there will be able to cut you down. Understood?"

Everyone slowly nodded.

"Good," Kruzinios said. "Follow me then."

I can't remember ever wanting to follow anyone less.

We passed into the barn, so filled with shadows I couldn't make out much at first, even though portions of the ceiling had fallen in and shafts of murky sunlight crisscrossed the dirt floor.

When my eyes finally adjusted, I saw that there were at least thirty or forty Syldoon soldiers inside. They were hardly in parade gear either, and looked more like a luckless mercenary company in mismatched pieces of armor than the former elite guards to an emperor. Though whether that was necessity or subterfuge, I couldn't say.

Kruzinios announced, "They are here, my lord."

A figure stepped its way through the heavy shadows and stark shafts. "So. The Jackals at last."

The deposed emperor stopped before us. Where Cynead was hardly ostentatious, that was its own kind of peculiar pride, as if he were so confident in his power and position he didn't feel the need to overawe with rich trappings or showy accoutrements.

But Thumaar was like an old lean wolf—tall, gaunt, tensed, a tight collection of spare muscle and hungry energy, lank hair down to his shoulders as fair as flax, gray stubble on his cheeks, and dark circles under his eyes that might as well have been tattooed there. He was dressed like a farmer in simple worn linens under his tarnished scale cuirass, but there was no mistaking him for one of them. Even with only a simple longsword angled at his side, the hilt weathered, the pommel unadorned, and no trumpets or leopards on chains or massive drums or chariots heralding his arrival, the man carried himself like one who had ruled vast tracts of the known world.

He was shorter than Azmorgon, of course, but would have been nearly of height with Hewspear, and so he looked down on the rest of the retinue, eyes slowly taking each of us in, and it felt like a cold assessment. If he paused when he came across me or Nustenzia, I didn't register it, despite our being very much out of place and depth here. Thumaar rubbed his large hands together, a dry, almost rasping noise. "Darzaak's Jackals, come to pay their respects to their former ruler at last, is it?"

The Jackals all saluted, and then bowed slightly at the waist, and Braylar said, "Your Majesty, we—"

"No," Thumaar said, and rarely had a single utterance been more definitive. "Not now, Captain. There is nothing majestic about wasting away in the wilds, pining for what is rightfully mine. I am no Emperor right now. It is a mockery of nomenclature. When you have helped me retake Sunwrack, reclaim my empire, then you may revert. Then it is 'Your Majesty' this and 'Your Majesty' that. But not now. Not today."

Braylar replied, "As you command. What would you have us call you instead, my lord?"

"'My lord.' Even that is spoiled fruit, but it will suffice." Thumaar looked at Soffjian again and then back to Braylar. "That is why you are here, is it not? To help me seize what is rightfully mine. Reseize, as it were. That was the message Darzaak sent. Though it is curious why you are so negligent in arriving to get started."

Braylar paused briefly before replying. "My lord, the Jackals have ever been your faithful men. We supported your bid to the throne, worked at your behest in Anjuria while you were Emperor, and continue to be your staunchest supporters today in helping you reclaim what is yours. That is precisely why we are here."

Thumaar replied, "How very stalwart of you. And yet, years have come and gone since I was ousted, and what have you done for me, eh? I will tell you. Nothing. Nothing and less. In fact, I was beginning to suspect the Jackals were tonguing Cynead's asshole with all the rest."

Kruzinios said, "My lord, they came here at great risk, and have endured—"

Thumaar raised a long single finger. "Do not speak to me of risk, General. Or endurance." He addressed the captain. "So why the delay arriving?"

Braylar replied, "I am sure Tower Commander Darzaak included this in his report, but Cynead drove us from the city. He cut down a significant number of my men before we even cleared the gates. His troops hounded us as we rode hard to deliver ourselves to you, and attrition was no less kind. You can be sure, if I ever see Cynead's asshole, I will drive a suroka into it."

Thumaar smiled, but it was a grim, thin thing. "Are you telling me you were unable to throw off a little pursuit or dispatch your foes, and this is what kept me waiting? You have served me well in the past, Captain, it is true. One of my finest operatives, in fact. I expected better."

Braylar glanced briefly at Kruzinios, who said nothing and only gave a barely perceptible shake of his head. Which Braylar ignored. "Commander Darzaak sent us to you for two reasons, my lord. One, he did not want this"—he reached down and shook the flail heads at his hip—"to remain in the puckered Emperor's possession. And two, he believes there might be a way to reverse Cynead's control of the Memoridons, to tether them to you. But if you have no use for either, please let us ride on our way. My lord."

As ever, I wished the captain had a modicum more sense of self-preservation. But if Thumaar took offense, he gave no sign. "Oh, yes. The Memoridons. I did have some with me a few days ago. Several tried to slip away in the night, to return to Sunwrack when they felt the bonds shift. I cannot say I blamed them. After all, what would I do in their place? Of course I cut them down, those I could catch, anyway. And yet"—he gave Soffjian a pointed look "unless I am mistaken, you have one in your employ just now. Curious. Most curious. Are you sure you are not licking the Great Leopard's ass, Captain?"

Before Braylar could offer a reply, Soffjian said, "I am bound to Cynead. Bound. There is no choice in that. But I am aligned with my brother."

Thumaar gave her a long look. "You would have me believe you risk husking out of familial loyalty, even while my own Memoridons abandoned me?"

Soffjian didn't back down. She and her brother surely had that much in common, if little else. "Absolutely not. I do not even care for my brother. You can confirm this with anyone."

"Plaguing true," Mulldoos said, slurring a little.

Soffjian said, "I owe him no loyalty at all. And you only marginally more, truth be told. But commander Darzaak promised me my freedom if I assisted him and you, and I am exceptionally loyal to myself. So there it is."

Thumaar nodded once. "Honesty at last. You and these Jackals have done it then? Discovered a way to undo Cynead's treachery?" There was an urgency there, underpinning the question, that was impossible to miss.

Braylar said, "We believe so, my lord." He pointed at me, "My scribe here has been translating ancient Anjurian texts, and we believe we have uncovered a method to reverse what Cynead has accomplished. To bind the Memoridons to you."

Thumaar laughed. "Anjurians? What could they possibly teach us about Memoridons, Captain? We are Syldoon."

Soffjian stepped into a shaft of light, motes dancing all around her. "And the Syldoon are the most arrogant creatures to stalk the earth, my lord. They did not invent the methods or the binds. They simply adopted them and improved them on a scale unimagined."

That seemed to take Thumaar off guard. "You are truly suggesting Anjurians pioneered this, then?"

"Not suggesting. Stating," she said. "Stating it as an unassailable fact. Cynead uncovered similar Anjurian texts and performed his own research. That is how he broke the binds each of the Tower Commanders had."

There was a stern set to the deposed emperor's jaw. "So, what are you suggesting? That some Anjurian lords learned how to control Memoridons and failed to utilize it?"

"Not precisely, no," she said. Thumaar's eyes narrowed and she continued, "Arki is the scribe, and I will let him explain it, as he is more familiar. Though, and forgive my impudence, 'stating' will still be more accurate."

The gaunt man turned his hot stare on me. "What of it, then? I have no use for mummery or games, boy. What is this plaguing witch going on about?"

I cleared my throat, no less comfortable around this man than Cynead, and possibly less so. "Soffjian speaks true, my lord. The Anjurians did explore binding before there was even a Syldoon Empire. But these experiments were conducted by rogue priests of the Temple of Truth, not kings or barons. And that is why the efforts were kept secret and stricken from most records."

"And yet you claim to have uncovered texts that prove this, that document it?"

I looked at Soffjian and Braylar, and Thumaar took a step forward and grabbed my face in an unyielding hand. "It is unwise to break eye contact with an emperor, boy, deposed or not. I asked you a direct question."

"I could show you, if you like." I said, though my scrunched up mouth mangled the words a bit. When he released it, I continued, "The translations, that is."

The deposed emperor looked at Braylar again. "I would like to know your plan. Darzaak's message was somewhat sketchy, but he claimed that a number of Memoridons were husked or killed when Cynead broke the binds and stole them for himself. Even if these texts you found are accurate, serve as some kind of manual, how do you propose we reverse what that insidious bastard accomplished? We have only one Memoridon, correct?" When Braylar nodded, Thumaar said, "Even if we manage to infiltrate Sunwrack and covertly speak to Cynead's new pets, I don't see a group of Memoridons willingly sacrificing themselves to switch masters. Do you?"

Braylar smiled, free of twitching for once. "No, my lord. I do not. But we have discovered another way."

Thumaar said only, "Have you?"

The captain waved a hand at Nustenzia. "With her, we only need Soffjian to accomplish this. And she might not even get husked in the process. Which brings me endless relief and joy."

Thumaar looked at the older woman as if seeing her for the first time. "And who are you, crone?"

Mulldoos laughed and Braylar began to answer, but Nustenzia overrode both of them. "I am one of the High Foci, sworn to serve the Vrulinka-Antovia-Lilka, Matriarch of Roxtiniak, Guardian of the Veil, the Great Wielder. And I am here under duress."

"Aren't we all," Thumaar said, and then asked Braylar, "What is she babbling about? Is this some cult I'm unaware of?"

"Not precisely," the captain replied slowly, "but the answer is . . . complex. And will require something of another history lesson, I'm afraid. Though I will be brief."

I watched Kruzinios close his eyes, shaking his head as Braylar began. "This is the reason we are as delayed as we are, my lord. The Imperials had us trapped against the Godveil, and my archivist here, through a mix of fine translation and deduction, discovered an unorthodox escape."

"Which was?"

"To part the Veil."

Thumaar didn't change his expression, except for the tiniest tremor that crossed his face and disappeared. He stared, unblinking, and waited several seconds before saying, "To part the Veil. Of course. And how was that possible?"

Braylar slowly pulled Bloodsounder off his belt. "That is another long narrative, but the short of it is, this is an artifact created just after the Godveil was created. It allows the wielder to pass through."

"And to transport an entire company, no doubt."

"Not all at once, my lord. A small group held off the Imperials as we made our escape piecemeal." He looked at Kruzinios. "Your kinsman, Lieutenant Hewspear, died sacrificing himself to buy us time."

Kruzinios lowered his head. "I am grieved to hear it. He was a good man."

"None finer, General. None finer."

Thumaar was not overly concerned with grief or sacrifice. "You are claiming a . . . sorcerous flail . . . allowed you passage through the Veil." The deposed emperor looked at his General, who remained impassive. "From history to lurid romances and fairy tales. This is what you have brought me?"

Before Kruzinios could say anything, Braylar replied, "If I had crossed by myself, without witnesses, that would be a claim, my lord. As it is, an entire company accompanied me. Well over a hundred men. You are welcome to interrogate any one of them—I can assure you they will corroborate in full."

Mulldoos said, "And begging your pardon, my lord, but you paint Cap here a plaguing liar, you best get a bigger brush, because we all went over, sure as spit. Every man of us."

Azmorgon and Vendurro both said "aye" in unison, and for once, every Jackal was in agreement about something.

But Thumaar didn't seem especially mollified or convinced. "Well over a hundred, you say? And where are the rest, then. Hiding in the hills?"

"No," the captain replied. He paused, no doubt considering how to dress up the next part, but shockingly went with the truth instead. "We were captured on the other side."

Thumaar still sounded unbelieving, but like a skeptic who secretly longs to be proven wrong. His next question had less bite than I expected. "Captured, is it. By whom?"

Braylar took a deep breath and exhaled loudly at length out his nostrils before saying, "The Matriarch Nustenzia spoke of, my lord."

"So. You crossed over the Godveil using an ancient artifact. Only to discover that we are not alone in the world after all. Perhaps you can see why I am tempted to send a missive informing Darzaak that his operatives have gone stark raving mad with some mind plague and had to be hung as we feared infection."

Soffjian said, "While I can appreciate you being incredulous, again, every soldier in this company will swear to the veracity. No one is lying."

"Or you all are lying," Thumaar replied. "Either way, madmen or charlatans, there aren't enough trees to hang you, so we will simply have to shoot you."

Kruzinios said, "My lord. Please."

Thumaar looked at the captain again. "Very well. So there are presumably some humans on the other side, one of them a pretentious ruler who styles herself 'The Matriarch.' Is that right?"

Nustenzia blurted, "No. She is no human." She said this with the usual strange derision, as if being a Focus and close to the Deserters had somehow elevated her above the rest of humanity.

Braylar closed his eyes, Mulldoos shook his head, and Azmorgon said, "Shut your yappy hole, bitch."

But instead, she glared at Azmorgon and replied, "Vrulinka is not a human, as you well know." She addressed the deposed emperor again. "The Matriarch is what you foolishly refer to as a Deserter."

Thumaar's expression didn't change, but his voice was rough and low as he said, "The gods." Cold skepticism was replaced by hot yearning.

"No," Nustenzia said. "An elder race, and giant, powerful, but no, they are not gods."

Braylar surely felt that he was in a precarious position, just as Kruzinios warned. "We did encounter the race that spawned all the Deserter visages and statues on this side of the Veil, but while they are as Nustenzia described, and exceptionally dangerous besides, she is correct—these beings are giants, but not gods."

Thumaar's next question was barely above a whisper, and his eyes had a feverish cast to them. "Oh? And you know this how?"

Mulldoos spat sideways into the moldy straw. "We killed quite a few of the massive horsecunts. Though they killed a lot more of us. And without a whole lot of trouble. But they do bleed. They do die. And they ain't plaguing gods, whatever else they are."

Thumaar took a few steps back, out of the sunlight, back into shadow, as Kruzinios said, "My lord, the only thing that matters is they discovered a way to bind the Memoridons to you. To help you reclaim your throne. That, and nothing else. So—"

"I thought you might be charlatans or madmen," Thumaar said. "But I was wrong. That is too generous. You are heretics." He spat the last word, as if it were an ember on his tongue he couldn't get rid of fast enough.

Braylar and his officers looked at each other, and Vendurro made the mistake of saying, "Your Majesty, it's nothing but the truth, what Cap said. And your general there, too. We can—"

"Silence!" Thumaar all but roared, stepping forward into the sunlight again.

Kruzinios tried again. "They are our allies, my lord. The only ones who can help us counter Cynead. They—"

Thumaar pivoted and shouted at his general, "Would you be branded heretic as well, General?"

The general shut his mouth. The captain did not. "Are there gods beyond the Veil? I do not presume to say. There very well could be. But what I tell you with certainty is that the beings that inspired the images are fearsome, monstrous even, but not godly. But your astute general here is right—what is critically important right now is not a question of theology, but how can you usurp the usurper. That is why we lost most of our company and incurred the wrath of the sitting emperor. That is why we endangered our Tower, risked our lives, and abandoned Sunwrack. We can only return if we do so returning you to the throne room. That is the only thing that has any import or meaning. My lord."

Kruzinios nodded several times. "The captain is right, my lord. Let them assist you. This is what you have longed for, an opportunity to retrieve what was taken from you. A chance—"

"And am I to forgive heresy, then?" Thumaar said, eyes filled with something dangerous. "Dismissal of the gods? That is the only crime worse than betraying your sovereign, isn't it? Is either forgivable? If I reclaim my throne with the help of liars and heretics, I have doomed myself further. Better to be in exile until I turn to dust than achieve my goals with the assistance of unbelievers."

Braylar said, "My lord, no man here dishonors or denounces the gods, old or new. In fact, it's entirely possible they guided us, allowed us to pass through the Veil to discover the means to reinstating you to your rightful place. We might very well be their instruments, the tools provided to you just for such a purpose."

Thumaar was shaking, though with fervor, fury, or something else, I couldn't venture to say.

He regarded the Jackals again, eyes moving as slowly as they had when we first entered. "You denounce the gods with one breath and try to align yourself with them in the next. So is it charlatan or heretic then?"

Braylar replied, "Neither, my lord. I clearly do not know the minds of the gods. So it would be nothing short of blind hubris to claim they supported me." He held up a flail head. "I only say that the creatures who inspired this and images like it are not deities. That is all. We explored only briefly beyond the Godveil. Gods could exist. But these giants were the ones we knew in ages gone by, who left, who created the Veil; they are not gods. Beyond that, it is speculation. What I do know for certain is that this far-too-talkative woman has the ability to assist those wielding memory magic. To amplify what they can do. She can help Soffjian break the ties and bind them to you. That is what I know. And that is all that is important."

Thumaar considered that for a few moments, with his heavy breathing the only sound in the barn as he slowly paced. "Perhaps you are right," he said. "Perhaps you are unwitting tools. The old gods, the ones we failed, who denounced us. They are still out there. And they will return. Once I return, they return. I am to help pave the way. I have seen it. Perhaps these . . . giants, perhaps they are priests to the gods."

Nustenzia started to say something and Braylar grabbed her upper arm and squeezed hard.

Thumaar stirred up more dust. "Perhaps they serve them. I do not know either. But if I hear one word about the gods not being beyond the Godveil, I will execute that heretic myself." He abruptly stopped and said, "Two days. We meet here again in two days' time, Captain. You will finish whatever research you must needs finish, and you will present a plan to me at that time."

"A plan, my lord?" Braylar asked flatly.

"Aye. You will provide a detailed plan about how precisely you intend to syphon control to me, undo what Cynead has wrought. Then I will hear more and decide what to do with you." He pursed his lips, clenched his fists, released them again. "Two days. That is all. Understood?"

Braylar nodded slowly. "Understood, my lord."

"Good. Get started then."

Thumaar started to turn around when Braylar asked, "If I may, my lord?"

The deposed emperor spun back to the captain. "What is it, Captain?"

"We will present a plan, as commanded. A thorough, vetted, and strategic plan for leashing the Memoridons to you. But I feel I must ask one thing. How is it you intend to utilize them and seize the advantage completely?

Cynead still has a large contingent of Syldoon inside Sunwrack that are pledged to him. Even if—when—we reverse his control over the Mems, they will only be cut down in the streets the moment he realizes he has lost them. And while that would be detrimental to him, my lord, it would hardly assure you control of the capital or its soldiers."

Thumaar stepped forward, his shoulders tensed, the cords in his neck standing out, nostrils flaring. But his voice was at odds, his words crisp and controlled, but still oddly quiet, almost a harsh whisper. "Do you take me for a fool, Captain Killcoin?"

"No, my lord, certainly not. I only want to ensure that our own plan dovetails with yours as neatly as possible, but to do that, it would be beneficial to—"

"Because only a man taking me for a fool might ask such a question. That, or simply one forgetting his place. There are only two options, and neither casts you in a good light." His stubbly jaw rolled around, and his lips moved once as if to shape words, stopped, and then he went ahead and added, "We have other allies arriving in two days' time. Substantial allies. Some on the eastern shores of the Bonewash. Others by land. I am not a fool, and I do not expect you to somehow win my empire back for me yourself. You only play a part. So make no mistake, an army will be at my disposal. Now, is there anything else you need explained just now, or would you like to get started on what I hold you responsible for?"

Braylar replied, "Everything is midday bright, my lord."

Thumaar turned on his heel and strode back into the crumbling barn, through bars of shadow and sun.

The captain led us back out of the building, to the horses.

Vendurro swung his leg over the saddle, looked over his shoulder to make sure none of the Eagles were close, and said, "Plague. Me. What the hells just happened in there?"

Braylar said, "That is a most excellent question. To be debated at a later time."

Soffjian dropped her ranseur on her shoulder and said, "Brother, I will give credit where it's due. While you should have listened to Kruzinios and not mentioned the Godveil and what lies beyond, nearly got us killed by ignoring him, in fact, that last bit of dancing was deftly done. I do believe our deposed emperor might very well have fitted our necks for real nooses otherwise. So, a wash really. But we are still alive and that is all that matters."

Braylar said, "Many thanks for putting things in perspective, sister, and you indulge me with such lavish praise." He rode up the winding, weedy trail to the mean village and what passed for a road running through it, and his Syldoon fell in behind him.

We made camp a few miles away from Brassguilt and its red dust and mottled plants, and no one seemed inclined to say anything else just then, though Nustenzia had tried, only to have Soffjian order her to be silent. As had been the case since crossing back over the Veil, Braylar didn't allow any fires. I would have liked a fire—the nights were cold, hot food tasted better, and if the Deserters did cross and track us, the Syldoon would have a meager chance of defending themselves if they could at least see their towering foes.

But Braylar was more concerned about Imperial eyes that might still be scouring the land. I spoke quietly to the captain, mentioning that I hadn't caught a phantom whiff of Skeelana's scent. He bluntly reminded me that she might not be among an Imperial force that happened to be riding nearby and decided to investigate a small company huddled around fires, and also ordered me to stop mooning over a Memoridon or he would tie me to a twisted tree and leave me for Skeelana to find someday.

That was the end of that conversation.

So, with purple tendrils of clouds slowly undulating against the darkening dusk sky, Braylar and his officers sat around their nonexistent fire. Rudgi took Nustenzia off and tied her to something (likely a twisted tree) before returning to our circle.

Azmorgon shifted, turned, and shifted some more, like a hound unable to find the right spot to lie down in, though at least he didn't spin in circles. Then he shook his head, big beard swaying. "I'll say it if nobody else plaguing will. Needs saying. That ain't the emperor I plaguing remember."

Mulldoos laughed. "You and him real cozy, were you?"

"Shut your slobbery mouth, Mushrooms. Just saying is he's changed. Thumaar has."

Even Mulldoos couldn't argue with that sentiment, shaking his head. "Got more fervor than a plaguing priest, that's for sure. Never figured him for a zealous bastard, but exile does queer things to a man."

Azmorgon nodded. "Exile burned something plaguing out of him."

Vendurro said, "Might be though, something else grew in its place."

Azmorgon rumbled, "What are you plaguing talking about, Squirrel?"

"Just saying, is all, that yeah, the man's different. No question. Maybe got something burnt out of him. But just because something turns to ash don't mean something different can't grow in its place. And different don't always mean bad."

Azmorgon was hunched over, looking like a huge mound. "I say again, you squirrelly little bastard. What the plaguing hells?"

Vendurro replied, "Well, when I was a wee lad, there was a hermit lived on the outskirts of the village. Walked like a crab, talked to himself or spirits or the gods, eating bark or berries or whatnot. He'd show up in the village once or twice a year, during a wedding or funeral or on account of some hermity timetable no one else could make sense of, and he'd scream some pronouncement or other no one could fathom, then he'd disappear back into the brush, elders shaking their heads at the poor bastard, children mocking him."

"Ought to have put the poor bastard out of his misery," Azmorgon said.

Mulldoos shifted, moving his scabbarded falchion to try to reposition his weight on that hip. "So you're saying Thumaar's our plaguing mad hermit? That's who we're following? Real plaguing comfort that is."

"Nope," Vendurro replied. "Saying no such thing. Wasn't done. What I'm saying is, one year he stopped coming. The loopy hermit, not Thumaar. No one thought much of it for the first season or three. But after that, folks started speculating if maybe that poor devil went and died out there—fever, poison, eaten by a bear, whatever. He wasn't what you would call a real contributing member of the tribe, so no one was in a huge rush to go find out what. But come spring, me and my brother went out through the miles of woods to investigate. The hermit was gone. No body, no footprints, no sign. But his little hut was mostly ash and blackened thatch. We poked through it, hoping to find his bones, you know, like kids do. But there was no sign of the man. But, after pulling a panel of wood out of the debris, I saw something amazing."

Vendurro paused as if braced for the next mocking interruption, but when none came he finished. "In the middle there, somehow growing in the ash, was the most beautiful flower I ever laid eyes on, and like nothing else I'd ever seen. Weird almost square-shaped leaves, reddish coiled petals with flecks of gold everywhere, like the shavings from a fine illumination or something."

Azmorgon laughed and said, "So, you're saying we ought to let Thumaar burn hisself out so we can pluck ourselves a right pretty flower?"

Braylar cut off Vendurro as he started to respond. "Thumaar is not a hermit or speckled wild flower or anything but what he is: the deposed emperor we have pledged ourselves to bring back to the throne. It does not matter what has been burnt out or what, if anything, has grown in its place."

Soffjian replied, "I swore to assist you. And that is what I will do. I have no alternative at this point," she said, clearly hating the admission as it passed her lips. "But I must point out, your Commander gave you these orders without having seen the deposed ruler these last few years. Do you imagine he would hold you to it if he were here now, had he witnessed Thumaar's . . . zealotry?"

Mulldoos said, "Aye. Ayyup. We got our orders. Wouldn't be the first time soldiers carried out orders that didn't make any plaguing sense. But, Cap, your witch sister here might have the right of it. I'm guessing Commander Darzaak might be rethinking his strategy a bit if he saw the old wolf in that rotten barn, more suspicious than a sick cat, threatening the only bastards who might be able to help him on account of him suddenly getting serious about worshipping gods that ain't gods at all."

Braylar was staring at the flail heads in his palm, gently rolling them back and forth, listening to the spikes clink together. "He is not the only man to still secretly worship the old gods, the ones who allegedly deserted us, believing that if we can only prove worthy enough, perhaps they will one day return."

"But," Mulldoos said, "and this is kind of an important plaguing point— those gods ain't real. We know that. Seen it with our eyes, have the scars to prove it."

"The Deserters are not gods," Braylar replied. "Whatever else they may be, it is true. *We* know that. And we will need to be especially careful who we profess that to. Not everyone is going to want to learn that everything we have ever believed was erected on a foundation of sand and silt."

"It's more than that," I said, before realizing I'd actually spoken the words aloud as everyone looked at me. "For Thumaar, I mean. Whatever gods Thumaar prayed to before have turned a deaf ear—he has been cast out, lost everything."

"Still has swords and gold," Azmorgon said.

I shook my head. "Which do him no good, as Cynead has more, and now the mightiest power in the empire at his fingertips. Thumaar has no power, no legitimacy and, until recently, no hope of achieving it. He has schemed and wasted away, with something burnt out, as you say. Flames fanned by desperation and fury at the injustice of it all. So to him, the Deserters probably aren't deserters at all, but exiles. Exiles who simply required the right opportunity to return to their rightful home and assume their sovereignty of all things."

"And when Darzaak sent his message," Vendurro said, "and we arrived—"

"When we arrived, it was as if his prayers were being rewarded, the gods beyond the Veil had heard him and delivered us into his hands. That was, until you tried telling him they weren't gods at all."

Mulldoos said, "So, what, we follow the man even if he's loonier than a plaguing flower hermit?"

Braylar let the Deserter heads fall to his side. "We follow our orders. Commander Darzaak is not here to countermand them, and without Memoridons or a rookery, we have no way to communicate with him, so our only choice is to follow the orders we do have."

Azmorgon sat up and threw a large stone into the brush. "Don't like it, Cap. Not one bit. Don't. Like. It."

"What's that, Lieutenant, following orders? Because if that is the case—"

"Darzaak ordered us to do this, sure enough. But he also promoted every plaguing one of you—well, excepting Squirrel here, Cap here done that—because you got grit and initiative. Maybe, when we head back into Sunwrack, we break the witch binds Cynead got, only instead of rebinding them to this man, maybe we seize it for ourselves. How about that?"

Vendurro corrected him. "Our Tower, you mean?"

The large man said, "Ayyup, of course. The Jackals. Commander Darzaak."

Braylar's dark eyes were slits, and his hand was still on Bloodsounder. "There is a keen distinction between initiative and treason." He said this quietly, without heat or inflection, but there was no mistaking that something slithered in the hidden depths.

Soffjian chuckled. "Says the man who ignored an imperial mandate when it was convenient to do so, who nearly convinced Cynead to enact the Fifth Man, who betrayed his own flesh and blood."

The serpent broke the surface briefly, as Braylar rasped, "For Tower. All we do is for Tower, sweet sister. Something you could not possibly begin to understand."

Azmorgon slapped a massive thigh. "Exactly what I'm saying! We do it for Jackals, seize the Memoridons, the throne, for ourselves!"

Mulldoos gave him a hard look that one slightly droopy eye didn't undermine. "Forgetting one real big thing there, Ogre. Darzaak was the one who ordered us to assist Thumaar. Commander Darzaak."

Vendurro added, "Forgetting something else, too. If the Jackals could have seized the throne for themselves, would have done it years ago instead of pledging fealty to Thumaar. We don't got the men to hold it, even if we grabbed it, which we ain't, as it violates a direct order."

Azmorgon jerked a thick thumb at Soffjian. "Things change. That was before there was a way to leash all of them in one hand. Things change."

Braylar stood up slowly, and the serpent was gliding along the surface now, sinewy, dangerous, very much a threat. "Just now, we need to discuss how we intend to sneak into the greatest fortified city in the known world, bypass thousands of Imperials and a multitude of Memoridons without being captured or killed, and put my sister in place to rebind them to Thumaar. As ordered. If, in the middle of our daring and likely suicidal raid, you happen to bump into Darzaak and mention that perhaps the mantle should be his instead, by all means, do let me know. Until such time, we will follow the orders we have in front of us. I do hope that is unambiguous enough for you all."

He looked around at his assembled officers and his sister, clearly no longer in the mood to tolerate any more rebuttals, but giving anyone a fair chance to earn his wrath. When no one offered any, he said, "Very good. I wish we had ale or wine. A great quantity of ale and wine. But we will simply have to plan while dining on dried meat and brackish water. So. Let me hear some suggestions. As Azmorgon adroitly pointed out, you occupy your current positions because you are cunning and clever. Let us be cunning and clever together, yes?"

There was some silence as each of them considered the problem.

Vendurro went first. "Maybe we could slip a few of us through the gates, disguised, like. Reassemble in the city proper, make our way to the Citadel?"

Soffjian wasted no time striking that down. "Maybe any other time, but they will be looking for me, tuned to me. Cynead takes risks, but calculated risks. He is not wildly impulsive, and not prone to letting his guard down. We cannot simply walk through the gates. No."

Azmorgon said, "Can't go knocking the gates down and fighting our way though. Dead within ten steps."

"Or dropping into the Trench like our brothers," Mulldoos replied. I shivered as I remembered the Jackals falling to their deaths in the great yawning chasm that encircled the entire fortified city of Sunwrack as the Imperials ordered the bridges pulled out from under their feet.

Azmorgon stroked his thick beard the way some men gave an animal affection. "So what, then? Can't sneak in through the gates, can't fight through them. And no matter what army Thumaar has, won't be enough to storm the city. Kind of plaguing stuck good, ain't we?"

Mulldoos said, "Hate to agree with the big bastard, but we covered this already. Pretty horseshit proposition we got here, Cap. Can't take Sunwrack. Just ain't happening. You said it yourself, if we were laying siege to the place, the only chance, and it would be slimmer than a suroka, is maybe a coordinated attack on the water supply from inside. Plaguers who built that place made it near impossible to take."

Braylar had his elbows on his knees, hands steepled together in front of his face, but when he heard "water," he unfolded them, sat up straighter, and looked at me. "You are absolutely right. But then again, we are not attempting to take the city. We merely need to get a small party inside, yes? And I now recall one such suggestion that could work."

Everyone looked around, having heard no suggestions that could work. But then I smiled, thinking back on the discussion Mulldoos and Hewspear had as I entered Sunwrack for the first time with the company, crossing one of the great bridges spanning the Trench. "Mulldoos hit on it just now, with the water. The aqueduct. It carries water down from the hills, right over the walls and into the city. We could sneak in through the aqueduct."

Mulldoos said, "Uh-huh. And as I recall, I shot that idea full of holes, because even if we survived the aqueducts and killed the guards—which is plaguing tougher than it sounds—still have to kill a bunch more in the gatehouses, lower the bridges, and hold them against that big Imperial army inside the city, plus a few hundred witches as well. Ain't happening."

I replied, "That's not happening, no. But as the captain said, our objective is to get inside, not invade, correct? We'd only have to take out the guards by the aqueduct itself and make our way through the city."

Soffjian gave me an appreciative smile that still unnerved me a bit, as if she were perusing weapons and found the one she was looking for. "That could work."

Mulldoos shook his head. "And what about our holy liege out there? The objective isn't just to creep into the city somehow—and I still say we'd be more likely to fall and go splat than make it across the Trench alive, you whoresons—but let's say that works, we still got to get Thumaar's army into the city somehow."

Vendurro asked, "Why?"

"What do you plaguing mean why? Even if we rebind the witches to him, he's still going to have to take the plaguing city to oust Cynead."

Vendurro replied, "What I mean to say is, we got to get him close enough for the rebind to work, right? In the city with us, or just outside maybe, but he doesn't have to get his army in just then. Doesn't have to take it at the same time."

Mulldoos glowered, still effective with one lousy eye. "What the plaguing hells are you talking about?"

Braylar said, "Let's hear him out, Mulldoos."

Mulldoos looked at the captain as if he was daft too and then back to Vendurro. "Yeah. Sure. Love to hear how we're going to take the city without taking the city. Go on, then."

Vendurro said, "Our job is to get inside, get to the frame, and reverse what Cynead done, right? Be real helpful if there was some kind of distraction though, wouldn't it? Because just getting into the city is going to be plaguing tough enough, but breaking into Cynead's lair, well, that will be all kinds of impossible. Unless there's something big that's got his attention. Like an army marching towards the gates."

"An army," Mulldoos said flatly. "Outside the gates. Okay then. This must be where it gets good."

Vendurro replied, "Let's say Thumaar arrives at the gates, camps outside, just outside of range of trebuchets and Memoridons. Maybe even just gets sighted marching towards the city, assembled nearby, even. That'll get Cynead's attention won't it? He'll figure Thumaar has cracked, and is making one final big move to take him on."

Smiling, Rudgi jumped in. "Only now, Cynead's got more power than ever. He's an arrogant prick, he probably won't just sit behind his walls and wait it out, will he?"

"Nope," Vendurro said. "Even though that would be the plaguing smart play. He'll want to wipe his enemy out, parade out a show of force. It's a chance to try out his shiny new toys, show the world what all those memory witches can do under one hand."

Soffjian nodded once. "I think they're both right. Cynead won't be able to resist the opportunity, even if his generals and captains urge prudence."

Vendurro said, "But while he's deliberating, arguing with his council and whatnot, all his attention on Thumaar, trying to figure out the best way to smash him, we're making our way right to the frame, getting in position."

Azmorgon stopped stroking his pelt beard. "Then what?"

Braylar replied, lips just barely curving into a smile, "Then, we wait for Cynead to march his Memoridons out of the Citadel, at the very least as a show of force, but more likely to take out his threat, eliminate Thumaar once and for all with the greatest audience possible." He gave an appreciative nod to Vendurro. "It has promise, I'll grant you."

"Promise?" Mulldoos asked. "You think Thumaar is going to risk his whole army on plaguing potential?"

"Yes," Braylar said, as he gave in to a proper smile. "Yes, I do. You see, he has the smaller force—no matter who he has bought or won over, they cannot possibly exceed what Cynead has. And with the Memoridons in Cynead's hand? No, Thumaar recognizes that we might utterly fail inside the city and risk being wiped out for good. But he is hungry, starving even. And he was never cautious, even when he was emperor. He will venture anything and everything on this."

I couldn't help saying, "But what if Cynead's advisors convince him to hold, wait out Thumaar rather than risking huge losses simply to drive him from the field? Even with his Memoridons and a larger army, he certainly isn't invincible."

Braylar said, "A less arrogant man would recognize that. But Cynead is lesser in no things, arrogance chief among them, so he will see this as a glorious opportunity to demonstrate his superiority. What's more, Thumaar's forces will have been bloodied already as he dispatches smaller battalions on his way to the capital, and Cynead knows he'll appear fraudulent and weak if he does not utterly destroy his foe. But, as ever, we will prepare for all contingencies. Cunning and clever, yes?"

And so we talked as the color fled the sky and the stars winked on, arguing over a dozen strategies for getting us into the Citadel, discussing the merits and failure points of each.

I spent most of the next two days hunched over my writing case, going through the remainder of the texts I had left, scribbling and translating, ink-stained fingers moving as quickly as I could manage as I hoped to stumble across any scrap of information that would confirm what I had already pieced together. Braylar and his officers considered and discarded a dozen various plans, and I caught snippets here and there, but the captain made sure I understood that my priority was to make it through the final pages if possible. What we had already might be enough. Probably was, even. But it was also a tremendous gamble. No matter what they came up with as a final plan to infiltrate, it was going to be exceptionally dangerous. But doubly so if we risked it all on one account with no corroboration.

So I read and wrote, the pain in my head flaring back up like embers you assumed had gone out but only needed the right breeze to produce flame and heat again. But still, there was nothing—endless writs, larder accounts, cartularies, transactions, tariffs, and every mundane thing one person could use ink to record for posterity, despite the fact that no one would ever want to read them again, most especially me.

Vendurro came over as I slipped a ribbon over another scroll I finished with and stared at the small pile of pages left. I knew the question was coming before he opened his mouth. "No luck?"

"No luck," I said, trying to keep the frustration at bay. Though I must have failed.

"You can only do what you can do. It's in there, it's in there, and if not . . ."

If not, a great many men and women might go to their deaths because they had inaccurate or incomplete information.

I'd seen Soffjian huddled together with Nustenzia on a number of occasions, discussing, arguing, questioning, no doubt preparing to go forward with what I had provided in the event that nothing else showed up in the pages. Which seemed likely.

Vendurro handed me a flask, and I put it to my lips, taking a huge swallow as it suddenly struck me just how thirsty I was, and the dark wine caused me to choke. "What . . . I thought . . ." I sputtered and wiped my chin.

"We needed some provisions. Rudgi led a party out to get some. Wine might not be a necessity, but . . . oh, who are we kidding. Of course it plaguing is."

He took the flask back for another few swallows and then handed it back to me.

I said, "I probably don't want to know, do I?"

Vendurro watched me drink more competently this time. "Can't say for certain what you do or don't want. But yeah, I'm thinking you don't. Wine doesn't grow on a bush, does it? Well, a canteen or bottle of it, anyway. Grapes do. Grow, I mean." He reached for the flask. "Easy there. Ink stains Cap can handle, but you hand him a bunch of translations with wine stains, thinking it might not go well for you."

No one else bothered me for the rest of the day. Which gave me the time I needed to finish. Though I wished I hadn't. There wasn't anything else about Bloodsounder, rogue priests, early efforts to control witches, or any topic of interest.

I put my quill down, fingers cramping, back sore, shaking a little, unsure when I last stopped to eat something. But it was for naught.

Expected. But that did nothing to lessen the disappointment. And there was something else. It wasn't just a failure to discover what we wanted that left me feeling empty. It was completing the job.

Perhaps the captain still wanted me around to record the Jackals' exploits, or serve as a translator in some other capacity. But I couldn't escape the sensation that I'd finished what I'd been assigned to do. This had always left me feeling a bit melancholy before, when my assignment came to a close. But this time, it was a heavier thing, dangling around my neck, pressing into my chest and stomach.

I briefly wondered if finishing the translation meant I'd not only concluded my task but outlived my usefulness. Certainly I'd done enough since riding with the Jackals to prove my worth.

Certainly.

I wished Vendurro had left the appropriated wine. I could have used some more.

Still, I wasn't entirely finished. I found the manuscript that had all the details the priest had compiled about binding and decided to revisit it, to be sure I hadn't missed anything. The thought that Jackals could die due to my lapse or error made my guts twist.

I'd uncover nothing new, but at least I could be absolutely certain I hadn't misinterpreted the references I already found.

After closing the latch on my case and throwing it over my shoulder, I went searching for the captain.

He was off by himself in a gulch and the ruins of a river, the water having disappeared ages ago. Braylar was holding Bloodsounder, but at least not whirling it above his head. He heard me approach, turned around and, before I'd said a word, read my face. "You discovered nothing new."

I only shook my head, bracing for the worst, wondering if I knew what that was.

Instead, after a brief sigh, he clapped me on the shoulder. "You have done good work, Arki. What we have will be enough then."

He started to turn when I blurted, "Do you believe that? Truly?"

Braylar looked at me. "All that matters is that my sister and Nustenzia believe it. And Thumaar of course."

"And do you have a solid plan, then? For getting them into the Citadel? Getting Thumaar close enough to shift the binds to him? Provided it works, of course." He opened his mouth and I hastily said, "Which it will."

Braylar gave me a level, unreadable look. "Your overflowing optimism is wasteful. You should conserve some, lest this incredibly dry ground simply drink it up. But to answer your question, much will depend on the tight-lipped deposed emperor of ours and what he brings to the event. But yes, I believe we have arrived at as good a plan as any. All things considered."

He gave me a look that I interpreted as a dismissal, which I ignored. "May I ask you something, Captain?"

Braylar looked over at me, surprised I hadn't left already. "Judging from your tone, no doubt something of import that will make me question my judgment in allowing you to remain in this company."

After considering if there were a delicate way to begin, I chose directness instead. "You told me about the failed attempt to kill your father's murderer. But not about what ultimately happened to him."

Braylar stared off at some scrubby grass rimming the entrance of the gulch. "That was not a question. But I will respond as if it were. If life was a romance of old, I would have had a second opportunity once I achieved manhood, a rare double chance to right the wrong, redeem myself, and kill the man once and for all in an epic duel, yes?"

"But that isn't what happened, is it?"

He gave one short laugh. "Of course not, Arki. The bastard was killed by an Anjurian near the border during a skirmish many years later."

"And that didn't bring Soffjian some measure of joy, at least?"

The captain slipped Bloodsounder back on his belt. "It might have. But she never forgave me for failing to stick him a second time with a blade, as I had promised so many years before."

I thought back to what Soffjian had said before, alluded to, really, about other broken promises. I was reluctant to bring that up, but I wasn't sure if we would ever have another opportunity. "Your sister mentioned something else. In the plague village. About not only failing to avenge your father, but something to do with your people as a whole."

Braylar didn't reply right away, and took so long I was sure he didn't intend to at all. But then he finally said, "Our rift started after our father's murder. But that was only the start. After we were captured, during that tenyear before my manumission, hostilities had increased dramatically between my people and the Empire."

"Because of your father?"

"In part. Only in part. Also because the Jackals had taken us, as in the days of old, rather than during a proper Choosing. My uncle Sirk recovered from his grievous wounds, you see. And in time, he managed to unify the neighboring tribes. Well, conquer, if we aren't being coy. But Sirk eventually grew enough in power, and had so many tribal factions under his sway that he finally challenged the Syldoon when they came to the island again. My uncle slaughtered that small company, and sent word that the tribes no longer were any sort of vassals to the Empire."

"That must have gone over well," I said.

"Ha. Yes, the Empire wasn't accustomed to any region trying to throw off their yoke, hinterland or not. So they intended to invade, to squash this rebellion in full, to make an example of my uncle. And they sent the Jackals at the front of the army, as they had the most familiarity with that part of the world."

Even with Soffjian alluding to something like this, it was still chilling to hear. "You were sent to kill or capture your own people?"

Irritation bled in, profusely. "You forget. I had been with the Syldoon and Jackals longer at that point than I had with my own tribe. The Jackals were my people now. While I had no desire to see the Orlu destroyed or enslaved, they were distant, remote, and part of another life altogether. They were no longer my people. And they should have recognized that they were inviting their doom, demanding it, truly."

This was difficult to reconcile, since I possessed neither family nor homeland dear to me nor any system or culture that had totally absorbed me. "When Soffjian spoke of this before, she said . . ." I stopped, wondering where curiosity ended and dangerous transgression began.

Braylar narrowed his eyes. "Out with it."

"She said you could have stopped this, should have done more to protect your people. That is, your tribe, your old people."

Braylar watched a shadow fall over the gulch, looked up at a large galleon-like cloud. "Why, of course she did. Yes, a young green sergeant is infinitely instrumental in determining imperial policy. I should have only said the word, and Commander Darzaak would have halted the campaign and turned around immediately."

There was an edge to his voice that should have halted me, but I found myself asking, "Was this Emperor Thumaar who ordered the invasion?"

"Yes. Excellent point. I should have simply marched up to the Emperor himself and said, 'Your Majesty, I know you are intent on bringing the Orlu to heel, but I feel the need to tell you, you are making a grave mistake.' To which he would have replied, 'Oh? Why is that, Green Sergeant?' And I would have said, 'Because my older sister says as much. And there is no arguing with her.' Yes. Boundless negligence on my part. A tremendous oversight and unforgivable failure of character."

The bile there was unmistakable, but I got the sense that it wasn't directed solely at his impossible sister. "Did Commander Darzaak invite you, that is, were you a part of his council? Did he solicit your input on how to best proceed, given your familiarity with your—with the Orlu?"

Braylar said, "You've met the man. Does he strike you as the type to solicit overmuch? No. No is the answer. He commands. That is what Commanders do best."

"So . . . ?"

The captain looked like he might want to draw Bloodsounder again. "So, what, exactly, Arki? So, should I have done more to dissuade him? To try to encourage him to some course of diplomacy, rather than a brutal incursion into the tribelands to teach tribals a lesson, simply because I had been one of them long ago? Is that what you are truly asking, or failing to ask, for fear that I might strike you down?"

I forced myself not to take a step back as he advanced on me, stopping only when he was so close I could count the stubble on his cheeks. Quietly, I said, "I'm just trying to understand why your sister so profoundly holds this against you so many years later."

Braylar nodded twice, very slowly, nearly nose to nose with me. "I see." And I felt as if I had well and truly overstepped, expecting him to deliver a flurry of elbows at any moment.

But then he turned away. "As it so happens, Arki, I didn't plead. But I did try to convince the Commander that my people were experts at the small war."

"The small war?"

"Yes," he replied. "Fighting in the dark, using terrain, hitting supply trains, refusing pitched battles, especially against a superior force. The Orlu, like all the tribes in the vicinity, were sneaky bastards and would whittle an enemy down, sap their morale, attack with speed, and withdraw even faster. Rather than appealing from an emotional position, doomed to fail, I hoped to convince the Commander, and through him the Emperor, that it would be a costly and ultimately futile campaign. Not worth the loss of lives."

"But this didn't succeed in deterring them?"

"Deterring? No," he said. "It succeeded in preparing them for the small war. And mitigating loss. At Thumaar's behest, Commander Darzaak mined me for all the information he could, and while I tried to use my proximity to discourage, redirect, or stop the invasion, I only truly succeeded in ensuring they didn't get drawn into a small war with the Orlu."

Though I knew the story wouldn't end anywhere good, I asked, "What did they do?"

"The Orlu might be sneaky, but the Syldoon are relentless, cunning, and—with the exception of the Urglovians and their ridiculous reliance on war wagons—adaptable. Before our army arrived, the Jackals sent envoys to visit the other tribes, promised that those who sided with the Syldoon would be richly rewarded, and turned most of the island against the Orlu even before we set foot on tribal soil. Between that, and sending in Memoridons to assassinate the Orlu chieftain—"

"Your uncle."

"My uncle," he agreed. "The Orlu resistance was doomed. By the time we jumped off our boats, they were broken, scurrying for caves and mountain holdfasts, and no danger of waging a long series of small wars or any kind of war at all. The invasion was a wild success. We enslaved half of them, killed anyone else we could find." He said this flatly, as if talking about an incident in a dusty history tome. "The Orlu were wiped out that summer. And though I protested, Commander Darzaak promoted me to lieutenant."

It all made a horrible kind of sense. "So Soffjian assumed you not only failed to do enough to save your people, but aided the invasion to profit from it."

"How remarkably perceptive. You must be a scholar of some kind." Braylar started walking away as another cloud shadowed the area. "Now leave me, Arki. Wordlessly."

I didn't consider any other choice.

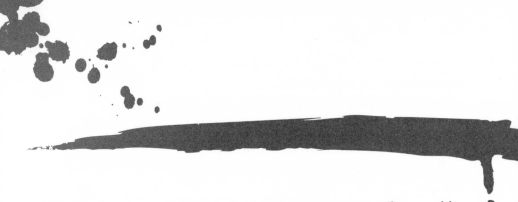

On that appointed day, I accompanied Braylar, his officers, and his sister as we rode back into the pisshole village of Brassguilt, taking a less direct route to avoid the flatly curious eyes of the villagers and tethering our horses behind the defeated and dilapidated barn—leaning drunkenly to the side with nothing to grab onto, it looked ready to tumble over for good at any moment.

It was cloudier than it had been the day before, so the shafts and bars of light were weaker inside, the gloom heavier, and the faces of the occupants more difficult to work out.

Kruzinios walked over as we entered and the Jackals saluted first, which he returned smartly, decades of discipline not easily outdone by gray braids. "On time today," he said. "My lord will be pleased to see it. Prepared as you are punctual, I hope."

Braylar nodded, and the general said, "Good. Very good. Follow me then." He stopped abruptly, and without turning around spoke more quietly. "And if you choose to ignore my warning again, I won't be advocating on your behalf. Enough with the deity business. Our liege requires a clear head and direct purpose just now. Do not cloud things. Understood?"

Braylar twitch-smiled. "Short of lying to our would-be-sovereign, it was hard to avoid, truly. Would you have me lie to the man then?"

Kruzinios spun on his heel, somewhat slowly but still with gravity and command. "You are one of the more gifted truthbenders I've ever met. It was why we sent you into Anjuria, after all. I'm sure you could have concocted some version of events that skirted close to the truth and still didn't fail to heed my warning. And if he presses you again on the topic, you will deflect and redirect as I know you are all too capable of. Tell me I am understood, Captain."

"Understood, sir."

The general led us into the barn. As before, a large number of Thumaar's soldiers were standing watch, not close enough to make out any conversations, but near enough to respond immediately if any threat presented itself. The deposed emperor was also standing roughly where he had been the other day, only this time there were six other figures just behind him.

Vendurro's eyes must have been the keenest among us, as he made one of the men there first and whispered, "Plague. Me. We're fucked, Cap."

Braylar didn't slow down and only whispered back, "Easy there, Lieutenant. Easy. Follow my lead."

He said it with a calmness and jocularity that had to be forced, given who was standing before us. I felt my legs wobble and had to resist the urge to reach for Lloi's saber, despite having little idea how to use it.

Baron Brune stepped forward, an oversized smile on his brutally handsome face. "Captain Braylar Killcoin! How very good to see you again! I was despairing we might never have such an opportunity." He turned and looked at Thumaar and gave a deep theatrical bow. "My humble apologies, my lord, for any broken protocols here. When you said the good Captain was going to be attending, I barely allowed myself to dream it was truly possible. I am so very anxious to catch up with the man. You see, he departed my barony rather suddenly and under such unusual circumstances."

"I am aware," Thumaar said, gruffer than quarry stone. "And you are aware, whatever grievances you have are dead and buried as far as I am concerned. Cremated even. Ash on the wind. Are you going to have a problem with that, Baron?"

"No, no," he replied. "None whatsoever. Well. Not directly with this man—he was merely a professional saboteur obeying orders at the behest of his Tower Commander. But I do hope some reparations are still in order. His shenanigans left me with a ripper running wild in my streets, which also happened to be littered with the countless dead, and—"

"I counted," Braylar offered. "I do like to keep track of my shenanigans."

Brune looked back at him, and his expression made it clear he wanted nothing more than to bundle us up and return us to his toyroom in the bowels of his castle in Alespell. "Do you? And do you know how many of my good paying Fairgoers were slaughtered in the streets, or how many escaped with their lives but took their coins with them, never to return? Do you know how much I lost when you and your men—"

"If anyone has a complaint here, it is me," Braylar replied. "The security in your city is atrocious, really. A large band of Hornmen walk through the gates to abduct and kill one of your guests and your men just assume they have a legitimate reason? I was sorely disappointed. Anything that happened from that point forward is on you, I'm afraid."

"*Me?*" Brune asked, voice rising.

"You," Braylar said, very calmly. "Or Captain Honeycock. Is he here as well, skulking about in the hay?"

Brune started to shout something I couldn't make out, but Thumaar thundered over him, "*Enough,* the both of you!" He walked up to the pair and scowled at the baron. "You can take up further reparations with Commander Darzaak, but the man promised to deliver Henlester's head to you, did he not? Help put down your little rebellion?"

The baron didn't back down. "I would have no rebellion to speak of it wasn't for his agent here."

Braylar said, "I merely hastened what was already occurring naturally on its own, Brune. Do not make the mistake of thinking for a minute that your priest caste would not—"

Thumaar jabbed a finger in the captain's sternum. "What part of 'enough' wasn't clear, Syldoon?"

I feared and expected that Braylar's tongue would only damn him more, but he wisely kept his mouth closed.

Thumaar looked back and forth between the captain and baron. "We are not here to mediate your differences. Baron Brune, you will receive your deviant priest as promised, and more importantly, you will be a hero to your people, an instrument that guaranteed the Anjurians were not crushed under Cynead's heel. If that doesn't constitute reparations, then nothing plaguing does. But none of that happens until I am back where I belong. And while that might taste like pickled asshole to you, you will keep your mouth shut and speak no more of it."

Mulldoos laughed at that and the deposed emperor rounded on the Jackals again. "And you will cease antagonizing the baron or his men. He is in my camp and among my council. Just as you are. And there's an end to it."

Azmorgon's voice resonated in the barn, and the soldiers furthest away likely had no trouble hearing him as he turned to Braylar and said, "Anjurians? Plaguing Anjurians? Sunwrack will collapse into the Trench before—"

Thumaar said, "Have you been an emperor, boy?"

Azmorgon shook his hairy head.

"No, of course not. You have no plaguing idea what it means to rule, to make difficult decisions. And what's more, you have no idea what it is to lose your throne, your empire, your ability to do those things. But I am reclaiming what is mine. And your captain here is helping me do it, boy. That is all you need to know or concern yourself with."

Azmorgon's huge chest rose and fell as he breathed heavily. "As you say. My lord. But I ain't a boy."

"Then plaguing act like a man," Thumaar said, maintaining eye contact for a few moments then turning away dismissively, as if the exchange had never occurred. "Now, Captain, it is time you explain precisely how you will help me."

Braylar replied, "Presently. But before I begin, it would be helpful to know a few things that will ensure the success of this plan. You mentioned your men had set sail, were landing on the eastern shores of the Bonewash, yes? And others were converging from land already. Were you referring to the Anjurians, my lord?"

Thumaar looked impatient and irritated as he said, "Yes, yes. Brune's men are marching from Alespell. My Eagles and the Confederates will have disembarked already and made for Sunwrack. What of it?"

Mulldoos and Vendurro looked at each other, and Soffjian asked the question they all seemed to be mulling, the lightning-bolt vein pulsing in her forehead. "The Confederates, my lord?"

Thumaar repeated it as if speaking to a young, slow child. "Yes. The Vortagoi Confederacy. Did you think I was simply licking my wounds this entire time? I have made preparations, Memoridon."

Braylar was often inscrutable, and no less so now, but I thought there was a tightness to his jaw as well as he said, "And what size host have you assembled, my lord? That will dictate the best operation for stealing Cynead's Memoridons."

"His days of usurping will be over soon. As to the men, there are twelve thousand Eagles, forty-five thousand Vortagoi soldiers, and from Alespell . . ."

Thumaar looked at Brune who replied, "Eight thousand. My lord."

Mulldoos tried to whistle, but it was mangled by his lips, and he cursed quietly to himself.

Thumaar called up the other men behind him. "These two men are from the Confederacy. They have pledged the necessary resources to help me regain my throne. Generals Tubarna and Luwatannis."

The Vortagoi generals wore matching armor, circular plates on their chests with bronze lamellar plates radiating away from the center like rays from the sun, tall domed helms with three feathers sprouting from the top, and long skirts that nearly covered their sandals. Each had a beard oiled in ringlets, though Tubarna's seemed to be hiding a weak chin and swollen neck.

Soffjian started to say something that sounded decidedly like an objection, but Braylar interrupted. "Well met. And very good. It is excellent to hear that you have gathered a formidable host. And it goes a long way to determining which strategy will work."

Thumaar's eyes were like turquoise stones under the silver brows, and equally as friendly. "Which is?"

"I was hoping you might finally ask that, my lord." That earned some grins from the Jackals, and even a hint of a smile from Brune, though he hid it well, but none from Kruzinios or Thumaar.

Braylar continued, "I suggest you order your forces to head to Sunwrack."

"Sunwrack," Thumaar said, quietly. "We can't exactly sneak up on them."

"No, my lord. They will learn of your advance quickly enough—they have the greatest intelligence gathering ability ever assembled now—and Cynead will order Thurvacian forces to oppose you, though he won't have much time. He will not believe you have risked late-fall storms crossing the Bonewash. So he might chance to order some army to try to impede you, but it will be difficult to do, given your decisive plan."

"You've told me nothing I didn't already know, and less about what you intend to do."

"Indeed," Braylar said, "I did in fact. I said 'command,' not lead. Kruzinios will personally lead your forces in the field."

Thumaar seemed decidedly interested now. "Will he? And where exactly will I be?"

"You will be with us, my lord."

"Will I? And where exactly will *you* be?"

Braylar smiled, and it seemed genuine and without edge. "We will be waiting for your forces to advance, closing in on Sunwrack. And about to sneak a small band through an aqueduct."

Brune laughed. When Thumaar looked at him, the baron said, "An aqueduct is an inspired choice, I will grant you that."

The former emperor said, "So. We sneak into Sunwrack through an aqueduct. Slay numerous guards. Likely in the middle of night, of course. And?"

"And," Braylar said, "We make for the Citadel. That is where Cynead's frame is, whence he derives central control of the Memoridons."

"And . . . he will be in the field, or en route, to destroy my outnumbered army, unwilling to hide behind the walls when he has the larger force and the Memoridons besides, is that right?"

He might have been burning from the inside out with ambition and vengeance, but Thumaar was a quick study, that was for certain.

"Exactly so," Braylar said. "He will relish the chance to crush you once and for all. So, timing is critical. We can only strike the Citadel when it's evident he's ridden forth, but we can't wait so long that he has time to engage and destroy your forces." He looked over at Brune and the Confederacy generals. "No offense meant, my lords, but Cynead does have the superior numbers, and, what's more, all the Memoridons."

"So we are merely bait?" General Luwatannis asked.

"Yes," Braylar replied, smiling broadly. "It is very good to see you understand your role. I was worried this might take some compelling rhetoric to make everything clear."

Kruzinios reached over and put a hand on Thumaar's shoulder. "My lord . . . you cannot risk this. One false step, and you fall to your death, or find an Imperial arrow in your neck, or worse, get captured and delivered into Cynead's hands. And everything you have waited for will be lost. Everything. You cannot."

Thumaar gave his old general a kind smile and looked at Braylar. "I am assuming I need to be close. To the frame, I mean. When you reverse what Cynead wrought and transfer control to me."

Soffjian said, "Yes, my lord."

Braylar agreed. "We believe that is the best chance of success, yes."

"Very well." Thumaar seemed to stand taller. "It is decided then."

General Tubarna's bulging eyes somehow managed to achieve froglike status, if frogs could go purple in the face. With that odd northern lilt, he said, "This is ridiculous, my lord! The Confederacy only agreed to assist you if you commanded the forces yourself. You cannot—"

Thumaar replied, "Do not dare to tell me what I can or cannot do, General. And do not forget who you are speaking with. Your Confederacy agreed out of greed. Nothing more. You want sovereignty over your own people. And I am granting that in exchange for the troops marching towards us now. But make no mistake, General—I *am* issuing the commands. And if my men here say this is the best means of achieving my goal—which means achieving your goal by proxy—then you will obey those commands, or I will bury you and find someone who will. I've expressed myself clearly, I hope?"

The general seemed apoplectic but forced himself to lower his bulging forehead and spit out, "As you say, my lord."

Brune said, "I would never be so bold as to tell an emperor, sitting or otherwise, his business. But allow an observation, if you will."

"Speak," Thumaar said. "Briefly."

"The last time this man concocted a plan in my presence, his oratory skills were equally sharp. And despite my own trusted advisor urging me not to trust him, I did so, against my own good judgment, even. And wished I hadn't. The man is a viper. How do you know he is not leading you into a trap in Sunwrack, or intends to turn you over to your fearsome enemy? That does seem to be what he does best, my lord."

I hoped Thumaar would shout him down or threaten him into silence, but he only looked at Braylar closely, seeming to suddenly recall he was branding the Jackals heretics only two days before. "Your response, Captain?"

"The man," Braylar replied, "is easily duped, both by me, his clerics, and likely anyone else in his inner circle, save the stalwart loyalist, Captain Gurdinn, but only because that man is too obtuse to be disingenuous. You, my lord, have only been deceived once, and through no fault of your own. Cynead is as cunning as they come, and makes any of my machinations seem the playthings of children. But if you require convincing—"

The deposed emperor seemed unmoved. "I do."

"Then I need only remind you: I fled the capital and was pursued by imperial troops for days, losing the majority of my company in the process, including Lieutenant Hewspear. We have bled mightily to meet you here, and are willing to bleed more to see you to the throne."

Brune said, "This could all be part of an elaborate ruse."

Braylar dropped his hand to Bloodsounder, and all glibness and charm disappeared in an instant. He rasped, "Say the death of my lieutenant is a ruse one more time, Baron. Please. Do. And it will be your blood staining this dirt floor red."

Thumaar raised a hand. "That is enough. I am satisfied." He looked at Brune, Kruzinios, and the Confederacy generals. "General Kruzinios, you will ride with the other esteemed officers here, and lead our troops south. Baron Brune, you will wait three days and then do the same with your army. Captain Braylar, where will we be that they can get word to us they are closing in?"

Braylar looked at his lieutenants, and Vendurro said, "There's an abandoned copper mine, close to the aqueduct in the foothills east of the Moonvows, west of a wee village. You know the one?"

"Aye," Thumaar said. "Any emperor who doesn't know the map of his own land isn't fit to sit the throne. And it's high time the rightful emperor reclaim his."

Braylar said, "Very good." He turned to Kruzinios. "Send a rider to the mine when you've advanced on Sunwrack, General. During the day. We will wait on your word. That night, we make for the capital."

Thumaar took a few steps back and addressed everyone. "We are unlikely allies. Maybe the unlikeliest. And you have misgivings. Doubts. Suspicious. I understand that. But you will burn them. Each of you. They are nothing. Let them go entirely. You are part of the grandest enterprise imaginable. You all risk much, but the rewards will be immeasurable. Do you understand me? In less than a tenday, each of you will receive what was promised." He took a moment to slowly scan each face in front of him. "That is all. Dismissed."

We all started to file out of the barn, the disgruntled Vortagoi generals and Baron Brune heading out the other entrance with Thumaar, and us walking back towards the north entrance.

Kruzinios called over to us. "A word, Captain."

Braylar stopped and waited for the old general to catch up. "You use what soldiers you see fit to accompany my liege, and your Memoridon. But you will take an equal number of Eagles."

Braylar tilted his head sideways. "Why, General, you do sound as darkly distrustful as a certain Anjurian who shall remain nameless."

"I do not like this course. Do not agree with it. But I trust you to do your job. Just as it is my job to protect our liege. I will not send Thumaar into Sunwrack without doing everything in my power to ensure his survival."

"Understood, General Kruzinios."

The older soldier said, "So. How many men will you require then?"

Braylar looked at his retinue.

Mulldoos said, "A hundred thousand ought to plaguing do the trick."

Vendurro took a more realistic tack. "We got to keep it smallish. Need enough blades to dispatch any Leopards we come across, but not so many to raise an alarm." He looked at Soffjian. "You know where the frame is, layout, guards, what have you. What do you reckon?"

Soffjian thought about it and said, "No more than thirty." She looked at Braylar. "Fifteen Eagles?"

Braylar nodded. "Fifteen it is. Send them to our camp. We will leave immediately after."

Kruzinios nodded. "And the remainder of your soldiers? Will they ride for our forces after you head to Sunwrack?"

The captain said, "Once we have mounted the aqueduct, they will hold that position. I would have them there if we need to escape. This is a gambit, for certain, but you knew every action would be. Still, I will abandon it and withdraw with Thumaar if it proves untenable."

The general nodded, they all saluted, and we left the pisshole village for what I assumed and hoped was the final time.

We rode for six days, taking goat tracks and seldom-trod paths and avoiding anything resembling a highway, and certainly staying well clear of any of the Syldoon's stone roads with all their heavy traffic. Our party was small enough that even with the fifteen new soldiers riding with us, avoiding detection wasn't that difficult, especially with the scouts ahead directing us around any populated areas.

With the translation complete, and little noteworthy happening on the journey there to require heavy recording of any kind, I mostly just observed and listened. Not surprisingly, Thumaar and the Eagles kept to themselves, and I made no overtures to introduce myself or join. I already had one Tower I barely fit into—that was enough.

So I tried to eavesdrop and occasionally sit and join Jackal conversations when I could. Braylar had shared our orders with the soldiers, and though I expected him to hold back the specifics regarding the other players involved, he did no such thing. So I frequently heard discussions and arguments about the merits or lack thereof of such a strategy. The prevailing opinion seemed to be that expecting foreign soldiers from the opposite edge of the empire to do Thumaar's dirty work would only end in betrayal or disaster, or, if he somehow managed to secure his throne again, it would be a tenuous reign at best, considering the deep hatred the Syldoon had for the Anjurians, and the gall and bile that would readily flow at the thought of giving the Confederacy any real kind of true independence, as seemed pledged.

More than one Jackal quietly pointed out that Thumaar's promises to Brune and the Confederate generals ran counter to all his previous agendas, but I heard Mulldoos shut that down quickly, stating the deposed emperor's agendas were no concern of ours, only our orders.

After listening to the thirtieth or so such debate, and watching the captain quietly observe the conversation as well, I asked him privately why he had divulged those things.

He seemed amused and irritated as he replied, "When you first joined us, I certainly cloaked much of my doings from you—you were untested, a civilian, and a foreigner. There was absolutely no reason to trust you. Whereas my men are the only ones I *do* trust in the known world."

I said, "Fair point. But aren't you worried that this particular bit of knowledge might poison the well, so to speak?"

"No. I am not. Would you like to know why?"

I nodded, and he continued, "Because the one thing the Jackals have in common with every Tower, every other soldier in the Syldoon empire, is that we are professionals. We do our duty. Our leaders will allow the soldiers to know the pertinent information that impacts their missions, their objectives, even give them rein to gripe and argue and brew some minor dissent in candid conversations. I allow it with my retinue, hear their complaints and objections, provided they do not question my orders when it matters, in front of the men.

"Our emperors give the commanders equal opportunity to air grievances, even that wily bastard Cynead, the last Caucus notwithstanding. But when it matters, and blood needs spilling, the Syldoon are thoroughly committed, and their loyalty is to their brethren and their officers in each respective Tower is manifest and unassailable. Professional to the last, you see."

I kept pace with him as we walked further from the troops, into a glade, though less wooded than regions further south in Anjuria. "And yet the Towers distrust each other, actively work to outmaneuver most of the others, and form uneasy alliances only so long as necessary."

"Yes," he replied. "You have spoken nothing remotely false."

"I doubt I will ever understand that."

"I share your doubts. You are not Syldoon."

We kept walking for several paces, and he added, "Though you have become far more embedded than I imagined possible. It has been interesting to watch. Exasperating, but also amusing and interesting. You have proven yourself to be far more competent than expected, Arki."

I was unsure how to respond to that spiky praise when Mulldoos intercepted us and grabbed my upper arm. "You and Cap about done with your little stroll here? Because if there's no quill in your hand, there sure as spit ought to be a sword. Come on, scribbler."

Braylar twitch-smiled. "You see? Who could have ever imagined that you and my gruff lieutenant would be getting along so smashingly now?"

Mulldoos replied, "Oh yeah, my sword is smashing into that stupid kettle helm left and right. And his thigh. And his sword arm. And every other place he can't seem to block worth a plaguing hell. We're really cozy now. Come on then . . ." The lieutenant dragged me off and continued administering welts and trying to teach me how to prevent them.

There was nothing cozy about it.

The following day, we started to encounter defunct smelting pots and furnaces in the hills. I understood little of mining and metallurgy but was aware that the contemporary smelting sites were once right alongside or in close proximity to the source of metals, and these looked old enough to confirm my suspicion that we had to be near our destination.

The scouts entered the site, circled it, and made broader circles in the surrounding wilderness, but saw nothing to give alarm, so our company rode down a gravel trail that was mostly overgrown. The trail wound around the lip of the excavation, and as we broke through some tanglebrush and creak-backed pines, I saw the abandoned copper mine below in the center of a large rock pit. There were wooden shacks that had rotted and fallen over, and larger, thicker timber structures, equally derelict, warped and broken and collapsed and rummaged through, decades earlier from the looks of it.

I saw flashes of the aqueduct in the hills not far to the west, the grey stones partly visible through the branches.

My saddle sores were gone, but I was still anxious to get off my horse. I had welts on my arms, chest, stomach, and the outside of my thighs from the beating Mulldoos had administered. While I was greener than any rank recruit he had ever seen—something he seemed to delight in repeating over and over, in as many foul ways as possible—and I apparently had a better chance of killing someone with a quill than with any bladed weapon (which also gave him great pleasure in declaring), he'd decided it was time to begin sparring. And while we were moving at half speed and three quarters most of time, we finished each session with full-speed sparring. He didn't have to exert himself much to demonstrate how I'd allowed my shield to drift open, or failed to step out of a blow even when it was clear it was coming, or stuck my sword arm out too far, exposing it, or a hundred other gaps in my defense.

My bruises had bruises.

It seemed so simple—you had a weapon in one hand, a shield in the other, and your feet to move—but notoriously difficult to put it all together. Occasionally I moved well, negotiating the space properly, and didn't do a terrible job of deflecting blows, but neglected to throw any of my own. Or I overextended, got too aggressive, and lost my balance, or forgot my shield work completely and took another clang to the helm or a stinging rebuke to the ribs.

"Welts are the best teacher of all," he'd said, hooking my shield with the edge of his to pull it out of the way and delivering a thrust to my thigh. "You're a real plaguing attentive student," he said, laughing, as I managed to block two blows in a sequence but lost sight of him, blinding myself with my own shield, and then heard a stout shot and felt the reverberations in my helm as he struck me when I tried peering over the edge. "I'm a crippler, you're a scribbler. Think you can change that any, pen monkey?" Another blow, another welt.

So it was a relief when I finally climbed out of my saddle at the abandoned mine site, especially since it was nearly dusk, so there would be no more training today. I was stiff, sore, and tired.

But, I reminded myself, at least I wasn't in a Deserter cell, waiting to be drained of memories and husked. Or a corpse. No matter how much my body hurt, it was better than the alternative.

Braylar trusted his men, but set out to explore the site as much as the fading light allowed, whether to assure himself it was a secure location, or simply to do something to stretch his legs. The rest of the company took care of their horses and made camp, and again the Jackals and Eagles gave each other space.

After a cold, unsatisfying meal of beans, hard bread, and of course the ubiquitous dried meat —it was so tough it was impossible to tell what animal it possibly could have been—I walked away from the abandoned mine, leaving the forgotten shafts and the miners' shades who might have still haunted them. The trees weren't as plentiful or towering as those in the southern tracts of land in clerical or royal forests, but they were woods, just the same. As I lost sight of the mine and soldiers gathered there, and headed out to empty my bladder, it was something of a relief to escape the low conversations, crude jokes, and wistful reminiscing about some soft maid or warm hearth or delightful diversion that seemed worlds away. The Syldoon might have been among the toughest men and women in the world, but they were not immune to longing for comforts, even simple ones like wine, now that the last stolen skins of it had run dry.

But that only made it less bearable. I was glad I couldn't see the aqueduct anymore either. The prospect of climbing up onto it soon, walking miles in the cold water to sneak into the most well-protected city in the known world on the most covert operation ever conceived, seemed only slightly less doomed than jumping into a bear pit with a blindfold on.

I heard some something scuffle through the dried leaves behind me and reached for Lloi's sword.

Rudgi laughed, its own scuffling sound. "You barely know which end of that thing to hold, but at least you have good ears. You might make a half-decent sentry. That's something."

She stepped out from behind a tree as I replied, "That has always been my life's ambition."

Rudgi said, "'Dream for the sky, or the horned moon in it,' right?"

I nodded, wondering how much of my face she could see. We were quiet for a few moments as she walked closer. It felt cold enough to see our breath ghosting, but it must have just been the brisk breeze stirring the trees, as there was no breath to be seen.

I stood there, she stood there, and it wasn't as awkward as I expected. Still, it felt like one of us ought to say something.

"So—" I began, just as she stepped in and kissed me, our teeth clinking together. Her hand was in my hair, on the back of my head, across my neck, exploring, and I started kissing her back, bringing my hands up, unsure where to touch, what she liked, so simply running them across her back.

Rudgi slid her tongue in my mouth, tentative, just a quick dart at first, then more assertively as I opened my mouth and responded, repositioning my head, suddenly feeling not the least bit cold at all.

Then I thought about the last time a woman was forward and kissed me and pulled back.

"What is it?" she asked, looking around. "Those keen ears hear something?"

"No," I said. And she reached for me again, but I stepped back slightly. "Did Vendurro put you up to this?"

She replied, laughing, "So, are you asking if I'm a copper-grubbing harlot, or if my commanding officer can tell me who I should be fucking?"

"No, I'm . . . I didn't mean . . . I just meant that, well—"

Rudgi reached her hand up, gently stroked my cheek for a second, then withdrew it fast to give me a quick slap. "For having a brain so big, you really don't have the first clue how to use it half the time, do you?"

"I didn't mean to offend you, Rudgi, I'm just not used to—"

"Oh, you didn't offend me, Arki. You think my skin's that thin? I'm a plaguing Syldoon. You amused me some, but didn't offend me." She stepped closer, and I braced for another slap. "Not used to a woman showing you what she wants, eh?"

I wanted to reach out, to taste her again, to stop us both from talking. She was hardly a lady who stepped out of a romantic mural—Rudgi was muscular and a bit stocky, with that bent nose like a busted adze, and there was no question that she was a plaguing Syldoon. But she also had a becoming smattering of freckles, an easy smile, and lovely eyes.

"Well, actually, I am," I said. "Used to it, that is. It seems that's the only kind of woman I attract, truth be told. Or maybe it's just that I'm usually too uncertain to initiate. Romance. To initiate romance." I cursed myself. "What I mean is—"

She put two callused fingers on my lips. "How about I talk. There's no romance going on here, Arki, never fear. And to answer your question, on the subject of who puts their fingers, tongue, or cock in me, nobody says when that happens except me, you understand? My Towermates respect that, and I'd gut any man who didn't. Now, I'm here to let you do those things. Are you going to, or do you want to go back to counting pine cones in the dark?"

Rudgi was right about the romance. I stepped forward, grabbed her shoulders that were only a little lower than mine, leaned in to kiss her. And bonked her on the nose. She adjusted deftly and turned her head and our lips were together again, and I forced myself not to flinch as she ran her hands over my sore ribs. She reached under my tunic, raked her nails over my chest, around to my back as our mouths met. I'd had little enough experience with women, so I wasn't sure if her forwardness was typical or not, but it was a far cry from Skeelana or the other girl I'd lain with. Rudgi was more animal than woman. A hungry animal. I wasn't sure why she wanted me, but just then didn't care.

I slid my hand over her tunic, circling one small breast, and she grabbed my fingers and pulled them under, positioning my hand where she wanted. I circled her nipple with the tips of my fingers and gently squeezed and she moaned and pressed herself into me, her own hand undoing my laces, nails scratching as she raked my stomach and then reached between my legs to grab me. "Mmmm, that's what I like about you young bucks—stiff as a staff at a moment's notice."

I didn't have a chance to wonder how many bucks she'd been with or to care, as she stroked me and bit my lower lip hard enough to draw blood. "Want my mouth on you?"

Nodding, I replied, "Yes. Unless you mean teeth."

Rudgi laughed and dropped to her knees. "No promises." I looked around, certain Vendurro or someone else would come crashing through the woods to interrupt us, but had no time to think about that either, gasping as she took me in her mouth.

I wished it were lighter out—I wanted to see her face as I ran my hands through her kinky twisted curls of hair, pulling hard once as she scraped her teeth along me, though she was only being playful.

I'd never had a woman do that to me before, and it was almost too much, too intense. "Whoa, slow down," I whispered.

Rudgi stopped long enough to say, "Please."

"What?" I exhaled hard as she teased me a bit more.

"You're a gentle lad, a scholarly sort. Use those manners, scholar. Say please."

"You want me to—"

She engulfed me again, and I didn't want this over too fast. I grabbed her head and said, "Please. Please stop."

She ran her tongue along my length and laughed. "Wrong time and place for manners, Arki."

Before I could say anything else, her head was bobbing again. "Stop," I insisted.

"Why?" she asked, between torturous licks.

"Because. I . . ."

"Because you want to put something else in me, is that it?"

I nodded, then realized she might not be able to see that. "Yes," I whispered.

"I bet you just do," she said, grabbing my hips, and got to her feet. Then she took one hand and guided it into her own breeches. "What do you think? Think I want the same?"

I touched her, amazed at how wet she was. Not trusting me to figure things out on my own, she nudged my hand further. I started exploring her, sliding a finger inside, and Rudgi leaned in, nuzzling my neck and then biting it, and not especially gently. Breathing heavy in my ear, she asked, "Ever given a woman a southern kiss, Arki?"

I almost admitted I had hardly done anything anywhere with a woman, but instead settled for, "No."

"Tonight's your lucky night then, scholar." With that, she wiggled out of her trousers. I started to reach for my own with my free hand, but she said, "On your knees, boy."

I was in no position to argue. I did as she bade, and she placed her hands in my hair and guided me again where she wanted.

Rudgi said kiss, so that's what I started with, uncertain, on her thigh, looking up, watching her throw her head back. "Good. That's a start. Now get a little more intimate, Arki . . ."

I'd seen drawings in illuminated manuscripts of this sort of thing, but that was the full extent of my experience. She seemed to sense that and told me what she wanted, and how.

Holding the backs of her thick thighs, I complied, using my lips, my tongue, trying my best to please her, and either I was wonderful or horrible, as it wasn't long before she pulled me back up to my feet, stepped around me, and leaned against a tree, looking over her shoulder. "I'm not some delicate lass you need to woo, scholar. Grab me like you plaguing mean it. Don't get shy on me now."

I did, moving over to her, squeezing her flesh in my hands, pressing my body against hers. While she was stocky and her legs were rippling with muscle, her bottom was soft and felt wonderful in my hands. She pushed herself back into me. "Now. I want you in me now."

I dropped my breeches, lowered my hips a little, missed the mark at first, and she reached back and took matters into her own hands, guiding me a final time.

She let out a long, low moan. "That's it. Yes. Just like that."

I held onto her tightly and reached forward to grab her hair as I took her, wishing she hadn't used her mouth on me, no matter how good it felt. I wanted her to enjoy this as much as I would, and knew I wasn't going to last long. So I slowed down, forced myself to focus on the ten thousand thousand stars in the black sky above us, trying to calm myself. Which only made her more enflamed. "Take me, scholar. Like you. Plaguing. Mean it."

And so I did, picking up the pace, pleasure the only thing that mattered. Not our unlaundered clothes or unwashed bodies, not the possibility of being discovered, not the likelihood that we might die tomorrow. Just the hot sticky moment and our bodies slapping together, the scent of ghost pines and sweat and sex in the night air.

I grunted as every frustration and fear and angry thing inside seemed to be released all at once, body shaking hard, my hands squeezing her harder, and Rudgi arched her back as she pushed herself into me, head dropping.

There was an awkward moment when I was still inside her, and I had no idea what to say or do, if she'd achieved the same sort of pleasure I had.

She moved forward, stood straight, and slowly turned around.

"Thank you," I said, and cursed myself.

Rudgi laughed and shook her head. "Like I said, Arki, this is no time or place for manners. Glad you enjoyed yourself, though." She leaned in and nibbled my ear and then kissed my mouth sweetly, tenderly, at odds with the coupling we just had.

As we pulled our trousers back up, she said, "Don't sprain your conscience any, Arki. It was just a night in the woods. Not expecting a betrothal, nor wanting it, when it comes down to it. Just two soldiers—well, one and a half, maybe—finding some small pleasure before riding into battle on the morrow. Well, crabwalking in an aqueduct for five miles. But you understand me."

Rudgi reached up and gave me a quick kiss on the cheek. "You left first, you go back first. I'll be behind a bit. And be ready to call out your name so one of the real sentries doesn't stick a bolt in your skull."

I started off towards the abandoned mine, head spinning even more than when the Deserter had rung my bell with a sling stone. You just never really knew what might happen when you walked off into the woods.

T he next afternoon Thumaar's rider arrived in our mine camp, horse frothing at the mouth, gambeson damp from wicking sweat off the man, breeches dusty.

The rider accepted a flask from another soldier and was about to take a drink when Thumaar marched up and stood before him, no more patient than Braylar was with any of his scouts. "Well? What is it, man?"

"Your army, my lord. On the move. Heading towards Sunwrack."

"Well of course it is," he snapped. "I didn't imagine they would ignore my orders and sit in a circle with their thumbs up their asses. What opposition? Were there imperial troops? How many losses?"

The rider reported, "Not imperial, my lord. Thurvacians. They were mighty surprised to see a bunch of Confederate ships dropping off troops."

"I just bet they were," Thumaar said, frowning. "That is one thing the Empire's been remiss about—our navy has never been especially good. Something I will remedy." He looked closely at the rider again. "And? How did the governor respond once he took notice?"

The rider replied, "Took him a few days to muster forces. Met them on the Galvanized Road, just east of the foothills of the Moonvows. Pitched battle. But we caught him flat-footed. Or, more accurate, that Baron Brune did. Flanked the Thurvacians while they were engaging your troops and the Confeds." The rider smiled, looking more boy than man. "Slaughter, really. Only lost a few hundred to their thousands."

If the deposed emperor was pleased he didn't show it. "And now? Marching fast for the capital?"

"Yes, my lord. Figure they'll run into imperial troops soon."

Thumaar seemed to notice the rider's condition for the first time. "Take a drink, lad. You've earned it." He looked at Braylar, and there was a sheen of what might have either been sweat or ambition on his craggy face. "We leave an hour before dusk."

Braylar nodded. "As you say, my lord. What could be finer than slinking across an aqueduct at night?"

Braylar pulled his normal retinue aside, though Rudgi and Benk were included as well. He looked around at his sister and his Syldoon and said, "In ordinary circumstances, I would leave a lieutenant or two behind to tend to the remaining soldiers—I do not relish the idea of risking all the officers on one mission. But this is something of an extraordinary circumstance. We will be leading our deposed emperor into the bowels of the capital—quite literally, as it happens, since we will finish our little journey in the cisterns.

"This is an unprecedented gamble. And I would have my best soldiers with me. But if there is a man or woman here who would like to volunteer to stay back with the remainder and ensure we have an escape route, speak up now."

No one spoke for several moments, until Mulldoos said, "Pretty plaguing sure I speak for one and all here, Cap, when I say plague that. Plague that left, right, and center. We're all going."

As everyone else nodded or said, "Aye," the captain smiled, one of the rare instances that seemed driven solely by mirth and not irony, spite, mockery, or pain. "I thought as much. Very good. Fifteen Eagles will accompany us, as mandated, and you may hand select the rest of the Jackals. Soffjian, you are entrusted with our resident Focus. I suspect she will like crawling through miles of aqueduct about as much as she enjoyed riding a horse for the first time, so your assignment is to ensure she does not panic, keeps her mouth shut, and never gives away our position or attempts to betray us. Understood?"

Soffjian nodded quickly, her own smile wry. "She is a bright woman, and wants desperately to return to her side of the Veil for reasons known. She will be compliant."

"Or dead," Azmorgon rumbled.

Soffjian regarded the huge lieutenant coldly, smile gone. "That did go without saying. So it is no surprise you said it."

Braylar turned to me. "You will stay with the Jackals. We should only be in Sunwrack for—"

"No," I replied, my mouth moving of its own accord.

The captain's smile disappeared. "What did you just say to me?"

I resisted the urge to lick my lips as I felt everyone staring at me. "With all due respect, Captain, I deserve to go as well."

"Do you?" The question was flat and all the more threatening for it.

"I do. I helped us cross the Godveil. I discovered the means of undoing Cynead's hold on the Memoridons. I suggested using the rain for cover to escape. The point is, I've served you admirably in every capacity, performing every task you have assigned, and gone beyond that, far beyond that, shooting people with crossbows, saving your life at least once, arguably more than that." I took a deep breath. "But the real reason I deserve to go is that is what you promised me."

Braylar's eyes narrowed, only a touch, but enough to let me know I was in dangerous territory. "Did I indeed? Refresh my memory, archivist."

I pressed on. "When you hired me, it was presumably to be exactly that, your chronicler, your archivist, to bear witness to every strategy and plot and mission you undertook. Obviously the main reason was to translate, but I have recorded, every step of the way. And I can't very well continue if you leave me behind."

Braylar's stare made me squirm, and it was Vendurro who might have saved me, saying, "Kind of has a point, Cap. He's your arc."

Azmorgon raised his bushy eyebrows. "Arc? What's a plaguing 'arc'?"

Vendurro replied, "Arc. Archivist. That's what he does."

"Look at Squirrel, doling out nicknames now. Huh."

"It's not a nickname, just short for—"

Braylar held up a hand, eyes still on me. "You have accompanied us every step of the way. That much is true. But this particular stretch of the journey is more fraught with peril than most."

I wondered at the folly of my reply but couldn't seem to stall it. "I've braved—well, endured, anyway—rippers, hordes of Hornmen, vengeful Brunesmen, not to mention massive Deserters—who could be demons or monsters, still to be determined. I'm not about to let a short crawl through an aqueduct scare me off now, even if there are eighty thousand Leopards on the other end."

Braylar gave one curt nod and then turned to Mulldoos. "Is Sergeant Bruznik up to the task of riding herd on the remaining Jackals?"

"Aye, Cap. If you hadn't picked Ven for lieutenant, I would have said Sergeant Bruznik. Good man, capable, respected."

Braylar said, "Settled then. Muldoos, Vendurro, Azmorgon, convey the orders, and select your men for our little jaunt through the aqueduct. Make sure those staying with Bruznik know their duties. The rest of you, check your gear, rest while you are able, and fill your bellies. We depart soon."

Our small company marched through the woods and gently rolling foothills in the late afternoon, warm in the autumn sun.

I had my gambeson and helm on, Lloi's curved sword on one hip—it was still impossible to think of it as my sword—the quiver of bolts on the other, carrying the loaded crossbow, with my writing case on my back.

Mulldoos had cursed me for a fool, and told me to leave the case behind, but whether it was superstitious or not, I was reluctant to let it go. The case had saved my life once, and if it did come to pass that I died on this attempted raid on the capital, I wanted a quill and ink close by, if not in my hands. It only felt right.

We saw the stone aqueduct on its arched tiers ahead. While it wasn't nearly as high as it would be near Sunwrack, with its quadruple set of arches putting it over one hundred and fifty feet tall outside the city—and higher still as it bridged the Trench—it was still an impressive construction out here snaking through the woodlands, so simple, and yet so sturdy.

I shaded my eyes and saw that the conduit at the top was covered in an arched stone roof.

I asked Vendurro, "I don't imagine we're walking along the top, are we? How are we going to get in?"

He replied, "They maintain these right regular. Every tenday or so, workers out here are inspecting, scrubbing any deposits clear along the channel the water runs through, fixing any leaks, other repairs or whatnot. So there are access panels every hundred yards or so. Somebody rode on ahead today, made sure we can climb right on in."

"But the inspectors, workers—"

"Not due again for a few days, at least."

I looked at the huge stone structure stretching down into the valley, towards the capital some five miles away. "But there are guards, correct? The Syldoon in Sunwrack know this is a potential weakness that could be exploited."

349

"There are guards, sure enough, but not out this way. Irregular patrols, but nothing permanent. The cisterns in Sunwrack, though, are something else. But Cap and Commander Darzaak have that worked out, got a surprise for them. So we ought to be able to get in. Provided it don't collapse, the wall guards don't see or hear us as we cross the Trench or crawl above the city." Vendurro was staring at the aqueduct, shaking his head. "But as to it being a real weakness? Nahh. Going to take all night to get thirty or so of us into the city, assuming the we-don't-die part—enough to cause a little mischief on our own if we had a mind, which we do, but not like we can take the city from the inside. Syldoon are real good about putting resources towards what matters and not worrying overmuch about the things that don't."

I thought about that. "So our big trick won't be getting into the cisterns and the city, but sneaking through the streets and into the Citadel."

"Nope. Getting in is going to be plenty tricky too. Lots of ways for this to go south in a hurry."

That was encouraging. "And assuming we do. Make it."

"Well then, ayyup, that's the easy part, which ain't any kind of easy at all. The rest is as plaguing difficult as sticking a pinecone in a bull's ass."

Our company stood near the bottom of one of the stone supports, even the most seasoned soldier looking up at the aqueduct and assessing it.

Thumaar was in an enameled lamellar cuirass, with bazubands and greaves engraved with eagles, but that was as ostentatious as he got. While his carriage and demeanor made it clear he was or had been an emperor, it would have been easy to mistake him for an uppity captain or modest general.

But the effect didn't last long.

Braylar and his men were wrapping their weapons and scabbards in felt, and the deposed emperor and the Eagles did the same. Then the Jackals starting handing out cloth covers for the shield faces and charcoal to cover up any exposed metal or helms. Most of the soldiers had opted for gambesons and hardened leather, and after some initial reluctance, Thumaar did as well, pulling off his cuirass and unbuckling his greaves and going with something less likely to catch moonlight. He gave his armor to a soldier that was going to head back to the camp.

Vendurro showed me the best way to disguise my gear and reduce the clatter.

When I looked up, Thumaar was surveying our group with a tight, hard smile. "We have miles to walk like trolls in a tunnel. In the dark. Anyone here afraid of the dark?"

That earned a few chuckles. He wrapped his hand around the long hilt of his sword and said, "Good. By this time tomorrow, the fate of the Empire will shift, and each and every soldier here will be instrumental. Let's get moving."

And then he started up, using the hand and footholds built into the stone so workers or inspectors could climb to the top, followed by the Eagles.

Braylar and Mulldoos exchanged a look. Mulldoos said, "Got to love someone leading from the front, eh?"

Braylar replied, "That all depends on where he is leading, doesn't it? I'll go next, then send my sister and her skittish charge. You and the other lieutenants after, then the rest of the soldiers. Have the good sergeants bring up the rear." He turned to a Jackal nearby who had been the only one riding. "Ensure Brudzik receives the orders—we need to be sure the way is clear from here to Sunwrack and there are no unexpected surprises, yes? Also, make certain that panels are cracked open on occasion along the way—we don't want to suffocate in the dark, do we? Oh, and I will personally flog you if anything happens to Scorn or any of our other horses. Understood?"

The soldier managed not to blanch. "Aye, Cap."

Then Braylar started up after the Eagles, followed by the lieutenants and myself.

I tried not to go too slowly but wanted to be sure I had a firm hold each time, also not wanting to fall and take someone below me down as well. While I had no fear of heights, and this section of the aqueduct was only twenty feet off the ground, I wasn't what anyone would call a good climber.

As I pulled myself onto the roof and away from the edge, I saw Vendurro holding the wooden panel before dropping into the conduit. It was clear even he wasn't going to be able to stand at full height inside, as it was designed for a man or men to move around but not comfortably. He looked up at Azmorgon, still on the stone roof of the aqueduct. "You might want to head back to the mine. Not thinking you'll fit in here."

Azmorgon said, "I thought the same thing of your mother, and made that fit fine. Well, after some struggle."

Vendurro shook his head. "Plaguing whoreson."

"She said the same of you." Azmorgon's yellow teeth were barely visible as a smile in his pelt of a beard, but the eyes were still hard and challenging.

Vendurro started to climb back out, but Rudgi grabbed his arm and pulled him inside.

Mulldoos gave the huge man a droopy scowl. "Always called you a horse-cunt and a half. Truth is, you're twice the horsecunt of any man I ever met, and that's plaguing saying something."

Azmorgon dropped into the conduit. Without looking back up at Mulldoos he said, "And you're a half-man with mushy mushrooms in his mouth." Then he ducked low and disappeared into the dark conduit.

Mulldoos was about ready to descend and looked me up and down, then pointed at my quiver. "Best buckle the quiver lid shut, scribbler." I was about to say thanks when he added, "Unless you want those bolts spilling every-where, tripping up the man behind you, and earning my big boot in your skinny ass."

I buckled the lid shut and watched as he crouched into the dark, though not having to bend as low as most.

After taking a final deep breath of clean air and feeling the last of the day's sun on my cheeks, I used the handhold built into the stone and climbed down into the conduit. The channel of water was in the middle, only a couple of feet wide, surrounded by a narrow walkway on either side, and covered with the vaulted curved roof that forced nearly everyone to hunch over, especially Azmorgon, which made me happy in a petty and mean-spirited way.

The first thing I realized as I started walking forward in a hunch was just how gradual and almost imperceptible the gradient was on the conduit and aqueduct. Just enough to keep the water moving towards Sunwrack, but not to a degree that it would result in rapid erosion of the plaster channel or any extra stress on the structure itself.

As I moved away from the open panel on the vaulted ceiling, my eyes tried to adjust to the dark, but we hadn't gone very far at all when that proved impossible. The roof was exceptionally well constructed, and there wasn't the slightest crack where the sunset above could penetrate.

We were in absolute dark before long and would be for the next several miles. The covered conduit echoed our slow shuffling footsteps, armor shift-ing, and steady breathing, and made thirty-five of us sound like ten times that number, with the only other sound being the steady and gentle noise of water moving in the channel.

One of the Syldoon had tried walking in the water at first, but jumped back to the stone walkway again when it proved too cold to tolerate for long, earning several curses from the officers ahead.

The company trudged along, obeying the command to maintain silence unless Braylar or Thumaar were issuing orders down the line.

The blackness wasn't quite as absolute as it had been in the pool in the bowels of Vrulinka's keep, but not far off either. We were bent over, feeling our way along the wall as we made halting progress, trying not to think about how we were like blind rats scuttling through a sewer pipe. Time seemed stretched out. The first hour felt like half the night. Breathing heavily from having my diaphragm compressed and only the stale and foul air to suck in and out, heavy with the reek of sweat and bodies and whatever rank odors came out of them, it was hard to ward off ferocious anxieties.

Silently cursing myself for arguing so vehemently about being included, I tried to keep my mind off the fact that it really did feel as if we might suffocate in there. I wondered about the previous night, my wild encounter with Rudgi. Clearly it didn't ripple beyond what had happened—we were not betrothed or amorous, not going to hold hands and whisper sweet sentiments to each other. But if you throw even a small pebble in a lake, there are some ripples. Assuming we lived through this, would we ever repeat that, twist our bodies together again? Or had it simply been a singular occurrence?

I had no significant experience with women, but even if I had been a frequent paramour, I doubt I would have met any like Rudgi, or had the faintest idea what to make of her. It's possible she hadn't thought twice about me since pulling her trousers back on last night, but I couldn't help hoping we had another chance.

I was dwelling on that when I finally smelled something pleasant and felt the faintest of breezes on my face. Not long after, I saw stars winking in a square of sky and realized we were passing an open panel.

Thumaar sent word back that everyone could straighten up for a minute as they came to it, take a quick drink of sweet air and whatever we had on our belts, and then it was back to it—we still had many miles to go.

I saw Mulldoos stand up ahead of me, rolling his shoulders back, stretching, grunting. He unstoppered a costrel, took a few swallows, and then looked over at me, hunched and waiting. "Let me guess. Didn't bring a flask, did you?"

When I shook my head he did as well. "Hopeless. Plaguing hopeless." Then he handed me his costrel and with a groan, bent down again and trudged forward.

The water was brackish in truth, but it might as well have been from a magic fountain, it tasted so pleasant. And the air . . . it was wonderful. Crisp and unpolluted. But the view was almost dizzying after being stuck in the aqueduct for so long, the immensity of the sky, the number of stars, the haunting cry of a bird in a tree nearby. Below us, I realized with a start. There was another tier of arches now, possibly two. While the gradient had only changed an incremental amount, the land must have dropped off quite a bit.

Lowering myself back into that conduit was twice as difficult as entering it the first time.

But there was no getting around it. Miles to go . . .

And so I bent over and caught up with Mulldoos, handing him his costrel again before being plunged into absolute darkness.

The rest of the night passed the same way, battling my mind and the sensation that we might end up stuffed in this conduit for the rest of our lives, enjoying the brief respite of another hatch, and then pressing on. While the gradient never changed, the contours of the aqueduct itself did, as it flowed over the roll of the land, carrying water down from the foothills of the Moonvow mountains to Sunwrack, filling cisterns, bathhouses, and fountains, and flushing sewage into the Trench.

The third hatch proved to be our last. As I poked my head up, the lights of Sunwrack were visible in Towers here and there, along the wall, lanterns or candles or torches. The city was asleep for the most part, but the guards were not, and the Syldoon were not, not with an enemy army marching towards their doorstep, and so while the city wasn't alive with lights, there were more than at any time I had seen in my brief stay.

Mulldoos pulled my arm. "Enough gawking, scribbler. It will all be up close and personal before you can spit. Get your last gulp of air and drop back in the hole."

I glanced down. Though it was hours from dawn, the sky was cloudless, and with the moonlight and starlight I could make out the silhouette of the landscape below. Far, far below. We had to be a hundred feet up now, possibly more. The aqueduct had to be high enough to cross over the colossal walls protecting Sunwrack, but that meant a very long drop and a squishy death at the bottom.

The air suddenly tasted less sweet, and I dropped back into the conduit.

⊕

It felt like hours more passed, but there weren't that many dark hours in a day. The air suddenly changed, and a breeze seemed to be blowing down the conduit. I'd been told there were no more panels open and wasn't sure what was happening before remembering how the aqueduct appeared in Sunwrack. The roof ended a hundred yards outside the trench. Presumably to make sure there wasn't an army hunchwalking its way into the capital.

I started to make out the shapes of the Syldoon ahead of me, just hints at first, but then their outlines, and though any steel or iron had been blacked as much as possible, there was still a faint dull glint of metal ahead as I neared the opening.

Mulldoos dropped down to a knee and looked back at me and the soldiers behind. "We crawl the rest of the way. Slow. Real slow. No noise. You hear me? You got to sneeze, you stick your head up your ass first. No noise, stay below the edge, and crawl like a snake. Don't even think of looking over either. Nothing gives away our position. Not a plaguing thing. And the man that does will be dead by my hand before any Imperials stick a shaft in his sorry ass."

Then he dropped to his belly and started slithering across the stones of the aqueduct, the starry vault of the sky the only roof now.

After letting him get ahead a bit, I did as he ordered, fighting the mad urge to stand and unfurl my muscles. The crawling pace was painfully slow, and difficult to do with a muffled sword on one hip and a quiver on the other.

Sounds carry queerly at night, but it was a while before I started catching the faintest sounds from the mostly-sleeping city ahead of us. A muted snippet of conversation from a guard on the wall. Someone whistling far, far away. I smelled wood burning, distant but somehow still tangy.

I was glad I couldn't look over the edge, as I probably would have only seen the Trench and vomited. I heard the hints of something scraping the stones in the dark below.

Head down, I kept moving slowly—every sound we made seemed ampli-fied in my ears, as if resounding across an auditorium and capable of reaching ears hundreds of yards away.

We continued on like that, making torturously slow progress, when sud-denly I heard something different, closer, a scuttling of some kind. I looked up, raised myself on my elbows, and saw some shadowy thing crawl over the edge of the conduit ahead.

There was a muffled sound, someone or something struggling. Mulldoos pulled his suroka off his belt and crawled forward.

I elbowed my way forward as well, wondering if I should pull the crossbow or not, but sure that wouldn't do any good, panic welling.

Vendurro was on his back, the thing on his chest—large, round, with mul-tiple legs—and his own suroka was plunging into its side, though it sounded like it was hitting a breastplate and not flesh, skittering off.

Mulldoos scooted alongside and grabbed at a leg, twisted it, pulled the creature back and turned it, then thrust his own suroka into the underbelly several times. The scuttling and scraping and muffled strug-gling was over.

I moved closer as Mulldoos hauled the creature off. It looked like a giant, bloated tick, covered in speckled chitin, and the front legs ended in thick terrifying claws that looked like they could have easily crushed a man's skull, maybe even in a helm.

Mulldoos whispered, "You okay, Ven?"

Vendurro couldn't sit up, but rolled over onto his stomach and looked at Mulldoos. He wiped some dark gore off onto his trousers and waved a shaky hand. "Vambrace took the worst of it," he whispered back. "Would have lost an arm otherwise. Thing clamped down good."

"That's a bull crab?" I asked, trying not to let my gorge rise as one of the creature's legs twitched, scraping on the plaster, splashing the water.

Mulldoos looked back over his shoulder at me. "Ayyup. Plaguing bull crab."

"Will . . . are there more?"

He wiped his bloody suroka off on his leg and said in a rough whisper, "Who plaguing knows. Don't usually come too far up out of the Trench. But there are hundreds, maybe thousands of the fuckers down there."

Azmorgon and a few Syldoon ahead had crawled back and the Ogre had to stifle a bristly laugh. "Looks like crabs got a taste for squirrel meat, eh?"

Mulldoos looked at the huge lieutenant. "Send word to any ahead to keep their surokas out. Might be more of the bastards on the aqueduct." Then he relayed the warning back to the Syldoon behind us again, adding, "Everyone shut your yaps. Got a ways to go yet. Anyone screams on account of a big bug, I'll gut the plaguer myself and drop him off the conduit."

I didn't doubt he meant it.

We crawled on, and while I didn't allow myself to look over the side, I knew we were nearly to the walls and Towers encircling the entire city, and had to be above the Trench. Even without seeing the massive chasm, I started to sweat more heavily, hearing the breeze whistle up from the depths below, carrying the stench of waste and rot and the things that roamed through it in the night looking for food. The bull crab might not even be the worst of them.

Gulping, I forced myself to focus on one elbow and knee at a time, moving slowly, and trying to be sure the scabbard and quiver didn't make any loud scraping sounds on the stones beneath me.

Finally, we passed over the wall and were one hundred and fifty feet above the mostly sleeping Capital of Coups, Sunwrack. The sounds were still infrequent, but louder, and though a trick of the ear or the air, sometimes seemed far too close—a snippet of conversation drifting up from guards on the ground far below us; the clip-clop of a horse moving down an avenue; the gurgling of a fountain.

Over the edge, I could make out the silhouettes of mostly dark Towers in the distance, a little taller than the aqueduct, but those fell away as we moved away from the outer wall. We kept going, one deliberate and maddeningly slow foot at a time. It felt like I'd spent half my life on this damnable aqueduct, hunched over like a troll or on my belly like a ferret, following the slow turn as it made its way towards the center of the city.

We pressed on though the last hour or two of darkness, progress in quiet inches. Finally, we stopped. I tensed, wondering if that meant another crab had made its way over the top or some other awful thing had happened. Even though the sun wasn't up yet and we were hidden from eyes below, one wrong noise or move might give our position away. I'd never felt so exposed and helpless before and reminded myself to keep my mouth shut the next time I was itching to volunteer my services on a dangerous mission into the heart of what amounted to enemy territory.

But there were no alarms raised, and no struggling ahead that I could make out. However, I saw a large dark shape ahead in the slate gray sky, about a hundred yards out, even higher than the aqueduct. And we appeared to be heading directly towards it.

I whispered to Mulldoos, "Lieutenant, is that—"

"Cistern tower," he said. "And shut your plaguing mouth."

I did and continued waiting. Then I heard a single noise that sounded like the warbling cry of a gulley wren. Only I knew somehow it wasn't.

And then, several second slater, there was a trilling return call, coming from the streets or somewhere far below, a cheery three-note blast of a bird that did not exist.

We waited there, and despite the imminent attack of bull crabs and risk of exposure and all the nerves that came with it, I was exhausted. I lowered my head for a bit, closing my eyes briefly and hoping they wouldn't spring open when a claw closed around my neck, listening to the gentle and insistent flow of water a few inches away.

I wasn't sure how long I dozed, but then Mulldoos nudged me with his foot and we were moving again, though even more slowly than before. There was a pale pearl light to the east, and the first sliver of color that meant dawn wasn't far off. I hoped we would be off the aqueduct soon. If not, the threat of discovery would increase tenfold.

I looked ahead and thought I saw the silhouettes of men on the roof of the cistern tower, but couldn't be certain. I clenched my teeth and kept moving, every slow incremental shift forward seeming to rub a welt or two the wrong way, dreading the moment we were found out and completely trapped.

We stopped again. There were definitely guards or sentries or men of some kind up there. Not many, three, four, a handful possibly. But figures for certain. We couldn't go any closer for risk of being spotted crawling, and yet we couldn't delay there much longer or the sun would eventually creep over the horizon to reveal us hiding there.

It seemed Thumaar and Braylar must have miscalculated, or we hadn't made the night-long journey quickly enough. Something was wrong. And there was no going back. And climbing down was not an option. I licked my lips, shifted my weight, and waited, sure we were doomed.

But then I heard something from one of streets below, around the cistern tower from the sounds of it, though it was hard to be sure—shouting, escalating, several different voices, then the clash of steel. A fight of some kind. The figures on the building moved away from the edge. And quickly, from the looks of it, though I was squinting to make it out.

Mulldoos looked back at me and said, "Now! Up!" And he got to his feet and started jogging, hunched over.

I stood as well and immediately wished I hadn't—the majority of the city that had been hidden below the rim of the conduit was suddenly unveiled, and it was all I could do not to fall right over the side.

Keeping my eyes fixed on Mulldoos's back, I started to jog, sure I would slip and tumble with every step, my body protesting every step of the way, muscles tightening and threatening to clutch up or cramp. We ran the slowly winding last stretch. Perhaps Braylar or Thumaar assumed that with the streets mostly deserted before dawn, and sound carrying strangely, no one would think to look up. Or maybe it was desperation and we simply didn't have the time to go slowly. Whatever the motivation, we kept going, and my thighs burned and there was a painful hitch in my side when we stopped, twenty yards out.

Everyone was panting, but the Syldoon in front had dropped to their knees and had their crossbows up. A few behind them were standing in a crouch, crossbows also trained on the roof.

Mulldoos ordered the rest of us down on our bellies as we waited.

Whatever was causing the commotion in the streets below had stopped.

The guards came back to the edge of the roof of the cistern tower and were filled with a dozen quarrels as the Jackals loosed simultaneously. The figures dropped behind the lip of the roof, dead or bleeding out of three or four holes each.

We jogged up to the wall, and then I saw the Syldoon ahead of me gathered at an opening. A very small opening. That had an iron grate over it. The conduit continued through the bottom, and the water flowed inside, but we weren't going to be entering the tower that way. These were stout bars and even Azmorgon couldn't pull them out of a well-maintained stone wall. A Deserter might have had trouble, it looked so sturdy.

One of the Syldoon ahead pulled something out of a sack, and another on the other side of the channel did the same. The pair worked quickly, assembling something, and then both took a few steps away from the wall. One soldier held the other two by their belts to steady them as they each threw some kind of a hook towards the roof with something trailing. Both hooks clanged against the lip of the roof and then fell. Another Syldoon barely managed to catch them before they hit the conduit or, worse, dropped to the street below.

On the second effort, they got both hooks to stick. I saw then it was a rope ladder that was trailing. One Syldoon tested the ropes, another Jackal knelt to weigh the ends of the ladder down and steady them, and then a soldier started climbing.

Two Syldoon waited below him in case he fell. Though if he did, it was just as likely he would take them down to their deaths in the street as they would stop his fall and save him. But while the ladder didn't behave like a wooden one and shook and wobbled, the soldier didn't fall. He climbed up to the roof edge, over the lip, disappeared, and then appeared again a few moments later to give some kind of hand signal.

Thumaar went next, and the rest of the Eagles followed him to the top, climbing slowly one by one. I stayed crouched low, watching the men ascend and glancing over the edge to the street below. Mulldoos caught me looking down and hisspered, "Scribbler! Quit gawking!"

I did, though I was sorely tempted to point out that if anyone looked up to see anything, it would be men climbing a rope ladder on the tower, not the top of my head peering over the aqueduct edge.

The sound of more scuffling or fighting in another street rose up to us, though it didn't sound as close.

"Jackals?" I asked.

Mulldoos only nodded.

I looked to the cistern tower and saw that Soffjian was struggling to get Nustenzia to start up the ladder. The older woman was shaking her bowed head, crouched down, leaning against the wall, any haughty composure utterly gone.

Braylar hadn't climbed up yet, likely sensing trouble there. He grabbed Nustenzia by the shoulders and pulled her to her feet. I couldn't make out what he said, but she shook her head, though less vehemently this time.

Braylar pointed up to the roof and this time I did catch the snippet, ". . . voluntarily or I'll tie you by the ankles and order you dragged up."

To her credit, Nustenzia rose to her full height, stuck out her chin, tucked some wisps of white hair behind her ears, and grabbed the closest rope rung.

She took another moment to compose herself, and then started up, going slower than anyone who'd preceded her, but going just the same. I found myself admiring her. She was in a captive in a foreign land, separated from family who needed her, and dragged along on a dangerous mission, with no hope at all of escape, and yet aside from that lapse before climbing, she rarely showed how difficult this must have all been for her, the strain she was surely under.

And then I reminded myself who she had served on the other side of the Veil—the admiration didn't lessen, but it was the kind reserved for accomplished foe rather than respected friend.

The ladder seemed to be even less steady the more hesitant or slow the climber, but she finally made it to the top, pulled over the edge by soldiers who had been ducking behind the lip.

Other Jackals went, with one slipping a little. Vendurro scurried up as if he practiced on rope ladders his entire life or actually did have squirrel blood. Azmorgon followed with a deliberate plodding ascent, and then it was Mulldoos's turn. I wondered how his arm was holding up, the strength in it, especially since he had lost some of it after Rusejenna's attack, but he managed to climb up without too much difficulty.

Then it was my turn. And I suddenly understood Nustenzia's reluctance. Even though it was only one story up to the top, the thought of leaving the sturdy stones of the aqueduct and trusting rope or the Syldoon below to catch me if I slipped suddenly made it seem like climbing a mountain.

I grabbed the rungs above me, put my foot on the one nearest the stones and took my first hesitant step. The ladder shimmied and shivered. I told myself at least it wasn't a single rope, took a deep breath, and started up, making sure I had one hand and foot on securely before moving the other. I suddenly wished I hadn't taken my writing case after all, as everything on my back and hips was throwing me off balance, but before I knew it I was at the lip.

As I pulled myself up, a hand grabbed either arm and pulled me the rest of the way.

Vendurro said, "Thought you decided to take a nap halfway."

I moved away from the edge and ducked down like everyone else. There were three dead Imperial soldiers lying in the gravel on the roof, bolts protruding everywhere, but the fourth wasn't among them.

I looked over and saw Thumaar and Braylar kneeling on either side of him, another Syldoon behind propping him up. The man had a bolt in his thigh, another near his collarbone, and a third in his belly, and his scale armor hadn't done much to stop any of them, as it looked like dark pools were all over his trousers. Braylar was giving him sips from a flask, and Thumaar appeared to be questioning him.

I heard Mulldoos behind me say quietly, "Gut wound. Bad way to go, that. Could be a long time dying. Never wish that on any man, even a plaguing Leopard."

Another Syldoon came over the roof edge, and I turned around and asked, "What are they interrogating him about?"

Mulldoos said, "Location of other guards, most like. Though knowing Cap, could be one of a thousand questions. Probably promising him a mercy death if he talks. Right about now, betting that sounds plaguing good."

Vendurro helped another Jackal over, grunting, and then said, "Lot of blood loss though. Might not be a long time dying after all. Man might hold out a stretch if mercy's got no leverage."

I looked back at the questioning. The man propping the Leopard up reached around and covered his mouth, and Braylar grabbed the bolt in his stomach and twisted. I winced at the muzzled scream.

"Ayyup," Vendurro said. "Looks like mercy ain't on the table anymore."

The Leopard shook his head, and Braylar released the bolt. After waiting a moment, the man behind him pulled his hand away from the man's mouth, though kept it close in case he cried out or screamed again.

Rudgi came over. I smiled, though felt foolish immediately and glad the dawn wasn't quite there yet.

I looked back, and the Leopard was talking quickly, though defiantly by the looks of it. Braylar nodded once, and the Jackal holding him brought his suroka across the man's throat and let him slide to the gravel on the roof.

Benk made it up and over and pulled the rope ladder up after him, bundling it in his arms and crouch-walking forward. We all did the same, moving towards the opposite side of the roof. There was a wooden trap door near Thumaar and Braylar. The deposed emperor seemed inclined to lead the charge again, but Braylar spoke a few words in his ear, and the older man relented, though grudgingly. Very grudgingly.

I was looking at the fourth dead Leopard, amazed and sickened by the amount of blood he seemed to have lost before his heart stopped pumping it out, when Braylar addressed the group, though still keeping his voice low.

"Well done. But the easy part is over. Our bloody Leopard here wasn't especially forthcoming or helpful, but we know already that there are still guards in the tower below, likely doing rounds. Thankfully, most of the building is full of cisterns, reservoirs, and pipes, so it isn't occupied like a Tower proper, but we still need to take out most of the Leopards in here quickly. The shift change will occur not long after dawn and we have to be on the ground floor to welcome them. So, we spread out and go floor by floor, eliminate most of the Leopards, and convene on the ground. Do note I said *most*. We need another prisoner. Preferably two or three, if possible."

Soffjian said, "I need to conserve myself for the frame, but when the relief shows up at dawn, I can take out one or two without killing them, or stun them long enough for you to subdue them."

Braylar looked at her and nodded. Then he addressed the small company. "Very good. New plan, yes? Kill anyone you encounter. Though do try to spare some Leopard armor and badges. We could use any that isn't soaked in blood." He gestured towards the trap door. "My lord, if I may?"

Thumaar was scowling but gave a curt nod.

s the sun flashed across the rooftop and began to light the edges of the city, the captain led us into the cistern tower. Vendurro poked his head inside the trap door, which seemed a good way to get it cut off, but safer than someone going down feet first, I supposed. He announced it was clear, then Braylar was the first down the ladder, with his lieutenants after, followed by the rest of the Jackals. There must have been someone Vendurro hadn't seen, as I heard a shout from somewhere inside, cut short by several twangs from crossbows, and then it was my turn to descend, with Soffjian and Nustenzia after me, and finally Thumaar and his Eagles. That must have galled him, to allow a mere captain and his troops to precede him, but it was the safest course.

It felt good to put my hands and feet on a solid ladder with only a short drop below, but the interior of the building was nothing like what I was expecting. For one, it wasn't poorly lit—the sunrise hadn't provided adequate natural lighting through the arched windows yet, but there were lanterns hanging from hooks all along the wall, lighting up the expansive basin the aqueduct fed into first. Still, there were broad patches of deep shadows, and that's where I saw the body of the next Leopard thirty feet away, filled with bolts.

The roof had corbelled ceilings, and there were countless pillars throughout this floor supporting it. The first huge reservoir on this upper floor was a settling basin, designed to sift any debris out of the water before it was transported to other basins for distribution to other portions of the city, but far larger than any I'd ever heard about.

Most of the Jackals had crossbows out, trained on the floor as they fanned out to make sure there were no more Leopards about, and the Eagles had their sidearms in hand—swords, maces, axes—as they spread out as well. If there were guards patrolling, they wouldn't be doing so for very long. I had my crossbow ready, hoping I'd have no cause to use it.

Soffjian had a tight grip on Nustenzia's upper arm, her ranseur in the other hand, angle up.

And so it went, floor by floor. There were two other guards, but they were cut down before raising an alarm or putting up a fight. I was stunned by the size and complexity of the tower. I knew this place provided untold gallons of water for bathhouses, fountains, flushing the filth from garderobes and drains out into the bottom of the Trench, as well as filling humongous cisterns and reservoirs. I assumed at least some of those were designed for drinking.

I was walking alongside Soffjian and Nustenzia, mostly to avoid getting in the way of the Syldoon as they cleared each floor. I turned to Soffjian. "Clearly infiltrating this tower wasn't easy, and it would be impossible to get a sizable enough force in this way to cause any serious mischief. So I can see why the risk outweighed the rewards and no one tried it. Until today, that is. But why wouldn't an enemy simply poison the spring in the mountains, or the water in the aqueduct on its way to Sunwrack?"

The Memoridon's head swiveling from one patch of shadow to the next, she answered, "First, so much water comes through daily that it would be difficult if not impossible to poison it to the extent of making anyone seriously sick, let alone dead. So there's that. But second, most of this isn't for drinking, and they have water tasters sampling those casks or cisterns daily."

"Leopards volunteer for this?"

"Dogs do."

"There is a Dog Tower?"

"No, the four-legged variety. Not everything relates to the Syldoon, you know." She flashed me a wicked smile. "And I suspect, being dogs, they are not aware they are volunteering at all. They are simply thirsty and drinking, as animals and some idiot men are wont to do. So, there you have it. Poisoning isn't especially practical or—"

Someone darted from behind a pillar we passed and ran for the ladder leading down to the next floor.

Soffjian spun, cocked her arm back, and while I thought she would splay her fingers and take the Leopard out with memory magic, she instead threw her ranseur like a spear.

The polearm struck the soldier in the lower back, but the tines didn't penetrate the scales, or at least not deeply enough to do more than slow him

down, as it fell to the floor behind him. The Leopard stumbled, reached back
by reflex, and then kept on running, speeding up if anything.

"Leopard!" Soffjian shouted. "The ladder!"

The running soldier slid on the stones as he tried to stop near the ladder,
regained his balance, and reached down to grab the iron loop on the trap door.

Azmorgon stepped out from behind another pillar, the oddly edged
polearm in both hands above his head, and he brought it down like an exe-
cutioner in a town square. Only instead of lopping off the man's head, the
long blade struck him in the shoulder and back, rending armor, breaking
the collarbone, embedding somewhere below it, ending the man's life in
one stroke.

I felt my stomach twist as Azmorgon stepped on the dead man's back and
wrenched his weapon free, then spit on the corpse before stepping away.

When the rest of the floor was clear and we were gathered by the
blood-splattered trap door, Thumaar addressed the troops. "The Captain was
clear, I thought. We kill all Leopards. That seemed clear enough to me. So if we
can't sweep the floor and manage that simple task without raising the alarm, it
won't matter what gods we have siding with us. They cannot abide men who
do not help themselves. The next man or woman who allows a Leopard to even
get close to another door will be executed on the spot. Is that understood?"

Everyone nodded or said "Aye," and from that point on, the Eagles and
Jackals were more thorough and painstaking in their searches, though we
didn't encounter any more Imperial soldiers patrolling anywhere.

We gathered before the trap and ladder leading to the ground floor, and it
was difficult to tell if I was more exhausted or hungry, as both led to my body
shaking and the return of an awful headache.

Braylar looked at the gathered Syldoon and said, "We do not know how
many men might be down there. Fewer than us is a sound guess, but still a
guess. We assemble by the ladder and sweep towards the main entrance, on the
eastern wall. Once we have secured that, we can eliminate any other Leopards
lurking amid the pipes and shadows, though I suspect most of them will be by
the door, waiting for their relief so they can go home and sleep. It should be
locked tight, so they can't simply run out into the street. But we also don't have
a large margin for error. Once they see us, especially if they are overwhelmed,
they will attempt to flee." He looked at his sister. "How many can you take out
without compromising your ability to undo Cynead's work on the frames?"

Soffjian put her hand on Nustenzia's shoulder. "With her aid? Likely all of them, provided you are correct about numbers. I won't have to expend nearly as much with her assistance. But if you are wrong about the numbers . . ."

Braylar twitch-smiled. "When have you ever known me to be wrong estimating numbers?"

She looked at the flail. "Before Bloodsounder came into your possession, quite frequently."

Thumaar said, "Enough squabbling. We do not have much time. Lead your men, Captain. Or stand aside."

Vendurro checked the ground floor as before, and nodded before stepping back to let Braylar past. The captain had Bloodsounder in hand as he climbed down, and everyone followed as before.

The ground floor was the first not to have open cisterns or pipes or channels leading out through all the walls. Instead it had rows of huge casks of water at least twelve feet high that must have been some kind of reserve, fed by pipes coming down from the ceiling. The whole tower was stunning in conception and execution, a marvelous feat of engineering unseen anywhere else in the world, at least on that scale. But I didn't have much time to appreciate that.

When our company was assembled, Braylar gave hand signals that meant nothing to me but everything to the Syldoon, and we started forward as stealthily as we could, some men in a small alley between casks, others hugging the eastern wall of the building.

But the casks ended as the room did, and we had to skirt the northern wall until we came to a closed door. Braylar cursed, clearly not expecting that. He looked at Mulldoos. "The entrance must be close, yes? Do you know the layout in that section?"

The lieutenant nodded. "Aye to the door, no plaguing clue about the layout. Never had cause to be in here."

Thumaar stepped forward. "It's been years, but unless they have rebuilt, the room beyond is open in layout. Rows of bunks and wardrobes, chests, a weapons rack. A desk or two and some tables and benches. A small barracks for the guards near the entrance." He pointed his sword at the door, frowning. "This is likely locked. Or should be if they aren't lax bastards disregarding protocol. That poses a problem. Tired or not, the men on the other side will probably notice us chopping a door down."

Azmorgon looked at the deposed emperor, smile mostly hidden in the pelt beard. "Who said anything about chopping?"

Thumaar looked up at the man, appraising. "The door is several inches thick, iron-bound, and secure."

Azmorgon nodded once, slowly. "Ain't never seen a door I couldn't knock off its hinges, unless you're talking about one at the big plaguing gates to Sunwrack. That might be a fix." He looked at Braylar. "But this? Nothing and less. I got this, Cap."

Braylar nodded as well and looked at Thumaar. "So, once Lieutenant Ram dislodges the door, we storm through, loosing crossbows at the closest Leopards. Soffjian, you and Lady Focus will need to come through quickly, prepared to take out the guards. This is when we need prisoners. At least six." He looked at the rest of the Syldoon. "Since clarity seems to be an issue, must I needs repeat myself here? Clean off any phrases for you? Prisoners. Six. More is better. But at least six. Understood?"

Thumaar said, "Assuming your big whoreson there is as good as his word, I will lead the first wave through."

Braylar stared, unblinking, before saying, "My lord, this entire operation will be for naught if you catch a bolt in the face or get cut down in this drippy tower. Might I suggest—"

"If I could piss on your suggestion, I would. Are you truly questioning the man who would be your emperor?"

Braylar still looked poised to argue the point or attempt a different tack, but relented. "My lord, the charge is yours and yours alone."

Thumaar and a handful of Eagles stood poised on one side of the door, and Braylar, Vendurro, Soffjian, and Nustenzia stood on the other. The rest of us cleared a path for Azmorgon, weapons ready.

He handed his polearm to Rudgi and said, "Hold this. Unless it's too big for you."

Then Azmorgon crouched down and put the fingers of both hands on the stone floor, narrow-set eyes on the door, breathing slowly, huge body rising and falling a few times before he launched himself forward.

Azmorgon ran ten steps and, just before reaching the door, threw himself forward, shoulder first.

With a splintering crash and the tortured scream of metal, the door flew into the room beyond and he fell on top of it, and then the Syldoon poured in after him.

I heard several crossbows release quarrels and a distant scream or two, and then I was in a wave coming through the door as well, crossbow leveled, trying to make sense of the scene in front of me.

We did outnumber the Leopards, but it was hard to tell by how much. Several Imperials were down already, but the rest were drawing weapons, or reaching for spears from the rack, some fitting arrows to the strings of their recurved bows. Some of the smarter ones who recognized the threat of crossbows jumped behind a large wooden desk. One ran for the massive double-arched doors in the nave of the building, fumbling with keys.

The other Syldoon had tossed their crossbows aside and drawn their sidearms, so I pivoted, taking aim, hand hovering along the long steel trigger. An arrow flew past me, though it was hard to tell if it was aimed at me or not. The Leopard by the door was about forty feet away, and I thought about trying to close the distance, but he was already drawing the oak beam out from the brackets on the door, so I took a deep breath and squeezed.

The bolt covered the distance in a blink, striking the Leopard in the back of the shoulder. He dropped the beam, staggered into the door, but then righted himself and started reaching for the beam again.

I cursed and reached for another bolt, knowing I couldn't possibly span it in time to stop him, ducking belatedly as an arrow flew over my head.

Then Soffjian pushed past me, one hand in a tight grip around Nustenzia's upper arm, the other in front of her, fingers splayed.

Two more arrows flew, one striking a nearby Eagle, another nearly hitting Nustenzia, who screamed as if it were buried in her chest. Soffjian only tightened her grip, and a moment later the Leopards in front of us were dropping their weapons, holding their heads, falling to their knees or onto their faces, screaming and writhing and twisting on the floor as if they were being flayed alive.

Thumaar marched forward, sword up, ready to silence them himself when they all dropped like puppets whose strings had been severed. The Leopards were all down, and quiet, even the ones who were injured and bleeding around the bolts in their flesh.

We'd taken the entrance. And if there were other Leopards hidden on the ground floor somewhere, they knew better than to try to help their comrades now.

Some Eagles and Jackals guarded the doors to the rest of the first floor on opposite sides of the chamber. A few tried to fit the broken door back in its hinges, but it was too late—the best they could do was prop it in place so on casual glance it might look like a secure door.

The rest of us put the room back together and stripped the fallen Leopards of their armor and surcoats. I was helping Vendurro turn the table back over, reclaiming the dice and leather cup, the copper decanter and wooden mugs, wiping beer off the table and then repositioning everything to look like a dicing game hadn't been interrupted at all.

I looked up as Azmorgon was dragging two limp Leopards in their small clothes by the arms towards an adjacent storage room, the same way a toddler might two stuffed toys. He hauled the bodies past the canvas and wood screen out of sight as other Jackals did the same with the other bodies. None of the unconscious men were bound.

Braylar grabbed me by the shoulder as I took a step towards the storage area.

I asked, "They're going to kill those men, the ones Soffjian subdued, aren't they?"

The captain was giving me a hard look, not quite wroth, but the one a teachers favors a very dense student. Very quietly he said, "You do seem to be having a very tough time with this lesson. Need I remind you—and it appears I must—the Leopards are our enemies, and slaughtered a large chunk of my company not so very long ago. And you would argue for what, exactly, clemency? Is that what the long look implies, Arki? Are you going to appeal to Mulldoos's tender nature and beg for them to be simply trussed up back there?"

I shook my head. "It just seems . . ." I struggled for the words. "They are unarmed . . . helpless."

The captain had moved to wroth. "While the Jackals bore arms, they were no less helpless on the bridge when they were cut down or dropped to their deaths. Measure for measure. And that's an end to it."

371

"You spared the blinded Hornmen," I said, knowing I was recklessly rowing into monster-infested waters.

Braylar said, "So I did. Because they were useful, if you recall. Those limp Leopards being moved out of sight? They have no utility for us whatsoever. And if we leave them bound, they will only be unbound sometime later to fight us another day. Or perhaps forgotten altogether while a coup is happening in the city around them. Perhaps they would starve to death. Is that your idea of mercy, archivist?"

I shook my head, feeling more tired, hungry, and empty than before.

Braylar released my arm and turned to Soffjian as another comatose Leopard was dragged past. "How long will the rest be out?"

Soffjian replied, "It is difficult to say. Had I taken them out alone, an hour, two perhaps." She glanced at the Focus. "But I'm afraid we might have overdone it a bit. It might be half a day. Longer. Let me guess—you need one of them awake now?"

The corners of Braylar's lips rose ever so slightly. "Why yes. How very astute of you."

"You might have mentioned that before I shook their brain boxes so hard, Bray."

"Well," he said, "our priority was taking the opposition out cleanly. I never imagined you would render them senseless for a day or two."

She nearly smiled as well. "Failure of imagination can be a dangerous thing. Who would you like me to try to rouse?" She looked at the Leopards pulled to the edge of the room and the few still in armor in the center.

Thumaar was walking towards the pair, wearing a relatively clean (or at least blood-free) tunic and Leopard cuirass, and was close enough to have overheard the last part. He pointed to a Leopard face down on the ground near the table. "That man. He has a sergeant's badge. Be quick about it. The relief could be here anytime."

Braylar glanced at me and then added, pointing, "And those two as well. If we are to pull this ruse off, they will need to see at least two or three of their comrades."

I wondered if they would be executed after they had served their purpose as well and tried not to think about it.

Nustenzia was staring straight ahead, almost as pale as Mulldoos, lips a tight thin line, and though it didn't appear she had been paying attention, she flinched as Soffjian approached and looked visibly relieved when the Memoridon moved past her to the sergeant facedown on the floor. Soffjian looked over her shoulder and beckoned the captain and former emperor forward, and Braylar called over Mulldoos and Azmorgon as well.

The small group was gathered around the Leopard sergeant while the rest of the company continued moving dead or unconscious bodies. Soffjian knelt down next to the man, closed her eyes, laid her hands on his head. Her lips moved slightly, as if she were about to talk in her sleep, and the lightning-bolt vein in her forehead throbbed.

The sergeant was somewhere in middle years, hair nearly routed completely, face a rough terrain of deep lines and brown gray stubble, like a furrowed fallow field. Soffjian's hand shifted on his temple a little, and then she barely moved back in time as the man sat bolt upright, eyes wide, darting, spit dripping out the corner of his mouth and onto his surcoat. He looked around at the Jackals surrounding him, and especially the tip of Thumaar's sword, only a few inches from his face. "Wha— . . . who the devils . . . ?"

Thumaar moved the blade in a very small circle just to be sure he had the man's attention. "Every Syldoon has killed an unarmed man before. So I won't insult your intelligence by promising you will be spared. But I will tell you I would get no joy of it. And that the only chance you have of not having your throat slit is doing exactly as I say. Does that sound like something you might be interested in, soldier?"

The sergeant looked away from the sword and up at the face of the man wielding it, started to speak, and then slow recognition stalled him. "Plague me. I know you. You're the former plaguing emperor, ain't you? You're—"

Thumaar brought the tip of the blade an inch closer. "Who I am doesn't matter just now. The only thing that should matter right now is if you can follow directions and not do anything glaringly stupid that will cost you your life." He pointed with his free hand to the bodies in the corner. "We are waking a few other prisoners as well. I can be done with you and put you in storage if you like." He pointed at a final Leopard being dragged into the other room, a bloody trail left behind. "The choice is yours. Choose quickly."

The sergeant chose quickly. And wisely. "Aye. You'll get no trouble from me, then. I've got a wife, kids. I'd like to see them again. Well, unless Cynead kills me dead once he learns I helped you. There's that." The sword moved a little closer, and the man swallowed hard. "But that's not right now, is it? Now is right now, and that's what you want me thinking on, ain't it? The here and now."

"The here and now," Thumaar echoed solemnly, nodding. "That's right, Sergeant. So, in this here and now, I'm going to need you to open that large door, just like you always do, when your relief arrives. Which should be soon, shouldn't it?"

The sergeant nodded, eyes focused on Thumaar. "Ayyup. That's true. Soonish. Only thing is . . ."

Thumaar's eyes narrowed. "What, Sergeant? What is the only thing? Speak."

The man swallowed again, wiped the back of his arm across his forehead. "Not usually me who opens the door. Fact is, not my job."

Thumaar glared at the cornered man. "Not. Your. Job."

"Nope, no. It's Nunce's."

"And would Nunce be one of those three over there?" He pointed the sword at the other three men Soffjian was standing over.

"No, Your Grace, he ain't—"

Mulldoos said, "Uh-oh."

Thumaar ignored him and the honorific for the moment. "Have you ever opened the door? Gone above the call of duty?"

The sergeant nodded. "Yeah, sure, just not in the ordinary is all. Just wanted to put that out there so—"

"Will opening the door yourself be an unspoken code that you are held captive against your will? Will it send your comrades outside running back to the Citadel like carrier pigeons? Will it, Sergeant?"

The man slowly shook his head. "No. Nope. Likely not. Just trying to be helpful is all."

Braylar said, "That is duly appreciated. But perhaps settle for truthful. Direct answers to direct questions. You can you manage that, yes?"

The man nodded and Braylar said, "So, would it be less suspicious if one of your minions there opened the door instead?"

"Aye. Maybe. Not that me opening it would be alarming, like you said, just a little peculiar, and guessing you want this to happen without anything peculiarish at all."

"That's right. So. We will have one of the other guards tend the door after you impress upon him the importance of following orders with no irregularities whatsoever. Now then, just a few more questions, yes? There is a tunnel below us that connects to the catacombs. True?"

The sergeant gave a quick nod and Braylar continued, "And these catacombs, there is an offshoot passage that connects to the old Well of Stairs in the Citadel, correct?"

"Aye," the sergeant said. "There is at that."

"And you can show us the way, after we have relieved the relievers of relief duty?"

The sergeant said. "Nope." And then quickly added, "Not that I wouldn't mind, mind. Would if I could. Just never had cause to go down there. Don't know the way or whereabouts whatsoever."

Braylar asked, "And who, pray tell us, dear Sergeant, could and would."

The sergeant looked around the room as he replied, "Ferret master could. Goes down there ratting from time to time. Old as the Trench he is, knows anything there is to know about earth and tunnels and—" He looked past Azmorgon's thick legs, stopped and then pointed at a figure in the corner with a crossbow bolt in his sternum. "Only he can't. On account of being real dead from the looks of it."

Braylar closed his eyes and sighed, perhaps anticipating Thumaar's rage as the deposed emperor shouted at the Jackals and Eagles, "Two dozen soldiers to shoot at, and you whoresons took out the bony old man with no armor on? Gods preserve us." He started to turn away and then spun back, the tip of the sword pressed into the sergeant's collarbone. "A map. There must be a map. Of the catacombs."

"Of course," the sergeant said quickly, breathily, "Of course there's a map. In the Citadel proper."

"I know about that one, you fool! Another map! Here! Somewhere else!"

The sergeant shook his head and closed his eyes, apparently fearing the worst, but the deposed emperor pulled his sword away, face purpling with impotent rage or frustration.

Mulldoos said, "Well that's a plaguing thorn in the shithole, ain't it. Guess we got to amble down the lane and knock on the Citadel gate after all, eh?"

Azmorgon looked like he wanted to stomp the sergeant to death. "Told you this was a fool plan. Let's kill the lot of them and climb back out of here."

Mulldoos said, "We ain't climbing anywhere just now, you dim bastard. Daylight. Going to have to wait for dark again. And—"

"Silence!" Braylar said. "The both of you. While there are miles beneath our feet, we know the general direction of the destination. This is a setback, but not defeat. We will simply have to do a little exploring."

Azmorgon looked down at the captain. "Without plaguing getting lost and wandering around down there for a tenday and starving to death? How do you figure we do that, Cap? We got no map, we got no—"

"We make one," I said.

Everyone looked at me, apparently having forgotten I was in the room. I reached over my shoulder and tapped the brass writing case. "I have paper, quills, ink. I can map our route as we go, keep track of dead ends, be sure we don't lose our way. At the very least, we can find our way back here. Provided we have time, we could find this well you are looking for."

Thumaar looked very much like he wanted to skewer someone with his big sword. "We have little time and less, scribe. Cynead is marching out to meet the Eagles and Confederates in the field. If we do not seize control of the Memoridons and begin this coup, they will be destroyed."

Braylar replied, "That is true enough, my lord. But our choices are to move with haste and try to find the Well ourselves, or give this up altogether and accept defeat." He looked around the room. "Does anyone else have any bright suggestions?"

No one volunteered any, and the captain said, "Very good. As soon as we deal with the relief, we head down and find our way."

Thumaar thrust the sword towards the sergeant again, pressing the tip into the wobbly flesh just under his chin. "If you or your men give anything away, I will let the Memoridon here have her way with you. She will peel your mind apart one slice at a time. It will be like getting skinned alive, but will last as long as I command it to, and I will command it to last a very, very long time. Do I make myself clear?"

The sergeant started to nod and must have nicked himself on the blade, then settled for, "Aye, Your Grace."

Thumaar turned the sword ever so slightly and made the sergeant gasp. "And if you call me 'Your Grace' one more time, I will chop you into bits and feed you to the bull crabs. Understood?"

"Aye, Your . . . Aye. Aye. Understood."

The deposed emperor drew the sword back and sheathed it, then turned to Soffjian. "Wake the other three."

Then he looked at his men. "Scrub any blood off the floor. Tidy up the desk and benches. Then half of you can break your fast in the larder over there. Take a respite. The rest of you, assume the Leopard mantles and do the same at the tables here. The relief will be here within the hour, and we want to be ready to welcome them."

Braylar, Thumaar, and several Jackals and Eagles were sitting at the table in Leopard surcoats and scale cuirasses. Azmorgon and Mulldoos had protested being excluded, but Braylar had rightly pointed out that they were hardly inconspicuous and would spoil the illusion immediately, and it was imperative all the relief enter the tower without any having a chance to run free and alert anyone.

The sergeant and two other Leopards were in position as instructed, with the two soldiers at the table, immediately facing the door, and the sergeant at the desk. Thumaar had repeated his warning once the soldiers came to, and neither of them seemed willing to defy him. But then they had to know they were likely dead either way. That was certainly the downside to such an absolute Syldoonian policy on prisoners—they didn't have much to lose. Though there was a wide difference between a quick death and one drawn out. Perhaps that would be enough to keep them in line long enough to lure the relieving Leopards into the room.

Bright rectangles of sunlight were on the floor from the arrow loops in the wall, but Braylar had ordered the lamps put out to make the room as dim as possible to cover anything that might have immediately looked out of the ordinary.

I was in the kitchen and larder with Mulldoos, Vendurro, some other Jackals and Soffjian and Nustenzia, and Azmorgon, Rudgi, and the remaining Jackals and Eagles were in the storage room. I much preferred this room—it had no dead bodies. And what's more, ever since growing up in an inn, I'd always found something comforting about the pots and pans hanging from hooks, the shelves with spices, the stone thrawl against the wall to help keep food cool. There were some small skinned animals suspended from a circular rack as well, but that was worlds better than being among the human corpses.

We all ate what we could, and the pantry and larder were well stocked with smoked meats and pungent cheeses, figs and pears, mushrooms and turnips, breads of various sizes. Vendurro even found himself a boiled egg, which brought a bigger smile to his face than I'd seen in a tenday or two.

There was a small buttery as well that only seemed to have small casks of weak beer. Still, that was better than nothing, and I gulped down a cup to steady my nerves.

While everyone else seemed to take this all in as a matter of course—seemingly enjoying their food, despite the fact that we were about to ambush a group of Leopards any moment—all I could think about was that more blood was about to be spilled, or brain boxes shaken beyond repair. I still ate, as I was famished, but I might as well have been chewing cud for all the pleasure it brought me. Nustenzia kept her gaze fixed straight ahead, eating only when Soffjian directly ordered her to. It was impossible to tell whether the prospect of being expendable or valuable weighed more heavily on her, as neither seemed likely to get her back across the Veil to unite with her son.

Assuming she had one. It could have been a well-wrought lie.

I was becoming more Syldoonian by the day, and that made my stomach protest as I chewed a wedge of salty cheese.

We all ate in silence, exhausted and still jittery. Or at least I was. It was quiet until Vendurro said, to no one really in particular, "When you fart, do you ever notice it smelling like dirt?"

Mulldoos gave him a queer look. "What are you plaguing talking about?"

"Farting. The air monkey, the belching spider, the bull snort, the ass salute—"

"I know what a plaguing fart is, you dim bastard."

Vendurro said, "Well, mine smells like dirt sometimes. But not all the time. Why is that?"

No one seemed inclined to answer, so I volunteered, "Someone I knew in university was studying to be a surgeon. They examined bodies, dissected corpses, and—"

Vendurro asked, "Cut people up, for fun?"

I looked at the falchion Mulldoos had across his knees. "You cut people up all the time," I said flatly.

"Aye," Vendurro replied, "but not for fun. That there's Jackal business, just something that got to be done. "

"Well," I replied, "surgeons don't do it for fun either. They do it to learn. And from what I heard, digestion, the way you feel, even flatulence, it has a lot to do with what you eat."

Soffjian said, "This is riveting. Do go on. Please."

So Vendurro did. "But I didn't eat any dirt."

Mulldoos said, "Maybe you did, just after your horse kicked you in the head again and you fell over. Accidentally ate some plaguing dirt. I swear, the fool questions that pop into your hollow head sometimes."

Vendurro ignored him. "So if it wasn't dirt, on account of me not eating dirt, what would do it?"

One of the Jackals sitting nearby said, "Probably roots. Do you eat a lot of roots then? Vegetables that been in the dirt a while?"

"He eats a lot of eggs," Mulldoos said, "which makes him smell worse than swamp gas. Dirt would be a plaguing improvement."

The pounding on the thick front door made me jump and spit out half a mouthful of cheese. I stood up, wiped some crumbs off my face, and tried to concentrate on breathing as I held my crossbow at the ready.

I heard the large wooden beam being pulled up and off the rack by one of the Leopards and gripped my crossbow tight, wondering what we would do if the prisoners inside gave any sign and the Leopards outside attacked or fled.

The sergeant called out with the line Braylar had told him to use, "Took you plaguing long enough. Come on in. Boys are tired."

I heard the sound of feet as soldiers walked in, and then a voice I didn't recognize, "Early if anything, you bastard. Always griping about something, ain't you?"

More footsteps then the same voice, "Plague me, but it's dark in there. Durgiss, light one of them lamps, would you? Light two. Can't see a plaguing thing in here. Say, where's—"

A crossbow string twanged, immediately followed by several more, then we were all moving, Mulldoos and Vendurro in the lead, sword and falchion out, with Soffjian guiding Nustenzia out right after. I darted out of the larder, crossbow up, and saw a chaotic melee.

The Jackals and Eagles had gotten the jump on the Leopards, and several were down already, but the relief was a dozen strong, and the armor and helms were doing their job. Even some of the soldiers who had been struck weren't down.

Bolts were flying from the crossbows of Jackals who had just come out of the storage room, but after that everyone was switching to a sidearm, so I did the same, having just as much chance of hitting an ally as a foe.

Soffjian was pulling Nustenzia along, raised her splayed hand, and swore, not being able to target the Leopards with everyone in such close proximity, then tried moving up along the wall to find a better angle.

And that's when the thrown spear struck Soffjian in the upper chest, piercing her scale armor and driving her back into the wall.

Nustenzia was staring down at her, half pulled to the ground as well.

I looked up, and the man who had thrown the spear had his sword halfway out of the scabbard when Azmorgon nearly decapitated him with his brutish polearm, the only thing stopping the blade from finishing the job being the scale aventail draped down from the helm.

Braylar was advancing on a Leopard with a spear and shield, buckler in one hand, Bloodsounder in the other. The spear flashed out; Braylar deflected it and stepped inside. The Leopard tried to back away to maintain the range to use the spear and hit a wall as Braylar came in fast. The flail heads whipped up and down, but the soldier was moving forward as well, and the Deserter heads only glanced off an arm as the Leopard swung his embattled shield, catching Braylar in the shoulder, knocking him off balance and into the wall.

But rather than try to step back again, the Leopard dropped the spear, pulled his suroka off his belt in one smooth motion, and stepped forward to stab Braylar.

The captain pushed off the wall, batted the long thing blade aside with his buckler and, because there was no room to swing Bloodsounder, launched himself into the Leopard, smashing the bottom of the flail haft into the man's face.

The Leopard stepped back, his nose a pulpy ruin, and blindly slashed with the suroka, but Braylar anticipated that and blocked it with his buckler before hitting the man again with the haft, this time shattering his teeth and likely breaking his jaw.

As the Leopard stumbled back, Braylar let him, using the space to whip Bloodsounder around, catching the man in the side of the helm with the flail heads, dropping him out of the fight.

One of the Leopards Soffjian had woken was reaching over to pick up a spear when Mulldoos chopped into the back of his exposed neck, dropping him to the stones as well.

I was about to step back to clear the way for the seasoned soldiers when I saw Vendurro retreating from two advancing Leopards.

I started forward, buckler up, curved sword ready the way Mulldoos had taught me. Both Leopards had embattled shields out, one armed with a sword, another with a knobbed iron mace, and they must have trained together before, because they were working well in tandem and not getting in each other's way at all.

Vendurro blocked a sword thrust, dodged the arc of the mace, and took another step back. His own sword slashed out, skipping off the top of one of the "merlons" on the embattled shield and then the helm behind it, but doing no damage.

The pair kept advancing, looking for an opening, and Vendurro backed into the table, tripping a little as the swordsman stepped in and threw a blow that Vendurro barely deflected.

Without thinking, I ran the last few steps, planted my foot on the bench, and launched myself into the air, slashing down at the Leopard wielding the mace.

He saw me and got his shield up in time, but my weight slammed into him and we both went spilling to the floor.

The wind was blasted out of my belly as I landed on another bench, and looked over at the Leopard, seeing him grab his mace as he made eye contact with me.

He was getting to his feet faster than I was, and my body didn't seem to want to respond, my lungs no longer working, and I knew he was going to brain me with that mace when Mulldoos stepped in, the falchion chopping down onto the man's elbow, between the bazuband protecting his forearm and the scale sleeve.

The arm snapped and was half severed and the man screamed, but not for long, as Mulldoos kicked him to the ground and struck him several times with the falchion.

I managed to get to my feet and looked back to see that Vendurro had dispatched the swordsman he'd been facing. In fact, seeing three Jackals corner and cut down another Leopard, it seemed the battle was over.

Nearly.

The Leopard sergeant was standing behind a Jackal, one arm around the soldier's throat, the other holding a suroka to it. His eyes were wild and darting as he looked around the room, surveyed the dead, the dying, the victorious. He stopped when he saw Thumaar. "You. Your Grace," he said, half snarling, half fearing for his life. "You were never letting me walk out of here. But you are now." He started sidling towards the front door, closed but unbarred, and the nearest Jackals and Eagles stepped back, waiting for a cue from the deposed emperor.

Thumaar lowered his bloody sword as he slowly walked towards the sergeant and the Jackal. "You are right about one thing. I am not letting you walk out of here."

The sergeant bumped into a stool, kicked it out of his way, and kept moving towards the door. "You do anything suddenlike, you or your men, and I'll cut this throat like it's nothing. I swear I will."

"I am sure you mean that, Sergeant," Thumaar said in an even tone, still moving towards the pair. "But then I would simply cut you down and make you suffer. Immeasurably. What does that accomplish? Nothing. Less. It is all loss. But you lower that suroka, surrender, and I will spare you. You and any of your wounded here. I will let you live. Test my patience on this point, and—"

The sergeant shook his head. "Lying. Spitting lies. That's what you emperor types do, ain't it. No way am I lowering nothing here. You're going to open that door and—"

He started screaming, eyes rolling back in his head, and I looked over at Soffjian. She was upright, face drained of blood but full of wrath, both hands outstretched and splayed.

The sergeant jerked and spasmed and screamed, and the Jackal reached up, grabbed the arm holding the suroka, and twisted and ducked, wrenching it away from his neck. Then he jumped forward as the sergeant dropped the blade, fell to his knees, blood dripping out his nose and ears, eyes rolled back completely, until his scream ended in a gargle as he bit his own tongue off and fell to his side.

Thumaar nodded and looked at his men, pointing to the wounded Leopards. "Kill those bastards."

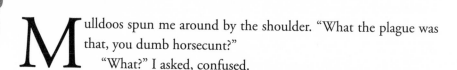

Mulldoos spun me around by the shoulder. "What the plague was that, you dumb horsecunt?"

"What?" I asked, confused.

"You know plaguing well what. Leaping in the air like a plaguing fire frog."

I slid the sword back in my belt. "Well, it distracted the soldier long enough for Vendurro to take out the other one. I saved him."

Even the droopy eye was full of anger. "And I saved you. Never leave your plaguing feet in a fight unless you are grappling on the ground. No jumping around like a plaguing idiot. You hear me?"

I nodded, looking at the soldier he had smashed and slashed into sludge. "Yes. I hear you."

"Do it again and you can fend for yourself after." Then he moved away. Mulldoos was slowly recovering from the aftereffects of Rusejenna's attack, but it was clear he favored his right side and still suffered in silence a great deal. I wondered how many fights he could scrape through before his limitations got him killed.

Of course, the same could be said about me every time I made the foolish decision to wade into a battle.

I glanced over at the Leopard sergeant, the blood leaking out of his mouth and trickling out his ears, forming a pool around his head, and shuddered.

Soffjian was sitting on a bench, and Rudgi was bending over her, dressing her wound with makeshift bandages torn from cloth. The spear hadn't penetrated deep enough to take her out, but there was blood around the wound and seeping into the bandages. I wondered how much blood someone could lose before they fainted or dropped.

When Rudgi finished, she gave a single small nod and helped the Memoridon slip back into her scale cuirass. It was clear then than Soffjian had little to no use of one arm, as getting into her armor was an ordeal. I wasn't sure how that would impact her ability to use Nustenzia when the time came.

But there was no turning back now.

The Jackals and Eagles finished bandaging their wounded. Two men had been killed, and there were several other casualties. One Eagle who was sitting on the floor and leaning against the wall had taken a wicked blow to the side of the neck. It might not have severed a major artery, but the wound was still bleeding profusely. Another stocky soldier with big ears was kneeling alongside him, pressing a wad of cloth to staunch the flow, but it was soaked through and he looked around, asking for more, something else to stop the blood loss.

The wounded soldier had a glassy look in his eyes and was breathing shallowly, his face covered in sweat, but oddly calm otherwise.

Thumaar walked over, standing above the pair, hands on his hips, face grim. "How bad?" he asked.

The Eagle tending the wounded man called out again, "Give me a plaguing tunic! Anyone!"

The wounded soldier waved one hand weakly and said, "That's all right, Bullipp. All right. You go on ahead. Got an emperor to crown, don't you? Go on now. I'll guard the cisterns."

Bullipp grabbed some more wadded cloth from another Syldoon and looked up at Thumaar. "My lord, we can't just leave him. We can't. Emmert here is—"

"He can't come with us, son. And we are too few and have suffered too many losses. I can't spare you. Bind him as best you can, and then we're off."

Bullipp looked poised to argue, but the wounded soldier reached up and put his hand on the man's arm. "We been waiting for this a long time. Long time. You ain't missing it. So . . ." he took a deep labored breath. "Go on. Get on with it. But fetch me a cask of that weak ass beer first. Crack open the top, leave me a mug. That'll do just fine. I'll be right here waiting for you when you're done."

Bullipp didn't respond, eyes fixed on the bloody wad of cloth on the man's neck as he wound several strips of cloth around it.

I looked away. That was somehow worse than the sergeant who had his brain shaken until it bled out his orifices.

Everyone was finishing up, wiping down weapons, readying lanterns, taking some food and drink from the larder, and throwing on whatever Leopard armor and tunics they could find that fit. There was nothing remotely close to fitting Azmorgon, but Braylar solved that deftly enough by telling him and a few others that they would be posing as prisoners.

That didn't sit well with Azmorgon, but once Thumaar supported the idea, that was that.

I was pulling on a cuirass of Leopard scale when I overheard Vendurro say, "What about the ferrets?"

I turned around as Mulldoos replied, "What about the plaguing ferrets?"

"Well," Vendurro said, as if the answer was as obvious as the sun, "They're in cages, ain't they?"

Mulldoos gave the younger man the disconcerting glare with one eyelid drooping, which would have ruined the effect on almost any other face. "And?"

"And," Vendurro said, lowering his voice as he looked at the soldier with the neck wound, "there's a real good chance we ain't coming back this way. No matter how it plays out."

Mulldoos shook his head, exasperated. "Real plaguing unlikely. So what?"

"The ferret master is dead," Vendurro said, "and depending on how things go, might not be any relief to this tower for a while. Poor little things could starve."

Mulldoos saw me listening to the conversation. "Can you plaguing believe this horseshit? About to sneak into the bloody Citadel and the skinny Lieutenant here is worried about some skinnier weasels."

I struggled to come up with something that managed to moderate or mollify, but it didn't matter. Vendurro started walking away, saying, "I'm letting them loose."

Mulldoos replied, "Dumb plaguer. We're about to—" He stopped when Vendurro walked past the screen into the larder, then waved his big hand in the air after him. "Every time I think there's no more foolishness to be plaguing seen, Ven comes up with a new one." He started towards the captain, presumably to tell him that Vendurro would be back shortly.

From behind me I heard, "Still glad you signed up that pen for Syldoon duty?" I hadn't even noticed Rudgi approach. Which wasn't surprising, considering how tired I felt. There was no overt affection or hint at all that the other night we had been copulating, but there was some wry humor there.

"Still? Who said I was glad in the first place?"

She nodded, looking straight ahead. "Saw you rescue the lieutenant. I have to say, you're not half as useless as any other non-Syldoon I've come across."

Making sure no one was paying attention, she gave me a quick wink, and then she moved off to check on Soffjian.

Given how little I understood women of any kind, it wasn't surprising that this lifted my spirits, embarrassed me, and confused me all at once.

Thumaar had the troops lined up, a few carrying lanterns, the rest with weapons out, and Vendurro made it back not a moment too soon.

Mulldoos said, flat as a blade. "Find your furry friends, did you?"

Vendurro replied, "Ayyup. Hard to tell with them bouncing all over the place, but I have to think they were plenty grateful."

"You have to . . . gods, but you're—"

Braylar walked over and addressed me. "Arki, are you ready?"

I had my writing case open and balanced in front of me, hanging from the strap. I wasn't sure how much more ready I could be. "Aye, Captain. I am."

"Very good." Then he looked at Vendurro. "Lieutenant—since you are inclined to be so especially helpful, you will hoist the lantern the whole way so our archivist has the proper light and does not lose our trail in the catacombs."

Vendurro nodded. "Beats latrine duty."

"Only because we lack opportunity, Lieutenant." Then he walked back to join Thumaar, and a moment later our procession was off.

As we headed towards the hall past the larder, I hazarded a look behind me at Emmert, expecting to find him slumped over or dead already. But he was holding his mug up in a shaky hand, his gambeson soaked with blood to the waist, offering a final salute.

We proceeded down the corridor, the captain and deposed emperor at the lead, with Vendurro and me somewhere in the middle. I noted any landmarks or annotation in the margins, but mostly I was just trying to be certain I captured the directions we took and the scale as best I could.

The first leg was simple enough, as we took a few turns, passing some mostly deserted storage rooms before arriving at a spiral stairwell that went down into what I presumed were the catacombs.

Footsteps echoing, we all descended, and even with lanterns lighting the way far better than torches, the sense of being underground heading towards the untold dead was somehow worse than navigating the blackness of the aqueduct. The stairs went down much further than I expected.

Having only read about catacombs, I wasn't sure what to expect. I imagined we would be in the thick of them once we stepped out of the stairwell, but of course it was just another empty unremarkable corridor. We proceeded down it until it turned north, and that took several more turns, hitting long stretches, passing intersecting hallways.

The featureless corridor we were in abruptly shifted as we passed through an arched doorway and into a corbelled hallway beyond. Where the walls had been large blocks of hewn stone before, now they were covered in their entirety on all sides by a horrible and dazzling array of bones, arranged by type. It looked like the ends of thousands or more likely hundreds of thousands of femurs filled the walls as far as the eye could see, creating a ghastly textured look that seemed to undulate as the lantern light washed over it.

As we entered the first hall of bones, Vendurro swung the lantern to get a better look and whistled. "Plague me, but that's a lot of legs, ain't it? I knew they carted skeletons down here, but always figured they repositioned them in their own compartment or cubby or whatnot. Never figured they'd organize them by . . . bone. Why do you figure they went and did it like that?"

I jotted down some hasty notes as I said, "I suppose with a city this size, built on a site like this, tombs or above ground cemeteries are reserved only for the most powerful commanders and emperors. So keeping the dead arrayed by, uh, person, wouldn't make best use of the space down here. Either way," I said, peering forward at the seemingly endless bones, "the Deserters would have liked something like this. The texture, I mean."

Vendurro nodded. "They'd have to crawl on their hands and knees, but ayyup, see what you mean."

We walked on, and while I kept waiting for the stench of death to wash over me, the only thing I smelled was age, mustiness, dust. The bones themselves were odorless, having been stripped of all flesh long before they made their way down here to the catacombs. And still, glancing back and seeing our pocket of light ending—the dark of the tunnel seeming to chase us along— and then the same to the front, our moving illuminated island seemed small indeed, and even without a foul stench, it was impossible to pretend we were anywhere but the halls of the countless unmarked dead, and equally impossible to ward off the dread.

After passing through another arched doorway, the corridor curved to the northwest, only this time, the walls were more modulated still, filled with nothing but phalanges of some kind.

We crossed a corridor and I marked out the options on the paper as we turned east, presumably towards the Citadel. However, it only went east for a small stretch before curving back south, and ending in a semicircular grotto filled entirely with skulls from floor to the barrel ceiling.

We backtracked and tried the other direction, and this went on for hours as I scribbled down notes and directions and tried to be consistent in ticking off distance in my head before jotting it down.

It was obvious Thumaar was getting more frustrated with every dead-end, or the recursive passages that wound back around and reconnected with other ones. Every time we seemed to be making some headway going east towards the Citadel, it seemed the catacombs intentionally thwarted us.

But the mapping did help, as there were a number of times we would have become hopelessly lost without the pages to refer to. A few times, I had to reorient myself or refer to marginal notes to be sure I wasn't misdirecting us, but no matter how arduous it was, I was confident I was at least saving us time.

We'd explored one branch trying to go east before coming to another set of spiral stairs heading down.

Thumaar was furious, wanting to double back and try one of the other corridors near the beginning that headed west.

Braylar said, "My lord, the passage you speak of is several miles behind us. Might I suggest we at least give the one below our feet a chance, and if it seems to be taking us further away from our goal, we abandon it and return to the other?"

Thumaar grabbed one of the hip bones and wrenched it free of the wall. "This goes down. The very opposite of up. Also the opposite of where we need to go."

"And yet we don't know that," the captain replied. "Perhaps the tunnel that ultimately leads to the Well of Stairs actually does so a level, even two or three, below. Unfortunately, we just don't know, and the resident Ferret Master's bones will be down here soon enough, so he is no help at all. But going back several miles to try a different route doesn't guarantee any better chance of reaching our destination, and will actually waste more time."

Thumaar was gritting his teeth, lower jaw rolling, sunken eyes seeming to sink further in the shadow. He turned to one of his men, a long-faced soldier as serious as a tomb. "What say you?"

The man, who must have been an officer of some kind standing in for General Kruzinios, nodded slowly. "Aye. I'm thinking Captain Killcoin has the right of it. Best to give the lower level a shot. If we make no headway, we climb back up here and head back to the beginning. Time's no ally of ours, my lord. But we got the mapmaker there, so we know how to get back to the other corridor at the beginning if needs be."

Thumaar deliberated for another few moments and then nodded.

We went down.

I started mapping on a different sheet, indicating the stairs up and down on both pages. Part of me hoped this level proved even more confounding or less likely to lead to the Well they spoke of. While there was no real difference between exploring deeper in the earth, something about having the bones of millennia above us gave me chills.

Cursing myself a fool, I kept scribbling as we found a corridor that headed in a mostly easterly direction, with a few small detours. The positioning of the bones changed on this level—where before each section of tunnel contained only one kind of bone, the sections here had strange patterns. One wall seemed primarily composed of bits of spine, but broken up by a row of skulls in the middle. We came across one of the rounded grottos that had the most elaborate pattern yet, with the curved wall mostly vertebrae interspersed with diagonal rows of skulls, and two columns supporting the roof that had a mix of every kind of bone, though the skulls were still the dominant feature the other types of bone all radiated out of.

Exhausted, and with eyes blurry and limbs heavy, it was difficult to gauge how much distance we traveled, and impossible to tell what time of day it was in the world above. Below, time was meaningless, or would have been if Thumaar hadn't insisted on pushing us hard, and reminding us after every new turn that haste was paramount. Cynead could be vanquishing his cosmopolitan army any time, and we were the only thing that stood a chance of stopping them. We'd gambled everything on our ability to sneak into the Citadel and reclaim the Memoridons.

As we walked down a curving corridor surrounded by ribs and skulls, I asked Vendurro, "When we were closing in on the cistern tower, someone exchanged a bird call type of signal to create a diversion. I'm assuming that was Jackals?"

He nodded, lantern bobbing in front of him. "Ayyup. Commander Darzaak knows we're on the move by now, and surely sent runners to some of the other Towers that still support Thumaar."

"To what end?" I asked.

Vendurro switched arms and shook some life back into the fingers of his free hand. "Part of the reason we got to hurry here. The Towers still loyal will throw in their support the second we seize the Memoridons. But only then."

I marked down a side passage we chose not to take, as it headed southwest. "So . . . they'll know the moment Soffjian works her memory magic. The Memoridons Cynead tasked to still monitor the Towers, they'll feel it immediately, just as they did when Cynead stole them when we were in the Hippodrome."

"Ayyup."

"And then what? Cynead will know as well, won't he? He'll sense the loss of them. He might not know Thumaar orchestrated it, or how, but he'll know his Memoridons have been stolen."

Vendurro glanced at the new part of the corridor as we passed through an arched doorway. "Plague me. Are those all . . . teeth?"

I looked at the wall. They were indeed. "It would appear so. But back to Cynead. What will—"

"Nothing all that original. Bloody coup."

I reached the edge of a page and swapped it out for a clean one. "But he'll still outnumber Thumaar's forces in the field. Even without the War Memoridons helping him, or the others giving him rapid intelligence, he could still prevail."

"Could," Vendurro agreed. "But he'll still lose Sunwrack. Well, should anyway. Still plenty of Towers loyal to the bastard in here too, but Thumaar's supporters inside will rally once they know he's in the city and has the Mems with him. Capital of Coups is going to get real bloody today, but once it all gets mopped up, Thumaar ought to be the one standing with the crown on his head."

I thought about all the priests and their attendants with a never-ending parade of carts laden with new bones coming down here, filling new corridors somewhere, arranging the last evidence of the dead in obscure patterns for obscure reasons perhaps only they understood. Would Thumaar send Cynead's skull down here, to be an anonymous testament to the never-ending struggle, treachery, and bloodletting in the world above?

The tunnel of teeth gave way to a corridor of tibias, which ended in a grotto and required more backtracking, but we found another hall heading east.

Still, while we seemed to be making halting progress, the number of recursive passages and dead ends was maddening. There was no guarantee that any of the tunnels on this level, or one below, or any we might actually traverse, would actually lead to the Well. We'd been down here for what must have been half a day, stopping only briefly to rest our legs and swallow some quick mouthfuls of food, but there was nothing to say we were any closer to where we needed to be than when we started.

No one spoke of it. No one had to. Not even curmudgeonly Mulldoos, snide Benk, or the most vocally critical of all, Azmorgon. There was a heaviness about traveling here, an unyielding leaden dread, that made conversation seem like an abomination. And that, with the growing doubts about us being able to actually break into the Citadel, silenced everyone.

But not long after our break, there was a change as we continued east, passing walls of alternating scapulas and skulls, when they suddenly stopped. We hadn't passed through an archway, which was the usual demarcation, and they weren't replaced by a new kind of configuration of bones. The stone walls on either side beyond were blank.

It was almost startling, after so many miles of the remains of the dead. The passage continued for a hundred yards, and then we passed through a square doorway. The space was bigger beyond and I sighed, expecting to have to pen another grotto, but this room was square, boneless, and only an antechamber to another larger space seen through an open doorway ahead.

Thumaar kissed his fingertips and lifted them towards the sky. The ceiling anyway. Then he turned and looked back at us. He had a beatific smile that seemed horribly out of place on his normally stony face. "We are close. The gods have willed me to return to my proper place. And when I do, that will be a harbinger of their own imminent return. Come."

Mulldoos looked back at us and rolled his eyes as we pressed forward.

Passing through the door, we entered a domed rotunda, the walls filled with carvings that appeared to be a millennium old. The dome itself was covered in alternating ceramic tiles of black and white.

There was a doorway on the other side, but Thumaar marched immediately to the left, seeming to know exactly where he was.

We all followed into a large rectangular chamber filled with columns carved in the same style as those of the Hippodrome—spiraling panels depicting ancient battles, victories, losses, discoveries, treaties, statesmen, soldiers.

In the center of the room there was a rectangular sarcophagus, the lid inlaid with alternating rows of lapis, turquoise, and carnelian, forming a border around a remarkably lifelike effigy of a hawkish looking man. Thumaar ran his fingertips over the surface, tenderly, reverently.

I whispered to Vendurro, "What is this place?"

He whispered back. "Never seen it. Heard tell of it. Chamber of First Emperors they call it. Expect that's the tomb of the first Eagle emperor. Three hundred years ago, or thereabouts."

"How many have there been?"

"Eagles? Two," he replied. "Well, Thumaar would make it three if he retakes the throne. Thumaar Twiceking, they ought to call him."

The chamber of the Eagles' first emperor gave way to ten more in succession, each filled with a single sarcophagus.

If we'd had more time, I would have taken a bit of charcoal out of my case to try to take a rubbing of the effigy. But time was certainly our enemy rather than ally.

We navigated around the remaining dead emperors. There was another rotunda beyond, identical to the first, a short passageway past that, and then a set of spiral stairs heading up.

Thumaar was moving like a man possessed and had already started up the stairs, apparently knowing exactly where they led, as half the company had already disappeared above us.

I jotted a note about the stairs as I stubbed most of my toes on one of them, and then just paid attention to the wild flashes of lantern light on the walls above me, like something alive and trying to escape this place.

We had gone up what felt like a thousand stairs but couldn't have been a third that when they abruptly ended, and Thumaar and Braylar were already halfway down the unadorned hallway ahead of us.

Unlike all the halls of the catacombs, this corridor had torches in brackets, lit and well maintained, and from the flickering flames it was clear we were about to taste open air again soon. The walls were a black smear behind each one. But even if the wind didn't take them, someone had to replace or relight them every hour or two, so we could be expecting company at any moment.

I watched the figures ahead, and saw Soffjian laboring a bit. While the injury might not have been life threatening (yet, anyway), she had obviously lost a fair amount of blood and was woozy. She matched her brother for stubbornness and pride, so if she was allowing anyone else to see the effects, it was only because she was completely unable to mask them at all.

Considering that the success of this mission was entirely on her bloodied shoulders (and Nustenzia's bonier ones), this was fairly concerning.

As we reached the end of the corridor, we turned to the right. But it was clear from the natural light ahead that we were entering a far more open space than we'd seen in what felt like forever, and I had to force myself not to rush ahead.

When I came to the end of the hall, the torch flames danced so much I thought they might go out as a gust caught them. I stepped out onto a small stone landing, catching my breath. We were in a giant brick cylinder that disappeared into the darkness below, seeming to sink into the earth even deeper than the Trench that surrounded Sunwrack, and rising several stories above us where light poured down from a large circular space in the middle of the domed atrium roof.

The rest of the small party was already moving up, walking the single set of stairs that spiraled up the interior of the stone cylinder to the top.

Vendurro was looking back at me and must have seen the look on my face. "Well of Stairs. Guessing you guessed that already, huh? I've only been up there looking down. Right different perspective going the other way, ain't it?

Well, you can't say, of course, never having seen it before from any direction. Anyway, mind the stairs. No rail, and it does get gusty."

He started up, and I said, "Does anyone use this anymore? For water, I mean?"

"Nah," he called back. "Used to be a major source of water for the Citadel, years back. Springs or underground river of some such thing, down there in the deep."

"What happened?"

"Can't say for certain. Be better off asking Cap or Hew or—" He stopped himself, then spoke again as if he hadn't said the other lieutenant's name at all. "Cap. But the only important thing is climbing out of here without letting a big old breeze suck you down into the black."

He was right about the wind—it seemed to be flowing both up and down, dragging at sleeves and anything projecting off the body. The stairs were three feet wide, but even keeping as close to the wall as I could, I felt the incessant tug towards that indeterminate fall in the center.

Round and round we went, up towards the light, until the steps finally reached the rim at the top, which was the most treacherous moment, with no wall to cling to as I practically jumped off the stairs. I hazarded one look back down into the depths, and even without wind swirling around the Well, I still felt as if I might be drawn in.

I stepped away and looked around. The building we were in housed a fabulous garden and collection of small trees and shrubs and what appeared to be a diverse collection of medicinal plants I recognized from university— feverfew, lavender, sage, peppermint, tansy—as well as many that weren't even vaguely familiar. It was obvious why so much of the roof had been left open to allow sun and the occasional rain in.

Thumaar's band hadn't drawn any weapons yet, which I thought odd before remembering that we had all donned various Imperial badges, sur-coats, and embattled shields with the Suns and Leopards each occupying half the field. Still, Nustenzia obviously didn't belong, and a number of soldiers had wounds, Soffjian in particular looking as if she just had just visited a battlefield surgeon.

Everyone swatted the dust off as best they could, with most walking off to a narrow irrigation trough that delivered water from some aqueduct piping or other hidden in the wall and rinsing off.

I splashed some water on my face and forearms as well, which helped wake me up for a brief moment, and turned to Vendurro, whispering, "What's the plan now?"

He was gargling some water out of his cupped hands, and Rudgi chose to answer, despite my not having even seen her sidle up next to us. "I expect we are going to walk through the Citadel like we own the place, make for the frame room when opportunity presents itself, and head to the streets when the festivities kick in."

I looked at her, blinking water off my eyelashes. She must have been as exhausted as the rest of us but managed to seem both alert and somehow looking forward to what happened next. I said, "We do look decidedly . . . beat up."

"Ayyup," she replied. "Not a handsome group, that's for certain. But Cynead just rode out of the capital to meet an enemy in the field this morning, the Jackals have been causing a ruckus all over the city all night, staging fights here, there, and everywhere, and the populace has got to be right nervous I'm guessing, especially with rumors of Thumaar's return flying faster than hungry hawks right now."

"Which means . . . ?"

Vendurro said, "Which means, war is in the wind today. The short sergeant has the right of it. Blood is being spilled. Not in every street just yet. That'll come later. Gallons of it. But it's still dribbling just now here and there with a lot of folks suddenly real restless, so some nicked-up soldiers won't be causing any raised eyebrows today. Besides, I'm sick of skulking around like a plaguing ferret, ain't you? Or were you hoping we'd crawl up Cynead's shitty garderobe? Come on."

Rudgi gave me a punch in the upper arm. "Just act like you belong. It'll all work out fine."

I nodded, completely lacking confidence in anything she said. I didn't believe for a moment that everything was going to be fine. In my relatively short stint with the Jackals, even when things went perfectly according to plan, the results were never what any non-Syldoon would think of as "fine."

We all started walking towards a door on the far side of the garden. I whispered to Rudgi and Vendurro ahead of me, "What if someone recognizes Thumaar? Or Braylar? Or anyone? I mean, it's not as if the emperor has been gone a tenyear or two."

Vendurro replied, "Well, Thumaar is presumably out there in the field, so it ain't as if anybody in their right skulls would be thinking he's like to stride down a corridor in the Citadel, all dressed up like a Leopard. And anybody looks like they are slowly parsing all that out are like to be hitting the stones dead before they finish."

Rudgi nodded. "Anybody recognizing somebody here is going to be awfully bewildered, even if only for a hot moment." She snapped her fingers. "And that's about all it will take. We got this, Arki."

I remained unconvinced. "So, we're just going to stroll through the Citadel, killing off one bewildered Leopard after another until we reach our destination?"

She looked at the lieutenant. "You were right on that score. He sure as hells does ask a lot of questions, doesn't he?"

Vendurro nodded. "Ayyup. That he does." He looked over his shoulder and gave me a crooked grin. "Cap and Thumaar got it worked out, Arki. Well, provided Soff doesn't bleed out on us. That would throw a big fat turd in the soup, wouldn't it?"

There was no arguing that point.

We were exiting the garden when we passed a Thurvacian servant carrying a bucket with shears and a spade, and other small tools I didn't recognize. I held my breath, but the servant kept his eyes low, bowing once as we all filed past.

I looked back at him as we started down a hallway with a tall corbelled ceiling, but if he though it odd passing a group of armed "Leopards" in this part of the Citadel, he kept about his business and disappeared among the twisty trees.

The first thing that was immediately clear was that the Citadel was adorned and decorated in far more grandiose fashion than the rather austere and simple Jackal Tower. The walls were draped with rich tapestries that seemed imported from every corner of the empire, and also broken up frescoes and murals and small alcoves with marble statues designed to impress upon the viewer the power, wealth and, to some degree, absurdity of the Leopard and Sun Tower. There were fabulously carved triptychs and rich paintings that stretched for a tenfoot or more. Even the most basic and functional of surfaces or elements of construction were decorated, engraved, to ridiculous degree, as if the artisans commissioned had been promised payment only if they managed to outdo the sculptor, carver, or painter on the previous panel.

Which meant every hall was filled with priceless artifacts, which also meant we would be encountering armed occupants at any moment.

And so we did. Rounding a corner, Thumaar still leading at a relentless pace, we nearly collided with another group of ten Leopards walking in the opposite direction.

Braylar addressed one as he helped steady him. "My apologies, good man."

The one similarity the Citadel had with the Jackal Tower, and I presumed all Towers in the Empire, was that they were occupied primarily by Syldoon, slave soldiers waiting for manumission, and the indigenous Thurvacian servants, clerks, and staff. Spouses and families seemed to be housed in residential buildings in the vicinity, but out of the way so as to avoid throwing silt or shit in endlessly turning gears.

This was no different—there were eight slave soldiers, not yet with inked nooses or surokas, but clearly bearing themselves in a way that would have gotten Thurvacians executed for insolence, and two armed Leopard escorts.

The soldier Braylar helped gave a curt nod. "You best watch yourself," he glanced at the pewter badge on Braylar's gambeson, "Sergeant. I'm a forgiving sort, but that would earn some odorous tasks from practically any other officer you nearly knock over. Maybe even some lashes, if you truly got unlucky." The officer looked over the rest of our bloodied company, stopping when he saw Soffjian and Nustenzia. "Unless you have reason for such haste. Looks likes you just had yourselves some action." His amicable demeanor clouded over. "The streets?"

"Aye, Lieutenant," Braylar replied. "Some plaguing Thurvacians were being . . . disruptive."

"I heard there was some trouble brewing this morning. Serious?"

"No, sir. A protest over fruit prices or some such thing. Turned a little ugly, and the City Watch needed a bit of help. Useless bastards, one and all. The Watch, I mean. And the Thurvacians, so long as we're counting idiots. But we cut down the leader and the rest dispersed quick enough. Still, I'm thinking the sooner Emperor Cynead rides back into the city the better."

The lieutenant was smiling again. "Go clean yourselves up. Get some wine." He looked at his charges. "You see. Stupidity begets stupidity, and power begets power. And some of you were grumbling things might be too easy for the Leopards now." He laughed. "Once you take the noose, we will be invading and civilizing some new part of the world, or putting down foolish rebellions on our very own doorstep. There is always action to be had."

Both parties kept moving in their opposite directions.

My exhaustion was getting the better of me—I had a moment of giddy relief that Braylar hadn't tried the unsuccessful "quills merchant" stratagem a third time.

We passed other soldiers or servants a few more times, and while our somewhat battered appearance raised eyebrows, it didn't raise alarms. We encountered one group of Leopards who appeared equally bloodied and unkempt and who likely had actually been quelling some small uprising in the streets, or fighting off Jackals, disguised or otherwise.

Every time we saw anyone else, I held my breath and kept my eyes on Vendurro's back, and in each instance, we made it by unaccosted.

We left the main corridor and its heavier traffic behind and walked down some narrower halls and I was thankful everyone else was familiar with the layout or I would have gotten hopelessly lost.

We took a right turn and headed into a broader hall filled with magnificent murals depicting the emperors who had occupied the Sun Citadel since it was built, with their blazonry split between suns and the charge of their particular Tower that they hailed from. I thought for a moment we might be heading to the throne room or a great hall, both of which would mean a lot more Leopards about and the chances of us escaping notice or questioning dwindling. Then I saw ahead that there were a number of guards in resplendent scaled cuirasses of gold and black guarding the stairwell to a tower.

As we walked closer, Braylar spoke quietly, "Sister, though this is not in your bailiwick, I suggest you look as docile and broken as possible."

Soffjian replied, "I am filthy, have lost a great deal of blood, and hope to remain conscious long enough to make all this worth it. It is not what one would really call a stretch."

"Very well," he replied. "And you other 'prisoners,' do your best to look defeated as well. Even you, Azmorgon. Though perhaps belligerent and irreverent will work in your case."

"Plaguing right it will," Azmorgon said.

When the party halted in front of the three steps and oak doors to the entrance of the tower, a Leopard with a gold and black plume stepped forward and addressed us. "State your business."

As agreed upon and to deflect any attention away from Thumaar, Braylar stepped forward. "We have apprehended a rogue Memoridon. She needs to be returned to the frame now."

The Leopard squinted as he looked at Soffjian, then seemed to recognize her. "This the one from the Jackal Tower?"

"The very same," Braylar replied.

"Who's the other then?" he asked, pointing at Nustenzia.

"Another from the Jackals, an initiate. This one escaped from their Tower. Seems they are all deserters there. And I have orders to return her to the frame immediately."

The Leopard was still eyeing Soffjian warily, as if he expected her to attack him with memory magic at any moment. "The Emperor's not here. And even if he was, I didn't hear anything about taking any rogue Memoridons to the frame."

"The Emperor's presence isn't required," the captain said. "Her sisters in the tower will deal with her. But she has to be returned immediately. Those were the orders. She cannot risk being separate much longer or she might just fall dead. And while I would be glad to see it, her sisters will want to put her to the question. Do you want to answer to the Emperor for allowing her to die right on the verge of entering? Because that won't be on me. You can be sure if my prisoner dies because you delayed, the Emperor will hear of it."

The Leopard looked uncertain, about to relent even, but then said, "I'll need to verify this, Sergeant. Protocol is all. I don't allow anyone up without express permission, and all I have is your word. And if that means your prisoner dies while we wait, well, I reckon we'll deal with that as it comes, won't we?"

I heard an all-too familiar voice from behind me and had to resist spinning around. "So, you have her then?"

Skeelana walked to the front of our group, smaller than everyone, including Rudgi, a pewter Sun and Leopard badge on the ash gray doublet she wore, the rings in her nose and ears catching the light. She stopped alongside Soffjian. "I'd heard you were apprehended but didn't really dare to believe it. Part of me hoped you'd escaped, I won't deny it. And part of me really just wanted to see the look on your face when we were reunited, and you saw just how badly you had miscalculated." Skeelana smiled crookedly. "And now that we are here together, it doesn't disappoint in the slightest. So rare when reality lives up to expectation, isn't it?"

Soffjian looked unsteady on her feet.

Skeelana ignored her and addressed the captain of the tower guard. "Let these troops through immediately, you imbecile. My sisters need to see this Memoridon right now."

The captain in gold and black hesitated, then said, "Fine. But these other prisoners got no reason to go. They stay. Leave the guards behind. The rest can go."

Braylar said, "Very good." He then assigned a split of Eagles and Jackals to remain behind with Azmorgon and the other "prisoners."

The Leopard captain looked over his shoulder. "Tell them to unlock the door."

One of the soldiers behind him rapped his knuckles on the thick door five times, and we heard wood scraping, and then the tumblers of the lock clinking loudly. The double wooden doors opened out, and the Leopards stepped aside as we entered. There were two soldiers inside who looked over each of us as we filed past, then dropped the broad beam back in the brackets behind us and turned the large key to lock the doors again.

Skeelana walked ahead of us down a dimly lit hallway as Braylar led us forward, with his "Leopards" in tow. I hadn't sensed the phantom smell Skeelana projected to me when we were trying to evade Imperial pursuit, so I was stunned she was here now walking among us, a dozen conflicting thoughts in my head, a third of them bloody.

We rounded a corner, and everyone remained silent until we'd gone far enough to be out of earshot of the guards at the door. We were nearly to the stairs when Skeelana started to turn around, but then Mulldoos was there, lurching, hunched a bit, not dexterous, but still fast, his suroka pressed against the Memoridon's throat.

He said, "One reason. Give me one reason why I'm not to slit this skinny throat right plaguing now. Got to be one, but having a real plaguing hard time seeing it."

Braylar put his hand on the lieutenant's big shoulder. "The reason is singular but compelling. We are in the tower of the frame. Without her and a battering ram, we would not be."

"Ayyup," Mulldoos said, still not moving the blade, "Got that much. But how? Why? I see a turncoat twat who needs to be offed. That's what I plaguing see."

Skeelana raised both hands slowly, licking her plump lips. "There are many of us—Memoridons, I mean—who didn't exactly appreciate being stolen. Darzaak wasn't the only Commander who didn't abuse us, who valued us."

Mulldoos reached up with his free hand and grabbed a handful of her dark hair. "You betrayed us. Led them straight to us, you little lying cunt. Straight. To us. You expect me to buy that you had a change of heart? Again?"

Skeelana looked him in the eye. "Cynead gave me a choice. Death, or spy on you lot. Forgive me if I erred on the side of self-preservation. But I always hoped we could undo what that bastard did. And when Soffjian helped you escape . . . I knew what she was up to. Thought I did, anyway. So yes, I led them close enough to you that they didn't execute me for abetting, but tried to buy you as much time as I could."

Her eyes darted to me. "I sensed you were in Sunwrack yesterday." And then back to Mulldoos. "I could have informed the Leopards. Could have led them directly to you and had you in real shackles if I had a mind to. But I reached out to Soffjian instead. So let me ask you, Lieutenant, does that seem like the sort of thing your enemy would truly do? Does it?"

Braylar still had his arm on Mulldoos's shoulder. "Soffjian told me the moment it happened. That Skeelana contacted her."

Mulldoos turned and glared at the captain. "And you didn't think it'd be a decent idea to share that little plaguing development with your officers?"

Braylar nodded towards the deposed emperor. "Like you, Lieutenant, I am but a humble soldier following orders."

Thumaar stepped forward, "Drop the blade, Lieutenant. You want to bark a complaint at anyone, direct it to me. But after. We have to move. Now. Despite her unexpected aid, those guards might still follow up. We have little time or less."

Mulldoos slowly pulled his suroka back and slid it in the scabbard.

We kept walking down the hallway, and I found Rudgi looking at me with an unreadable expression that might have been curiosity, irritation, confusion, disgust, or some other womanly face that was certain to remain a mystery to me.

"What?" I asked.

She jerked a thumb at Skeelana. "That's the one who made your knees turn to sand, so helpless you just had to kiss her?"

Hot in the face and neck, I replied, "I wouldn't describe it like that. But yes, that's the one I kissed."

Rudgi looked straight ahead again, grinning. "Huh. Figured her for a stately beauty. But it's clear you like shorties."

That was the extent of it before we reached the end of the hall and stopped in front of a set of spiral stairs.

Skeelana looked at Braylar. "Unless Cynead renovated last night, there is only one floor, several stories up. This is more minaret than tower. The frame is on that floor."

Thumaar addressed the Memoridons. "In my day, we kept a contingent of guards up there, as well as a war Memoridon. Has anything changed?"

"Yes," Skeelana said. "The frame is guarded by several martial Memoridons now. Four, possibly five. There are guards as well, perhaps double that, but the Memoridons will be the real trouble."

"Always plaguing are," Mulldoos growled, before turning to the captain. "What's the play, Cap?"

Braylar pulled Bloodsounder off his belt. "We cannot risk Soffjian. And I am the only one who has any immunity to them. I don't know if I can withstand four or five of them at once, or for how long, but I will attack them first, take out those I can and draw the attention of the others. The rest of you eliminate the guards and cut down any remaining Memoridons."

"Bold move, Cap. If you want to be dead right quick. Even if the Memoridons aren't enough to overwhelm you, the guards'll cut you down before you cross the room to wet that flail."

Nustenzia said, "I understand why Soffjian must conserve her strength. But why not have this one—Skeelana, was it?—use me to amplify her power and take out your enemies in the room? I have no wish to aid in your bloodshed, but no wish to die either."

Skeelana replied, "That's not really what I do."

"What is it you do, then?" Nustenzia asked, sounding mystified.

"Besides shank her allies in the back, you mean?" Mulldoos said. "Not a plaguing thing."

Soffjian said, "Skeelana is no offensive weapon, it's true. But she is excellent at obfuscation. She could use Nustenzia for that, confuse the Memoridons long enough for Braylar to close and dispatch them. With Nustenzia, any illusion you create will be absolute. At least long enough for us to enter and wreak havoc. That should be coverage enough for Braylar to approach them." She looked at Mulldoos and Rudgi. "And while it might have been a while since you shot anything besides a crossbow, I trust you still remember how to use a composite bow."

Mulldoos looked down at the quiver on his hip as if it contained snakes. "Probably no better than the scribbler here. Been a long time. Now's no time to practice. I'm thinking once you rattle their cages, Cap can lay into the Memoridons before they take out the lot of us, and we'll follow close, take any guards out hand to hand."

Thumaar had been listening quietly but reasserted his command. "We have it then. Skeelana, you will get them to unbar the door, with the same scheme that got us here. Nustenzia, you will be clasping hands or whatever it is you need to do to aid her. Create whatever illusion you see fit to allow the captain to enter and see to the Leopard Mems. The rest of us will eliminate the guards. My boys have no lack of experience with bows. They will fall back and plunk the Mems until the captain closes, then switch to melee. Questions?"

Skeelana raised her hand and looked at the older woman. "Nustenzia, is it? How exactly will you assist me?"

Nustenzia replied, "I will grab hold of you, and you can draw on me, as you would a well. Pull up the power you need."

Skeelana wrinkled her nose as if the notion were distasteful, or possibly just foreign. "Is there a . . . limit? Do I need to take care not to draw too much?"

"No," Nustenzia said with her haughty smile. "I am the Focus of a Grand Wielder."

"I have no earthly idea what that means," Skeelana said. "But I am sure it is mighty impressive."

Nustenzia frowned. "It means the well is not limitless, but it is too deep for you to threaten the bottom. I can assist you and Soffjian without worry."

Skeelana said, "If Soffjian vouches for you, that's enough for me."

Thumaar looked around, nostrils flaring on his narrow nose, eyes fever bright. "Other questions?"

No one said anything.

"Good." He closed his eyes and bowed his head. "May the gods of old preserve us, aid us, and help us rectify the wrongs brought on by false emperor Cynead, so that we can pave the way for their own rightful return, expunge the false god who has risen in their place."

Thumaar opened his eyes and abruptly started up the stairs as Braylar, Skeelana, and Nustenzia hurried to catch up, with the rest of us following them.

They reached the landing, which was large enough to accommodate most of our small group, with the remainder on the steps just below.

Skeelana looked everywhere around us, head pivoting with excruciating slowness, seemingly taking in each stone, crevice, crack, and shadow, just as she had in the streets of Alespell before working her weir skills on the Hornmen.

Mulldoos whispered as guttural as a whisper could be. "Get on with it, witch."

Soffjian hissed, "She is preparing, you fool. Do you actually want to survive this? If so, shut your mouth and let her be."

Skeelana continued examining methodically, then finally looked at Nustenzia. "You're sure this will work?"

The older woman nodded, tight-lipped, as she grabbed Skeelana's hand. Then Skeelana looked at the rest of us and quietly said, "Don't move. Not a one of you. I will have a difficult enough time making the illusion stick without interference. Understood?"

If Thumaar and Braylar rankled at being addressed that way, they gave no indication, maybe respecting her abilities even if the captain was itching to take off half her skull with Bloodsounder.

Soffjian was alongside Skeelana and looked down at her. "I didn't harry you before, but I'd suggest hurrying now," she said, her face drawn and pale, the lightning-bolt vein blue on her sweaty forehead. "If I fall over it won't matter how elegant the illusion you wrought."

Some of the Eagles disguised as Leopards had their bows out already, arrows nocked, but hadn't drawn yet. All the other soldiers had their weapons in hand and had moved to the side away from the hatch in the middle of the door. Soffjian and Skeelana would be the only ones immediately visible to whoever looked out.

Skeelana knocked six times, two quick knocks followed by four spaced out more evenly.

The panel opened from the other side and a woman's face appeared, bronze and harsh-looking. "Skeelana. You are . . . unexpected. Early. The check-in is in tenday. It has not been a tenday. This has been explained. What is it?"

Skeelana looked up at the open panel. "Is it? I have such a difficult time keeping track of these things. But that isn't the reason for my little visit."

The Memoridon on the other side wasn't amused. "You might be the Emperor's little pet just now, but that carries no weight with us. Be quick about it or be gone—what do you need?"

Skeelana replied, "Direct. I appreciate that. But speaking of Emperor Cynead, you might recall he sent his little pet out into the wild to track down some deserters. Especially a Memoridon deserter. Does that sound at all familiar to you?"

The bronze Memoridon narrowed her eyes and inspected Soffjian but didn't respond.

Skeelana said, "There you go. Powers of deduction. Yes, this is she. Soffjian, of the Jackal Tower. And while check-in isn't for a tenday, this one won't last ten more minutes. She is injured and has been separated from the frame for far too long."

The bronze woman looked back to Skeelana. "That could very well be the true. Likely even. But no concern of mine. Not unless you have Imperial writ granting her early entrance."

Skeelana blinked twice. "Given that Cynead is out there trouncing his enemies right now, I don't expect to be able to get his signature to satisfy you this moment. There simply isn't time. But you see, that's sort of the advantage to being a pet—I do have his attention. At least for now. So when I ride out to him, present this woman's corpse, and explain that she is dead because a guardian of the frame stuck to some ridiculous protocol instead of doing the smart thing and ensuring she was kept alive for questioning . . ." She shrugged her shoulders. "Well, I have a funny feeling he won't be amused. Call it a hunch. So, Lady Protocol, remind me of your name please. I want to be sure I do give an accurate account."

The woman started to reply but I heard a voice behind her. The bronze Memoridon stepped away from the panel, there was some muffled arguing, and then a minute later she appeared again. "You may enter, Skeelana. Just remember—Cynead is famous for changing favorites. You won't be a pet for very long."

"I guess I will take the belly rubs while I can get them, then."

The panel slid shut, and for that moment, my hatred of Skeelana was at odds with my reluctant appreciation—what she lacked in power, she made up for in deviousness, guile, plucky charm, and verve.

The soldiers all tensed as we listened to lock tumblers clink and clack and a large beam being drawn back on the other side.

The door started to swing in and Skeelana pushed Soffjian through first, holding tight to Nustenzia's thin wrist as she followed.

The bronze woman's eyes widened in surprise, clearly not recognizing or expecting the older woman, and when Braylar ran in behind the trio, she called out, "Breached!" and started to raise her arms.

Braylar was too quick, snapping her arm out of the way with his buckler and bringing the flail heads around, both of them striking her squarely in the side of the head.

I was glad I didn't have time to see the extent of the wound as she fell and the rest of us stormed into the room.

Skeelana had one hand out, maintaining whatever illusion she worked for as long as she could, drawing on Nustenzia to solidify it. Guards and war Memoridons inside the room all turned to face the door, and it was clear they couldn't see those of us behind Skeelana, as they focused on Braylar and the Syldoon immediately behind him.

He ran towards the next Memoridon, a tall woman with tempestuous gray hair and a copper scale cuirass who stretched her arms out, face intense as she splayed her fingers, and accomplished absolutely nothing.

Whatever she hoped to fell Braylar with failed, which she recognized too late, trying to draw her sword as he advanced but only getting it halfway out of the scabbard before the bloody flail heads came down. She tried blocking them with her arm, which proved a mistake as it wasn't armored and the flail broke her forearm. As the Memoridon fell back, broken arm still up, he brought the flail heads around again, and she didn't manage to get anything between them and her face, which erupted in red.

A Leopard stumbled and grunted behind them, an arrow sticking through his bicep just below the mail sleeve, and he dropped his spear. When he bent over and broke the shaft off, another arrow plunged into his neck, and he toppled over.

Like the battle with the Hornmen in the predawn streets of Alespell and the skirmish with the Brunesmen as we captured Henlester, this was a wild melee with pockets of combatants fighting each other all over the crowded circular room. While the Syldoon understood the benefit of forming up and fighting in units better than any soldiers alive, there simply wasn't much time, as Eagles, Jackals, and Leopards engaged each other as best they could, though we at least had the element of surprise. Judging by the looks on the Leopards' faces, we must have seemingly emerged from nowhere as we stepped out of the fabric of Skeelana's illusion and attacked.

I heard more arrows whizzing past as I followed close to Mulldoos and Rudgi as they moved towards a pair of Leopards who saw us and had locked the edges of their shields together, spears angling over the tops as they advanced on us.

Mulldoos raised his shield and had his falchion up, the blade resting on the embattled "merlon" as he called out in his slurry growl, "Behind me, scribbler, you dumb whoreson!"

I kept directly behind the pair—the spears had range on us and we would have to close to eliminate that advantage. I kept my own shield up high, just below eye level, and positioned my curved sword across the top, for all the good it would do.

Both Leopards sent their spearheads flying—one slammed into Rudgi's shield with a thud and the Leopard pulled it out just as fast, while the other went between Mulldoos and Rudgi and right at my head. I managed to duck just enough that it clanged off the top of my helm.

Mulldoos and Rudgi moved forward together, deflecting the spears as the two Leopards retreated to try and maintain their range. One Leopard feinted a thrust at Rudgi's head, trying to draw her shield up, and then directed the real attack at her legs, but she didn't bite on the thrust, slapping the spear head away as she came in fast, and Mulldoos followed her lead, keeping pace as they closed.

The Leopards realized too late they had backed into the curved wall of the tower, and before they could fight for more space, Mulldoos and Rudgi were on top of them. The lieutenant caught the spear haft on the merlon of his shield, trapped the spearhead with his falchion as the Leopard tried pulling it back, then stepped in, the thick blade whipping out in a horizontal blow. The Leopard blocked it, but Mulldoos threw his weight behind his shield and slammed it into the other man's shield face, knocking him into the wall, pinning long enough for the falchion to come down low, driving into the Leopard's exposed knee. The man cried out, crumpling, and Mulldoos rained more blows on him, blasting his defenses aside and surely breaking bones under the mail byrnie with one wicked blow before the next caught the soldier in the neck and finished him. Whatever Mulldoos had lost in balance or coordination he made up for in being more vicious than ever.

Once the pair of Leopards was divided, Rudgi relied on her quickness, blocking a final spear thrust, then delivering a flurry of blows of her own, her sword a blur from high to low, left to right, back up, as she hooked the over-whelmed Leopard's shield with hers, pulled it aside just enough, and dropped down, driving her sword up into the inside of the soldier's thigh.

The Leopard threw his head back to yell, and Mulldoos's blade came into the opening, striking the mail coif but crushing the windpipe underneath as the man fell over bleeding profusely from his leg, choking and gurgling as he writhed on the floor.

Rudgi yelled at Mulldoos, "I plaguing had him!"

Mulldoos yelled back, "You're plaguing welcome, Sergeant! Now shut your—"

"Look out!" I cried.

Another spearhead shot out, striking Mulldoos in the meaty part of the shoulder just outside the lamellar cuirass, driving it into the mail byrnie.

Without thinking, I was already charging forward as the Leopard drew the spear back to thrust again, and I rammed my shield into his arm, swinging my curved sword wildly, striking nothing. But I'd knocked the soldier off balance, and as he started to recover, Rudgi was there, blocking his spear away, slicing the Leopard's hand just below his bazuband.

He dropped his spear, and I pressed forward against his shield, pinning it against his body just long enough for Rudgi to step in, thrusting into his thigh just below the hem of his scale cuirass, then bringing the blade around in a tight circle and hitting him in the side of his exposed neck, and another to the front for good measure. The scale aventail prevented his throat being cut, and she didn't strike him hard enough to break his windpipe, but he was stunned, gagging, and she stepped behind him, dropped to a knee, and drove her sword between his legs. The Leopard collapsed immediately, rolling on the ground, and I swallowed hard, stepping back and forcing myself not to look at the blood pooling underneath him.

Mulldoos spun me around by my shoulder. "You dumb shit! I told you—"

"You're plaguing welcome," I said.

There was blood around the broken links of mail, seeping through his gambeson, but not a huge amount.

He pivoted his head around, trying to assess who to take out next, and I looked around the room as well. The Eagles and Jackals had made good use of the initial confusion, occupying the Leopards so Braylar was free to advance and take out the other three war Memoridons. Well, two of them. Arrows from the Eagles brought down the third.

Thumaar was standing above a dead Leopard, his longsword in both hands, blood dripping off the last few inches of the blade, surveying the room as well.

We'd done it. We'd taken the tower. There was only one dead Eagle that I saw. I looked over at Nustenzia and Skeelana. We probably couldn't have even bluffed our way into the tower if it hadn't been for her, but even if we had, we surely would have lost most or all the men if she hadn't assisted us here.

After feeding a hate fire ever since Skeelana used me and betrayed us, it was hard to imagine putting the fuel down and letting it die out.

As Eagles walked around the room killing the wounded Leopards, Thumaar called out to Braylar, "Well done, Captain. Well done. Now it is your sister's turn."

Braylar was walking towards Mulldoos, the spikes on the twin Deserter heads hanging from the haft at his side, swaying as he moved, tiny drops of blood leaving a trail on the floor behind him.

The deposed emperor turned to Soffjian. "Are you ready, Memoridon?"

She looked over at Nustenzia. The older woman stepped away from Skeelana and joined her, and Soffjian said, "Yes, my lord. Let's do this while I'm still able."

Now that the chaos of combat was over, I finally had a chance to look around the room at the top of the tower. It was spare and simple, and not designed to be lived in. There were two small round windows letting in shafts of light, some tables and chairs along the wall, and that was essentially it.

Except for the large frame in the middle of the room on the small dais. I'd barely even registered it before, my heart in my throat, wondering if I was about to die. But now I was able to take it in, and it, too, was simple, but awe-inspiring as well. The frame itself was a charcoal-colored stone, inlaid with threads of white. At first glance I thought it was marble, but the pattern was unlike anything I'd seen before, wild whorls amid whorls. But what was so striking was of course what was in the frame itself—a rectangle composed of the same stuff as the Godveil and the dome around Roxtiniak—pulsing, shifting, waves flowing into themselves like a square taken from a turbulent mystic sea. But unlike the Godveil and dome, I felt no draw, smelled no vinegar, heard only the faintest hint of the thrum. The patch of pulsating energy was confined to such a relatively small space that it didn't produce the same effect.

Soffjian told Thumaar to accompany her and walked towards the frame with the lean Nustenzia alongside her. As the trio passed, I heard the Focus say, "The Deserters, as you call them, are the unquestioned masters of memory magic. But this . . . this is something even they did not fashion. It is . . . beautiful."

Soffjian replied, "That is not the word I would have chosen."

The three of them stopped in front of the middle of the frame, a few feet away. Soffjian took Nustenzia's hand in her own while the rest of us watched, then she looked over her shoulder and said, "Skeelana. Come."

The smaller Memoridon looked uncertain. "As I told you, this isn't my realm of . . . expertise. I don't think I can help you with this, Soffjian. In fact, I might actually impede you or get in your way. I—"

Without turning around, Soffjian said, "Skeelana, attend me now. My strength is not your strength, but I am attempting something it took multiple sisters to accomplish. Even with Nustenzia's consult and her considerable aid now, I will be not snuffed out because you neglected to help. Come."

Skeelana looked hesitant until Thumaar spun around. "Do it, girl. Quickly. Regaining control will be pointless if we are trapped in this tower because you dawdled."

Where before he'd always been lean and hungry, now that he was on the cusp of retaking the empire, his intensity seemed a raging fever.

Skeelana said, "Yes, Your Grace," and walked forward, and for once he didn't object to the usage.

She stood on Soffjian's other side, the three women holding hands, and they all raised their arms up. Soffjian had to keep her right lower to accommodate the shorter Skeelana, and she grunted once as she tried to extend her left, her wound clearly burning, but then said nothing else.

The two Memoridons and the Focus stood like that for a long time, frozen in front of the frame, a frieze of their own, three women so very different from one another but united in this one effort. They remained unmoving, except for some slight trembling in Soffjian's left arm, while the rest of us watched. Two Eagles checked the stairs for any signs that the Leopards were rushing up for us, though if they were, that meant Azmorgon and the others were dead and we were likely next.

Finally, Soffjian lowered both arms, and the other two women let go of her. She staggered briefly, reached out to steady herself on the stone frame, and then stood tall again. When she turned around, her face was as pale as Mulldoos's, almost as ashen as a Deserter's even, and her eyes were wet with tears.

There was a moment then as the Memoridons, Focus, and emperor stood on the edge of the dais, a tableau that felt momentous, the fate of the empire changing before our very eyes.

Soffjian said, "It is done."

Skeelana looked at her, smiling, tears streaming down her face as well. "You did it. You really did it."

"We did," Soffjian corrected.

But Thumaar reached up slowly towards the pulsing field in the frame. "What . . . I don't . . ." He looked at Soffjian, one finger pointing towards the frame as if in accusation. "Nothing feels different. It is not even as before, when I had my own Memoridons. I feel nothing."

While the Memoridons looked triumphant and the deposed emperor looked confused, Nustenzia alone seemed shocked, stricken, horrified even. She turned to Soffjian very slowly and quietly said, "You are . . . free. And you are doomed."

The field of warping weaving energy in the frame flickered, vibrating, the tang of vinegar emanating strongly, producing a thrum even louder than that of the Godveil, and for a moment I thought it might explode or flood the room, but then everything abruptly stopped.

The Veil energy and stench and noise disappeared as if it had never been captured at all. All that was left was an empty stone frame.

Thumaar started to draw his longs word as Braylar reached for Blood sounder. "Soff. What have you—"

"What needed doing, brother," she said. "I will only tell you this once. You should run."

Then she grabbed Nustenzia's wrist again, faced Thumaar, and her other arm shot up like a weapon, fingers splayed. The deposed emperor flew back away from her, dropping his longsword, and unlike the other times she had used memory craft to drive a man mad, shredding his veils and assaulting him with too many sensations for his mind to withstand, Thumaar didn't flail or shriek or tear at his eyes or face—he simply staggered back and then fell to the stone floor like a puppet whose strings had been abruptly severed.

Skeelana grabbed Nustenzia's other wrist, and it was as if the trio disappeared completely. While I'd always seen trace hints that my mind was being fooled when Skeelana had done this before, a warping as she moved, the illusion was flawless this time as she drew on the Focus for power.

They were completely invisible.

That didn't stop the Eagles with their bows from drawing arrows and loosing them. Two shafts flew through the air where the women had been a few moments before but only bounced off the curved wall behind the frame, one shattering.

The rest of the Syldoon drew their weapons but had no idea what to do next. Braylar called out, "Block the door, you fools!" as he started running for it himself.

Two more arrows flew but again only ricocheted off the wall, clattering to the floor in broken pieces.

One of the bowmen shot the next arrow more slowly, not blindly loosing, but gauging the distance from where the women disappeared and where the other arrows had missed, and then released. This arrow bounced off the wall, sparking, but it must have nicked Nustenzia or Skeelana first, as the illusion was spoiled for a moment and the three women were visible right before the door.

Both Eagles by the door were startled the trio were so close, and that moment of inaction was too much. Soffjian drew on Nustenzia again, arm outstretched, and the pair of Syldoon flew back as if physically struck, slamming into the wall as if buffeted by an invisible Deserter.

Skeelana must have thought they were clear and reached for the door instead of reestablishing connection with the Focus. Mulldoos pulled his throwing axe off the back of his belt, cocked his arm, and let fly—the weapon spun three times and struck Skeelana in the upper back. She cried out, letting go of the door, falling to her knees.

Soffjian stepped past her, looking down at Skeelana as she pulled Nustenzia after her through the opening, as two more arrows thunked into the heavy wooden door.

Braylar called out, "Rudgi, check Thumaar," but it sounded as if he knew the effort was pointless, and then ordered, "Eagles, Jackals, after them, you shrunken cocks! Run them down! Alive if possible!"

Several soldiers ran out of the room, their stolen Leopard gear jingling and rattling as they pursued Soffjian and Nustenzia down the stairs.

Rudgi looked up as she knelt next to Thumaar, slowly running her fingers over his still-open eyes, shaking her head. The exiled emperor had returned, but the empire would forever elude him.

I heard a scraping and looked over and saw that Skeelana was still alive, sitting up as she leaned her shoulder against the wall, breathing heavily, coughing a little, red spittle on her lips. The throwing axe was lying next to her in a small puddle of blood.

Mulldoos stalked towards her, wobbling slightly, falchion in hand, and Braylar called out, "Mulldoos, no! I want to question her."

The pale boar looked back at the captain as if he were mad. "She just helped your bitch sister kill the rightful emperor and fuck us all in the arse. What's to plaguing question?"

Braylar ignored him and squatted down in front of the wounded Memoridon. "I have to say, Skeelana, while I have done my share of betraying and been betrayed in turn, this is a first. I have never been betrayed twice by the same person."

Skeelana looked up, eyes glassy, and smiled, her teeth bloody. She wiped away some red spit bubbles with the back of her hand and coughed before replying, "First for me, too."

Braylar watched her, lips tight. "You were working with Soffjian this entire time, weren't you?"

Skeelana nodded once and coughed some more.

"Who has control? Of the Memoridons?"

Skeelana's chin started to drop but Braylar cupped it in his hand and tilted her head up. "Who. Has. Control?"

She swallowed hard, her entire body convulsing, and she said, "You just don't get it."

Braylar squeezed her chin, and she dripped bloody spit on his palm.

I said, "No one. No one has control. The Memoridons are free. Aren't they?"

Skeelana looked over at me, laughed and coughed immediately, a deep, racking thing. "Reason I knew . . . reason I knew I . . . liked you . . ."

Mulldoos repeated the word as if it was totally foreign. "Free? What are you plaguing going on about, free?"

Braylar released Skeelana's face and stood up. "I was a fool. Of course they are free. Everything she told Darzaak, us, it was simply to keep her close in case a way presented itself to sever all the bonds. She never intended to hand the tethers to Thumaar or anyone else. Every Memoridon in the empire . . . they are beholden to no one but themselves now."

Rudgi said, "But . . . what did Nustenzia mean, going on about doom like that? It sounded like she was as surprised as we were."

Braylar started towards the door. "I have no idea. Let's go find out, yes?" He looked back at Skeelana and then to me. "I leave her fate to you, archivist. Let her die slowly, or take pleasure in putting a blade in her, even if it gives her mercy she doesn't deserve. The choice is yours."

The captain, lieutenant, and sergeant rushed out. I listened to them taking the stairs quickly, descending, their footfalls growing distant, then looked over at Skeelana.

Her eyes were locked with mine. I bent down to one of the Eagles Soffjian had slain with memory magic, pulled a suroka off his belt, and stared at the unbloodied blade.

Skeelana said, "Probably been hoping . . . for this reunion, huh?" Then she hacked and wiped her bloody mouth again.

I nodded slowly, hoping to stoke my anger again, to build it into a furious bonfire, but it wouldn't light. There was only ash. My feet moving of their own accord, I walked towards her, limbs heavy.

Skeelana tried to smile and only spit up a little blood instead, then said, "Saw you . . . fighting. Come a . . . long way."

"I nearly got myself killed," I replied, realizing those were the first words I spoke directly to her since she first betrayed me in Sunwrack.

"But you . . . didn't. I did." She convulsed again. "Dying . . . hurts."

"Dying slowly, yes," I said. "The others, that Soffjian slew, they died quickly. For once. At least there's that."

Skeelana looked at the suroka in my hand. "I don't . . . deserve it . . . I know. But—" She swallowed hard, and it looked like even that was agony. "Please."

I crouched down. Shooting a man with a crossbow was one thing. So was trying to kill a man who was trying to do the same to me in the heat of battle. But this . . .

Skeelana said, "I . . . I just wanted to say . . . for what it's—"

I drove the blade into her chest, pressing hard with both hands and all my weight, keeping it parallel to the ground to avoid getting it hung up on a rib. I closed my eyes after it punctured where I aimed, just left of her sternum. I felt her jerk twice under me, her legs kicking out into mine a few times quickly until they suddenly stopped.

I pulled the suroka out, ignoring the small sucking sound it made coming free of her flesh and stood up without bothering to look at her or close her eyes. She might have deserved a merciful death, but she didn't deserve anything beyond that.

And then I headed down the stairs after the others.

I exited the tower door and was confronted with the scene I'd hoped not to see but feared the most. Soffjian and Nustenzia were nowhere to be seen. And the Syldoon—Leopards, Jackals, and Eagles—were lying everywhere, as the Memoridon must have drawn deep into the Focus well to fell them all so quickly. It looked as if she had slain the Leopards and one or two Eagles, but had only stunned or debilitated the Jackals, as Braylar and his men were rousing several, slapping faces, shaking them hard as if they were just experiencing a drunken stupor.

I had to bite my lip to avoid laughing. Not the natural laughter that comes from witnessing something truly funny, but the nervous, hiccupy, unhinged laughter borne of madness or mania or exhaustion.

Vendurro was already awake, but disoriented, leaning against the wall, his legs not ready to support him. Some of the other Jackals were in the same condition. Azmorgon was one of the last to rise, but he seemed to recover his wits the fastest, perhaps for having so few. He looked at Braylar, eyes beady under his eyebrow shelf. "Bitch sister. Betrayed us. Just like I done told you she would."

The captain said, "So she did." He addressed the rest of the Syldoon. "We have to get to the Well of Stairs. Now."

One of the Eagles stepped forward. "Where is Lord Thumaar?"

Another soldier who had been with us in the tower replied, simply, "Dead," as he glared at the captain as if he had slain the deposed emperor himself.

Braylar breathed heavily out his nostrils. "We were all betrayed. But him most of all."

Azmorgon shook his head. "Thumaar, dead, us, betrayed. All on account of you." He walked towards his captain, towered over him, beard seeming to bristle as he said, "This is on you. All of it. Every last bit of it. On you. Every last plaguing dead soldier, your own Hewplaguingspear, boys we lost to those Deserter cunts, and now the emperor who trusted you to set things right. All—"

Mulldoos stepped forward. "Watch your tongue, Ogre."

Azmorgon looked at Mulldoos briefly. "What are you going to do about it? Plaguing nothing. That's what. You know I'm telling it true." He looked at Braylar again. "This plaguing bastard has a lot to answer for."

Mulldoos laid his hand on the hilt of his falchion. "This plaguing bastard is your plaguing commanding officer, and no matter what you got to say, you'll say it with respect, you hear me?"

Azmorgon shook his head. "Not any plaguing more he ain't." He snapped an elbow out, catching Mulldoos in the side of the head, sending him spinning onto the floor, then took one step and grabbed Braylar by the neck, pushing him against the wall, lifting him onto the balls of his feet. "You ain't Cap of nothing no more. You hear me? You're done."

Braylar grabbed Azmorgon's wrist, not to pull it down, which was impossible, but to pull himself off the ground, and used his legs to push off the wall, kicking out at the lieutenant's groin.

But Azmorgon must have expected it, as he turned and caught the blow on his thigh and then grabbed Braylar's neck with the other hand and held him dangling in the air, ignoring the captain's kicks and punches.

Vendurro drew his sword, as did Rudgi, but Benk and an Eagle stepped between them and Azmorgon, weapons drawn as well, and then everyone was pulling steel, several Eagles siding with Azmorgon, some uncertain, and the rest of the Jackals standing alongside Vendurro.

I pulled my sword from the scabbard as well, but yelled, "This is madness! We're in the Citadel surrounded by enemies! We have to get out of here, not kill each other!"

Braylar's face was turning purple as Azmorgon choked the life out of him.

Then the huge man screamed, dropped the captain, and nearly fell over himself. Mulldoos had rolled over and driven his suroka through one side of Azmorgon's knee and clean out the other. The Ogre instinctively tried to kick Mulldoos, but his leg buckled and he staggered back several steps.

And then chaos erupted, blades flashing as Benk and some Eagles fought Vendurro, Rudgi, and the remaining Jackals.

I pulled the buckler off my belt, kept my sword hand behind it, and shuffled sideways to move closer to Vendurro.

Braylar was on his side, clutching his throat, sputtering, as Azmorgon pulled the suroka out of his knee, bellowing as blood started to flow freely down his leg. The blade looked tiny in his oversized hand, and he threw it aside, bent over with effort to retrieve a discarded spear on the ground, then staggered forward towards the captain again, dragging his damaged leg behind, beady eyes full of murder.

I circled behind the Jackals, barely catching one sword blow with the buckler but breaking one of Mulldoos's first rules, blinding myself with it. I stepped back as I lowered the buckler to see my assailant, sure that I was about to be cut down by the next blow, but a Jackal interceded and slashed the Eagle across the forearm.

I scooted around behind the other combatants but wasn't going to make it there in time. I called out, "Mulldoos! The captain!"

Mulldoos was getting to his feet unsteadily, embattled shield strapped on his left arm, the falchion in his right hand, and turned to see Azmorgon nearly on top of Braylar.

The pale boar stepped in, deflecting an Eagle blow on the way, and yelled, "Azmorgon, you horsecunt!"

The huge lieutenant turned, and even though he was bleeding profusely and hobbled, he came at Mulldoos, spear held in two hands like a quarter-staff. Mulldoos not only waited for him, but retreated a few steps, and a huge grin split Azmorgon's beard, ugly and the color of ear wax. "That's right, you little cunt, I'm going to kill the lot of you!"

Mulldoos's retreat shocked me until I realized he was drawing Azmorgon away from the prone captain, probably hoping the huge lieutenant would bleed more and weaken.

I was moving to help Mulldoos when an Eagle knocked into me, driven back by the Syldoon he was fighting. As he turned to see whether I was friend or foe, I instinctively swung something. I had poor form, worse aim, and had inexplicably chosen to attack with the buckler over the sword. But it clanged off the man's helm, sending reverberations up my arm, and distracted the Eagle just enough for the Jackal to send him backpedalling, trying to deflect a combination of blows.

I looked up and saw Azmorgon beating Mulldoos back, gripping the spear in the middle, the spearhead and buttspike lashing out from either end, high, low, keeping Mulldoos on the defensive. Mulldoos blocked the spearhead with the shield, and the falchion came out in a blur but Azmorgon caught it on the haft and stepped in more, spreading his grip as he slammed the haft into the shield and sent Mulldoos flying back into the wall, his helm banging off the stones.

I stepped in, sword high, screaming, knowing I was going to be too late, as Azmorgon ripped the shield aside with the lugs on the spearhead and drew back to drive the spear into Mulldoos's exposed belly.

And then the left side of Azmorgon's head exploded in red mist, as the flail heads caved in the huge lieutenant's skull and took off a good chunk of it as they ricocheted away.

But to be safe, Braylar whirled Bloodsounder around and struck Azmorgon again as he was falling over, the spiked Deserter heads thankfully hitting him in the back of the skull this time, so I couldn't see the damage.

The huge lieutenant was on the stones, blood pooling around his head and knee, and Braylar stepped over the body without another glance. He looked at me. "Stay on my shield side."

I nodded, obeying, and the captain looked at Mulldoos, who was shaking off the effects of being slammed into the wall. "Lieutenant."

Mulldoos pushed himself off the wall. "Cap."

And the three of us waded into what remained of the melee. Only a few Eagles and Benk still fought on, backing towards the entrance to the frame tower. When they saw they were outnumbered and that Azmorgon was dead, they ran into the tower, slamming and bolting the door behind them.

Mulldoos and some Jackals started after them, but Braylar called out, "Leave them. They are trapped. Leave them for the Leopards."

The lieutenant spit against the wall. "Gods and devils, but this sure turned to shit in a hurry, didn't it?"

Braylar twitch-smiled and rasped, "Are you about to lead another mutiny, Lieutenant?"

Mulldoos shook his head. "Are you plaguing kidding me? I got enough trouble just keeping the sergeants in line. No desire to wrangle mouthy lieutenants on top of it. Your throat OK?"

Braylar looked down at the blood dripping off the flail heads. "It wasn't the first time I've been choked." He looked at Mulldoos and nodded once. "Thank you."

"For what, Cap? I gave you a hand, you gave me one. We're square. But you mentioned something about getting out of here."

"So I did." The captain turned to the remaining Jackals. "To the Well of Stairs. If anyone attempts to intercept us, we kill them all and keep going. Stealth is no longer our objective; survival is."

We navigated around the bodies of Jackals, Eagles, and Leopards scattered around the tower door and ran down the corridor, weapons out, gear clattering, our mission in shambles.

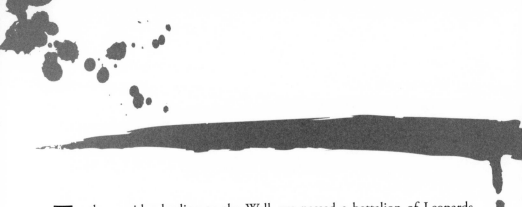

In the corridor leading to the Well, we passed a battalion of Leopards heading the other way at a jog, their own weapons and gear jangling, clacking, slithering. My heart was lodged in my throat, but even though we had obviously been in a fight, we were still dressed as Leopards, so they didn't stop us.

The closer we got to our exit the more I felt like my nerves were tied in fiery knots. As we descended the Well, I looked up, half expecting to see Benk or Soffjian or someone else looking down, ready to fill us full of arrows or knock us off the stairs with memory magic, but no one appeared. But we made it through the garden and down the stairs along the wall of the Well without incident.

After swapping out our gear and leaving behind the Leopard arms and armor, we made our way through the emperor crypts and more generic catacombs, reversing the path we'd taken and I'd mapped out. No one said a word for a long stretch. There was only the clomping of feet and heavy breathing.

But I knew if anyone had a comment it would be Vendurro. He was ahead of me and turned to Rudgi as we rounded a corner. "He was a right proper giant bastard—mean, belligerent, nasty piece of work, sure as spit Nasty. But this? Just never . . . just never figured is all. A Towermate? Plague me." He shook his head.

Rudgi kept pace but didn't respond. But I said, "Is it really that strange?"

They both glanced back at me, and I continued, "What I mean is, the Syldoon are sort of experts at infighting, aren't they? Betrayal is something of second nature. Is it so strange that Azmorgon would—"

Rudgi replied, "Gods, but you don't know anything. *Towers* betray *Towers*, Arki. Natural order of things. That's how the Syldoon function. You can barely even call it betrayal."

Vendurro said, "But Towermates? The men you hung with, fought with, squabbled with? Doesn't matter whether you hate the bastard next to you or not, he's your brother—"

423

"Or sister," Rudgi amended.

"Or sister. You defend your Towermate to the death. Against any and all." He sounded forlorn just talking about it. "And before you ask, it ain't just a Jackal thing. It's a Tower thing. True for Eagles or Leopards or Serpents or Wheels or whatnot. The Tower is . . . everything. You obey your commanding officer, you obey your Tower Commander, and you fight for your Towermates, no matter plaguing what."

Rudgi agreed through tight lips. "No matter plaguing what."

I watched the lantern light flicker over the countless bones as we passed the compartments and rounded another corner. "Has a Jackal ever—"

"No," Vendurro said. "Never. Not plaguing ever. Not until that giant whoreson nearly killed Cap. Wish he had died slower. A lot plaguing slower."

"Aye, Lieutenant," Rudgi said. "Bastard got off easy."

They seemed intent on not naming Azmorgon at all.

I looked at racks of skulls alternating with vertebrae in an arrangement that might have been called aesthetically pleasing. If it had been a mosaic and not the remains of the dead. Stymieing a shiver, I said, "And what of Soffjian and Skeelana's betrayal? Wresting control of the Memoridons, breaking the frame?"

Vendurro replied, "No clue. Mems always been controlled by the Towers. And then Cynead. Hoping for Thumaar next. But with no masters to answer to . . . who plaguing knows?"

He didn't stymie a shiver, and Rudgi started to say something, but Mulldoos had heard enough, shouting, "Shut your plaguing holes, the lot of you!"

He was clearly angry, there was something else there as well. Hate? Fear? Fury for allowing himself to feel uneasy over unshackled memory magic? I imagined he would rather face a freed ripper on his own with no weapons than engage a Memoridon now.

While Azmorgon's mutiny had thrown the Jackals' concepts of Tower and self wildly off balance, it could be written off as an aberration. But the prospect of the Memoridons being truly free, operating independently, unchecked, creating their own agenda for the first time in history . . . That seemed to unnerve all of them.

⊕

With my map, heading back to the cistern tower took less time than going the other way, though it was still a matter of hours. We discovered it in exactly the same state as we left it, bloodied, full of bodies, and in total disarray. At least the Leopards hadn't discovered it and closed off our escape route. The only real difference was that the Eagle Emmert had joined the ranks of the dead, having bled out as he leaned against the wall. It was just as well his Towermate was trapped with Benk in the Citadel.

The captain commanded everyone to raid the larder and pantry once more. "It has been a long day already. But will be longer still. Rest a bit and fill your bellies."

Mulldoos pulled the captain aside and pointed towards the door that led to the cisterns. "Even if we're waiting on dusk, ought to get up to the roof, away from the front door here, Cap. Let's get topside."

Braylar replied, "No, Lieutenant. We will have use of the front door."

Mulldoos blinked, though one eyelid wasn't cooperative, and it appeared more of wink. "Use? What plaguing use? We got to clear out of here."

"We do indeed. And that is precisely what I mean to use it for."

Mulldoos looked at the barred door and then back to Braylar. "What are you plaguing talking about, Cap?"

"We have to get to Darzaak, to let him know what has occurred here. And we will not do that jumping from rooftops. We walk. And to do that, we must needs walk out the front door."

"We walk." Mulldoos repeated it slowly, still slurring the edges a little. "Out the front door. Down the street. To Jackal Tower. That's what you are plaguing telling me, Cap?"

"That is precisely what I am telling you, Lieutenant."

Vendurro and Rudgi had heard the conversation as well and approached, and Mulldoos appealed to Vendurro. "Never been much good at talking sense into this man. Pretty plaguing lousy at it, in fact. Unless Hewspear was siding with me. But . . . it's on you now, Ven. Tell Cap here that moseying down the thoroughfare is about the worse plaguing idea you ever heard."

Perhaps just more diplomatic by nature, or more cautious given Azmorgon's recent betrayal, Vendurro said, "I've heard a lot of lousy ideas. Said a lot of them myself. So it's steep competition." He looked at Braylar. "Cynead might have lost the Memoridons. But he's still emperor. Leastwise, right now. And he'll have us hung without reprieve if we get captured, assuming we don't get murdered good on the spot. So . . . why are we walking out the front door, Cap?"

Braylar looked at us and said, "We have no idea what is happening out there. And—"

"We know your sister shat in our soup," Mulldoos said.

"So she did," Braylar replied, biting the words off. "And eloquent as always. But we have no idea what effect it has had. Did Cynead's Memoridons abandon him in the middle of battle or turn on him? Did Thumaar's troops, trusting that he was alive and undercutting Cynead, overcome the long odds and defeat the emperor anyway? We do not know. But even if Cynead proved victorious and is marching back to the capital, he is considerably weakened now, vulnerable, and we will need to inform Darzaak and act immediately.

"Will our Commander make a play for the throne? Will he throw the Jackals in a coalition of other Towers to seat someone else on it? We simply . . . do not . . . know. But Darzaak cannot operate blindly, and won't—he will wait until he has obtained intelligence. And I *do* know we are the only ones who can supply it, yes? So we perform our duties, aid our Tower, and see our way through this, no matter how we have been betrayed or how frayed the original plan is."

The captain looked at all the Jackals still alive. "So. Unless you have some pigeons in your packs that can carry word to our Commander, we resort to the one recourse we still have available. Our feet. *That* is why we walk out the front door."

Mulldoos wasn't one to talk with his hands much, but he did just then, waving one around as if trying to dispel a stench. "Fine. Somebody can. Just send a runner."

Rudgi smiled. "I'll go. Got nothing better going on just now."

"You most certainly will not, Sergeant," Braylar replied. He looked at Mulldoos. "I am down enough officers as it is, but more importantly, while we can get word to the man, do you really believe Commander Darzaak is going to believe a runner who tells him our company made the critical mistake of trusting my sister and were all betrayed on the cusp of securing Thumaar his throne again, so now all Memoridons are free to do gods know what? 'You might have noticed the ones Cynead assigned to your Tower slipping away quietly. Oh, and Thumaar's dead, our apologies and regrets. As is the vile whoreson Lieutenant Azmorgon who tried to strangle Captain

Killcoin and organize an impromptu mutiny with the Eagles, who will surely be our enemies now if word gets out that we led Thumaar to an ambush.'

"Is *that* what you intend our presumptive runner to say to Commander Darzaak? Assuming the good Commander hasn't also been struck down by the unbound Memoridon in his employ?"

Vendurro said, "He's got a point, Mull."

Mulldoos ground his jaws together. "Gods and devils, but we're in a bad spot."

"Yes," Braylar said, "on that point we definitely agree. But we cannot afford to make it worse by delaying or taking half measures now. We must get to Darzaak immediately to verify his safety and to inform him of what has occurred so we can plot our way clear of this. Yes?"

Grudgingly, Mulldoos nodded. "We go out the plaguing front door. Fine. But how about this, when we get close to Jackal Tower, we send a runner ahead?" Braylar started to object but Mulldoos pushed on. "Not to deliver the plaguing news, but to make sure we ain't walking into a worse situation. Get the lay of the land, and if Darzaak is alive and kicking like we all hope, then the rest of us follow."

Braylar nodded. "Very good. Now get some sustenance. But quickly. We leave soon."

Mulldoos walked away shaking his head, scowling, looking more likely to chew stones than food.

Vendurro said, "You don't have to tell me twice. Come on, Sergeant. Grub."

Rudgi looked at him in amazement as they walked towards the pantry. "You eat like a plaguing Deserter but you're barely bigger than Arki there. Queerest thing."

"What's queer is how plaguing hard it is to find a boiled egg when you want one. Really shouldn't be this plaguing difficult. . ."

Even exhausted and starving, I couldn't suppress a smile. There was a man who lived in the moment.

True to his word, shortly after we'd stripped off any Leopard paraphernalia and eaten something, Braylar had us assembled by the door. I'd thrown some oatcakes and the salvageable parts of a wrinkled apple down my throat and followed it up with a small beer, so I felt halfway human again, but the heavy tension and lack of sleep made me want to just find a spot on the floor with the fewest blood splatters and fall into the deepest pit in my mind that I could manage. I had a weary revelation then that waking and dreaming were like the drain lake in Roxtiniak, one ever flowing into the next in an endless, mysterious, inexplicable cycle.

Two Jackals pulled the bar clear of the brackets on the door, and Braylar looked at Rudgi. "Send two out, take stock of the street and surrounding area, ascertain what they can, and report back."

She nodded and walked over to the soldiers by the door, talking quietly to two of them.

My heart was hammering hard when a Jackal pulled the door in, giving the pair enough space to slip out, and closed it behind them. Perhaps nothing had changed out there in the streets of Sunwrack at all. But too many momentous things were happening, and it was impossible not to imagine the horrible ripples today's events would have.

The rest of us waited. And waited. And waited some more. Finally they knocked on the door five times and were let back in. They walked up to the captain and the shorter scout said, "Way seems clear enough, Cap. But rumors are flying wild. Overheard soldiers and Thurvacians. Some are saying Cynead routed Thumaar in the field and had the old wolf's head on a pike. Which were impossible, him being dead back there in the tower, and not having lost his head at all. Others are saying Cynead was the one who got crushed."

Braylar asked, "And what of Thumaar's allies in the field? The Anjurians, the Vortagoi Confederacy?"

The short scout replied, "Some say they were destroyed. Others claim they got wind things were turning, thought of somewhere safer to be and let out. All I know now is, not knowing who is emperoring, or what's happened with the Mems, the Thurvacians are getting right panicky, smelling blood in the air, heading indoors, bolting their doors."

Braylar nodded. "Yes. As they should. While they often get the narrative wrong, Thurvacians have been under Syldoon rule long enough to have a sense of when things are about to erupt, and historically have been fairly accurate in predicting bloodletting." He looked at our small group. "Out we go, then. We do not draw weapons unless a threat presents itself. Whether Cynead is alive or dead, the Leopards do not know we have returned yet. They likely discovered the bodies in the Citadel, but will just as likely assume it was a coup attempt by the Eagles. Still, we do not have much time. So we nonchalantly but fairly quickly make our way to Jackal Tower to see what we see. Understood?"

The Jackals all nodded or said "aye," and I found myself echoing them. Then the door was opened again and we filed out.

I half expected to see the city on fire or madness reigning as Tower battled Tower from street to street. Instead, it was eerily quiet. Dusk was coming on, the sky gray behind the charcoal clouds like a huge tattered and torn flag draped over the world. During any normal day, we still would have seen Thurvacians heading to their homes, merchants closing up shops, men heading to a tavern or brothel or theatre for some form of entertainment, some filing towards the gates before curfew was called. But except for a few stragglers darting inside to some hiding place, we didn't encounter any of the native inhabitants, and there was a tension in the air. And for the first several streets, we didn't see Syldoon soldiers of any Tower either.

It was as if the City of Coups was holding its breath, dangerously still, and it felt like we were walking among the catacombs again. That was unnerving, but at least it meant we made quick progress. And then, almost at once, things changed.

Rudgi and another scout who had been checking the streets ahead returned from different directions at the same time. Rudgi said, "There's a battalion ahead, smallish, but a lot bigger than us. Couldn't tell which Tower, though. They were moving fast, harried by another group."

Braylar pulled Bloodsounder off his belt and adjusted the straps on his shield as he looked over his shoulder at our small company. "The order to walk unarmed has been rescinded."

I slid the curved blade out of the scabbard, careful not to slice myself or anyone around me. The captain asked Rudgi, "How many streets ahead, and heading which direction?"

As if in answer, we heard the distant sounds of battle and shouting as Rudgi said, "Four or five streets, moving west, so not hard to skirt around them. Let the smaller group retreat and make our way behind the bigger."

Braylar turned to the ginger-haired scout. "And you, soldier? Let me guess, grim tidings as well, yes?"

The Jackal nodded quickly, starting straight ahead, looking uneasy. "Aye, grim and grimmer, Cap. Saw a party near the tanner district. Shields say Falcon Tower, for what that's worth. Though we know blazonry don't always mean shit. About thirty, forty men maybe. Got wiped out. Fast."

The way he said *fast* made my skin crawl.

Braylar asked, "By which Tower?"

The scout gulped quickly. "Leopards. But they had it easy, Cap. Real easy." He clearly didn't want to say more but had no choice. "Two war Mems brought the Falcons to their knees first. Leopards only had to wade through and slit throats. Finished them quick and kept moving east."

Mulldoos gave Braylar a look that could have been imploring or furious, it was hard to tell, which the captain pointedly ignored.

Vendurro said, "Doesn't make any sense, Cap. Falcons support the Leopards."

"Supported," Braylar corrected. "They *supported* them. And Cynead in particular. But it appears the Memoridons were not content with simply throwing off their invisible shackles. They are orchestrating a power move here. So until we know the particulars, we cannot trust anyone outside our own Tower."

No one mentioned Azmorgon and the fact that even that loyalty might be suspect, as the wound was raw and fresh, but I'm sure I wasn't the only one who thought it.

The captain said, "So. We will have to be doubly sure the route forward is entirely clear. Sergeant Rudgi, take three more men, fan out, and be sure we do not have any unexpected meetings with Syldoon or Memoridons."

After Rudgi ordered Jackals to accompany, they set off at a jog—three exploring the streets ahead, one falling back to be sure no one came up from the rear.

Vendurro moved closed to Braylar, but I was near enough to hear him say, "Even if we run into another company, Cap, we don't have numbers. But if it's the Mems, then—"

"That is precisely why we have scouts, Lieutenant. And our chances of getting trapped or caught treble if we stand here under an awning arguing. We move. Now."

No one else protested and we started forward again, winding our way slowly towards the great Towers, sometimes having to change direction when one of the scouts returned to report fighting somewhere ahead.

Still, it wasn't long before we saw the massive curtain wall around the city and the Jackal Tower looming above the much smaller buildings and residences around it. We stopped and sidled alongside a building, waiting for the scouts to investigate the immediate area around the Tower to be sure the way was clear.

Mulldoos moved close enough to the captain that Vendurro and I were the only ones who heard him say, "You know my mind, Cap, and I know knowing it ain't changing yours none, but I've got to say one more time, we ought to hunker down somewhere, cistern tower maybe. Exposed out here. Real plaguing exposed. And I don't like this one plaguing bit."

Braylar drummed his fingers on the haft of the flail. "What is to like, Lieutenant? A deposed emperor is dead, a sitting emperor very likely could be, some of our own turned against us, and the Memoridons severed a thousand years of Syldoon control as easily as cutting a single throat. But our Tower still exists, and I would learn what state it is in, and if our Commander yet lives."

Mulldoos didn't have a direct answer for that, good or bad, and simply rubbed the back of his neck several times with his big hand, pale eyes hard, the droopy eyelid seeming more weighted down than ever.

And so we waited, backs against the wall of a granary as night came on. Then Rudgi returned. I thought she was alone, but then several Jackals stepped out of the shadows after her, ten or twelve.

The captain approached them, and the closest soldier saluted and stepped forward. He was a thin man with a round moon face and one chin too many. He said, "Plaguing glad to see you again, Cap. Sergeant here told me you and your company were back, but good to see it firsthand. Me and the boys thought—" then stopped himself when he saw how small our group was. "Gods, Cap, are the rest—"

"Winnowed." The captain stepped forward. "Report, Syldoon. How do things stand?"

Moon-face replied, "Not good, Cap. Not plaguing good at all."

"Expound. Immediately. Does Commander Darzaak live?"

The soldier looked bewildered as he said, "Aye, Cap. Leastwise, last I saw him. Can't speak for the interim. But the Mems that used to be ours, then Cynead's, well, seems they ain't nobody's now. They just ain't nobody's no more and—"

"Yes, I am painfully aware of that. What of the Commander?"

"They took him, Cap. Him and some of his captains. Captain Grizzwik, Captain Julvers, Captain Bikmoss. Those bitches husked and killed their guards, holed them up in Commander's quarters. Me and the boys here got out, right as orders come out by way of Julvers to lock the Tower up tight."

"Took initiative, did you?" Braylar asked, eyes narrowing.

The soldier suddenly froze as if he realized he was standing right next to a hissing viper.

The Jackal said, "We made for Otter Tower, Cap. Figured they might lend a hand. Lieutenant Bortniss told us to. To head to the Otters, that is, to see—"

The captain stepped forward so he was nearly nose to nose with the soldier. "And did Lieutenant Bortniss consider that given that only a handful of Memoridons are holding your most senior captains and Commander captive, it is a reasonable assumption they will not take kindly to your absence, that you are in fact actually risking the lives of your brothers and officers to deliver me this most unwelcome news?"

The solider could only nod once more, round face bobbing. "I can't speak for what the Lieutenant thought or didn't thought, Cap. Just followed orders. But it made sense. At the time leastwise. Until we got to the Otters."

The captain rasped, "Let me guess—that Tower was locked down as well, yes?"

Moon-face said, "Aye, Cap, aye. Tighter than a priest's—"

"That is all, soldier. Join the others."

Moon-face nodded twice, fast, glad to be moving away from another incensed officer, and led the other Jackals past.

Rudgi approached Braylar, Mulldoos, and Vendurro. "Seen the same thing up and down the wall, Cap. Towers are buttoned up. I saw a group of soldiers slipping out the front of the Serpent Tower, but a Mem struck down most from a window halfway up. The remainder scattered."

Braylar replied, "If there is one thing my sister's ilk can do well, it is coordinate and communicate immediately. It seems they have adopted the same strategy across all Towers. Capture the senior officers, order the soldiers to stand down. A clever if dangerous stratagem."

"No one is likely to storm a Commander's room, if the Memoridons did exactly that," I said. "But they also don't have Bloodsounder."

Everyone looked at me and I resisted the urge to shuffle my feet as I added, "We took the frame tower because the captain was immune to the memory magic, so long as he wielded his flail. Couldn't we do the same in the Jackal Tower? Raid Commander Darzaak's quarters, free him and the others."

As expected, Mulldoos was the first to shoot the idea down. "Ayyup, sure, easy. If we had an engineer, a squad of sappers, and six months to mine under the solid rock beneath Jackal Tower."

"I imagined walking through the front door."

Mulldoos replied, "Might as well imagine ten pretty flying ponies carrying us to the roof. Didn't you hear? Gate's locked down tight. Even with a battering ram, you couldn't break it, as it's up all those stairs. No plaguing way in the front gate, scribbler."

"Wouldn't someone inside be willing to let us slip in?"

Braylar shook his head. "The Memoridons will have one of their own watching the door, Arki. While I applaud your willingness to risk all our lives on a doomed rescue mission, it starts and fails with gaining entry, and that is simply not possible.

"There must be some way," I said. "Isn't there some sort of, what is it called, postern gate? Sally port?"

Mulldoos glared at me. "The witches ain't exactly in unfamiliar territory, scribbler. They know every entry point in the plaguing Tower, down to the stinking garderobes the gong farmers plaguing harvest. Not. Happening."

I must have inspired Vendurro though. "What about the grappling hooks back at the roof of the cistern tower? Maybe we could sneak in a window somewhere, get into the Tower that way?"

"And maybe," Mulldoos said, slurring only a little, "we could just throw stones up at a window and get all the witches to poke their heads out at the same time and shoot them in their dumb plaguing faces?"

Rudgi shook her head. "Lieutenant Mull is right—we'd clank those hooks against the stones ten times before getting them to latch. This isn't the lip of the cistern ten feet above us, and even that took more than one try. And the stones aren't like that Deserter keep—almost no hand or footholds to speak of on Jackal Tower. So climbing just isn't going to happen. If we get in, it'll have to be some other way."

Braylar was staring over the rooftops at the visible portion of Jackal Tower, the Deserter heads clinking together as he moved Bloodsounder to point with the haft. "It is immaterial. As difficult as entry is, that would be the least of our concerns. Even if we could somehow get inside without raising an alarm, and even if we could somehow sneak up every floor to the Commander's chambers, also miraculously without alerting the captors, unlike the Memoridons guarding the frame, these witches will be highly alert, prepared for just such a reckless attempt to free Darzaak and the others. And you can be sure that my sweet sister has alerted them to the properties of this flail, on the very remote chance I would be a large enough idiot to attempt just suck a foolish rescue. So they would not waste time trying to bring me down with any memory magic.

"What's more, you surely recall that we had Skeelana helping to confuse them in the frame room as well. No, we will not take them unawares twice. They would strike anyone else down with memory magic, and me with very mundane weapons, but even if I somehow got close enough to slay even two or three Memoridons, you can be sure one hanging back would be more than willing to cut down the Commander and the other captains."

He turned and looked at all of us. "As much as I would love to rescue the Commander and free the Jackals, it will not be here or now." Through clenched teeth, he said, "Until a better possibility presents itself, we must withdraw."

Mulldoos slapped his meaty thigh. "About plaguing time!"

"Where to then, Cap?" Vendurro asked, sounding and looking as tired as I felt. "Holing up somewhere in Sunwrack?"

"Impossible," the captain replied. "Soffjian told me to run, and I suspect she actually intends to let us, but she cannot delay tracking us long."

Mulldoos said, "That cunt's got nothing good for us, and less. She betrayed the whole Empire, and she'll blast our skulls open or see us hanging from our entrails the first chance she gets."

Braylar gave him a long unreadable look. "You are incorrect on one point, Lieutenant. Soffjian can track nearly everyone here, and her bind to me is incredibly strong, much as I wish it were otherwise. She can sense I am still in Sunwrack, even now, I am sure of it. And while she is no doubt busy conducting the largest coup in history this moment, if she wanted us dead today, she could snap her fingers and make it happen. But you can be sure our grace period will run out very soon. So we have to leave Sunwrack. Tonight."

Rudgi said, "But the bridges are hauled in, and the gates shut tight, Cap. Nobody is leaving through the gates tonight, and probably not anytime soon."

Sometimes it was difficult to catch the twitch smile in the sunlight, and twice as hard in the dark, but I felt certain I saw it. "I never said we were walking out the gates, did I?"

It took everyone a moment to realize what he meant, and then Mulldoos groaned and Vendurro said, "Cap, your sister knows how we came in. Sure as spit she'll have posted guards at the cisterns by now?"

"Not if she truly is offering us one chance to escape."

"But why would she do that, Cap? Mull is right, doesn't make any plaguing sense."

Braylar replied, "The draining lake of Roxtiniak is less mysterious than the inner workings of a woman's mind, Lieutenant, and none are more perplexing than my sister's. I make no boasts about divining the meaning there, but she is giving us a small opportunity. And we will seize it." He clapped Vendurro on the back. "At least we will be leaving a city without having to kill everyone first, yes?"

Then Braylar looked at Rudgi. "Guide us back to the cisterns, Sergeant, and be sure we do not run afoul of any patrols or inexplicably homeless Syldoon roaming the streets. Once there, take three men inside and be sure there are no traps awaiting us."

She nodded and set off into the shadows with the other scouts.

My legs wearier than at any time I could remember, I followed the captain and his retinue back to the cisterns and the aqueduct that connected them to the outside world.

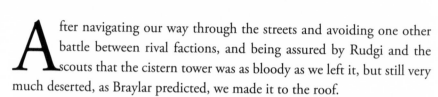

After navigating our way through the streets and avoiding one other battle between rival factions, and being assured by Rudgi and the scouts that the cistern tower was as bloody as we left it, but still very much deserted, as Braylar predicted, we made it to the roof.

The prospect of another all-night crawl through the aqueduct was daunting, and my muscles already quailed at how grueling it would be, but the captain assured us that we wouldn't have to hunch our way the entire stretch back up into the foothills and the abandoned mine—once were a mile or two out from Sunwrack, we could descend and make our way through the darkened hills by foot. That was something. A slightly less exhausting and odorous something, but something, just the same. After allowing us a small break to fill our bellies and briefly rest, it was time to leave Sunwrack yet again, albeit by the most underused road possible.

The descent down the rope ladder was uneventful (it would have been far more eventful if Vendurro hadn't grabbed my belt as I nearly lost my balance and plunged to the stone streets below). We got on our bellies again, the Jackals drew their surokas to ward off any other hungry bullcrabs, and we started crawling. Thankfully, we didn't have to kill any of those either as we made our slow exit from the City of Coups, never more aptly named than this day.

Occasionally the sounds of some combat floated up from somewhere, but distant, and infrequent now that it was deep into the night again. Whoever resisted was either cut down or determined to carry on the fight once the sun returned.

I felt the emptiness of the Trench beneath me, and then we were back on our feet, trudging forward, backs aching, eyelids heavier than stones. In the deep dark of the aqueduct, it was so incredibly tempting to simply sit down and lean against the wall, listening to the water gurgle past as I closed my eyes and didn't open them again for three days, but the captain drove us on.

True to his word, once we got to the first access station, a scout climbed out and checked the terrain, and when we got the signal it was clear, we all followed, taking the built-in stone ladder down to the earth below. After seeing nothing for such a long stretch but the utter blackness of the aqueduct, the stars above looked radiant, brighter than torches, and the cool night air was a welcome and refreshing change from being forced to smell nothing but our own stink and the stale air trapped inside. The ability to stand up straight was also an undeniable relief. I was still exhausted, but we were clear. There was always the chance some mounted Syldoon might show up at any moment and kill or capture us, but for the moment, we were free.

Braylar led us on through the night, one foot after another as we traversed the hills, keeping the aqueduct in sight but ourselves as hidden as the infrequent trees and brush allowed.

The next miles went quicker than the ones in the aqueduct had, but we still moved slowly and cautiously, partly to be as quiet as possible and avoid detection, and also to prevent anyone turning or breaking an ankle on the uneven ground in the dark as we put one tired foot in front of the next.

When we finally sighted the mine, I exhaled so deep and long I felt like it might never stop. And when I overheard the captain send a runner ahead to let the remaining Jackals know we were coming and not to shoot us, I nearly wept. I'd feared he was going to order us to saddle our horses and ride to some other site, and when Mulldoos asked him why we didn't, the captain replied, "My sister is not coming for us. Not yet, at least. But if she chose to, riding ten or fifteen miles further would not prevent her from tracking us. We would have to ride through the Godveil to prevent that. Which it might come to yet. But not tonight."

I expected the lieutenant to grumble and growl a bit, as he was wont to do, but he had to have been as weary as I was, because while he clearly didn't agree, it didn't seem he had the energy to argue.

We walked the remaining distance to the abandoned mine, and though it was a rocky bed, I'd never been happier to lay my head down to sleep in my entire life.

Dawn came and went without anyone shaking me back to life, as did noon. It was only midday when I felt Vendurro's hand on my shoulder and finally woke, ravenous, disoriented, and hoping it was all a mad dream, that maybe we hadn't even taken the aqueduct yet, that the deposed emperor was alive still, a Jackal hadn't turned on his own, and the Memoridons hadn't captured or killed every significant leader in the capital city, and quite possibly all the provinces where Towers resided.

But one look on the young lieutenant's face dispelled that notion immediately. While he must have gotten some rest as well, he had the dark circles and haunted look of someone who also felt like he was stuck in a nightmare, or feared falling back into one. He tried a half smile as he handed me a hard heel of bread that must have been soaked in bacon fat hours earlier, as even cold it tasted like something fit for an emperor.

I tore into it as he handed me a flask of warm water, also tasting far better than it had any right to.

Vendurro squatted beside me as he said, "Rough going the last day or two, eh?"

I nodded and spit crumbs as I said, "Rough going," wondering if he could understand either word. After taking another swig, I tried again. "What are we going to do now?"

Vendurro spun a pine cone in the dirt. "That, Arki, is one plaguing tough question that's got no kind of answer at all. Or none Cap saw fit to share with me. I expect he'll give us our marching orders soon enough." He looked around at the abandoned and rusted equipment. "Unless he figures we're going to take up mining. Then it'll be digging orders. Though after yesterday, can't say that that would be the worst idea ever."

I looked over at the other Jackals gathered nearby, all looking uneasy, anxious, and for the first time, not very Syldoonian. It was one thing to be driven out of their home city by a rival faction and to see their brethren who couldn't make it in time cut down on a bridge. As awful as it was, that was at least somewhat familiar territory. But this . . . this was something else altogether. Not unlike crossing the Veil for the first time. They had no idea what lay ahead, or how poorly they might be equipped to handle it.

Rudgi walked over and said, "Sorry to interrupt the feast, but Cap wants us all to attend. Well, the officers and you, Arki. Come on."

Vendurro stood and dusted his hands off on his trousers. "Time to get marching or digging."

He forced a smile, but it was weak and unconvincing.

We both followed Rudgi away from the mine, and in the same general direction as where she and I had had our brief but all-too-memorable encounter what felt like another lifetime ago. I wondered if I truly pleased her, if there were any chance of it ever happening again, and then cursed myself.

Braylar was standing, pacing slowly, and Mulldoos was sitting on a fallen tree, apparently transfixed by the pale hairs on the back of his hand. There was another somewhat familiar Jackal leaning against the tree, looking up at the slowly passing clouds as if watching the most magnificent galleons on the most fantastic sea imaginable.

The captain stopped pacing as we navigated around the trunks of some thin weeper pine and watched us until we joined them in the small glade. "Well. Our council has grown small indeed." Braylar looked at us and then over to the other officer. "You remember Sergeant Bruznik, of course? Well, perhaps not Arki. Arki, the sergeant, Sergeant Bruznik, Arki." He looked at Bruznik, eyes looking mossier than usual in the midday sun. "You no doubt felt slighted not being included in our little raid the other day, Sergeant, but I do hope you count yourself incredibly lucky. For you are."

Sergeant Bruznik stepped away from the tree. "Not one to question your orders, Cap, but still wishing I had been there to lend a hand. Never did much like the Ogre. Would have been glad to stick him a time or two, chance allowing." He spit in the dirt.

"I appreciate both the sentiment and the novelty of such fierce loyalty, you can be certain. It is more rare than it should be these days." The captain waved a hand, inviting us to join the small circle.

Sergeant Bruznik gave me a brief nonjudgmental nod, and if he wondered why I was included in the captain's retinue, he didn't ask.

Vendurro asked, "Any word about what happened to that bastard Cynead?"

Bruznik replied, "Nothing to be said for certain. Looked like he was about to flank and overwhelm Thumaar's troops out in the field when he stepped in a big pile of cowshit. All sudden like, his army halted, lost cohesion, seemed confused or operating under conflicting orders or whatnot. Then it seemed to fray at the seams, the center couldn't hold. Some battalions kept marching on the Confederates and Anjurians and Thumaar's boys, some fell back, others broke off completely. From what you all said, the Mems had something to do with that. But still no word on whether they threw him in chains or offed him right there."

I asked, "How did the battle play out then?"

Sergeant Bruznik looked at me, and while it was flat, there was no obvious hostility there. "There were heavy casualties on both sides. But Cynead had the upper hand. His big forces broke down right when they had things in hand. We figured your plan worked out just like you hoped."

"You figured wrong," Braylar said. "But from what you said, I imagine they did in fact capture the emperor. Deposed emperor, now. If not, news of his death and the Memoridon betrayal would have spread like brush fire, and his imperial army would have been in total disarray. General Kruzinios might have been able to rout them, even, or at least drive them from the field, victorious. But from what you said, they regrouped after a time and started a guarded retreat back to Sunwrack."

"That's right, Cap," Bruznik said. "Some Confederate skirmishers harried them, and the imperial army, well, Memoridon now, I reckon, they engaged, slowed down to protect their flanks. But there was no question they were quitting the field."

Mulldoos said, "Those cunts are no better than Azmorgon when it comes down to it, but they are ten kinds of clever. Got to grant them that. Bold move, seizing all the leaders. Might not pan out in the long run, but in the short, they grabbed the Towers by the jewels, slid a suroka right close, and dared them to squawk."

Braylar dropped his hand to Bloodsounder, not in a threatening manner, but slowly, deliberately, as if checking a divining rod for signs of an underground stream. "Is it so very strange they seized this opportunity when it presented itself?"

Vendurro asked, "What do you mean, Cap?"

"I mean," he said, watching a passing cloud, "are they so very different from every one of our emperors in history? They saw weakness, and methodically took the initiative to pounce. And from their perspective, they are not only power hungry, but righting a millennium of wrongs, of slavery."

Mulldoos's good eye nearly bugged out of his head. "Wait . . . are you plaguing *defending* them, Cap?"

"Defending? No. I merely point out that had roles been reversed, had it been us bound to serve with no possibility of release, with no—"

Mulldoos pushed himself off the log, and it creaked under his weight before he rose. "Those vicious slits have Darzaak, the other captains, the other

Commanders across the whole plaguing Empire under the knife just now, and you're plaguing talking about the horsecunts' plaguing *motivation*?"

Braylar turned and regarded Mulldoos but said nothing right away. Everyone seemed to tense up, but then the captain smiled. Not the twitchy kind or the mocking version, not the mummer's kind as he attempted to win over or play an Anjurian mark, but the very rare, earnest, and prolonged smile he only favored a staunch ally with. "You are right, Lieutenant. Their motivations do not matter, whether we agree about them or diverge. All that matters is what we do now. Which is why you are here."

He looked around our small group, taking us each in in turn, and stopping again when he reached Mulldoos. "You are fond of saying that I seldom solicit your input, and often disregard it even when I do. But I am inviting it now. And will dismiss nothing out of hand. So. While I am not relinquishing my post and will determine our direction, I ask you, what do you suggest, oh erudite and practical retinue?"

Mulldoos looked at Vendurro. "Is this a trap? Sort of feels like a plaguing trap."

Braylar replied, "I assure you, while I am fond of setting traps, this is not one of them. Speak. The floor is yours."

No one spoke at first, perhaps stunned, but then Rudgi said, "Well, we can't stay here, that's for certain. Maybe Soffjian let you flee Sunwrack, maybe she didn't—another divergent debate no doubt—but even if she didn't, that's not to say the other Memoridons will. We have no idea who truly rules right now, but if it's not her, others might press her on our whereabouts."

Vendurro said, "If for no other plaguing reason than to get their witchy hands on Bloodsounder there. The weapon, not the wielder, I mean."

Sergeant Bruznik understandably looked confused, but Rudgi continued, "So we got to get moving. Only question is where."

Mulldoos sat back down on the creaking tree, his forearms bulging as he steadied himself. "No place far enough. Not if they come hunting. Not unless we got back across that plaguing Veil, but we all know what kind of fun to expect on that side."

Vendurro said, "What about trying to find General Kruzinios?"

Mulldoos gave him that droopy but still incredulous look. "Oh, yeah, the Eagles will be real plaguing happy to take us in. Especially after we explain how we led Thumaar into a trap, saw him done in by witches supposed to be helping him retake the throne, and then had to fight off some of his guard to get free of the Citadel."

That shut that line of inquiry down in a hurry. When no one else said anything else for a few moments, I cleared my throat and offered, "Mulldoos, you mentioned the Veil. But we don't have to cross over, do we?"

He turned the droopy skepticism my way. "We do if we got to run from the witchslits. Which we got to do sooner or later, likely sooner. You heard Cap—his bitch sister can track us anywhere, if she has a mind to. Only thing we can do is go far enough to make it not worth their while. At least until we figure out what to plaguing do next."

Braylar gave me one of his calculating looks. "In the spirit of hearing things out, explain what you meant, Arki."

"Well," I said, "We could find a secluded spot near the Veil, hole up there. If the Memoridons or Memoridon-led troops come for us, we can cross over if we have to." Mulldoos started to object, but I pressed on. "Not far into the territory, mind you, for obvious reasons. Just on the other side. But then we'd know if they intend to hunt us down. And it allows the only true means of escape we have if they did."

"And if they don't come . . . " Vendurro said, figuring out where I intended to go.

I said, "Then at least we are still relatively close to Sunwrack, to the Jackals, until we gather more intelligence and figure out the next plan of attack."

Vendurro grinned, and it seemed less broken this time.

Bruznik looked closely at me again and turned to the captain. "I like this skinny bastard, Cap."

Mulldoos rolled his eyes (well, the one really) as Braylar said, "It took him much longer to grow on me, but yes, he is more astute than he looks."

Rudgi said, "It's a good idea. But where?"

Vendurro tapped the side of his nose. "Got the place, as it happens. Little deserted village north of here four days, probably five if we're moving stealthy. Called Ondolyr. Nestled up close to the Veil."

"Another plaguing plague village?" Mulldoos asked.

Vendurro replied, "Nahh. Saw it on patrol years ago, hunting some Urglovian rebels. Hadn't been used at all in half of forever, overgrown, only a few stone buildings still standing. Probably cleared out after the Veil went up, I'm guessing. It's close enough they must have lost some to the draw of the thing and got tired of having their own wander on over to their deaths."

Mulldoos rubbed his stubbly cheek. "Yeah, sounds plaguing lovely. Maybe we could grow some peonies and raise rabbits."

"Wasn't saying we ought to settle down there, Mull," Vendurro said. "But you want a place not on any map, close to the Veil, affording the kind of escape only Cap there can provide, you'd be hard pressed to find a better site."

Braylar said, "If you have any objections or better suggestions, I would hear them now."

Mulldoos looked like he was ready to roll out some more rebuttals, though out of pure habit or pique it was hard to tell, but then surprisingly held his tongue, shrugging his big shoulders. "Heard lousier plans."

"A resounding endorsement," the captain said before turning to the others. "Anyone else? Other alternatives? Critique? Asinine remarks?"

After another few moments of silence Braylar slapped the buckler on his belt. "Very good. It is settled then, yes? To the abandoned village at the edge of our world."

Put like that, I wished someone else had objected, but once settled, the captain was not easily unsettled.

W̲e avoided main byways for the first two days, winding through sparse woods and along the edges of farmland, but then we joined Carper's Road heading north. I was riding next to Mulldoos and asked why and he jerked a thick thumb over his shoulder. "Two words for you, Arki. Bitch. Sister. If she or any of her ilk are after us, no amount of zig-zagging or skirting through the brush is going to do any plaguing good, and will only slow us down. We'll make for this weedy hamlet as fast as we can now. Not as much chance of running into patrols now, and scouts are scouting. We're good."

And so we rode for the next four days, moving off the small dirt track a few times when a scout brought back word of an approaching wagon, a group of pilgrims, or small caravan, but otherwise undisturbed. There were no troops ahead or behind, Syldoon, Confederate, or Anjurian. We made camp, Mulldoos continued leaving welts up and down my body as we trained (slightly less numerous than before, though my welts had welts, so it wasn't much of an improvement), and I listened to the soldiers. The sense of malaise was heavy, partly because we were a much smaller group than when we had escaped Sunwrack the first time, and partly because we had a mission then, an objective, a sense there was still something worth moving forward to. Now there were only questions and uneasiness.

It was mid-morning on the sixth day when Vendurro led us off the rutted road and through the sparse woods for several hours. Rudgi took another rider ahead to be sure the area was safe and not housing bandits, rebels, or any other troublesome occupants. We watered and rested the horses and waited, and two hours later they returned, stating the abandoned village was well and truly abandoned.

The sun was still up when we sighted Ondolyr, or what remained of it. Winding around trees and a hundred yards out, I might not have even known there were buildings ahead. While this region was dryer and less green than anything in Anjuria, a thousand years of vines, lichen, weeds, creepers, and moss had overtaken any structure left standing. I expected some stone buildings to have withstood the years—there were manor houses, and what looked like a mill— but was surprised to see so many of the wooden ones still admirably bearing the weight of so many centuries.

We rejoined a road leading to it that must have been an offshoot of Carper's further north. Squirrels skittered and chattered at us as we passed, and some black quilltails burst out of a small grove to our right and flew off, but we were without question the only humans in the vicinity. As we got closer, the road split off around a small plaza and what remained of a fountain near the entrance to the villa. The stones in the plaza surrounding the fountain had been broken up by roots erupting through them, and were covered in the natural detritus of ages. As we circled the round, cracked, and useless fountain, it wasn't hard to imagine that it had once been beautiful, as the enameled tiles inside were still largely undisturbed, and the statue of a fox jumping a log in the center would have looked nearly as good as new with some maintenance.

It appeared a wind storm must have swept through here at some point after the villa was deserted, as the roofs of several wooden buildings had been torn free, and several red tiles from the manor houses were scattered and broken all around the buildings. The structures that had lost some or most of their roofs had suffered considerably, exposed to the elements, everything inside deteriorated by warp and rot and mold, but again, even after the passage of so many years, it was easy to see that this had once been a thriving and beautiful villa.

Before the Deserters erected the Veil.

It was impossible to miss, not far beyond the edge of the villa, pulsing its way up to the sky, and even fifty yards out, I felt the first tentative tugs, the faint urge to keep riding towards it. Even though I had seen the Veil several times now, it still inspired a terrible kind of awe, this wall of memories spanning the world designed to keep us and our plague on this side.

Braylar turned his horse around and pointed back at a manor house we had passed thirty yards back. "We stay there." Then he pointed at a stone well off to our left. "If you cross this marker, you are already too close. As you well know, the Veil solicits any and all, and the invitation is a powerful one. We go no closer unless we are penned in by Memoridons, and even then, you will accompany me. Is that understood?"

There was a chorus of ayes, and the captain said, "You best get comfortable, and clear this place out. We won't be renovating the villa and moving in, but we could be here for a while."

I helped Vendurro and several other Syldoon haul out debris from one of the manor houses. Most of the roof was intact, but there were a few holes and the interior immediately below had weathered poorly, though the frame, timbers, joinery, and overall appearance were remarkably good—it was hard to image this had been abandoned nearly a millennium before.

Especially since, similar to the plague village we stayed in, there were countless artifacts remaining in Ondolyr—things left behind by the villagers who had presumably suffered enough losses to the Veil and realized that every moment they stayed here put someone else in jeopardy. I imagined they loaded their wagons and horses and oxen with their most important valuables, but left behind a great deal of furniture that had been mostly protected from the elements that was still recognizable—even the fabric, while faded, mildewed, torn, and no doubt home to a thousand beetles and spiders over the years, was in fairly good shape when not in the vicinity of the holes above.

There were also cabinets, some still filled with dust-caked candlesticks or wooden cups, an empty wardrobe containing the stained and threadbare fabric that had been clothes of some kind but was largely unrecognizable now, and on and on, the remains of the terrified populace that vacated and never returned.

I was filling my arms with some red shingles and looked over at Vendurro. "It's still hard to believe the Memoridons betrayed Thumaar like that. Well, all of you Syldoon, really."

"Ayyup," he replied, kicking a beam to see how heavy it was. "That whole business with the frames. Got to hand it to the witches. Mighty manipulative."

I tossed the debris out a window. As I moved over to help him with the other end of the beam, I said, "Well, in that sense, it isn't surprising at all. They don't lack for cleverness."

Vendurro chuckled as he kicked some shingles towards the wall. "Aye. Sure as spit." He gave me a long look. "Been meaning to ask, about Skeelana that is . . ."

The unspoken question hung there, and I sighed. He started to say something, maybe withdraw the question, but I said, "I wanted to let her suffer. Truly. I thought I would. But I couldn't."

He nodded. "You got a bigger heart than me."

"No," I said. "That's not it. Do you know why I finished her off?"

Vendurro dusted hands on his pants and looked at me, waiting. I said, "Not to give her mercy. Not really. But because part of me worried that if I left her alive, then Soffjian or some other Memoridons might return, find a way to save her. It didn't seem likely. But then, neither did the Memoridons overthrowing Syldoon control with our help. She had caused enough damage, and just then, I hated her, and wanted to be done hating her. So I finished her off."

I hadn't expected to admit that to anyone. But there it was.

Vendurro asked, a small, sad smile on his face, "And how's that working out for you? The not-hating part?"

I shook my head. "Not so good."

He patted me on the back, raising dust. "Well, good thing you got some other diversions then, eh?"

"Other diversions? What—?"

Vendurro winked. "At least she's not a Memoridon. That's something. Even Mulldoos can't argue with that one."

I felt my cheeks grow hot, and not from the exertion of cleaning. "It was just—that is, just the one time. I don't know if, don't even know—"

"Nobody does, Arki." He gave me a big toothy grin. "No matter what you read in any prettified romances, nobody does. Might only be the once, might be the first of a thousand. Got terrible luck with women, myself, so I ain't offering any advice. But she's not Memoridon, and you can't die like Rokliss, so I'd say you're off to as good a start as any."

I thought about that poor smother bastard and laughed, then coughed on some of the dust. Looking around, I lowered my voice as another Syldoon pushed a chaise out of the way nearby. "How long will she be off? Scouting?"

Vendurro said, "She's off gathering intelligence while we hunker down here, her and a few others, riding off in different directions. Hard to say when they'll be back for certain. Until then," he pointed at a crumpled and broken chair under a hole in the roof, "we clean this place up and hunker down for a bit. Let's get to it."

⊕

As it happened, two of the other scouts returned two tenday later, reporting mixed news. They heard from more than one source that confirmed that Thumaar's temporary allies, Baron Brune and the Confederate generals, had survived the battle outside Sunwrack and slunk back to their homelands. They wouldn't be players in any immediate action, so that was one less thing Braylar had to contend with.

The scouts also declared that they heard conflicting reports from those who had left the city of Graymoss, but more often, it sounded as if Memoridons held sway over the provinces just as they did over Sunwrack, though it was impossible to tell how long they could sustain that position. Mulldoos thought every Tower would rise up at the first chance they got, while Braylar maintained that the Syldoon were drawn to power as much as anything else—just as they would support a strong emperor, they would throw in their lot with the Memoridons once it was apparent they weren't going to be ousted anytime soon.

One unfortunate rider had the task of trying to get a message to Commander Darzaak and hadn't returned from Sunwrack. Rudgi and another scout hadn't returned either.

Our small company was anxious and restless as we waited for more word to come in to piece together our next move. We couldn't return to Sunwrack, and we couldn't appeal to the Confederates or Anjurians, so until we somehow got direction from Darzaak, we were adrift and listing.

Mulldoos continued welting me, sometimes enlisting another Syldoon as a sparring partner to raise bruises in new spots, and small groups of Jackals roamed the countryside away from the Veil, hunting, foraging, exploring the area.

More than once, Braylar pulled Bloodsounder off his belt and approached the Veil, disappearing for long stretches each time. I caught up to him as he returned from one such outing and said, "Are you all right, Captain?"

He was oddly calm, which was disturbing in itself. "When I killed those Memoridons in the Citadel, it washed all the poisonous memories clean. Even after striking Rusejenna out, I hadn't felt so wonderfully empty, myself again. The last time I was so cleansed was the moment before making the egregious error of taking this wicked thing out of the earth."

Braylar stopped himself, trailing off a little. I said, "But?"

"But," he replied, fixing those mossy stone eyes on me, "then that mutinous bastard's memories began flooding into me. With no rogue witch to attend me, and no Memoridons to strike down, I began to think . . . But then, I remembered something you said, after translating."

I looked at the shimmering Veil in the distance and then back to him. "And what did I say?"

"The Priest of Truth. The Grass Dog witch. She claimed visiting the Veil cleansed her. So I visited."

"And?" I asked, more loudly than I intended.

Braylar smiled. One of those prolonged, unnerving, rare genuine smiles. "It is slower than killing a Memoridon, but I will never need a witch to attend me again. Provided I can get to the Veil." He glanced down at Bloodsounder. "It worked, Arki. Slowly, for certain, but it worked."

"That is fantastic, Captain! I wish I had—"

We heard hoofbeats, coming fast.

Rudgi and another scout rounded the bend, galloping hard for the villa.

I had Lloi's sword on my hip but no crossbow. "Should we arm ourselves, Captain? Should I raise an alarm—"

Braylar put his hand on my shoulder. "Easy there. I do not believe we are under attack. Yet. Or it would be sentries with frothy-mouthed horses, not our Sergeant of Scouts. But do round up Mulldoos, Vendurro, and Bruznik and meet us by the fountain." I nodded, and he gave me a shove. "Today, Arki!"

I ran off and found the officers and told them to head to the fountain. Vendurro was the last one—he was taking a nap—and the pair of us joined the others by the fountain.

Rudgi was sitting on the cracked ledge, still breathing heavily in between taking swigs out of a costrel.

When Braylar saw Vendurro and me, he said, "Very good. Now, Sergeant, report."

Rudgi looked at the captain and nodded, sweaty, tired, shoulders slumped, but it was the look in her eye that made my hairs stand up straight. One part haunted, two parts morose. "It's Graymoss, Cap. The plaguing city . . . it's dead now."

That did nothing to settle my nerves. Braylar said, "What do you mean, Rudgi? How is it *dead*?"

She took a deep breath, steadied herself. "I was heading north, just like you said, keeping close to the Veil, just like you told me. Planning on heading further west once I got closer to Erstbright. But six days out, I—" then she pointed at the scout, who appeared no less shaken. "That is, we. We saw the Deserters. An army of Deserters."

Even Mulldoos seemed taken aback by that. "Through the Veil?"

"No," she replied. "They crossed over. Wielders, staffslingers, clubbers, those legless bastards on their backs, supply wagons pulled by rooters. There were a lot of them already forming up on this side when we saw them, and Junti and I, we hung back, really far back, and watched the rest come through." There was awe in her voice as she said, "Thousands of them, Cap. Between ten and fifteen, so far as I can tell. Filled up a whole valley. Once they assembled, they headed west, and we shadowed them."

I looked at Rudgi. "Well. The Deserters must not be overly concerned about the edict anymore."

She didn't reply, but Vendurro asked, "What's that? What edict?"

I replied, "Rudgi and I asked Nustenzia if the Deserters could cross the Veil. We were worried about her following us. She told us she wasn't sure if they could or not, but there was some edict or other that prevented them from even trying. Clearly they can."

The other scout, Junti, turned to Braylar. "They move fast, Cap. Even without horses. And don't need rest like we do. It was hard to keep up, but we did."

Mulldoos said, "Let me plaguing guess. Grand Bitch Mother Vrulinka was with them?"

Rudgi nodded. "Saw plenty of Wielders with her, but ayyup, the Matriarch was there all right, trailing dead flowers behind, flying her colors. This was her force."

"And?" Braylar asked, hand drifting down to Bloodsounder. "She headed to Graymoss?"

"She did," Rudgi replied, before taking another drink. "They surrounded the city. Folks inside must have thought the gods themselves were back, maybe even that they were the chosen ones. They sent an envoy out, to parley I imagine. But the Deserters, well—"

Braylar said, "They didn't come to this side after all this time to parley, did they?"

"No," Rudgi said. "They sure plaguing didn't. Smote that poor bastard and then the Wielders set to work."

Vendurro asked, "What does that mean, 'set to work'?"

Rudgi capped the costrel with shaky fingers. "They built a dome around the city. Just like Roxtiniak."

"We thought they were just trapping folks inside, like a prison," Junti said.

Rudgi shook her head. "Only that wasn't what they intended at all. We were fixing to ride back here, just about to kick up some dust, when I noticed something. The Veil dome they built, it was getting tighter, smaller, contracting like."

"Contracting?" Braylar said, fist closing around Bloodsounder's haft.

Rudgi looked at him and nodded once, quickly. "Aye. Contracting. We sat and watched, gods help us, we did. But there was nothing we could do."

"We thought," Junti said, "hoped maybe, that they were just threatening Graymoss, making them surrender."

Braylar said, voice cold. "But they didn't want surrender, did they?"

"No," Rudgi replied. "They didn't plaguing want surrender. That dome just kept getting smaller, closing in on the people inside, passed the outer walls, kept on going, contracting."

Junti was staring at his feet, hands in his lap like a small child. "Even up on our hill, we heard that city screaming when the people in it realized what was happening. Never heard anything like it."

Rudgi said, "Those Wielders just kept tightening that dome down. Took two and a half days, the Wielders with their arms outstretched, never moving. The Veil just getting closer to everyone inside, herding the people further in until there was nowhere else for them to run and nobody left to scream." Her voice broke. "Sorry, Cap. It's just, they wiped them all out. Every last one. The whole plaguing city. We sat on the hill and watched it happen, to make sure we were reporting true."

Vendurro said, "Plague. Me. Graymoss must have had, what, sixty thousand people?"

"More," Mulldoos said, looking north. "Plaguing more."

No one said anything else for several moments until I blurted, "That's what Nustenzia said. In the frame tower in the Citadel."

"When she said what, exactly?" Braylar asked, voice a rasp.

"That we were doomed," I said. "Right after she realized Soffjian had freed the Memoridons. A strong and united Syldoon Empire was probably the only thing keeping Vrulinka from crossing over. But now, with it broken, the possibility that Memoridons could lose control completely, that the Empire could fall into civil war with no powerful emperor to hold it together . . ."

Braylar held his hand up. "That is quite enough. We deal with the here and now, and the very real problem before us."

"And how are we dealing with it, Cap?" Mulldoos asked.

The captain turned to Rudgi. "You did good work. The both of you. I assume you stayed long enough to ascertain where the Deserters marched off to next?"

Rudgi nodded. "Aye, Cap. Once the dome disappeared, they got moving again. The giant bastards are heading south. Towards Sunwrack."

He addressed Junti. "Dismissed, soldier. Get yourself some rest. We leave on the morrow."

Junti saluted and led his horse away. When he was out of earshot, Mulldoos asked again, "Leaving, huh? What are we doing, Cap? What do you got planned?"

"We return," Braylar said.

Mulldoos rolled his lower jaw around. "Return? What do mean, plaguing return? Sunwrack? Your sister will have us hanging or husked before we get even ten yards into the city."

Braylar released the haft and plucked up one of the horned Deserter heads, examining it in his palm as he turned it over. "We will not enter Sunwrack. Not yet. But we have to alert the Memoridons, apprise them, prepare them. We know what is heading their way."

"You want to *help* the plaguing Memoridons? After what they done? Are you plaguing serious?!"

Braylar stared at the ugly eyeless visage in his hands. "Arki is right—the only chance we have of stopping the Deserters is being united. Being an Empire. We have to help them. If the Memoridons aren't prepared, the entire Empire could fall. Our Tower included. You do recall we have thousands of our brothers in Sunwrack, do you not?"

"Of course I plaguing recall!" Mulldoos said, slurring the edges of a few words again. "But there's got to be a better way. Get word to Darzaak and—"

"And what? Hope he can convince the Memoridons of this danger, despite him being in lockdown and having no way of knowing what befell Graymoss?"

Mulldoos slapped his thighs and stood up. "They're plaguing witches! They have to know already. Graymoss had some Mems inside. Sure enough, someone sent message to your bitch sister and her ilk already."

"If they hadn't been under siege by Deserters and Wielders, you would be right, of course. But are you willing to risk all of Sunwrack, perhaps the entire Empire, on the presumption that the Wielders couldn't have intercepted any such messages and destroyed them, or that the Veil didn't prevent them from being sent in the first place? I am not, Lieutenant. I am not."

Rudgi said, "We saw them do it to a biggish city, wipe out every living soul inside. But Sunwrack is nearly ten times the size. We don't know they can manage that, Cap. And not from so far away. They'd have to be out of trebuchet range to manage it."

"And again, I ask, are you prepared to be responsible for the loss of two hundred thousand lives, and the fate of an Empire, if we gamble incorrectly? Because again I say, I am not." Braylar dropped the Deserter head with a loud clink. "We will set up a meet with Soffjian and a few of the other key Memoridons outside the city. We will convince them the walls of Sunwrack provide no safe haven, as the Deserter siege isn't concerned with gates or Trenches or trebuchets. The Syldoon and Memoridons must meet the enemy in the field and destroy them or be destroyed in turn."

Mulldoos shook his head. "She'll never go for a meeting, Cap. She'll assume it's a trap and stay clear, or she'll set a trap of her own and take us in. She won't meet us in good faith. Never plaguing happen. She won't do it."

"She *will*," Braylar said. "I will compose the message myself, make the urgency crystal clear, and set the terms of the engagement."

"She just betrayed the whole plaguing *Empire*. You think a little *note* is going to keep her honest?"

The captain took three slow strides over to Mulldoos, who got up off the fountain and stood up to meet him. Braylar said, "You overstep, Lieutenant. Perhaps I confused things by inviting input right after Sunwrack. But I am not doing so now. This is not a discussion. We are meeting my sister and impressing upon them the immense danger heading for them so that the Empire can stand united against it. That is all."

Mulldoos seemed to be biting back a number of rebuttals and further objections, as his pale face had gone crimson and his teeth were clenched. But whether he suddenly remembered Azmorgon or simply realized the captain was not about to be swayed by any more arguments, he nodded once. "Aye, Cap. Meeting the plaguing witches. Saving the plaguing Empire from giants and bigger witches. Got it."

Vendurro said, "Where, Cap? Where are we meeting her?"

Braylar spun around and said, "The abandoned mine outside Sunwrack—we are all too familiar with it. We will arrive there first, have sentries in position to alert us if it appears the Memoridons have any foul intentions." He looked at me. "Arki—bring me your pen and ink. I am no great supporter of the epistolary arts, but I have a very pressing missive to write just now. Attend me."

The captain said, "The rest of you, prepare yourselves and say goodbye to this charming villa—we leave at dawn."

W e rode as hard as we could to the abandoned mine without blowing the horses. Part of this was likely due to the Syldoon affinity and affection for the animals, but undoubtedly it was utilitarian as well—a crossbow cavalry member without his or her horse just wasn't going to be as useful.

The first day, scouts reported a fairly sizable force camped ahead, suspected to be Eagles, though they certainly weren't flying any colors. So we added some time to ride well clear of them, and that only seemed to incense the captain to spur us on more. Other than that, we didn't encounter anyone else besides some civilian travelers on the road heading in the opposite direction, but they moved aside and kept their heads down as we rode past.

When we were two days out, Braylar gave his letter to a Jackal and sent him galloping towards Sunwrack. Mulldoos shook his head, looked over his shoulder to be sure the rest of the troops were out of earshot, and said, "Cap, I know you're set on this. I still think it's a fool plan, but you're the captain, and so there it is. But as much as you like to lead from the front—and you know I plaguing respect the hells out of that—you really ought to stay clear on this one. Me and Ven, we can handle the meet. If your bitch sister has any other nasty surprises, it'll spring on us, not you. And if not, we can deliver any news after. Stay clear, Cap."

Braylar patted Scorn's neck as he said, "If I am not there, Soff will assume it is us setting the trap. That will never do."

"Maybe you come down out of the hills if I give a signal," Mulldoos said. "Thumaar liked to lead from the front too, and look where that plaguing got him. That's all I'm saying."

Braylar sat straight in the saddle again, rolled his shoulders back. "As much as I trust you in most things, Lieutenant, being my proxy in this matter simply isn't one of them. If this plays out as planned, there will be several Memoridons in attendance. And accurate or not, when they are called

455

bitches, witches, and cunts, it does tend to make them far less amenable."
Mulldoos started to say something else, and Braylar continued as he rattled
Bloodsounder's chains, "And what's more, I am the only one protected from
them. I have to be there, and there's an end to it, Lieutenant."

Mulldoos spit into the brittle grass. "Aye, figured you'd say as much. Just
had to try."

"You wouldn't be you if you hadn't. Let's ride."

And so we did, making excellent if exhausting time.

The camp was in the same condition we left it, the same rusted tools
strewn around the same gaping hole in the ground exactly. It wasn't full
dark as the captain led our small company into the area, but the moon was
already up, its ever-present ring bright and shiny, as if it had been recently
polished. I tried to pretend that portended good things, but just couldn't
muster the optimism.

Still, I assumed the Deserter army marching through the Syldoon Empire
just now couldn't see it—the crowned moon, the sun, the stars, probably even
the clouds were all visual pleasures only humans could appreciate. No matter
what wars we fought, what hatreds we harbored, what vendettas we nurtured,
humanity all existed under a single sky that was ours alone. No matter how
powerful they were, the Deserters could not claim it.

As I climbed off my horse, muscles weary, eyes heavy, and started uncinch-
ing the saddle, I tried telling myself again the shiny ringed moon was in fact
a good portent and nearly believed it that time. Perhaps we could be united
under it, at least long enough to drive the invaders back.

Perhaps.

Two days later, Rudgi rode back into camp and reported a small party
approaching from Sunwrack. Braylar addressed his company. "Vacate the
mine. Head up into the hills. Eighty yards or so, yes? And stay visible. Keep
your crossbows spanned and within reach, but do not present them or otherwise arm yourselves.

"This is not an ambush. Let me repeat that, for those prone to hearing
what they want—today is not the day we lure these Memoridons into a trap.
Whatever grievances we have with them—and we clearly have massive ones

just now—we set them aside for today. And all the days to follow until we have either dispatched the Deserters or died in the attempt. But we can only do so if Syldoon and Memoridons fight together. That is the purpose of this meeting. If any man or woman sours it with an untowards action, I will personally visit my wrath upon them. Is that understood?"

The Jackals all replied in the affirmative, but one freckled soldier near the front asked, "And what if the Mems betray us? Again, I mean. What if they try anything?"

Braylar twitch-smiled and replied, "Then, soldier, I expect you will be shooting your crossbows until your quivers are empty. But do not come storming down the hill. Do not engage. There will be several War Memoridons here, and if you attempt to close, they will utterly destroy you. Is that understood?"

There were more "Ayes," and then the captain ordered them to mount up and maintain their positions.

Braylar's retinue remained behind. He looked at me and said, "Arki, I suspect I know what you will say, but I would be remiss as your patron if I didn't tell you that your presence here is not required. Mulldoos could very well be right—this parley could easily end with all of us in chains or in tombs."

I made sure I wasn't slouching as I said, "As tempting as it would be to ride off, I think I will stay right here just the same, Captain. At least there are no aqueducts or catacombs."

"As you will," he replied, the smile on his lips a ghost, but at least not disappearing quickly.

I saw his officers looking at me as well with what I thought and hoped might be respect. That was at least some sort of balm for my undeniable foolishness.

When Mulldoos opened his mouth, though, I expected him to gut my small moment of satisfaction. Instead, he closed it again, clapped me on the back, and then moved aside to speak quietly with Vendurro. Bruznik had gone into the hills with the other Jackals. The captain was running his hand down Bloodsounder, eyes closed, perhaps waiting for the tremors of memories to come that foretold violence here.

That left Rudgi, who was still looking at me. As usual, she didn't dawdle coming to her point. "I'm not one to regret laying with a man, or riding him, or however it plays itself out. I make my choices, live with them too. But sometimes, I feel better about it than others. This is one of those. You have more grit than any non-Syldoon I can recall meeting, Arki." She grinned, her top lip disappearing. "That sounds like mixed praise, I know, but I mean it in the best way. The lieutenant is right on that score."

With my limited experience, I barely knew how to handle any compliment from a woman, let alone one couched in such terms. I nodded a few times, stalling for the right words to come, when I saw a group of horsemen ride up to the rim of the mine. Horsewomen, more than half of them, anyway. There were five Memoridons, including Soffjian, the Focus Nustenzia, and three Syldoon. I shaded my eyes and squinted before I realized they were now-deposed emperor Cynead, Command Darzaak, and what I assumed was another Tower Commander.

Mulldoos said, "Plague me, but you drew them out, Cap. Kind of wishing this was an ambush right about now."

"It still very much could be if we mishandle the situation," Braylar replied, watching the riders dismount and start walking their horses down the incline. "While I ordinarily admire your independent bent, I'm going to insist you don't speak unless I clear you to do so. Understood?"

Maybe watching Azmorgon orchestrate a mutiny had changed the lieutenant slightly, or maybe Braylar simply caught him in a rare acquiescent mood, but rather than offer an immediate or abrasive rebuttal, Mulldoos simply said, "Aye, Cap."

Next to me, Vendurro leaned in and said, "Something about our lives hanging in the balance always makes me real hungry. Even before my manumission—when I really got hung—my stomach was growling like a bear beforehand. You get like that?"

I shook my head. "Right now, I sort of want to throw up. So I'm glad my stomach is pretty empty."

He watched the Memoridons and Jackals approach, put his hand on the pommel of his sword, caught himself, and removed it quickly, fiddling with his belt instead. "Not easy, being hungry all the time."

I couldn't argue with that.

The group was about thirty yards away, and I had to resist the urge to look over my shoulder and up the hill at the Jackals watching as well.

While Cynead had been stripped of the crown, the Memoridons still allowed him some of his pomp, even if he had been demoted back to Tower Commander of the Leopards again. He wore a dual-colored cotehardie, black on one side, gold on the other, and the plaque belt had leopard heads only now, no suns, but was no less impressive and gaudy. He still bore a scabbarded sword, which surprised me, as did the gnarled Commander Darzaak, looking much more plain in his simple gray tunic.

The other Syldoon, who I assumed was a Commander, was the shortest in the group and had one large malformed ear that looked like a pale vegetable, and a close-cut blond beard.

The War Memoridons were outfitted like the ones we had met in the frame tower—scale and lamellar cuirasses, blousy trousers, one with a sword, another with a svelte-beaked warhammer on her belt, a third with a military fork propped on her shoulder, and Soffjian was again in her usual scale cuirass, though the bandages underneath were clearly visible on her shoulder. She had her customary ranseur as well, but clearly was in no condition to wield it.

Nustenzia was the only one who looked truly out of place, as she was—unarmed, balanced precariously between haughty resignation and fear, with the carved flesh on her face marking her as an outsider even a distance.

When the group stopped ten feet away, Braylar and his officers saluted Darzaak, fists twisted and hitting their chests, and he returned it briefly, saying, "You lads alright then, Captain? Your sister here was tight-lipped on the particulars."

Braylar said, "That is not altogether shocking. As to our condition, Commander, most of our men are dead." He turned and pointed up to the hills. "No doubt you marked those there. That is all that remains of our company."

Cynead wore a hard smile. "The great provocateur, Captain Braylar Killcoin, unwitting pawn of the Memoridon ploy to undermine everything that underpins our Empire. The irony is thicker than whale oil, really. But still, I had rather hoped that the next time I saw you, your head would be on a pike or some such thing. So very disappointing, truly. I am also surprised my new lieges here have not blasted your skull apart already. I would rather enjoy that, though perhaps they recognize the part you played in abetting them."

Braylar replied, "Ah, it's such a treat to see a deposed emperor in the flesh. They so often are only bones. First Thumaar, and now you. I do wonder how long before these Memoridons see that you will only be a magnet for unrest so long as you yet live. They are exceedingly clever. It can't be long."

Cynead started to respond, but one of the War Memoridons, a tall woman with her red hair pulled back into a severe bun, turned to the former emperor. "You are here as a courtesy, Syldoon, and have no authority. Do remember that."

Cynead looked at her, head tilted ever so slightly to the side. "That would be such a difficult thing for me to forget, Memoridon."

The Commander with the cross-cropped beard nodded at Braylar coolly and said, "Captain. I do not know you except by reputation. But I know Commander Darzaak here, and that is enough for me."

"Many thanks, Commander Meodrik." Braylar returned the nod and then looked at Soffjian. "So, as a matter of protocol, how should we address you? Are you a bevy of Empresses, then?"

Soffjian replied, "How we style ourselves is not particularly important. I will only say we are not Empresses. But what is entirely more important, Bray, is that you have called us here, requested this meeting, when you truly should be anywhere else in the world just now. I do recall advising you to flee, did I not?"

"You did indeed," Braylar said. "And I was eager enough to follow such sound advice. But as you have read in my missive already, that is not possible. Not now."

Soffjian said, "Yes, yes, a matter of urgency, fate of the empire, so you said. And yet—"

"And yet," the Memoridon of austere features and bun said, "our sister here made the mistake of allowing you to leave the Citadel in the first place. So we regard her recommendation to meet you here at all to be suspect."

Braylar replied, "I am quite sure you do, Latvettika. Though I must admit, given that you would not even be the unnamed and multitudinous rulers of a fractured Empire right now but for Soffjian's expert manipulation of us, I am rather surprised you did not name her Empress for all time and kiss her gilded toes. And as to her allowing us to leave"—he flicked Bloodsounder's haft up—"I am quite sure you have been briefed—this snake is not to be charmed by the likes of you. So if anything, I allowed her to escape. Pray I do the same with you."

Latvettika began to reply but Braylar cut her off. "But neither party is here to issue threats or ultimatums or proclamations. We are here because we possess knowledge that might very well save our Empire if we work together. And you are here because your Memoridons in Graymoss have gone utterly silent. So however suspicious you are of my intentions, you would not be here or have brought with you the Commanders as I requested, unless your suspicions that I was telling the truth were greater still. So. Let us try this again, somewhere north of amenity and south of acrimony, yes?"

The other Memoridons glared at him, particularly Latvettika; Soffjian had difficulty curbing a smile, Darzaak didn't bother hiding his at all, and even Cynead had to appreciate the captain needling his captors from a position of some leverage, even if he wanted the man dead.

Braylar nodded. "Very good. Now, I presume you have all read my brief manifesto on the vast danger currently marching towards you, which means you surely have questions. Ask. But do so with haste. Every moment we spend here discussing the veracity is one less we have to prepare. And there is so very much to do."

Latvettika said, "How did you do it? That is all I wish to know. Was it that cursed flail?" She looked at Bloodsounder as if it were a real serpent that might strike her at any moment.

"Sadly, no," Braylar replied. "I had nothing whatsoever to do with it. While I could have slain several of your sisters in Graymoss, I had no desire to, at least no overt desire or plan. But even if I had, there is no way I could have managed such a thing unless they all took supper in a beer garden and imbibed a great deal first. Are they prone to that? I suspect not. So someone would have sent word to you if I had gone on a methodical Memoridon assassination spree. Next question."

Darzaak all but barked, "I enjoy your machinations as much as the next man, Captain, and hope you have a doozy up your sleeve to justify all this. But cut to the point and be done with this charade."

Braylar looked at his sister as he replied, "With all due respect, Commander, there is no plot this time. No wheels within wheels. It is actually quite simple. And dire. But before these women can arrive at their own conclusions and act decisively, I require corroboration. And there are only two here who can do so."

The lightning-bolt vein pierced Soffjian's brow and she suddenly paled. Very slowly and quietly she said, "I imagined it was Bloodsounder as well. I assured my sisters you had discovered a way to use it to stopper our communication. But that isn't it. Is it, Bray?"

"Would I possessed such power, blood sister, but no," Braylar said. "And when you eliminate that, as well as the extremely unlikelihood all your Memoridons contracted the plague on the same day and died before sending word to Sunwrack"—he looked at Nustenzia—"that leaves only one real possibility, does it not?"

Nustenzia closed her eyes and sighed deeply.

Soffjian saw the Focus's reaction and whispered, "Gods. They are here."

"Not gods," Braylar said. "That much you know all too well. But yes, the Deserters are here."

Latvettika's lips were so pursed they nearly puckered, and her brow was as wrinkled as a fallow field.

Mulldoos laughed, looking at Soffjian. "Oh, that's blooming rich! You didn't plaguing tell them, did you?"

Commander Meodrik was a man of few words, but asked, "What is it I'm missing here?"

Soffjian started to reply, but Latvettika spoke over her. "On that score you are entirely wrong, Lieutenant. Soffjian revealed everything she knew. We merely hoped that she was mad." She looked at Braylar. "But you are claiming she spoke true? Is that it?"

Braylar replied, "If we had the luxury of time and I trusted you a great deal more, I would simply let you sift through the memories of one of my men and confirm this for yourself. But she spoke truly. The Deserters exist. But the Godveil is a misnomer. While they are incredibly powerful, wield memory magic far beyond your reckoning, and are giants besides, they are not gods. They bleed. They die. At great cost, but they can be defeated. But thanks to your impressive coup, they must believe the Empire is weakened enough to strike now. A large host of Deserters has crossed the Veil. And they are coming for Sunwrack."

The short-haired and long-faced Memoridon with the military fork said, "Then they are incredible fools as well. Even if these creatures could defeat us in the field—and I am sure you are overestimating them doing even that much—Sunwrack it the most fortified city in the world. It cannot be taken."

Braylar gave her his most withering look. "And here I thought Memoridons considered themselves paragons of perception. Perhaps you missed the beginning of the conversation, Wenna, when I mentioned where you lost contact with all your sisters in Graymoss? The implication was not especially subtle, but I will spell it out for anyone else obtuse enough to have missed it—the Deserters not only wiped the Memoridons out, but every inhabitant in the city as well. Without engines, sappers, poison, starvation, or any other conventional means of siege craft. In under three days, they killed every man, woman, and child inside, without losing one of their own. Nay, without even knocking down so much as a cup inside. The city itself is untouched, the stones undamaged. It is the most perfectly conceived and executed siege ever carried out, I assure you."

Wenna all but spat, "Preposterous!"

"I assume," Braylar said, ignoring her and looking at Latvettika, "that you have already dispatched riders to investigate so you can verify this for yourself. Provided they managed not to run directly into the army of Deserters now headed this way, that is."

"We are not fools. Of course we did," Latvettika said.

Of everyone in attendance, only Cynead seemed unrattled by any of this. "So, at the risk of being *obtuse*, let me see if I apprehend correctly. You somehow crossed the Veil"—he pointed at the flail—"with that, I am guessing, obliquely as it were. And on the other side, you discovered giants—"

"Eyeless horned giants," Vendurro added.

"Of course," Cynead said. "Eyeless horned giants, that for a millennium we assumed were the gods who abdicated the realms of men. Only it turns out they are nothing deified at all. That could be seen as a boon or a disaster, depending on who you ask, only you didn't. Not surprising, but you and your men offended or angered them. That alone might not have been problematic, except for the part you played in upending the powers that be and fracturing the Empire as never before. So they have finally returned, and they mean to destroy us. Is that the sum of things?"

Braylar smiled, remarkably without a twitch. "That is mostly on the mark. Only it isn't the entire race that has crossed the Veil. Only a small army. Of giants."

"Well. That *is* a relief," Cynead replied.

Commander Meodrik said, "This all sounds like the poorly-drawn panels in a bestiary, and yet you all speak of this as if it is in fact . . . fact. Do you expect me to believe this is true?"

Braylar said, "True, yes. And what's more, the Deserters do very much possess the means of destroying us. We fought them on the other side, and lost ten men to one of their warriors, but that isn't the worst of it, being a numbers and strategy game after all. You see, they have the equivalent of Memoridons called Wielders who can do things that would put these women to shame." The captain looked at his sister. "I imagine you told them of the dome Veil around the city of Roxtiniak?"

She nodded slowly, color draining from her face, looking as pale as Mulldoos, and then Braylar stared at the other Memoridons in turn. "You are all exceptionally familiar with how the Godveil operates, yes? Well, these Veildomes are no different." He looked at Darzaak and Cynead. "They fashioned the fabric of the Veil into domes around their cities as a means of defense. Only it seems they have learned a new trick."

The captain addressed the Memoridons again. "My scouts witnessed the Wielders constructing a dome around Graymoss, enveloping the city in its entirety, just as they had their own. Only this dome was not built to defend, but to annihilate. They closed it down on the city over the course of several days, shrinking it, collapsing it in on itself. The dome passed the city walls, growing tighter, and tighter still. They herded every inhabitant to the center of the city, the people inside trampling themselves in vain to try to escape the Veildome closing in around them, until there was simply nowhere left to run. They executed more than sixty thousand without a single loss on their part."

I looked at the Focus and couldn't resist saying, "Do you still consider your masters so very superior, Nustenzia?"

Before she had a chance to reply, Braylar turned back to Soffjian. "So. You see, then, that perhaps tearing off your leashes just after paying the Deserters a visit might have been a bit ill-conceived."

While Soffjian had looked somewhat stricken by the realization of a Deserter laying waste to an entire city a moment ago, her expression hardened. "Do not speak to me of timing, brother. Your kind has a manumission. Ten years a slave? Nothing. You can't possibly—"

Darzaak interrupted. "We don't have time for sibling rivalries and spats. What's done is done. How do we stop them? That's all that matters."

"No," Latvettika said, "that is not all that matters." She looked at Nustenzia. "Why now? I don't mean Vrulinka attacking—I saw it on your face; you agree with the Captain's assessment. And there is no denying that we are in a precarious position." Wenna started to interject, but Latvettika pressed on. "But if what he claims is true, and the Wielders can envelop and destroy a city with memory magic, why wall us in behind the Godveil in the first place? Why didn't they simply destroy us all when they realized we posed a threat? Why wait until now to unleash it?"

The Focus looked tired, and suddenly as old as her years. "The Godveil draws memories to it. My masters have ever used it to scry on you. But even if that told them nothing, they are tuned to the channeling of memory magic on this side, and the fetters that contained it. Between those, they felt or saw your Memoridons free themselves.

"And as to why now? The answer is simple. Discovery. Much as you yourselves only recently learned how to untangle a millennium's worth of invisible chains. My masters have skills far beyond yours, but as has been established, they are not gods. They discover things, just as you did. Vrulinka has long sought a means of manipulating the energies in this way, though I had no idea what she intended to do. I assumed she intended to use such an ability against rival city-states on the other side of the Veil." She tucked some hair behind her ear nonchalantly and said, "Clearly, she has mastered it now. And found an unexpected use for the tactic."

Wenna wasn't convinced. "Even if this is all truth, who is to say they could possibly envelop Sunwrack with such a . . . Veildome. The city is ten times the size of Graymoss, and the trebuchets on the walls would prevent any giants from getting close. Do you really think they are capable of such a feat, creating a dome that massive, or from such a distance?"

Soffjian replied, "Yes, it is ridiculous. It's not as if these Deserters created a wall of memory magic that encircled and ensorcelled the entire world. Clearly they lack the ability a thousand years later to engineer something on a much smaller scale. How absurd."

Darzaak said, "Which brings us circling back to my question. How do we plaguing stop them then?"

Braylar replied, "That is precisely why I summoned the bevy here and asked them to include you, Meodrik, and Cynead, as Commanders of three of the most influential Towers." He looked at Cynead, "And before you disparage the Jackals on size alone, recall that Commander Darzaak is still one of the most respected Commanders in Sunwrack."

Then he turned to Latvettika again. "You see, while you have control just now, it isn't exactly the kind that inspires loyalty. While some Towers have openly thrown in their lot with you, many have no desire but to see you fail and slaughtered in the streets."

"He does have a point on that score," Cynead said, smiling.

"So," Braylar continued, "in order for our stand against the Deserters to succeed, you will need the major Towers to stand as one. And that will only happen if you have respected Commanders such as these three to sway and lead."

A Memoridon with wide-set eyes and a broad nose, who looked as if she might have been hit by a shovel, spoke up. "He is a known liar. And this is simply a ploy to empower the Towers against us, to set us up for nothing but slaughter or slavery again."

Braylar regarded her coolly. "It is true, I do have a gift for deception. And I speak the truth only when it directly serves my purpose. As it does here. You will ascertain for yourselves in short order, again assuming your investigators survive. But we need to begin preparations. The threat is very much a reality. The Deserters are here, they are capable of killing off entire cities—large cities—even without bloodying their giant hands, and whatever Vrulinka's larger agenda, she certainly feels the need to wipe out the Syldoon. If we do nothing, the Empire is doomed. We have fought them. We know their strengths and weaknesses. And we can help marshal the forces to drive them back. That, and that alone, is why I am here. But we must start immediately."

The flat-faced Memoridon started to reply, but Latvettika held up a hand, and she shut her mouth. "Captain, for what it is worth, I do believe you are correct about the threat. What I fail to understand though, is why you are even here. You fled Sunwrack. Officially and formally, you are no longer even *of* the Empire. Why return and risk your lives on our behalf? What is it you hope to gain? And before you spout off some creaky platitudes about loyalty to Tower and Commander, need I remind you, you abandoned your Tower in the night, scurrying away like rats."

Mulldoos looked ready to finally disobey the order about minding his tongue, but it was Braylar's turn to hold up a hand before replying, "Given your disparate natures, and festering hatred of your former Syldoon overlords, I am sure this will be difficult for you to comprehend, Memoridon. But to a Syldoon soldier, the only thing that does truly matter is one's Tower. Creaky or not, it is reality, not platitude. And after we inadvertently helped my sister break the binds of the frame . . . " He paused and then looked at Soffjian. "Lest I forget, I must give credit where it is due—that bit of manipulation and theater was deftly done—I never suspected you were capable of such treachery."

Then he turned back to Latvettika. "After that, we saw that Jackal Tower was under your control, along with the rest, and we did leave Sunwrack. We didn't know what we could do to undermine you, but it was clear it would not happen with us caged or executed. That is why we scurried, as you say. And as to what we want—"

She interrupted. "I do hope you aren't going to suggest we relinquish or revert anything."

"Of course not," Braylar said. "I am not in a position to make suggestions. I am, however, in a position to make demands."

Latvettika was not amused. "Oh? Soffjian knows as much about these Deserters as you do, and this Nustenzia knows a great deal more. We need only their counsel to adequately prepare a defense, now that you have truly warned us. The way I see it, you don't even have enough leverage to *suggest*—"

"You are neglecting some significant facts," Braylar replied. He raised his index finger and then pointed up behind him without looking. "Fact one, my soldiers have orders to shoot you to pieces on my signal or if you make any aggressive move. Fact two"—he patted Bloodsounder with two fingers—"even if you take out everyone else in this small company and manage to strike out at the crossbows on the ridge as well, I am immune to your witchery and can take out several of you on my own. I would start with Soffjian and Nustenzia.

"Which brings us to the rather large fact three." He held up three fingers and spun them in a slow circle. "If we kill each other here, well, there you go, but the Empire is doomed. No one wants that. And if we do kill you all here, that won't free the Empire—you are obviously a multi-headed snake—but it would still leave the remaining Commanders and Memoridons clueless about the immediate danger threatening them. And we would have to begin this whole exercise again with new Memoridon envoys, and less chance of winning them over, given your corpses off to the side. And since we are short on time, that simply won't do. I would much rather we negotiate here and now. Wouldn't you? By the way, the signal to shoot you is me holding up four fingers."

Soffjian's lips were curved in the faintest beginning of a smile, and Latvettika was as silent and still as an effigy, but the other three Memoridons couldn't talk over each other fast enough, explosive objections coming so furiously that it was impossible to parse them out.

Finally, Latvettika raised her hand and silenced them. While she might not have been an empress, she clearly had their respect if not their deference. "In typical Syldoonian fashion, you overreach. But let us hear these demands."

Braylar said, "There are only two. First, your amnesty of all my men. Assuming we all survive, you will not hunt, impede, attack, or attempt to capture any of them, whether they stay or go."

Latvettika replied, "Considering that you were instrumental in ousting Cynead here, that is not an outlandish request. And the other?"

"After we help you fend off the Deserters, you allow any Tower that no longer wishes to be part of the Empire to secede."

"Secede?" she said, with a harsh laugh. "Now *that* is a rather exorbitant request."

"Demand," Braylar corrected. "But it's not so exorbitant as it first sounds. The Syldoon are practical by nature. Utilitarian. They recognize strength, power, and rally to it. Surely several Towers will pledge themselves fully to your banners, not out of fear or extortion, as is the prevailing condition now in the aftermath of your coup, but because they understand that their own future and success is more fully guaranteed if they align with the strongest faction. Which is unquestionably you. And for those Towers that don't, you would be better off jettisoning them, as they would only conspire at all times to undermine or betray you. I speak from experience."

Wenna said, "Towers have never been allowed to break off. Never."

"And Memoridons have never ruled the Empire," Braylar countered. "But today is a new day."

Latvettika looked at Darzaak and Cynead. "And does Captain Killcoin claim to speak for you?"

Commander Darzaak answered first. "This is the first I've heard of it. But it's a sound idea. And I say that not knowing if the Jackals would stay or go."

Cynead was toying with the leopard heads on his plaque belt as he considered the question. "I would never allow this man to be my proxy in any matter. But on this particular point, I find myself agreeing with Darzaak." He flashed a big smile. "Though I might keep the Leopards inside Sunwrack to reseize power, should you provide the slightest opportunity, I do think that sometimes culling the herd serves to strengthen it."

Latvettika said, "The Memoridon Assembly allowed us to treat with you here, and empowered us to weigh your information and act accordingly. But not to make promises of this magnitude."

Braylar was undeterred. "Memoridons do not have to be in the same room to convene. Certainly one among you can communicate with your sisters in

Sunwrack. I expect they are waiting to hear from you in fact even now. But I would urge you not to deliberate long."

The Memoridons rejoined the Syldoon, and Latvettika said, "The Assembly does not object in principle."

She was calm, and her delivery was unhurried, but Braylar either saw some tell or guessed as he said, "Your investigators sent word, then. They have seen the multitude of unbloodied corpses in Graymoss."

Latvettika's voice had a new edge to it. "They have. And report the same occurring at Erstbright. The city was untouched, and the populace was decimated by memory magic." She maintained her composure as she said, "So. You claim to be able to help us defeat these horned bastards. Explain yourself. Quickly."

Commander Darzaak said, "How big is this Deserter force? Around thirty thousand you said? Even with the Leopards and some allies taking heavy casualties recently, and limited time to recall any soldiers from the provinces, we can still field more than two hundred thousand. That's a huge plaguing disparity." As he watched Braylar's reaction, though, the deep lines in his face only deepened. "But something in your eyes says that won't mean what it should."

Braylar replied, "I'm afraid not. One Deserter warrior can take out ten Syldoon. And the Wielders are far more dangerous than the Memoridons. We will outnumber them, outflank them, and hopefully select terrain and ground of our choice to engage them. But we will not be able to muster a large enough force to negate their inherent advantages."

Vendurro said, "But they got weaknesses." Everyone looked at him, and he blushed a little. "Well, not many, but they have them."

"Such as?" Latvettika said.

I hadn't intended to speak, but the words were out of my mouth of their own accord. "They obviously have no eyes, so they can't perceive the world as we do, but they do see it in a way we can't. Only it does have its own weaknesses."

Latvettika favored me with a look normally reserved for the arrival of unexpected rodents. "Who is this speaking, and why should we be listening?"

Braylar looked irritated, though whether by my interruption or Latvettika's demeanor, it was difficult to say. "This is my company scholar, Arkamondos. He was the one who first uncovered the means of crossing the Veil, and was instrumental in our escaping the Deserters, based on his learned speculation and supposition."

"Very well," she said. "Proceed, scholar. Enlighten."

I took a deep breath and sought the words in my head this time before blurting them aloud. "How their senses work isn't really worth going into right now, but suffice it to say, the Deserters do not see light or color. However, they do perceive textures, contours. The physical shape of everything, in all directions at once. It is quite powerful. But also limited in some ways."

Latvettika seemed intrigued. At least marginally. "Limited how?"

"Rain, for instance," I said. "Raindrops are nothing more than tiny objects moving at great speed. They perceive those, and it confounds their senses, effectively blinding them."

Cynead looked up at the cloudless sky. "Unless your learned scholar here knows how to manipulate the weather, that Deserter fact, while utterly fascinating, is less than helpful."

Though I wasn't accustomed to arguing with emperors, deposed or otherwise, I still replied, "With respect, I was merely using that as an example. Their odd vision can be used against them. Surely there are other ways of befuddling them, confusing them, at least briefly so as to seize an advantage."

Cynead looked at Darzaak and Latvettika. "Peculiar vision that is not vision. Well. That is something we will need to consider tactically at length. Pending the Grand Memoridon's tacit approval, of course."

She barely hid a scowl as she said, "What else?"

"Well," I replied, "as I said, they do not see colors at all. You could choose to fight them in some tall grass, arrive the night before and paint areas ahead of time that are filled with caltrops, for instance. Your men would know which areas to avoid, but the Deserters could never see the paint or whitewash."

Mulldoos grinned or snarled—it was hard to say with the left side of his lips still not cooperating fully. "More devious every day, scribbler. I like it." He looked at Latvettika. "Another weakness: big bastards don't use shields that we saw. Not any. They got brass and leather armor and skin as thick as a rooter's but the fuckers are susceptible to arrows and bolts."

Darzaak tapped his sword hilt. "So back to the numbers game—we strike from range and take them out before they even get close."

Braylar said, "Bear in mind, they have staff slings. With the Deserters' size and strength, and the length of the weapon, the slings are essentially siege engines—they can launch rocks or lead shot the size of your fist from a greater distance than we can shoot our bows."

"Fair enough," the Commander said. "They strike first. But I'm guessing not all their thirty thousand have slings. We get within our range, we will have numbers again, can mow the big bastards down."

Mulldoos replied, "Stands to reason, Commander. Only these huge rootercunts got their own tricks. Besides big plaguing stones and lead, the staffers shoot pods at the onset, release a hellish smoke that brings visibility to zero and leaves you sputtering and hacking. We engaged them with crossbow cavalry just on the other side of the Veil, thinking we could just peg them to pieces from range, but they disabused us of that notion right quick."

"And what's more," Braylar added, "as the lieutenant said, they have armor of brass plates and rooter hide, and skin ten times as thick as our own. Beyond their obvious size and strength advantage, the reason they can take out so many men before falling is that they can absorb a tremendous amount of punishment. The ones we killed with crossbows looked like hedgehogs."

Soffjian said, "And let us not forget the Wielders. We fought them when they only had one or two, and we were soundly trounced. With such a sizable force, the Deserters undoubtedly brought more than one or two to this side. We will have to contend with them."

Vendurro jerked a thumb towards Nustenzia. "But we stole one of their Foci. That ought to help you Memoridons take out some Wielders, or counter them or whatever."

Nustenzia replied, "You forget, Syldoon—I am but one of many. The Matriarch will be here with her full contingent of Wielders and Foci."

"Huh," Vendurro said. "Ayyup, that's bad."

Braylar said, "And precisely why we need to explore all the ways we can take advantage of the few weaknesses the Deserters do have and begin making preparations immediately. We have many weaknesses, but time is chief among them."

Latvettika said, "Then let us conclude this clandestine meeting and return to the capital to continue discussions of strategy."

Braylar twitch-smiled. "You will forgive me, Grand Memoridon, if I do not accept your exceptionally gracious offer. We will continue discussions here about tactics and terrain and what affords us the greatest chance of achieving victory. And my company will remain outside the walls until the Jackals and other Towers march forth to engage the Deserters." He looked at me. "Arki, let the others know we will be rejoining our Jackal brethren soon enough."

I nodded and turned to go and heard Mulldoos add, "Might leave off the bit about us marching off to do battle with a huge host of Deserters to save a plaguing Empire. Leave that message to Cap. He'll deliver it so it sounds like we'll be toasting our victory over Vrulinka's corpse before the day is done."

fter we met with the Memoridons in the abandoned mine, they returned to the capital, and we remained in the hills. Two days later we rode down before dawn and waited outside Sunwrack for the bridges to roll out and the gates to open. The merlons on top of the Towers caught the first rays of light first, their fanciful and stylized representations of the various charges on display: foxes and moons, pikes and beetles, elk and horses. Having entered and left the city under the cover of night the last two times, I had forgotten just how impressive it was.

But as the gates opened and the lines of soldiers started to ride out, I realized that I didn't really know what impressive was.

Before riding with the Syldoon, I'd seen only fisticuffs or the odd knife fight in a tavern. But since joining Braylar, I'd witnessed intense combat in a wagon, bloody skirmishes in ruins and deserted streets, melees in the woods and the fringes of a town, larger battles between the Jackals and both Imperials and Deserters.

None of that prepared me for the spectacle of seeing the full might of the Syldoon Empire assembling on the broad plain around Sunwrack.

Even though I expected a massive army was going to file out of the largest city I'd ever seen, knowing it is going to happen and making your eyes accept it are two totally different things.

I was on horseback with the rest of Braylar's small company as the Elk Tower filed out of Sunwrack first, all mounted, even the infantry, their banners snapping in the morning breeze. As they left the bridge, they began forming up into columns fifty men wide and twenty deep. Even working with haste, it took time to assume their formations and continue making room for the next column and the next and all the ones after.

Vendurro was watching me watch and laughed. "Something else, ain't it, seeing a Tower ride out in force?"

473

I nodded, counting soldiers, calculating, in awe at the precision they managed even with their ranks filling out more by the minute.

Rudgi was alongside us and said, "That's nothing. This is a smallish Tower. Just wait, Arki. You're in for a real treat today. The Empire hasn't sent out an army this size in a hundred years. Maybe more."

With the sun cascading golden down the hillside, only a few wispy clouds above, and the Tower forming up as if on parade, it was easy to forget that we were all riding to face the greatest threat the Empire had ever seen. I would have been happier if storm clouds were on the horizon, as those would have at least favored us.

But Rudgi wasn't wrong. More and more Towers rode out of the four bridges of Sunwrack as the day wore on, forming up, their supply wagons with weapons and provisions and pavilions and who knew what else rolling up at the rear. The plain filled up quickly, and it was truly a spectacle unlike anything I'd ever seen, as the smaller Towers (relatively speaking—the Otters looked to be just shy of three thousand, the Hawks, around five, but both still far larger than any force I'd ever seen outside of an illuminated manuscript) gave way to the middle-sized ones, such as the Foxes, Ravens, and Jackals. I assumed the Leopards and a few of the largest would be coming sometime later, but we were done watching.

Our small company rode down, passed under the aqueduct we knew all too well, and filed in with one of the lead columns of the Jackals. Commander Darzaak was at the fore, looking grim and determined as ever, and the captain and his officers saluted him. Soffjian and a handful of other Memoridons were now a close and permanent part of his retinue, making sure their presence and control was felt. That must have galled the old man fiercely, and the other Commanders as well, but as Braylar noted at the mines, the Syldoon loyalty, unbending to their own Tower, was very malleable when it came to pledging fealty to the power of the day—some Towers had likely already sworn allegiance to the Memoridon rule, and even meant it.

Still, I didn't imagine Commander Darzaak was going to be one of those. Assuming he lived. Or that any of us did.

Part of me feared Braylar would leave me behind with the supply wagons, and part of me hoped he might. That must have registered on my face as Vendurro leaned over and said, "You'll ride with us until we get close. A few days or so. Then you'll hang back with the Commander's column. Safest place for you, really. Just stay close to Commander Darzaak. Cap and the rest of us, we'll be ahead, skirmishing and harrying the big bastards, but you'll be good back there."

Mulldoos overheard and said, "Don't coddle him, Ven, for plague's sake." He leaned out of his saddle and jabbed a finger in my chest, and I was thankful I had the gambeson on. "Listen here, scribbler. After we engage, there won't *be* a safe place. Jackals will be in the center, and right up front, and this is a plaguing Deserter army we're talking about. Not trying to make you shit yourself, but don't go into this thinking you'll be out there picking flowers or counting clouds, either.

"Could be, after we piss the huge bastards off and ride back, Cap'll want you with us, if we dismount, anyway. You can't ride for shit. Could be, though, he'll order you to stay with the Commander. Either way, you'll probably need to use that crossbow and sword before the day is done. Do what I trained you to do, and you have a halfway decent chance of not dying immediately."

As inspiring and encouraging as ever.

With several Towers ahead of us, the next three days involved a lot of eating dust and looking around repeatedly, marveling at the sheer size of the army as we made slow but steady progress through the hilly country between Sunwrack and Graymoss. One thing that became immediately apparent was that the romances and manuscript pages were completely inadequate in capturing the immense smells that accompanied a huge host on the move. The wafting stench of sweaty humanity, the multitude of horses, shit from both creatures, meat sizzling on spits, oil from the wagons. It was nearly overpowering at first.

So, too, the endless sounds of harness and armor jingling, wagon axles creaking, horses whinnying, men shouting orders up and down the lines or calling for Syldoon slave boys and girls who hadn't undergone the manumission ceremony to attend them or fetch this or that.

And in the divisions of every Tower where the Commanders and officers rode, there were always the Memoridons, silent, watching, alert, some that were surely War Memoridons, and some with more subtle skills like Skeelana, silently communicating with their sisters.

We weren't going to be on a prolonged campaign, which I was grateful for, but the number of supply wagons was also staggering, most laden with food and weapons, but some with the pavilions for the Commanders and smaller tents for their officers. For the rest of us, it was fairly simple—after horses were picketed, patrols and scouts sent out to roam the countryside far ahead, and guards posted, the nights meant a restless sleep in a bedroll on the hard cold ground. And for me, anyway, a growing dread about the battle looming ahead and a morbid curiosity about whether the Deserters had finished executing the inhabitants of Erstbright with their Veildome.

Rudgi joined me for a few hours on the second night, snuggling up against my body and falling asleep almost immediately. Exhausted from scouting, she had no interest in coupling, but the closeness of her body was a greater comfort than I imagined. She was gone before I woke up, and I might have thought I dreamed it, except her smell was still there with me.

The fourth day, we entered a broad shallow valley that sloped down below us, with the highest hills to the east and west. The ground was largely brown and tan, with a patchwork of green scrub here and there and some short, stiff (and apparently stubborn) grass growing in long winding swaths, with a stunning array of purple flowers hugging the hills to the west.

But what really stood out, and had to be the reason the army halted its march with orders being shouted and conveyed again and again like an echo, was the pattern of glaring rectangles of white across the middle of the valley floor, the whitewash practically glowing in the sun. The rectangles marking the place no man or horse should go. They took my suggestion to heart.

And then it hit me. This was where we were going to make our stand.

The army spread out across our side of the valley, the Towers maintaining integrity as they moved down to slightly more level ground, operating independently under the orders of their respective Commanders, but obviously connected by the Memoridons accompanying them, relaying silent communications across the valley to coordinate effectively and precisely.

We had to be thousands of yards across, and several hundred yards deep. The Jackals were positioning themselves roughly in the middle of the center divisions of troops, composed primarily of heavy infantry who would dismount and take up their long spears and composite bows when battle was imminent. Commander Darzaak and his officers and a small block of troops took up position behind the front divisions, I assumed because it afforded a better view with somewhat better elevation, though the incline was still very gradual on this end of the valley. The other Tower Commanders did the same, to better communicate orders.

Far off to our west, the Horse Tower in their thousands had their armored cavalry as one wing along the bottom of a fairly steep incline at the base of the hills there. I looked to the east, the brim of my kettle hat providing good shade, and there was another wing far to the east, likely also cavalry, though I couldn't make out the Tower that settled into that spot. There were hills there as well beyond the right wing, but more gradual.

Glancing to our rear, I saw the other Towers moving about, keeping their cohesion, ready to deploy their infantry, and behind those the auxiliaries and supply wagons.

It truly was a staggering sight.

I'd stopped moving, and another Jackal shouted at me. I apologized, nudging my horse along with my knees and some less hostile words of encouragement.

Vendurro was nearby and rode over. I looked around as roughly two hundred thousand Syldoon and Memoridons slowly overtook the southern expanse of the valley. "So," I said, "this is it, then?"

He nodded, grinning. "Ayyup. Good a place as any, am I right?"

I forced a nod but coughed on some dust, so was spared trying to look overly brave or confident.

He had enough for the both of us. "Kind of glad the giant bastards showed their ugly faces on this side. They killed off plenty of Jackals over there, so there'd be some revenging in store just on that account. But wiping out two whole cities? They owe us more blood than they can ever repay. Once we litter this valley with their corpses, I hope Cap leads an expedition across the Godveil again so we can kill every last one of the hulking whoresons."

I glanced around again, at the lines of soldiers spreading out, reforming, the largest host assembled in living memory and beyond. But almost none of them knew what really was heading this way, no matter how they were briefed or what the Commanders and Memoridons actually revealed. I hoped they weren't overconfident in their advantage of numbers. Numbers alone would not destroy this enemy. But they couldn't possibly understand that before fighting them.

"How's that for timing?" Vendurro pointed at Tower slaves moving among the ranks, handing out scarves. Every soldier took one and tied it around his or her neck.

I accepted mine and asked, "What is this?"

"Might only help a little, but Cap thought it would be good to have something to keep from choking to death if the Deserter whoresons launch those smoke gourds at us again. Speaking of," and he popped the last bit of egg in his mouth as Braylar and Mulldoos rode up, their faces obscured by the aventail drapes on their helms.

The captain said, "Lieutenant, it is time we reintroduce ourselves to the Deserters and show Matriarch Vrulinka some of our hospitality." He pointed to the sky. "It is an exceptionally fine day for crossbows."

"Aye," Vendurro said, dusting his hands off on his pants and turning his horse about. "That it is." He tapped the brim of his own helm and said, "Be seeing you, Arki."

Whatever words I might have chosen dried up in my mouth, so I only nodded as they rode off towards a division of crossbow cavalry that dwarfed the force the captain had led when we fled Sunwrack the first time after Skeelana's betrayal. There had to have been at least a thousand Jackals, and further up the line, another division led by another captain was forming up as well.

Both groups rode away from our line towards the north part of the valley. I watched as they carefully trotted around the squares of earth and grass ahead that had been painted white, taking the alleys between. I wondered if they were littered with caltrops.

The day was warm, but not especially hot, and still the sweat began to pour in earnest as I watched the Jackals disappear over the slight ridge at the other end of the valley.

The next two hours crept by with excruciating slowness. I kept scanning the other end of the valley, hoping to see the captain and his men return. But as it turned out, the only arrival was from the rear. The Urglovian Syldoon had sent a large contingent of war wagons to join us, and they slowly made their way to the center to help anchor it against whatever Deserter onslaught came.

They set up at least eighty war wagons there, just ahead of the Jackals, alongside Cynead's considerable Tower forces. Like all Syldoon, they knew their business and worked methodically—I watched for hours as they lined war wagons up, chained them end to end, arranged the wooden walls, set up ballistae on the wagon beds, and handed out the glaives, halberds, long spears, and extra sheaves of arrows for the composite bows as soldiers took up their positions.

But after that distraction passed, I again had to suffer my thoughts and fear. Rudgi was off scouting, Braylar and his retinue were skirmishing with a Deserter host and trying to draw them here, and while I was standing in the middle of a huge Syldoonian and Memoridon army, I felt more alone than I had in a long time. Even when I saw the wounded Hornman at the Great Fair in Alespell, it had only been me wandering for a bit, trying to clear my head. But now, for the first time since joining the captain and his company, anyone I had known for more than a few minutes was either dead or could be.

Almost everyone.

I heard her voice coming from a few feet behind me, "I am a bit surprised to see you here, young scholar. At this point, perhaps I shouldn't be—you do seem to have a habit of courting danger."

"Or," I said, not turning around, "danger just has a way of finding me."

She moved up alongside me and also looked across the scrubby floor of the shallow valley towards the other side. "Are you concerned? For the well-being of my brother? You look concerned."

It was said in such a way that I couldn't determine if she was earnest or simply trying to needle me, so I didn't reply.

"You shouldn't be worried," Soffjian said. "He is exceptionally gifted at taking care of himself."

There it was.

While I knew all too well what she was capable of, and she still made me very uneasy, I no longer quavered in her presence, and her demeanor actually irritated me enough that I replied, "It must have been satisfying."

She looked at me, eyebrows raised ever so slightly.

"To strike down Thumaar like that," I said.

Soffjian didn't change her expression, stance, or tone. Which was more than irritating. "It was necessary. I didn't take pleasure in doing it, but neither did it offend any sensibilities."

"Hmm. That surprises me a little. I mean, regardless of what hatred you harbor for your brother or whatever culpability you think he had, Thumaar was ultimately responsible for ordering the decimation and enslavement of your people. So, having the chance to not only completely thwart him, but to actually be the one to strike him dead . . . I'm surprised it didn't bring you greater satisfaction."

She spun her ranseur in the dirt, the tassels whipping around like a dancer's skirts. "By that token, you must have found it satisfying to see Skeelana killed?"

I considered a few different responses and opted for the truth. "I was the one who dealt the blow that finally killed her. And I hoped it would make me feel a great deal better than it did. She was probably going to die either way, and I could have left her to it. But I chose not to."

"Mercy," she said, rather neutrally.

"No," I replied. "Not especially. I just didn't want to hear her talk anymore."

Soffjian laughed, short and clipped.

"You have a terrible sense of humor," I said.

She replied, "I am sorry. It's just a bit ironic, is all. I was just thinking that while killing Thumaar felt a bit empty, perhaps it was because I really wanted him to know what it meant to me personally. I didn't have the time to explain. It wasn't just part of a political maneuver, or simply the transaction of another coup, but some vengeance I'd held onto for so many years it putrefied."

Soffjian favored me with a smile that didn't seem envenomed, predatory, or a disguise for calculations. "So, it struck me as funny. I wanted more time. To draw out Thumaar's suffering, to express why I did so, to convey something to the man as he writhed in pain, and was just thinking that it never works out that way. There is never enough time, and we don't often get to the words we most want to say. Whereas you just wanted Skeelana to stop talking."

I found myself smiling in return. "Well, we were in a bit of a hurry." I didn't admit that I really didn't want Skeelana suffering anymore, even if part of me felt like she deserved it.

Soffjian returned her attention to the opposite ridge of the valley. I did as well. We were both quiet until I said, "May I ask you something else?"

Soffjian said, "That depends. May I kill you for talking too much?"

I replied, "Well, you did approach me, after all."

"Point taken. What is it you wanted to know?"

I looked around at the endless soldiers everywhere, walking, lounging, napping, playing dice, arguing, looking off in the valley exactly as we were. Nearly two hundred thousand of them, with Memoridons mixed in their midst everywhere. That would be enough. It had to be.

I thought about dropping it, but then decided that with doom very possibly marching towards our position, getting husked by a Memoridon might not be the worst thing that could happen. "You used us to break Cynead's hold on the Memoridons. Do you think it's possible, when Vrulinka and her Wielders examined us, that they sensed what you planned, and wanted it to succeed, to pave the way for their own invasion? They didn't pursue us the way I expected. Maybe they allowed us to return for a reason."

Soffjian didn't reply right away, and I feared I had misstepped, but then she ground the ranseur in the earth. "Latvettika and my other sisters, they have asked me the same thing. At length, in light of recent events. I will answer you as I did them. Yes, it is entirely possible the Deserters were hoping the Memoridon coup would succeed. But also, it's immaterial.

"We are not about to rebind ourselves to the Syldoon Commanders. And the Deserters are here. They have attacked us. And we must eradicate them all, or at least defeat them decisively, to send a message to any of Vrulinka's kind that they must never venture on this side again. Or at least not for another millennium. That is all that matters just now. And if—"

She stopped as I pointed to the other end of valley as the first horsemen began to gallop over. I said, "It looks like we will have our chance soon."

"That it does, Arki. That it does. Come, let's join the Commander."

After the crossbow cavalry avoided the gleaming white patches of grass and what appeared to be dirt in the valley, I tried to calculate their numbers, but they weren't in as tight a formation as the infantry and moving fast besides. Still, it was obvious they had suffered some casualties, as the unit could not have been the size it was when they left.

Most of the mounted Jackals then veered off and rode to join the left wing of Syldoon cavalry, while Braylar and his officers made for our position. After riding through the ranks of infantry ahead of us, they dismounted near Commander Darzaak, his other officers, and the handful of Memoridons, and I was relieved to see that Braylar and his retinue were all still alive.

After the Jackals saluted, Commander Darzaak barked, "Report, Captain!"

Braylar pulled his helm and aventail off, his face red and sweaty. "As our scouts indicated, the Deserters are indeed ahead of us and heading south. And as we expected, they had their own advance party, a few hundred as it were. We harassed them, exchanged some volleys, maintained our distance, but did not engage directly."

Darzaak scratched the white stubble on his face around the prominent sideburns. "These eyes aren't what they were, but looks like you lost some men."

"Aye," the captain replied. "Only a few injuries in the first exchanges. But we harried their scouts as they made their way back towards the main host. And that's when another party came out of a nearby ravine, flanked us, and hit us hard. Only this one had a Wielder." He looked at Soffjian. "And you know just how devastating those are." He turned back to the Commander and said, "We managed to take her out, as well as half that scouting party, but we lost close to two hundred men fighting through them. As I said, our numerical superiority is not so superior as all that."

Darzaak's face grew more splotchy the angrier he got. "We best hope that sacrifice was worth it and they follow you this way. We won't get a chance to set up in another valley."

Braylar accepted a proffered costrel of water from a soldier as Mulldoos replied, "We nipped at their heels and pissed them off pretty good. The only upside to getting slaughtered so fast is we probably gave the giant horsecunts all the encouragement they plaguing need. They'll come."

"They better." Darzaak looked at Soffjian and another, pastier-looking Memoridon who wasn't kitted out for combat. "Best let your sisters know. Relay the word."

The doughy Memoridon pursed her lips but nodded as Soffjian said, "A most excellent suggestion. You do recall, however, that you are offering us your suggestions and military expertise, but not orders, Commander. Not ever again."

The Commander flushed nearly purple and looked ready to chew rocks into pebbles, his jaws were grinding so hard. "Aye, Memoridon. I'm not quite as sharp as that Cynead, though. I'll probably need to hear it a few more times before it sinks in."

Soffjian said, "Who better to remind than one with exemplary memory?"

"Quite," the Commander replied, the word nothing but gravel.

The pasty Memoridon moved away from the Syldoon officers and then stood still, eyes closed, no doubt relaying a message coded in memories to her sisters with the other Towers.

Braylar asked Darzaak, "When the Deserters arrive, do you want me to lead the crossbow cavalry on the wing, Commander?"

Darzaak replied, "Aye. You and Lieutenant Mulldoos there. Sergeant Bruznik as well. Anyone else you need. The rest can stay with me."

"As you say, Commander."

Darzaak looked at the much younger captain, rolled his shoulders back in his lamellar cuirass, and said, "It's good to have you back with us, Killcoin. Didn't really have an opportunity to say as much before."

The captain nodded. "It is good to be back, Commander."

Some younger Syldoon slaves came up to Braylar and his officers to lead the horses back to a small picket behind the Jackal column.

One of them, a stocky lad who must have been nearing his manumission, reached to take Scorn's bridle.

Braylar said, "Do take care. She is notoriously ill-tempered. Assuming you ingratiate yourself and she does not bite your face off, you will need to rub her down properly. She has ridden hard the last two days."

The Syldoon slave blanched a bit and said, "Aye, Captain," as he cautiously led Scorn away, looking at the beast as if it were a ripper rather than a horse.

I asked Braylar, "Is that something you tell grooms to keep them in line, or is she truly as vicious as all that?"

He looked at me. "Worse, in fact. Scorn bit a stable boy's ear clean off not long before we met. She is aptly named, Arki."

And well-suited to her master, I thought but did not say. I'd grown comfortable in the captain's presence, but not *that* comfortable.

Up and down the lines all around and in front of us, the infantry put their embattled long shields and long spears on the earth at their feet near the extra sheaves of arrows and had their composite bows out. I saw the ballistae operators on the war wagons in the front begin to crank their windlasses to draw the wooden trough back, the large iron-tipped arrows the size of small spears being slotted in place.

As it turned out, the anxiety and preparation were premature. It was dawn the following day before Rudgi and some scouts returned to rouse the army and announce the approach of the Deserter army.

The Deserter scouts stood tall on the horizon of the valley, massive silhouettes, even from thousands of yards away. The morning sun lit their white skin, winked on the brass plates on their hardened rooter hide armor, and flitted across those strange spikes in their great clubs.

I was with Braylar and his retinue alongside the Commander, and there were a number of curses, exclamations, and even gasps as Jackals saw the massive eyeless enemy for the first time.

More and more of the Deserters crossed the ridge, and it looked like some were gesturing in our direction.

Realizing the giants could inexplicably see with no organs to do so had some Syldoon uttering louder curses and more than one "plague me."

The Commander put his hands up to his mouth and called out, "Listen here, Jackals, this is your Commander speaking. The Deserters might be big and freakish, but our own Captain Killcoin and his boys have killed them by the score. The giants bleed. The giants die. And we're here to be sure they do both. Now quit your jabbering, steel yourselves, and do your plaguing duty, or by gods, the Deserters will be the least of your worries."

In the romances and even some of the histories, there were accounts of stirring and even lyrical speeches preceding battles, instilling courage and resolve, but that was the extent of Darzaak's. Still, it had the desired effect. The soldiers in the ranks around us shut their mouths.

It looked like other Commanders were taking the same tack, with Cynead being the most demonstrative, resplendent in his jet and gold enameled scale cuirass, the horsehair plume waving in the breeze as he rode his stallion back and forth in front of the Leopard divisions.

Latvettika was one of his Memoridon keepers, and looked on sourly as he made his showy speech that I wasn't close enough to make out.

Rudgi was nearby and said, "Gods, what a pompous ass he is. Bet Cynead wishes the Deserters actually *were* plaguing gods—more glory in the victory."

I had my crossbow in hand and was chewing on my lower lip, near to eating it as I watched half the Deserter scouting party come down the incline on the opposite end of the valley, while the remainder returned to report.

Vendurro said, "Easy there, Arki. It will be a spell yet. The huge whoresons aren't going to come screaming over the ridge and running into our spears just yet. They got to be a way out yet, and once they do show, stands to reason they got to assemble."

I forced myself to try to breathe more slowly as I looked up at the sky. It was a perfectly cloudless day, the azure above almost brilliant in its purity. "I have to admit, I was hoping for a spot of rain."

"Me too," Vendurro said. "Or at least some shade. It's going to get warm today. Little rain would sure feel good."

Rudgi said, "I have to hand it to you, Lieutenant—never seen a man more worried about creature comforts, no matter what the conditions."

Vendurro replied, "Well, I'm a creature, and I like to be comfortable. If my basic needs ain't met, I tend to get cranky. At least there's time to break our fast. That's something."

We watched along with the rest of the assembled Syldoon army as Vendurro proved prophetic—the main force of the Deserters showed up mid-morning, walking over the ridge and down the slight hill, and it was midday by the time their whole host was there, with the rooters pulling their colossal wagons behind them.

The Deserters formed a long line across the floor of the opposite end of the valley, several ranks deep, with the staffslingers mostly on the wings.

I asked, "Why aren't they in a block, or other formations like the Syldoon?"

Vendurro replied, "Them not being Syldoon, can't say for certain, but it's actually smart. They probably imagine we'll try to flank them at some point, given how we got the numbers. A long line makes that tougher."

With the sun glinting off the brass plates on the hulking warriors, and the female Deserters being shorter and much thinner, it wasn't difficult to make out the Wielders in their ranks. And with an army of more than thirty thousand, it wasn't surprising that that included hundreds of Wielders.

We had numbers, but as the captain said, that guaranteed nothing at all today.

The ballistae were prepped and loaded, the more than hundred and fifty thousand infantry had their bows ready, and with any luck, the Deserters would fall prey to whatever traps the Syldoon had prepared. We were fighting them on ground of our choosing, we were as prepared as we could be, we had a huge numerical advantage, and yet my heart felt like it might burst through my rib cage and fly free like a bloody hawk at any moment.

"What if they wait until dark?" I asked. "Wouldn't that be smart as well, given that they can sense us but we will be the blind ones?"

Soffjian walked up unnoticed, as she was so talented at doing. "That would be problematic, it is true. But we anticipated as much, and brought thousands of lanterns and torches. You can be sure every one of them will be lit if the Deserters hold for nightfall."

"Not ideal," Vendurro said, "but then neither is fighting giants at all, really. We'll do what needs doing."

But then the line of Deserters started to slowly advance across the valley, the warriors and Wielders, as well as the rooters pulling the wagons.

"Hmmm," Soffjian said. "Strange. I actually assumed they would wait."

Rudgi replied, "Are they worried about being penned in? Is there another Syldoon force riding from the provinces?"

"An astute question. There is, in fact, another force coming," Soffjian replied. "But it is several days out yet. And even if their scouts sighted that army, it is considerably smaller than the one in front of them, and not likely to startle them into acting rashly."

Vendurro said, "Anvil's a lot bigger than the hammer, but the hammer does the pounding. Maybe they did a forced march and are coming in from the rear. Like you said, the smart play would be to wait for dark, but here they come . . ."

Witnessing a huge force of Deserters marching across a valley towards us was more terrifying than I imagined. Perhaps it was good there were only a few handfuls of us in this host who had seen what the giants were capable of.

With their huge legs and long strides, it didn't take them long to cross half the valley.

When they were still more than six hundred yards out, the line stopped.

Some Deserters moved among the human slaves that were helping drive the wagons, and I wondered if Bulto were still alive, and if so, if he was hoping his masters might be destroyed or we might for breaking our promise and leaving him behind.

The Deserters were unloading something, though we didn't have enough elevation to make out what it was.

Rudgi said, "What do you suppose—"

But the answer revealed itself before the question was done. The Deserters were passing out huge rectangular sections of wood that were bigger than barn doors, like massive sections of palisade walls, and twice as thick from the looks of it. The warriors slung their great clubs and staffslings on their backs, hefted the huge panels, and then positioned them so the edges overlapped as they created a wall as well as a roof for the entire line.

"Plague me," Vendurro said, "but that's clever. They know how many bows we got on this side, just aching to use them. But that there is better than any shield wall. We were hoping to shoot them to pieces, but guessing we could loose a hundred million arrows now and it wouldn't make a difference. Plaguing clever bastards."

The line started to move forward again, leaving the wagons behind, progressing more slowly, but inexorably towards us.

When they were five hundred yards out, I saw the infantry in all the blocks pull arrows out of their quivers at their sides, Tower after Tower of them, as far as I could see. Then I heard the strain of the composite bows as they drew them back, bows titled up, not aiming towards targets, but intending to hit the area the Deserters were marching into at the extreme edge of their range.

As the Deserters came a few strides closer, I heard officers call out "loose," and it was nearly one voice, as a hundred thousand arrows filled the sky, their dark shafts thicker than rain, blackening the blue, and the sound of their flight like a storm wind.

Thousands struck the earth in front of the Deserter line, tens of thousands maybe, but the majority slammed into the giant wooden rectangles thicker than any human shield. And while the Deserter line had suddenly sprouted over fifty thousand shafts, the wooden barricade they held aloft and before them protected them completely.

The Syldoon drew back and unleashed another volley, and another, but the Deserter host kept coming, warriors and Wielders both safe behind and under their makeshift portable palisade.

Suddenly, the crossbow in my hand felt as useful as one of the ink quills in the writing case on my back. But that didn't stop the Syldoon from sending more volleys, and still more, until I heard Darzaak scream, "Hold, lads! Hold!"

I thought he must have realized the futility of shooting still more arrows, but when I looked across the valley I understood. The earth all around the Deserter line had so many arrows sticking up it looked like they were walking through thick reeds. But twenty or thirty yards in front of the line, the first rectangles of white were untouched—the earth and scrub that had been whitewashed were free of arrows.

The ballistae on the wagons began launching their projectiles, and they arced much less than the arrows, slamming into the wooden face of the makeshift palisade wall the Deserters had in front of them. The line suddenly slowed. I hoped it was because some of the spear heads had penetrated deep enough to damage the giants holding the panels, but more likely, it was because some of the shafts dipped and jammed into the earth.

Gaps started to form in the line briefly, but the Wielders ordered them to form up again, as the warriors holding the giant plank protection broke the shafts that had lodged in the earth, or dislodged them.

Then they were moving forward again.

And that's when I heard several loud thumps in quick succession.

I looked to my left and saw the long arms of ten trebuchets appearing above one of the hills just past the wing of cavalry, the slings empty and the huge round stones flying high through the air. These weren't the massive siege engines on top of the Towers along the walls of Sunwrack, but still large enough to drop stones half the size of barrels.

The trebuchet teams were winching the arms back down even before the first huge projectiles struck. Most of them hit the earth behind the Deserter line, bouncing until they nearly struck the rooter wagons far behind them. Two hit the ground before the line, bouncing high twice and then crashing into one of the front panels.

But two hit several rows back, shattering arrow shafts, smashing the wooden panels underneath, and creating holes in the coverage.

Commanders everywhere ordered the infantry to loose their arrows again, but while some inevitably made it through the gaps and injured Deserters, they were quick to shift their line and close them up.

Still, they recognized the danger the trebuchets posed and the Deserter line began to move faster.

And that was when they hit the first patches of whitewashed ground three hundred yards away.

Suddenly the cohesion of the front line broke completely, as several Deserters disappeared, breaking through thatch mats that covered pits.

"Spikes!" Vendurro called out. "Fall on them, you fuckers!"

He got his wish, as several Deserters in the rows behind them carried into the pits as well, unable to slow their momentum in time.

That was far more devastating than some caltrops.

Vendurro whooped and orders went up and down the line before the infantry resumed unleashing volleys of arrows that struck Deserters by the hundreds or thousands, now that big sections of their wooden wall had disappeared into the pits and their line was broken.

I heard a series of loud whumps off to the east as several of the trebuchets shot their large stones into the Deserter host, again collapsing sections of the makeshift roof, creating more openings for arrows to rain down.

Four more trebuchet arms flew up as the counterweights dropped, but this time they shot what looked like large sacks high into the air.

Forty or fifty arrows flew from behind the hill, many missing the mark, but several struck the sacks at the apex, and suddenly they erupted, pouring ash down on the Deserters, and the sacks that hit the ground exploded into an ashy cloud as well.

Rudgi said, "It's not rain, but it's not half bad, either." She punched me in the arm. "Looks like you gave them some good ideas. Having no eyes might do these huge bastards in before they even get to this side."

The Deserters closed the ranks again quickly, reforming lines as another volley of arrows flew across the valley. But it was obvious we'd done some damage, and now some of them might even be blinded or disoriented by the ash as they tried to navigate around the pits. It looked like Rudgi was right.

And that's when my flesh went pebbly with goosebumps as a chill washed over me.

A hundred yards ahead of us a Veil suddenly appeared, spreading in both directions until it covered the valley floor, the weft and weave of energy like a mystical tapestry unrolling. While it wasn't close enough to directly affect the Syldoon host, it did cut across the hill exactly where the trebuchets were and I heard shouting carrying briefly from that direction, faint and warbled, before it was cut off completely.

The infantry kept filling the sky with arrows, but they disappeared from sight when they passed through the Veil, so there was no way to tell how much damage they did.

A few moments later, thousands of projectiles flew out of the Veil in our direction. I instinctively lifted my shield, as did the soldiers around us, and thought they had to be the stones launched from the staffslings before realizing they were the gourds or clay canisters that released the thick oily smoke when they struck the ground or shield faces in the Syldoon divisions.

Being among the Commander, Memoridons, and Jackal officers, we were back far enough not to be hit directly, but the smoke wafted back towards us, and I heard the coughing rolling back with it as most of the Syldoon squares were lost from view.

Even though I didn't endure the worst of it, my eyes immediately began to water and my throat burned, as this smoke or gas seemed even more potent than the kind the Deserters had used when they captured us on the other side of the Veil. I pulled the scarf over my nose, but even some distance from the most concentrated clouds, it didn't help a great deal.

Another volley of canisters followed, smashing into the lines and releasing still more clouds of the noxious stuff among the Syldoon. The entire army wasn't affected—the Deserters simply didn't have enough slingers to blanket the entire side of the valley with the smoke—but enough that the deluge of arrows suddenly cut off to a sprinkle, as most of the Syldoon were struggling to see or breathe.

Tears were pouring from Commander Darzaak's eyes as he yelled through his scarf, "Soffjian! You've seen this! How long until it clears?"

She had her own scarf in place, red of course. "If they ever run out of ammunition, you mean? Several minutes. At least."

"Fall back!" Darzaak ordered.

The doughy Memoridon closed her red-rimmed eyes, and Soffjian didn't rebuke the Commander this time.

A moment later, Doughy said, "Latvettika concurs. We fall back."

"Plaguing right we do." Commander Darzaak barked the order, and a soldier next to him pulled his scarf down long enough to fix his lips to the end of a complex horn that curled around his shoulders, then he blew and gave three short brassy blasts.

I heard the same signal repeated up and down the line, and then we were all retreating, trying to put some distance between us and the canisters that continued to suddenly appear through the Veil and drop out of the sky.

Slaves broke down the horse pickets and led the beasts away, and the Tower Commanders and personal retinues followed, least affected by the smoke. We walked backwards, and I watched as the staggered lines of Syldoon came, many dragging their brethren along, trying to maintain order while shaking off the effects of the wafting blue-gray smoke.

When we'd gone thirty or forty yards up the gently inclining hill, the Commanders ordered the trumpeters to relay another order with two short blasts, and the lines tried to reset.

Tens of thousands of Syldoon still seemed to be struggling, maybe as many as half our host, even with the relatively cleaner air, but they were still hardened professionals. While they faced an enemy unlike anything they had ever seen, decades of drilling and training seemed to break the engagement down to things they knew and understood. Even the ones who could barely see through their tears dropped their spears and shields on the earth again, took up their bows, and began nocking arrows. A moment later, another substantial volley arced through the air, into the Veil, and hopefully into the pale skin of the enemy on the other side.

The next volley was heavier still, as more Syldoon obeyed the command to loose.

More clay canisters came our way by the hundreds, possibly the thousands, but the majority struck the ground we had abandoned. And after a few more volleys, the canisters stopped coming altogether.

Vendurro said, "Think they're out?"

"Maybe," Rudgi said, "or up to something else."

The infantry kept shooting arrows by the tens of thousands, blocking out most of the sky each time, and I watched them disappear into the Veil again and again, wondering what they were striking. Had the Deserters made it past the series of pits? Surely their protection must have suffered to do so.

The doughy Memoridon looked at Soffjian, then the Commander, then back to Soffjian again, clearly uncertain about the protocol before announcing to both of them, "Latvettika wants to strengthen our position. Reclaim the war wagons and the ground we gave up." She said this as a flat declaration rather than a decisive order or even a question.

I looked at the hazy smoke below us, thinner and dissipating, and saw the shadows of the war wagons, now unmanned.

Darzaak pulled his scarf down away from his mouth, face going crimson. "We have no plaguing idea where the enemy is right now. Not a one. They could be retreating, they could be moving up into the hills. So unless the

Grand Memoridon can squeeze her eyes real tight and make *that* go away"—
he pointed at the Veil shimmering across the valley floor—"maybe we ought
to hold the higher ground here and not fret so much about the godforsaken
wagons until we get some real intelligence."

Soffjian started to reply when I heard shouting from several quarters and
looked ahead.

The Deserters walked through the Veil, undamaged by the shimmering
warp and weft of memories that composed it, their mobile palisade bristling
with so many arrows it was difficult to see the wood they were buried in.

But no many how many Deserters had been caught in the pits or struck
by arrows or trebuchet stones, they had regrouped, reformed, and were now
coming for us again.

"Will that suffice for reconnaissance?" Soffjian asked. "Order the advance,
Commander. Now."

Darzaak gave the trumpeter a brief nod, and he blew one long, hanging
note, and the Jackals began surging forward, the lines mostly even as they
moved at a quick march to reclaim their initial position, the second and third
blocks of infantry behind loosing arrows at our foes while waiting for the first
divisions to advance.

Everywhere around us, trumpets blew the same extended blast, and the
Syldoon army moved forward as the Deserters continued to emerge through
the Veil.

Commander Darzaak said, "Two hundred wagons. Giving up good position for two hundred plaguing wagons. Makes no—"

He stopped as he saw what we all did—a volley of stones arcing towards
us, released by Deserter staffslingers. The Syldoon didn't need a trumpet to
tell them to halt and bring their embattled shields up, locking them edge to
edge as thousands of stones larger than fists rained down.

Most struck the squares of troops ahead of us, and I heard screams and
shouts and curses from the Jackals and the Otters alongside them. While
the stones weren't launched from a trebuchet, they still had more than
enough weight and momentum to batter through any shields that didn't
make it up in time to bear the weight with the rest. I saw one Syldoon bent
over, fumbling to get his composite bow in his quiver while slipping his
arm inside his shield, and a large stone turned the top part of his head to
red mist.

A few of the stones flew further, some landing near us, and one striking a Jackal in the shoulder, crushing bone and likely knocking his arm from its socket.

Vendurro and Rudgi pulled me under their shields. He said, "Get your shield up there, Arki!"

I did as he commanded, but the first barrage was over and already the Syldoon were answering, volleys of arrows flying free.

Looking down the incline, I saw the Deserters had closed the gap considerably, and were nearly to the empty war wagons. They split around them, makeshift palisades still up, absorbing most of the arrows as they picked up speed, their huge legs churning.

The front lines of the Syldoon formed their phalanxes, bows back in quiver cases, shields up, long spears angled over them, prepared to withstand the charge, while the squares behind kept shooting over them, but hitting very little but the wooden panels or the arrows already embedded in them.

"So much for not having plaguing shields," Vendurro muttered.

I thought about Mulldoos and Braylar and glanced over at the crossbow cavalry. They were still holding their posting but shooting crossbows at the staffslingers who had fallen back behind the ranks of warriors holding the palisades. Dozens went down, bolts sticking out between the leather and brass armor, but that didn't stop another vicious volley from heading our way.

Most were aimed at the infantry still wielding bows and came whistling in a nearly flat trajectory. All across the line, those blocks of archers didn't have time to duck or grab their shields and were struck down, bones crushed, helms stove in, sometimes two or three soldiers taken out by a single stone.

I looked around my shield, just as the Deserters closed in on the first line of Syldoon, sprinting now. I expected them to discard the wooden walls in favor of their weapons, but they kept the palisade ahead of them and charged.

Spears struck the wood and shattered, and then the giants hit the phalanxes, smashing into the first line, the second, sending bodies flying as they used the huge panels like a ram and knocked soldiers into their brothers and sisters or trampled them under.

I heard myself gasp, watching the ranks of Syldoon mowed down and battered out of the way, spears completely ineffectual, screaming, cursing, dying by the hundreds. The Deserters smashed their way ten men deep in each square, twenty, into the next square, and then starting laying about with the huge palisade pieces, swatting Syldoon in all directions, annihilating the integrity of the lines and formations, bellowing inexplicable war cries or simply expulsions of rage as they did.

The squares behind loosed as best they could, but they were down to their final sheaves now, and while they eventually took Deserters out, it was only after each one had killed dozens of Syldoon and broken the ranks to pieces. The giants waded into the huge gaps in the lines, most of these with their great clubs out now, spikes bloody as they wreaked havoc, smashing and puncturing bodies on all sides.

Deserters that stopped to swing the palisades or switch to their clubs were struck by arrows or stabbed with spears and eventually fell, but only after devastating even more of the Syldoon ranks. And the arrows seemed to be nearly exhausted now.

While the heavily armored archer phalanxes might have been a tremendous formation against nearly any other foe in the world, the giant Deserters had outwitted them, and everywhere I looked, the lines were fractured and buckling, in disarray, with thousands of Deserters still ramming their way through the tight ranks of men, palisade pieces obliterating anything that stood in their path. And while the Syldoon might have been able to quickly maneuver against any human army, pivoting and bringing those thousands of spear points to bear, once the Deserters blasted through the first ranks, the weapons were nearly useless.

To our right, a Deserter made it through the first squares of infantry and kept on going, charging towards the Otter Commander and his household guard. The Syldoon formed up quickly, wielding melee weapons and shields. I thought they would all be trampled and destroyed, but a Memoridon stepped out of the retinue, held her hands aloft, and then attacked exactly as Soffjian must have instructed, bombarding the giant with human memories.

He slowed, staggered, dropped the wooden wall, and then fell to one knee as the Syldoon surrounded him and hacked him to pieces. After he had slain no less than thirty soldiers.

The warriors, armed with wood and clubs, many with legless javelin throwers on their backs, were greatly outnumbered at the start of the battle, but they changed the red ratio quickly, tearing through the Syldoon squares and decimating the army. It happened with horrible and brutal speed.

Darzaak gave a hand signal, and the trumpeter blew four undulating blasts. This was picked up by other trumpeters and repeated.

Soffjian looked at the Commander. "Latvettika will not be pleased."

"Latvettika can plaguing take it up after," the Commander said.

The Deserters had spread their line as wide as they could to prevent being flanked, but now that the center of the Syldoon had wavered and been driven back, the wings of cavalry and outer battalions of infantry rode and charged forward, curving towards the outnumbered Deserter host like a crescent or the pincers of a bull crab.

I glanced over as the crossbow cavalry wheeled towards the edge of the Deserter line, loosing hundreds of bolts at the warriors and Wielders, and saw that the same was happening with the cavalry on the right wing.

If the center could hold out, we could overwhelm the Deserters and strike them from the sides and rear.

Darzaak said, "And here's something else she won't like. The Memoridons have to get in the fray. I saw your sister bring a Deserter to his knees. We need to take it to them. Now."

Soffjian rubbed her injured shoulder, breathing heavy, indecisive for a moment, and then she nodded and looked at her doughy companion. "He's right. If the center breaks, we all die. Tell her to commit us to battle."

And that's when the Deserter Wielders went on the offensive.

We were moving forward, my hands sweaty on the hilt of Lloi's sword and the strap of the shield, blood pounding in my ears, running towards the Jackals who were fighting the giant Deserters in their midst, when the Wielders demonstrated their power.

The right wing of cavalry, at least eight thousand strong, was charging the Deserter flank, striking them with lances, riding off before the Deserters could close and destroy many of them, when large pockets were suddenly trapped in five Veildomes, the memory energy pulsing, nearly opaque, flowing like oil over water, and slowly growing smaller.

The remaining horsemen rode clear, wheeled away, and in some cases didn't have time to stop themselves from running right into the shimmering walls of the domes, and were struck dead immediately.

"Plague me . . ." Vendurro said as we jogged forward.

Commander Darzaak called out, "The task at hand, Lieutenant!" as we reached the rear ranks of a square of Jackal infantry in complete disarray, the Syldoon soldiers still struggling to form up to use their spears against the Deserters.

Out of the corner of my eye, I saw more glowing domes appear out of thin air, capturing or killing large chunks of the left wing, but the Commander was right—our threat was much closer.

Thirty Deserters ahead were fracturing the lines, destroying the ranks, some still swinging the wooden palisade pieces about, but most having switched to their spiked great clubs.

Either way, the phalanx formations were not serving the soldiers well—once the Deserters blasted past the initial forest of long spear points, the Syldoon were getting destroyed.

The Commander called out, "Sidearms, you dim bastards! Sidearms! They get close to you, drop your plaguing spears and draw your sidearms!"

The Jackals were caked in blood and sweat and the residue from the smoke gourds, and the reek of near panic was in the air, but seeing their Commander armed and wading into battle seemed to steel their resolve. The soldiers formed up a shield wall, with the first two ranks wielding spears, but the ranks behind drawing their swords, warhammers, maces, and axes.

Soffjian had her ranseur in one hand but was so haggard, it looked like she might fall over or rip her wound bloody again the moment she tried to use it.

I was standing between Rudgi and another Jackal. A group of ten soldiers from the war wagons saw us advancing and sidled in behind the spears, their glaives and halberds and bardiches at the ready.

The Deserters dispatched the remaining pocket of soldiers ahead, one of them kicking a body off his great club, when they sighted us and charged.

The spearmen dropped their stances, dug in their heels, grounded their spears as best they could, and braced for impact.

Soffjian stood tall, arms outstretched, fingers splayed.

Nine Deserters in the front of the wedge faltered and then fell, stunned, tripping up some behind. The rest came on undeterred, knocking spear points aside or snapping the hafts with swings from their great clubs.

Some Deserters were struck, one or two impaled and not making it to the men holding the spears, and one was run through, a spear bursting through the flesh above his hip and out the other side. But the others bludgeoned their way in and then kicked at the shields or threw their huge forearms into them, breaking the line completely before swinging their clubs into the men, driving them back.

The Syldoon from the war wagons rolled out from behind the shields and attacked the Deserters on the edge with their polearms, drawing some off, and those of us with sidearms moved forward to fill the gaps and attack.

A Deserter hit a Syldoon in front of me with the backswing of his club, impaling the man in the neck, but there was a moment he had trouble shaking the body free. Commander Darzaak came in and buried the blade of his axe in the outside thigh of the giant.

The Deserter roared, jerking back, pulling the axe with it, finally ripping his club free from the dead Syldoon, and raised it high to bring it down into Darzaak. Rudgi and I both moved in at the same time—she thrust her sword into the creature's knee, and I slashed at the hip above the axe.

The giant tottered, lost its balance, grabbed the edge of a shield, and pulled two Syldoon with it. Rudgi darted in, as did several other soldiers, and attacked the giant before it had a chance to regain its feet or fend them off.

I looked at Darzaak as he bent over to retrieve his axe, and then behind him, past the Deserters, to a group of Wielders fifty yards away, surrounded by a handful of human females who could only be Foci.

The Wielders had their thin, pale arms outstretched, horned heads tilted in our direction, robes flowing in the arid breeze.

And then I realized the one in the center had on a cloak of dead flowers, and I could almost sense Vrulinka looking at us—Soffjian, me, the others she'd held captive in Roxtiniak—and heard a ghostly whisper, *"You carry the plague . . . it is who you are . . ."*

Then the air around us crackled, and was replaced by the warping Veildome, some fifty yards across, blocking out the blue sky. And growing smaller. I could feel it even if I couldn't see it at first.

The Deserters fought on, smashing into the lines of Syldoon around me, ahead of me. And it was everything I could do not to throw my weapon on the ground and drop to my knees.

We were doomed. Even if we somehow defeated the giants in there, the dome itself would crush us with its memory storm soon enough.

Doomed.

But then I saw several things almost as a frieze, exactly as Braylar had once described sometimes happening . . . Vendurro spinning away from a spiked great club, shield up, working with three other Jackals to try to flank the giant and force it to take on only one of them . . . Rudgi slamming the pommel of her sword against her shield and trying to get the attention of a Deserter standing above the body of a fallen Syldoon, one huge leg rising up as it prepared to drive it down to crush the soldier to death in the dirt . . . Soffjian stumbling forward, face ashen but for the pulsing blue lightning-bolt vein, leaning on her ranseur with one arm, the other outstretched, hand shaking, fingers not quite splayed, trying to summon the energy to combat the dome or stun more of the Deserters.

I threw my sword at the Deserter about to step on the soldier. It spun end over end, and the pommel hit the giant in the shoulder before the sword dropped to the ground next to the wounded Jackal. The creature put its foot down and turned to face Rudgi, changing the grip on his great club, the translucent spikes seeming like a mix of milk and oil.

She circled it as it came for her, and I looked around wildly, picked up one of the spears on the ground, and ran forward.

The Deserter swung the club and Rudgi managed to dance away from it, still in a crouch, sword tucked behind the shield. She drew it towards her, and I drove the point of the spear into the back of the giant's neck with all my weight behind it.

It froze for a moment, and I was sure I had somehow slain the Deserter, but then it reached back, plucked the spear out of its neck, and turned to face me.

I instinctively started backing away and reached behind me to try to pull the crossbow to the front, but the strap caught on the edge of my writing case, and I nearly laughed and yelped like a madman at the irony.

But then Rudgi darted behind the Deserter, slashed it across one exposed hamstring, moved with it as it tried to turn to face her, and sliced the next as well.

The Deserter fell forward, breaking its fall with one arm, but then three more Syldoon hacked at it from behind and finally took it out.

The remaining Syldoon formed up and faced the Deserters in our dome. Soffjian had managed to stun a few more and looked ready to drop, mostly held up by the Commander. We were down to fifty soldiers, and there were at least ten Deserters about to charge us again.

I had been wrong. The dome wouldn't have time to shrink enough to kill us after all.

And then I did laugh as I worked the devil claw and dropped a bolt in.

Vendurro looked over at me, questioning, and I pointed up at the dome. "A good day for crossbows, am I right?"

He laughed as well as the Deserters came for us, only the dome suddenly disappeared—the bright blue sky above was so brilliant I gaped and felt more laughter bubbling up.

And then I saw why it had vanished.

Vrulinka had a crossbow bolt buried in the side of her throat and was reaching up, running her long fingers over the fletching gently, as if it were part of a necklace she was about to reposition for better effect. Then Braylar rode past, throwing his crossbow behind him and pulling

Bloodsounder in time to strike her on the back of the head, dropping her to her knees.

Mulldoos galloped past as well and sliced off the top of her skull with his falchion for good measure, thick strands of mane fluttering to the ground before she toppled over.

One of the Wielders turned and swung the elongated translucent spine at Braylar as he passed, striking him across the chest and vaulting him out of the saddle.

And then hundreds of Braylar's crossbow cavalry rode into the rear of the Deserters attacking us and I lost sight of the captain and the Wielder who struck him.

The Deserters took out a dozen more Syldoon and half as many horses, but they were quickly overwhelmed and cut down from all sides.

There was still fighting occurring up and down the line, but the Syldoon wings, while depleted, managed to flank the remaining Deserter forces now that the Wielders were taken out. And the Memoridons stepped in, stunning huge pockets of Deserters with the abundance of toxic human memories at their disposal.

With the Matriarch dead, the tide turned quickly. I walked among the giant corpses of Deserters, the punctured and mangled corpses of human soldiers, moved past shattered spears and broken bodies, ignoring the moans from the injured and the sounds of combat near and far.

The captain was lying on his back, with Scorn standing nearby, and Bloodsounder a few feet from his hand. I ran over to him as he struggled to sit up and fell back to the ground.

"My helm . . ." Braylar said, voice loamy. "Take it . . . off."

I knelt next to him and called over my shoulder, "Water! Get me some water!"

"Wine . . . make it wine . . ." He coughed as I undid the strap and pulled the aventail up.

Bloody spittle was all over his lips and chin. "What part of *off*. . . do you not . . . understand?"

"I'm sorry," I said and slowly pulled the helm free.

Braylar turned and looked at the body of the Wielder nearby. "Her face . . . bitten off . . ." then he grunted as he looked at Scorn. He gasped and said, "Told . . . you."

I nodded slowly as I smiled and tried not to cry, vaguely aware that others had joined us.

"Gods, Cap," Mulldoos said, his slurry voice catching. I looked up at him as he ripped off his own helm and yelled, "Vendurro! Over here! Now, you skinny bastard!"

I passed the captain the only flask I had. He took a small drink of water, swirled it around his mouth, then turned his head and spit pink water out. "Better. Now . . . wine . . . yes?"

"I don't—" I said, then looked at Mulldoos and Vendurro and Rudgi as they joined us. "Wine? Does anyone have wine?"

Vendurro slowly knelt down as well. "Cap?" he asked, quietly. "Are you—"

Braylar nodded at Vendurro. "No. My ribs are . . . shattered." He spit up some more blood. "Some in my . . . lungs."

Mulldoos turned and yelled, "Wine, you plaguing whoresons! Give me some wine now!" to no one and everyone.

Braylar looked up at what remained of his retinue. "If I die . . . waiting for wine . . ." he said through shallow breaths, "I will haunt . . . every one of you . . ."

A young Jackal who must have only just had his manumission ran up to us, handed Mulldoos a flask. The pale boar unstoppered it, eyes wet, then said to the soldier, "Good lad. Now get the fuck out of here."

The Jackal nodded quickly, backing away. Mulldoos knelt and brought the flask to Braylar's mouth, tipped it up.

A great deal of red didn't make it anywhere, but at least it disguised the blood as it ran down the captain's chin.

Braylar coughed, sputtered, and tried to raise a hand, but then dropped it as Mulldoos took the flask away.

"Gods be . . . cruel," the captain wheezed, chest rattling, "but that is . . . bitter . . ."

That was the last thing he said just before Soffjian approached, leaning on Commander Darzaak.

She saw him and stumbled. "Bray . . ." The Commander kept her on her feet, but she pushed away from him, nearly falling again before jabbing the ranseur into the earth. "Braylar?"

Captain Braylar Killcoin stared unblinking into the brilliant blue sky.

Mulldoos stood, tears leaving jagged tracks on the dirt on his cheeks. "Too plaguing late."

The Lieutenant walked over to Bloodsounder, stared down at it, fists clenched, chin on his chest.

I wiped the wine of the captain's face as best I could, though it was difficult to find any cloth clean enough not to make things worse, and it was hard seeing what I was doing through the tears in my eyes.

Finally, I gave up and rose just as Soffjian used the ranseur to lower herself to the ground, clenching her teeth. She reached out, closed his eyes, then put her hand gently on the captain's chest, and closed her own eyes.

She stayed like that for a long time before finally whispering, "I warned you to go, you fool . . ."

"And if he plaguing tucked tail and left Sunwrack behind," Mulldoos said, standing over her, "you'd all be dead. Syldoon would all be dead. Witches, Towers, every last plaguing one of us. He saved our sorry asses." His voice broke, but he kept talking. "It were me, I would have killed you a long time ago. Half tempted to do it right now. But he saved you. So there it is. Not undoing what he did. Not today."

He shook Bloodsounder, watched the Deserter heads clink together. "But if you and your bitch sisters don't honor your promise, I'll kill every last one of you. If Commander says the Jackals are pulling out, or any other Tower for that matter, and you try to stop them, this plaguing flail will be the last thing you see. You understand me? Don't think the promise died with him. Because it didn't."

Vendurro said, "Mull, maybe—"

"Don't feel anything yet," Mulldoos said. "Not even sure it'll work for me. Maybe it was just Cap. Maybe it won't protect me from witchery. Maybe it will." He looked back at Soffjian. "But you don't honor your plaguing word, you can be sure we'll all find out in a real plaguing hurry."

Soffjian sighed and nodded. Then she slowly got to her feet. I reached out a hand to offer her help, and she shook it off, using the ranseur to support her weight instead.

Then she turned and looked at us each in turn, eyes wet. I expected her to say something, anything—profound, inane, uncharacteristically revealing, biting. But instead she wiped her face, gave a small cryptic smile that seemed both sad and amused at something only she could appreciate, turned, and hobbled away.

Rudgi looked at Bloodsounder, then up at Mulldoos. "Is that . . . do you think it might not be a, you know, a bad idea . . ."

Mulldoos was staring at Braylar, the tears still coming, and he sucked the snot into his throat, turned, and spat it into the dirt. "Terrible plaguing idea. No two ways around it," he said. "Maybe I'll live to regret it, maybe not. But if it grants immunity to memory witches . . . " He shrugged his big shoulders, then tucked Bloodsounder in his belt.

Mulldoos looked around at us and wiped his face again. Then he slipped his head back into his helm and buckled it on, before pointing across the valley at some of the fighting that had moved off. "Those giant rootercunts are trying to desert again, looks like. Cap was a rigid bastard sometimes. Lot of things he didn't budge much on. Chief among them, though, was doing your duty. And he might just haunt the lot of us if we skirt ours. So let's go hunt some Deserters down before they make it to the Veil, and come back and give this man the proper sendoff he deserves after we plaguing earn it."

Rudgi and Vendurro both said "Aye" quietly, and Mulldoos and the sergeant walked off to get their horses.

Vendurro looked at me then, wiped his eyes with his forearm. "Gods . . . first time in my life I might have lost my plaguing appetite." He looked up at the sky as the tears came, then slapped his face. "Like Mull said, got duty to do, yet. Got to ride. What about . . ."

"What about me?" I asked.

"Ayyup," Vendurro said. "What about you?"

I thought about it, looked over at Braylar, then around at the incredible carnage and death everywhere in the valley. "Well . . . you're all still here. Bloodsounder is still here. The weapon and the man, looks like."

Vendurro grinned and then seemed to feel guilty, as it disappeared. "He'll plaguing hate that, he will."

"And I'm still the Arc. I'm a horrible rider. I'd only get one of you ki—. I'd only get in the way. But I'll be here when you get back."

I looked around at the battlefield again. "There are a lot of wounded. I'm sure I can make myself useful."

Vendurro started to turn to look at Braylar, then forced himself not to, looking instead at the Deserters fleeing the valley, eyes full of wrath. "Aye. Duty all around, then."

"Duty all around, then."

Vendurro ran off to find his horse, or any horse, and when I saw Scorn still standing over the fallen captain, I nearly wept.

But I forced myself to look away as well. Plenty of time for that.

Duty all around.

I t felt like years had passed since Captain Killcoin originally solicited my services. I distinctly remember his words in that dingy inn in Rivermost, when he assured me I would accompany him on an exceptional venture with far-reaching consequences that involved the expiration of a way of life, the death of a kingdom, and the redrawing of a map.

Somehow, I doubt this was what he had in mind.

Braylar intended me to chronicle the downfall of the Kingdom of Anjuria, I'm sure, but instead, I witnessed what lay beyond the Godveil for the first time in human history— irrevocably altering the map—and saw the most significant coup the Syldoon Empire had ever experienced. Would that result in the death of a body politic? Was the Empire truly crumbling now, right before our eyes, because we had unwittingly assisted Soffjian in freeing the Memoridons? Was it truly the Syldoon Empire anymore now, or was it now the Memoridon Empire? Could it last, as crippled and compromised as it was? The army had survived the Deserter incursion, driven them back across the Veil, but at horrendous cost.

All the lives lost along the way, and the widowcoin being doled out fast enough to empty the Tower coffers as Syldoon and Memoridon alike buried their dead and tried to make sense of the aftermath.

Braylar had no heirs, no widow or fatherless children left behind. A blessing and a curse, really. No one understood him like his men, so it was just as well they were his only family—if he had any wife or offspring, I imagine their mourning would have been suffused with bitterness, just like Glesswik's widow.

The captain had been exceedingly difficult to deal with on the best of days, and I had questioned him past the point of safety on numerous occasions, had been mortified at some of his decisions—many, in truth—but I knew I would never meet a man of his ilk again.

Perhaps that was also a blessing and a curse.

Glesswik, Lloi, Hewspear, and of course the captain, dead. Thumaar, Skeelana, and even the traitor Azmorgon, dead. Countless Syldoon and Memoridons, gone.

So I was bitter when I learned that the Focus Nustenzia had survived when so many hadn't. Still, I wasn't surprised to learn that she wasn't allowed to cross the Veil and return to her slow son. Soffjian and her sisters recognized her for the resource she was, both in knowledge of the Deserters and how they operated, and in magnifying the power the Memoridons had. Nustenzia would be their prisoner indefinitely. While the rulers might have changed in Sunwrack, the Memoridons were no less coldly pragmatic than the Syldoon. Possibly more so. And they would use any advantage they had to survive. She would never return to her kin or her homeland. Perhaps that was worse than death.

But even if the Deserters never crossed the Veil again in our lifetime, the future of this new Memoridon Empire was uncertain and fraught with human dangers within and without, especially as the Memoridons proved true to their word. Whether Mulldoos's threat was compelling or they merely thought it prudent to cull those factions most likely to try to actively work against them, the Memoridons allowed those Towers who wished to leave to do so unmolested.

There were certainly some Syldoon who marched out of the capital or principalities around the Empire, but not as many as I expected. I supposed if the City of Coups imparted any lesson, it was that nothing at all was set or certain forever—bloody change was inevitable. I found myself oddly relieved that Commander Darzaak opted to keep the Jackals in Sunwrack. Perhaps he was aligning the Jackals with other Towers to check the power of the Memoridons, or maybe Darzaak considered the prospects outside the Empire even more grim than those inside.

But beyond the borders of the Empire, there were plenty of threats even if the remaining Syldoon and the Memoridons established a dynamic that persevered. The Anjurians and Vortagoi Confederacy hadn't thrown their support behind Thumaar out of the goodness of their hearts, after all, but because they perceived rewards in the gamble. And they had doubtless heard by now what had occurred in the Empire. They might not have believed it—stories of eyeless gods or giants storming through the Veil to destroy cities and nearly undermine an empire were probably difficult to swallow if you had not seen the events firsthand. They were difficult to believe even if you had.

But the Vortagoi and Anjurians knew the Memoridons had seized power, and likely attributed the extreme casualties and attrition to that. Men like Baron Brune were still out there, opportunists who wouldn't hesitate to strike if they saw how weakened the Empire was now. Brune would gather the support of his baronial brothers. Who knows, even the weak boy king might be convinced to invade.

Still, as Vendurro liked to say, a soldier's lot was to do only what he could do, follow orders, and eat as many eggs as possible. An archivist's lot wasn't much different, really. Well, except for the eggs. I didn't have the hankering for them that Vendurro had. But those larger shifts and schemes and politics were above me, beyond me, and I wasn't in a position to do much about them anyway.

Immediately after the battle with the Deserters, Darzaak promoted Mulldoos to captain. And Captain Mulldoos agreed to keep me on as Tower archivist. He said (and I didn't even need to write it down to remember it clearly), "You're still a shit combatant, and get in the way half the time. But you're twice as loyal as I ever expected. And you got stones, scribbler. Likely to get you killed, but you got stones, have to grant you that. Plus, it would be too much plaguing work to teach another pen monkey not to trip over his two feet. So you're staying."

That was as ringing an endorsement as I was ever likely to get. Mulldoos was no less difficult to deal with than his predecessor, but no worse when it came to it. More crass, perhaps, but he'd protect his own with a ferocity and single-mindedness that was equal parts inspiring and terrifying.

So, I would worry about the next assignment, the next orders to follow, whether or not Rudgi and I would have a chance to repeat our rendezvous, and if I had enough ink and quills to record everything. Only what was directly in front of me. At least, I would try. It was difficult to keep my mind from spinning over the possibilities.

Captain Killcoin hadn't predicted what had come to pass in Sunwrack, but he had been absolutely right about one thing—I'd seen things so far beyond the pale they made me dizzy to think about. Joining the Syldoon was surely the most remarkable adventure I could have embarked on, no matter how things turned out.

There was a knock on my door. I was starting to get up from the table when Vendurro poked his head in. "Come on, Arki, Commander called us to a meeting." He was about to withdraw when he looked down at my feet. "You got no shoes on. It's the middle of the day. Why don't you have any shoes on?"

I replied, "My left ankle. It's a little swollen."

"Twist it in the library, did you?" Vendurro smiled, and for the first time since Braylar died, it didn't fall off his face right away.

I returned the smile. It felt good. Surprising, but good. "No. I turned it in the yard the other day."

"Captain Bloodsounder using you for pell practice again?"

"My pellishness is one of my defining features," I said. "But I thought Mulldoos wasn't too taken with that name. 'Captain Bloodsounder.'"

"Oh, he hated it plenty the first time he heard it," Vendurro replied. "Still looks at the wicked flail on his hip like it's a two-headed snake that might sink its fangs into him any second. Which, come to think about it, is pretty much on the plaguing mark. But still, it's a good name, 'Captain Bloodsounder.' Sounds right fierce, don't it? Mulldoos'll come around, given enough time." He shook his head. "But that's something in real short supply, just now. Commander wants us in his quarters yesterday. Sounds important. So get some shoes on your plaguing feet, and you best hurry. Maybe you failed to notice, but Commander's not real big on truancy."

"Really?" I said. "So shocking. Syldoon are paragons of patience." I limped around, looking for my shoes. "I'll be right behind you."

Vendurro nodded, still smiling, and pulled the door shut behind him.

I finally found my shoes and then fetched my writing case. Whatever else happened to the Jackals, to the new regime, or to the Empire itself, I would be there, to play what part I could, to try to avoid accidentally shooting an ally with my crossbow, and as ever, to witness and record.

The End

ACKNOWLEDGMENTS

I'm not going to lie—I struggle with writing acknowledgments almost as much as doing a damn synopsis, and for a similar reason: too much to say, too little space to say it. But in this case, it's too many people to recognize, not just my garden variety verbosity.

As always, I need to thank my wife right out of the gate. Writing might be challenging or frustrating at times, but it's not a hard job, not really; teaching junior-high kids, defusing bombs, removing a railroad spike from someone's skull on the operating table—those are hard. But so is living with a writer (or at least *this* writer), and Kris manages that better than I deserve, encouraging, understanding, and calling me out on my shenanigans.

My agent, Michael Harriot, has always been a tremendous sounding board and beta reader, gently nudging me away from dumb ideas and offering fantastic feedback on stuff in process at every stage. He does all the nuts and bolts agency stuff, too, but I value his input and critiques as much as anything.

Jeremy Lassen, my editor, once again helped shape this book into the final form, offering great substantive suggestions for improving the manuscript, eliminating inconsistencies, and refining things. He has been my editor for all three books, and his keen insights certainly made them all stronger.

The Night Shade/Skyhorse team did a marvelous job as ever on *Chains of the Heretic*. Jason Katzman and Lauren Burnstein deserve a special shout out for coordinating the whole production and publicity shebang, and ensuring everything progressed according to plan. As with every book, there are tons of people who worked behind the scenes on composition, proofreading, interior design, marketing, and printing that I don't know by name, but who deserve kudos for doing such a fine job.

The cover artist, Ryan Pancoast, totally captured the tone I was hoping for—menace, mystery, hulking monstrosity—and created an amazing and evocative cover. He also endured my blitz of ideas and arms and armor references, and incorporated everything on my wish list.

And William McAusland was a glutton for punishment again, signing on to create the new map for *Chains*, once again proving himself not only talented, but patient and flexible as well. I really lucked out on the art front with the covers and the maps for the entire series, and I know not every writer is so fortunate.

Writing Bloodsounder's Arc has been a crazy and wonderful journey, and I hope you enjoyed it half as much as I did. So finally, thanks to you, dear reader.